THE LACK BROTHERS

THE LACK BROTHERS

MALCOLM McKAY

BANTAM PRESS

LONDON · NEW YORK · TORONTO · SYDNEY · AUCKLAND

TRANSWORLD PUBLISHERS LTD
61–63 Uxbridge Road, London W5 5SA

TRANSWORLD PUBLISHERS (AUSTRALIA) PTY LTD
15–25 Helles Avenue, Moorebank, NSW 2170

TRANSWORLD PUBLISHERS (NZ) LTD
3 William Pickering Drive, Albany, Auckland

Published 1998 by Bantam Press
a division of Transworld Publishers Ltd
Copyright © by Malcolm McKay 1998

A catalogue record for this book is available from the British Library.

ISBN 0593 042042

Typeset in Century Old Style by
Phoenix Typesetting, Ilkley, West Yorkshire

Printed in Great Britain by
Clays Ltd, Bungay, Suffolk

For my mother and father

PART ONE

SOHO

$$1$$

The angels were cold. Neither their coats nor their flesh were thick, merely standard issue to keep up appearances. They shivered as they looked down from the top of the old mustard warehouse on to the roof and upper floors of the Sunset Hotel opposite them. It was a concrete block of a building, fading grey and stained deep with the bad rain of London; the city of Charlie Lack, the subject of their inquiry.

Sorush, their leader, was disgruntled. She had huge black angry eyes, an explosion of hair and a threadbare black coat. She was perched by a chimney, quite still and skinny, with her feet splayed to grip. Her concentration was intense, and she held her head cocked to one side like a vulture. She shuddered and looked back to Kasbeel, the ancient. He was even colder than she was, hugging his big book to his collapsed chest and muttering some incantation that was only heard by the vague forms that surrounded them. These were other angels with even less substance, who were mostly translucent against the grey sky. They moved against each other and their rags rustled, almost the only sign of their existence, as they tried to keep warm.

Sorush stared into a particular window on the top floor of the Sunset Hotel over the street from them. Beyond the window was a hallway leading away from her. It had rooms off either side. She leaned forward. She seemed to be waiting for something and tensed as she heard the hum of a Hoover coming slowly towards her. It was being pushed by a cleaner, now visible, in a grey dress. She was coming slowly down the corridor, ever closer to the window that the angels looked through. From behind the Hoover there was another sound. This was a second cleaner, also in grey, who was pushing a wicker basket with squeaking wheels. She went in and out of the rooms, gathering dirty laundry. She was coming towards the angels too.

Suddenly the door opened from the last room on the corridor, the one nearest the window. A woman came out of it, but kept her back turned to the angels. All they could see was a curvy figure huddled in a dark coat, a pair of shapely legs and high-heeled shoes. She walked away from them down the corridor and receded quickly from view, elegantly stepping over the Hoover cable and skirting the wicker basket with a swish of her coat. Neither of the cleaners paid much attention to her.

Sorush glanced again at Kasbeel. He too was intent and the rustling of the forms behind them had stopped. This seemed to be it. They watched and waited as the cleaner with the Hoover came closer. The angels were by now completely still and quiet. Even the vaguest forms amongst them seemed to have gained definition in the silence. The second cleaner took a pile of fresh sheets from her wicker basket and opened the door that the woman had come out of. The angels watched as she went into the room.

They didn't react as she stopped short and screamed, nor when the cleaner in the corridor dropped the Hoover handle and also hurried into the room. She joined her colleague and screamed too. Slowly their panic began to subside, and first one, then the other, began to smirk. This rapidly became embarrassed giggles, as they glanced at each other and then down at the body by the bed. Soon they were laughing out loud, leaning on each other's shoulders and gasping for breath.

Neither Sorush, Kasbeel, nor an angel moved. Perhaps they had no sense of humour. The sight of Charlie Lack, stark naked in his pale and bony carcass, with a bright-red pair of woman's panties stuffed in his mouth, heart stopped dead, didn't seem to have amused them at all.

Sorush looked at Kasbeel, who opened his book and began the incantation. As he did so, the various forms behind him became more visible, giving shape to wings, faces, slow-moving hands and black material that rubs and mutters. And in front Sorush uncoiled. Her head raised, she became more beautiful and human by the minute.

Kasbeel the ancient rasped in a voice heavy and wavy, as if it was an echo of time, 'I require thee, O Lord Jesus Christ, that thou give by thy virtue and power over all thine angels, which were thrown down from heaven to deceive mankind, to draw them to me, to tie and bind them that they may give me a true answer of all my demands.'

Sorush straightened, her black coat rippled then fluttered open in the rooftop breeze, revealing breasts forming, fluid and poised, and a long body of limbs and thighs uncurling. Her eyes were black and deep set through life to death. She was wary, alert and the essence of some great power. She knew things had begun. This is why she'd come. The death of Charlie, and Mihr. Especially Mihr.

2

Charlie's funeral was five days later. As Father Cassidy officiated, a no-hope ex-Jesuit called O'Dare gave a running and drunken commentary from a side aisle. Forgetting he was defrocked, O'Dare had taken the view that Cassidy, as usual, was cocking up the mass, and he began to issue loud instructions from the buttress that supported him. There was a holy pause from Cassidy, himself thinking of the wine in the chalice and the taste on his tongue, and a ripe stagger or two from O'Dare. The church was awash with the red prickle of embarrassment.

The Lack Brothers were in the front pew. Arnie, the eldest, coming to his fortieth year, was furious. He might have known, his father's funeral and this was the usual fuck-up. The priest was tottering, O'Dare was worse, and the girls up the back were either howling their grief too loud, hitching their underwear, or just not paying enough attention. Arnie's big nose started to sweat and twitch. He'd have taken off for a farthing; less. But some sense of propriety kept him enpewed, the back of his knees hard against the scraped brown wood of the seat behind him. He wasn't feeling too good, the old man had gone and he wanted to ask a few questions like, 'Dad, would you care to comment on the manner of your parting in a ten-bob hole-up in the Sunset, with some tramp's knickers in your gob? People talk, you know; they snigger!' He looked at the coffin, his irritation increasing, then he suppressed it with the thought that at least he'd be able to sit in the restaurant or down in the club without having to listen to any more of the old man's wild plans for the place.

He rolled his shoulders back and watched Cassidy rambling through the more pertinent points of the service, and to his left O'Dare, quieter now as he concentrated on remaining upright. He thought, Things can only get better. After a pause, he thought again, But they won't, will they? He sighed and listened to the murmurings from the rest of the packed congregation. His nose twitched again as he heard a cackle and a thump from the back. Had someone passed out already? He couldn't believe it. He glanced along the pew at Bernie, who at twenty was the youngest of the brothers. He'd hang around for him anyway.

Something had stopped Bernie's brain growing when he was eight, but whatever it was, it hadn't stopped the rest of him. He was now six feet four and fifteen stones. Auntie Harriet insisted his bones still hadn't reached their full size and there were probably still a few inches to come. He was a handsome giant of a young man, even now with his mouth hanging open and a hint of spittle on his lip. He was trying to imagine his daddy's body in the coffin just a few feet away from him. He knew he was sad and had tried to cry, but there was too much else going on. He was thinking, What's all these gits doing here then? My dad's dead. He's in that coffin. What's he doing in there?

He clutched at the dog-eared copy of his huge picture book, *King Arthur and the Knights of the Round Table*. Bernie was never seen without it. It was his succour and his bible and it had good pictures. He wanted to open it and take a peek at his favourite one of Galahad, as he had done in moments of stress or confusion for as long as he could remember. The book had been given to him by their mother, Violet, as a last bequest before she'd picked up her suitcase and taken off, never to be seen again. This was roughly how Bernie perceived the death of his father. He'd done a runner like Mum, except you could still see his body lying there, or anyway you could have done when it was down the undertaker's, not breathing, at least not when you was looking anyway. 'My dad's dead. Can't breave in that box. He'll get assixiated. My dad's dead.' He reached down for Mirabelle's hand.

Mirabelle, small, teenaged, pretty, Scottish and pert, stood by him, dwarfed by his huge frame. She looked up and smiled. 'Nearly done.'

'Thass it, Meebelle, keep your pecker up.' Bernie grinned back and

12

then decided for no reason at all to turn and beam his lighthouse smile at all the cold and shivery sundry on the back pews.

Ronnie Lack, at thirty, precisely the middle brother of the three, gave him a gently disapproving look. Neat and dapper, with a head full of thoughts he could never quite keep up with, Ronnie was also the smallest of the brothers and a good foot shorter than the youngest by his side. He craned his neck up so that Bernie could see his frown, but the big boy had decided to switch the beam off and was whispering out of the side of his mouth to Mirabelle. 'Got to have a pee, Meebelle.'

'Won't be a minute.' She gripped his hand.

Ronnie smiled at her, then mouthed, 'Hang on, Bern. We're nearly done.'

'I'll hang on, Ron, don't worry about me, mate.' Bernie looked stalwart and proud as he grasped his balls with his right hand, making sure his King Arthur picture book was tucked especially securely under his massive arm. Even Arnie couldn't help a grin. At which point, Father Cassidy, as if to help Bernie out, brought the service to an end.

3

The big black cars churned through heavy rain up to the cemetery in the east of the city and drew up beneath the spire of the vast, gothic, brown and abandoned church of St Aldgate, which sat square, pointed and threatening amidst the three square miles of decrepit gravestones. They came to a halt and the mourners spilled out into the wet and mud. These were the drunks, whoring girls, shopkeepers, street traders, layabouts, has-beens, mobmen, barmen, betsmen, cocksmen, and other assorted trash, charm and peculiar attitude, that were getting Arnie down.

He went round to the back of the hearse and waited while the under-taker's men lifted the hatch. They seemed to be half-cut as well. Arnie shoved the professionals to one side and yelled to Ronnie and Bernie. 'Here, we'll take him up the hill. Me an' Ron will get the front, and Bern you bring up the rear. And don't drop him.' They heaved the coffin out of the hearse, and the staggering, mud-stuck, cursing mêlée formed behind them to begin the trudge up to the graveside.

O'Dare, having failed in the church, seemed determined to take over at the burial. He turned and shouted at a butcher still in his pinstriped apron, urinating behind a huge headstone, 'Don't piss on the dead, you eejit! Can't you see it's tipping down? Get him in the ground before he drowns the lot of us!' And with that he turned and tramped in bad temper up the muddy path, trying to catch Father Cassidy in front of the coffin, where perhaps some long-past sense of priesthood suggested he should be himself.

As he went up he passed the brothers slipping and sliding on the turf with the weight of their father pressing down on their shoulders. Mirabelle, who was following immediately behind them, could see that Arnie was angry, Ronnie was looking sad and confused and Bernie was struggling. Even for someone of his bulk the coffin was heavy and his shoes were so caked with mud that every step was a struggle. He said, 'I'm really sad, Meebelle.'

'I know. So am I.' She had to shout it through the rain.

'You got the Arfer?'

'Don't worry.' Mirabelle smiled and held up his picture book, as O'Dare, the strands of his grey hair stuck to his watery forehead like devil's prongs, finally overtook Father Cassidy and made it to the head of the procession just as they reached the open grave.

O'Dare turned and shouted, 'That's it. Gather round! Hurry up!' Then he looked up to the bursting heavens. 'Jesus Christ, couldn't you give us a sodding respite for ten sodding minutes?'

Cassidy mildly turned to the brothers. 'Arnie, would you use the straps laid out for the purpose and lower your father into his grave.'

'And quick before it becomes a pit to drown us all,' added O'Dare.

Arnie gave the ex-priest a black look as Blue Lucy, his sometime girlfriend and all-time stripper, with a borrowed coat over her well-built undress, gave a hoot as her heels sunk into the mud and she fell back into a puddle that maybe God had put there for the very purpose.

'For Christ's sake, Lucy! Straighten up, will yer? Straighten up!' Arnie yelled. 'Sort yourself out! This is a bloody funeral!'

Lucy was helped to her feet by the beautiful Mathilda, the soulful black girl who took the cash in the peep show where she worked. 'Thanks, Tilda. Sorry, Arn.'

Arnie glared. 'Right.' Then he and his brothers, with the help of one of the undertakers, gathered the straps to lift the coffin and lower Charlie into the grave. They awkwardly manoeuvred him over the hole. Maybe it was because the wood was cheap and had soaked up the rain, or maybe Charlie had gained weight since death, but whatever it was, Arnie's and Ronnie's strap broke precisely at the moment the coffin was in the perfect position to be lowered. Seeing the other end go down, Bernie naturally heaved upward. There was a dull thud, then silence as the congregation stood in the pouring rain, staring at Charlie's coffin, standing head down and perpendicular in the grave.

Arnie moved fast. If anyone cared to laugh they could join his old man doing headstands in the pit. He glared round. 'What difference does it make? Hey? It don't make no difference. We'll lie him down after, won't we, Father?' The congregation stood silent with guffaws, smirks and snickers frozen on their wet faces as Father Cassidy stepped forward.

'I knew he wouldn't go easy,' Harriet Lack, elder sister to Charlie, whispered to no-one in particular.

'Ah . . . brothers and sisters, parishioners, ahem . . . friends of the dear departed . . .' Cassidy began.

'He done all this in church,' Harriet noted.

'Charlie, a gentleman of note, friend to the ladies and font of generosity, occasional churchman, holy brother and single parent to Arnold, Ronald and Bernard.' Cassidy appeared not to notice that he was addressing the coffin-encased feet of the deceased. 'May the Lord on High take you up and fill the void in us all with the grace of his good self.'

Looking at the upended coffin, Arnie couldn't help thinking that his old man was diving head first into hell.

' May you rest in peace,' Cassidy concluded.

'Amen,' said Mirabelle, as she peered up at the church spire. She seemed to be looking for something.

4

The Lacks' restaurant was on the first floor of a tall narrow building standing in a wide alley off Dean Street. In the Fifties it had been a Soho wine warehouse, with giant wooden vats and sherry-soaked walls, until Charlie had had his vision and painted the place yellah. It was the same peeled canary that was greeting the mourners now for his wake. They were pouring in, having shaken the hand of rueful Ron or angry Arnie at the door, and were grabbing sandwiches and ancient chairs, the respectable desperately trying to separate themselves from the disreputable. Unfortunately, as the tables were hardly knee room apart, there wasn't much chance of that, so trader found himself next to chancer and spinsters crossed legs with tarts.

Harriet Lack went quickly through the gathering crowd, up the stairs at the back, and climbed to the room above the restaurant which had once been designated by Charlie as the tearoom. Having not really understood the delicacy of the idea, he had never given a thought to dainty china, cake stands and filigree serviettes. Instead he'd poured thick brown tea into cracked pint mugs and handed out plates of broken digestives, so it was not surprising that the room remained largely vacant. By now it was used more as a storeroom. Cases of beans surrounded by Vim, Andrex straddled by Johnny Walker, Persil covered in ketchup, and boxes of cutlery, crockery and a pile of broken furniture were among a twenty-year-old inventory of discards, all piled in no apparent order from one corner of the room to the other. There was, however, one remaining table and two plastic chairs by the window and Auntie Harriet covered one with her coat and placed her handbag on the other, reserving them both for herself and Sayeed Sayeed, honorary uncle to the boys and ancient Bengali, mystic pal of Charlie's.

Harriet was about to sit down when Mirabelle hurried behind her towards the stairs leading up further into the building. The tearoom was also a thoroughfare to the Lacks' flat above, which was jammed, tiny room by tiny room, on to the next two floors. None of the family had ever given a thought as to how it was that so many people, with all their laughter, moans, dreams and stench; so much furniture, scratched, shredded and worn, and such a quantity of junk of every

16

conceivable colour, size and degree of uselessness, could be crammed into such a pixielike labyrinth of life. But so it was. This was where the Lacks lived, packed tight together, limb curled into limb and breath on breath. Except for Mirabelle. She was above, in the pokiest attic in Soho, tucked beneath the eaves with her truncated tallboy and tiny bed.

She rushed breathless up the wooden ladder from the hallway in the flat and began to change out of funereal black into workaday white. She had Bernie to look after and half the district to help feed. They were all bound to show up for a quick bite (as much as they could thieve) and tot (ditto), to toast dear old Charlie, their much mourned soulmate, late landlord and chalker of their slate.

She dashed back out and down through the crowded flat, then descended the stairs again, past Harriet in the tearoom (now comfortably seated, taking a furtive swig from her hip flask and still waiting for Sayeed Sayeed), quickly through the restaurant (already packed with dross), and down, even further down, to the basement of the Lack domain, where Charlie had created his dream of dreams, his very own club.

Papered in deep damp red, covered in faded portraits of Fifties filmstars – Doris Day was the favourite – and with a tiny well-stocked bar in the corner; this was where the father of the Lacks had plied his trade of charm and chat for eighteen hours of the day and night; where he'd handed out doubles, bad deals, worse jokes, stories and ineffectual threats to anyone who cared to listen; where he'd ruined his marriage and educated his boys, and where the motley crew of his life were now beginning to gather, to wet their throats and dry their limbs.

Mirabelle went straight out the back to the kitchen, the home of the greasy pan, and the source for over twenty years of every fry in the book, dumb-waitered up to the restaurant tables above. As the door swung behind her, the club not only felt good, it smelled good too, impregnated as it was with the stench of two decades' worth of grease and fat that had emanated over the years from the kitchen next door.

Not that Luis Riss would have agreed. Standing by the bar he puckered his little Maltese snout in distaste as Mirabelle passed. He turned carefully, not wanting to crease his impeccable double-breasted, even while standing still. 'Kitchen right next to the bar. Fucking disgusting. Stink of fried egg in your gin. No idea, these people, no idea. Things got to change.' This last statement surprised him. Why had things got to change? What had this dump got to do with him? He considered for a second, trusting his mouth more than his brain, and realized an idea was forming. It was still vague and blurred, but was definitely growing foetuslike in the damp mess beyond his hairline. He looked round the club and said it again, more quietly this time, 'Things got to change.'

'Sure. Thass right. Thass right.' This was Emil Riss, only son to the self-styled mobster, Luis. He spoke in a contrived mid-Atlantic accent and was, in his own view, of a different class to the old man. He had no idea what his father was talking about, but agreed nevertheless. He shot his cuffs. 'Thass right. No problem.'

Raphaella Riss, Luis's voluptuously beautiful, sex-obsessed and over-protected daughter, hadn't been listening. She dabbed a tear from her eye with a perfumed handkerchief, being careful not to distress her mascara. 'You got no feelings. None of you got no feelings.'

'Shuddup, Raphaella.' Luis was still thinking and didn't want any interruptions at the moment from one of life's deepest problems: his daughter.

'And why don't we go to the grave, Papa?' she persisted.

'Go to the grave?' Luis looked startled, like someone had just walked all over his own. The last thing he was going to do was get shit on his shoes at St Aldgates. He had fully intended to make an impressive entrance into the club when it was packed full of mourners, but the priest's non-existent sense of time, propriety and the waiting Riss ego had outfoxed him, and so they'd arrived early. Luis was upset at the thought of being seen waiting for a Lack, but what else was he supposed to do? Walk up and down the alley outside for half an hour and get soaked?

'I want to see Charlie get buried.' Raphaella sniffed, affecting grief.

'Go to the grave? Are you kidding? It was raining!' Luis waved a pudgy, diamante-covered hand in Raphaella's face. 'I go to the grave for my own mother, OK? Charlie Lack? Are you crazy? Hey? And blow your nose.' He caught sight of her well-charged cleavage and suddenly remembered something else. 'And I still don' know where you were, half-past ten last night!'

'Oh, Papa.' Raphaella pouted. Although Luis considered her a virginal twelve-year-old, she was at least twenty-eight and rising. As usual, she played her trump of childish charm, took her father's hand

and literally twisted it round her little finger, causing a twinge in his wrist. 'Don't be angry with little Raphaella, Papa, I look in the shops, thass all. All night I look in the shops, 'cos I don' have no money. Give me some money, Papa.'

'Cover yourself up.'

Raphaella pulled her blouson up half an inch over her breast curve and pouted prettily again. 'Just a fifty, Papa.'

'Hey, you think we're made of the stuff, Raphaella?' Emil pulled his shoulders back and placed his feet apart like he was a man who was.

'What's it got to do with you, Emil! Shuddup!'

'Don't you tell me to shuddup!'

'Shuddup!' Luis topped them both, then for reasons he still didn't quite understand, he pulled out his wallet with a flourish. 'What's a fifty on a day like this?' He flicked a crisp note under his daughter's nose. 'Look around you.' These words were coming out of his mouth, but he still didn't know why. Nor did his son and daughter. They obediently looked round the club as he said, 'You like it? Maybe soon you get more than a fifty.' He laughed, again for no apparent reason, and then turned quickly and maybe just a bit shiftily, as Mirabelle came back out of the kitchen balancing four plates of sandwiches.

'Hey waitress . . .'

'They're for the restaurant, Mr Riss.' She gave him a hostile stare then headed for the stairs.

'Some other things going to change also!' Luis laughed again, his brown teeth shown up by his crisp white shirt.

'Thass right, Papa. Thass right!' Emil laughed cluelessly, as Raphaella, snuffles forgotten, tucked her fifty into the heavenly crevasse between her breasts and Luis tried to work out what was happening in his head.

Up top in the alley, the crowd was multiplying. Arnie feared the worst; those electric words 'free booze' were connecting the streets and there was hardly a juicer who remained unplugged and wasn't following the flow right to the socket of the Lacks. 'We're going to have to close up in a minute, Ron.'

'Should never have opened in the first place, Arn.'

The crush got worse. A crowd of street traders and shopkeepers swept past them. Then came the shriek of the ex-priest O'Dare. 'Out of the way, you bastard heathen! It's the Church! Make way!' He shoved his way towards the brothers at the door.

'That Irish prat is pissed worse than usual,' Arnie, pushed back against the wall, croaked to Ronnie.

'And he's not coming in neither,' Ronnie yelled back.

'Where are the tarts!' O'Dare shouted and then disappeared into the crowd. Five seconds later he reappeared halfway through the restaurant door and was sucked into the interior maul before Ronnie could do anything about it.

'Wait a minute . . . !'

'Don't know why you bother, brother. Being once a priest, funerals are his game, aren't they? Today is mayhem, Ron, let it be.' Arnie had decided to be philosophical and drink himself into oblivion. In fact, he could already hear the sound of the ice chinking in that oh-so-friendly way at the bottom of the glass he was about to take, when suddenly the light seemed to change for a millisecond. Sayeed Sayeed, the old Bengali pal of Charlie, in his usual yellow, stood in front of them. His diamond smile shone out from his old brown face.

'Your father was a very popular man.'

He was certainly popular in the kitchen. Porchese, the little Italian chef, one bottle of whisky to the bad, staggered in uncontrolled grief away from the tin of tuna he was supposed to be mashing on the table. He tipped backwards into a rack of kitchen trays and sent them crashing to the floor, tolling his own personal bells for Charlie. As he slowly slid further down to the tiles, his tears of sorrow mixing with whatever was coming out of his nose, he raised his eyes to the heavens and shouted up to God, 'Make eats on a day like this? Who you kidding, huh! Do it yourself! You take! You make!'

Sophie Lighterman, the fifty-year-old, very fat and very shiny, Jamaican kitchen assistant and vegetable specialist, sitting mountainous on a stool at the other end of the table, was unperturbed. 'Where's that tuna, Porkie?' She was neatly and expertly filling the sandwiches that Mirabelle was taking upstairs by the plateful.

'Drop dead on hotel floor! Why? Why you leave Charlie on the carpet?' Porchese howled from the floor. His dialogue with his Maker and Taker wasn't done yet.

Sophie crammed four plates of egg and cucumber, neatly decrusted, into the dumb waiter and pulled the rope to haul them up as Mirabelle ran in behind her. 'Sophie, wait!' She skidded to a frustrated halt as the dumb-waiter doors closed and the food ascended.

'Thought you was upstairs, dear,' said Sophie blankly.

'Oh God.' Mirabelle turned fast and ran back the way she'd come, hoping to intercept the sandwiches as they arrived in the restaurant above, before they disappeared into the great gob of the uninvited.

'The dead is slow and life is quick.' Sophie sat back down and attacked another loaf with the marge.

Porchese moaned, 'Charlie! Oh, Charlie Lack! Holy saint of Soho. Where you gone?'

'That's enough of that, Porchese.' It was Harriet. Her hip flask had run out while waiting for Sayeed Sayeed in the tearoom, and she'd descended to the bar for a top-up. Now a little on the tilt, she leaned against the kitchen door. 'Respect for the dead, dear. Get up, wipe the vomit from your whites and help Sophie with the sandwiches.'

Porchese put a hand up on the sink. 'I lost my gumption.' He tried to haul himself to his feet, as more kitchen trays clattered to the ground, doing no favours for Harriet's headache and tinnitus.

'You're going to lose more than that, dear,' said Harriet wiggling her finger in her ear, 'Up. Up, Porchese. We are the Lacks of Soho, and Charlie or no Charlie, as such we shall remain.' Porchese vomited in the sink. 'Not on the celery, dear.' Harriet raised her eyebrows at Sophie and, turning with just the hint of a stagger, went back through to the bar, as the little Italian heaved the last of his love and affection for his erstwhile employer into the sink, trying to avoid Sophie's washed vegetables.

Harriet stood still for a moment and viewed the club. Even in her few seconds of applying propriety to the chef, the human content of the tiny room had roughly doubled. She took a moment to consider. Was this as it would always be? Would Charlie's world never change? Were these her fellow travellers? The thought thrilled her faintly and at the same time made her feel slightly sick. She dismissed it, pushed her way through the throng and grandly ascended the narrow stairs to the restaurant above, leaving her nephew to deal with the rabble below.

Arnie's idle thoughts of a quiet and solitary descent into alcoholic stupor had already been shattered by what was fast becoming a riot of bereavement, and he was close to being stark pissed off as Luis Riss fine-tuned the hang of his double-breasted and moved in on him at the bar. Luis smirked and said, 'Take advice, my friend, clean your house.'

'Correct,' Emil, the snappy son, agreed loudly.

Arnie wasn't having any of that from Emil. 'As a matter of fact, my father always informed us that people were more important than custom.'

'He was an arsehole.' Emil played it tough.

'You what?' Arnie glared.

Luis, being brighter than his son, realized that it wasn't always best practice to insult the dead within an hour of the funeral. He interposed his oily head and smarmed, 'Charlie was a generous man, Arnie.'

'I wouldn't say you had the cat's nippers down your slot shop, Emil. And a peep show's not exactly the bleeding Odeon is it?' said Arnie.

There was a silence. Luis stared at Arnie for a moment and then said, 'Frankly there's too much fucking humanity in here for my suit.'

Arnie couldn't think of a reply to that and Emil ostentatiously picked a piece of fluff from his sleeve. 'Anyway,' said Arnie, about to move away.

'Don't you say hello to me, Arnie?' Raphaella looked up, meltingly sympathetic, into Arnie's eyes.

'Hello, Raphaella. Ah?' Arnie looked meltingly sympathetic back. 'Would you like a drink?'

'Babycham. No cherry. Thank you, Arnie.'

This was too much molten sympathy for Luis. 'Shuddup, Raphaella, and grieve.'

'Hard,' added Emil.

There was a pause. The chit-chat appeared to be over. That left just the business. Although Luis still had no clear idea what it was. He raised his glass. 'Here's to Charlie. RIP. And we talk another time.'

'Talk? What about?' Arnie couldn't remember any encounter with Luis that had resulted in anything that could have been described as talk.

'Talk, Arnie, talk!' Luis repeated the word, as if aware of its strange taste.

'You know, open the mouth, let shit fall out,' Emil interpreted.

22

'What do you want to talk about?' Arnie looked from one to the other.

'Nice place you got here.' Luis looked round. The thought was coming. Soon he'd have it solid and true in the front of his brain.

'What?'

'Sleep the dream of dreams, my friend,' said Luis mysteriously.

'Hey?'

'Night, Arnie.' That was it. The talk was over. Luis downed his drink, grabbed Raphaella's elbow and began to turn towards the basement exit.

'Night, Arnie.' She gave him another molten look.

'Good night, Raphaella.' He returned the look, then wished he hadn't as Emil thrust his long nose and big lips up close. 'Hey! None of your old man's gameroonies on my sister! You get me?'

Raphaella broke from Luis's grasp and shoved her teeth at Emil's ear like she was going to bite it off. 'Emil, you clut! You think I'm four years old! You think I'm kiddiwinks? You find out, big dumb brother!' She poked him hard in the chest and stared briefly into Arnie's eyes, 'Bye Arnie,' then she went after her father.

Encouraged by the girl, Arnie got braver. 'My old man never touched her.'

Emil rubbed his breast bone. 'But he tried, Arnie, he tried!' He gave a mocking laugh and raised his drink. 'To Charlie and all he leaves behind.' He dropped his glass on a table and followed his father and sister. 'See ya.'

Luis stood by the basement door, framed by his son and daughter, and raised a proprietorial arm to what he fondly imagined were his people. 'Good night my friends.' No-one took any notice and he went out. Arnie watched through the window as the party climbed the basement steps outside. There was something about Raphaella's backside that he didn't want to talk to her father about. His brief reverie was interrupted by shouts from the bar.

Mirabelle was being accosted from all sides by hands grabbing for sandwiches as she hurtled out of the kitchen, once more heading for the inside stairs to the restaurant. Arnie decided not to get involved. It was all too much, this day was dark enough as it was. He swallowed his drink and pushed towards the bar for another. Mirabelle finally extricated herself and the sandwiches from the throng, and bounded up the stairs. Halfway up she met a hired waiter coming down. 'Look out for O'Dare,' he warned, as he descended to the gloom below. Mirabelle's heart sank as she went warily on up to the light above.

O'Dare was sitting at a table in the restaurant with Mathilda and Lucy, Arnie's girlfriend, who, having rid herself of her coat, was now bursting out of her dress. The ex-priest, drunk beyond his ex-order, had his hand along the back of her chair and was beginning to grope her upper arm.

'Get off, will you! You're a bloody disgrace!' Lucy snapped.

'Show us a garter. Go on. Show us anything, or I'll bust me trouser, yer tart.' O'Dare grinned his horrible, half-toothed grin.

'I'll pray for you, Vicar.' Lucy turned icily away.

O'Dare tried another tack. 'Would you like a confession? Come on, I can still do it. What have you got to confess?' He moved his hand to Lucy's thigh.

'Take your hand off, you dirty beast!' Mathilda, the beautiful peep-show till girl, swiped at O'Dare's hand on her friend's leg and then, as if afraid the sound of the slap would cause offence, looked longingly over at Ronnie, who was sitting with some local traders at another table. He was watching as Mirabelle took what was left of the sandwiches over to the girls' table.

O'Dare seized his chance as Lucy stood and bent forward to take a quarter prawn from the offered plate. He swept both his hands up the side of her legs and roared with delight as he revealed her stocking tops and pantie bottom.

'Get off, you bastard!' Lucy straightened fast, sending the sandwiches flying up into the air as O'Dare pulled at her suspenders, trying to get a tune.

'Oh Jaysus, pluck them like the strings on a cherub's heart!'

'Piss off!' Lucy screamed and suddenly slipped as the sandwiches fell to the floor. O'Dare rasped with delight as she landed flat on her backside in a spread of sliced bread, sending a spurt of mayonnaise across the lino. She slowly looked down between her legs at her ruined dress and wailed, 'Sod you, you blasphemous prick! That's mud and mayo! And all in one day!' She'd have burst into tears if she hadn't caught Ronnie's eye. 'Beg pardon, Ron.' She went crimson in the silence.

'Get up will you, Lucy?' asked Ronnie tiredly.

Mathilda, anxious to please, tried to catch his eye. 'Shall I brush the lino, Ron? Shall I get a mop?' She helped Lucy to her feet.

O'Dare, iconoclastic as ever, broke the mood of apology and swooped to the floor to pick up a squashed sandwich. 'Jaysus, I never seen a sarnie so flat. Up your bum!' He popped it into his mouth.

Lucy, mustering as much dignity as a woman could with half a plate of seafood stuck to her arse, grabbed her coat from a chair and yanked open the restaurant door. She turned back to O'Dare and shouted, 'You are ... you are ... a disgusting cleric!' Then, her eyes brimming with tears, she slammed the door behind her and stomped away down the alley.

Mathilda hung about for a second, desperate for a kind look from Ron. He stared down at his tea, pointedly ignoring her. She ran out after Lucy as Mirabelle yelled down the hatch of the dumb waiter, 'Sophie! Sandwiches, mop and bucket, ground floor!'

Ronnie suddenly felt a surge of anger. 'Things are going to have to get changed!' He'd said it to no-one in particular. The day was getting to him too. 'And bloody quick as well!' He looked up in surprise as Mirabelle dropped a dustpan. 'Sorry, I didn't mean you, Mira ...'

But it wasn't Ronnie that was bothering her. 'Bernie! I forgot Bernie!' She chucked the dustpan quickly into the hatch and ran towards the stairs.

'Anyhow,' continued Ron. 'Anyhow ...' his voice trailed away.

Harriet had finally connected with Sayeed Sayeed. They sat opposite each other across the table by the window, surrounded by the junk of the overflow room. She poured whisky from her flask into her teacup and raised it. 'Here's to sudden death. Here one minute and unreturned the next. Don't know why it is, but there you have it. He had no heart to speak of, probably.'

'He had plenty of heart, Auntie. Charlie had plenty of heart.' Sayeed Sayeed smiled as Mirabelle suddenly appeared in the room from the top of the restaurant stairs.

'More tea, dear, for the whisky.' Harriet lifted her cup, but Mirabelle was already mounting the stairs to the flat above. 'Nice girl. Scotch, you know.' Harriet pondered the link between the nationality and her almost empty cup for a moment and then returned to the contemplation of her dead brother. 'One thing Charlie didn't have, Sayeed, was his wife. I often pondered whatever became of Violet.'

'It's a mysterious world, Harriet.'

'You can say that again.' Harriet drained the dregs. 'I lose a brother in a blink and Sayonara wins the four-thirty at Epsom. Beats me.'

Sayeed Sayeed smiled again. He knew that there were more things in this world than the Lack Brothers would ever dream of.

Bernie had been a good boy. He'd changed into his jim-jams all on his own and was cleaning his teeth in the tiny bathroom, which was all but filled by his huge bulk, when Mirabelle squeezed into the doorway, holding his King Arthur picture book.

'You should be in bed by now.'

'I'm late tonight, 'cos my dad died.'

'I know.' Mirabelle leaned against the woodwork and watched him as he meticulously brushed his teeth one at a time. 'If you're not going to take all night, I'll read to you.'

Bernie grinned, going even slower. He knew she'd read to him whatever the time was. Even in the bloody mist and snow and rain, even at bloody four o'clock in the morning, even if they were starving to deff and the house was falling down, she'd still read the Arfer.

Half an hour later he was in his bed with his feet sticking six inches over the tailboard. Mirabelle perched on the tiny ledge of available space by his side and put one foot up on Ronnie's bed, which ran parallel with Bernie's. She angled the book on her knee so that he could see the pictures and he looked knowledgeably at the faded colour. There was Lancelot leading the knights away from Camelot, as King Arthur stood, grief-stricken, by the castle gate.

'For today was the day when . . .' Mirabelle began.

'King Arfer's crying.' Bernie pointed at the picture.

'You always say that.'

'That's because he's always crying.'

'Anyway. Today was the day when Lancelot . . .'

'He was the best of the lot. Except for Galahad.' Bernie spoke seriously. This was his subject and he knew everything about it.

'Do you want me to read, or not?'

'Well don't say in words what it says in the pictures.'

'How do you know what it says in the words? You're not looking at them.'

'I know and that's that.' He screwed up his face and farted as if to prove his point. 'Another bun, Vicar?'

'Bernie!'

'Are you going to read or what?'

'Don't be so rude.'

'Sorry.'

'For today was the day when Lancelot led all of the knights of the Round Table . . .'

'Including Galahad.'

'That's not in the words.'

'Well it should be.'

'Including Galahad. In search of the . . .'

'Holy Grail. Thank you.' Bernie closed his eyes.

Mirabelle kissed him gently on the forehead. 'And they rode away from Camelot, fully armed,' she read as he began to snore quietly.

5

A few hours later Arnie locked the door on the empty restaurant and stood in the lamplit alley, looking down the basement steps to the club. There was still laughter and light coming from the window below him, but he'd leave Harriet to deal with that. He sighed and turned to Ronnie, standing beside him in the moonlight. 'They'll be down there all the bloody night, won't they?'

Ronnie shrugged. He'd never been that much of a boozer and the bar-room bonhomie below, previously encouraged, not to say whipped up by Charlie, and now seeming to develop of its own alcoholic accord, mystified him.

Arnie put the keys into his pocket. 'Emil Riss was going on about the old man and Raphaella.'

'Nothing new about that, Arn.'

'Old bugger did try an' all, didn't he? Never stopped bloody trying, did he?'

'So why don't you?'

Ronnie always seemed to ask questions that Arnie didn't want to answer. 'Because I fancy her, Ron, that's why. And if that old bastard could sniff about, why can't I?'

Ronnie sighed. 'I think I'll go out for a bit.'

'See Mathilda, Ron?'

'See Lucy, Arn?'

'Yeah. Night, Ron.'

'Night, Arn.'

They went in opposite directions down the alley. As he walked, Arnie wondered why he'd brought up the old man and Raphaella in the first place. As he walked into the neon of the streets he decided that if he had anything to ask, he'd ask Lucy. She never knew what he was talking about.

After a couple of minutes he stopped in front of Emil's peep show and looked through the lurid red of the entrance. He could see one of the Riss minders, Scotch Jock, a psychopathic, punch-drunk idiot, leaning back in a plastic chair, reading a paper. Mathilda wasn't in her usual place in the pay booth. There was some other tart polishing her nails and yawning. Arnie knew that both Lucy and Mathilda had taken the night off for the wake, but was prepared to bet that Lucy, having left early and for want of anything better to do, had decided to put in some overtime in the barrel. He walked past the girl in the booth and Jock on his chair, straight into the gloomy interior of the peep show.

'Hey! Whoa!' Jock yelled. 'Where do you think you're going?'

'Fuck off, Jock,' Arnie yelled over his shoulder. He felt belligerent, and anyway, he only wanted a word with Lucy if she was there.

'It's only half a quid!' Jock gave up and sat back down under the mocking stare of the girl with the nail varnish. Without the support and irritating bullshit of his boss, Emil, Jock could surprisingly often opt for the easy life. Not always though, and the girl in the booth was taking a risk with her superior grin. So, for that matter, had Arnie. Jock was a fully disturbed, up-to-the-minute, top-of-the-range, expertly diagnosed psychopath. He could just as easily have gone berserk when Arnie passed him, as sat down and read the results of the day before yesterday's racing. His violence was entirely instinctive and he took great pleasure in the fact that he had no foreknowledge or responsibility for its ignition. This, on occasion, made him truly dangerous. He glanced up at the girl, who didn't know how lucky she'd been, and lit a cigarette.

Lucy, naked except for a G-string, was dancing languidly and bored inside the ten-foot diameter barrel of the peep show. She glanced at her watch and then up at a pair of eyes staring at her through one of the slits in the side. They opened, then closed, then opened again. Lucy knew, with that natural sense of man that somehow she'd been born with, that soon she'd be hearing the rustle of tissue paper (provided free by the house). Like the true woman she believed herself to be, she gyrated her hips towards the slit in the wall and dabbled her fingers on her crotch in a rough approximation of masturbation. The eyes were opening and closing faster. There was no denying that Lucy was feeling a vague thrill of excitement for this unknown wanker, when she heard a voice, hardly distinguishable over the thump and pound of the shit soul music, which Emil fondly imagined was good to dance to. 'Fancy a hotel? Oi! I want to go to a hotel!'

Lucy didn't like this. Anonymous eyes in slits could elicit her sympathy, even occasionally work her up, but a punter reflecting humanity, not to say making demands and asking for dates was definitely not on. She shouted, 'Piss off!' Then yelled towards the exit, 'Jock, I got a donkey in the stalls!'

But the voice persisted. 'Lucy! It's me! Arnie!'

She spun round fast and the pair of eyes behind closed in ecstasy as the longed for prospect of her G-strung buttocks suddenly reared out of the dark-red light. 'What d'you want?'

Arnie was standing in a booth, ankle deep in used Kleenex. 'How can you come in this? It's disgusting.'

'Do you mind, Arnie! This is where I work!' Her rear cheeks quivered as she shouted above the music, giving the eyes behind a second, albeit smaller, spasm.

'Just tonight, Lucy. Help me out, please. Do me a favour, will you? I want to go to a hotel.'

Lucy turned back. The eyes were closed and receding. She'd done her job, and after all, it was Arnie who was asking. She dotted on her too-high heels towards the low entrance door of the barrel. Within seconds her coat was on and they were heading back up the corridor towards night light. They went past Jock in the entrance before he realized what was happening. He jumped up quickly. 'Lucy! Blue Lucy, you bitch! Come back!' He followed them onto the street, shouting at their backs as they walked away. 'What are they supposed to peep at?'

'There's no-one there, Jock!' Lucy yelled over her shoulder.

'There'll be some coming soon!'

'Not without me, they won't!'

'They're tossers, Jock!' Arnie took his second risk of the night as he strode down the crowded pavement with his girl on his arm.

'Lucy, I'll massacre you!' Jock stood outside the peep show. There was a part of him that was idly wondering whether he was going to go psycho, inhabit the scream and watch Arnie disintegrate in blood and shit. Apparently not. He turned and prodded a filthy finger at the girl in the booth. 'Your turn in the barrel. And don't fucking argue.' He took her seat by the cash drawer and didn't even bother to watch her arse wiggle as she disappeared sulkily into the interior. He picked up the paper and reread the racing results, dead calm.

Arnie felt better now he was with Lucy. She was comfortable, like an old overcoat. She never inspired him, or changed his mood, but she took the edge off things and made him feel warmer. The fact that at this moment she was striding by his side, stone naked except for a G-string under her coat, made him smile.

'What hotel, Arnie?'

'I'll show you.'

They moved on through the thinning late-night crowd, across wet pavements that reflected the West-End lights above. They didn't talk much as they walked, and as they passed the Kundora Coffee House they didn't look in.

If they had, they'd have seen Ronnie, who was sitting up the back on a white plastic chair at a white Formica table under white neon light opposite Mathilda, who was very black, heart as well as skin. She was close to tears. Her longing for Ronnie was so intense and so eternal that the pain had become almost entirely what she was.

'Come back with me, Ron.'

Ronnie took a look round at the late-night disasters propped against the tables and showing their cracks in the bright light. He was hunched and isolated as usual. 'I'll go home, thanks.'

'I'm sorry about this afternoon. That O'Dare . . .'

'It wasn't your fault.'

'You can't go back to Bernie farting in your ear in that little tiny room for the rest of your days.'

'It's quite entertaining sometimes.'

'Ronnie?'

'I'm a bit upset.'

'Because of Charlie?' She leaned forward. Even the slightest glimpse of a feeling from Ron was raindrops in the desert.

'What upsets me is . . .' He stopped and she leaned even closer, wanting to take his hand. 'I don't think I loved him.' He took a sip of cold coffee.

'I didn't love my dad either.' Mathilda was trying to empathize. 'See, he took too much rum and ran off when I was eight.'

'I know, you told me before.'

'But what I mean is, Ron, I put him to one side, you see?'

'Perhaps I'll do that too.' He put down his cup.

'In time.' Then she took his hand. 'Come home with me.'

Ronnie looked away and watched as a drunk slowly slid to the floor. A coffee cup smashed leaving a brown pool on the white tiles. The saucer spun for a long time before it settled, and then Ronnie looked back to Mathilda and said, 'I'll go home, thanks.'

Lucy might have guessed. She looked round the room in the Sunset Hotel. 'I mean, when you said hotel, Arnie, I should have thought, and I would have said, well if that's what you want, it's all right, but the actual room he died in, Arn? I mean is that the actual bed?'

'He would have been down there. On that bit of rug.' Arnie pointed at a cheap piece of tufted pale blue. 'That's where he had the attack.'

'In this very room.' She took another look round, hoping for some kind of clue that would resolve the eternal mystery of existence and its opposite, but it was just curtains and chipped hotel furniture. 'Are you sure it was this one?'

'That's what they said. But they all look the same, don't they?'

'Well it's a morbid affair, isn't it? Push that rug under the bed.'

Arnie stared at the pristine pillows. 'That's the last thing he lay his head on.'

'This is giving me the bleeding shivers, Arnie.' Lucy looked at the wardrobe, half expecting Charlie to materialize through the door. 'Why'd he come here anyway?'

'That is the question.'

'We should have gone to my place.'

'I wanted to have a look.' He sat on the bed.

This was no good for Lucy. She had a talent for closing the door on the past the instant it was passed. Sometimes she even closed it while the past was still present, which could be construed as a capacity for self-deceit, especially as it usually happened in the middle of some of her more slanted sexual experiences. But she would have said, what you don't look for, you don't see, and what you don't think about, isn't there, so why not get on with something else? And she'd had enough of death for one day. She looked at Arnie, shoulders hunched, on the bed. 'Well. Looking's done and doing's on.' It was her favourite mantra. In her mind the sadness was over, past dissolved and future perfect. She smirked. Now for the fun. 'How do you want it then? In the shower, nice and steamy? Hmm? Or there's ice in the fridge.'

Arnie didn't move. 'I feel a bit flat, Lucy.'

'All right then, in bed with the telly on.'

'Come here.'

'Oh, Arnie . . .' She was on his knee and had his nose in her cleavage before he could change his mind.

6

Mirabelle was perched on the window sill of her attic high over the alley. She smiled as she heard Bernie snoring in his room below, and then looked up at the dark sky. The hard stone of the alley below seemed to be welcoming her as she leaned further out, but she seemed unaware of the danger as her eyes swept the darkness above. One small hand gripped the wooden window frame as her body slowly extended from the window, parallel to the ground, then, incredibly, she lay back and let go of the frame altogether. Only her heels rested lightly on the ledge, as she seemed to float thirty feet off the ground, staring up at the stars. An observer, perhaps, may have thought that she was a magician of some kind practising a trick, or that she was a member of some Eastern sect who had mastered the art of levitation. The truth, depending on the observer's faith, was either more strange or more ordinary than either.

Mirabelle was simply, and in fact, the earthly form of an angel descended. In the orders of the celestial, she was Mihr, the ancient and bright. The very same Mihr sought by the Dark Angel, Sorush, who had witnessed the death of Charlie at the Sunset. For a million years Mihr had sat in judgement on the Bridge of Sighs with Sorush, and ever since flying that place and descending to terra firma as waitress and nursemaid to Bernie, she'd waited for the Dark Angel to come in search, and as soon as Mirabelle had heard the news of Charlie's unfortunate and sexual demise, she'd known Sorush would appear soon – the death would be her excuse.

She stared up at the sky. By now she had no contact with the building at all and was suspended horizontally, lying in the air, looking up into the darkness. She was imagining the grief and the violent vows of vengeance she was sure the Dark Angel would have sworn once she had discovered her disappearance. But still the sky seemed empty.

Slowly she curled in mid-air and floated back to the window ledge. She could hear Bernie snoring in his bedroom below her and counted it as a blessing. He was her special charge, but as his well-being was so deeply connected to the essence, or more to the point, stability, of his brothers, she became effectively responsible for them as well. In her angel's eye she had seen Arnie go into the hotel room with Lucy, and that meant there was one brother still unaccounted for.

Not for long. She looked down as she heard footsteps and saw Ronnie come slowly down the alley to the restaurant door. He stopped for a moment, looking up at the building and then down to the darkened club in the basement. He unlocked the door and went into the building below as she looked further along the alley. Mathilda was standing under the lamp-post on the street corner. She was watching the lights going on and off in the building as Ronnie made his way upstairs inside. Mirabelle could see the distress in the curve of the girl's body as she turned and walked out of the light and away into the darkness of the street.

Mirabelle sadly watched her go and then looked down into the quiet and deserted alley. Today the father had been buried and she sensed that everything had begun. She knew the death of Charlie would cause an upheaval, exploding certainty and scattering habit, and any of it might threaten Bernie. He was her mission and she had to be prepared. Already she knew she was too involved in these brothers. Their hearts, minds, dreams and spirit were the continuum she rode, and despite her great powers as the angel Mihr, she began to doubt she had the strength. She breathed in, calming herself, and prayed against the weakness of her human being. It is at such times that we are tested. The Dark Angel had come.

'I am cold, Mihr.' Sorush, black-eyed, pale and beautiful, had appeared sitting astride the roof across the alley. The night sky behind her was filled by faintly moving shapes and murmurs. Only Sorush knew for sure how many angels there were. They would divide or multiply according to the function she gave them.

Mirabelle immediately exploded into the brilliant light of Mihr. Her face was hard. She said, 'Why have you come, Sorush?' Her voice had a metallic edge.

There was a silence then Sorush said, 'I am a free spirit.' She shrugged as if there were no more to her appearance than that.

But Mihr knew better and asked again, 'Why have you come?'

Sorush said simply, 'The father is dead.'

'You investigate the father?'

'What else?'

'Why should such an ordinary death concern you, the great Sorush?'

'All death is recorded and the life is evaluated. Have you forgotten the Bridge? Have you forgotten me, Mihr?' Sorush's sound became plaintive. 'Why did you desert me?'

'I have other business.'

'What business could take you from me?' The eyes of Sorush were full of pain.

' My mission is not yours.' Mihr's porcelain skin and piercing blue eyes blazed light into the enveloping and subsuming darkness of her ancient opposite. 'You are not required, Sorush.'

Sorush, moving fluid and infinite, smiled sweetly as she said, 'As you will not explain your new duty, I shall remind you of the old. The father is dead. We shall seek the picture of his life and make our judgement. As we have always done.'

'No, Sorush.'

Kasbeel, the Ancient Angel, had remained still and hunched in the shadow of the roofs. He spoke; the sound was of shifting sand. 'Mihr, Angel of Light. Sorush, Angel of Darkness. In eternal conjunction on the Bridge of Sighs.'

'I have flown that place!' There was anger in Mihr's voice.

'And I have followed after, Mihr. You can never separate from me.' Sorush seemed to be moving closer, enveloping the White Angel's light. 'You shall for ever plead mercy and I shall for ever condemn. You shall for ever show them across the Bridge and I shall for ever hurl them down.'

'Be that as it may, I am not of this investigation.'

'You have no choice!'

'None.' Kasbeel spoke again.

'Kasbeel . . .'

'In eternal conjunction, Mihr.' The voice of the Ancient Angel quietened Mihr. She felt the black pulse of Sorush and retaliated with bright shafts of her own, as they fought their time-honoured battle of light and dark.

The Dark Angel said, 'Shall we begin? The father?'

'No . . .' Mihr made one last attempt, but it was too late, Kasbeel had opened his book. Her flight had failed, Sorush had come and the judgement of Charlie Lack was upon them. She accepted it as heaven's way.

Kasbeel began the incantation, 'I require thee, O Lord Jesus Christ, that thou give by the virtue and power over all thine angels, which were thrown down from heaven . . .'

Sorush smiled, triumphant, 'See, Mihr.'

'Adonay, Horta, Amay, Mitai . . .' Kasbeel began the litany of fallen angels.

And Mihr looked down at the brothers' father in the alley.

It was a midday, sometime in the 1950s, and Charlie Lack, a strong powerful man in his thirties, stood, sharp-suited, with his hands on his hips, looking up at the old wine warehouse, his eyes alive and shining with brute happiness beneath his trim and snappy trilby. 'What do you think, Vi?'

His wife, Violet, was a beautiful bottle blonde, with fashionably permed hair and a strong well-kept body, that even after the birth of her two boys (Bernie was, as yet, unborn) was slim and moved with a muscular ease. Her most extraordinary feature was her eyes, deep green or blue, depending on the light, which were alert and sad at the same time. She often exuded a sense of vulnerability, but not at the moment. She was angry. Dressed in a well-cut navy-blue coat, she viewed her husband with distaste. 'Charlie, for Christ's sake!'

He laughed. 'Give it a chance, Vi!' He was looking up at the old warehouse, but Violet's attention was distracted. Three-year-old Ronnie had picked up a discarded gin bottle from the gutter and raised it to his mouth.

'Ronnie, put that down!'

'At least have a look, Mum.' This was Arnie, aged around twelve, standing next to Charlie, copying his hands-on-hips pose, and sensing, like his dad, that he was going to have to deal with a stupid woman.

'And you can be quiet, Arnie.' Violet had taken the gin bottle from Ronnie and didn't know what to do with it. 'I'm not interested and that's that.'

'Come on, Vi, Sayeed's gone to a lot of trouble!' Charlie turned and winked at the Bengali, who stood smiling in his deep yellow dhoti at the side of the alley.

'It's not the place, Charlie, it's where it is! Look!' She held up the gin bottle and threw it into the gaping and collapsed interior of the warehouse. 'That's what you get around here, isn't it?'

'It's not a dangerous area, Mrs Lack. I promise you.' Sayeed Sayeed made a little bow.

'Dangerous! It's perfect!' Charlie was on one, his voice was getting louder. 'Violet! Trust me!' He was leering, full of his own charm, coming towards her, arms outstretched. 'Do me the favour of having a look at what I propose.' She turned away and his voice hardened. 'Let yourself go, girl. Undo a string or two on that corset will you?'

'Shut up, Charlie.'

'Come on, fuck it.' Charlie strode past her into the warehouse. Arnie followed gleefully as Sayeed Sayeed touched Violet's shoulder.

'It will be all right,' he said gently.

The place was in ruins, musty and dark, and the first-floor ceiling had fallen in. Charlie looked round with delight at the wrecked vats, caved-in barrels, splintered shelves and years of garbage strewn across the floor. He sniffed at the clammy smell of ancient alcohol that still hung about the place. 'It's a dream come true. What do you think, Arnie?'

36

'It's a dream come true, Dad.'

Charlie turned. Violet had picked up Ronnie and was standing in the doorway with him in her arms, backlit and silhouetted by the sun.

'It's where it is, Charlie! Why can't you listen! Look at this place. Who do you think walks up and down this alley at midnight? I don't want the boys to see that!'

'It's Soho, Vi! They come to the theatre, they go to the flicks, they come from everywhere to go snouting all about round here, don't they? And then what?' He grinned. 'They're starving hungry! Look, we put a counter over there. Tables here and here.' She could see his vision growing in front of her and her depression deepened. This was it. Oh God, this was where she was going to bring up the kids.

'Is there a basement, Sayeed?' Charlie asked.

'Oh yes. Very big. The same as this.'

'Well there you are then. That's where the kitchen will be, won't it Arnie? You can pull the rope on the old dumb waiter. You want to do that, son?'

'Oh yeah, Dad!'

'And if there's room down there, Vi, what about a little club? We can have a glass when we feel like it.'

'Can we go home, please?'

'Sayeed, you're my man, you colourful bastard, tell my wife for me, will you?'

'It's very cheap, Mrs Lack, a very good investment.'

'In us, Vi!' Charlie really wanted her to go with him. He was pleading, but Vi knew that behind this plaintive tone there was a will she couldn't defy, and this begging was just an act. She would have to do what he wanted and she hated him for it.

'Tell her, Sayeed. I'm a success in everything except my wife. Tell her how I will do this place out. Tell her how I'm going to paint it, will you? Go on. Listen, Vi.'

'He wants to paint it yellow, Mrs Lack.'

Violet walked out of the warehouse with Ronnie in her arms. She'd lost and she knew it. She walked quickly to the end of the alley and out into the traffic, moving as quickly as she could away from the place she'd hated the moment she saw it. A news-vendor cried out and the brakes of a black saloon squealed as she disappeared into the chaos of the street.

The eyes of Sorush sparkled in the night. Even if it wasn't the Bridge, she was back where she knew she should always be, in the absolute balance of opposition to the White Angel.

'I've seen enough,' said Mihr.

'We've hardly begun,' said Sorush. Mihr looked down as the angels shifted to another vantage and time.

The walls and ceiling of the warehouse had been renovated and plastered, and Charlie was splashing yellow paint above the new restaurant window. 'There you are, matey. A nice drop of canary.' He took a step down the ladder to admire his handiwork and winked at young Arnie below him. 'Brightens the old heart, don't it?'

'Yeah, Dad.' Arnie was painting below the window, trying to keep up with his old man.

Charlie began to sing as he painted again, 'You are my sunshine, my only son shine! Come on Arnie, keep up! You make me happy when walls are yellah!'

Arnie tried to keep pace. 'You are my only son shine!'

'You're behind, son.' Charlie continued the song as Arnie dropped the brush and ran up the stairs to the flat above. He was full of excitement and covered in paint. He loved this new place, everything about it was brilliant, and it wasn't pokey like the old flat in the south for a start. There were loads of different rooms and there was a restaurant and there was going to be a kitchen, and Dad had said he could earn himself a few bob by pulling up the dumb waiter and helping, when they got the cook, and running errands. He shouted out in sheer delight as he took the stairs two at a time.

'You are my son shine, Mum! You are my son shine, Mum!'

Violet was on edge. The argument was done; she'd packed up the old flat, said her goodbyes and had even looked smiley and keen as her neighbours in Streatham had turned their noses up and mouths down when they'd heard of Charlie's hopes and plans. She'd pretended she would be in touch, but in truth was glad to be rid of them, with their grimy hands and foul mouths. She'd never liked them or what they'd stood for, but where they'd come was worse because she sensed it was the summit, the fulfilment of her husband's dream, and no matter what became of it, there would never be another move. This was what she'd married. She could see her future in the collected junk that was overflowing from the cardboard boxes and beer crates that surrounded her in her tiny new living room. It was the trash of her past and the bedrock of what would be. It was Charlie, just Charlie, and she was nowhere in sight. She felt listless as she unpacked. She had no idea of where to put it all and even less idea whether she wanted it anyway.

'Ronnie, come here! Get out of that!' She pulled the three-year-old out of the box of old newspapers and coiled brown twisted electrical flex that Charlie had insisted they keep in case it came in useful.

'Mum, Mum!' Arnie ran in.

'Arnie, look at your bloody clothes!'

He looked up at his mother's angry face. He sensed a fight going on between his parents that he didn't understand, but he knew whose side he was on. He sang defiantly. 'You make me happy when walls are yellah!'

Violet snapped and suddenly shook him. 'Shut up! Bloody shut up!'

Arnie burst into tears. 'I didn't mean it.'

She instantly regretted what she'd done and hugged him. 'I know, I know. I'm sorry.'

He wiped his face with the back of his sleeve, leaving a smear of yellow. 'We done it, Mum. Dad wants you to come and have a gander.'

'A look, Arnie. I'm not a duck!'

'Vi, come and have a butcher's.' Charlie had walked in behind Arnie with a big grin on his face.

'A look, Charlie! A look! I'm not a piece of meat!'

'Whatever you want, darling. Just come and rest your eyes on it. Canary yellah.' He put his arm round his son, sensing the tension in his wife.

Arnie sang again, 'Don't take my canary yellah walls away!'

Violet looked at the pair of them covered in paint. 'He thinks he's going to be just like you, Charlie.'

'What's wrong with that?'

'Tell him how to make pennies when you spend your life giving pounds away!'

'What?' Charlie was baffled. He'd taken months to raise the cash for the move and renovation. What was she going on about now? 'What's up, Vi?'

'I've had enough! I've had enough, Charlie!' There were tears in her eyes. She sat down quickly on a chair, facing away from him. 'I don't want to be here! It's all wrong. I know it's wrong!'

Charlie glanced at the boys. Arnie was already getting upset. 'Here y'are son, pick up your brother and go for a walk.' He handed Arnie a few coppers. 'Show him the yellah. Teach him how to sing it and go and buy a yellah lollipop. Go on.'

He waited as Arnie took Ronnie's hand and led him out. He heard them singing in their high voices as they went down the stairs, then he went and crouched quietly behind Violet.

'Go away, Charlie.'

'Nothing's wrong, everything's right.' He touched her shoulder and sang softly. 'You'll never know dear . . .'

'It's too much, Charlie. You're too much.'

He finished the line of the song, '. . . how much I love you.' She turned back to him, crying now as he carried on singing, 'Please don't never, not no how, take my sunshine away.'

'Charlie . . .'

'Give us a kiss, my sweetheart.'

She looked at him, her eyes dark blue with tears, then she leaned forward and kissed him, forcing her tongue into his mouth, as if getting inside the cause would somehow take all her doubt and pain away. He began to unbutton her blouse.

'. . . Surunat, Ysion, Ysesy and by all the holy names.' Kasbeel closed the book as he came to the end of the incantation.

Mihr's light was dimmed. The Dark Angel was molten darkness moving within and beyond intense black eyes and a suddenly voluptuous mouth. 'We shall see more, Mihr.' Then she gave a look as if she were a lover spurned and was gone.

Mirabelle was shaken. The thought of investigation and judgement of those she knew and had known through mortal form, horrified her. 'Oh God, please give me the strength to withstand Sorush.' She looked up at the sky and saw no sign that she had been answered or even heard. She settled back into the hard wood of the window sill and the rock of her own faith, in the hope that whatever Sorush may show her, the Dark Angel would never discover the real reason for her flight from the Bridge. Or at least she hoped that Sorush would never discover the heart of her mission before she knew it herself. This was the cause of her confusion. Her instruction had been only to protect the youngest brother, but she didn't know why such an ordinary mortal had been given such an extraordinary safeguard as she, Mihr, the Angel of Divine Mercy? She stared up at the quiet sky as Bernie snored beneath her. Even in her brief time in this place, she'd begun to sense that there was something in him that would never be truly understood by those he lived amongst – and perhaps never by herself either.

$$7$$

Bernie counted his breakfast. Eggs, three; sausages, four; bacon, four; tomatoes, five; black pudding, one; fried bread, two; beans, a hundred, and six toast. He was satisfied and began to eat. 'Fanks, Meebelle.'

She was already exhausted. The brothers' breakfasts were done, but Harriet wasn't down yet, no doubt suffering from her excess at the wake the night before. The old aunt had slept in Charlie's bed, and Mirabelle could tell she was preparing to move in on a more permanent basis. The brothers wouldn't complain. Harriet had become such a fixture in the restaurant and club that no-one noticed whether she came or went; she seemed to always be there as just another fact in the life of the Lacks – like huge breakfasts. Mirabelle sat down under the restaurant window and watched Bernie and Ronnie hack their way through the fry.

Arnie sat at the other end of the table reading the paper. He'd left Lucy asleep in the Sunset, paid their bill and wandered around the streets for an hour at dawn. The comfort of his woman was fine while it was fine, but at the precise moment it got that way, he felt obliged to leave. He'd given her a kiss, though, before he went. Then he'd idled his way back home. He'd been first for Mirabelle, had eaten most of her spread, and then buried himself in the sports pages.

Ronnie, halfway through his eggs, was pensive. Something would have to be done about Mathilda, but he didn't know what. She was the most beautiful girl on the streets and everyone fancied her. Why didn't he? And there was something else stirring too. When he'd looked up at the building last night, he'd felt a weird desire. He hadn't known what it was, and then as he'd walked upstairs a word had occurred. This word hadn't so much come into his mind as kind of turned in his stomach, like some old worm that had lived there for years and finally popped up to introduce himself. The word that said hello was 'design'. For anyone outside of Ronnie it would have seemed obvious. Design? What else? He was the snappiest, sharpest dresser around. Ronnie was design, wasn't he? But to himself, the word had never meant a thing. Until last night, when he'd looked up at the place in the moonlight and he'd thought about what he'd said in the restaurant that afternoon, about changes that would have to be made. 'Change', there was another word. They were coming thick and fast, sometimes doubling up like 'move on', or 'lifestyle', and even turning themselves into incomprehensible phrases such as 'get another life' and 'who are you, anyway?'. He hadn't been able to sleep. Was it to do with Mathilda? If it was, he couldn't work out how. He'd got up early and done some thinking, then gone for a little walk. When he'd come back, he'd got a pencil and a piece of card and had begun to . . .

Bernie farted. It was long, rich, low, and he was proud of himself.

Arnie looked up. 'I'm trying to read the paper, Bernie.'

'It weren't me, Arn. It was Ron.'

'I never fart at breakfast, Bern. It ruins the day,' said Ronnie.

Arnie turned a page. 'Spurs lost.'

'Oh no!' Bernie was devastated.

'See what I mean?' said Ronnie as he shovelled more egg into his mouth.

Bernie was considering the connection between his arsehole and the Premier League when Harriet walked in holding her head and looking very pale. 'Pour me some tea, Mirabelle dear, I'm on the shake.' She sat down and turned nauseously away from Bernie's plate of grease. 'Thank God we only die once in a lifetime. What's my stars, Arnie?'

'I shouldn't bother.' Ronnie gave Bernie a sad look.

'A bad day. Don't get up,' Arnie read.

'What I tell you, Bernie?'

'You're having me on, Ron.'

'How am I?'

'I dunno.' Bernie paused, then grinned. 'It was a good one though, wan' it?'

'Shut up, Bernie, will you?' Arnie raised his nose over the paper.

'Sorry, Arn.' Bernie jammed a whole sausage into his mouth.

'Were those really my stars, dear?' asked Harriet.

'Yes.'

'I'll see Freddie tomorrow then.'

'He'll say the same thing if you see him today, tomorrow or next week.' Arnie's mood was sour.

'Who's this geezer, Freddie, then?' Bernie wanted to know.

'He's our solicitor, dear,' said Harriet.

'Oh. What's a solicitor then?'

'A necessary evil, dear.'

'Oh. What's he going to say to us then?'

'It's about your dad's will, dear.'

'Oh. What's a will then?'

'Oh, shut up, you prat!' Arnie glared.

'It's about us takin' over the restaurant, Bern, so we can have ambition and not fart, and things like that.'

'Fanks, Ron.'

'And we can change it too.' Ronnie said this with a sideways look at Arnie.

'What for?' Arnie's nose began to twitch.

'Because we have to progress, Arn. Dad's gone, so it's us now, and we're different. Aren't we?'

'You might be.'

'I intend to be, Arnie.' Ronnie wasn't entirely sure where his new-found certainty was coming from and was already beginning to feel faintly uneasy. 'I mean, I don't mean the walls. I think we'll keep the walls yellah. I like the yellah.'

'Yellah's fine by me, Ron,' Arnie agreed.

'Comes in handy if someone frows an egg at it,' said Bernie.

'That's right.' Ronnie was relieved to revert for a moment to a bit of banter. This design was hard work.

'No good for red sauce though.'

'Nor for gravy neither, Bern.'

'No, yellah's only good for eggs.' Bernie liked his jokes and he began to chuckle. It began as a rumble in his bowels and chugged up like an old slow train through his ribcage, bulged in his throat and then burst in low, deep, rhythmic pulses from the bottom of his face. Mirabelle smiled and Ronnie decided to go for it.

'You see, Arn, bein' as this is a restaurant, then the food's the thing.'

'What?' Arnie looked up from the paper again.

'In my view that's where the ambition starts. You think Porkie's up to heightenin' the menu?'

'Finds ham, egg and chips a bit of a handful don' he?'

'He was vomiting on the celery the last time I saw him,' Harriet thought to mention.

'I mean, he's Italian, in' he? Must mean somethin',' Ronnie pushed on.

'What are you talking about?' asked Arnie.

Ronnie produced the piece of card he'd worked on in his bedroom before breakfast. 'This.'

'What's that?'

'It's a new menu, Arnie. What do you think?'

'Oh fuck.'

8

Porchese wasn't impressed by Ronnie's idea either. 'No! No! No! No e no!' He was white with sickness and was leaning on the bar in the early morning club. He'd furtively swallowed a leftover cocktail he had found from the night before in the hope that it might pick him up. It had. Then it had tossed him in the air and hurled him straight back into the last moments of the drunken haze that he could barely remember from the kitchen the previous afternoon. At least that's what Ronnie hoped had happened as he sniffed Porchese's glass and prodded the rapidly hardening, sticky green residue left at the bottom. This extreme reaction from the little chef couldn't be entirely due to his new menu. Or could it?

Porchese stared at Ronnie's scrap of card on the bar. 'Spaghetti Napoletana? Spaghetti Milanese? Pizza quattro formaggio!' He stared up at Ron, pissed, perspiring and eyes bulging. 'Are you crazy! I am from Leytonstone! You know how long bus is from Leytonstone? One hour and one quarter! Every day for ten years! I don't do this for no Eyetie spaghetti joint! I do it for Charlie!' He picked up his coat from a bar stool and began to pull it over his off-whites. 'Charlie! You get me?'

'Just a thought, Porkie. I got it from Giuseppe down the road . . .'

'No, no e no!' Porchese staggered towards the basement door, then turned, waving his hand at the discarded menu. 'And I don't do no veggie bar neiver! No veggie food for veggie people! I am Porchese Dimarco! Egg and bacon!' He opened the door and half fell up the steps leading to the alley.

'Porkie . . .'

'I don' do nothing, no more!'

'Wait a minute, Porkie . . . !' Ronnie considered following him, but knew it was useless. There was the determination of drink about Porchese, that would almost certainly carry him as far as Leytonstone and probably further, as he'd undoubtedly fall asleep before he got there and miss his stop. Anyway, even if he did come back he'd only be sick again in the kitchen. Ronnie watched the little chef go up the steps outside on his knees.

'Egg and bacon!' Porchese's heels disappeared from view.

Ronnie sighed, then turned as he heard a step behind him. Arnie was standing at the bottom of the inside stairs. 'Porkie didn't think a lot of you heightenin' the menu then, Ron?'

'I agree with you there, Arn.' Ronnie wandered back towards the bar, looking round the place in a way Arnie didn't like. 'You ever thought about alternative cabaret?'

'You ever thought about who was going to do the lunch trade now we don't have a chef?'

'I was thinking about puce.'

'What?'

'For the walls, Arn. It's an option. Think about it.' Ronnie looked around again, letting colour charts slide idly across his mind before vaguely wandering up the stairs to the restaurant, his new world growing by the minute in his brain.

Arnie stared at the club wall and then shouted up the stairs, 'What's wrong with maroon? I like maroon!' But Ronnie had gone and he leaned over the bar and poured himself a surreptitious double, then, what the fuck, treble Scotch, and sat on a bar stool. 'Puce!' He sank the whisky and then realized he'd just done exactly what he'd seen his old man do, at exactly this time, every day of his life. The thought so depressed him that he needed another drink. He was reaching back over the bar towards the optic when he heard a sound on the basement steps behind him. That was all he needed, some drunk at ten thirty in the morning. He shouted without looking round, 'We're closed!'

'You kidding?'

Arnie turned, then nearly fell off the stool. Standing just inside the door was the radiant vision of Miss Raphaella Riss. Like a curvy madonna, her form was neatly haloed by the golden sunbeams gloriously flickering through the inch-thick dust on the basement window.

'Raphaella?' Arnie's mouth hung open.

She smoothed her dress slowly from breast to thigh, waited a second and then said, 'Hi, Arnie.'

'Raphaella?' He said it again.

'Hi.' She just stood there, sex on wheels with no brakes. She puckered her lips and enquired nonchalantly, 'You want a quick screw in the little yard out the back between the garbage and the old cupboard where Charlie kept the paint?'

'Raphaella?' Arnie's throat went dry.

'Look, you want it or don't you?' She was in no mood for debate.

Did he want it? Did he want the moon in his pocket? Something around that size was there already. 'Yes.' It was a croak, the best he could do.

'You do.' She considered him for a second, then, 'Not now, OK?' (It definitely wasn't OK.) 'See, Papa's upstairs and he go crazy if he go for pee-pee and see his little baby pantie down and leg up on a trash can.'

'Would he?' Arnie didn't understand how he could go so high and fall so low in the time it took for Raphaella to change her mind.

'Sure, stupid.' She smoothed her dress again, this time from thigh up, bunching her breasts together as she got to the top. 'So I go to Wonderland and win maybe two hundred on the slots. See you, Arnie.'

'See you, Raphaella.' He watched as she walked up the steps outside. She went up one foot in front of the other. Just like that. What a miracle she was. He sniffed the perfume still hanging in the air and raised his eyes to heaven. 'Thank you.' Then he poured himself another treble. 'For nothing.'

*　　*　　*

The drunk Arnie had imagined to be descending to the club, had in fact manifested himself in the restaurant. It was Martin, an acid Welshman who'd made a fool of himself with O'Dare in the club the night before. Having slopped his way through part of a breakfast, then forgotten how to eat the rest, he stood swaying in front of Harriet at the till. His pockets were turned inside out and his palms were up, coinless. 'Wednesday, Auntie. I promise.' He spoke with a camp Welsh trill.

'Martin, most of us have breakfast before we have a drink.'

'Uncle didn't send my cheque.' There was something about Harriet that reminded Martin of his mother. He began to look like a little boy, getting younger by the second.

Harriet could see she had to move fast. 'We all have to pay what we owe, dear, from the midwife to the undertaker and probably after. As far as you're concerned, Wednesday never comes.' She stuck out her hand. 'I want it now.'

Martin stared at her hand as if he didn't know what it was, then leaned slowly forward and whispered in Harriet's ear, 'Nirvana. Two o'clock. Newmarket.'

'Are you sure?'

'As I'm standing here.' He staggered backwards.

'I don't know how you hold it down, dear.'

'Wednesday.' Martin used the continuing momentum of the stagger to make a sideways lurch towards the door, which was fortunately opened at that precise moment by Mirabelle coming in. Finding air where he expected glass he fell, unimpeded, through the gap, and didn't stop until he hit the wall on the other side of the alley with the top of his head. He remained motionless, bent over, with his arms hanging limp at his side. After about five seconds, he suddenly stood straight, ruffled the brick dust out of his hair and strode away whistling. Then he fell over.

'Oh dear.' Harriet looked up expecting to see Mirabelle, but she'd dashed through the restaurant and up the stairs. She'd been replaced by Luis Riss, smart and unruffled in a pale-green, box-cut single-breasted. He'd observed the whole scene.

'Oh dear is correct, Harriet.' He put his hand in his pocket. 'One Danish, one coffee. No sugar.'

'We don't charge for sugar, Mr Riss. Why don't you have some?'

Luis missed the irony. 'Thank you, very nice.' He paid her and looked round the restaurant. His big idea still hadn't fully formed. By now he knew it was to somehow take over the restaurant. Now Charlie was gone, the boys wouldn't be too much of a problem. But precisely how to do it? That was the question. 'Nice place, nice food. Good possibilities, but . . .' He stopped with a sad shrug, looking up the alley to where Martin was struggling to get up. 'Non-payment for services rendered. Bad business. Maybe possibilities not so good.'

Harriet was ruffled. 'Our prospects are excellent, Mr Riss. My brother was a generous man, an honourable man, and all his obligations will be paid in full by his three sons.'

Luis gave her a look. This was interesting. 'Obligations? You mean debt?' A little spasm of excitement tickled the root of his spine and shot brainward. He contained it and asked innocently, 'Charlie got a lot of debt?'

'Our slate will be scoured, Mr Riss.'

Luis shook his head. 'Bad business.' He looked away, hardly able to keep a straight face. Bad business! It was all falling into place! Debt! It was the best news he'd had for a week! He yawned and dropped tuppence into the tip jar and then, as usual, his moment was ruined by Raphaella. He noticed her coming up from the club room and walking away down the alley in a manner that anything with a penis would have considered as soliciting. He smirked at Harriet, caught between the dizzying brilliance of the business plan that had arrived fully formed in his brain, and his fury at his daughter. He coughed twice, said, 'Ah,' and then hurried out without saying goodbye.

Harriet gave him a sour look as she watched him through the window. He had lost Raphaella already and was scuttling up and down Dean Street, craning his neck in the traffic. 'We all have our crosses to bear, Mr Riss.' She smiled to herself and picked up the phone by the till and dialled. 'Mr Mercedes? It's Harriet Lack. How are you, dear?' She waited for a second as the bookie grunted a response at the other end of the line. 'Ten pounds on the nose. Nirvana. Two o'clock. Newmarket. Thank you.'

9

Raphaella had craftily ducked through St Mary's passage, cut fast across Wardour Street, shot through the market, and had already made fifteen pounds in her brother's slots arcade before the owner pounced. 'How you do it?' Emil looked down in amazement as the coins crashed into the bowl.

'Don't be stupid, big brother, don' you know how to play the slots yet?' She was about to insert another coin when Emil grabbed her by the collar and yanked her away. 'How many times I tell you? You don' play no bandits! And especial, you don' play none of my bandits!' He dragged her towards the small office at the back.

Raphaella struggled violently. 'Get off me, Emil, or I stab your eyes out!'

'Shuddup!' He dragged her through the machines. 'You don' cream no profit off your own family! You're banned! You get me? B–A–N–D. Banned!' He pushed her through the narrow brown door and into the office, where Lucy and Scotch Jock were sitting in front of an electric fire, eating their lunchtime sandwiches. 'Out!' Emil yelled into their faces, still holding the wriggling Raphaella. 'Out! Out!' He glared at Lucy. 'Don' you got no tits to swing round? Don' you got no-one to peep?'

Lucy was indignant. 'I'm entitled to eat, you know!'

Jock could see that this wasn't the best time to explore the rights of the female worker and pulled Lucy up. 'Shut up.' He grovelled to Emil. 'Sorry boss.' Then he went out, but Lucy jerked her arm out of his hand and stood by the door with as much dignity as she could. She opened her coat and flicked the sandwich crumbs off her bare thigh. 'I don't see why I should be treated like . . .' Her tone was a mistake. Emil grabbed her coat with one hand while still holding Raphaella fast with the other. 'You want to talk? So tell me. Where you go last night?'

'What?'

'You piss off from the peep with Arnie.'

'I had to go to the dentist.'

'At midnight?'

'Emergency.'

'What emergency?'

'Root treatment.'

'You listen to me.' He pulled her into his face so she could feel his foul breath up her nose. 'You take off when you're working and you see that Lack again and . . .'

'I kill you!' Raphaella finished the sentence for him.

'Shuddup!' Emil grabbed his sister harder, and pulled the two women nose to nose with his own in between. 'Arnie Lack ain't in no picture I paint. You get me?'

Neither of them did, but their sheer proximity, lip gloss to eyelash was enough. Their rivalry was street legendary. They growled, spat and parted like two alley cats on a wall, fur up and backs arched. Emil took a pace back, wishing he hadn't started it. Lucy hissed, 'Bitch!'

'You stupid silly slag.' Raphaella's voice was high and her tone patronizing. She tossed her mane and pouted her lips in a pose she imagined to be superior. Lucy stayed cat and moved towards the door, never taking her eyes off her prey. 'Bitch!' She hissed it again, her sibilance like gas, lasting until the door-slam cut it off.

Disconcerted by the electricity of the silence where once there'd been a peep-show worker, Raphaella attempted a small smile. Emil took his chance and grabbed her again. 'Don' I never see you in here, no more! No more slots! No more bandits! Go home and watch TV!'

'I don' want to watch TV! I seen everything!'

'So watch repeats!' He pushed her away, but before she could go the door opened and their father came in fast, followed by his main minder, Razor Jam, a blanked-out Sikh from Birmingham. Scotch Jock, who obviously hadn't gone back to the peep with Lucy as he should have, was still standing just outside the door, trying to look busy and impress Luis.

'Hey, Papa, you know what?' Emil pointed a long finger at his sister. 'This girl been on the slots again.'

'So what? I don' have no money!' Raphaella shouted.

'And what you doing swanning all over with a tight skirt on your backside outside the Lack place?' Luis wanted to know.

'I was looking for you, Papa. I don' have no money! Give me some money, Papa. Please.' As usual she used the big eyes and pouting lips of a ten-year-old, but couldn't believe her luck when Luis suddenly produced two fifties out of what seemed nowhere. This was at least twice as much and twice as fast as she'd expected.

'Wha . . . ?' Emil's mouth sagged open.

'My angel,' Luis bared his brown teeth, 'my sweet little angel. Here, for you, go an' buy something pretty.' He pushed the money at Raphaella.

'Oh Papa!' She pursed her lips and threw her arms round his neck, but her legs were already moving and dragging her upper body towards the door, so the kiss went unconsummated.

'Go with her. Buy the dress. Get her home,' Luis shouted to Jock across the flash of Raphaella's departure. 'Don't let her out of your sight!' Even staying only to hear the end of the instruction, Jock had to run to catch up with her.

Luis barked at the Sikh. 'Close the door.' Razor Jam did so with a thud, as Emil sank onto the battered chair by the desk.

'What is this? A free world?'

'Shuddup!' Luis grinned. 'Shuddup and listen!'

'Shuddup, he says. He just give the crazy bitch a ton, don't you?'

'Shuddup Emil! Listen to me. I give her a ton, I give you a grand, I take a million! We got business, Emil!' He was so pleased with himself, he started to shake. 'What business we got!'

'What business?' Emil looked at Razor, who remained blank.

'I know how to do it! One small Danish and I got a restaurant! And a club! And a house!'

'You talking about the Lack place?'

'What else?' Luis took the pause and beamed, feeling magnificent. 'He got debts!'

'So what? Who don't?' Emil was still sulking.

'Why I got such a stupid offspring? Debts? Don' you get it? Debts is liability. Debts is door to paradise!'

'Wha . . . ?'

'Shuddup.' Luis hadn't got time to waste on Emil's snail brain. 'Don' think. Do what I say.'

'Do what?'

'Go find everyone who trade with Charlie. Everyone! They sell him vodka, they sell him potatoes, you find them!'

'Ah, Papa, excuse me, but . . . ?'

'Shuddup! Do it!'

Emil got up. He'd only seen his old man like this once before and that was when he'd pulled the junction scam and got a filling station for free. It was worth 100,000, Emil remembered. As a matter of fact they were still living off the proceeds.

'Get out! Do the business! Debts! Find the debts of Charlie Lack!' Luis sat down after they'd gone. His hands were on the table, his squat little legs open wide in front of him. Then he began to wriggle his shoulders, shaking himself out, getting prepared. This was it, the game was on. 'I always wanted a restaurant.'

10

The place Luis coveted was packed. The lunch trade had been carefully built up by Charlie who knew the value of a cheap chip and cheerful service. Mirabelle pushed through the crowded tables, crashed a pile of dirty plates into the dumb waiter and yelled down into it. 'One liver and bacon and chips. One sausage and tomato and beans and chips.' She pulled the rope and sent down the empties.

Ronnie was on the grill, turning eggs and burgers as the crockery landed in the corner of the kitchen. He quickly pulled it out of the dumb waiter and dumped the lot into the sink, breaking three saucers, then he slammed two meals into the hatch. 'Here's egg and black pudding and beans. And egg and two sausage and tomato! And no omelette, no Porkie!' He reached for the rope.

'Wait a minute.' Arnie jammed in another plate before Ronnie could pull the dumb waiter up. He shouted up to Mirabelle. 'Two eggs and one sausage and beans and fried bread!'

'That should be two sausages and one egg,' Ronnie said as he moved back to the grill.

'What?' Arnie turned and yelled up the hatch. 'One or two sausage?'

Mirabelle's voice echoed down, 'Which one?'

'The one with the beans and fried bread.'

'Which one with the beans and fried bread?'

'The one before the liver.'

Mirabelle flicked through her order pad and yelled down, 'Which one before the liver? The one with the tomato, or the one with the black pudding?'

All she heard was, 'Bollocks!' and then the sound of the kitchen hatch being slammed. Arnie walked back to the stove. 'All tastes the same anyway.'

Sophie sat on her usual stool carving the chips. 'When's Porkie coming back?'

'Might be better if he didn't.'

'Make me laugh, Ron, just make me laugh, will you?'

'All revolution involves struggle, Arn.' Ronnie carefully turned a burger.

'You what?'

'All revolu . . .'

'I heard you the first time!'

Mirabelle shouted down again, 'Two poached eggs, yolks runny.'

Arnie decided to ignore it. 'What revolution?' But Mirabelle wasn't going to go away. Her voice reverberated from the hole in the wall. 'And Harriet says you've got to go and see Freddie the solicitor.'

Arnie stuck his head into the hole and yelled back up. 'Tell her we're too busy to go and see Freddie because we don't have a chef! And don't tell me how to poach an egg!' He pulled his head out and faced Ronnie, his nose twitching.

'See, Arn, I thought we might go . . .'

'I am! I am going myself! I'm going on the bus to Leytonstone and I don't care how long it takes, and I'm going to offer Porkie lira, Ron!'

'No, Arn. See, I thought we might go French.'

Arnie's mouth sagged. He couldn't believe it. He looked round the grease and chaos. 'French!' He was starting to splutter.

Mirabelle yelled down again. 'Harriet says good about Freddie 'cos her stars are bad, and two eggs and three sausages and tomato and a fried slice and beans and black pudding and double chips!'

'And what about snails? And what about fucking *escargots*?' Arnie slammed the hatch door shut. 'Who eats this stuff anyway?'

'The whole world, dear.' Sophie dropped a handful of chips into the frier.

11

And as the chips sizzled, so the Riss mob slid their greasy fingers into Charlie's fat. Luis stood in the shadows at the back of the Polish deli belonging to Otto Petrowski and his wife, Tanya, who'd both been grieving at Charlie's wake less than twenty-four hours before. Tanya was slicing Armenian sausage on the counter. She cocked her ear towards her husband, who was standing by the cheese rack, half hidden in shadow, as Luis whispered to him, 'Two thousand, Otto? Charlie owed you two thousand? You're kidding me?'

Otto shrugged, the rolls of fat on his waist rolled up and down. 'How you keep a business and friends also, huh?'

Luis looked concerned. 'You think you get it back? I mean from Arnie or the other brothers? Or Harriet or what?'

Tanya shot a glance as Otto answered. 'Charlie don't have it, why come his boys get it?'

Luis took a little circular walk. The smell of the cheese was making him feel sick and he'd have preferred to talk by the cooked meats, but it was too near the front of the shop. He turned back, bottling the nausea and affecting distress. His eyes filled with tears. How was Otto to know it was the Danish blue? 'I tell you something.' He looked directly into Otto's eye. 'I love Charlie. And on my heart, I want to help out his poor boys. I got two kids myself. What's Emil without me, huh? Just a lost little boy in a double-breasted, you know? Otto, I ask you? What's a kid without a papa?'

Tanya knew what was coming. Maybe Otto did, but he hid it in his chins and wiped the sweat from his eye with a tea towel.

Luis went on, 'Look, I tell you what I do. Just to help out these boys, you understand? I take your two thousand debt for five fifty, OK? Then I say to the boys, give me what you got and we all get back to friendship after the grief. What you think?'

'Five fifty isn't too much when the debt is two thousand.' Tanya had said it so softly that at first Luis thought it was Otto without his lips moving. 'A thousand five hundred.' Tanya spoke louder this time.

She was asking for too much, but Luis knew he had them. She was dealing and that meant they didn't expect the cash back. Who would? Charlie didn't pay up when he was breathing, what hope now he was six feet under? 'Tanya, Tanya, listen to me. I am a generous man, but I got a family to keep, and I don't have no wife no more.' He shrugged as if this explained everything.

'A thousand.' Tanya had hardly looked up, but Luis noticed that the entire Armenian sausage was now in a hundred exact slices. There was something about Tanya and her knife that worried him. But he looked on the bright side, she'd come down 500. They obviously, for sure, didn't think they were going to get a penny out of the Lack Brothers. This would have to be his line, too, as precise as the sausage slices.

'OK, let's be honest. These boys don't pay nobody. You, me, nobody. Why? Because they don't have no currency in the back pocket. So what I do? I take your debt for a grand and I don't get it back and I'm light one grand, right? But I am generous. I love them. So I give you five hundred. What you think?'

Tanya was thinking how come he talks about a grand then comes down to five hundred from five fifty? Otto was thinking, he liked the brothers and this little Maltese prick stank worse than the Camembert, but business was business. He looked at Tanya. She said, 'Eight hundred. That's it, Mr Riss,' then she picked up her knife again.

'Seven.' Luis hadn't come this far by being intimidated by a Pole.

'Tanya?' Otto was feeling bad, his wife would have to do it.

She smiled. 'Take it. Help out the boys. What else but friends?' Luis nodded sadly. She said, 'Cash, Mr Riss.'

Luis had come prepared and unloaded his wallet onto the counter. Tanya turned away and jumped as she saw Bernie across the street. He was loping along, talking to himself, carrying a white plastic bag and making her feel very bad. 'Poor darling,' she said as she watched him come to a great galumphing halt outside Emil's peep show opposite.

Bernie leaned back and poked his head forward at the same time, then with a sudden jackknife curve of his neck and shoulders, stuck his nose round the bright red doorway of the peep emporium and boomed, 'Hello Tilda!'

Mathilda came running out, as usual gorgeous in a tiny skirt and T-shirt. Jock had spent months trying to get her into the barrel, but Mathilda wasn't stripping for nobody (except Ronnie, who didn't want it) and she stayed resolutely on the cash drawer, looking after Lucy and giving the punters erections before they'd entered, which even Emil could see wasn't bad for trade. She gave Bernie a smile that half of the street would have died for, and a kiss on the cheek that stopped the rest.

'Look what I got, Tilda.' He put his hand into his bag. 'It's lots of paint in little tins. Ronnie says we might go French. Umm?'

'What do you mean, French?'

'Well see, it might be like this colour, or that colour.' He held up a couple of sample paint pots. 'What colour's French?'

'I don't know, Bernie!' Mathilda laughed.

'Got to get a shift on though, 'cos these are important and trying times, Tilda.' He pushed the top half of his body forward, his huge legs followed and he lumbered off, towering over everyone else on the street.

'Bye, Bernie. Tell Ronnie you saw me!' Mathilda looked sad as she watched him go.

'Get on the till, you slag!' Scotch Jock swaggered out of the peep. He was in more of a psychopathic mood and his brain was full, having been infected by the excitement and energy that was surging through the boys. The Riss mob was moving and it wasn't a pretty sight. Jock felt proud. And then prouder. At that very moment his boss hurried out of the deli opposite. He shouted across the street, 'Mr Riss! Mr Riss! It's me, Jock!'

Luis turned furiously. The last thing he wanted at this delicate stage in his affairs was to be perceived as a man with a mob. He laughed as if he was delighted to see his old friend, the northern maniac. 'Jock! I've bought the sausage!' He held up his hand with nothing in it and walked quickly away, intent on firing the Scotch prick at the first opportunity.

'What a man!' Jock turned to where Mathilda had been. 'Come back out here, you slag, I'm talking to yer!'

12

A few hours later Luis sat at the dining table in the huge brown living room of the Riss apartment. He picked up the phone and dialled another number. He'd been on the blower for most of the day and half the evening. It was tough; he'd sweated, he'd talked fast. Sometimes he took the sympathy line, as with Otto and Tanya, but usually it was a more straightforward offer. Charlie wasn't famous for probity. He was a *mañana* man and tomorrow never came. He'd make you laugh, buy you drinks all night and invite you to be his pal for ever, but he never came up with the notes, the spondulicks, the stuff you needed for the mortgage and the kid's new toy. Charlie had spent most of his life running on financial empty, and as Luis was rapidly discovering, there were more than a few who could have filled him up – preferably with petrol and then lit his mouth. They thought Luis was crazy. Why'd he want to buy worthless debt? It was sometimes a difficult question to answer. With most of them, he couldn't get away with pleading help for the bereaved family – they'd never have believed he was a sucker for succour – so he just told them straight, 'Mind your own fucking business. I'm offering twenty-five in the pound. You want my money or don't you?'

Which is roughly what he'd just told the grocery wholesaler from the market who was on the phone. The affirmative was immediate and Luis barked delightedly, 'Don't worry, Moshe, I'll get the cheque round in the morning.' He glanced up happily at his son counting invoices on the polished mahogany of his table, and his daughter watching a truck-size TV at the other end of the room. 'What, Moshe? You want it right now! You think I change my mind? You have the paperwork?' Luis winked at Emil. 'On your desk! I get someone round. Thank you, Moshe.' He put the phone down and reached for his chequebook. 'They can't get out quick enough! How can you run up six grand with a potato seller?'

Emil thought it was a test. 'Chips!'

'Compound interest, shithead!' Luis thumped the table in front of him. 'That's how, Emil, compound interest!'

'Right, compound interest.'

Luis handed the cheque to Razor, who'd been sitting by the door. 'Moshe. The market. Fast. Come back with invoices.'

'Yes, boss.' It was rare that Razor Jam spoke, which was just as well because the Maltesers had trouble with his Brummie accent, not to mention his turban. Was there anything beneath it? It was difficult to tell. If there was, his face wasn't letting on. They hired him because he did what he was told, and he had a razor, which he'd once used to slash a rival's face into confection, hence the nickname. He took the cheque carefully and walked out as Scotch Jock came in.

Luis held up a stack of envelopes. 'Smithfield, Gray's Inn, Warren Street, Covent and Hatton Garden. You remember where they are?'

'Sure, Mr Riss.' Jock was on his best behaviour. He'd come close to being fired for saying hello to his boss on the street, and although he hadn't understood the charge he was happy enough with the acquittal.

'Bring back invoices.' Luis handed him a stack of envelopes, some stuffed with cash. Jock hurried out as Raphaella took her thumb out of her mouth and turned from the monster screen.

'Papa, how long I got to watch TV?'

'The rest of your life!' Luis picked up the phone and dialled. He curled into the receiver, honey-voiced for starters. 'Gerald! Luis. Hey, Gerry, you hear about poor Charlie and the trouble his boys got into?'

13

'Ha, ha, ha, ha!' It was the club's first comedian up on a wooden box in the corner. He'd brought his own microphone and amplifier and was halfway through his act. Ronnie hadn't realized it could be so easy. One call and the talent agency wouldn't hear of letting him down; they'd have their very best top-line comic over there that very night, and he'd bring the bill with him, cash only please. It was a bit quick for Ron, but he hadn't known how to say no, and apparently he'd become an impresario overnight. Things were looking up. He checked his tie in the bar mirror, smoothed his suit and glanced up at the walls. The filmstar pictures would have to go, that's for sure, and what about purple instead of puce? His dream was interrupted by silence. He looked around at the bar.

They were all there: O'Dare; Martin, the acid Welshman and his leather-clad, overweight boyfriend, Geoffrey, the pompous poet and actor; a drunk and aged virgin called Michelle; a couple of friends of Lucy's taking half an hour off; John from the shoe shop; Pete the alley-man, and Arnie over by the wall. These were some of Charlie's gang, who'd probably be here drinking to the demise of the departed until their own. Now, however, they were all doing something they'd never done before, they were keeping their mouths shut. They couldn't believe their eyes. The comic was a sweet-looking boy of about seventeen, who looked more like a performing doll. He said, 'I lost my mind. It dropped out my head on the way here.' Silence. 'Anyone seen it?'

'What the fuck is that fucking eejit over there?' It was O'Dare.

'I got him from an alternative agency, Arn.' Ron smirked proudly.

'I'm not surprised, Ron.'

The comic continued, 'My mother-in-law died. Oh no!'

'Out! Out of here, yer brainless arsehole!' O'Dare was moving threateningly towards the wooden box in the corner.

'Don't worry, dear, Uncle knows how hard you try.' Geoffrey's leather trousers squeaked over his blubber and his actor's voice boomed as he moved along the bar and squeezed Ronnie's hand.

'And so does Uncle Martin.' The Welshman moved over too and touched Ronnie's shoulder.

Things quickly got worse. O'Dare went and stood beneath the comic and a physical attack looked imminent. A couple of aged toothless regulars, Barry Boy and St Jude, were beginning to sing the 'Grenadier's Lament', Michelle screamed at O'Dare to sit down, and even inoffensive Shoe-shop John started mumbling obscenities into his gin. The volume level was rising and Arnie had had enough. He was moving towards the centre of the room to sort the whole thing out when Harriet suddenly appeared at the bottom of the inside stairs. 'Arnie, Ron, I think you'd better come up to the restaurant, dears.' She looked pale.

'Ha, ha, ha, ha!' The comic was at it again.

'Will you shut your fucking trap?' O'Dare leaned back as if he was about to flob. Arnie gave O'Dare a warning look and then followed Ronnie up the stairs to the restaurant.

It wasn't often Harriet looked worried and it wasn't long before they saw why. The place was closed up for the night and Luis and Emil Riss were sitting at a gloomy table at the back. Razor Jam stood threateningly in the dark by the door and Arnie could feel Scotch Jock behind them in the shadows by the dumb waiter.

59

'It's this, dear.' Harriet handed Arnie a sheaf of invoices. 'They're all ours.'

'Mine,' Luis corrected her with a grin. 'All signed over to me.'

'What?' Arnie took the sheaf from Harriet and shuffled through the grubby scraps of paper. 'What's this?'

'Invoices, dear. They're our debts.'

Arnie held them up so he could read them by the lamplight through the window. He looked at Ron and then at Luis. 'How come you got these?'

Luis shrugged. 'Commerce, Arnie. They sell. I buy.' He shrugged. 'With these, only you owe me thirty-two thousand.'

'You what?' Arnie looked again at the invoices and handed them over to Ron one at a time as he read them out. 'Johnny Beck? Goldstone and Company? Ollie Barton? What's this? Otto and Tanya?' He looked at Harriet. It was everyone they'd ever dealt with, everyone they knew. 'They've all sold us out?' He stared at Riss. 'Thirty-two thousand?'

'No.' Luis said it simply. Arnie and Ronnie waited. The Maltese dropped his shoulders in exaggerated sorrow. 'You know me, I want to help you all I can, but . . .'

'Get on with it.' Arnie's nose was twitching.

'You know a loan shark called Walker-Pearcey?'

Arnie did. His heart skipped a beat. 'What about him?'

'Charlie borrowed every year, maybe three, maybe five thousand. All take and no give, know what I mean? Every year. Hear my words, Harriet.'

She was, and not without a certain amount of dread. 'I hardly see what it's got to do with you, Mr Riss.'

'I bought this debt also.' Luis could hardly contain his excitement as he carefully spread the relevant documents on the Formica table top in front of him. He furrowed his brow and jutted his chin in what he imagined was the manner of the fiscally sound. 'You see, Harriet. Arnie. Ronnie. And Bernie if he was here. With this,' he tapped the Walker-Pearcey invoice, 'and the inclusion of the previous, inasmuch as those what you are holding in your hand. You owe me,' he paused, 'one hundred and thirty-seven thousand pounds.'

Silence. Just the sound of the drunks downstairs. Emil couldn't hold it. 'Compound interest, right, Pa?'

'Shuddup!' This was Luis's moment and he wasn't going to have it stolen by a shit in a suit, even if it was his son.

'Wait a minute. Excuse me!' Arnie's nose was sweating as well as twitching. 'Are you telling me that you have been sniffing around in the gutter, buying up our debt, so you can sit in our house and tell us ... tell us ... ' he stopped and looked at Harriet and Ron.

Luis paused and leaned back in his chair. 'How much you think this place is worth?' It was all going better than he could have dreamed. It was game, set and match point. He could afford to expand, open up, smile and yet be a villain. 'If you want, I make you a very generous offer. If you want, I forget this debt you got to me and I give you fifty grand and you clear out the place.'

Harriet turned as if in slow motion. 'What, you take it all, dear? Lock, stock and barrels? Restaurant, club and flat?'

'And we move out?' Ronnie was catching up.

'What do we want you in our house for?' Emil grinned, ruining the sense of occasion as usual.

'Shuddup!'

'You're a very generous man, Luis.' Arnie's eyes were beginning to bulge.

'So I recover the finance through the law? Give solicitors funds for Alfa Romeos? Who needs it?'

'You get out anyway, right?' Emil couldn't remember when he'd had such a good time.

'And how about we go down the bank, get a mortgage and pay you off?' Arnie was beginning to use his head.

'Arnie, Arnie, you think bank manager's a circus clown? How you going to pay off a loan when the business is pissing money down the drain every week? Huh. Tell me?' Luis raised his hands and grinned.

'We have changes in mind, Mr Riss,' said Ronnie plaintively.

'We all got changes, Ronnie, but you don't paint the door after it is bolted, you get me?' Luis sighed elegantly and picked up the loan shark's debt from the table in front of him. 'Charlie, you know, a good friend, but I'm sorry, no head ... '

'All prick.' His son finished it off for him.

'Shut up!' It was Harriet this time and Emil jerked backwards in shock. There was none of the old man's familiarity in her tone and it scared him.

Luis continued as if nothing had happened, 'So I do Charlie a favour. For his boys and for old times. What do you think?'

'You do us a favour by kicking us out of the home and business we've had for over twenty years?' asked Arnie.

Luis offered up the papers. 'So pay full value.'

Harriet could see that Arnie's rage was on the point of getting the better of him. She stood quickly. 'We'll talk it over amongst the family, Mr Riss.' She glared at Emil. His remark about her brother's centre of gravity had shocked her more than a loss of a home ever could. She was outraged, but at least blood was running through her veins again. 'Good night.' Her lips were clamped tight.

'The offer don't last for ever.' Luis pushed himself up from the table and put on his hat. 'Nothing lasts for ever.' He moved towards the door.

'Maybe we'll sell it to someone else,' said Arnie.

'Won't get a better price, I guarantee you that.' Luis grinned. 'I come again tomorrow.' Razor held the door for him. 'I want to help you. For your father.' He laughed, then he went out into the yellow light of the alley, followed by Emil and the minders. The door swung closed behind them.

'What was all that about then?' Ronnie looked bemused.

'Fucking hell, Ron.'

The sound of a piano came from downstairs.

Geoffrey swayed on the box in the corner. The wood was creaking under his weight, but he was long past caring. If the comic's performance had been worth anything, it had been to give the drunks the idea of performance. They'd been queuing up for the box and even the piano, which had gone unplayed for years, and now Geoffrey had decided on his Shakespeare. He cleared his throat. The sound was round and portentous, 'Why did thou promise such a beauteous day, and make me travel forth without my cloak?'

'Shut your filthy fat gob, Geoffrey!' shouted Martin.

Geoffrey ploughed on. 'To let base clouds o'ertake me in my way ...'

Arnie put his hands over his ears. He was standing next to his brother, hunched over a drink at the bar. 'Game's up, mate.'

'Keep the hope up, Arn. Always do that.' Ronnie was wary. He could see the rage building in Arnie with the alcohol.

'The offender's sorrow lends but weak relief to him that bears the strong offence's cross.' Geoffrey thundered on, 'Bastard!'

Martin had thrown a pint over him. 'You pretentious wet-piss!'

'Ha, ha, ha! Look at the homosexualists!' It was O'Dare again and Arnie finally flipped from black to crimson.

'Shut up! Fucking shut the fucking well shut up!' His shout stopped the piano and the poetry in one. 'And fucking well go home!' There was silence as he glared round the club. Go home? These words had never been heard before. At least not before midnight. All movement ceased, including the flies round the cheese rolls.

'Ah? Arnie, may I suggest?' It was O'Dare. 'With regard to your father.'

Arnie, as if in aspic, turned his head the slightest fraction to fix O'Dare with a malevolent stare. 'What?'

It took nerve, but O'Dare had it. He slowly raised his glass and said, 'I could borrow a church. A treble Drambuie buys a mass for the dead.'

Arnie exploded. 'You fucking Jesuit!' Before he knew it O'Dare was off the ground and flying like a black bat over the bar. He yelled 'Dominus' in mid-air and 'Vobiscum!' as he landed with a crash in the empties. Arnie, hardly aware of what he'd done, looked down at the broken glass and the black suit of the ex-priest as he lay spread-eagled under the counter, with pale ale dripping into his big ears and a slice of lemon perched on his spit-stained gob. After a second the eldest Lack, pained to his root, raised both his arms above his head and roared like the elephant in the pit, 'I'll piss on Riss!' Then he sat heavily on a bar stool and stared at his shoes until everyone had gone and Harriet had locked the door.

14

Luis popped a chocolate in his mouth and looked across the wastes of his sofa at his daughter, who was removing her make-up with pink tissue and a gallon of astringent. She had spent another useless evening locked in the brown sitting room surrounded by nothing more exciting than heavy oak furniture. She scrubbed her face and moaned, 'In the morning it goes on, midnight it comes off. What happens in between?'

Luis could afford a smile. The master of the alley, tomorrow's land-lord of the house the Lacks built, leaned over four feet and patted a cushion between them on the sofa. 'Tomorrow we got our own apart-ment, we got our own restaurant and we got our own club. You can stay in and go out at the same time!'

'Will Arnie be there?'

Luis choked on his coffee cream. 'No he don't! That boy don't have any property except himself. And who wants it?'

'Not me! I want a restaurant!'

'So why you got a papa, my angel?' Luis began to cackle.

Raphaella tossed a tissue onto the pile on the carpet and began to laugh along with her father. She had a feeling everything was going her way.

$\boxed{15}$

It was the early hours and Mirabelle sat high on her window ledge. The alley below was deserted and the lamp-post at the end spread a lonely circle of light. All was quiet and she wrinkled her nose and raised her face to the moon, making her nightly trawl through the hearts and minds of the brothers. Bernie, as usual, was snoring in the bedroom below. Ronnie was sleeping in an armchair in Mathilda's room, as the girl herself lay beautiful in her bed, watching him with such love in her eyes that Mirabelle sighed. Then she smiled as she heard the grunts and moans of Arnie as he had sex with Lucy. Mirabelle always enjoyed witnessing Arnie's sex life. If only he could feel happier about it himself. She wanted to tell him, on the highest authority, not to feel so guilty. Have faith, Arnie. She was about to say a little prayer for him when the air suddenly froze.

Sorush was standing, wings unfurled, on the apex of the roof opposite. Kasbeel sat sternly on the sloping tiles six feet below her, and around them both were the half forms of her transparent legion filling the air and flickering the lamplight with the soft flap and beat of their moving. Mirabelle was immediately transformed into the silky translucence of Mihr, moving bright across the front of the building. She spat light from her blue eyes across the alley towards the Dark Angel.

'Such fury, Mihr.'

'I've told you, my mission is not yours.'

Sorush moved easily across the roofs. She seemed unconcerned and made no further enquiry as to the substance of this mission. She reminded Mihr that she had come to this place only to re-establish the balance they had once enjoyed on the Bridge. She was there to do her celestial duty and investigate the father, Charlie, no more.

'You ask me to make judgement on him?'

'What else?'

'I will invoke no judgement.'

'You cannot fly judgement.' Such a thought was heresy to Sorush.

Kasbeel spoke. 'Judgement is to retain the distance between Man and God. If there is no judgement, there is no God.'

Sorush moved closer. 'And no angels. And no light, nor dark. No Mihr, nor Sorush. Our existence is to judge.'

Mihr knew that what she said was true. It was this balance between them, between mercy and justice in eternity, that provided the measure of the mortal. But how could she judge those she loved? She was placed in an impossible contradiction and could feel the darkness, as it began to envelop her, making her blaze brighter and involuntarily restore this balance she rejected.

Sorush turned to the ancient. 'Kasbeel.'

His book was already open. He began the incantation. 'I require thee, O Lord Jesus Christ, that thou give by thy virtue and power . . .'

Mihr waited as Sorush stared into her eyes, black into the brightest blue, and the investigation resumed. She looked down into the alley as she heard a baby cry.

It was sometime in the 1960s, eight years after the family had moved to Soho. Charlie reeled out of the restaurant door. He was drunk and fell forward into the arms of Sayeed Sayeed, dressed in his usual yellow dhoti. He put his hands on the old man's shoulders and said, 'It's a boy.'

Arnie, aged around twenty, stood in the doorway behind his father.

He had shoulder-length hair and maroon velvet flared trousers. He was pale-faced, stoned and looked as if he had been crying.

Sayeed Sayeed laughed as Charlie began to lunge around the alley, half dancing, hardly able to stand up. 'At my bloody age! A new son!' He staggered towards Arnie and put his arms round him. 'Don't sulk, old boy! You've got a new brother!' Arnie pulled away from the hot beer breath and watched as his old man half fell back through the restaurant door. He could hear him as he made his way through the diners, cheering, back-slapping and offering drinks to anyone he passed.

'New baby bring luck.' Sayeed smiled at Arnie.

'What kind of luck, Sayeed?' Arnie leaned back against the wall and looked up. He could hear the baby crying in the flat above as Sayeed Sayeed went in after Charlie. Then he heard Charlie's voice from the bedroom. 'My boy! My lovely little boy!' Arnie waited for a while with his head leant back against the wall of the building, then he slowly pushed himself forward and walked away down the alley with his head low and shoulders hunched.

'He didn't come back for ten years.' Sorush folded her wings in sour contemplation and watched as Arnie walked away. Kasbeel continued the incantation.

Violet lay back in her bed. She was exhausted. She didn't react as her drunken husband staggered towards the midwife and chucked the chin of the baby in her arms.

'Nine pounds, three ounces. He's a big one,' said the midwife.

'Course he's a big one, he's my boy!' Charlie gently took the child into his hands and looked down on him, pride bursting out of his every pore. 'This is Bernie! Aren't you, boy?' Then he looked up at the midwife, very serious for a second. 'He's called after my brother who got it in the war.' He looked back to his baby son, grinning with tears in his eyes. 'You're Bernie, you are. You're Bernie Lack! And you're going to be the best of all of them!' Bernie slept; he was solid, silent and almost unnaturally still. Charlie took him over to his wife. 'Here you are, Vi, put him on your tit.'

Violet looked at the child for a second and then turned her head away. 'Take him out of here.'

'What?'

'Take him away!'

Charlie turned to the midwife, who put her finger over her lips. 'Ssshh.' He looked back to where Violet lay with her eyes closed, then he turned to Sayeed Sayeed who had come up after him and was standing in the doorway.

'Leave her, let her sleep,' the older man said.

Charlie understood and was suddenly pissed again. He moved back over to the midwife with an exaggerated tiptoe and handed the baby to her, then put his finger to his lips, and still on his toes went over to Sayeed Sayeed. 'Sssshhhhh. Let's go down the pub.' He left the room, as Violet opened her eyes and stared at the dark wood of the wardrobe door.

Mihr looked up as the clouds passing the moon cast a shadow across her face – and Sorush shifted time again.

It was night-time, a couple of days later. Violet was up and dressed. She ignored her puffy and pale face in the dressing-table mirror as she quickly swept a hairbrush and her make-up into her handbag. She turned and looked at the two-day-old Bernie lying in his cot. His eyes were open and he was looking up at her with an unblinking stare. Her face was expressionless, too, as she stood above him. Then she turned and put on her coat. She glanced again at the baby, and stooped to pull a package out of the bottom of the wardrobe. She stared into her son's eyes as she unwrapped it. It was a child's picture book, *King Arthur and the Knights of the Round Table*. She placed it at the bottom of the cot, picked up a small brown suitcase and left the room. Bernie didn't move. He remained staring at the place where she had been.

Violet went quietly down through the tearoom, then slipped quickly down the stairs into the dark and deserted restaurant. She stopped for a second and listened to Charlie's laughter coming up from the club below, then she unlocked the door and went out into the alley. It was cold and she shivered. She locked the restaurant door behind her and looked down the outside steps to the light from the club-room window. She could hear Charlie's voice quite clearly, rising above the racket.

'Bye, Charlie.' She threw the restaurant keys down the basement steps and waited until they came to rest at the sill of the club-room door. Then she picked up her suitcase and walked towards the lamp-post at the end of the alley. She didn't turn or look back. She walked through the lamp's circle of light and disappeared into the shadows of the street.

'. . . *Surunat, Ysion, Ysesy and by all the holy names.' Kasbeel closed his book.*
'Witness, Mihr, a mother and a son go forth within days of each other. She never came back; the son took a decade to return.'
'You investigate the death of the father, Sorush.'
'It was him they left,' said Sorush, and then she was gone.

Mirabelle looked out over the empty roofs. She had witnessed the birth of her charge and was beginning to feel even more uneasy. Were these scenes she was seeing being chosen? If so, why? And on what grounds? The selection in itself didn't surprise her. Sorush had always picked those episodes that would justify her judgement of a wrongdoing. But there was something more now. Mirabelle was beginning to feel with dread that perhaps the Dark Angel was seeking more than the mere judgement of the father, and perhaps had her own agenda. What was it? Did Sorush know herself? In the same way that she, Mirabelle, didn't know the full extent or ultimate purpose of her mission, was perhaps Sorush also seeking something as yet unknown to her?

$$16$$

The next day, Bernie clattered down the stairs into the restaurant and stopped dead. The table was laid out for breakfast and Mirabelle was holding his plate of food. He was in the hugest of dilemmas. He did a quick count. Sausages, four; bacon, three; eggs, scrambled (couldn't count them but there was a lot); tomatoes, six; beans, a hundred and fifty; black pudding, two, and two fried bread. 'See, Meebelle, I dunno what to do. Downstairs is me bruvs with an important meeting! I didn't wake up, see. Oh no! What about me brekkers?'

'You could eat it first, then go down.'

'But it might be over! See, it's panic stations, Meebelle. The time is flying past and the tides don't wait for no man!'

'Well go on down then.'

'Oh no!' He stared at the breakfast. Then he suddenly looked up and said, 'I see Galahad last night in me dreams.'

'Did you?'

'He was playing for Spurs at White Hart Lane.' He raised his hands in the air and chanted, 'Come on you Spurs! Come on you Galaahaad!' Then he stopped as suddenly as he had started and became very serious again as he looked down at his breakfast. 'Sometimes Galahad rode for weeks and weeks without any food in his stomick essept leaves and honey from the bees.'

'Do you want it, or not?' Mirabelle held up the plate.

'No.'

'You sure?'

'Just gis a sausage.' He took one and popped it in his mouth. 'Thass like the bees and the honey.' He turned and ran down the stairs to the club.

'So you got my offer, what more do I say? I don' say no more.' Luis Riss leaned back on one of the rickety club-room bentwoods and winked at Emil, who was sitting next to him. Raphaella was a little further away; she'd caught the sunbeams coming through the dust of the window again. They were flickering around the black curls of her hair, giving her a halo: St Raphaella of good times. She crossed her legs in the silence. Arnie caught the sound of her stockings brushing against each other on her inner thigh and felt the slight bulge of a mild erection. He saw Raphaella's breasts rising and falling under her white cotton shirt and realized he needed to concentrate or he was in trouble.

Ronnie was looking at him. 'Arn?'

'What?' Arnie pulled the bottom of his jacket over his groin.

'I said, I don' say no more,' the Malteser repeated.

Before Arnie could say anything they were interrupted by the clump of Bernie's entrance. Massive feet, huge bones of legs, then the bulk of the rest of him appeared at the bottom of the stairs and stopped like a mountain of arrested development. The summit was a swivelling head with half a sausage sticking out of its mouth. He saw the Riss mob and went bright red. He'd known he was going to a very important meeting with his bruvs, but hadn't thought that someone else might be there. And they were all staring at him. And he'd forgotten to comb his hair. And his mouth was full. 'Sorry.'

'Sit down here, mate.' Ronnie pushed a chair out for him. Raphaella giggled as Bernie sat down. 'Anything wrong, Raphaella?' asked Ronnie.

'Are you kidding?' Her tone was triumphal. Like the rest of her family she knew they had these crazy Lacks by the pubics.

'So? What you want?' Luis gandered round at them. 'No home plus fifty grand or no home plus nothing?'

Arnie's head was still full of the residue of last night's twenty-three Johnny Walkers. It felt like they were taking a run round his skull in hobnailed boots.

'It's not a lot of choice, Arn.' It looked like Ron was caving in.

Luis leaned in, his moment was near. 'So?'

Such was the state of Arnie's brain and trousers that he was about to say, fuck it, let the arsehole have it. But in the millisecond before thought became speech there was the ring of high heels on stone, and they all looked up through the window at Harriet in her best fur wrap clipping down the basement steps outside. She came in quickly through the door and into the centre of the room. 'I beg pardon for my laxity, Mr Riss,' she said slightly breathlessly, 'but I thought it best to have a word with our solicitor, Mr Frederick Wart.'

Emil smirked. 'Frederick who?'

'Wart.' Harriet sat down under the sepia Doris Day and glared at him. After his remark about her brother and genitals the night before, Emil was her enemy number one and she could have cheerfully stabbed the ignorant little sod in the front trouser with a knitting needle.

'Harriet!' Luis raised his hands. 'What you want to see a lawyer for? What can a brief do, except take for ever?' He sniggered at his own little joke. No-one else got it, so he went on, 'The offer's on the table.' He banged the one in front of him in case anyone had any doubt as to what he meant.

Harriet had no doubt at all. 'I'm sure it is, Mr Riss, but unfortunately you're making it to the wrong persons.'

'What wrong persons?' Luis felt a slight twinge in his chest and sat marginally forward.

Harriet adopted a slightly bored, neutral tone. It was her own brand of triumphalism. 'The boys don't own the restaurant, the club or the flat.' She then sat back. This was front-page news and everybody wanted their own version.

'You what?' Ronnie and Arnie said it together.

'You what?' Bernie added.

Harriet smiled. 'Charlie, in all his wisdom, left the lot of it to his departed wife.'

It was Luis's turn. 'What?'

And then Emil. 'You what?'

Raphaella was more original. 'His wife?'

Harriet sat back. 'So if you want to collect your debt, I suggest you ask her.'

Luis's twinge became an intense jab. He looked at Emil, who had his mouth hanging open. For a second he observed his son's teeth and wondered what he'd done to deserve such an heir with fourteen fillings and no wisdom. He turned back to Harriet. 'His wife? She got the debt?'

'Inherited it with the building, Mr Riss.' Harriet brushed her fur nonchalantly.

'So, where is she?' It was nearly a shout. Luis's jab was becoming permanent pain.

'I don't know, dear, I haven't laid eyes on her for twenty years. She could be anywhere. And according to Mr Wart,' she eyed Emil, 'that's W–A–R–T, there's nothing to stop the boys living in their mother's house for the rest of their natural.'

'But she owes me!' Now it was definitely a shout and Luis stood up.

'Then I'd go to the courts, Mr Riss. Long and expensive business though, suing someone whose whereabouts are unknown.'

'Sue? Hire legal eagle? Me? You kidding? What are you talking about?' Luis was sinking back down, the pain in his chest was spreading.

'If you like we can discuss repaying the debt. As friends.' Harriet didn't bother to hide the sarcasm. 'I'm sure we can raise a loan, Charlie had many friends and some perhaps even you don't know about.' Luis was going pale, Harriet had stolen all his colour. 'I have no doubt we can make you a very generous offer. Shall we say we'll give you twenty in the pound?' She narrowed her eyes and tilted her head back. Harriet

71

hadn't spent thirty years in betting shops without learning a thing or two about percentages.

'Aaah!' Luis gasped; it could be a heart attack.

Arnie had no concern for the collapsing Malteser. He was outraged. 'You mean the old man didn't leave anything to his sons?'

'He made the will a long time ago. Freddie thought he must have forgotten to make another one,' said Harriet.

'Lucky he did really.' Ronnie grinned. This was more like it and he hadn't had to say a word.

'What's up, Ron?' Bernie had his serious face on. He produced a big furrow where his eyes met.

'Means we don't have to move, Bern.'

'Oh. Shall I go and have my brekkers then?'

'If you want, mate.'

'No, I fink I'll stay until the meeting's over.' Bernie sat back and folded his arms. Whatever was going on, things were looking up.

Not for Luis, but he was recovering enough to ask, 'Where is this will? Let me see it.'

Harriet opened her black patent-leather handbag with a brisk click of the clasp, took out a photocopy of the will and handed it to him with crisp and exaggerated efficiency. 'All above board, Mr Riss. Witnessed by Mr Sayeed Sayeed of the Bengali Star, Isle of Dogs, and Mr John Flaherty who still manages the shoe shop on the corner. Charlie left everything to his wife.'

'That's me.'

Luis took the will and read it. 'Everything to his wife.' His eyes began to fill with tears.

'That's me.'

'Shuddup, Raphaella!' He read it again, hoping the little letters in the little words would leap up, jump around and metamorphose into other little words that might make him feel better.

'We got married the day he died.'

'Shuddup!' Luis had shouted across to his daughter and turned to confront Harriet again, but the old girl had her mouth open and there was a kind of sticky silence in the room. Luis's heart began to pound again like some big bass drum in an ancient cavern. He creaked his face back round to Raphaella as if he was in the middle of some kind of slow-motion replay on *Match of the Day*. 'What you say?'

Raphaella didn't bother to repeat it, she just went on. 'Then we go to the Sunset Hotel.' She checked her nail varnish.

Luis had the weirdest mixture of feelings, half drowning in a sea of rage, half gulping the air of salvation. 'You marry Charlie Lack and then you go to the Sunset?' He began to push himself up from the table.

'Then we go on the bed, and he got to gasping and groaning so bad, I shove my pants in his big gob.' Raphaella blew on the varnish, although she knew it was dry. 'Then he drop dead,' she added.

Luis was beginning to shake. 'You sleep with him?'

Raphaella looked up from her fingernails with the eyes of a natural-born killer. 'Course I do! I'm twenty-eight!'

Luis's neck bulged bright red, his heart was beating a tattoo on his ribcage. He screamed, 'You sleep with Charlie Lack! You sleep with . . . !' He spluttered to a standstill, spit dribbling down his chin. 'Thank God for that. You got a marriage certificate?'

'Sure I got a certificate. You think I'm a whore?' She looked blandly at her father, clicked open her handbag, fumbled for longer than necessary in order to increase the drama, and then carefully placed the certificate on the table in front of him.

It was Arnie's turn to rise. 'He married you? My old man married you?'

'In the register office.' She winked at Arnie. 'We din't do no white wedding. Just my little red number with the red silk panties.'

'He married you!' Arnie roared it again and then sat back down slowly, holding his head as the Johnny Walkers in his skull decided on a clog dance.

'Hey, wait a minute?' Emil had been thinking. 'Charlie owes us. Raphaella marry Charlie. This mean we got to collect a hundred and thirty thousand off our own family?'

'Wha'?' Luis thought about it too. For a second, dread was descending again. Had he spent an entire day collecting his own debt? Then it came to him and he leaped up. 'Ha! Don't be crazy! We just cleaned our own slate! Half price! Hahaha!' He walked around, his hands flapping in joy. 'Hahaha!'

Arnie looked at Ronnie. 'You know what this means, don't you?' He pointed to Raphaella. 'That tart's our stepmother!'

Luis didn't like that. What did it make him? Step-grandfather or something? To the Lack Brothers! He screamed at his daughter,

'Raphaella! How you do this? Marry Charlie Lack? What you done to me?' And then there was the moral position. 'What you doing sleeping around with a husband I don't know you got? You don't go out again for six years! I am your papa, Raphaella, your papa!' He looked like he was going to burst into tears, but then he suddenly laughed again, the pound in his pocket weighing more heavily than the pounding in his heart. 'Haha! Hey, Arnie! Get out of here! Get off my property!'

It was Raphaella's turn to stand. 'It's not yours! Charlie left it to me! It's mine!'

'Shuddup, Raphaella, you're in big trouble! Hahaha!' Luis could have done a little jig.

Raphaella was outraged. Not only had she saved the family finances, she was a widow! She was in deep and terrible trauma. She whipped out a tiny lace handkerchief and wailed, 'My husband is dead! It was my secret sorrow! You don' know how much I suffer. In secret! We was going to live in Majorca and drink pina colada!' She burst into tears. 'You don't understand, none of you!' She whirled round, a dizzying picture of grief. 'I am a black widow, what's the matter with you? Don't you got no pity?' There was no response. 'I hate you! I go down Wonderland and play the slots!' She said the last mainly to Emil, then walked quickly towards the door, ferocious in her sadness and desire to get at the machines. 'I hate you!'

Her brother turned fast. 'Hey, Jock, go with her! And keep what she wins!'

Jock had to run to catch her. She was already halfway up the basement steps, howling into her handkerchief. 'Charlie!'

Luis grinned. He'd gone from triumph, to heart attack, to torment, back to heart attack, to hysteria, back to triumph in three minutes, and he was still here in one little piece of gloating Malteser. He looked at the Lacks, sitting incredulous and shattered before him. 'So. My daughter owns the property. When you going?'

Harriet still had her wits about her. 'When you can prove the marriage is legal, Mr Riss.'

'Legal? Whaddya mean, legal? We got a certificate!'

'It's only legal if Charlie divorced Violet, which he didn't as far as I know. Or if she's dead, Mr Riss. Otherwise his marriage to Raphaella is bigamy, isn't it? And unlawful.'

Arnie looked up. Was there still hope?

Not according to Luis. 'Bigamy! You prove it!' He slammed Charlie's will onto the table. 'This says property belong to wife!' Then he slammed the marriage certificate on top of it. 'And this says wife is Raphaella Riss! That's it! You got one week to get out of here! And don't never insult the name of my daughter again!' He walked quickly to the door.

'Or my sister!' Emil followed. Razor Jam, being polite, closed the door after them, and within seconds they were gone.

Arnie got up and walked slowly over to the bar. 'The old man was going to piss off to España and do cocktails with Raphaella?'

'Still fancy her, do you?'

'No I don't, Ron, as a matter of fact.' Arnie poured himself a very large drink.

'What's up then? We got a problem, bruvs?' Bernie was hoping he could finish his sausage now.

Arnie stared at the optic as it drained into his glass. 'He forgot his own sons. Frankly I find myself amazed.'

'I think you'd better find yourself a mother, dear.' Harriet got up slowly and went towards the inside stairs. 'Come on, Bernie, we'll see if we can get Mirabelle to make you some breakfast.'

'Don't matter, Auntie, I can live on leaves and honey like Galahad.' He looked round at his brothers, but they weren't looking back.

PART TWO

EAST

1

Harriet had needed to talk everything over with somebody and she'd called Sophie up from her vegetables in the kitchen. She was immediately comforted by her friend's big Jamaican body and huge smile. She explained the problem to her. The boys had to find their mother to prove she was alive and had never divorced Charlie. Sophie was shocked by his clandestine marriage to Raphaella, but amused by the potential bigamy.

Harriet hadn't found it so funny. 'If Charlie was here, I'd give him a good kick up his back end, Sophie. Serve him right, too! Going off to Spain! How did he think he was going to get away with that?'

'Thinking ain't what you do with Raphaella!' Sophie laughed again, showing her mouthful of long white teeth.

Harriet wasn't in the mood for that kind of talk and hoped she wasn't going to begin to regret asking Sophie up. 'Anyway, we have to find Violet.' She pointed to an old cardboard box on the sofa. 'She's in there somewhere. It was on top of Charlie's wardrobe.' She heaved the box onto the living-room table and tipped it up. A cascade of old letters, postcards, photographs, valentines, Christmas decorations, calendars, hairpins, tubes of glue, fluff and dust showered down onto the table-cloth. 'Not much to show for thirty years of a family, is it?'

Sophie held up an old newspaper picture of a racehorse. 'What's this?'

'Mr Moody! That was my biggest win, Sophie! Four hundred and eighty-five pounds. I was going to pin him to my headboard.' Harriet looked longingly at the horse as Sophie swooped into the pile again.

She pulled out the coloured likeness of a young woman.

'This her?' She gave the picture to Harriet, who blew the dust away from the surface, and then held it up to the light coming in through the window. It was a large 1950s photograph of Violet. It had been taken at around the time they'd moved into the flat. Her hair was still blond and short, and the technicolour processing had given her eyes the same colour as her name.

'That's her.'

Sophie took the photograph and stared at it. She was impressed. 'She stun you by lookin' and she stun you by leavin'.'

'And if her mother had had anything to do with it, she'd have never come in the first place.'

'This is one girl for the fellers.' Sophie held the picture at arm's length to get a good look.

'And what a mess was the result, Sophie.' Harriet took the photo back and studied it. 'Charlie adored her.'

'Can see why.'

'Treated her bad though. Or she treated him bad. Who knows? Thank God I never married.' Harriet put the photograph back on the table and picked up a tattered white envelope with an old lady's ornate scrawl on the front. 'This is what we want. It's from her mother. It's got the address.' She handed the letter to Sophie, as if she didn't want to touch it any more than was necessary. 'The whole thing gives me the shivers, Sophie, if you really want to know.'

Sophie quickly put the envelope back onto the table. She was a superstitious woman and shivers meant shivers. 'If it's as bad as all that, I don't.'

'Well you're going to have to, aren't you, dear? We all are.' Harriet went to the door and shouted down the stairs. 'Mirabelle, get the boys. We've found it!'

2

Raphaella jerked the handle. Silver clattered into the bowl, the sound mixing with the snorts and splutters of her grief. Her cries drowned even the massed bass thumps of the five-card stud and high-pitched jingles of the fruit machines in Emil's slots arcade. 'Oh my Charlie! Charlie's dead!' She jabbed the hold buttons and watched the fruit spin. At precisely the right moment she hit the joker with split second timing and exact pressure. She didn't pause as more coins crashed down.

Scotch Jock leaped forward with a plastic bag and scooped up yet more handfuls of cash. The bag was already getting heavy and he could see it splitting and a thousand fifty-pence pieces scattering around fifty slot machines and fifty teenage tearaways trampling all over him in the scramble to pick them up. Realizing it was pointless trying to talk to Raphaella, he nervously considered his options: 1) Leaving her for a moment and getting another plastic bag from the fast-change booth – but that was to risk her doing a runner with the latest handful of cash. 2) Stopping the cash flowing altogether by stopping Raphaella playing, which would involve a punch-up and either he'd go psycho and kill her, or he wouldn't go psycho and she'd kick the shit out of him, which would be embarrassing. 3) Chat up Raphaella, take her to the back room and fuck her. Hmmm? Jock wasn't good at handling situations like this. His natural state was crisis and he could feel the panic needle rising towards the red zone.

Raphaella wasn't helping, her yelps and gulps were getting louder. 'I could have been Mrs Lack with a husband and a diamond on my cutesy! In a Spanish night with my little blue number with the split skirt!' She hit at the buttons again, more silver splashed into the dish and Jock scooped it up into the bag, which was splitting worse. He'd decided on a run to the cash desk for another one when he saw Razor Jam standing just inside the door. The Sikh pointed at Raphaella and mimed a lunge. It was option two! Put the grab on the boss's daughter!

'And what about the sun and the sangria, and up the mountain for the monk's blessing! Oh, Charlie!' Raphaella continued to wail.

'Excuse me, Miss Riss.' Razor tapped her on the shoulder.

'Aaagghh!' She screamed as she fell backwards. They hadn't given her a chance. Jock grabbed her feet and tipped her. Razor caught her bulk as she fell, and they carried her fast and horizontal out of the arcade. Jock held on to as much of the cash as he could, but most of it burst through the bag and scattered on the floor. It instantly disappeared beneath a heaving mound of fighting, shrieking boys as they carried Raphaella out. The pavement outside flew past a foot beneath her nose, and before she'd gained breath to scream again, she'd landed flat and spreadeagled on the back seat of the Riss Daimler amidst a shower of silver. Razor came in after her and held her down as Jock went round the car and got in the other side. They heaved her upright and held on to her in a whirlwind of pointed elbows and blood-red talons as she screamed at Luis behind the wheel. 'Let me go! You don' do this to me! I got a restaurant!'

'Shuddup, Raphaella!' Emil turned from the front passenger seat.

'I don' shuddup!'

'Shuddup! I say shuddup! What I say? I say . . .'

'Shuddup, Emil!' Luis put the Daimler into gear and they pulled away fast into the traffic, causing chaos as a black cab behind skidded to avoid a bicycle messenger who'd swerved to avoid Luis.

The horns and curses from the street didn't stop Raphaella. 'You're banned! All of you! You're banned from my restaurant! You don't get no slap-up on the house! And Emil, you don't cruise no tables in no bow tie!'

'And you don't get no restaurant anyway! What kind of sister go marry a bigamister so she get a screw in the Sunset?'

'Well it ain't the first time!' yelled Raphaella.

'What!' Luis, apoplexed, slammed his foot on the brake; the car came instantly to a halt, and the cycle messenger behind didn't escape this time. His front wheel hit the Daimler's bumper, and he flew over the handlebars and landed on the boot with a bone-jarring crash. Luis hardly noticed. He turned to Raphaella from the driver's seat, his face white with rage. 'What you say?'

'I said it ain't the first time!'

'What you saying? You saying you had sex when you ain't married!'

'Sure I had sex.' Outside the car was mayhem; all traffic had stopped, the cab driver was hurling obscenities and a small crowd was gathering to look at the cyclist flattened on the boot of the Daimler. Inside it was the icy calm of a family about to disintegrate. Luis stared at his daughter, his eyes very small. 'So tell me, Raphaella.'

'So you want to know, huh?' She released herself from Razor and Jock and began to count on her fingers. 'OK. One, I screw the techie who fix the slots behind Freeway Fantasy. Two, I screw O'Dare in the graveyard.'

'You screw the fucking Jesuit!' Luis spluttered and began to claw at the back of the leather seat, his body moving involuntarily towards her.

Raphaella continued in calm and deadly fury, 'Three, the delivery driver from Harrods. Four, the pizza boy. Five, the plumber who came for waste disposal. Six, the man from the Pru . . .'

Luis began to yelp as he tried to get at her over the seat. 'Hold her! Give her to me!' He got his knee up on the armrest and his feet on the steering wheel to give him purchase as he swung his fists. 'Hold her! I want to kill her!'

And still Raphaella didn't stop. 'And plenty more I can't remember! There was . . . Aaagh!' Luis had caught her with a haymaker on the side of her face. She scrabbled back into the leather away from Luis as he struck out into the space between them. 'I screw everybody! And my husband Charlie gave the restaurant to me! You get it? He gave it to me!' She pushed herself back further.

'Hold her down! What's the matter with you? I got to smash her face!'

Luis had climbed halfway over the front seat and was beginning to fall into the space behind as Raphaella kicked out, fighting him off with her legs and feet. Razor and Jock desperately tried to hold on to her as she levered herself up onto the shelf behind the back seat. Suddenly her body went rigid and she began to scream. She'd come nose to nose with the bloody face of the cyclist through the back window and thought it was her own reflection. She screamed again as the cyclist passed out and his head dropped, leaving a wide smear of fresh red blood on the window. Raphaella thought she'd just deconstructed. Where once there was pure flesh and pale beauty, now there was just red stuff. She felt she was going to faint. 'Blood! Aaah! Go away!' She slid back down the back seat, her sudden terror and vulnerability taking the steam out of Luis's attack. 'Blood! Oh, Papa!' She ended as a crumpled, curled-up mess between the two minders, with her skirt round her thighs. Jock was desperately hoping she'd struggle again to give him the chance of a quick feel, when she screamed again. She'd noticed a bright-red stain on her white shirt. More blood and this time it was definitely her own! It had been pouring out of her nose since Luis had hit her and now it was being joined by a flood of water and mascara. 'Papa, my face! Do something! It's my face!'

Luis suddenly froze as he became aware of where he was and what he was doing. He was halfway over the front seat of his Daimler with his fist raised at his daughter, who had her dress round her arse, and her face covered in blood and snot, and a crazy bicycle guy with a plastic helmet also covered in blood was half dead on his boot, and a traffic warden was hammering on the window, and Emil, his useless son, had his hands over his eyes, trying to pretend he didn't exist! And it was the middle of Brewer Street, and probably everybody he knew was out there laughing at him! He had to pull himself together fast. First things first. He yelled at the warden, 'Shuddup! Get off my car! You crazy guy or what?'

'Papa, my face! What about my face?' Raphaella kept it up.

'It's OK! OK! Keep the blood off the upholstery!' Luis tried to turn and get himself back into his seat, but it was more awkward than he thought and he couldn't seem to get his knee out of his face. The traffic warden hadn't been listening and was still banging on the window. Luis yelled, 'Touch this car and I sue you!' He managed to get both legs into the right order and shouted at Razor Jam, 'Don't just sit there, do something!'

Razor's blade flashed with the speed of light and the traffic warden leaped back six feet from the window, but this wasn't what Luis had in mind. 'Not that, you prick! The upholstery! There's blood on the leather! Do something!' He got his feet onto the pedals and reached down to turn the ignition.

'I got a handkerchief, Mr Riss.' Razor produced a square foot of crumpled white cotton stained with green and brown.

'Papa, please, please, get out of here.' Emil, ten years' hard-earned street cred spent in seconds by his stupid sister, had sunk as far down the seat as he could and was trying to get his head into the glove compartment. 'Please, Papa!'

The Daimler's engine, a perfect machine unperturbed by any human blood, greed or riot, purred into life, and Luis slipped it into gear. 'Shuddup all of you!'

'Don't forget, it's my restaurant.' Raphaella straightened herself up on the back seat as they pulled away, leaving the cyclist to slip slowly down the boot and fall into a crumpled heap on the street. 'You understand? I am the wife and the restaurant is mine!' Her voice bounced around the leather trim and walnut dashboard as the Daimler swept round the corner and disappeared from view.

3

Mirabelle hadn't been able to find either Arnie or Ronnie. They'd both disappeared to deal with the morning's events in their own way.

Ronnie had wanted to walk. He needed to think. Forty-eight hours ago they'd buried the old man, and this time yesterday he'd been planning the great leap forward. The entire continent of cuisine and decor had seemed at his elbow, and designs and plans for the restaurant had been tumbling into his mind faster than he could cope with. For the first time in his life he'd felt clear about what he wanted to do. Now, instead of going forwards, they were having to go backwards just so that they could stay where they were. Now they had to find a mother. The thought made him jittery. She'd gone when he was ten and he thought he'd put her out of his mind. She was too many questions he didn't want to answer, or even ask.

He walked about, breathing the monoxide and giving the streets half a shufti with one side of his brain, while with the other he considered pissing off and leaving the whole lot behind him like Arnie had a few years back. Where would he go? South America, Toronto, Cardiff? But what was the point? He'd only take himself with him, including his new impulse for change, which was the only impulse he could ever remember having that made him feel good. He wanted to sort out the restaurant, didn't he? Change it all about, give it the old hokey-cokey. So what was the point of running away when the only thing he wanted to do was here? He had a feeling that he could make it all work out, too. But it was more than that. The truth was that he wanted to make the decisions about the restaurant because he wanted to make up his mind about himself. Be the guvnor of what was outside, so he could be the guvnor of what was inside him. Be his own man for a bleeding change.

He stopped in the street as he thought about it. He could see a crowd up ahead. They were watching as a cyclist in a plastic helmet was being carried into an ambulance. Several of the crowd were drunk and one of them fell over the kerb and split his head. A medic had to attend to him, leaving the cyclist groaning, half in and half out of the ambulance. Someone laughed, someone cheered, someone else obstructed and another gave useless advice. It was the usual chaos. Ronnie watched and, in spite of himself, smiled. This shit-hole was his life and he knew he'd have to give it a go, even if it did mean finding his mum again. He turned and walked back, feeling a bit better.

Arnie had helped the temporary chef with the lunch trade. Porchese still hadn't shown up and he was beginning to wonder if the little Italian hadn't gone for good? Maybe he'd have to get the bus over to Leytonstone after all? But what for? The way things looked they wouldn't have the place much longer, and at least they wouldn't have to pay Porchese redundancy. Or at least Luis Riss wouldn't. He grabbed a half-bottle of Scotch and went to sit by the garbage in the backyard to work things out in his usual way.

Mirabelle decided he might need a bit of time to himself, at least until Ronnie returned. So she left him there, his snout in the bottle and his rage churning. Having finished the Scotch he'd heaved himself up, brushed the potato peel and yard-dust from the back of his trousers and gone upstairs to find someone to moan at.

He was already in the living room, reading the old letter from Violet's mother, when Ronnie walked in. He was saying, 'How can you have a name like Green and call your daughter Violet? I mean what kind of woman's that? That's what we're dealing with.' His irritation was getting refocused. He tried to read the address at the top of the letter. 'It's Kitchener Square. That's east, isn't it? The ink's run. I can't see the number.'

'I could try the phone book,' said Ron.

'If she was in the phone book, we wouldn't need the letter, would we?'

'I could have a look anyway, couldn't I?' Ronnie went over to the sideboard.

'Phone book, thass a good idea, Ron.' Bernie was sitting at the table, looking all about and getting excited. This seemed like some detective story for real.

Arnie gave him a filthy look and then read out the letter. 'Dear Violet, the episode in the café with your husband was quite offensive.' He looked up. 'What episode? What café?'

'The café Mum and Dad had in the south,' said Harriet.

'What, Dad had another café?' All this was news to Bernie.

'No, dear,' said Harriet, 'my mum and dad, your dad's mum and dad.

Your grandparents, Bernie. Charlie and Vi lived with them for a bit before you were born. Arnie was there. You remember, Arnie?'

'I prefer to forget.'

'Didn't Vi say that her mother went there once and gave you five bob?' asked Harriet.

'I don't remember.'

'Who's Bob?' Bernie wanted to know.

'Shut up, Bernie.' Arnie returned to the letter. 'The incident quite ruined the holiday for Albert and I . . .'

'Who's Albert?'

Arnie ignored him. 'I think it best we do not meet again whilst you are married to this ignorant man. Your mother, Lucretia.'

'Who's Lucretia?'

'Violet's mother. Your grannie, dear.'

'Oh. So who's Albert and who's Bob?'

'Bernie, will you shut your bloody mouth?' Arnie tossed the letter back onto the table. 'Lucretia bloody Green.'

'What a letter to get from a mother.' Sophie was disgusted.

'Charlie had a good laugh when he showed it to me,' said Harriet.

Mirabelle had been sitting by Bernie at the table, looking through the photographs. She held one up to Harriet. 'Is this Mrs Green?'

Harriet took the picture from her. It was old, grey and faded, and the photographer, whoever he was, hadn't held his camera straight, so the three women standing in front of a pretty Georgian house looked as if they were on an incline. She turned the picture over and read the faint pencilled inscription on the back. 'That's right, dear. Lucretia Green's the one in the middle.' Harriet pointed at a thin, middle-aged woman with a prim, tight-lipped smile. 'That one on the right is Vi, and on the other side, that's her sister, May. She's three years younger, but looks like Vi, don't you think?' She held the photograph in front of Mirabelle. 'And that's where they lived up east. It was gentry then, over there. Not like now.'

Bernie had a gawk. 'Which one's Mum?'

'That one, dear. And that's your Auntie May. No it's not, it's the other way round. Is it?' Harriet studied the picture trying to tell her Violets from her Mays.

'Dad says Gran was a horrible cow 'cos she wouldn't tell us where Mum was,' said Bernie.

'And if she wouldn't tell us then, she's not going to tell us now, is she?' Arnie had settled on the sofa, the Scotch out in the yard was beginning to get to him.

'She's not on the blower, anyhow.' Ronnie put down the phone book.

'Look at this, Ron.' Harriet had picked up another photograph and Mirabelle had a quick peek. It was of Charlie, Violet and a middle-aged man with thinning hair. Harriet held the picture up to the light. 'That's Tom Cherry, isn't it?' She showed it to Sophie. 'He was a Dandy Kim, dear. He gave a ten-shilling note to a taxi driver once. You remember him, Ron.'

Ronnie didn't seem to want to go into it. 'Why don't we get the Snipe out the garage, go over to Kitchener Square and see if she's there. Get it done and over.' The resolution he'd discovered on the street was beginning to evaporate and he knew he had to act on it before it disappeared altogether.

But Harriet had found another photo of Tom Cherry. 'Here's one of him with you, Ron. Remember his dress shop?' She turned to Sophie again. 'He started with a little place on the corner and ended with a dazzling success.'

'I don't want to hear it now thanks, Auntie. I want to do what we got to do. Arnie?' Ronnie looked at his brother, who was beginning to drift into sleep on the sofa. 'Arnie, do you want to wake up?'

'Yeah, let's go and see Mum.' Bernie was ready to go, right then.

'She won't be there.' Arnie's eyes half opened.

'Might be, you never know in this game of soldiers.'

'You're not coming anyway, Bernie.' Arnie closed his eyes again.

'I am. I bloody am.'

'You're not.'

'I am! I bloody am! I bloody am!'

'Bernie . . .' Ronnie could see Bernie was going to be a handful any minute.

'I'm bloody coming, geezer! That's my bloody mum, that is! I'm bloody coming!' Bernie stood up and his bulk seemed to fill the room.

'Cut it out!' Arnie had not only woken, he'd roared. Bernie shut up immediately, his eyes filling with tears.

'Arnie, why can't the boy have a nice ride east in the Snipe?' asked Harriet.

'I'm coming,' Bernie said stubbornly.

Arnie was closing his eyes again. 'This isn't going to do any of us any good.'

'Got to stick together, bruvs!' Bernie raised his fists in the air and began to chant, 'Totten-ha-aam, Galaha-aad! Got to stick together!'

Arnie didn't hear. He'd fallen asleep on the sofa.

4

The Riss sofa was brand new, fluffy pink, about four yards across and five feet deep. Raphaella was drowned in cushions, holding a hand mirror and tentatively prodding her nose. 'Don't no-one bonk my conk! I'm telling you!' She dabbed it again with a cream tissue. The colour had been carefully selected to show up the blood – greens, oranges and especially dark blue had all been rejected as tonally inefficient. She turned and glared at her father sitting behind her at the huge table poking at a Chinese takeaway and feeling more and more guilty by the minute. 'Could've been a fracture! You know what this is? This is my face!'

Emil looked up with his mouth full of egg foo yung. 'So don't hump with plumbers.'

Raphaella leaped up and threw her mirror into the pile of a hundred or so used and faintly pink-smeared tissues that surrounded her on the sofa. She'd already squeezed three apologies out of her old man, plus what looked to her like a substantial loss of appetite as he morosely picked at the fried rice. Now it was time to see what material gains she could make out of the incident. Since being left the restaurant, her ambition had soared. She sought the personal freedom to do what she liked in future, plus no less than a radical shift in the family power structure – and looking at her dumb brother smearing his big lips with sweet and sour sauce, she realized it wouldn't be too much of a problem. Number one, he wasn't going to talk to her like that about plumbers. 'I screw what I want!' She looked down her faintly swollen nose at him. 'You don't see no Raphaella with no takeaway come home in a paper bag! I got my own restaurant!'

'OK, OK, angel, and I make sure you keep it.' Luis couldn't cope with much more of this. He'd discovered that what he thought was his virginal daughter had in fact fucked half the city; and now, instead of leaving her well whipped, shunned, shamed and locked in whatever was the Soho version of the woodshed, he was actually apologizing to her, smarming like a shifty pussy cat and prepared to offer his left arm and right leg if only she'd shut up and not make him feel so bad. He tried a friendly, conspiratorial smirk. 'That place with a lick of paint, worth maybe half a million.'

'Three-quarter.' Emil had moved on to the deep fried oyster.

Raphaella eyed her old man. 'What do you mean, I keep it? Course I keep it! Why don' I keep it?'

'Maybe Arnie and the boys find their mama, that's why.' Emil chewed.

'What?' Luis looked round. He'd been so preoccupied with punching his daughter's face and its aftershock that he'd forgotten to give the morning's events his full and proper consideration. 'What you say?'

'So they get hold of this Violet and bring her back.' Emil picked up a prawn cracker and poked the air with it, making his point. 'Maybe she say she don't ever get no divorce and so she gets the restaurant. And maybe she say she don't pay no debts. And maybe she don't pay no compound interest, right? Maybe we got to go to court and fork out a fortune and don't win nothing. And so maybe we rest our case, know what I mean, and maybe we lose what we already paid on the debts and the other half million we didn't get because we don't own the place anyhow. Right?'

'What?' Luis hadn't eaten much but he still choked.

'I mean, maybe, Papa.'

'Maybe you're right.'

There was a silence. Luis looked at his son's mouth. There could have been a universe in that grain of fried rice on his lip; a universe of loss and worse, a whole eternity of local humiliation. Emil smugly crunched his cracker. It wasn't often he was taken seriously, except by Jock, and that didn't count.

'So what you going to do about it, stupid brother?' Raphaella was a woman of immediate action.

'Hey, I . . . ?' Emil raised his hands.

'So, Emil?' Now Luis wanted to know too.

'Listen, I don' buy no debts. I don' carve up no restaurant.' Emil shrugged. 'I got a peep show.'

'So peep!' Luis stood up at the table. This had gone far enough. He was close to one of the best deals of his life and he was sitting there listening to his idiot son with a mouthful of China, and feeling guilty about a nymphomaniac daughter who he should have slapped around years ago. 'What am I doing? Losing the marbles? You!' He thumped Emil on the back, sending a spray of half-chewed cracker across the table. 'You hear me? Peep! Go down the Lacks' place and watch those brothers. They find a mother, you make sure you find her first! You get me? Anyone picks a Violet, it's us! Take Jock, take Razor. Don't take my car!'

Emil was on his feet and suddenly ecstatic. Now they were moving again. And, plus, he knew something good was going to come out of all this. 'Hey, Papa, and they go anywhere, I take the Corvette! I take Miss Brown and White!'

'Get out of here! And leave the king prawn, what's the matter with you?' Luis's appetite was back.

'Hey! The Corvette! Don't worry, Papa, I find her for you.' Emil picked up his hat and went out happy, leaving the door open.

Luis roared after him, 'Shut the door!' Emil came back and slammed it. 'What's the matter with him? He knows I like king prawn.'

Raphaella went back to the sofa. 'I don' know how you got two kids, Papa. One who got a restaurant and one who don' got a brain.'

'Shuddup, Raphaella!'

She did, and leaned back in the cushions, then dabbed her nose and thought about it. Emil was bound to make a mess of it. It was about time she started to consider what was going to happen next.

5

Razor Jam stood in the alley for two hours before there was any sign of a Lack. It was early evening before Ronnie and Bernie came out of the restaurant. They were followed by Harriet and Mirabelle. They all waited a couple of minutes until a sleepy-looking Arnie joined them, and then walked across Dean Street. Razor hid behind a phone kiosk and watched as they went to an old back-alley, lock-up garage. The moment he saw Ronnie slide the door up, he slipped inside the kiosk. He lifted the receiver and searched in his pocket for some change. He hadn't got any, so he replaced the receiver and walked round the corner to tell Emil personally. It looked like the Lacks were going somewhere.

Bernie looked at the big, black, shiny Snipe tucked cosily in the dark of the lock-up and felt as excited as he always did when he saw it. Charlie had bought the car years ago and for Bernie it meant special occasions. A trip to the seaside, going somewhere for Crimble, or even visiting some old geezer and his Mrs who'd probably give him a cake or an apple and then a shilling when he went home. It always involved dressing up, your best flute and all that. Arnie and Ronnie had put on shirts and ties and double and single breasteds, so Bernie had put his on too. He looked like a corker, even if the suit was a bit small. It was charcoal, that's what Auntie said, but as far as he was concerned it was dark black, and he had his best white shirt on with no tie. He didn't like ties; they were too tight round his neck.

Ronnie started the motor. The Snipe purred forward out of its concrete lair and sat, glistening black and silver under the street lights. Bernie couldn't wait and leaped straight into his place in the back. Mirabelle got in the other side.

'Speak well and up, dear.' Harriet spoke over the roof of the car to Arnie as he got into the passenger seat. 'We all bow to charm.' She leaned into Ronnie at the steering wheel. 'Tell it to your brother, will you? It doesn't matter what we think of Mrs Green, nobody turns a blind eye to kindness.'

'Thank you, Auntie. I'll bear it in mind.' Arnie was suffering his first hangover of the day and that was before he'd had an evening drink. He turned sourly to Ron. 'This is not a good idea.'

'Might see Mum.' Bernie poked his head forward over the front seats. He was, as always, clutching his Arfer.

'That's what I mean.'

'Oh.' Bernie didn't get what Arnie was talking about, but he didn't mind because he knew his big bruv was usually right about most things.

The Snipe pulled away down the alley and they turned into the neon streets.

'Look at that, it's the Scotch prat.' They were passing Emil's peep show and Arnie could see Jock and Razor in animated conversation.

Jock looked up as the Snipe passed and then ran into the dark-red interior with the Sikh not far behind. 'Boss! They've come! They've gone!'

Mathilda in the pay booth watched as Emil came running out. He was dressed in his best brown suit and loafers. He stopped under the red bulb and quickly scanned his chain-store gangland exterior in the huge mirror on the side wall of the entrance. 'How do I look?'

'Er . . . you look fantastic, Mr Riss.' The Sikh knew how to please.

'You kidding me?'

'No, Mr Riss.' Razor never lied.

'Let's go! Miss Brown and White!' shouted Emil.

Mathilda watched as they ran out to the two-tone Corvette, colour coded to Emil's suit, that was parked proud and badly outside the peep show.

'They're still up by the lights!' Jock got in behind the wheel and his boss eased himself in beside him, careful not to crease his trousers or knock his hat off. The car roared away in a cloud of blue smoke as Mathilda ran from the cash till into the gloom of the interior and Lucy.

.

6

Arnie stared through the windscreen of the Snipe at the wet, chaos and gathering gloom of the Great Eastern. It was like the road to hell: packed with screaming, stinking traffic all rushing at the speed of light from red light to red light through dark-grey mist, like mad dogs let off their leash for the last sprint of their desperate crazy lives, just so they could get home for tea.

Arnie flicked on the radio. It was a weather forecast. '. . . there's a depression heading east.' He looked at Ronnie, hunched over the wheel and driving like a maniac just to stay alive. 'You hear that? What's new?'

Bernie was snug in the back. He'd got bored with reading number plates, looking for the magic BL of his initials, and had opened his Arfer. He held it up and could just make out one of his favourite pictures in the glare of the passing headlights. It was a luridly coloured drawing of Galahad and two other knights riding swiftly through a lush forest glade with their shields up and lances lowered. He poked Mirabelle with his elbow. 'See that? That's Galahad. That's me.'

'And who are the other two?'

'Well, that one's Sir Perceval, who is Ron.' The picture disappeared from view, then suddenly came brilliantly alive again in the blinding light of an eighty-ton pantechnicon flashing past with the tops of its wheels out of sight in the gloom above them. Everyone ducked except Bernie, who stared at the picture unperturbed. He pointed at the third knight. 'And that one is Sir Bors, who is Arnie.'

'You what?' Arnie turned.

'It's us, you see, Arn,' Bernie said in his most serious voice. 'We are leaving Camelot, which is like the restaurant and my bedroom, to go looking for something, which we don't know what it looks like but we know what it is.'

'What is it?'

'It's Emil Riss!' Ronnie was looking up into the rear-view mirror. 'He's following us in his flaming Corvette!'

'What?' Arnie turned fast. 'Wipe the back window, Mirabelle!' They angled their necks and saw a brown-and-white, low-slung American car sending up more spray than a double-decker, one foot from their back bumper, and being driven by the maddest Scotsman in London.

In the front seat, Emil was talking into his mobile phone. 'Don't worry about a thing, Papa! We're right on their tail!'

'Oh no we're not!' Jock shouted. The Snipe in front had suddenly accelerated away.

'Go! Go! Go!' Emil yelled, then turned back to his mobile. 'No not you, Papa! We're right after them. Don't worry!' He grinned. 'Nobody loses a Corvette.'

The Snipe plunged ahead fast through the traffic, Ronnie steering her crazily left and right as the horn count doubled. He shot past two buses, a Jag, a Cortina and a prick in a Porsche who'd never knowingly been passed before, and that was before he'd made the outside lane.

'Whass up! Whass up!' Bernie was getting scared.

'It's all right.' Mathilda laid a hand on his arm.

'Why we goin' so fast? Whass up?'

'Put your foot down, Ron!' Arnie yelled. 'Stop!' They were heading straight for the twelve-foot-square, solid-steel back of the pantechnicon that was coming to a sliding halt at red lights thirty yards ahead. Ronnie knew he'd never be able to stop in time and wrenched at the wheel, desperately trying to squeeze the Snipe into the left-hand lane ahead of the Porsche, who was coming up fast and very furious on their inside. It was tight but the old girl had been here before with Charlie, and although her body swung at an alarming degree, creaking and threatening to detach herself from her chassis, the suspension held and she made it, missing the pantechnicon by one inch and defeating the skidding, braking Porsche by two, before leaping across the junction on fading amber. The weather forecast continued on the radio. 'All in all, it's going to be a stormy night, folks.'

'And you can fuck off as well.' Arnie turned it off with a shaking hand, as the Snipe shot down the road, showing their pursuers a nicely shaped, old-fashioned back end.

The Corvette burned rubber coming to a slidey, juddering halt at the lights on the inside lane. 'What you doing, crazy guy? What you stopped for?'

'The lights are red, boss.' Underneath it all Jock was a practical man.

'You don't stop on red!'

The Sikh leaned forward. 'Yes you do, Mr Riss, or you get caved in you see, from an on-coming vehicle cross-wise.'

It was the thick Brummie accent, with a stress on the thick, that got to Emil. He screamed, 'You traffic division or what?' then he shouted into his mobile, 'Hey, Papa! Give me the tools and I do the job!' He suddenly became aware that the Great Eastern decibel count had risen. It was as if he had disappeared into a huge black hole that was made up entirely of car horn. It was all too much for Emil. The electric windows he was so proud of were jammed, so he turned and screamed through the back, via Razor's flaccid face. 'Beep me, I blow you away!' Then he yelled at Jock, 'What's the matter with them?'

'The lights are green, Mr Riss.' Razor never lied.

'What?' Emil turned. They were. 'So go, go, go!'

Back at the Riss apartment, Luis held the telephone receiver away from his ear and then looked at it as though he was listening to outer space. It was a mess of the high revs of the Corvette and shouting, panicking voices, one Brum, one Scots and one inadequate, and Luis knew well who the last was. They were confused, they were arguing, they were stupid and they were lost. 'They went that way! . . . No! . . . This way! . . . That . . . Mr Riss, I believe we've seen that building before . . . Are you kidding me? . . . Go there! . . . What? . . . That way!' Luis slowly replaced the receiver as the yelling and static got louder. He looked up at Raphaella. All he could see was the back of her head as a huge black silhouette against the brilliant colour of the giant TV screen. Then he looked back at the phone. He was amazed by what he'd heard. 'This is the son of Luis Riss? This son is from me?' He shook his head. Some things are simply unfathomable.

'You got a daughter, Luis.' Raphaella spoke from the direction of the TV. Luis? She'd used his Christian name, but her father hardly noticed. He sat at the table and stared at his hands, wondering what life was for and why he was doing it.

'And you got to protect her interests,' Raphaella went on. She stood and turned. Luis looked up and gasped. Her profile against the bright light of the TV seemed vast and somehow mythic. She had proud breasts, jutting chin and flyaway hair. It seemed to him that she was the image of some goddess he'd seen in a commercial somewhere. 'Or else,' she added.

7

It had stopped raining and Bernie looked out of the window as the Snipe purred through the darkness. He thought it looked like a canyon in a cowboy film. He could just make out a tiny strip of starlight about 100 miles up, separating the tops of the huge black warehouses as they loomed up from either side of the narrow road. 'They was in a dark and angry forest and they was seeking adventures.' He'd said it to himself but knew Mirabelle was listening, so he gave her a wink, then tapped the glass of the car's side window. 'Do not fail me, faithful charger.'

Mirabelle smiled and looked over at him as he stared up at the huge buildings sliding by in the silent night. She realized that she loved him very much and wasn't too sure whether that was allowed. Her thoughts were interrupted by Ronnie. 'It's somewhere near here. I think it's by a river.'

'What river?' The second Arnie asked, Ronnie slammed his foot on the brake. Directly ahead was the water shimmering in the moonlight. Wheels locked and tyres squealing, the Snipe slithered, then stopped inches from the edge of the concrete bank.

'That one,' said Ronnie.

The dark road had come abruptly to an end on the docks themselves, and the Snipe sat surrounded by the giant shadows of ancient cranes and derricks. Bernie peered out into the silence. 'And all around were the forces of evil.'

'Shut up will you? This is a bleeding fool's errand, in' it?' said Arnie. 'Reverse, Ron, for Christ's sake.'

'We got to find her, Arn.' Ronnie shifted gear and the car rolled back away from the water.

'We could try further along,' Mirabelle suggested. She agreed with Ron. Violet had to be found. She sensed there was an inevitability about it all.

The Snipe moved slowly along the dockside. There were decrepit buildings to its left, and bright shining water to its right. Bernie turned from his Arfer and looked through the back window. And there he was, just as he knew he would be. Galahad was behind them, sitting astride his white charger, his armour reflecting the silver moonlight shafting through the black shadows cast by the rusting cranes and catwalks above. He didn't follow as the Snipe pulled away and Bernie watched through the window as the silvery figure receded, slowly becoming a tiny brilliant dot in the darkness behind.

The Corvette had finally found its way onto the warehouse road, either through luck, argument, or Razor's insistence that always turning right was the route to success. Emil was becoming increasingly worried. 'We lose them, Papa will kill me! Faster!'

'I'm doing sixty, boss.'

'Faster!'

Jock pressed down on the accelerator and the speedometer needle edged up to seventy, then eighty. The sheer speed seemed to lighten Emil's spirits. Getting nowhere faster was better than being somewhere slow. He tapped the dash. 'OK, Miss Brown and White, you show us the way!' Then he sat back as the warehouses either side suddenly disappeared, and where there had been black there was a flash of moonlight and . . . 'A white horse!' yelled Jock. He didn't even have time to brake.

'Stop . . . !' Emil had seen the water and knew there was no chance. The Corvette came across the dock at around eighty-five. It hit the embankment and took off. Inside the car it was a quiet flight. They stared ahead, mouths hanging open and their lives passing in front of their eyes as Miss Brown and White winged it fifteen feet above the mud, like some skewed and filthy albatross coming in to land. The back wheels hit the sludge first, and after twenty feet of spray and furrow, the front came down with a splash in two feet of foul water with the tide coming in.

The crash landing had been surprisingly gentle and all three, having silently congratulated themselves on being alive, looked down at their feet. They were ankle deep in slime. Emil jerked his loafers out of the rising fetid flow and looked out of the window as Razor stated the obvious. 'We lost them, Mr Riss.'

Emil turned slowly to the Sikh in the back seat. 'Can't you see what has happened?'

'Mr Riss?'

'My Corvette is in the fucking river!' Emil began to cry.

8

Kitchener Square was deep fathomless black. The weak circle of yellow light cast by the lamp-post at the far end seemed only to exaggerate the impenetrable darkness of the rest. Ronnie drove slowly around. Even the road was potholed and cracked. They could see in the headlights that all that was left was devastation and destruction surrounding a patch of overgrown green that must once have been the garden at the centre of the square. There were gaps where houses used to be, and where the gaps were filled there were only broken windows, half-hinged doors, peeling paint, collapsed walls, sunken roofs, piles of rubble and a million weeds that were nature's fingers up to the big joke of past civilization. Ronnie brought the car to a halt and hitched the handbrake.

'There ain't even a bloody light on,' said Arnie. They looked round the square. He was right, not a glimmer.

'And they came to a ruined city and it was all ruined. Sir Galahad, Sir Perceval and Sir Bors . . .'

'Bernie,' Arnie was using his reasonable tone. 'Will you be quiet? Mirabelle will you shut him up please?' He turned to Ronnie. 'What now?'

'Could wait till morning, Arn. Might be able to see something in the daylight.'

'Spend a night in the Snipe?'

'Done it before, haven't you?'

'The company was more amenable, Ron.'

'Let's have a look round anyway.'

'What at? The rats?'

'How should I know?' Ronnie got out of the car.

Arnie waited a second then angrily opened his door. 'You stay here, Bernie.'

'No! I'm not staying anywhere!' Bernie was out of the car before anyone could object further.

Arnie turned to Mirabelle alone on the back seat. 'You stay then.' He got out, took Bernie's arm and followed Ronnie into the gloom.

Mirabelle watched them go. She'd already seen the house they were looking for. It wasn't as badly damaged as the others and was in the middle of the row on the other side of the square. She knew it was the house because Sorush was sitting on the roof.

9

The Dark Angel was astride the broken tiles with the strange flutter and rustle of the rest of the legion around her. She looked down on Kitchener Square and then over towards Mihr, who had become a blinding nexus of brilliant light centred on the brothers' car in the middle of the green. Neither angel spoke. Mihr had unwillingly accepted the inevitability of the investigation into Charlie and Sorush had no other apparent purpose. Below her by the gutter was Kasbeel with his book already open. He began the incantation, 'I require thee, O Lord Jesus Christ, that thou give . . .' And night turned into day.

The square was as it had been over forty years ago. The houses were Georgian, in need of a paint, but solid and pretty. Many of them had already been converted into flats, but Lucretia Green's was still a single residence, and although beginning to decline, was one of the most impressive houses in the square. It had green curtains and a green door. The small front garden was well tended.

It was early morning and the sun was shining. Two children in school uniform and with satchels on their backs came quickly out of the house next to Lucretia's and raced down the road, late for class. Then the green door opened and Violet, in her early twenties, came tripping down the steps. She hurried away down the road. She too was late.

Sorush looked down from the roof and said, 'That's how she was.'

Mihr hardly had time to respond before Sorush had gone, shifted in time and space, and they were looking down into the saloon bar of a public house.

Violet was pulling a pint. She was a typist by day and a barmaid by night. Her mother objected, but the war wasn't easy for any of them and Violet pretended they needed the few extra shillings she earned. More to the point, she was vivacious and bright, she liked the chat, and most of all she needed to get out of the house.

She handed the beer to a uniformed veteran with a badly scarred face. He shifted on his crutch to take it and gave her a bitter and angry look. Violet smiled and quickly looked away. There were a lot of things about this bloody war that no-one liked and there was no need to keep reminding her of them. Anyway, there was a nice-looking man in a navy-blue suit and black trilby standing at the other end of the bar. He winked at her and raised his empty glass. It was the first time she'd laid eyes on Charlie. She was aware of his eyes on her as she pulled his pint, then felt the touch of his palm as she gave him his change.

He leaned forward over the bar, and after a quick glance at the piano player dropping desultory notes over in the corner he sang softly, 'Sentimental Journey.'

'Thank you, Count Basie.'

'Ames Brothers as a matter of fact. What are you doing later?'

'You should be in uniform, shouldn't you?'

'I'm a spy. There's some vital installations around here. The canning factory for a start.' He grinned but never took his eyes off her as he spoke. He was making her nervous and he knew it.

'Are you in the black market then?' She affected disdain.

'Want a pair of nylons?'

'You're beneath contempt.' She wanted to move away but couldn't.

'I'm on sick leave.'

'Malingerer.'

'I'm in the Royal Engineers, chasing up spanners for the war effort.'

'Oh, you're a mechanic. I can't stand oily men.'

The quip made him smile and the smile gave her the confidence to move away. She picked up a cloth and wiped the back of the bar and then wished she hadn't. The distance she'd put between them was giving him a chance to run his eyes over her whole body. If the back of her legs could have blushed they would have done. She half turned to see him smile and wink at the scarred veteran. 'Next one's on me, mate.'

The veteran looked at Charlie's civvy suit with loathing. 'Swine like you.' Charlie's grin froze, but he kept it constant as the injured man paused then said, 'You're the wise ones.' He moved away from the bar towards the piano. The sound of his crutch was loud on the wooden floor.

Charlie looked up at Vi and his smile unfroze. 'See you.'

They hadn't spoken again and he'd finished his pint and gone. Violet was careful not to look up as he ambled towards the door, but she couldn't resist a glance as he opened it. He went without looking back. She leaned on the bar and wished she'd forced him into making a date. That was what it was like around there. People came and people went. Most of the time you never saw them again.

Charlie wasn't like other people. Two hours later Violet came down the steps from the Black Owl and into the blackout. She hated it. She couldn't see a thing and imagined worse. It had been a quiet night and she'd been bored. A cloud passed over the moon and what light there'd been immediately vanished. She put a hand out to touch a shop window and steady herself.

'Walk you home, Miss Violet?'

She jumped. A match flared and she saw Charlie's face as he lit a cigarette. She couldn't help thinking he looked good with his face illuminated yellow for a second beneath the brim of his hat. 'You gave me a shock, you did! How d'you know my name?'

'I made enquiries, Miss. In my experience it's always an advantage to know the moniker of your future wife.' He'd let the match burn and she could see his confident smiling eyes as he grinned at her.

She was taken aback. 'You what?'

'You're the most beautiful woman I've ever seen.'

'Bugger off!' She moved away as quickly as she could. Then the cloud passed from the moon and she increased her pace. There was no-one around and all she could hear for a while was her own footsteps echoing in the deserted street. Then she became aware of another sound. He was somewhere behind her, singing 'You Made Me Love You' softly. She stopped and looked back. It was difficult to see anything in the darkness, but slowly she could make him out, moving in and out of the shadows on the street. She hurried on, but could still hear the sound of his voice in the blackout behind her. No matter how quickly she went, the song always seemed the same distance away and was always sung in the same measured, relaxed tone. She had to admit to herself that she quite liked it. Then it stopped and so did Violet. She looked back and waited. There was nothing except the eerie silence of the dark streets. For the second time that night she felt disappointed and then turned and continued her journey home. She walked quickly along the side of the square and took out her door keys as she climbed the steps to her mother's house.

He was sitting on a bench in the middle of the square, but now he was singing at the top of his voice.

'Ssshhhh! You'll wake everybody!' She went quickly back down the steps to the pavement. 'How did you know where I lived? How did you get here?'

He carried on singing.

'Will you be quiet!' He stopped. 'And will you please go away.'

'Sweet dreams, Violet. I'll see you in the morning.' He lay back on the bench and put his head on the armrest, then he tilted his trilby forward over his eyes and folded his arms to sleep.

Violet couldn't believe it. 'You won't!' She turned, climbed the steps again, unlocked the door and went in, slamming it behind her.

Charlie grinned under his hat. The bang of that door would have woken the dead. He must have got to her. He was experienced enough to know that this kind of approach to a woman had to be unwavering. You couldn't say you'd marry the girl and then look as though you didn't mean it. Charlie had no idea whether glances across crowded rooms, instant recognitions, love at first sight and all that were true, but he knew that women thought they were. And given that she was attracted to him, which he could see was so, then if there was no deviation in his intent and no hesitation in his pursuit, she would finally come to understand that he was the man of her life, and if she wasn't certain, he was – his very persistence was proof that it was so. And who knows, maybe it was all true, maybe he did want to marry her? Whatever else, he was reasonably confident he'd fuck her soon enough. He shifted again on the bench and decided that once he thought she was asleep he'd go and have a kip on the back seat of the car.

Violet stood in the darkened hall. Her mother and May had gone to bed. She didn't want to turn on any lights in case he came banging on the door, so she felt her way quietly up the stairs. She could hear her mother snoring as she passed her bedroom on the landing, then she went into her own room, dropped her handbag on the bed, lifted the corner of the curtain and peeped out of the window. He was still there. He'd put his hands behind his head and was whistling. If nothing else she was flattered. She undressed and got into bed. Five minutes later she got up and looked out of the window again. He was still there. This time she felt angry. Who did he think he was? She got back into bed and decided to forget about him.

The next morning he was gone. Violet couldn't make up her mind as to whether she was relieved or disappointed. Finally she decided that he couldn't have been serious and tried to put him out of her mind. She ate her breakfast too quickly as usual, said ta-ta to May and her mother, and walked through the square to work.

She didn't see him all that day or in the Black Owl that evening, although every time the door opened she looked up, half hoping it was him coming in. Finally she decided that he'd had his chance and that was that. She had enough men buzzing around for her to worry about an idiot who didn't wear a uniform and hadn't even fought for his country. Anyway, there was James, her fiancé. He was a good man and he loved her and he should be enough for any woman. She looked up again when the door opened. It wasn't Charlie. He'd probably just been acting the fool the previous night, or worse, was playing hard to get. Either way, sod him. By closing time she'd given him up entirely. She washed and wiped the last of the glasses and stacked them neatly behind the bar. Then the sirens started. The landlord, who'd sat his fat self on a high stool all night and hadn't moved a muscle, got up and went to the cellar door. 'You coming down?'

'No, I'm going to risk it.'

'Please yourself.' He shrugged and waited while she put on her coat, then turned all the lights off as she ran out into the blackout. She didn't give a damn about aeroplanes and she'd spent enough time sitting on damp beer crates in the basement with her grubby employer looking at her the wrong way. Sod him and sod Adolf. The street was deserted and she wanted to walk home and think about the dance that weekend. She was going with James . . .

'Give you a lift?' It was Charlie. Violet couldn't believe how he managed to show up at almost exactly the moment she'd stopped thinking about him. He was smoking and nonchalantly leaning on an almost new black Morris. He had a different suit on. It was difficult not to be impressed.

'Is that your car?'

'It's an old one. I'm swapping it over tomorrow.' He dropped his cigarette on the pavement, crushed it with the sole of his shiny shoe and opened the car door. 'Jump in, I'll take you home.'

'You can go and swap yourself over!' She went to move past him and he put a hand out and touched her arm.

104

'Come on, Violet. There's an air raid on.'

'I don't care!'

'You're like me, girl. I don't give tuppence either! When it's got your name on it, it has, and when it ain't, well what's all the fuss?' He looked up to the sky. The sirens had stopped and there was the low sound of distant bombers. 'Ain't for us anyway. They're going west.' He hadn't moved his hand from her arm and she hadn't moved away. He was very close. It was the smiling eyes and the certainty she couldn't stand. 'Why don't you face it? You like me, don't you?'

'Why don't you go and take a jump!'

'I can see it. I can see what you feel.'

'What do I feel?'

'You're in love with me.'

'I don't even know you!' She turned away angrily, but he pulled her back.

'What's that got to do with it? It's inevitable isn't it? I'd say it was fate.' Neither of them had heard the plane, but the bomb seemed to explode very close. Violet said afterwards that she'd felt the wind blow hot on her face and would swear that the Morris had been blown a good foot along the road. She remembered running and she wasn't sure how she'd got there, but she found herself in Charlie's arms in a shop doorway.

'What did I tell you?' He leaned in and kissed her cheek. It was very gentle, not much more than a peck, and she didn't try to pull away. 'See, even Hitler knows.' He smiled and she looked up at him, waiting for him to kiss her again. This time it was on the mouth and she felt her arms going up around his neck to pull him towards her, and then, instead, push him roughly away.

'I don't care about Hitler! I'm engaged to be married!' She turned and ran.

Charlie watched as she disappeared down the street. The bomb had hit a cinema, already there were shouts and men running out onto the street with buckets of water. He could see Violet silhouetted by the flames for a second and he suddenly felt very bad. He walked over to his car and ran his finger over the roof. It was covered in soot. He opened the door and sat in the driver's seat. She'd said she was getting married. Now he knew that he'd been serious from the moment he'd laid eyes on her. He started the engine.

Mihr was silent. She'd let Sorush unravel.
  Time shifted again.

*   *   *

To a dance hall. It had been a week since Charlie had seen Violet. He'd been surprised by how much he'd thought about her. He had a big deal on and usually the parley, the stalk and the strike, with the occasional bint of an evening, would have occupied him, but every day there seemed to be something that conspired to remind him of her: a flower seller, an advertising hoarding, even another girl in a pub. Violet, Violet, Violet. He had to face it, he was becoming obsessed by the thought of her. He'd gone back to the Black Owl three days later, but was told she'd packed up the job. He hadn't even bothered to stop for a drink and had stood outside wondering whether to call at her house, but then he thought she might not be there, or worse she'd catch him hanging around waiting for her, which would make him look weak and feel like a supplicant. He knew for a fact that he wouldn't win her that way. He had to be on top form, blood up, confidence rising, punchy with the gab and rocking with laughter. In other words he had to be normal charming Charlie, not a sap suckered by love. And anyway there was something else. He somehow knew that this thing would happen. Him and Vi would go together down the road, horse and carriage, love and marriage. He knew it. He was sure he'd been right; it was their fate. The thought filled him with fantastic delight and it scared the seven shits out of him.

He waited until the following weekend and then put on his best grey with a silk tie and went to a dance at the town hall. He'd never felt such a strong instinct. He'd have bet his mother's life that she would be there, and she was. He saw her dancing with a tall bloke in a cheap blue suit and knew immediately that this was his rival, her fiancé. His spirits rose. The bloke was clearly a prat. He looked uncomfortable, his hair was thinning, and worse – it would have been obvious to a corpse – he loved her too much. That would be no good to Vi; she was a colt, the fastest on the track; she was pure energy and craved a harness, a pull on the rein, not a cuddle and lovey-dovey. If Charlie knew anything, he knew power sought power, and compared to him the prick in blue didn't stand a chance. He went to the bar and ordered a whisky. This was more like it; he was feeling like himself again.

The dance came to an end and he watched as Violet left her fiancé and moved through the crowd on the floor towards him at the bar. This was his chance and he hid behind a crowd of soldiers as she approached, then suddenly stepped out in front of her. 'Care for a caper?'

Violet stopped dead. She'd thought about him all week and here he was, looking everything she'd dreamed of. 'No! Not here! You can't be here. Go away!' She walked quickly past him and went into the Ladies at the corner of the bar.

Charlie looked around. Nobody seemed to have noticed the rebuff and he was thankful enough for that. He went to the bar and ordered another drink. The fiancé was waiting like a lonely fool on the dance floor. Charlie sensed he was a walkover and felt no pity. The band struck up another number and he decided on his next move. He had a quick look round and saw immediately what he needed. She had dark hair, a nice figure and more importantly was looking over at him. Another lonely lady in time of war; it was all too easy. He winked and crossed the bar towards her. Her name was Phyllis and he made sure he was giving her his most vibrant smile when Violet came out of the Ladies. She, of course, ignored him and went straight back onto the dance floor, followed within seconds by Charlie and his new enchanted friend.

He made sure that he and Phyllis danced within a few feet of Violet and her boy in blue, and every time he found himself facing her over the shoulders of their respective partners he winked or smiled. At first she looked away, then she began to giggle, and finally he could have sworn she was manoeuvring her partner so as to be in sympathy with the turns he was making. At one point her fiancé caught her look and turned sharply to look at him. Charlie grinned and winked at him too. The fiancé went bright red and before Charlie could register his astonishment, not to say slight twinge of guilt, the number ended and Violet was being led from the floor.

Charlie dumped the disappointed Phyllis with a mock bow, and he was heading back towards the bar, pushing his way through the increasingly raucous crowd of military drunks, before she could say anything. Violet and her beau had taken a table in the corner and Charlie was wondering what he should do next when, as usual in his life, fate intervened. Six feet away a squat corporal with dots for eyes was looking up and down at Charlie's suit with a sneer on his spittle-wet gob. 'Oi! Who are you fighting for, mate?'

107

Charlie decided to smooth it. 'A barmaid.'

'Colonel fucking Conchie, I reckon.' The corporal put down his glass and several of his mates, too ugly for dates, began to crowd in. Out of the corner of his eye Charlie could see Violet's fiancé coming towards them at the bar. Was he going to join in too? With a seamless move from fear to advance, Charlie realized that a trouble doubled could well be a problem solved. He frowned and leaned into the corporal. 'Listen. Mind if I have a word in your lug?' He whispered for no more than ten seconds. The fiancé came closer to the bar and never knew what hit him, or more to the point, why it hit him. The soldiers parted to let him through and then two of them grabbed his arms while the corporal kneed him in the groin. Charlie slipped quickly away as a third soldier punched the fiancé in the face. By the time he'd fallen to the floor Charlie had crossed the bar to Violet, who'd stood to see what was going on. He said, sharply, 'Come on, I want to get you out of here.'

'What's happening?'

'It's war, in' it?' Charlie turned. As usual the fight had spread and the bar was already a khaki tumult of flying fists and boot caps. 'And your feller started it.'

'Where is he?'

'Who cares?'

'I want to know!'

He grabbed her arm. 'Vi, I've done pubs, bombs and now I've done the British army. How much more do I have to do?' He'd meant every word and looked down into her eyes. 'Are you going to come with me? Please.' A chair hit the wall a few feet from where they were standing and Charlie didn't wait for an answer, he took her hand and pulled her out. She only half resisted as they ran across the car park. The thought of going with him was too exhilarating and she didn't want to think about anything else. He opened the door of his car. 'Get in.'

'Charlie?'

'Just do it, Violet. You want to, I know you do.'

She knew that if she paused any longer she wouldn't do it, and he was right, she did want to. She got in as he went round to the other side and came in next to her. She was conscious of refusing to allow herself to think as he started the engine. She watched the high street pass, concentrating on the gleam of the dashboard and the smell of the leather seats. She began to make excuses in her mind. She'd tell James she'd lost him in the rumpus, had looked all over for him but couldn't find him. She could even pretend to be angry with him for deserting her while the fight was going on. After all it could have been dangerous, she could have been hurt. She was halfway to convincing herself when Charlie passed her a half-bottle of Scotch. 'There y'are, girl, that'll make you feel better.'

She unscrewed the cap and took a long swig. It made her cough. 'I don't know what I'm doing.'

Charlie took the bottle back and took a swallow himself. 'Don't worry about it. I do.' He was feeling more nervous than he'd ever felt in his life, but knew that whatever he was doing, it was somehow right. This was it and whatever happened he would have to push it through. Now or never, Charlie.

Violet couldn't stop herself, she needed to know. 'Why did they suddenly attack James like that?'

Charlie glanced at her and decided honesty could be the only policy. She had to know it was all for her. 'I told them I was an investigator from Catterick on the lookout for deserters.'

Violet could see it already. 'Charlie!'

'They must have thought your bloke . . .'

'He's a policeman!'

'What?' Even Charlie hadn't thought of that one. Perhaps it was because of the momentary look of panic that crossed his face, making him look like a five-year-old, or perhaps it was just sheer nerves, but whatever the cause, Violet burst out laughing. Charlie was caught between fear and delight as he looked at her. What was she laughing at? Then he realized, he'd done it! This girl was his! 'What did I tell you! Fate! It rules our lives, Violet!' He changed up a gear and put his foot down. The car shot forward and the streets passed in a dark blur.

Violet watched him as he drove. His hands were strong and his manner easy. Now she knew and she could admit it. She'd wanted him from the moment he'd walked into the pub. And she'd go with him wherever he took her.

'You're going to have to take me home to your mum some time,' he said.

Kasbeel closed the book and brought the incantation to an end. Sorush had already gone from the roof. She had no further words for Mihr.

*   *   *

Mirabelle looked up at Lucretia's house. She knew for a fact that the brothers were now going to find their grandmother. Sorush wouldn't have been here otherwise. Even as she thought it a light came on in an upper window.

10

'Up there!' It was Arnie's voice.

'Whass up? Whass up?' Bernie boomed.

'Why don't we go and ask?' asked Arnie. He was close to Mirabelle as she sat in the open door of the car.

'It's a bit late, Arn,' said Ronnie.

'It's the only light in the bloody square, isn't it?' They looked up as a second dim light came on in the house. 'Let's have a look.' Arnie began to cross the green.

'This where Gran lives then?'

'Shut up, Bernie.'

Hardly had they arrived at what was left of the gate, when the front door of the house opened. A small, ball-like man in his seventies, wearing an old, worn, plaid dressing gown, stood in the darkness of the doorway. He spoke in an affected tone. 'Mrs Green does not appreciate these pandemoniums and shenanigans.'

'Mrs Green?' Ronnie looked at Arn.

'That's what I said.'

'And who are you?' Arnie was pretty sure he already knew.

'Albert Rollins.'

'I thought so.' He turned to his youngest brother. 'This is him. This is Albert, Bernie.'

'So, who's Bob?' Bernie never forgot a question.

'Up there.' Ronnie pointed up to a first-floor window where the hunched silhouette of an old woman had appeared. She was lit from behind by a dull yellow bulb and seemed to be looking down on them. 'Is that her, Arn?'

'Course it is.' Arnie turned to Albert at the top of the steps. 'Remember me? I was about ten the last time you saw me. In the café in Streatham? Remember?'

'We know who you are. We saw you get out of your car. Mrs Green has decided she will see you for a few minutes in the hope that you will then go away and not disturb her again.' Albert took a step back into the hallway.

'And nice to see you too, Albert.' Arnie started to walk up the steps towards the faded peeling paintwork of the green door. Albert stepped to one side and they trooped past him into the dilapidated hallway. Bernie shivered as he looked up at the mould-covered walls and Albert motioned for them to go on up the stairs.

'Galahad don' half get himself in strange adventures, Meebelle.'

'So he does, Bernie.'

'And these bloody stairs are bloody spongy.' Bernie was scared his feet were going to go straight through the crumbling wood, but looked ahead and saw that Arnie didn't seem to have the jitters at all, so he followed. The only light on the landing, apart from the bare bulb above their heads, was coming through a half-open doorway ahead of them. Arnie went carefully along the creaking, half-rotten floorboards and slowly pushed the door open. Lucretia Green lay propped on mildewed cushions on a huge four-poster directly in front of him. He went in slowly with Ronnie and the others behind.

Bernie had never seen so much junk in his life. There was chairs covered in falling-apart drapes, with holes in them, that were stacked on tables which were then stacked up even higher on some old sofas. There were these boxes full of stuff that was overflowing and there was dark pictures and trunks all in huge piles around her big old bed that had like tree poles round it and tatty old curtains hanging up, and these also had holes in them. Everything had holes in it, and it all stunk of rot. It was like the rats had got in or something. And on the bed was her. This must be his gran. She must have been nearly ninety at least, and looked like it too. She had hundreds of wrinkles and deep cracks in her face, and she looked disgusted, like she'd just smelled something horrible or something. And she stunk herself too.

Once they were all in the room Albert shut the door behind them.

'Hello, er . . . Gran.' Arnie was the only one of the three of them who'd ever really met her, but even he was unsure of what to call her.

The old girl croaked and pointed a withered finger at each of them in turn. 'You must be Arnold. You, Ronald. And you, Brian.'

Bernie was nonplussed. 'What?' His big head seemed to revolve on his neck as his eyes bulged. 'I'm not Brian.'

'It's Bernie, Mrs Green,' Mirabelle helped out.

'Bernard,' Lucretia corrected her. 'Ah, yes, the defective one.'

Bernie's head revolved again. 'You what?'

Lucretia ignored him and eyed Mirabelle. 'Are you his nurse? Violet left them because of this idiot.'

'What idiot?' This was not what Bernie had expected at all. He looked at his bruvs.

'It's all right, Bern.' Ronnie half sighed. He was beginning to wish they hadn't bothered.

Lucretia glared at them. 'Why have you come? And at this time of night?'

Ronnie could see that Arnie was beginning to glaze over, a sure sign of impending aggression, which he didn't think was going to do any good at all. He decided to be diplomatic. 'How are you, er . . . Gran?' She didn't answer. 'Er . . . We need to find our mother, you see, er . . . Violet, and we hoped you might . . .'

She cut him off. 'I don't know where she is, and if I did I wouldn't tell you.'

Ronnie didn't know what to say to that. Arnie was more positive. 'Why wouldn't you, Gran?'

His irritation was like a red rag to a sacred cow. She pushed herself up in the bed and leaned forward on scarecrow arms. 'I hear your father's dead.' Then she sneered. 'Good.'

There was a silence as the brothers looked at each other. Finally Arnie managed to say, 'What?'

Lucretia seemed to be satisfied by her evening's work and lay back on her disgusting pillows. 'Show them out, Albert.'

'Hang on! Wait a minute! Do you mind?' Arnie had thrust his nose forward and Ronnie could see that there wasn't much that could be done to stop him now. 'Why'd you let us in then? Just so you could insult us and insult our bloody dad?'

Lucretia's mouth snapped into a line. 'To stop you pestering me!' She turned to her rotund companion who was smirking. 'Albert, show them out!'

'Who do you think you are?' Arnie's neck was beginning to crane, another bad sign. He looked around the wall-to-wall debris. 'Is this your house? I know homeless people who are better off than you!' Listening to all those years of the old man's resentment at this old cow had taken their toll.

'Albert!' Lucretia tried to shout, but it was more like a terrible racked wheeze. Her breath was coming quicker.

'Anyone with any manners would have offered their grandsons a cup of tea!' Arnie was working up to full fury. 'My dad was right, you're a bloody monster!'

Lucretia replied with a venom that belied her years, or perhaps had grown because of them. 'Your craven father destroyed my child, and I have no time, let alone cups of tea, for the cretins he created! Now, Albert, will you show them out!' She lay back on the pillows waving her ancient talons in front of her withered face, her pigeon chest heaving with the effort of a violent disdain.

'Thank you very much, Mrs Green.' Ronnie decided enough was enough and turned on his heel. Arnie clenched his hands by his side, stared, made a conscious effort to clamp his jaw tight, then walked after Ronnie without a word.

Bernie stayed rooted to the spot, staring at the old lady. He hadn't quite understood what had happened, but he was sure this couldn't be his gran. Mirabelle took his hand. 'Come on, Bernie.'

He made up his mind that there'd been some mistake. This definitely wasn't his gran. This was some other geezer. He swivelled his head on his neck again and pursed his lips. 'You got up the nose of my bruvs, Mrs.' He blinked hard and didn't know what to say next. 'So anyhow . . . I'm going.' He went out after his brothers, leaving the old girl tight-lipped and silent.

Mirabelle forced a smile. 'Good night, Mrs Green.' She turned and went. Lucretia wanted to lie back alone, poison-perfect and triumphant in her revenge, but instead felt a blast of freezing air and shuddered as the young waitress left her bedroom. Had she but known it, she'd just experienced the cold pity of an angel.

Ronnie slammed the car door and turned the ignition. He couldn't remember the last time he'd felt so angry. 'I thought grannies were nice old girls who gave you tenpence when your teeth fell out.'

'I'm amazed we're so fucking sane,' Arnie slammed his door too, 'with ancestors like that . . .'

'We should all be barmy!' Bernie completed it for him with a deep chuckle. 'That's right in' it, Arn? We should all be barmy!'

'I heard you the first time, Bern.'

Ronnie put the Snipe in gear and they turned out of the square. 'You didn't help, Arn, giving it to her like that.'

'You heard what she said! What else was I supposed to do?'

Ronnie didn't answer. He'd felt insulted too, especially when she'd called Bernie defective. Remarks like that didn't so much hurt as shock. Bernie wasn't defective; he was Bernie. And what may have been unusual or comic or even disturbing to outsiders was perfectly normal to them. He shifted into top gear and the Snipe purred away from Lucretia and her horrible lair.

Mirabelle could feel the disturbance in Arnie and Ron. She knew they hadn't deserved the treatment they'd received from Lucretia. She wondered what Charlie and Violet could have done to have so destroyed her mother.

Bernie suddenly spoke into the gloom. 'For crying out loud, I'm starving hungry! I could do with double eggs, double bacon, double tomato . . .'

'How about a ruby?' Arnie turned in his seat with what seemed like relief and a sudden grin. Bollocks to Lucretia, he wanted to have a drink, and he knew just the place.

Bernie was ecstatic. 'Sayeed Sayeed! Oh yes! Oh yes! Double curry! And double chips! And double bacon curry! And double tomato curry . . .' He kept it up for the next three miles.

11

Emil stood on the dockside and watched as Jock and Razor, up to their knees in mud and water, tried to push the now more brown than white Corvette out of the river. He'd kept them at it for as long as he thought they'd wear it. The only alternative was a call on the mobile to Papa and that wasn't an alternative, it was suicide. 'Push! Push! Whatsamatter with you? My Corvette! I don't believe it!'

Razor stood back from the car and, having placed all his weight in one spot for longer than two seconds, immediately sank another six inches into the ooze. 'We need help, Mr Riss.' Simplicity was truth and Razor was telling it like it was.

Emil stared at the mobile. His time had come and he knew it. He took a deep breath and tapped the number into the phone, as if each touch gave him an electric shock, then he walked up and down the riverside in deep and personal terror as he waited for the connection. He wailed back to the boys in the river, 'My papa is going to kill me. My car could be dead. My brown and white car! Push! Push! You crazy, crazy guys!' It was a last and futile exhortation and he knew it. He shouted at the stars, 'How am I going to pull the Fräuleins now, huh? This is three inches off my dick!'

Jock, aware of Emil's despair, could only cry lamely from the water, 'Honest boss, I swear I saw a white horse.'

'You don't see no white horse, you drink it!' The phone rang at the other end and Emil jumped as if someone had just punched him in the back. He held the mobile away from his ear as though it was going to explode. Then he heard his father's voice. This was it. His infantile psyche was about to be shattered. 'Hi, Papa! What's on TV? You having a good time?' There was no answer and Emil knew he may as well put his head on the block, load the rifles and tie the noose. He adopted a deep, rather businesslike tone. 'Papa, I got some bad news...'

Luis went up the wall, across the ceiling and down the other side. If he'd been a volcano the city would have been brain-deep in lava. He went red, pink, white, black and then red again, like some surrealist traffic light. He shouted, he spluttered, he stuttered, he went ballistic, destroyed the target, came back, destroyed his launch pad and went sky-high again. Luis was mad as hell. 'What! You what! You prick! You what? . . . I got a prick for a son! Next time I want a screw, I use you!' He looked up at Raphaella, his face white in disbelief. 'You hear this? This prick Emil put the Corvette in the water!'

Raphaella was, on the face of it, unconcerned. 'When you going to learn?'

Luis was back on the phone, or in it might have been a better way of putting it. If he could have squeezed himself into the receiver, elbowed his way down the line and jumped out of the mouthpiece the other end and beat the living prickness out of a son, he'd have done it. 'No!' he screamed. 'You don't do nothing about the Lack Brothers! You get a tow truck for the car!'

This struck hard at Emil's self-esteem. He was no longer big boy in a hat and Corvette, he was the jerk who called the garage. 'Hey, hey, Papa, listen to me. I mean, who you got that's better than me to fill in a Lack?' The screams at the other end were so intense, even at full-arm stretch from the ear, that Emil put the mobile on a rusting anchor near the water's edge, walked five yards away and waited. After a couple of minutes he sidled back, crouched two feet from the mouthpiece and was as amenable as he could be at that distance. 'OK, Papa. I accept your wisdom. We get someone else and we give it to these brothers with compound interest, right?' This was his attempt to be ingratiatingly witty. It didn't work. The mobile, true to its name, jumped off the anchor and bounced around on the ground as the electronic pulse from the other side of town burned the plastic.

'Compound interest! What's the matter with you? Every time you open your mouth, you say compound interest! Never, ever, ever, say that to me again! Learn something else! Learn "capital investment"! Learn "high finance"! Learn "corporation tax"! Learn how not to put a fucking American car in the fucking English river!' Luis slammed down the phone and stared at it. He was shaking badly. 'I am wounded in a part of me that don't know how to talk.'

Raphaella was cool. She moved slowly towards the remains of the Chinese meal still spread over the huge table. 'So what you going to do, Luis?'

He erupted again. 'Don't call me Luis! I am your papa! How come I got a son who got no brain in his mind and a daughter who got no respect?'

Raphaella was unperturbed. She was moving mysteriously towards the cold egg fried rice. 'So what you going to do, Papa?'

Luis sat at the table with his head in his hands. 'How should I know?'

'I got a restaurant and I'm gonna keep it.'

'I know you got a restaurant, Raphaella! You don't have to tell me every five minutes! I know you got a restaurant!' Luis was beginning to babble.

'So, Papa, what we do is this.' She sweetly lifted the brown-paper carton from the Chinese restaurant and plonked it under his nose.

'What you talking about?'

She pointed a long fingernail, painted in pink of your dreams, at the logo plus telephone number printed at the bottom of the bag. 'Take a look at takeaway, Papa.'

'Huh?'

She moved the bag closer. Luis was no wiser. She held it up three inches from his eyes. 'Take a good look.'

A pause. Luis had looked and he had understood. He gulped, 'You mean?' He stopped; he couldn't believe what she meant. He couldn't believe he even thought she meant it. He couldn't believe she even knew who they were! 'You mean Chan? You mean Chan and Gerard McCarthy? How you know about the twins?' He stared at her. The McCarthys were only known by rumour and the cream of the streets like him, not stupid girls who spent their life buying nail varnish. 'How you know about the twins?' He was beginning to feel very nervous.

'I hear.'

'Where you hear from!'

'From the snipper in the haircutter who screw the brother of Gianni Morelli.'

'Morelli?' Morelli was even bigger than Luis. This was getting serious.

'So you going to call them?'

'Are you crazy?' He'd asked her nicely. He sat with his head sticking up out of his neck, just like a little boy at the table looking up at his mother.

Raphaella loomed over him, 'Are you Papa? Or are you Luis? Or maybe you are little prick brother who sink a Corvette?'

'I am Papa!' Luis the little boy roared, his eyes wide and round.

'So prove it.'

'Wha . . . ?'

'You heard me.' She prowled above him. Her scent was beginning to envelop him and he could feel he was going a little wacko.

She asked again, 'Who are you?'

'I . . . I am Papa.' For some reason he was very scared.

'So.' She sat by him and put a perfumed arm round his sloping, shivering shoulders. 'And you are good Papa. You are sweet Papa. You are big and brave Papa.' Her voice was cold. She didn't mean it; he knew she didn't mean it; she knew he knew, and she didn't care. She had him by the sacred ancestral foreskin and was about to tweak. She pulled the paper bag closer and pointed again at the phone number. 'And so I got a restaurant.' She waited.

Luis just stared at her and gulped again. 'You want me to call Chan and Gerard McCarthy?'

She didn't bother to answer. Why was she related to such dickheads? She picked up the phone and dialled the number.

'You know what it means when you call the twins?' Luis was shaking now. 'You're talking about a contract, you get me?'

'I don't care what you sign.' She stared with bland unblinking eyes. 'See, Luis, point is, if first Mrs Lack don't get no divorce and is still breathing when second Mrs Lack get hitched, then second marriage don't get nod from legal eagles. And Charlie's will don' do me no good. So, second point is, first Mrs Lack got to disappear final so no-one knows if she's alive or dead when I marry Charlie. Get me?' Luis didn't. Raphaella winked at him. 'With a pot of paint, restaurant worth maybe three-quarter million.' There was a click as someone picked up the phone at the other end, then a Chinese voice. Raphaella held the receiver up to her father's mouth.

'Hello. Ah?' Luis's throat was dry and he was beginning to sweat.

Raphaella pulled a pink tissue from her sleeve and dabbed his forehead. 'My dear Papa . . .'

12

Sayeed Sayeed had given the brothers a warm greeting. Charlie's sons were always welcome in the Bengali Star. It had once been known as the last restaurant in the east, but in recent years the wasteland around it had begun to be built up again. Small communities surrounding hypermarkets and petrol stations had appeared like beacons in the rubble. Nevertheless, progress wasn't quick, and the Bengali Star still stood in about twenty square miles of nothing. You got there by a web of short roads, turning right and left and right again every fifty or so yards. These had once been terraced streets, but the houses were long gone and now there were just heaps of brick and concrete. So indeed the star above the Bengali did shine bright. It was twenty feet in diameter, fringed by yellow bulbs and wired to a fifty-foot pylon high above the restaurant. In some directions you could see it from ten miles away across the low black silhouettes of the piles of debris.

Sayeed Sayeed had immediately sat the brothers at one of his best tables in a bright-red velvet alcove beneath a vibrant mural of a tiger. Bernie had asked for double curry and chips before he'd sat down; Arnie wanted a quadruple Scotch and a couple of bottles of house red, and Ronnie had used the phone to call Harriet. Sayeed smiled at Mirabelle, his special friend, and told her to leave it all to him. Within minutes Bernie found himself looking down at a huge pile of curry and potatoes on the biggest plate they could find in the kitchen. Arnie swirled the ice in his glass as Ronnie opened the wine.

'Who's Bob?' Bernie asked with his mouth full.

'Dunno, Bern.' Arnie drank again. 'Could be anyone. Bob the Bobbie, Bob-a-job, Bob Hope.'

'Could be Bob's your Uncle!' Bernie honked with laughter and stuck his fork into the curry. Arnie and Ron watched him eat. 'You want to go on with all this, Ron?' asked Arnie after a minute or two.

'I don't know, mate.' Ronnie stared at the wine in his glass. That seemed to be the end of the conversation for a while. Sayeed's smiling waiters plied the table. Bernie had some more, and then some more with some paratha, then he'd belched and farted twice and said he wanted to go to bed. Sayeed Sayeed had a couple of the waiters make up a bed for him in the upstairs storeroom and Mirabelle led him away, yawning, through the empty restaurant. Then the old Bengali sat down at the table. Most of the food he'd provided hadn't been touched. Mirabelle had virtually no appetite, Ronnie had picked at it and Arnie just drank. 'You got any idea where our mum might have gone, Sayeed?' he asked.

'If I could tell you, I would. I remember the day she went. Charlie cried many tears.' Sayeed shrugged sadly. 'He had lost the beautiful Violet.'

'Thank you for the Eastern wisdom.'

'Arn?' Ronnie gave him a look.

'Sorry, Sayeed. I'm feeling a bit black.' Arnie drank again.

The old Bengali touched his hand. 'These things mean great pain for all the family. Charlie was crazy with pain. One night he came here. He was very drunk and said he knew there would be blood on his hands. I said, what do you mean? He said, nothing. I said, what are you going to do, Charlie? He said, nothing.'

'What was he talking about?'

'I don't know. Ronnie. Sometimes, after, he'd say it was just his fate. Another time he said she'd gone away with Tom Cherry. I don't know.'

Arnie looked up. 'Cherry? Harriet found a picture of him this morning.'

'She won't have gone with him,' said Ronnie.

'Why not?'

'I don't know.' Ronnie was pulling back from the table. 'Cherry was married.'

'No he wasn't.'

'He was, Arn.'

'How do you know? You were only ten.'

'I knew about him.'

'What did you know?'

'I didn't know anything.' Ronnie obviously didn't want to talk about Cherry.

'She may have gone to him for help, or for a job in one of his dress shops,' Arnie persisted.

'She wouldn't have.'

'How do you know?'

'I thought you didn't want to find her!' Ronnie was getting agitated.

'I didn't say that!'

'Come on, Arnie, you didn't want to get in the Snipe and you didn't want to come over here!'

'What's up with you?'

'Nothing.' Ronnie looked away. 'Anyway no-one knows where Cherry is.'

'I do.' Sayeed Sayeed smiled.

They both turned to him. Ronnie seemed nervous. 'Where?'

'I can show you.' The old man pushed himself up from the table and walked to the door of the restaurant. Arnie and Ronnie stood and followed him out. It was a bright night with a high moon and Sayeed Sayeed seemed to gleam in his yellow dhoti. He pointed across the wasteland to distant blocks and office towers on the edge of the city, rising against the starlit sky. 'There.'

'How do you know, Sayeed?' Arnie was beginning to feel nervous himself.

'He came to eat here once. He is a very rich man. A very charming man.'

'He mention Mum?'

'No. But he showed me the tower where he had his office.'

'Which one is it?' Ronnie asked.

Sayeed Sayeed pointed to a block standing separate and to the right of the others. 'That one.'

The two brothers didn't move. They stared at the tower, each wrapped in his own thoughts and his own reasons for packing in this quest right now. 'You want to go, Ron?' asked Arn.

'I don't know. You?'

Arnie didn't have time to answer. From out of nowhere came the beep of a car horn and then an echoing shout. 'Whooeee! Surprise, surprise!' A taxi was coming across the wasteland. It was still about half a mile away and they could clearly see Lucy hanging out of the back window. Arnie grinned. Harriet must have told the girls where they were. They could worry about Tom Cherry tomorrow.

'Give Auntie another bell, Ron, it looks like it's going to be an all-nighter.' He gave the old Indian a big grin. 'All right, Sayeed? One for the old man?'

13

It was after midnight. Luis was exhilarated. He walked quickly up Great Stuckey Street. 'Emil, you want to see what your papa can do?' He chuckled to himself. 'Lacks don't you mix with no Riss!' He laughed out loud. He felt good. Raphaella had shown him the way. Now he knew who he was again, and he was going to do what he should have done from the beginning. He was going to hire the McCarthy Twins! He was a new man. He was his daughter's father!

He suddenly stopped. His heart was in his mouth. He was terrified. He was about to hire the McCarthy Twins? Was he crazy? The fear caused his body to crease. His gut began to churn and he was in physical pain as he slunk slowly down Peterborough Alley. Get it straight. In order to impress his daughter, teach his son a lesson and terrify the Lack Brothers, he was about to press the inner city's equivalent of the nuclear button? Was he out of his mind?

No. He straightened. He was doing the right thing. A man of his cut, cloth and double-breasted should do whatever was necessary. Didn't he have clout and muscle, shouldn't he show these pygmy Lacks that he had his loafers well astride their globe? He turned left smartly up Broadhurst Street. His head was in the air, his nose aquiline and his mouth grim. He was Caesar, leader of men.

Aaah! The pain hit again. 'What are you doing, you stupid fuck!' He stopped in his tracks. He couldn't move. Ahead was the Peking Palace, the deepest bunker in town, the steamy hide-out of the McCarthys. He felt in his inside pocket. The cash was there in brown envelopes, each containing 500 pounds. His safe in the apartment was empty. How many envelopes would he have to shell out? You never knew with the twins. Aaah! The pain was getting worse. He staggered forward. Could he do this? It was like unleashing the holocaust, and how much was it going to cost him? He stopped. His legs began to turn him round to the left, his torso still pushed forward and his head spun to the right. 'What are you, some crazy fucking contortionist? Stand up!' He did. 'Breathe!' He did. 'Be calm!' Impossible. He was stuck halfway down Broadhurst Street, by the dry-cleaners, his knees knocking and his mouth opening and closing with no sound.

Then he heard it, like it was a voice out of a drain, 'What are you? Are you Papa or are you little prick, Emil?' It was Raphaella, clear as day. Aural hallucinations were something new to Luis and for a moment he marvelled at the sheer genius of his own insanity. Then his mind cleared and he saw the truth. For twenty-eight years he'd thought his daughter was his pooch, his lickle-dickle spoiled brat, his half of him, his excuse for being a daddy, his reason for living for God's sake! But in this piercing instant he knew different. He could see now what he'd really raised. She was Boudicca, Medea and Cat Woman all rolled into one! The ugly duckling had turned into the great fucking female monster!

He loosened his collar, trying to breathe and work it all out. There was no chance. But he knew he had to go on, because if anything in this world scared him more than the McCarthy Twins, he knew for holy-roly certain now, it was Raphaella! He staggered forward and grasped the handle of the door to the Peking Palace. He pushed it open and staggered in, feeling something like relief.

He passed by the velveteen chairs, pink cloths and sullen waiters in the dimly lit interior, then pushed through the double doors at the back. The twins were waiting for him through the kitchen hatch. He'd heard this. They were never there unless you came for business and then they appeared precisely one second before you did. Some said they were prescient, most didn't care to speculate.

He faced them through the hatch. They were Chinese/Irish, but their Hong Kong mother's genes had predominated, and it was two shining and identical oriental faces that stared inscrutably back at him. Maybe the McCarthy Twins communicated between themselves in some psychic twinspeak, but who would know if it was in English or Mandarin? No living soul had ever heard a word from them. The dead? Well that was another matter.

'Ah. I appreciate your silence, Chan, er . . . Gerard.'

Two plates of chicken chop suey came from the hiss and clatter behind the twins and were picked up by a brusque waiter on Luis's side almost before they'd landed on the ledge between them. Luis moved forward to speak but was interrupted again by three fried oysters and a Peking duck. Taking his chance between a set meal for five and a ham omelette, he quickly whispered his problem. The twins said nothing. Luis hadn't expected a response but was still non-plussed. 'You see my predicament. Uh?' He waited, the twins' stare was unwavering, then he caught on. He took a brown envelope out of his pocket and put it on the ledge. He remembered someone had told him that this was the procedure. If they picked up the money, the deal was done. If they didn't, you had to keep going with the envelopes until they did so. If you decided that their price was too high and wanted to pull out, you could leave with all the envelopes except one. This was the price of the conversation.

He stared at the envelope, the twins didn't move. It was covered briefly by a plate of chilli fried beef, which didn't seem to affect their reaction. Luis placed another envelope on the ledge. Still no move. A third and a fourth went down. Shit little bricks, this was 2,000! A fifth and a sixth, a plate of sweet mango, a seventh, a pot of Chinese tea; he was beginning to sweat, how much was the Third World War? The twins stared implacably. He thought, A lick of paint and the place is worth three-quarter million. He put down another one. Eight envelopes, four grand, this was getting serious. Another envelope and there was still no movement from the twins. It was getting crowded on there, nine little pre-packed half grands; there was hardly room for the sweet and sour wonton and the clear soup. Someone was obviously starting a meal in the restaurant. Luis wished he was them. Why couldn't life just be ordinary and nice? Fuck it, he was out of there. The decision was made. He was actually reaching down to clear eight of the envelopes out of the way of a set meal for six and put them back in his pocket, when he heard her voice again. 'Are you Luis, or are you Papa?'

It was so clear, like she was standing next to him. He felt his blood freeze and pulled his hand quickly back from the ledge, then he shakily reached into his coat pocket and put his last envelope down. Five grand, was he insane? For a second he had the pleasing thought that he was, so everything must be all right, but the relief was brief. Reality intruded in the form of a large plate of assorted dim sum. When it was lifted from the ledge, the money was gone. The twins had accepted the contract. Luis felt like he'd won a heart attack in a poker game. He stepped back. For the first time in five minutes there were no dishes coming through, no waiters brushing past him and the kitchen had gone quiet. He remembered a film about the war and men in trenches experiencing a suffocating hush before the final deadly assault. He couldn't bear it and spoke just to make a noise. 'Thank you. Violet Lack. Once was Violet Green. OK?' The twins didn't move. Luis turned and walked out through the restaurant. If Violet lived, she was dead.

The Bengali Star was dark and quiet. Arnie's all-nighter had become an hour and a half of heavy and then maudlin drinking. No-one had much heart for it and they'd all slowly left the table to find somewhere to sleep. Sayeed Sayeed had locked the door and turned off the lights. Then, as host and temporary guardian of the family, he'd sat himself upright in a chair facing the door and closed his eyes. He never really slept, he merely rested his conscious mind for a few hours, and he hardly breathed as he slipped from this world to some other, known only to him. If he could hear Mathilda in the corner of the room it was only as a distant accompaniment to the soft beat of his heart. She was sitting above Ronnie, who was lolling, half asleep, three-quarters drunk, on a padded corner seat.

'Ron?' He opened his mouth, but didn't say anything. She leaned in closer. 'Ronnie? I know you're awake. Do you love me?'

'No.'

'What?' He didn't repeat it and she decided he hadn't said it. She said, 'I love you. I always have done, you know? I'm full on, Ron. I always was since I saw you in that maroon suit and weird tie at the ringmaster's party. I knew for sure, and it wasn't just the suit, Ron. It was 'cos you looked like a frightened man. Sorry to say so. I love you true, Ron.'

Ronnie raised his head. 'I forgot to phone Auntie.'

Mathilda looked away. 'There's an end to love, you know.'

Mirabelle looked down on Bernie as he snored in his temporary bed, with his Arfer still open across his chest. Then she turned to the window. The storeroom was at the top of the old building and she could see out for miles across the wasteland. She'd heard Sayeed Sayeed tell Arnie and Ronnie of Tom Cherry's tower and she could see it glistening in the starlight. Tomorrow they would go to it, she was sure of that.

She looked down. Below her was the shining roof of the Snipe. The car was carelessly parked with its front tyres awkwardly turned against a pile of brick and rubble. It was very quiet. Arnie was asleep in Lucy's arms on the back seat. He'd gone out there with her an hour before. The intention had been sex, but after a perfunctory feel of her breast and a brief journey on her part into his open fly, they'd both realized that nothing that soft was going to have the hardness of purpose to take on two quadruple Scotches, three bottles of house red and the coldness of the Snipe's leather seats, so they'd cuddled down under Lucy's coat. Arnie had fallen asleep almost immediately. Now he was dreaming of his mother. Mirabelle shifted her view and saw his dream.

Violet was leaning against a wall. She was older, perhaps in her early forties. She was crying, her face was covered in blood and her dress was torn. She was groping and feeling her way along the wall towards a door. Mirabelle couldn't quite make it out, but it looked like a wall in the flat above the restaurant. Arnie shouted in his sleep. Violet pushed the door open and half fell through . . .

And suddenly the sky was full of angels. From where Mihr sat, straight ahead to the far-off tower, from the horizon on the left to the horizon on the right, from ground level to a height of fifteen miles, the air was filled with the beat of the legions. Sorush had come. She showed her power and stood forty feet high, wings half extended, on the wasteland 500 yards from the restaurant. Her eyes were on the same level as Mihr, who had risen, bright, to the roof of the Bengali Star. Sorush's pale skin glistened, and her deep black eyes shone. Mihr could see that the Dark Angel was pursuing this investigation from deep within herself. Mihr was required to accompany her. First they would gather the information they required. Any dispute would come later. Kasbeel began the incantation. 'I require thee, O Lord Jesus Christ . . .' And Mihr looked down on the east of the city forty years before.

Charlie and Violet had married. They'd done it quick in the register office, with a town-hall cleaner and the registrar's secretary as witnesses. It was drunken and a kind of madness. Violet hardly knew where she was. After signing the book, they'd gone on to the Black Owl and drunk gin. Now they were staggering down the steps out of the pub. Charlie's suit was new and he had a carnation in his buttonhole. He laughed and stretched his arm back towards the door as Violet came stumbling down after him. She was dressed in a lilac suit, a pretty hat with a white half veil and she carried a small bouquet of flowers. Charlie beamed up at her. 'You've got to throw it, darling, you've got to throw it!'

'We don't have a bridesmaid, Charlie!'

'Chuck it anyhow!'

Violet looked up and tossed the bouquet towards an old lady who was passing the pub. She made no attempt to catch the flowers and they bounced off her shoulder into the road and disappeared under the wheels of a red bus. Charlie laughed as the conductor hung off the back of the platform and gave them a thumbs up, then he turned and led Violet down the steps and into his arms. 'That means that there's no-one ever going to be married like you've been!' He kissed her and then he kissed her again. There was hardly a more delighted man in the East End.

'Oh my God, I'm scared, Charlie. I can't believe I've done it.'

'Well you have, and I promise you, you'll never wish you hadn't.' He grabbed her in a bear-hug and gave her another huge kiss on the mouth. She responded with her tongue. They could have coupled there and then on the pavement. There were cheers and Charlie turned back to the pub. Half the saloon bar was standing in the doorway and the rest were looking out of the windows. They were clapping and laughing.

Charlie bowed. 'Thank you, thank you!' He took Violet's hand, and she curtsied as he raised his trilby and bowed again. 'What a send-off, girl, hey?' They both waved as they turned from the pub and then stopped dead.

Standing in front of them was Violet's fiancé, James Hooper. He was in his police constable's uniform and on duty. He still had a plaster on his nose from the battering he'd taken in the dance hall the week before. There was a horrible silence. Violet looked away and then at Charlie for support. He grinned. 'Afternoon, Constable.'

His voice gave Violet courage. 'Charlie, this is James.'

'James.' Charlie extended his hand. It was a friendly enough gesture, but there was a smirk of triumph on his face that wasn't lost on Hooper. 'We just got married, James.'

Hooper didn't say anything for a moment. He felt like he'd been hit. His body was very heavy. Then he whispered, 'Why didn't you tell me, Vi?'

'I . . .' There was no real answer she could give. This was an act of cruelty she knew she would pay for some time. Her face hardened. 'I didn't have time, James.'

Hooper saw nothing except the superficial; her lilac suit, her face powder, her lipstick. He couldn't look into her eyes. He dropped his head and mumbled, 'You will regret this day.'

'What are you talking about, mate?' Charlie stepped forward.

'Charlie . . .' Violet put her hand on his arm.

Hooper didn't look up. His heart was too full of pain and he knew his face showed it. He stood with his head bowed. He could see his uniform buttons and his police boots below him. Somehow they gave him courage. He looked up again. 'You will regret it. Both of you. Because what you've done is bad.' Then he looked directly at Violet. She'd never seen so much love and hurt in anyone's eyes. If Charlie hadn't been there she'd have hugged him. He straightened his shoulders. 'Good afternoon, Violet.' Then he turned and walked slowly past them.

'Can't stand bad losers.' Charlie grinned.

'Shut up!' Violet snapped. There were tears in her eyes.

Charlie took her hand. 'Vi?'

She could see that she'd hurt him, and for the first time she did something she'd do for the rest of her life: she buried what she felt and made the best of it. She looked at her new husband. She could see he'd suddenly become unsure of himself. She decided there and then that what she'd done, she'd done, and that she loved this Charlie Lack and always would. By an effort of will her eyes dried. She kissed him on the cheek and smiled. 'Wait till you meet my mum.'

Lucretia's mouth was tight. She stood amidst the polished furniture and aspidistra of her living room. She couldn't speak. A clock ticked. The silence seemed endless. Her daughter was married. She'd not been informed. There'd been no proper ceremony, or at least none that she knew of. Violet was standing in front of her in an appalling lilac suit with a man quite clearly from the lower class. And they were drunk. And she'd married him. Lucretia could have cried or fainted. She did neither. She placed her hand on the shining mahogany of the table to support herself and kept her mouth clamped shut.

'Mum, are you all right? I said, this is Charlie.'

'How do you do, Mrs Green? I realize it's a bit of a shock, but you'll get over it and love me. I guarantee it.' He smiled.

For a second Lucretia was aware of his charm, but shut the thought from her mind. She was in deep shock. She could have been told that Violet was dead and it wouldn't have been worse. Her younger daughter, May, came into the room. She was as pretty as Violet but smaller and darker. She stood by the door grinning, wanting to giggle. Violet took her hand. 'May, this is Charlie. Charlie this is my sister, May.'

'If she's your sister, she's mine an' all. Come here, my darling!' He went over to the door and hugged May where she stood. Her face flushed and she laughed. 'Honoured I'm sure, Mr Charlie.'

He turned back to Lucretia. 'Mrs Green?'

She spoke at last, her voice barely above a whisper. 'You have married?'

'Mum?' Violet had expected this. It was the unadmitted fury she'd known from her mother all her life. She'd known her mother was never going to accept Charlie. He was an energy her mother could never entertain. He could really love and she could only preen; he could hate and she just seethed, like she was now, standing with her hand on the table, as if she was the pained mistress of some manor house. And Violet knew exactly why she'd done what she'd done. It was to get her own back on a mother who'd never seen her for what she was. She looked at Lucretia across the gleaming mahogany and could see that she was shaken to the very core. She was white in the silence. Vengeance was powerful, but nothing's ever that simple, and Violet realized too late that pity was stronger. She said, 'Mum?'

Lucretia spoke. 'I'll see to dinner.' Then she walked out of the room. Charlie waited until she'd closed the door. 'Hello, Mum!'

May collapsed in nervous laughter as Charlie grabbed Violet's hand and pulled her towards him. It was his first kiss in Kitchener Square and he intended to make it one worth remembering. Violet went with it. She arched herself into him, and for the second time that day she buried her feelings. She told herself he was the true cause and she'd never wanted anyone so much in her life. And she needed to kiss him now to wash away the sour taste and guilt of her mother. She'd have fucked him on the dining-room table if her sister hadn't been watching.

Lucretia's shock had turned cold. An hour later she sat at the head of the table poking at her dinner plate and glanced up at Charlie eating heartily at the other end. She'd seen him cover his plate with salt and pepper, then ladle mustard onto the side. He sat with his shoulders hunched and his elbows on the table. He sliced the beef as if it were a carcass, he held his knife like a chisel, he used his fork as though it were a spoon and shovelled up peas and poured them into his mouth, which remained open as he masticated. He even belched, grinned and said *pardonnez-moi*. She loathed him.

'Nice place you've got here, Lucretia . . .'

'Mrs Green.' She regretted it even as she said it. Pettiness was not the way.

'Nice place, Mrs Green.' He smiled, then retaliated. 'I thought what with Violet being a barmaid . . .'

'My husband was a director of Lawrence and Deakin Amalgamated, Mr Lack.'

'I heard of them. Plumbers, weren't they?'

'A sanitary-ware company.'

'I intend to be my own man. No-one's director, Mrs Green.' Now he was using her name as if it was a joke. Even Violet was smirking. 'But my, you did have beautiful daughters. Perhaps I should have met May first!'

The girls laughed. Lucretia looked down at her food. Violet poked him. 'You look out, Charlie boy!'

'With an angel like you, what more do I need?' He kissed her hand with his mouth full, then he looked up at Lucretia. 'An' what grub an' all!'

'Excuse me.' She placed her knife and fork neatly on her plate, picked it up and went out. No-one turned or spoke as she left the room. She went into the kitchen, put down her plate and held on to the sink. She looked at the drain and saw it as Charlie Lack's great, gaping, foul mouth and everything she'd valued was pouring down into it. She cursed herself for being so stupid and forced herself erect. She stared at the green of the garden through the window, trying to stop the tears coming to her eyes.

'Mum?' She turned. It was Violet. She'd collected the others' dishes and was standing by the door.

Lucretia looked away. 'How could you?'

'I love him.'

'You don't. It's sex. Nothing more. Sex.'

Violet hardened. 'How would you know?'

'You're such a fool, Violet! Such a fool!'

Violet didn't want to look at her. 'We've all been that, haven't we?' She could hear the sound of singing from the dining room and went out quickly. Lucretia turned back to the garden. It was beginning to rain.

Charlie was holding May's hand across the table and looking into her eyes when Violet came back in. He was singing, 'Daisy, Daisy, give me your answer do! I'm half crazy all for the love of you . . . Vi!' He saw the flash of jealousy in his wife's eye immediately and filed it away under useful. He got up and hugged her. 'My darling, don't you go away again!' He pulled her to the table and then took both their hands. 'Daisy, Daisy, give me your answer do . . .'

Violet looked at her new husband as she sang. Husband. The word, for a second, struck terror in her heart. He was too big, too strong, she would never be able to contain him. Then she was proud. He was big, he was strong and he was hers. She sang louder, 'I'm half crazy, all for the love of you!'

Lucretia didn't sleep. She sat stiff and upright against her walnut head-board and stared at her walnut wardrobe. An hour earlier, she'd been aware of the faint thump of a bedhead against a wall. The ape and her daughter were having intercourse. She hadn't moved at all since she'd heard it. The room was very still. Next to her was a small bedside table with an alarm clock on it, to her left a silver-backed brush and mirror on the dressing table, and her overnight gown hung on a hook on the back of the door. These were the only contents of her bedroom and they were almost as lifeless as their owner. The one difference being that within her was a slow beating hate. She'd made up her mind.

The next morning she came down early, but as she came to the top of the stairs she smelled bacon and knew he had beaten her to it. She went slowly down to the hall and pushed open the dining-room door. He was sitting at the head of the table in her place gobbling a huge fried breakfast. He looked up and winked. 'Morning, Mrs Green.'

'I see you've made yourself breakfast.'

'Early bird gets the worm. I'll have to educate the sleeping princess.' She stared at him for a second and then sat down. 'I'd like to talk.'

He forked the yolk of an egg into his mouth. 'Better to lance the boil, hey?' He chewed. 'I know you can't stand the sight of me. People like you never can.'

She clasped her hands on the table. 'I appreciate your honesty.'

'What else is there? Want some tea?' He held up the teapot.

'No, thank you.'

He watched her while he ate. 'What did you want to talk about?'

'I saw you flirting with my younger daughter last night.'

'May? Why don't you call her May? It's her name isn't it?'

'I saw you flirting with her.'

'I know you did.' He wiped his plate with a piece of bread. 'Tell you the truth, half the time I did it because I knew you were watching.' He grinned. 'Lust is lust, isn't it? I know that and I know you know that.'

'Do you?' She set her face.

'I do, Lucretia. You don't mind if I call you Lucretia as this is getting personal, do you?' She didn't reply. 'I know you think I'm stupid, but I'm not. My attraction is sex. We speak openly, am I right? They want to have it – sex – with me.'

'Mr Lack . . .'

'Don't blanch, Lucretia. Sex is in all of us, including you. I can see it.' His eyes seemed to pierce her. 'I am primitive.' He allowed himself a smile. 'I know you'll agree with that. Well, we're all primitive. I am, you are and so is this wonderful life. It didn't take me long to work that out.' He put more fat-soaked bread into his mouth. 'So, that's where I stand. What can I do for you?'

She raised her head. She was surprised that what he'd said hadn't shocked her more. 'How much to see the back of you?'

'How much you got to offer?'

'A hundred pounds.'

'I knew you thought I was cheap, Lucretia, but that hurts me.'

'How much do you want?' He didn't reply. He was wiping his plate very clean with the bread. 'I want you out of this house.'

He grinned. 'I've been honest with you, why don't you be honest with me?' He was very still for a second. 'Where'd it come from? This house?'

She was affronted. 'My husband.'

'Where is he?'

'As you probably know, he is buried.'

'What'd he die of?' Charlie leaned forward on the table.

'This is impertinent!' She was ready to rise.

'What about the truth, Lucretia? My husband was a director of Lawrence and Deakin Amalgamated? Yes, he was, wasn't he? He was also done for fraud and committed suicide in Wandsworth Prison a year after May was born.'

'That's a lie!'

Charlie didn't bother to reply for a moment. He sipped his tea. 'No it isn't, darling, I check everything. Tell me your investments, I'll drink a gin with your stockbroker. Tell me your shoe size, I'll chat with the cobbler. Detail is the art of success, Lucretia.' He looked her in the eye. 'What I've just said is true. I've told Violet by the way. She's very shocked. She thinks you should have mentioned it to her.'

Lucretia was pale. This wasn't how she'd imagined it. He went on, 'I'd like you to know something else. I wouldn't leave Violet for a million pounds. I love her. I'll say it again, so you hear. I love her. However much I flirt, whatever you think of me, I love your daughter more than my life. She's mine. It's written in the stars. And she's going to have my boys.'

She stood. 'Get out.'

'She wants me and I want her. We can do a deal if you like. We can pretend we like each other. I'll buy you a nice present every Christmas.'

'I'm waiting for you to go, Mr Lack.'

'I want her body to swell with my child, Lucretia.' He popped a last piece of dry bread into his mouth. He was enjoying himself.

'You are disgusting!'

'Honesty? People like you give me a pain in the neck.'

He wasn't going to be bought out and he wasn't going to get out. He sat there sipping his tea. It was all over. Lucretia had lost and she knew it.

'Mum?' Violet had come in behind her.

Lucretia turned and walked quickly out of the room as Charlie smiled at his wife. 'Get me some more bacon, please, Vi.'

Kasbeel closed the book.

'Primitive. He said it himself, Mihr.' Sorush rose, beginning to fade.

Mihr's blue eyes flashed across the darkness of the wasteland. 'To see is to understand, Sorush.'

'To understand is to plead. I am to condemn,' said Sorush. Then she was gone and the sky was clear.

Mirabelle was unsettled by what she'd seen. She sensed a power in the beginnings of this relationship that frightened her. It was as if a bad seed was being planted. She thought again of the blood of Violet in Arnie's dream and shuddered.

She looked down at Bernie. He'd turned onto his shoulder and his picture book had slipped from his stomach to the floor. She bent and picked it up. By the light from the Bengali Star above she saw that it had fallen open at a picture of a huge dark castle surrounded by an impenetrable forest and with a bright yellow moon above. The portcullis was raised and two black knights were galloping out on deep dark chargers. Their pennants were made of rags and their chain mail glistened with evil intent.

$$15$$

Harriet yawned and looked at the clock on the living-room sideboard. It was nearly half-past two. She'd spent the last twenty minutes clearing the club and locking up. There'd been the average tantrums, bitterness, jokes and fights. She'd decided a long time ago that this family of Charlie's was indestructible and would probably live for ever. Perhaps she put up with them because they made her feel as though she'd always be there too. And there was no doubting it, they made her laugh sometimes.

She could hear Sophie in the kitchen. She was such a sweetheart. She'd insisted on staying with her when the boys had left that evening and had spent the whole night in the flat waiting up for her. Harriet had no idea what her friend did with herself most of the time. She never watched TV or read a magazine. She had an extraordinary talent for doing nothing (except for the veg downstairs) and then being there when you needed her. Now she was making their bedtime cocoa. Harriet shouted through to her, 'That club closes at midnight from now on.'

'Can't hear you, dear!' Sophie called back.

'That club closes . . . !' Harriet had raised her voice, but Sophie came in with a tray. 'I'm having no more drunks and dreamers keeping me up this late, and those buggeration boys didn't telephone me again, did they? Just like their father. Go out looking for a mum and end up in a curry house.'

'Don't talk to me about families.' Sophie looked up. There was the sound of breaking glass coming from the alley below. 'What's that?'

'Life in the city, dear. A customer returning his beer mug, I imagine.' Harriet picked up her racing paper. 'Doppelgänger, four o'clock, Newmarket.' She marked it with a pen. 'I'll need reminding.'

Sophie was on another track. Families were a big concern to her. Her own had broken up in a mysterious feud that had started back in Kingston and spread with the black diaspora to the big city overseas. She didn't see any of them any more, and while never elucidating the cause of the disruption, never stopped harping on its effect. 'Families, they just one big upset, you ask me, Harriet. You get born with claws in your heart and you can't never take them out.'

'Yes, dear.'

'I forgot the sugar.' Sophie went back to the kitchen.

'At least then you know you've got a heart, dear.'

'What?'

'At least then you know . . .'

'Oh I know that all right.' Sophie was pouring the sugar from a bag into the bowl. 'It pumps this and it pumps that, Harriet, and it never lets me be.' She picked up the sugar bowl and went back to the living room. 'I sometimes wish I didn't have a heart at all . . .' The words dried in her mouth. Harriet was no longer sitting on the sofa. She was suspended above it between Chan and Gerard McCarthy.

While the twins may have inherited their facial features from their oriental mother, they'd taken their height and build from their un-known Irish father. It was something Luis hadn't seen as they sat in the steam behind the hatch in the Chinese restaurant. They were an identical six feet five and a quarter and it was no great effort for them to hold the five-foot Harriet eighteen inches off the floor like a puppet on a line. They stared inscrutably at Sophie who stood by the door with the sugar bowl. Harriet thought her shoulders were going to break and her breath was constricted, but she managed to gasp, 'Don't say a word, dear.'

Sophie was made of sterner stuff. 'I would appreciate it, please, if you wouldn't handle my friend like she is a piece of laundry.'

There was a silence, the twins did nothing and Harriet dangled. Then suddenly, as if they were one and the same being, they moved. Chan, holding Harriet with his right hand, let go. Gerard, holding her other shoulder with his left hand, swung her towards him and, keeping her off the ground, turned her to face the wall behind them. At the same time Chan moved fast to the telephone on the sideboard and ripped the cord from its socket.

'Oh no!' Sophie's fingers slipped on the sugar bowl, as Chan swung the heavy old-fashioned phone by the cord, and Gerard grabbed Harriet's hair and pulled her head back. Then three things happened simultaneously: the sugar bowl hit the ground; Chan cracked the heavy phone hard against the side of Sophie's skull, and Gerard smashed Harriet's face into the wall. There was a pause for a second and then, as if choreographed, the two women were wheeled round and thrown onto the sofa. Harriet's nose was badly broken and her face was covered in blood. Sophie was dazed and hardly knew what was happening as Chan pulled her upright again and Gerard punched her violently in her ample stomach. She fell back onto the sofa, retching.

Both women were too shocked and hurt to cry out. Chan stood over them as Gerard went quickly to the table where the family photographs and memorabilia were still jumbled and spread. With a strange and mysterious speed he found what he was looking for and held the items up for Chan to see. The first was the photograph with the pencilled inscription on the back of Lucretia standing between Violet and May outside the house in Kitchener Square, and the second was the letter from Lucretia to her daughter complaining of Charlie's behaviour in the café. Gerard looked at the address at the top of it and slipped the photograph into his pocket. Chan moved quickly past the two women and Gerard followed him to the door. They closed it quietly behind them.

Harriet heard them go down the stairs and closed her eyes. It seemed an age before she became aware of the smell of Sophie's vomit and then the feel of its hot wetness on her thigh. She reached up and touched her face. It was sticky with blood. Slowly Sophie pushed herself up from Harriet's legs. She lay back on the sofa breathing heavily, then her hand groped for Harriet's and they both began to cry.

It took them twenty more minutes to help each other up from the sofa and stagger to the door using the chairs as supports. They descended the stairs, one painful step after another, and by the time they'd got down to the restaurant Sophie was virtually on her knees. Harriet couldn't bear to go a yard without her and helped her to a table next to the telephone by the till. She picked up the receiver as Sophie dialled and then Harriet spoke her first word since the attack: 'Ambulance.'

It took another twenty minutes for the emergency services to arrive, and by that time Sophie had passed out on the restaurant floor. A young police sergeant called Fairfax tried to get some sense out of Harriet, but she couldn't stop sobbing and holding her shaking hands in front of her battered face. Fairfax watched as the medics heaved the two women on stretchers into the back of the ambulance. Then he went up to the flat to have a look round. Forty minutes later Sophie was sedated on a ward and Harriet was lying on a stretcher outside the operating theatre waiting for a surgeon.

In total, one hour and twenty minutes had passed since the assault, which is exactly the amount of time it took the McCarthy Twins, driving at high speed through the deserted city and then along the Great Eastern in their black Mercedes van, to reach Kitchener Square. Perhaps they were helped by the dawn beginning to break, or perhaps it was just their inspired and frightening hunter's instinct, but they had found Lucretia's house within a minute.

Neither she nor Albert woke as the sledgehammer smashed into the rotten wood, or even as the door crashed down flat onto the disgusting hallway floor. That was their last chance to call for help because they wouldn't have heard the twins come up the stairs even if they had been awake.

The first Lucretia knew about it was when she was dragged from her no doubt hateful dreams, hurled backwards and upwards and felt the rough edge of a sheet being wound around her neck. Within a minute she was suspended on the headboard of her bed, facing the blank face of Gerard. He stepped aside to reveal the pyjama-clad Albert, who was being carried into the room by Chan. Her companion's thin white limbs had been forced agonizingly through the legs and supports of a kitchen chair and he was immobilized as effectively as if he had been roped. Chan dumped the bentwood-entangled old man onto the floor and pulled from his pocket the bottle of household bleach he had found in the kitchen. He crouched by Albert and forced his head back over the seat of the chair until his mouth yawned open involuntarily, and then he began to pour the bleach.

Gerard held the photograph of Lucretia and her daughters in the old girl's face and pointed to Violet as the bleach bubbled in Albert's gullet. The old girl tried to scream, but Gerard merely pulled the sheets tighter round her throat. He held the picture and waited as Albert spluttered and howled. Finally Lucretia croaked, 'Tom Cherry.' Chan continued to pour the bleach into her companion as she gave the details of the tower.

16

The next morning Ronnie hadn't wanted to call Cherry. He sat at Sayeed Sayeed's table with Lucy and Mathilda as Arnie reluctantly picked up the phone and dialled. Tom Cherry's company had been in the book. It looked as if it was going to be easy. The phone rang at the other end as he watched Bernie come down into the restaurant with Mirabelle. 'What you doing, Arn?'

'Sit down and have your breakfast.' Arnie waited while the phone rang.

'Yeah, curry for brekkers!' Bernie sat waiting for his food and keeping one eye on Arnie.

A receptionist had picked up the phone the other end. 'Can I speak to Mrs Lack please?' Arnie was beginning to feel nervous and was almost relieved to hear that the receptionist had never heard of his mother. He cupped the receiver and called over to Ronnie, 'They don't know her.' Ronnie looked away. That was that then.

'Try Violet Green, Arnie,' Mirabelle suggested.

Arnie glanced at Ron, but he was looking down at Sayeed's saffron table cloth and saying nothing. Arnie had no choice. He asked, 'Do you have a Miss or Mrs Green?' He waited, listening while the others watched. Then he put the phone down.

Ronnie looked up. 'Arnie?'

'She's there; or will be at ten o'clock. Miss Green apparently is the managing director of Tom Cherry Limited.' This, for some reason, made Arnie angry. He stuck his hands in his pockets and walked towards the door. He was about to go out when he turned. 'Managing director! She couldn't even use our fucking name, could she!' He walked out of the restaurant into the dull stench of the wasteland outside.

'Whass up?' asked Bernie.

'Your breakfast.' Sayeed Sayeed put a huge plate of bread and curry on the table and the big boy immediately filled his mouth.

'Nothing for me thanks, Sayeed.' Ronnie was surprised to see himself take Mathilda's hand. He could have just proposed marriage by the smile she gave him.

'Did anyone think to call Auntie?' asked Mirabelle.

$$17$$

Harriet lay back in her hospital bed. She was still groggy after the nose straightening, as she called it, and both her eyes had gone black. They'd put her in a private room and Sophie's bed had been wheeled in next to her. The young police sergeant had insisted. Temporary protection, he called it, although he doubted that their attackers would return, as he was of the opinion that it was a straight up and down burglary with assault and probably battery. Fairfax was a good copper who was usually stationed in the east. He was up in Soho for his CID course. This was his last day and he wasn't sorry to be going back home to the love of his life, his motorbike, a fully reconditioned Norton with . . .

Sophie moaned and he decided he ought to get on with the matter in hand and at least give his Soho successor on the case a good set of notes. In his opinion this was almost certainly a waste of time, because most of them over here didn't have a clue as to the proper and rigorous use of procedure. They seemed to think that police work was based on obscenity, beer and laying a few pounds in the snout's mouth in the pub after hours. They were hopeless in Fairfax's view. But it was decidedly their problem. He was out of all this at six o'clock that night. He was looking forward to a cup of tea and a reasonable conversation with his superintendent when he got back to his station in the east. He was sure the superintendent wouldn't fall asleep like last time. He looked down at his notebook. 'So the intruders made off with a photograph of one Miss Violet Green?'

'Always used to say what a terrible colour.' Harriet might well have been hysterical from the after-effects of the anaesthetic.

'And then she married Charlie Lack.' Sophie felt sick and had a terrible headache, but if Harriet could joke about it, so could she.

'I beg your pardon.' Fairfax didn't get the point. He wasn't really listening anyway. In fact, most of his mind was engaged on a certain set of procedural changes he'd like to make at the station in East Ham. He was having an imaginary conversation with the superintendent when the same walked into the room, nodded and said, 'Sergeant.' For a fraction of a second Fairfax was about to continue the fantasy debate, but then he realized that the superintendent was actually standing opposite him. A lesser man might have quailed at the coincidence. Not Fairfax. 'Ah, sir. Good morning, sir.' Then he queried, 'Sir?' This was Soho, what was his superintendent doing over here anyway?

'Introduce me if you will, Sergeant.'

'The victims, sir. Miss Lack and Miss Lighterman, Superintendent Hooper.' If his name rang the faintest tinkle of a bell in Harriet, then hers was already a Sunday symphony in the mind of the man standing at the end of her bed. For it was him, the very Hooper, the actual ex-constable, now superintendent, James Hooper, who'd loved Violet, wanted to marry her and lost her to Charlie on that terrible day on the steps of the Black Owl. The pain of that memory was etched into his heart. He'd never got over the humiliation, never married and never a day had passed when he hadn't been obsessed by the thought of his long-lost sweetheart. And now, so many years later, this was the second time in less than two hours that he'd found himself facing a member of her family.

The first had begun when he'd received information about an attack in Kitchener Square. He knew the address, of course. For several years, every weekend, he'd walked past the house wanting to knock, renew his acquaintance with Lucretia and enquire after Violet. But he'd never dared. After a while he'd begun to avoid the square altogether, so when the call came he hadn't been near the place for over twenty years. Several cars were already on their way to Lucretia's and there was no real need for him to go, but he found himself getting up from his desk and putting on his coat. His heart was beating very fast as he drove.

He'd recognized Lucretia immediately, although she'd forgotten him. She was too ill to talk much and they'd taken her out to the ambulance. Having untangled the old man from the chair, a constable had managed to get from him a rambling story of bleach and some kind of Japanese giants after 'the girls'. What girls? Lucretia's girls? May? Violet? Could this be contact with her again?

Hooper had to sit for a few minutes on the front steps of the house, trying to take it all in. He was due to retire in three weeks' time and this could well be his last case ever, and she could be involved in it! Oh God. He smoked his first cigarette in twenty-nine years and was doing his best to calm himself when he heard from a colleague that there'd been a similar attack earlier that night on Central. Two orientals had battered a couple of old ladies. Hooper asked immediately for the names of the victims. One of them was Miss Harriet Lack. The pounding in his heart got worse.

He'd demanded a car on the spot and on the drive from the east he'd discovered that his protégé, Fairfax, was at this very moment at the hospital talking to the lady in question. As soon as he walked into the room he could see in her, despite the bruising, a strong resemblance to her brother, Charlie. Hooper breathed in sharply. There was still such an ocean of Violet in him that he doubted his capacity to stay afloat. He waited while Fairfax made the introductions, then said as coolly as he could, 'Good morning, Miss Lack, Miss Lighterman.'

Both women nodded. Fairfax was still trying to work out what his superior was doing there. 'Sir?'

'Tell me what happened, Sergeant.'

'Two men, oriental appearance. They stole a photograph . . .'

'They were after Violet,' Harriet interrupted him.

Although Hooper had suspected, as soon as he'd got the call from Kitchener Square, that his world was about to be turned upside down, Harriet's statement hit him like a sledgehammer. He'd never felt better, or worse. It *was* Violet. She *was* involved! His blood seemed to be heating, his skin cooling and his knees felt weak. He sat down quickly on a hospital chair.

Fairfax was amazed. 'Are you all right, sir?'

Hooper wasn't. The swelling sea inside him was becoming more turbulent by the second. He could barely speak. There was only one thing to do; he had to let some of the froth and boil out of his heart. 'I know Violet, Miss Lack, I was once engaged to be married to her.' The statement brought him out in a cold sweat, but he couldn't stop. His voice was shaking. 'Perhaps she mentioned me to you.'

Harriet looked at him. Even in her state she could see his. Always full of sympathy for the afflicted, she lied. 'Do you know, Superintendent, I believe I do remember her saying something about you. And at times with regret.'

Hooper could have cried. 'I'm touched to hear that, madam. The regret is reciprocal.' There was a silence as he listened to his heartbeat. He knew he'd have to ask and he did. 'Do you know where she is?'

'Unfortunately, I don't.'

'None of us do,' Sophie added. Frankly she thought more attention should be paid to her. There was no glamour in being hammered, but they might have spared a thought in the aftercare.

Hooper looked down. This was as far as he could go at the moment. He was relieved to hear Fairfax picking up the questioning. Through a mist he heard of the death of Charlie, Violet's three sons, the restaurant and their quest for their mother. Hooper couldn't listen any more. Violet had been separated from Charlie for twenty years! Luckily he managed to get to the gents before he was sick.

$$\boxed{18}$$

Mathilda and Lucy waved as the Snipe pulled away from the Bengali Star. Arnie had decided they should wait for them there.

'Only wants me after midnight.'

'Ronnie doesn't even want me then.'

They walked back into the restaurant as the Snipe crossed the zigzag roads of the wasteland towards the tower gleaming silver in the distance. Sayeed Sayeed watched through a restaurant window as the car receded from view, its roof shining in the early morning sunlight. As the girls came towards him, negotiating the puddles and mud in their high heels, he whispered to himself, 'Fate, Charlie. Whose fate?'

Arnie in the passenger seat was thinking on roughly the same lines. Except it wasn't his father's fate that was concerning him, it was his own and his mother's all mixed up. He stared at the flattened piles of black rubble passing through the window, and knew in some dull way that he'd never really grown up and out of his mother and that she'd never really grown out of him. No matter how much he ran she was somehow still there inside, and sooner or later they were going to have to face each other as full and separate beings. And he'd taken off for years to avoid all that! He'd spent ten years in some drugged-up, doped-out blackness in the west just so he could forget it! All right he'd come back and he'd worked it out with the old man. He'd grown out of the father by knowing him. But his mother wasn't there, was she? And he never wanted to see her again. That was the truth. And now he was fucking well looking for her! This was his fate, as Charlie would have said. He was going to see her one last time. He badly needed a drink.

Ronnie's nervousness in Sayeed's had been more to do with confusion than anything else. For the first time in his life he'd thought he'd got himself clear. He was going to sort out the restaurant and sort himself out at the same time. Then, suddenly, he didn't have the restaurant. And on top of that there was his mum. All that had to be looked at too, didn't it? The truth is he couldn't remember her that clearly. She was a bit of a goddess done out in a ball gown up the back of a dress shop. He was thinking maybe he could have a chat and ask her a few things. Like Tom Cherry for example. And perhaps she'd like to explain . . . ? The towers were coming closer. He put his hand up to shield his eyes from the sun.

Bernie was thinking about it too and looking at his Arfer all at the same time because he was very excited. 'So there was this castle, see?' He prodded the picture with his huge finger. 'See that. Thass a pretty maiden. And thass another one. Look, they're all hanging out the winders. And see them, they're all villains and they're dressed in black and they got pointed helmets, and there's thousands of them all round the back of the castle, which you can't see. And see, there's Galahad, riding up with his fellow knights. "Now you all let them maidens go at once," says Galahad, "or me and Sir Bors and Sir Perceval are going to have something to say about it. I hope you bloody get that, you!" Bernie poked at the picture of a villain on the page. Then he looked at Mirabelle with big eyes. 'But he didn't, did he? None of them got it. They didn't know Galahad always meant what he said. So there was a big sword fight and the wicked villains had to do a runner.'

'Good idea.' Arnie had said it half under his breath. He sat motionless, watching as the towers came closer and got higher, filling the windscreen.

'How much longer then?' said Bernie.

'We're here.' Ronnie turned into the car park. He stopped the Snipe and turned off the engine. The sun had gone in and the tower was vast and silver against the grey sky.

'I got to have a pee, Meebelle. I'm busting,' said Bernie.

'We'll find somewhere inside.' They got out and Mirabelle hurried after Bernie, who was loping after his brothers and already holding his crotch.

The reception area was huge, high and marble-floored. The receptionist was rude. 'Miss Green's secretary will call down as soon as she has spoken to Miss Green. Until then you will have to wait, Mr Lack,' she said to Arnie. 'Over there.' She pointed to a nest of leather sofas at the foot of the thirty-foot tinted windows. Then her jaw dropped and her imperious face and finger froze as she noticed Bernie. She'd never seen anyone so big and, let's face it, so good-looking, hopping around from one foot to the other with both hands holding his balls and groaning, 'Got to have a pee quick!'

Arnie gave the receptionist the smallest of smiles. 'Got any ideas?'

The receptionist was still pointing at the sofas. She didn't speak. She swivelled her whole body until her finger was pointing at a pair of double doors at the side of the reception.

'Go on then, Bern, piss off.'

'That's what I'm doing, Arn.' Bernie started to chuckle.

'Do you want me to come with you?' Mirabelle was already following him.

'No, I bloody don't!' He half hopped away. 'Who's Bob?'

'Do you know?' Arnie smiled at the receptionist again.

She dropped her arm and stared at him. 'Know what?'

'Bob? Is he in?' Ronnie grinned.

*   *   *

Bernie came quickly through the double doors and his confidence went. He couldn't see his brothers or Mirabelle no more and it was all different in here. He walked down the quiet corridor. There was a kind of hum and there was a phone ringing somewhere. And then there was someone carrying some papers. And then another woman. Was that his mum? No, probably not. He remembered he wanted to have a pee. And then this geezer said, 'Going up?' and he said, 'Yeah, all right,' and he went into this little room where there were two other people. One of them was carrying papers as well. And then it starting humming again and there were some lights flashing and it was a lift. The doors closed and opened again and the man with the papers got out and another woman got in. Was she his mum? No, probably not. And then it went up and it stopped again. And lots of people got in and some woman looked at him like he was mad and started laughing. He really wanted to piss bad by now, but he didn't know where the pisser was so he didn't know where to get out. Maybe his mum would come and tell him where the pisser was, but she didn't. And the doors kept opening and closing and people kept getting in and out and he didn't know what to do. Then there was no-one in the lift at all! It was a bit lonely and then the doors opened again and he walked out. Perhaps this was where the pisser was, but there was no-one around. It was really quiet again, which he didn't like much. He really wanted to look at his Arfer, but he wanted a piss too bad, so he just kept walking and this woman came up to him. 'Can I help you?'

'Umm?'

'Who are you looking for?'

'Umm? My mum.'

'Your mother?'

'Yes.'

'Oh, I see.' This woman was just looking at him like he was mad and she didn't tell him where the pisser was. 'What's your mother's name?'

'Mum.' She just smiled like he was double, double mad, and he'd seen that smile before and didn't like it much.

'But her name. What is your mother called?'

'Oh.' Why didn't she say that in the first place? 'Miss Green.'

'Miss Green?' The woman looked like she'd just had a shock off the electric. 'I didn't know Miss Green had a son.'

'Well you do now, don't you? Where's the pisser?'

'I beg your pardon?'

Now he'd buggered it all up. He was never going to get to the pisser at this rate. 'I'm sorry. I didn't mean to say that. I mean where's my mum?'

'Well?'

'She's called Miss Green.'

'I don't know if I . . .'

Whass she looking at him like that for? 'She said she was here.'

'Well, that's her office.'

'Fanks.' He walked on down the corridor, then he went into the door of what she said was the office. There wasn't no-one in there. But there was a sandwich on the desk, so he picked it up and took a bite. It was prawn and lettuce, which he quite liked, but not as much as tomato and Marmite and onion. He took another bite and saw that there was another door further back, so he went through. There was a woman sitting in a chair with her back to him. 'Hello.' She didn't say nothing, so he had another bite of the sandwich, then he saw a knife on the floor and thought it was all covered in tomato ketchup, so he picked it up and licked it, but it wasn't ketchup, it tasted funny. 'Hello, whass this on this knife then?' But the woman in the chair didn't say nothing. Maybe she was deaf or hard at work or something, so he said it louder. 'Hello, whass this on this knife then?' She still didn't say nothing, so he thought he'd go over and give her a prod. He didn't want to touch her back, so he pushed the chair and it spun round like it was one of those revolving ones or something. He liked having a go on them. But even when she was facing him, he couldn't see the woman's face because she had her head down. Then he noticed she had ketchup all down the front of her shirt. Perhaps it had come off the knife. He tapped her on the top of the head. 'Excuse me, whass this on the knife then?' But she still didn't say nothing, so he just touched her hair and moved her head up a bit and saw that there was ketchup all over her neck. And then he realized it wasn't ketchup at all, it was blood, and she was probably dead. He stared at her. Was this his mum? He hoped not. Then there was this woman screaming like mad at the door. He turned and had a look. It was the lady from the corridor. She must have come poking her nose in again. She was screaming and screaming and giving him an earache. And then he remembered he still didn't know where the pisser was, so he just started to have a piss anyhow. If she was going to scream, he didn't care, he'd wet his pants, wouldn't he? She just screamed some more and then she ran away as he kept on pissing.

In the reception, Mirabelle leaped up from the sofa. 'It's Bernie! Tenth floor!' She was running towards the stairwell before Arnie and Ron had got up.

'What?'

'Bernie! Hurry! Ten!' And she was gone, through the double doors and flying up the stairs.

'What's she on about?'

'How do I know, Ron?' Lift doors suddenly opened behind them and they ran in, unnerved by Mirabelle. Arnie punched ten.

Mirabelle was two flights up the stairs before she raised her eyes, whispered a brief apology and then disappeared. She materialized outside the office. The woman was still screaming. Two men were standing by her, trying to calm her down. Mirabelle went quickly into the outer office, then through the door into the inner to find Bernie. He still had the sandwich in one hand and the bloody knife in the other. The woman on the chair was slowly revolving. Her head had fallen backwards. Her throat had been cut.

'Sorry, Meebelle.'

'Oh my God!'

'Sorry. I didn't mean it. I couldn't find a pisser!'

'What?'

'So I done it on the carpet! Sorry.'

'Oh, Bernie!'

'Whass up?' He was getting panicked. 'Whass up?'

'We've got to go, Bernie.' She approached him slowly. 'Just do as I say?'

He started to pull back from her. He'd never seen her look at him like this. 'Whass up? Whass up, whass up?'

'Come with me.'

Arnie and Ronnie ran in. 'Sorry, Ron, I pissed on the carpet!'

'What have you done, Bernie?' Ronnie stared at the woman revolving slowly towards him with the huge gash in her throat.

Bernie held the sandwich out. 'I just found it on the desk. I din't nick it!' He was close to tears.

Ronnie walked slowly towards the woman. 'Mum?'

'It's Miss Green, Ron.' Bernie was trying to be helpful.

Ronnie turned. Arnie was still by the door. He was very pale. At first he'd thought it was his mother, too. He said, 'It's May. It's her sister. It's your Auntie May, Bernie. What are you doing with that knife?'

Bernie dropped it quickly. 'I don't know.'

'He wouldn't do that!' Mirabelle shouted.

Arnie stared for a second then made up his mind. 'Come on! Out!'

Ronnie wasn't so sure. 'Arn . . .'

'Talk about it fucking later!' Ronnie's uncertainty had immediately firmed up Arnie. 'Out, Bernie!' He grabbed him by the arm and pulled him towards the door. 'Come on!' Bernie lumbered after Arnie into the outer office. Two men and a woman were standing by the door. Arnie screamed. 'Out of the fucking way!' And charged at them. Bernie followed, all elbows, knees and tears. The office workers scattered. A crowd was gathering in the corridor, but they backed away too. No-one tried to stop them. The woman was still screaming at the end of the corridor as Mirabelle ran past, getting ahead of Arnie and Bernie.

'This way!' She led them to the stairwell and they clattered down after her. She looked back. Arnie was holding Bernie's hand and pulling him down as fast as he could. Fire alarms were ringing. Ronnie followed looking white.

Bernie started to howl, 'I din't do nothing! Whass up? Whass up?' The stairwell rang with the echoes of their flying footsteps.

In the reception area the alarms were deafening. A security guard was shouting into a telephone, but he couldn't hear much over the bells. 'What? What are you talking about? I can't hear you! They're bloody fire alarms! Where is it?'

The brothers and Mirabelle came quickly from the stairwell and stopped at the double doors leading into the reception. Mirabelle looked through the glass panel and could see the guard taking a fire extinguisher off the wall and running towards the lifts. She turned back to the brothers. 'They think it's a fire.'

Arnie was breathing heavily. He faced Bernie. 'All right, drop the sandwich. Put your hands in your pockets. Can you hear me, Bernie?' He shook the sandwich out of his brother's hand. 'Put your hands in your pockets and stop crying. Just walk slowly by me, all right? Ronnie's the other side.'

Bernie put his head up and tried to stop the tears as Mirabelle held the door and they went into the clamour of the reception area. A security guard ran past them. 'Clear the building! Clear the building, please. Assemble in the car park.' He ran back across the reception to warn others coming from the lifts.

Arnie and Ronnie walked closely either side of Bernie as they passed the reception desk. The receptionist was throwing her cigarettes and make-up into her handbag and didn't look up. More and more security men were running from the back of the area as Mirabelle held the doors again and the brothers left the building. They only started to run when they were in the car park. Ronnie began to fumble with the car keys. 'Give them to me!' Arnie opened the driver's door and yelled across the roof to Mirabelle, 'Get him in the back!'

'Sorry! I didn't mean it!' Bernie was crying again as Arnie started the Snipe and shoved it into gear. He pulled away with a squeal of tyres and they turned fast out of the car park, leaving the tower behind, looming high against the grey sky.

19

Arnie took the Snipe off the arterial and onto the zigzags of the wasteland on two wheels. He was taking each right-angled corner with a screech of the tyres. The car bounced and rocked on her ancient springs, throwing them up and down inside.

'They thought it was a fire!' Ronnie shouted.

'They won't for long. There'll be a murder squad all over the place in ten minutes.'

'So what are we bloody doing, Arn!' Ronnie was very frightened.

'How should I fucking know?' Arnie took the car fast round another corner throwing Mirabelle onto Bernie in the back.

'Well I don't know either!'

'Well shut up then!'

'Whass up? Whass up?' Bernie was beginning to panic again.

Ronnie felt it and tried to calm him. 'It's all right, Bern.'

'Who killed Mum?'

'It wasn't your mum.' Mirabelle wanted to take his hand against the jolting of the Snipe, but he pulled it away. 'It was your auntie . . .'

Bernie wasn't listening. It was all starting to get clear. Someone was dead. And they was all scared stiff. And it was all his fault! He shouted and began to heave himself up. 'I din't do nothing!'

'Sit him down, Mirabelle!' Arnie yelled from the front.

Mirabelle tried to hold him. 'Bernie!'

His hands and legs were jerking as though he was about to have a spasm. His sheer size in the back of the car was getting frightening. She tried to grab him, but the car hit a pothole and she was thrown up and away from him. His legs were thumping against the back of the front seat. 'Whass up? I'm in a state, I am!'

'Bernie!' yelled Arnie.

'I'm in a bloody state! Whass up!'

'Hang on, Bernie!' Ronnie leaned over his seat and tried to push down on his brother's legs.

'Whass up! Whass up! . . .' Bernie was going out of control.

'Shut up! Shut up, Bernie, all right! Shut the fuck up!' Arnie's voice was frightening and cut through Bernie's panic. He suddenly and immediately clamped up tight, but as if to compensate for the lack of sound from his mouth, huge tears spurted from his eyes. He sat shaking.

'That's better. Thank you.' Arnie turned and took a quick look at him. 'Don't worry, we'll sort it out. All right?'

Mirabelle took Bernie's hand in both of hers. He was still shaking but he was quiet. Arnie would sort things out, he knew that.

'So where we going then?' Ronnie asked again after a second or two.

'I don't fucking know! I told you!' Arnie, having cooled Bernie, was in danger of blowing it all again. 'We're just getting out of it for a start, Ron!'

'Sayeed.' Mirabelle stated the obvious.

'That's it! Ask Sayeed, Arn. We got to ask someone!' said Ronnie.

But Arnie had another idea. 'Mathilda!'

'What?'

'She's with Sayeed! She can take us south!'

The Snipe, that good old girl, purred on at high revs, skidding, squealing round the angles, her great bulk rolling, then righting herself on burning rubber. She was mechanical perfection, burnished and nurtured, and she would contain and deliver her fragile, panicked cargo of Lacks until no longer needed. The sun wasn't out any more. Just a grey day on the wasteland as Arnie brought the old motor to a skidding, sliding halt outside the Bengali Star.

PART THREE

SOUTH

1

Superintendent Hooper had remained in the hospital toilets for a long time. For several minutes his mind had gone absolutely blank. The white wall of the cubicle became, as it were, himself. In the years since Violet had abandoned him on the steps of that pub he hated more than any pub in the world, he'd done nothing but work. If he involved himself in it enough, buried himself in paperwork and crime, he could forget her for hours at a time. But after the labour of his days came bare and desperate nights. He'd passed every evening doing nothing but stare bleakly out of the back window of his maisonette with the flower of his love carved into his heart. Slowly this window had become a frame for his thought, and the white walls of the cubicle were likewise coming alive as a screen for his dreaming. He was seeing again what he'd seen night after night for over thirty years, the construction in his mind of an entire life for himself and the Violet he'd lost.

In this ever-growing fantasy, they'd married and had five children. He'd given each child two Christian names, a school life and a career. They'd moved four times; every new house being a step up the ladder of prosperity. He could tell you every bright room in every new house, every shining piece of furniture, every pretty flower in every well-kept garden. Hooper's dreams were sunshine and wholesome, cut grass and bacon. He'd kept up with progress, too, nothing was too much for Violet. Every new product had been obtained as soon as it had come on to the market. They'd started with a Ford Prefect and a three-piece suite in a small flat above a hardware store. After this it was a terraced house in a better area, with a record player for the kids, a new fridge and an exchange on the car for a Zodiac. Years later there'd been another larger terraced house, and he'd added a patio, central heating and an account at Burton's. Then along came an electric blender, a workshop, a quadraphonic stereo and insurance policies, all fitted seamlessly into the third house: a semi-detached with two elm trees in the garden and a Cortina neatly parked outside. Lately he'd moved on to a Granada and a four-bedroomed property with microwave, a computer for the kids, a little business for Violet, holidays in Florida and savings accounts for the grandchildren. The list was endless and added to every night. Over the years there was no part of modern life that hadn't imposed its reality upon his invention; there was no issue or talking point he hadn't discussed with Violet, no problem unresolved and no night when their sleep wasn't sweet. The years of his dream passed, as did the seasons of his life, as he stared through his window 200 yards from the East Ham police station where he worked. Sometimes he'd sat in his chair and cried with joy at the pure sentimental loveliness of a life he'd never had.

He began to cry again as he stared at the white cubicle wall, trying to will himself into action. He knew if he didn't work, his days as well as his nights would become nothing but fantasy, which he was sane enough to know was madness. He should have retired five years ago, but had pleaded with his superiors for an extension. He was a good officer, firm and kindly to his men, and as they were short of experienced senior ranks at the time, they'd allowed it. But now his time was well and truly up and in two weeks' time he'd no longer be a police officer. He could hardly face the thought. Retirement for him was an abyss waiting and there was nothing he could do to prevent himself falling into it. He knew, with absolute certainty, that in a fortnight he was going to lose all touch with reality.

But wait, what was he talking about? The white walls were buzzing. The colour of the fantasy had gone and with it the dread misgivings of its ending. Something else was appearing. It was called actual life. But what was it? If the dream of Violet had been his reality for all those years, then her real life could only be a dream, couldn't it? But it wasn't, was it? Her mother had been attacked, hadn't she? Her sister-in-law had been assaulted. His mouth hung open, the walls swayed. What was the reality? Was Violet in the rose garden of the fourth house or was she being pursued by a couple of Chinese? And what about Charlie? He hadn't given him a thought for over three decades because as far as he was concerned Charlie didn't exist; now, apparently, not only did he exist, but he was dead, and not only was he dead, but Violet had left him and seemingly disappeared.

His knuckles went white as he tried to grasp this new reality in the shape of the toilet-roll holder. The paper was wet with the sweat from his hand, there was a banging in his head. Had he finally tipped into the abyss? No. He realized with a glazed relief that Sergeant Fairfax was thumping on the cubicle door. 'Sir, are you all right, sir?'

Hooper looked up. He had no idea whether he was or wasn't, but the sergeant's voice began to stabilize him. It was a proper police voice. It was stern, it meant procedure, action and the possibility of a head as clear as could reasonably be expected in the circumstances. He said, 'Wait outside, Sergeant.' Then he stood and was amazed for a second to find solid ground beneath his feet.

He left the cubicle, went to a washbasin and splashed cold water onto his face. He began to consider the events of the morning in a way that, although it might not have been entirely rational, was at least in a language a policeman could understand. Violet had disappeared. That was true, wasn't it? Yes. Was she dead? He didn't want to think about that. She therefore, in rejection of consideration of the opposite, was alive. If she was alive, would she remember him? And if she did, would she . . . ? Hooper hardly dared ask the question, even in the cracked privacy of his own mind. Would she . . . want anything to do with him? He stared into the mirror. He knew that even to ask this was the beginning of renewed fantasy, and if he wasn't careful he would be back in the fourth house, drinking lemonade with his non-existent children. But he had to be a policeman now and whatever the outcome, he was, he had to face it, like her sons, part of the quest for Violet.

New information had come in almost immediately. As Hooper was leaving the hospital with Fairfax, they'd received a call on the car radio. Lucretia Green had whispered to a WPC from her hospital bed that she'd told the orientals of a man called Tom Cherry, who had employed her daughter. It hadn't taken long to trace Cherry, and they were on their way to his office in the tower when the first reports of the killing came over the radio. Although these initially suggested that it had been a random attack, Hooper's heart pounded when he heard that the victim had been Cherry's managing director, a woman called May Green; Violet's sister. He told Fairfax to put his foot down.

2

Crime officers were in the process of sealing off the office and a police photographer was beginning his work when Hooper and Fairfax arrived at the tower. They went quickly through the cordon into May's office. The corpse was still seated upright in her office chair. Her hands hung loosely at her side, her skin was alabaster white and the blood had congealed around her throat. Hooper's stomach knotted as he saw the physical resemblance to Violet. In that moment he knew instinctively that his love had been the killer's target.

'At least it's ours now, Sergeant,' he said, as he looked down at the dead woman. He'd have fought tooth and nail to head this inquiry, but now that the third incident, and by far the most serious, had occurred on his patch in the east, he could legitimately claim the case as his. He breathed in deeply. He was no longer a lovelorn constable outside the Black Owl, he was a superintendent with all the powers of the Met at his disposal. He may not have been much of a romancer, but this was crime, his territory, and this was the investigation he'd rehearsed for all his life.

The first thing he did was to ask to speak to this Mr Cherry, May Green's boss, but was told he'd taken a few days off. They didn't know where he was and he wasn't expected back until the weekend. Hooper asked that he be informed the moment Mr Cherry got in touch. His brain was at last beginning to function and he pushed his shoulders back and stood straighter.

Fairfax noticed the change in his demeanour and was relieved. He'd heard his superintendent's admission at the hospital that he'd been engaged to Violet, and on the journey from there, he'd looked at his superintendent's pale face and begun to worry. He thought he should ask, 'Sir, this isn't too personal is it?'

Hooper glared and Fairfax wished he hadn't opened his mouth.

'This is a murder investigation, Sergeant. Proper statements, professional procedure.' He emphasized the last adjective and Fairfax, suitably chastened, was about to turn away when a local detective constable came up to Hooper. He'd been one of the first officers to arrive at the scene. He looked down, checking his notebook.

'Three men, sir, and a girl. They were seen in the office at the time of the attack. One of them . . .' The DC was about to describe the witness accounts when Hooper interrupted.

'Three men, Constable?' Hooper had been expecting two and both of them oriental. He looked at Fairfax. 'Is this the brothers? Did Harriet Lack mention a girl?' Apparently she had when Hooper was in the hospital toilet. Fairfax explained Mirabelle. Hooper looked again at the corpse of May and said vaguely, 'That's their aunt.'

'I beg pardon, sir?' The DC didn't know about any of this.

'They wouldn't kill their own aunt, would they?' Hooper said.

'Sir?' asked the DC.

Hooper explained. 'Last night a further aunt, plus a West Indian friend, were attacked. This morning a grandmother and her companion were also considerably put out.'

'Three brothers did you say, sir?' The DC was trying to catch up.

'No, two twins. Chinese apparently. It seems to be related.' Hooper was trying to work out the connection himself.

'Sorry, sir?'

'The brothers are called Lack.'

'I'm not surprised.' The bemused DC looked at Fairfax, who winked.

Hooper paced the floor. 'Names, addresses, witnesses, Sergeant. Everyone. And check all known associates of the brothers.' In times of confusion, the clear line of operational procedure was the only one to hang himself on. 'We need to find these Lacks, don't we?' But even as he said it, he was aware that professional operational procedure hadn't prevented him from thinking that he was pursuing them for her – in the hope that she'd like him for it.

3

The brothers Hooper was seeking were heading south in the Snipe. It had been hysteria all round at the Bengali Star. Ronnie had jumped out of the car when Arnie had just wanted Mathilda to get in so they could piss off, but Ronnie insisted they talk to Sayeed and had walked over to the old man at the entrance to the restaurant. Arnie had refused to get out of the car and then Lucy had jumped in and refused to get out as well, so Arnie had got out and tried to get Ronnie to get back in. 'Ronnie?'

'Talk to Sayeed, Arnie!'

'Mathilda, at least you get in, will you?'

'What for, Arn?'

'Get out of there, Lucy!' Arnie was beginning to lose it.

'Arnie, Bernie's covered in blood!'

'I know that, Lucy!' He turned in exasperation to Mathilda. 'Do you know somewhere we can hole up in the south?'

'Is Ronnie coming, Arnie?'

'Yes, Mathilda.'

'I could talk to my aunt.'

'Where's she?'

'She's in . . .'

'Arnie, will you talk to Sayeed?' Ronnie shouted over.

Arnie ignored him. 'Will you get out of that car, Lucy!'

'I'm coming with you!'

'You're not!'

'I bloody am!'

'You're worse than bloody Bernie!'

'I don't care, I'm bloody coming!'

'Bollocks!' Arnie had got back into the car and started the engine. 'Ron, we got about half an hour before the law puts an alert out on this vehicle!'

'Arnie, talk to Sayeed!'

'I'm bloody going! I'm going now!' Arnie shoved the car into gear and started to pull forward. No-one wanted to be left behind and they'd all jumped in. Arnie pulled the Snipe out from the Bengali Star car park, sending up a spray of water from a huge puddle as they took the road south. Sayeed Sayeed had placed his palms together as they left and prayed. 'Oh, Charlie. The bloody end has come.'

As they drove, Mirabelle told the girls what had happened at the tower. Bernie just held on to his Arfer and tried to curl himself into a ball through all the inevitable questions. Finally Lucy, crammed next to him in the back, put her arms round him and gave him a big hug. 'I know you didn't do nothing, Bern. We'll all go down the nick and they can throw away the key before we let them touch you.'

'Oh, Christ.' Arnie was finally admitting to himself that he didn't need Lucy in daylight. He took a corner too fast out of irritation. His state of mind wasn't helped by the fact that they were coming into that dosser's delight and vagabond's paradise, the industrial dereliction of the south of the south.

'What's next then, Arn?'

'You don't have to take that sarcastic tone, do you, Ron?' Arnie stared ahead out of the windscreen.

'So, what's on the agenda, Arn?'

'I don't know! It's fucking hidden!'

'Well have a think, mate. I mean the Old Bill's going to be a bit down in the mouth, aren't they? They consider doing a runner on a murder charge is not on.' Ronnie gave Mathilda next to him in the front a serious look.

'Well make a suggestion will you?' said Arnie.

'Making a suggestion now's just pissing in the air after the horse has bolted.'

'Don't get intellectual with me, mate.'

'I was trying to talk about it with Sayeed, Arnie.'

'What's it got to do with him?'

'He would have helped us.'

'How can he do that? How can anyone do that?' Arnie accelerated through streets that didn't deserve the name. There was hardly a house that was lived in. 'I see a little brother standing over the corpse of an auntie, covered in gore, waving a blade, pissing his trousers and eating a prawn sandwich! What do I do? Tell me!'

'I din't do nothing!' Bernie shouted. 'I only nicked a sarnie! I didn't get no breakfast! Them Indian ones at Sayeed's don't have no egg!'

Arnie was having to slow down. They were passing through an old deserted housing estate and the roads were shorter. 'Well, why don't you tell us, Bern? Tell us what were you doing standing there with a knife?'

'What? I din't have no knife!'

'Yes you did. We saw you.' Arnie glanced over his shoulder and asked seriously, 'I want to know what you done, Bernie.' His gentle tone had silenced everyone and Bernie could see that they were all waiting for an answer.

'I give in.'

'It's not funny, Bern.' Ronnie turned from the front seat.

'Who's Bob?'

'All right, mate, if you're not going to tell us, shut up.' Arnie was hardening.

Bernie panicked. 'I don't want to go down no nick! I don't want to go . . .'

'You're not, you're not . . .' Mirabelle had to calm him again.

'You're not. Don't listen to him!' Lucy weighed in. 'Leave him alone, Arnie.'

'All right, Lucy.' Arnie knew it was hopeless. 'Don't worry, Bern. You're not going anywhere. So put a bucket over your head and shut up.'

Bernie was close to tears. 'We got to stick together, bruvs. That's the whole point.'

Ronnie smiled. 'Just don't fart and ruin anyone's day, will you?'

'I won't, Ron. Sorry, Arn. I din't do nothing. Promise.' They drove on in silence.

'We're here. She'll be here somewhere.' Mathilda was looking around the desolate industrial estate they'd come into. Arnie stopped the car by an empty factory. 'That's where she usually is.' Mathilda looked round. The estate was surrounded by row upon row of derelict houses, most of them blackened by the fires of an itinerant population. On a patch of waste ground ahead there were about half a dozen of them sitting around a caved-in day centre.

'Don't they know it's closed?' Arnie felt morbid.

'Tilda! Tilda! What you doing?' There was a bang on the window. 'You come here to me and let me grip that gorgeous body!'

An old black woman had appeared from nowhere. She was dressed in what seemed to be the remnants of several dresses and had brightly coloured scarves, slides and pins all over her huge head of hair. 'It's my auntie.' Mathilda was more than a little embarrassed by her relation. Ronnie shifted so that she could get out of the car.

Her aunt put her arms around her on what was left of the pavement and yelled in delight, 'Why didn't you tell me you was comin'?'

'These are some friends of mine.' Mathilda leaned in through the car window. 'This is Auntie Two-pin.'

'Who?' Arnie had taken one look at her and felt even more depressed.

Two-pin squeezed her head through the passenger window, forcing Ronnie back onto Arnie's shoulder. 'Two-pin! Even a poor black know how a pretty pin is cheaper than out o'reach garment material!' She gave them all a wide grin and took a look round the inside of the car. 'You boys in trouble?'

Arnie wondered how she'd spotted it. Maybe everyone down here was. He decided to take the bull by the horns. 'Know anywhere we can stash a Snipe?'

'I know where you can hide the Tower of London!' She pointed to the old factory across the road. The brothers craned their necks. The place looked like a bombed-out Gothic cathedral. It had huge padlocked gates across the front. 'And I got the keys!' Two-pin produced a massive jangly bunch from somewhere in her dresses. 'You want to come in?'

She ran quickly across the street with Mathilda, and they unlocked and then hauled back the gates. Arnie drove the Snipe through them and into what was once the factory loading bay. He stopped the car and they looked ahead through to the vast cavern of industrial gloom beyond. It was the size of a football pitch and had obviously once been the main factory floor. There were relics of machinery scattered across it and old damp offices fifty yards away at the other end. A rusting catwalk ran thirty feet above their heads round three sides of the building, and there were gaping holes in the roof. Bernie shivered. Two-pin laughed. The gold at the back of her mouth glittered for a second like the pins in her hair. 'Welcome to shut-up shop! How long you going to stay with me?'

4

The killing was in the papers and on the lunchtime TV news. Raphaella was, as usual, on the sofa and Luis sat at the table, staring at the giant screen over her head. Emil, hair still wet from his three-hour vanity bath, prowled the room in a white dressing gown, watching as a reporter interviewed Superintendent Hooper.

'So what? Some crumb cop.'

'Shuddup!' Luis leaned forward. He'd never seen Hooper before, which was unusual. Luis had put a few ton in the pockets of all of them at one time or another. Hooper looked as if he meant business. His natural, heavy-browed sadness and air of sincerity made him surprisingly photogenic. The reporter asked him about the three men seen running from the scene of the crime.

'We wish to interview them and are following a number of leads.' Hooper was being very professional, but what he said next was more difficult. 'We are also seeking the victim's sister, a Miss Violet Green, also known as Violet Lack.' He'd almost stumbled there. In his mind she'd always been Violet Hooper. He controlled himself and continued. 'We are asking her to come forward in order to help us with our inquiries.'

'What?' Luis couldn't believe it. 'The boys in blue want her too!' He got up quickly from the table and snatched the remote from Raphaella's sticky paw. He switched off the TV and Hooper's melancholy face faded from the screen. 'What is this? What I got? The whole world want this woman!' He prowled the room. 'Hospitals! Murder Squad! What next, huh? What I pay for? The dogs of war?' He realized his hands were shaking and jammed them into his pockets. 'I go to these twins and I say *Violet* . . . Is this difficult? One word, one person!' His hands came out of his pockets again in a gesture of despair. 'Harriet, Sophie, grandmother, sister! These are three persons and none of them is Violet!'

Emil ignored the mathematics and said, 'So why don't you leave it to me?'

'You! Look at you! You drown a Corvette! What is this? I make payments on a sunk car?' Luis was verging on the hysterical.

'OK, so how much you pay McCarthys for the holocaust?'

'How much I pay is a matter of finance not for birdheads!'

'OK, so how much you pay when the flatfoots come knock, knock, knocking on the front door with the bracelets? How much you pay legal buffs, huh?' Emil relaxed himself onto the table. His hours of humiliation were forgotten. His own incompetence seemed dwarfed by that of his old man. He gave Luis a superior smile and asked what he knew already. 'So how much you pay twins, huh?'

'Shuddup!' Luis was coming to the end and he knew it. He'd abused his son and daughter so many times over the years that the verbals were just bouncing back and echoing round his own head. Insult a child, insult yourself. If they were inadequate, what was he who was responsible? He wanted to sink into the sofa and watch game shows for the rest of his life. He made one last valiant effort. 'I stop these twins, pronto!'

Emil could smell the blood of his father and moved in like the piranha he was. 'You stop the McCarthy Twins?' He laughed. 'You crazy guy, or what? No-one stops the McCarthy Twins. Get me?'

'Shuddup!' It was no good, Luis was weakening and Emil could see it.

'Stop the McCarthy Twins?' Emil raised his hands in a gesture of amused amazement. He was beginning to enjoy himself. 'Stop breathing, crazy guy!'

'I say shuddup, so shuddup . . .' Luis was getting pathetic. He was seeing conspiracy to GBH and accessory to murder raps pass like the spaces between bars in front of his tired, frightened eyes. 'Can't you see I'm a sick man?' He just made it to a chair by the table and collapsed in a crumpled heap.

'OK, Papa, so here's what we do.' Emil stood as his father fell. But he didn't do it quick enough.

'You listen to me, is what you do.' Raphaella had risen from the sofa. An aura like a sweet pink cloud with the scent of bubblegum suddenly filled the room. It had taken the entire morning, but she was now, without doubt, the biggest cosmetic job in town; a she-giant of lip gloss, pancake and hair gel, mounted on six-inch heels.

Unfortunately for him, Emil didn't seem to notice the change that had taken place. 'Sure, Raphaella, we listen to you and what happens?' He flicked his dressing gown over his bare legs and smirked. 'We buy Max Factor, or what?'

Raphaella walked slowly towards him. Her hips swayed and her underwear swished, her cheekbones were armoured and her tits were pointed. The Amazon stood over her irrelevance of a brother and stared at him with eyes mascara'd for war. Emil's smirk froze. He asked himself, Why was he so scared of his sister? He didn't know the answer, but could already feel a need to cross his legs. When she pulled the cord of his dressing gown he wished he had. It fell open and Raphaella looked down on his small soft coil, shrivelling by the second. 'Call that a dick?'

'Hey, sis!' Emil scrambled to cover himself.

Raphaella wasn't interested. She'd seen better appendages on pizza boys, or, come to that, Charlie Lack. She'd already moved to the other end of the table and looked down on her father. She put one hand on her hips and checked the nails of the other; today's colour, blood red. She half yawned and said, 'Don't worry, Papa. I do it. You want it efficient, ask Raphaella. I can screw anybody.'

'Shuddup! No more!' Luis cried. He looked longingly at the sofa. All he wanted to do was curl up like a baby child and disappear into the soft plump cushions. 'Please, you break your dead mother's heart!' He looked up to the ceiling. 'Oh, Josephina, what I do wrong?'

Raphaella looked down with clear, hoodlum-brown eyes. Appeals to buried mothers cut no ice with the coldest heart on the block. 'Learn something, you prick.'

'Wha . . . ?' Luis's jaw sagged.

Raphaella spun on her heels. This was it. Her true self, life and purpose was about to be revealed. 'Take a look!' She stood with her hips, breasts and chin thrust forward. 'Didn't you notice? When my husband die I am a widow! And I got a restaurant! And I don't listen to you no more. You give cash to Chinese!' Both father and son wanted to remind her that this was her idea, but they had no time and even less courage. Her head turned fast and it seemed to Emil that her hair flew in curves like a hundred whirring machetes. He instinctively ducked. 'And you, little brother, you think swanky car is submarine and let Lacks get lost! Huh!' She spat the last with the contempt of an empress. 'You ask me and I pick Arnie Lack with my pinkie nail.' She flicked her inch-long talons towards him. 'This is Raphaella world! OK? Who murder the slots? Who give heart-attack screw in the Sunset? Who? Raphaella!' Then she added, 'Me!' in case they weren't clear.

'Raphaella?'

'Shuddup!' she snarled, and Luis noticed that in her mouth the word held the truly violent and steely ring that had once been exclusively his. 'You don't talk no more, Papa! You watch TV.' She pointed a finger at the screen and as if by magic a game show came on. Luis looked up at the bejewelled and perfumed glory of his daughter standing over him and suddenly began to laugh. It was hysteria. It was relief. It was over! From his loins he had borne forth a true image of himself after all! It wasn't the male he had expected, but who cared? If this warrior queen had sprung from him, maybe he hadn't been such a bad dad after all? Was his work done? He prayed silently to his dead wife that it was so and looked over at the sofa again. He wanted them all to go so he could lie on it and watch the game show. It was a rerun of *Take Your Pick*, he noticed.

Emil wasn't quite finished. 'Hey, sister . . .'

'Shuddup.'

'Hey, sis . . .'

'Shuddup, shuddup!'

'Hey . . .'

'Shuddup, shuddup, shuddup!' She used the magic word three times and it was hers. Emil was finally cowed and proud. He held a brief silence to show respect and then said, 'Hey, sister, what a crazy guy.'

'And I find this Violet.' Raphaella took a turn round the room. 'I don't like no rival, even for a dead husband. It's a Raphaella world!' She liked the ring of it, so she repeated, 'You hear me, a Raphaella world! And she don't take no shit from nobody. Get your clothes on, brother, and get Jock and Razor. First thing we do is go and tell McCarthys they're off the case. Right now.'

'Uh? What?' Emil gulped.

'You heard me.'

'Wait a minute.' Emil tried to smile, but this was very, very serious. Having his sister carve him up was one thing, having the McCarthys do it was something else altogether.

'You're not with me, brother, you're against me.' Raphaella picked up her coat and walked to the door. 'See you at the slots. Ten minutes.' Then she was gone.

'Hey, Papa, you got to do something!' Emil suddenly felt very naked and vulnerable in his thin dressing gown.

Luis got up and slowly walked to the sofa. 'Emil, you seen the TV guide?'

5

Raphaella didn't walk, she strode. The kingdom of the streets was hers. Emil tried to keep up. Scotch Jock lagged behind. There were few enterprises of mayhem or violence that he hadn't either participated in or dreamed of, and this was one of them. The McCarthy Twins? Was this woman off her fucking head? And to make matters worse it was Razor's afternoon off and he'd gone on his weekly visit to his father in the nuthouse. All the brain cells Jock had left were telling him to tender his resignation.

Emil was getting breathless as he ran after Raphaella. 'Listen, sister, please listen to me. You can't do this; it's against the rules. These people are for ever!'

'And I am for longer.' Raphaella walked on, scattering a small group of workmen who turned back with their mouths open.

Emil skipped to dodge a lamp-post and a hot-dog seller. 'Oh, little sister, you don't know what you do! You hear me? On the heart of my holy mother! You don't stop the McCarthy Twins, are you kidding? These guys are the sea. I mean, you don't stop the sea, right? I mean, what do you think you are? King Neptune?'

'Shuddup!' It was the S word again. Emil was beginning to understand. In other families, it was the person who held the sword, the sceptre or the crown who reigned supreme. In his, it was the one who held the 'shuddup' – and it wasn't him. It was her and she just kept going, leading them all to possible, near-certain, definite death.

She stopped outside the Peking Palace. This was it. Emil's last chance. He pleaded, 'Hey, sister, I beg you . . .'

'You don't like heat, don't play with matches.' She pushed open the door and went into the restaurant.

'Oh no, crazy guy . . .' Emil turned in desperation to Jock.

'Excuse me, boss. I have to . . . uh?' The Scotsman's bottle had emptied. He knew his feet wouldn't carry him over this threshold. 'Uh, you know?' He stepped off the pavement into the traffic. Two taxis, a bus and a Honda all screeched to a halt, horns blaring and drivers screaming obscenities. Jock didn't notice. He wandered away pretending he was thinking of what to do for Christmas.

Emil screamed, 'Don't leave me, you arsehole!' But Jock was gone. Emil looked up at the door of the Peking Palace and felt the first sign of slippage in his bowels.

Raphaella stood in the back room with her hands on her hips. 'May is May and ain't Violet. So, shitheads, you got the wrong sister.' The twins, as usual, had appeared at the hatch exactly one second before business arrived and were now looking at Raphaella through the steam. They said nothing and no gesture of face or hand betrayed them as they listened to her go on. 'This is Raphaella world, OK? So you're fired, end of picture.'

'Oh no . . .' Emil had crept in through the restaurant and was cringing by the door, by now badly wanting to shit.

Raphaella sneered. 'And you owe me five grand. You got twenty-four hours to give it back, OK? And something else, China Twins, sell this place up. Bean sprouts is over. You want to eat the best, come to my place.'

'Sis?' As soon as he'd said it, Emil wished he'd kept his mouth shut.

Raphaella turned to him, bringing with her the flicked eyes of the twins. 'Don't shake, cutie boy. Raphaella rules OK? Peking is for ducks and we got Lacks to locate. Ciao, boys.' She winked at the twins and walked out of the door, past her brother, who didn't seem able to move. The twins' stare was unwavering and Emil, like a hare, was stuck in the double headlights.

He tried a nervous smile. The twins didn't move. Emil knew he had to before he filled his trousers. 'See you, boys. Maybe we eat chow mein. Spring roll?' He shrugged as if the only thing on his mind was the menu for their forthcoming dinner. The twins stared. 'Have whatever you want! On me.' That was the end of his words and he didn't know what else to do. He was still caught in the headlights and his rectal muscles couldn't cope much longer. Then God intervened and a waiter came through the door. In the instant that he passed between Emil and the stare, the hare had fled. The twins' faces were slowly obscured by the steam from the kitchen behind.

6

Bernie had been sitting in some crummy old office at the back of the factory for bloody hours. They'd made him have a wash in dirty water out of a drain or something to get the blood off his hands, but it was still on his shirt and he didn't like that. Mirabelle and Mathilda and Lucy kept trying to cheer him up, but they was as cold as he was and no-one knew what was going on, which was the worst thing. He'd kept his big gob shut for most of the time but every now and again was feeling really bad, especially as Ronnie and Arnie didn't come in and talk to him. 'I'm in dead total panic, Meebelle. It's a fit-up. I din't do nothing! I'm an innocent party. God help me!'

'He will.'

'I'm not so sure about that, mate. I dunno about that.' He shook his head, then jumped. Something had flapped in the doorway. 'Whassup?' Two-pin came in holding a massive white shirt. 'You could have given me a bloody heart attack!'

'That's enough of that language, boy. You learn some manners and gratitude.' Bernie went into a sulk as Two-pin held the shirt out to Mathilda. 'Come from Uncle Horn's own personal wardrobe.'

'Uncle Horn! Oh no! I told you, keep your mouth shut, Two-pin!' Mathilda looked horrified.

'Any boy need a priest, this blood-stained one do.'

'I don' need no priest!'

'You cover your body with this pure white, boy, and leave knowing better to them who do,' said Two-pin.

'Bernie, say thank you to Two-pin.' Mirabelle had already started undoing the buttons of his blood-spattered shirt.

Bernie mumbled a quick 'Ta'. He didn't like that red stuff on him and was pleased to get the shirt off. 'I ain't no sinner. I don' need no holy man and I don' have no stains neither. Not once I got this off.' He stood and took the shirt from Two-pin. She was impressed by his huge body.

'Where'd you get those muscles, boy? You use them dumb-bells?'

'I'm just natural strong.' He put the white shirt on and stood with his hands hanging down by his side like a miserable gorilla.

'You look like Galahad.'

'Not no more, Meebelle.' He sat back down on the chair, depressed. 'I don' think this world's what it's cracked up to be.'

7

Razor Jam hadn't seen his father at the nuthouse. The old boy had stabbed a fellow patient with a fork earlier in the day and was sedated in solitary. The Sikh was unperturbed. So far as he was concerned every adage was true and so there was no reason to think that 'like father like son' would be any exception. Consequently any violence on the part of his father that involved a knife, or indeed fork, was a confirmation of his own chosen career. He was feeling quite content as Jock grabbed him on the street outside the slots arcade and mumbled in incomprehensible and no doubt obscene back slang that they had to go up to see the boss immediately. Jock pulled him along by the hand, which Razor had to concede was unusual, but said nothing. He also didn't react when he heard about the McCarthys. Jock couldn't work out whether this was foolhardy courage, or deafness caused by the Sikh's turban. He was tempted to persist until he got a response, but there was no time. They were already on the stairs up to the Riss apartment and the great brown door was approaching fast. It seemed only yesterday that they were running out of it with big grins, bearing wads of Luis's cash and returning triumphantly with Lack Brothers invoices. Those were the days.

A few minutes later they were standing by the door of the living room as Emil came out of the bathroom again. He'd been four times in the last hour and still didn't feel the needle was on empty. He sat at the table, holding his stomach and groaning. 'You see what happens when you mess with McCarthys?'

Jock wasn't listening. He'd been attempting to justify his cowardice outside the Peking Palace as merely the entirely necessary precaution of keeping a lookout against McCarthyite reinforcements suddenly taking them all by surprise with a kamikaze attack out of Peterborough Alley. Not surprisingly, this hadn't been accepted, so he stood upright and acted tougher than he felt, desperate to revive his credibility as a hard man, not only for the sake of his reputation, but also because he was now totally in awe of Raphaella. This was the kind of woman a man could put his cock on the block for. He could even feel the beginnings of a hard-on as he watched her standing in the middle of the room thinking with her back turned symbolically to the TV.

'So where are these brothers, huh?' asked Emil. Raphaella ignored him, so he turned on Jock, catching him adjusting himself down the front of his trousers. 'Why don't you stop playing with yourself and do something?'

'Like what?'

'Well.' Emil spread his arms wide and sneered. 'Why don't you locate the Lacks like little sister, big boss, tells us?' He doubled the sneer and aimed it at Raphaella. 'Hey, so what's next? So far you got us on the triad death list and given the old man a nervous disaster!'

Luis popped his head up from the sofa. 'What? Don't talk to me. I watch TV. It's better than life.' He disappeared back into the cushions and the game show.

'Papa, see what's happening, why don't you?'

Luis suddenly sat bolt upright and pointed at the TV. 'See that! That chicken farmer just won a Fiat Uno, six suitcases and four weeks in Albania!'

Emil looked round in despair. Razor stood vacant by the door and Jock was looking adoringly at Raphaella, who was still deep in thought. Unusually for Emil, he tried reason. 'Listen, Raphaella. I mean like, uh? I am your big brother, right? Am I or ain't I? I am. Right. So, there are places I've been, you don't, right? There are things I seen, you don't, right? You hear me?' She clearly didn't, but he persevered. 'There are things I am, you ain't . . .'

'Shuddup!' Raphaella used the word with vehemence. Emil quailed. 'Don't you see I'm trying to think!'

'So think quick, sister. Two twins don't play chopsticks!'

'So,' she thought out loud. 'To get Violet, we got to get to the sons. So?'

'So what?'

'So, shuddup!' There was a silence as she began to move up and down the room thinking some more. 'Detail!' she said suddenly. 'Detail is the art of success. My dead husband told me.' She looked round at

Razor, Jock and Emil, who stared back vacantly. 'I want everything about the Lacks. I want where they go, where they been, what they think. I want detail . . .'

'Listen, Shylock Holmes . . .'

'Detail, brother, detail!'

Emil shut up and there was a silence as the boys tried to think of a detail. Razor thought of one. 'They got a restaurant, Miss Riss.'

'Genius.' Emil sat back on his chair.

'They don't got a restaurant! I got a restaurant! Gimme another detail.'

Jock tried to be helpful. 'Arnie goes out with Lucy.'

'I don't want to hear about no Blue Lucy. She's a fat whore!' There were some details you just didn't mention to Raphaella.

Razor had another try. 'They got an auntie.'

'Who's in hospital.' Emil was beginning to enjoy the charade and wondered how long his sister was going to last in pole position. 'Guess why?'

'They got an auntie.' The thought seemed to have triggered something in Raphaella. 'Auntie Harriet. So?' Her walk around the room was getting a little quicker. 'So where does Auntie Harriet come from? Huh? Same place as Charlie come from.' Was this getting somewhere? She wasn't sure and increased her pace. 'Where's Lucy come from? I don't want to talk about no Lucy!' She was as hard on herself as everybody else. 'Mathilda? Where's Mathilda come from? Huh?' This was better. She moved even faster, going round and round the table. 'Where's Mathilda now? Disappeared. So why she disappeared with the brothers when Ronnie don't want her at best of times? Hmm?' She stopped dead. 'Only one reason. So she can help them disappear! Why not? So where they disappeared to? I tell you!'

'Huh?' She'd lost Emil on the second lap.

'They disappeared to where Mathilda come from, which is same place as Charlie and Harriet come from. The south!' She'd shouted it. Jock and Razor were amazed. It was either brilliant or stupid, but they weren't qualified to tell, and anyway who cared, she was the boss and she was moving round the table again.

'Thank you, sister.' Emil was getting dizzy. 'The south. How about some other detail? Like a door number? Hmm, genius, Alfred Weinstein, ratface?'

Raphaella spun on her heels and stood over him. She pointed a dangerous-looking fingernail and spoke through her cleavage. 'You get detail, don't worry, Emil. And you call me ratface again and you don't got no mush for a face at all for ever onwards. You get me?'

Emil was amazed to see Jock and Razor take a threatening step towards him. This was when he finally knew he'd lost. 'Sorry, sis.'

She spoke down to him like he was something she'd found up her nose. 'You go to Lack place and see what you find from the south.' She changed her mind immediately. 'No. Lack place is Harriet. Is hospital. Is dogs of law all over it.' She thought again. 'Yes! Mathilda place! You know it?'

'Why should I know it?' Emil was sulking.

Jock stepped forward like a proud schoolboy. 'I do, boss.'

'So, go. Take Razor. Get everything you see and bring it back. We find where Mathilda come from in the south and whatayagot?' She leered down at her defeated brother. 'So, we got the Lack Brothers. And so whatayagot? We got Violet! And so whatayagot? A restaurant!' She stepped back and smoothed her skirt over her thighs. 'This girl's got it made, and she's only twenty-eight.' She pulled her blouse tighter over her breasts. Jock could hardly stand it. 'China Twins. Forget it.'

8

Bernie had waited for hours, hanging around in the old office, but still his brothers hadn't come and talked to him, so when Mirabelle wasn't looking he sneaked out. He saw Arnie and Ron talking with Lucy on the factory floor and went quietly up the steps to the catwalk above, where he stood, thirty feet high, looking down on them.

Ronnie had his hands in his pockets and was walking round the rusted machinery. They were going round it all again. 'So who done it, then?'

Arnie was leaning against an iron pillar with his arms folded. He'd just come back from listening to the radio in the Snipe and had heard they were wanted men. He breathed out hard in exasperation. Wanted men! He was a rational, nearly ordinary, non-tax-paying

174

subject of the realm for fuck's sake! He'd hardly listened to Ron. 'Done what?'

'Who killed Auntie May, Arnie!'

Lucy slipped off the base of an old lathe. 'It was Riss, Ron. It's that bloody Indian with his razor.' She looked to Arnie for affirmation.

'Because', said Arnie like he'd been through it all too many times, 'they thought she was Mum.'

'I don't believe it.'

'She looked like Mum, didn't she?'

'They want the restaurant that bad? Come on, Arnie, it's a bloody café!'

'It's the property! Think about what that's worth.'

Ronnie changed tack. 'How'd they know where she was?'

'They were following us over on the Great Eastern, weren't they?'

'So they were behind us up east at Gran's, they waited all night outside Sayeed's and then followed us to the tower, except they got there ahead of us. Come on, Arnie, it don't make no sense.'

'How the fuck do I know how they found her!'

'Riss isn't up to it! He's all trouser and no fly, isn't he?'

'So who do you think done it then?'

'I don't know.'

'Come on, Ron, spit it out.'

'I said, I don't know!' He walked away towards the end of the workshop.

Up above, Bernie stood on the catwalk, huge in his white shirt. He wasn't hidden. Any of them could have seen him if they'd looked up.

Arnie turned to Lucy. 'Well, you know who he thinks done it, don't you?'

Ronnie's voice echoed around the factory. 'I haven't said that, Arnie.'

'It's what you think. You think Bernie done it, don't you?'

'I don't know.' Ronnie moved slightly towards his brother. 'Look, Arnie, he can be strange sometimes, you know that.'

There was a silence for a second. Neither Lucy nor Arnie could deny it. They were all going to have to face the inevitable sooner or later. Arnie spoke quietly. 'So you're saying we should call up the constable?'

'No. I don't know what to do!' Ronnie was in agony. He walked round in circles, his shoulders hunched, then he kicked at a piece of rag on the floor. He stopped and seemed to come to some kind of decision. He looked up at Arnie. 'What else is there, mate?'

Arnie moved towards him. Their voices were lower but Bernie could still hear every word.

'Ron, the constable takes one look at Auntie May with her throat hanging out and thinks, This ain't a normal deed. Then he takes one look at Bernie and he thinks, This ain't a normal boy.' There was a silence. Ronnie knew Arnie was right. 'So what happens next? Bernie's in the slammer whether he done it or not.'

'And Riss has a good laugh,' added Lucy.

'So what do you want to do then?' Ronnie asked the pertinent question. 'You want to go fugitive in a charabanc? Who's going to have a good laugh about that? The constable! And that makes us all accessories, Arnie.'

'So who are you worried about then? Yourself or Bern?'

'I don't know!'

'He's our brother, mate,' said Arnie.

'I know! And I know we got half the Old Bill and his dog out looking for us!'

'So what do we do about Bernie?'

Neither of them knew. There was a tension, as they both faced the intractable. The silence was thick and horrible. It was suddenly broken by a desperate howl booming around the concrete walls. 'I don't want to go down no nick!' Bernie ran along the catwalk above them like a giant, crazed, clumsy bear. 'I don't want to go down no nick!'

'Bernie, come back here, you prat!' Arnie shouted up, but it was too late. Bernie had come to the end of the catwalk and disappeared onto the stairs beyond the far factory wall. They could still hear his cries: 'I don't want to go down no nick!' coming through the brickwork and slowly becoming indistinct as he disappeared.

Mirabelle came quickly from the offices with Mathilda behind her as Arnie and Ronnie ran to the iron stairs up to the catwalk at the office end of the factory. Mirabelle kept going forward and went quickly in the same direction but on ground level. She listened, but couldn't hear anything except their echoing footsteps on the catwalk above. She went quickly into the loading bay at the front of the factory. There was nothing but the Snipe, grease, rags and old wooden boxes. She ducked through a small door at the side and came to the bottom of a flight of concrete steps. This must have been the way Bernie had come. The stairs ended in a small hall that had a corridor running off it. Mirabelle went quickly along it, desperately resisting her desire to use other powers to find her charge. Although she'd used them in the emergency at the tower, they were technically forbidden and there were heavy penalties, including the revocation of her mission. She went faster. She could hear the shouts of Lucy and Mathilda somewhere behind her as she came into a small yard that looked as if it had once been the office car park, and saw what she'd been dreading. There was a small open judas door in the locked gates on the other side. She was running towards it when Arnie and Ronnie came into the car park behind her.

'He's gone out here!' she shouted back to them.

'Oh fuck! He's on the street!' Arnie in turn yelled back to Lucy and Mathilda.

They went one at a time through the low door and stood outside the factory, facing row after row of derelict council terraces. They could see four men in beaten-up combat gear and berets pulling apart an old Transit van for no discernible purpose, and a female scarecrow in black and brown rags was aimlessly wandering in the middle of the road ringing a bell, again for no apparent reason. Otherwise it was peaceful. Bernie was nowhere to be seen.

He was on the run. He was getting out of there bloody fast because he wasn't going down no nick. Not for bloody no-one. He didn't know where he was running to and no-one cared less, did they? His bruvs didn't, that's for sure, and all these geezers out here were too mad to bother about it anyway. And this bloody shirt was too big an' all. And he definitely wasn't going down no nick, so he just kept running down the streets.

'Bernie! Bernie!'

That was Ron; he was on some other street over the houses, well bolix to him, he wasn't taking no notice, he was keeping running, because he wasn't going down no cop shop with them coppers and all what they do and chuck you in the slammer and lock it up. Bugger that for a game of soldiers. He hadn't done nothing, just nicked a prawn sandwich, and he didn't want to think about pissing on the carpet because he thought you might have to go in the nick for that, and so that was another reason he was just going to keep running.

'Bernie! Where are you?'

Bolix, that was Arnie and he was on the other street over the houses on the other side. What's up with Arnie, why didn't he sort it all out? Then he heard Lucy's voice shouting out his moniker too. They was all surrounding him to take him down the cop shop with bracelets and badges and silver buttons. He was getting super-panicked and his head was going up the wall and round the bend and off its rocker. He ran straight down a passage between two houses and ended up in someone's garden, which was just a bloody big mess with weeds and rusty gear and old crisp packets and papers. Didn't they have no waste-paper bins round here? He leaned against a wall and began to cry. 'I ain't done nothing. You baskets! You're supposed to be my bruvs! Things I had to put up with! I've bloody had it!'

'Bernie!' It was Tilda now. She seemed to be getting closer.

'Oh no. For crying out loud, I can never get away. This is a disaster!' He turned to run back through the passage.

'Ain't no use running. God always catches up.' And there was this big black bloke with a big black hat, who'd come out of the back door of the next house and was staring at him over what was left of the garden fence. 'And that's my shirt you got on. Where'd you get it?'

Bernie took a step back. If he'd been bothered before, now this was twice as bad. 'I din't nick nothing. I got it off an old black girl!'

The black man smiled in a superior way. 'I know you did, 'cos that's my sister and that's what's left of her house you're standing in.' He pointed a long elegant finger at Bernie. 'And you're one of those big criminal brothers she was telling me about.'

'We ain't no crimbos! We're dead clean, we are!'

'Not what I heard.'

'Well buzz off then! You blessed, blinking bloke! Buzz off!'

'You think you're talking to a bee, brother?'

'I don't care what you are! Buzz off!'

'It's all right, Bernie, don't worry about him.' Mirabelle had come through the passage and was staring at the black man with a wary eye.

Mathilda came up behind her. 'Mirabelle, this is my uncle.'

The man extended his hand to Bernie and said suavely, 'The Reverend Harvey Horn, pastor to the Lord. I've been waiting to meet you.'

Bernie took his hand but didn't like it. 'We ain't no crimbos, Vicar.'
Mirabelle stared at Horn. Her dislike was instant.

Mathilda and Mirabelle walked Bernie back through the streets. The female skeleton was still ringing the bell but the men in combat gear were gone. Only the chassis of the Transit remained on a patch of wasteland like the skeleton of some monstrous, prehistoric insect. They met up with Arnie and then Ronnie on the way and escorted Bernie back to the factory. He was still very frightened. As he reached the judas door, he said, 'I ain't going down no nick, Arnie.'

'You're not going anywhere, don't worry about it, mate.' Arnie was worried that Bernie might balk at going back into the factory and his tone was comforting. He was also feeling guilty that Bernie had over-heard him saying the things he had.

Ronnie felt equally bad. 'That's right, Bern. We'll look after you.'

Bernie ducked through the door but still wasn't completely re-assured. 'You said you was going to call a constable.'

'No constables, no sergeants, no bluebottles whatsoever.' Arnie knew he was making up his mind as he said it.

'You promise?'

'Yeah.' Now he'd done it. They weren't taking Bernie in, and that was that.

'You said I wasn't normal.'

'I'm sorry, Bern. I apologize for that.' They'd come into the work-shop and the Reverend Horn, who'd followed them from the streets, went into the offices at the end with Mathilda to look for Two-pin. Arnie put his arm round Bernie. 'Listen. I am going to see Luis Riss and knock his block off.'

'What's Luis Riss got to do with it?'

'We think he's the one who got Auntie May done in.'

'Oh.'

'So that's another promise. And it don't matter what you done.'

'Only a sarnie, Arnie.'

'Don't matter. Like you said, the bruvs will stick together. Right, Ron?'

'That's right.'

'Right.' Bernie grinned. He felt better now. They all did, and although neither Arnie nor Ron knew what they were going to do, at

179

least they would do it together. Bernie already had other concerns. 'I'm starving hungry.'

No-one had much to say to that because no-one had thought to bring the picnic hamper. The problem was solved by Horn, who appeared in the doorway to the offices with Two-pin behind him. 'Two-pin, what you waiting for? You got bread and I got water!' He produced two bottles of Jamaican rum with a magician-like flourish from voluminous pockets inside his coat.

'Oh no,' said Mathilda. Her uncle's ferocious and wounding nights on the booze were famous throughout the family.

He laughed. 'You think I don't see what these boys require, Tilda?' He passed a bottle to Arnie, who accepted it gratefully.

Two-pin put in her twopenn'orth just to make Mathilda feel even more ashamed. 'You think being a priest ain't full of laughter? What's the point of being a priest, he don't enjoy himself? A priest is life, girl!'

Arnie reflected for about half a second on the seemingly eternal connection between booze and the clergy and then took a swig of rum. It was very strong. He gasped. 'God bless you, Reverend!'

'That's me, Mr Horn of Plenty! Get these boys some meat in a pot, Two-pin, and Tilda you wipe that disparaging look off your face. You been running rootless for too long, girl, and I got words to say to you!'

'Oh shit.' Mathilda wished she was home in bed.

9

She wouldn't have if she'd known who was standing over it. Scotch Jock stared at the crumpled sheets and looked down at the shattered door smashed flat beneath his feet, then round at the broken lamp-shade, emptied drawers, open cupboards and clothes and papers tossed around the room. The entirety of Mathilda's life seemed to be spread across the floor. 'Untidy bitch.'

'I think someone got here first,' Razor noted.

'And perhaps you'd explain why you came second?' Jock and Razor turned with their mouths hanging open as two men came into the room. Three uniformed police officers stood in the doorway behind them. 'I am Superintendent Hooper and this is Sergeant Fairfax. Who are you?'

'Eh? Ah? The name's McFadden,' said Jock.

'What are you doing here, Mr McFadden?' asked Hooper politely.

It had been a long time since anyone had called Jock Mister. He immediately puffed himself above himself. 'I'm the manager of the peep show. I was looking for the keys to the Kleenex cupboard.' He grinned superciliously.

'Don't mess about, sir.' Fairfax sounded proper but threatening. In Jock's view the straight copper was invariably more of a problem than the bent. They tended to gaol you if you broke the law. Fairfax shoved his jaw forward. 'Because we're not. You are under arrest.'

Jock slumped. 'Eh, wait a minute . . .'

'Why are you here?' Hooper looked directly at the pair of them. There was a light in the back of his eyes that pierced the melancholy of his voice and Jock had the feeling he meant business. He said, 'We were looking for the girl, sir. She didn't show up for work.'

'Where is she now?' Fairfax moved closer.

'We don't know.' Razor never lied.

'Did Luis Riss send you here?'

'Who's Luis Riss?' Jock, in truth, was no Razor.

Fairfax turned to Hooper. 'It looks like breaking and entering to me, sir.'

'We may have entered, but we didn't break anything!' Jock's indignation was marginally less than what it could have been, since what he said was fact. It was only in guilt that his protest was extreme.

'Take them to the station, Sergeant. We'll talk to them there.'

'I demand a solicitor!'

'Be quiet, Mr McFadden.' Fairfax turned to a uniformed officer. 'Constable.'

Jock and Razor were led away, but not before Jock in his innocent anguish spat out, 'And if you see her fat friend, tell her she's fired!'

Hooper watched them go. 'Fat friend?'

'Could be Lucy Legg, sir. Works in the peep show. Known associate of Arnie Lack.' Fairfax had done his homework on the brothers. It was this that had led them to Mathilda's bedsit.

'And this?' Hooper had stooped to pick up a framed photograph of Mathilda. Somebody had obviously trodden on it and the glass was smashed. 'Is this Ronnie Lack's girlfriend?'

'Seems so, sir.'

'She's a beautiful girl.' Hooper stared at the cracked glass and thought aloud. 'How far is Mr Riss prepared to go in his pursuit of this restaurant?'

Fairfax shrugged. 'We know someone was here before them, sir.'

'And if I were to hazard a guess, I'd say they were Chinese.' Hooper handed the photograph to Fairfax. 'Check her; and her friend, Miss Legg.' He looked up at the window. 'There has to be an end to this violence some time, Freddie.'

Fairfax always rather liked it when his superior used his Christian name. He beamed. 'Yes, sir.'

10

Jock and Razor were taken into a gloomy and abandoned office, situated down amongst the old pipes and reject furniture of the basement at the Central Police Station. Hooper was meeting obstruction all round in Soho and it was all they would give him. No-one was happy. The coppers at Central still thought it should be their inquiry and if it wasn't, why didn't the eastern law fuck off back east and use their own toilets? Hooper and Fairfax would have been happy to oblige, but at the moment had no alternative other than to accept what was offered, so Jock and Razor were brought in and searched. Razor's razor was confiscated, and they were sat, handcuffed, by the boilers. They weren't too upset because they knew they couldn't be done for robbery. All they wanted to do was get out, face Raphaella, get sacked and go down the pub and get drunk, until they were reinstated by the mob in the morning. But they'd have to wait until Fairfax had finished.

Despite the razor, which would have to be checked by the scientists, the sergeant made the big but understandable mistake of thinking that the Sikh was hardly bright enough to interrogate and had therefore spent most of his time confronting the lying Scot, who didn't know the difference between a porkie and his elbow, which were both, as far as he was concerned, legitimate means of defence. No, he didn't know no Chinese men; no, Luis Riss was not involved in nothing; no, he had not broken into Mathilda's; no, he was not a Celt; yes, he came from Berwick (Jock was cunning; he told the truth every now and again, like a feint with his left boot), and what about getting them a solicitor? Fairfax looked despairingly at Hooper, who was proving to be no help at all. In fact, after ten minutes his superintendent left him to it in order to make a few inquiries of his own upstairs.

Having failed to get any of the day-shift officers to give him the time of day, Hooper finally tracked down an old sergeant who had a grand-mother from East Dagenham, and in familial sympathy let Hooper know what every other policeman at Central knew, or thought, or thought he thought, on these matters. Namely, if they were after two orientals suspected of murder it was bound (or not) to be the McCarthy Twins. These were legendary assassins whose fame was based on either fact or myth, depending on which informant's rumour you believed. Although certain characters of a dubious nature had laid claim to having been associated with them, no-one had ever come forward with any reliable evidence, either because the potential witnesses were too scared, or because the twins had never committed a crime, or because there weren't any twins at all. All right? The old sergeant left it at that, apart from mentioning that, if they indeed existed, they were rumoured to be found at, or via, or through, or were possibly associated with, or might have been seen in, if they'd been seen anywhere at all, the Peking Palace Chinese restaurant in Broadhurst Street, where on the production of a warrant card you could get a 10 per cent discount on parties of six or more. Full stop. As to Luis Riss, the sergeant was more useful. He was a known character with a record, who apparently was not too well at the moment. He had been seen that very afternoon behaving strangely at his son's slots arcade. Hooper thanked the sergeant and then went back to the boiler room to see what Fairfax had come up with.

His sergeant had got somewhere without realizing it. In desperation he'd asked the Sikh a simple question. 'Do you know, have you ever known, or have you had cause to know, if there is, was, or has ever been any kind of connection, including physical or electronically trans-mitted conversation, between Mr Luis Riss and one or both of two men with oriental appearance?'

Razor had replied quite simply, 'Yes, Mr Riss hired them and his daughter fired them.' Unfortunately he'd said it in his mother tongue, which Fairfax wrongly took to be Hindi. As it wasn't a language he was familiar with he decided the Sikh was taking the piss and let it pass, although he made a mental note to find an interpreter and take up the matter later, if only to teach Razor due respect for his betters in blue. At this point Hooper walked in.

The superintendent sat on a wooden stool he'd found behind the boiler and watched his sergeant getting nowhere for ten minutes. The Scot knew nothing and the Sikh didn't speak unless it was in his own tongue. Hooper was restless, his heart had begun to leap again and the temperature of the room was going to his head. He was getting what he'd started to call Violetitus. (This, he felt, was a kind of a relief. To name the disease was at least the beginning of a cure.) He knew he needed more time to contemplate the profundity of all these matters, and squatting in this heat and squalor with a couple of deadbeat street scum, who wouldn't understand a philosophical inquiry unless it was made of wood with barbed wire wrapped around it, wasn't going to help him much – and anyway he'd failed to procure a cell for them. He rose from his stool and took Fairfax to one side. He instructed him to release the pair on police bail and warn Razor that a charge for the possession of a dangerous weapon was imminent. They weren't to leave the city. Then he watched his sergeant lead them away up the stairs.

He was about to follow when the phone rang. It was an old black 1950s Bakelite model, sitting dusty and isolated on the bare top of a battered wooden desk in the empty office behind him. The switchboard upstairs had finally co-operated and put through one of his own constables from the east. He gave Hooper the first actual news of the real Violet he'd had for forty years. Since that morning's media appeal, the police in Hammersmith had received several calls. Apparently they'd been told that there was a woman who went by the name of Violet Green, who worked, and indeed was quite well known, in the fashion trade. Hooper's heart leaped. The police over there had even discovered her address. Hooper's heart leaped higher. They'd been to her apartment, but it was empty. None of her neighbours or the telephone contacts knew where she was. It seemed as if Violet had suddenly, or at least temporarily, disappeared.

Hooper replaced the receiver. He sat slowly on the chair recently vacated by Scotch Jock and tried to take in what he'd heard. He shook his head. She was alive! At least up until a few days ago. She was using her maiden name – Violet *Green*! She hadn't remarried! His thoughts were whirring as Fairfax came back down the stairs. He made a few quick decisions. He'd send Fairfax to investigate the Peking Palace and these twins, if they existed. As for himself, if he couldn't see his soul's desire, he could do the next best thing. He'd go to where she'd been and sit close to one who'd known her. He resolved to visit Harriet again as soon as she was released from hospital. He'd see this restaurant for himself. He glanced at his watch. It was seven thirty; he still had time to steady himself. Two cups of strong coffee, he thought, and as many cigarettes as he needed. What the hell, life this intense could be short. He even considered alcohol. There was a distant crack of thunder.

11

The storm may have been developing for Hooper, but for the Lack Brothers it was overhead. They'd all made themselves as comfortable as possible in the damp offices at the back of the factory. Two-pin, with the help of Mirabelle and Mathilda, had boiled up her own Caribbean stew on a Primus and they were sitting around on old boxes and broken chairs watching Bernie eat most of it. The candles around them flickered in a hundred draughts as Arnie shared the rum with Lucy and Horn. There was more thunder above them and they could hear the rain pounding on the corrugated-iron roof of the factory. Arnie took another swig of the rum and passed the bottle to Horn, who was sitting higher than the rest on an old desk. 'I hear you brothers been on a rocky path.'

Arnie didn't want to talk about it. 'Thanks for the rum, Rev.'

But the alcohol was running and alcohol was Horn's key to the door of the soul of the wicked. In rum they opened up, and he could see the malevolence revealed. He'd been born with an unfortunate mixture of personal rage and a genuine talent for the perception of weakness in others. At times like this he knew he'd been put on this earth for one reason only, and that was to point the finger of righteousness at the darkness that surrounded him. His purpose was truth, which in his terms was blame, and rummed up in mind and mouth, blame he would. 'Two-pin here say to me, come and see this boy with blood on his hands.' Bernie looked up from the stew nervously. Horn winked at him. 'So I come and what do I see? I see an innocent child in the body of a man. I drink to you, brother.' He raised the bottle to Bernie and took a long pull of the rum.

Bernie was relieved and so he farted. ''Scuse me, Vicar, it's the stew.'

'You're welcome.' Horn took another drink; his juices were beginning to flow. He looked slowly around the room. 'But I see guilt also.'

'What?' Ronnie had been fairly irked with Horn from the beginning, but the priest had come with the food, so he'd kept his mouth shut.

'I am a man of the cloth and I speak plain.' Horn slipped off the desk and stood over them. 'I see guilt here in this place.'

'You're pissed, padre.' Arnie had been here before with one or two other bitter drinkers, who'd used their insight to needle anyone who seemed happier than them. He also knew that booze was the beginning of rage and the cause of the attack – and he didn't want Horn to drink it all. 'Pass the bottle, will you?'

'Wait a minute, Arnie.' Ronnie turned to Horn. 'Who's guilty?'

'Guilt is a coat of many colours, my son.'

'Don't call me my son. What are you talking about?'

'Ron . . .'

'Shut up, Arn. What's he on about? We're not guilty. Who's bloody guilty?'

'Here! Right here!' Horn pointed his long finger at Mathilda. 'Look no further than right beside you!'

'Tilda? What's she done?' asked Ronnie.

'I see a desperate quest for a love unfulfilled.'

'Uncle Horn, you shut your mouth!' Mathilda was uneasy. She knew Horn and what he could do.

'And why is this girl in such a piteous state? Because here is an irresponsible child punishing herself for running out on the true love of her own blood and family!'

'That's a lie, Uncle!' Mathilda stood up. The truth always hurt.

'Who by her own disgraceful behaviour sent her one father, my own good brother, Horrie, back to Kingston full of drink and despair!'

186

Two-pin, as usual, made it worse. 'I never heard a word more true.'

Mathilda was horrified. 'My dad didn't go back to Kingston because of me! He went full of rum from your own bottle, Uncle!'

Horn raised his finger high. 'Guilt, girl! I see guilt in your face!'

'Wait a minute. Hang on . . .' said Ronnie.

But Horn was in full flow. 'And here, Tilda, as if I don't see everything in you plain as day,' his finger came down witheringly into Lucy's face, 'here I see it in your companion plainer!' He breathed in to give himself full volume for the pronouncement. 'Here I see hell and harlotry!'

Lucy couldn't believe it. 'You what?'

'Here is all the stench of Babylon on unclean streets, in short skirt with suspenders snapping, bosoms protruding and red lips pouting!'

It was a pretty accurate description of Lucy. She said, 'Piss off!'

'Excuse me, Reverend . . .' Ronnie would have been at his most prim if Horn had allowed him to finish. He didn't, he stared directly into Ronnie's face. 'And what do I see here?'

Ronnie was caught. He wanted to tell the priest to go to the hell he surely came from, but something in him needed to hear what he had to say.

'I see a man unresolved.' He looked down at Mathilda. 'And you know it. You know I see a faint-hearted man, a coward of a man, a man who promise and don't deliver, a man who deals out pain 'cos of his own dishonest nature!' He stared, eyebrows arched, into Ronnie's eyes, daring him to disagree with him.

Ronnie was stunned. He said weakly, 'What me?'

It was enough for Arnie. In booze, violence was never far from his surface. He stood fast, grabbed the bottle from Horn's hand and stuck his big nose into the reverend's face. 'Thank you, Uncle. Now why the fuck don't you get lost?'

Horn, to give him his holy due, was unmoved. He stared unwaveringly back and stated calmly, 'But I say guilt. Didn't I say guilt, Two-pin?'

'That's what you say, brother.'

'And that's what I see here in all its foul glory, right here in front of me.'

Arnie shoved him away. 'Who is this arsehole?'

Now that Arnie had made a move, Bernie knew where he stood.

'Dunno, bruv, he came out of a door of a house and was just standing in the bloody garden like a prat in a hat!'

Horn ignored him and pointed his finger at Arnie. 'Hear this, sinner! Only two choices a man can make! One, let the good spirit wash your blood. Two, let the evil demon poison your soul!'

Mathilda could feel that her vile relative was about to reach into the true pit of his venom. 'Shut up, Uncle!'

'Shut me no shut-ups, girl!' Horn stared at Arnie with his eyes bulging. 'Only one thing to do, brother. Spill the beans! Get that bad deed out where the Lord can see it! Get it out before it festers in the heart and destroys the soul. Rid the curse, brother! You hear me? Come clean!'

There was a horrible silence. Lucy was expecting Arnie to explode, but he didn't. He stood in the centre of the room, the candlelight flickering over his face, looking directly at Horn. The only person who moved was Mirabelle. She edged slightly towards Bernie and the stew.

Horn looked in triumph at Arnie. 'I see you hear me, brother. So do it. Spill the beans before the Almighty come down from his heaven and take you bad.'

Arnie still said nothing. Lucy stood up by him. 'Arnie? Arnie, we don't have to stay here. This bloke's a lunatic.' She looked around. It seemed as if Horn had succeeded. Everyone was unmoving and quiet.

'So what I tell you, Two-pin? Here in this one place,' Horn's conceit was unbearable as he pointed at them all, one by one, 'the innocent lamb, the ungrateful child, the street-walking whore and the coward!' Then with a great grin of self-congratulation he stared at Arnie, who seemed to be in some kind of trance, 'The unclean man!' He stepped forward and took the bottle from Arnie's hand, then tipped the last of the rum into his mouth. 'What I tell you, Two-pin? Guilt!'

'What about me?' Mirabelle stepped forward into the light.

'You?' Horn looked faintly perturbed for the first time.

'What am I, Reverend?'

Horn went to drink again, but remembered the bottle was empty. His act was over, no coda necessary. Who was this impertinence anyway? 'You? I don't know you.'

'You seem to know everybody else. What am I?'

There was something about Mirabelle's bearing that was unsettling

Horn. He attempted to dismiss her. 'You're like the rest of them. You're evil!'

He'd hardly got the words out before Mirabelle had lifted the pot from the Primus and emptied its contents over him. 'There's no such thing, Reverend.' She viewed him covered in the last of his sister's stew. 'Now get out.'

It was all Arnie needed. Mirabelle's action had freed him from Horn's spell. He grabbed the priest by the lapels and propelled him to the door. 'Spilled enough beans for you, Reverend?' Horn didn't answer as he was pulled away. There was something about Mirabelle that had completely shut his mouth.

The others heard their footsteps as Arnie dragged Horn across the old workshop floor. Then there was the distant sound of a yell and a door slam as Horn was ejected. Lucy looked at Mathilda. 'Bleeding hell, Tilda, what next?' No-one said anything. After a while they could hear Arnie coming back as the rain still pounded on the iron roof above.

12

Raphaella wasn't pleased. She viewed Jock and Razor with distaste as they stood bedraggled by the door of the apartment. 'Dickheads!'

Jock belched. He'd had five pints and five chasers in the Empress. He'd known they were going to get hammered. Mind you, there was something about being taken apart by Raphaella that he quite enjoyed. 'Sorry, boss.'

'So who got to Mathilda's place first?' she wanted to know.

'We came second.' It was the best Jock could do, but Emil wasn't impressed.

'And the coppers come third and you could have cost us one grand fifty in bail finance!'

'You didn't pay nothing, boss.'

'I said could, didn't I?' Emil sneered.

'Shuddup!' Emil jumped. Raphaella had spoken. 'What's the matter with you?' she snapped. 'I got to think, and how can I think with birdbrains flapping?'

'Huh?' Emil pushed his luck. 'What I tell you about twin terror, sister?'

'What are you talking about?'

'We don't get to Mathilda first, who does? Huh?'

'I say shuddup, so shuddup!' Raphaella got up and straightened her skirt in a movement that went straight to the bottom half of Jock's problems. He sincerely hoped his trousers hadn't become transparent in the wet. 'So?' Raphaella began to pace, thinking out loud as was her new and boastful fashion. 'So, these Chinese is still working. So? They get to Mathilda's place. So? Now they get to Mathilda, the girl herself. So? They get to Lack Brothers in person. And so?'

'And so they get to Violet in person and cut her up for chop suey!' Emil finished it for her.

'Correct!' Raphaella snapped up her painted, blood-red first fingernail with a look of triumph. Emil was pleased to be right, but somehow he felt he'd got there for the wrong reasons. Raphaella sat down again and unscrewed the cap of her nail varnish. A new realization deserved a new colour. 'And I got a restaurant, stupid brother! It's obvious. These twins do it for me!' She'd decided on flamingo pink and started to paint.

'Wait a minute, sister. What about Papa? Didn't he slip them start-up finance?' Emil looked over at Luis, who was leaning forward with his head only inches from the TV.

'Papa?' Raphaella didn't seem to know who Emil was referring to.

'Yeah, Papa! The guy who married Mama! What happens to him?'

Luis suddenly yelled, 'Take the money!' He pressed his nose flat against the screen. 'Take the money!'

Raphaella looked over at him dispassionately. So this was who Emil meant by Papa. 'He go to gaol for murder accessory, I got a restaurant. And Lack Brothers? They got McCarthy Twins.'

Emil looked at his sister, who went back to painting her pinkie, and then across to his sad old man flat against the TV. He felt like the rain on the window, dribbling down the pane into nowhere.

13

The same rain was also pouring onto the roof of the taxi as it came to a halt in the circle of lamplight at the end of the alley by the restaurant that was causing so much grief to everyone. Porchese leaped out of the cab with an umbrella.

The little Italian chef had been drunk since the day after the funeral and then had lain sweaty and hung-over in his bed, tossing and turning over in his mind the deepest darkest problem of his existence to date, which was: Charlie was his life and Charlie was dead, so what therefore was his life? In front of him was his chef's tunic and trousers draped over his old armchair and covered in vomit. He stared at them for two hours, then slowly heaved his torso to a sitting position. He'd done this because an idea had taken root at the bottom of his spine and slowly worked its way up to his head, taking in the rest of him on the way. When he was, as it were, full of an idea, his body had risen like a loaf puffed by yeast. Because Porchese was a very simple man, his idea was also very simple. He had realized that he personally wasn't dead. He stared at the daylight coming through his filthy curtains and pondered the ramifications of the thought. The first was that he would remain not dead, so to speak, until he was. In turn he realized this meant that there was a kind of waiting time. He began to understand that this was what people usually called life. His problem then became quite clear. How should he fill in this gap called life until he became what he had realized he wasn't, which was dead? He stared at the sick on his whites for another hour. Whites? Wear whites? Why wear whites? Ah? Because he was a little chef. Chef? He raised his head higher and thought about it. That was the word he'd been waiting for.

Not long after, he got out of his bed, put on a clean tunic and trousers, looked at himself for ten minutes and caught the bus. Chef he was and chef he would remain until he had filled in every second of the waiting time, and then he'd be dead and he wouldn't do it any more. Simple.

Charged by the functional purity of this idea he had walked into the restaurant and discovered from Geoffrey that the boys had gone east and Harriet had been half killed by a couple of Chinese. What had been so simple had suddenly become complex and then horrifying. Oh

Madonna mia, the little man shook. It was all too much. He realized that chefness wasn't all. He was also full of love and sorrow – and the dreaded guilt. How could he lie in his bed when *multo amico* Charlie was dead and Auntie Harriet battered? He was mortified. He raised his fist high and punched himself so hard on the forehead that he knocked himself out. Geoffrey had been very sweet and made him a cup of tea, but there was no time to lose. He made a dash to the hospital and prowled the corridors, no longer just a chef, but an extremely angry and upset chef, until Harriet and Sophie were released. He'd kissed their hands, cried, then ran into the rain and called them a taxi. He'd even insisted on paying for it.

So now, as the cab came to a halt at the end of the alley, he was the first to leap out. He opened the umbrella he'd borrowed from Geoffrey and held it over Harriet as she stepped down. 'So welcome back, Auntie. Forgive me. Porkie don't never disappear again. I promise you.'

Harriet did her best to smile, even though her nose was in a splint. 'Don't worry, dear. A pain in the hooter I can stand, it's the pain in the family . . .' She stopped to help Sophie out of the cab. 'Give me your hand, dear. And don't get your turban wet.' This was a reference to the swathes of white bandage around the black woman's head.

Sophie didn't respond. She'd noticed that the lighting in the restaurant seemed to be different. It was flickering. 'What's going on in there?'

They looked through the window. All the tables were covered in white cloths, on top of each was a white kitchen candle on a saucer and by each saucer was a teacup full of small wilting flowers. Standing in a line amidst all this were Geoffrey the actor, Martin his boyfriend, and O'Dare, waiting to greet them. They were all wearing aprons, had dirty tea towels draped over their arms in a waiterly manner and were having difficulty remaining upright. Sophie was all for hailing another cab and heading back to the hospital, but Harriet pushed open the door and they went in.

'Auntie!' Geoffrey beamed.

'We have prepared a welcome.' Martin helped the old girls in. 'We found the cloths and candles upstairs.'

'The flowers came from the graveyard,' added O'Dare.

'Thank you, Martin, they're not tablecloths dear, they're bed sheets.'

Harriet sat down. She was almost past caring. She'd heard by now that her nephews were fugitives and had never felt such shame, or anger. All she wanted to do was lie in her bed and curl up until this dreadful time had passed.

'I am in the process of preparing the O'Dare special.' The Irishman rocked slightly. 'It's an event of a culinary nature.'

'Wha . . . ?' Porchese sniffed the air. Culinary? What was cooking?

'It involves bacon and it involves eggs. In fond memory, I call it good morning Dublin.'

'It's half-past ten at night, dear.' Harriet tried to be polite.

'Wha . . . ? Wait minute. You go in my kitchen?' Porchese's colour was beginning to rise.

'We were under the impression you'd resigned, you Neapolitan trollop,' minced Martin.

'You go in my kitchen? Don't you never go in my kitchen!'

'Porkie, we were merely trying to help.' Geoffrey was about to huff.

'Don't no Porkie me! I am chef! Don't you not never go in my kitchen!'

'Oh dear.' Sophie sunk onto a chair, holding her head.

'That's enough! Thank you.' Harriet held her head up, the splint on her nose adding to the authority of her profile. 'You've even paled Sophie and that's an achievement. Blow out the candles, put on the lights, take the bedding and the foliage from my tables and go downstairs. Thank you for the thought. Good night.'

'Auntie, we have read the papers.'

'And so have I, Geoffrey. Good night and down to the club where you belong.'

'Ah, Harriet, in your troubles, can you not accept . . . ?' O'Dare began.

'Down! I'm not up to it.' Then she added, 'Have a drink on me.'

'Ah well . . . ?' O'Dare considered negotiating.

'We know they are innocent!'

'Snuff the candles, Martin, and go.'

'Yes, Auntie.'

The lights came on as the candlelight was pinched and the boys took the stairs. O'Dare was the first to go, having discerned accurately that their attempt at kindness had given them the moral high ground and therefore the bar below was theirs for the night. Sophie held her head against the thump of their feet as they went down.

'A pot of tea please, Porkie,' said Harriet.

'You want good food. Ham, egg . . .'

'No thank you, dear, just the tea.' She gave him the wannest of smiles as he went quickly out. She was beginning to feel a touch tearful. 'I'm collapsed, Sophie. I think my fire's gone out.'

Sophie took her hand. 'Oh no, dear. In sickness, health and bad, bad men, you'll burn bright for ever.'

'In hell I suspect.' Harriet pushed herself up from the table. 'I'll leave Porkie to close and bring up the tea. I shall retire . . .' She looked up as the restaurant door opened and Superintendent Hooper walked in.

'Miss Lack?'

It was the last straw. 'I don't know how you've got the nerve to put your foot through that door!' Harriet could feel the blood rush from her nose.

'May I have a word?'

'Wanted men? Those words are in every newspaper! What have you done to our family name? You, Superintendent, are a sod!'

Hooper was shaken by this. 'These are very serious matters, Miss Lack.'

'You accuse those boys . . . ! Whoever heard of a nephew damaging an aunt? Am I not an aunt? I can tell you that those boys have never so much as glanced at me with intent!'

'May I sit down?'

'You may not.'

Hooper looked away. He badly wanted to talk. Although he could easily convince himself that this visit was in aid of the criminal investigation, he knew what he was really doing there. Like someone parched for thirty years, all he wanted was to drink in every drop of the life Violet had lived without him. His only source was Harriet and she appeared to hate the ground he walked on. 'Harriet . . .'

'Miss Lack.'

'Miss Lack, there is no family in the world . . .' Hooper stopped. He knew he was coming close to admitting his personal distress and his innate professionalism balked at that.

Fortunately Sophie could see what he was going through. She looked up through her bandage at Harriet and then said, 'Let him sit down.'

'Thank you.' Hooper did, then wasn't sure what to say. He glanced at the door. Fairfax was in the alley talking into a radio receiver. He leaned forward towards Harriet. The game was up and he might as well admit it. 'Miss Lack, this is as personal for me as it is for you. I haven't seen Violet since the day she was . . . married. I . . . I was given to understand that pain ebbed with time.' He couldn't go on.

Harriet remained cold, but Sophie was warmer. 'Weren't we all?'

Harriet cut in quickly. 'My nephews are innocent, Superintendent.'

Hooper leaned forward, desperate to make this woman his friend. 'I will catch the killer of Violet's sister. I can promise you that, Miss Lack.'

'Innocent, Superintendent.'

'Tell me about Violet.' Hooper realized he was begging, but couldn't help it.

'What about Violet?'

'Anything.' It was one word, but it spoke his world. 'Anything at all. I'd appreciate anything.' Hooper said it again, digging himself in deeper. He waited. Harriet was still giving nothing away. He ploughed on, 'We believe she is in the west.' Harriet raised her eyebrows. He went on, 'I must get to her.'

'Why?'

'I believe the men who attacked you are seeking her.' This was easier. He was feeling like a copper again.

'So my nephews were not involved?' Harriet wanted her pound of flesh.

'I must talk to them.' Hooper avoided her question.

The phone by the till rang. 'Excuse me.' Harriet got up to answer it. Hooper, his head full of Violet, vaguely heard her say, 'Hello, Mr Mercedes.'

By then Fairfax was in the doorway. 'Sir?'

Hooper stood and nodded to Sophie, as Harriet spoke again into the phone, 'Three o'clock, Newmarket . . .' She didn't even give Hooper a smile as he went out to talk to his sergeant.

Fairfax had got nowhere at the Peking Palace. They'd never heard of the McCarthys and then had ceased to be able to speak English. Having resolved to move to a city where his native tongue was understood, Fairfax had had a stroke of luck. The Criminal Records Office had finally come up with something on Ronnie Lack's girlfriend. She'd been done for shoplifting five years ago and they had an address. 'The girl, Mathilda, sir. We've traced her uncle . . .'

Hooper wasn't listening. He was watching Harriet as she glared at him through the window, and then she put the phone down.

14

Ronnie heard the dialling tone. Harriet had cut him off. He was standing outside the phone box as an old girl was living inside it. It was weird, in other parts of town they destroyed the phones and lived in houses, here it was the other way round. He handed the receiver back to the resident and turned to Mathilda, who asked, 'What she say?'

'She said, three o'clock, Newmarket. Runaway.'

'What?'

'It was the name of the horse.'

'What are you talking about, Ronnie?'

'She couldn't talk, could she? She's telling us to get out of it.' He looked bleakly up the street. 'Then she said, gone west.'

'What's that mean?'

'I don't know, Tilda. Perhaps she was talking about us. How long are we supposed to run away for, that's what I want to know?' He looked at her. She didn't know either. There was nothing for it but to start the long walk back to the factory before it started to rain again.

'Ron?'

He could tell by the tone in her voice. 'Don't start, Tilda. I ain't in the mood.'

'Ron?' She was going to start anyway. 'Don't be scared.'

'I am scared. I'm bloody scared of everything. That bloody reverend was right. I'm just a bloody coward.'

She tried to put her arm round him. 'No, you're not.'

'Don't, Mathilda!' He shrugged her off. 'I am and you know it.' He walked on quickly, getting ahead of her for a moment. 'You know the truth.'

'What truth?' Mathilda caught him up.

'And I'm just too scared to admit it.'

'Don't take no notice of Uncle!' She was terrified he was going to say something she dreaded to hear.

'I'm like Bernie, aren't I? I'm not a normal boy.'

'No!'

'It's the truth!' He was walking very quickly now, as though he wanted to get away from her, from himself, from the whole bloody thing.

Mathilda, having brought it up, wanted to change the subject. 'My dad didn't run off because of me like he said! He went off because he saw Uncle Horn in bed with my mum! That's the kind of bastard he is, Ronnie. Don't take any notice of him!' She was walking behind him getting breathless. She wanted to talk and talk, fill him up with her words so he wouldn't need to talk himself and wouldn't need to say things she didn't want to hear. 'I can tell you a lot of things about Horn. And Two-pin . . .'

'How long we been together, Tilda?' It was because he knew that she didn't want him to talk, that he was.

'Over a year. One year and three months. We met in April, so that's . . .'

'So why haven't we had any sex?' Ronnie was driving on. Whether it was true or not, he was going to say it.

'Ronnie! Don't listen to Horn! He's . . .'

'Why haven't we?'

'It takes time!'

'You know the truth!'

'I don't!'

'You do!' He stopped and faced her. This was it. 'You do, Tilda.'

She stood a few feet from him. His face was pale and his hair was dark and he was so sad. She'd never felt so much for him in her life. It didn't matter any more about her own dread, all she wanted to do was make him happy again. 'What are you telling me, Ronnie?'

He looked down. It seemed to be a very long pause. 'I don't know.'

She waited; he didn't say anything else. They'd come close to something, but the moment had gone. She touched his shoulder. 'I don't care what you are. I love you.'

He turned away quickly before tears came. 'All I know is I'm bloody scared!' He was walking quickly again. 'I should call the law, shouldn't I? Get all this over with. But I'm too scared. I'm even too scared to wear that red and yellow striped shirt you got me.'

She took his arm. 'Don't matter. I'll just get you a different one.' They walked away quickly as the thunder started up again.

15

The cause, or at least the narrator, of Ronnie's consternation, Reverend Horn, still drunk on Jamaican rum, was staggering along the glistening wet pavement. He didn't know whether to feel triumphant at the impact of his revelations, or irate at the stew splattered over his suit and his ejection from the factory. Who was this Mirabelle? Some dumb waitress of a girl, he concluded, and his greatness couldn't be diverted by her ignorance, so he decided to revel in his triumph as he remembered the pain in Arnie's eyes and the fear in Ronnie's face. He was what he'd always known himself to be, the soul scrubber, the sin scourer, the street cleaner! What would the world be without his piercing stare and finger of guilt? He was without a doubt becoming a holy legend in his own lifetime. He chuckled to himself and hardly noticed as the black Mercedes van came slowly past and stopped twenty yards ahead of him.

Two men in shiny black shoes got down from either side of the van. They both wore identical navy-blue suits. One waited on the pavement as Horn approached and the other circled the van and waited just out of the reverend's sight. Not that he was looking anyway. He was considering his next sermon, or assault, as he sometimes called them. The path of genius never ran smooth, and if anything the grab of the collar and Arnie's boot in his backside were both mere proof of his perception and brilliance. Now, far from being dejected at being ejected, the rev was revved! He laughed again and was suddenly flying through the air. For a second he considered the physical uplift to be little more than an earthly manifestation of his heavenly glory. It wasn't until his face crunched into the pavement and he heard the sharp crack as his nose broke that he realized his beans had been well and truly spilt once and for all.

The man who'd circled the van, and venomously tripped him, screwed his heel into the back of the reverend's neck and pushed down with the sole of his shiny shoe onto the back of his head, as if to smear Horn's face into the stone. The second man reached down to pull him up and then punched him hard in the stomach, causing him instantly to puke and fall down again. By the time Horn had tasted the blood in his mouth, heard rather than felt the horrendous crack of the iron bar on the side of his skull and looked up at the inscrutable violence in the faces of Chan and Gerard McCarthy, he knew he'd left heaven for the deepest hell. The twins threw him into the back of the van. He lay looking up at the black metal roof. If he was right, and pain and mortification were proof of genius, then he, Horn, with rum in his gut, stew on his suit and hot shit running down the back of his legs, was the man who was going to change the world for ever.

16

Bernie looked up as he heard the thunder start again. He was still in the office, sitting on the floor, wrapped in an old tarpaulin that Mirabelle had found. He was flipping over the pages of his Arfer by candlelight until he came to his favourite picture of the three knights in the forest. 'See, Sir Galahad, Sir Bors and Sir Perceval was doomed in the big, dark, green forest. And there was slime on the trees.'

Mirabelle was perched on a desk above him with her knees under her chin. She smiled. 'Slime?'

'Yeah. And it was sticky and it ran down and it was horrible. So they couldn't climb up and look about. See, that's the point of the slime.'

'Is this in the book, Bernie?'

'No. This is true life. I'm making it up.' He looked very serious. 'They was all very uncertain about future plans. See, their swords was sharp but they didn't know where to stick them.'

'So what did they do?'

'How should I know?' He yawned and lay back against the wall.

'Good night, Bernie.'

'Night, Meebelle.' He closed his eyes. 'Who's Bob?'

Mirabelle smiled as she watched him sink into sleep. From behind a door to her left she could hear Two-pin snoring in her own private cubicle. Ronnie and Mathilda had found a smaller office further towards the back. She looked up as the rain began to beat again on the roof. She jumped lightly down from the desk, walked quickly to the door, and with a last glance at the sleeping Bernie, went out of the room.

Her intention was to go up into the roof of the factory, but first she ran quickly past the dark iron pillars and the giant hulks of rusting machinery on the workshop floor to the front of the factory. She wanted to check on Arnie. She stopped by the high entrance to the loading bay and looked through. The Snipe was parked in the middle of the greasy floor, its black paintwork gleaming in the wet moonlight. She could see Arnie's profile through the rear window of the car. He was sitting on the back seat with Lucy. Mirabelle inched forward and listened as they talked. Arnie was saying, 'Coppers or no coppers, we'll have to find her before Riss gets to her, won't we?'

'How are you going to do that?'

'Back to the tower, isn't it? Ask Tom Cherry. Has to be, doesn't it? We'll do it tomorrow and then, hello Mum and how's your father.'

'What?'

'Don't matter.' Mirabelle watched as Arnie looked out through the side window. The condensation on the Snipe's windows was making it difficult for her to see them inside the car. She edged closer and saw Arnie's jaw move. He said, 'Sometimes I think I make the rain.'

'It'll clear up,' Lucy whispered. Mirabelle could see the white of her arm as she put it along the back seat and around his shoulder.

'That's what worries me.' Arnie moved away from Lucy.

Mirabelle went quickly back across the floor, then up the steps to the catwalk and looked down at the giant shadows cast by the ancient machines. She stood for a moment and wondered about her feelings for these brothers. She loved them all and was becoming increasingly worried by the consequences of Charlie's death that seemed to be working in them. Arnie seemed more hostile than usual and she'd seen that Ronnie, when he'd come back with Mathilda, had been quiet and upset. She had deep doubts as to whether she was qualified to help them. She looked up at the broken glass of the sixty-foot factory window and then down through a smashed pane. A street of deserted terraced houses ran at right angles to the factory and Mirabelle saw immediately what she'd expected to see.

On the roofs of the twenty or so houses either side of the street were thousands of angels. They were silent, black and unmoving, silhouetted against the moonlight, glistening in the rain and staring solemnly up at

Mihr as she exploded into light and looked down through the factory window.

At the far end, over 100 yards away, standing on the broken street, was Sorush herself. She was wingless and black-coated. Her dark hair was matted by the falling water and her huge eyes flashed with threat and intelligence. She moved as a woman, secure and confident in the massed power of her angels above. 'You are a special guardian, Mihr.' There was a venom born of jealousy in her voice and the angels above flickered their rage in a million tiny movements of wing and feather.

'What of it?' Mihr knew she was on the downward path of admission.

'Who is it you protect?'

'This is not your concern, Sorush.' Mihr stared down, her blue eyes implacable. There was a deep silence in the chasm where light met dark. Neither angel would give way.

Kasbeel, who sat on a rooftop directly above Sorush, spoke. 'Mihr, as a guardian you love, but such love cannot be the eternal, benevolent love of the angels. To be a guardian is to love one more than the other and is therefore to invoke the divisive love of mankind.'

'My purpose is not your concern, Kasbeel.'

Sorush exploded in fury. 'Guardian or not of whatever spectacle of humanity, I am here, and I shall discover what it is you hide, Mihr!'

The legions on the rooftops seethed and their movement swelled until it had expanded 500 feet above Mihr, surrounding her light, blocking the moon and filling the black sky with erratic wings and the heavy, dull beat of implacable anger. Sorush glared up at the factory, then turned to the roof above her. 'Kasbeel!'

The Ancient Angel opened his book and the incantation began once more.

The street below became the same street forty years before. The gaping holes in the doorways were filled with chipped wooden doors, some with bright brass knockers and letter boxes. A black car came from beneath the factory windows; its headlights, blacked out but for the narrowest of slits, cast thin yellow beams onto the surface ahead. It was Charlie's Morris. He had left Lucretia in the east and come south with Violet.

*   *   *

After Lucretia had tried to buy him off and failed, Charlie knew he couldn't stay. The old girl's wounded pride and bitterness would have worked its way into Violet and slowly destroyed her love for him. He'd looked round the house in Kitchener Square with some regret. He could have put his feet up by the fire and planned his deals and refined his moves, served by his adoring wife, her beautiful sister and their respectful mum. It was a shame to let it all go, but Charlie had his pride too.

It had been easy enough to reject the bribe, but although he didn't like to admit it, the fact that Lucretia had tried to get rid of him had made him feel small. As he sat at her table waiting for Violet to bring his bacon he stared at his clenched fists. He could take the lot of them in one hand and squeeze the squealing, sniping life out of them. So why could she still get to him? How could she still make him feel bad? No matter what you were, how much you succeeded, these bastards still did it to you! For a second he felt a wave of hatred. He waited to let it pass, then calmed as he realized how he'd take his revenge. He'd remove Lucretia's future from her. He'd take her daughter and teach her that life according to the old fool of Kitchener Square was dead, and fit only for fools and sponges. This now was a time fit for heroes, real men and women who stood alone, who had been given nothing and who earned what they were with their brains and hands. He would wrench from the mother the love of her daughter and turn it into at best pity, at worst hate. And he would do it not because Lucretia had tried to bribe him, but purely and simply because she had turned her nose up at him.

He stared down at his hands on the white tablecloth. He'd made his decision and was clear. Violet walked in with the bacon and he said, 'We'll take a walk, have a drink in the Black Owl for old times, sleep it off for an hour or two and then we're leaving after dinner. I think your mother would prefer that, don't you?'

Violet looked down at him. She could smell the bacon on the plate she held. The grease was burning her fingers. His eyes were kind and full of love. What else was there but him? She'd married this man and that was all there was to it. And so they did exactly as he said. She packed everything she owned into the car. May waved from the front window, but Lucretia didn't see them off. She'd gone to bed with a migraine as her daughter had left her.

Charlie parked on the corner of the blacked-out street, and Violet looked up at the darkened windows of a small café. 'Gone to dreamland, haven't they?' Charlie winked at her. The whole place wasn't much more than the house at the end of the terrace and Violet couldn't see how she could stay with in-laws she'd never met in the couple of rooms above the café. Charlie seemed to read her mind. 'There's more rooms at the back. You can't see them from here.'

'Charlie, it's too late to arrive now.'

'Never too late. As long as you get there in the end.' He opened the car door as air-raid sirens started up in the distance. 'All right, Herman, don't drop one on us now.' He walked over to the café door and banged hard on the glass. 'Come on, Vi, come and meet the old man and me mum.' He grinned, but Violet could tell he was nervous.

She'd hardly had time to join him at the door when it opened. Arnold, Charlie's father, stood in the dark of the café. He was wearing a dirty vest and hastily pulled on trousers with old striped braces hanging loosely down the side. He was shorter than his son, but had the same barrel-chested, powerful build. He looked at his son with anger. 'What do you think you're doing? I don't bloody lay an eye on you for four bloody years and you turn up at midnight with a bloody woman!'

'Wife, Dad. This is my wife.' Charlie smiled.

'What?' The old man gave his son a hard look.

'We got married yesterday. Vi, this is my father, Arnold. Dad, Violet.'

'Hello, Mr Lack.' Violet offered her hand.

There was a pause as Arnold looked Vi up and down. 'Christ all bloody mighty.' He didn't take her hand, just carried on looking at her.

'Any chance of letting us in, Dad? Or shall we stand out here all night?'

'You got married? What's your mother going to say?'

'I'll make some nice tea.' A voice came from behind Arnold.

Violet peered into the darkness and could just make out a woman coming slowly towards them in a nightdress and curlers.

'Mum!' Charlie moved quickly past his father and gathered his mother into his arms. 'Mum, my bloody old mum!' He squeezed her tight to him, and as he rocked her, Violet could see his eyes were wet.

'Come in, come in off the street.' Arnold addressed Violet for the first time. There was still the drone of planes high overhead as she moved past him into the unlit café. She caught a glimpse of half a dozen battered tables, neatly surrounded by wooden chairs and benches, then she followed Charlie through a dark passage into the scullery.

His mother hadn't spoken since her offer of tea. She'd accepted Charlie's embrace limply and then walked ahead of them slowly, her pale nightdress just visible ahead of them. When Arnold turned on the light in the scullery, the old woman stood in the middle of the room, smiling and looking down as if she would have been quite content to have remained in the darkness. She seemed to be in another world. Violet wondered if she'd upset her by arriving so suddenly and unannounced as Charlie's new wife.

'Vi, this is my mum. Edna, that's all right if she calls you that, isn't it, Mum?'

'I'll put the kettle on.' Edna turned away without looking at Violet and began to fill the kettle at the sink.

'Mum?' Charlie grinned. Violet could see that he was as confused as she was by his mother's demeanour. He glanced at his father, who looked sourly away, then looked back to his mother. 'Mum, come here, give us a kiss.'

Edna didn't turn to face them. She was shakily pushing open a box of matches. 'It's a relief to be out of that bedroom, dear. He won't go to the shelter. Wants everyone to get shrapnel with him I suppose.' She lit the gas as Charlie looked again at Arnold.

'You'd better sit down, hadn't you?' Arnold roughly pulled a chair out from the table and Violet sat, perched on the edge of it. 'It's a bit bloody much, son. Midnight. She don't get much bloody sleep, you know.'

'Sorry, Dad.' Charlie was still trying to make out what was going on. He heard the distant crump of a bomb falling and took a second out to peer through a crack in the blackout curtains. 'Buggeration. That's a big one. It's over by the river.' He turned back. Arnold was standing behind Violet's chair and Edna was spooning tea into a pot. They were like shady figures in a dark yellow half-light. It was an image that stuck in Charlie's mind for many years, like some kind of slow-motion nightmare, because of what Edna said next.

'It's a shock to see you though.' She looked at Charlie and gave him a childlike smile. 'Like Bernard was a shock.'

Charlie didn't pick it up. 'How is he, Mum? Still avoiding the military police?' He grinned.

Edna carried on spooning the tea into the pot. She didn't look up as she said, 'He ran away from the Army for all those years, then all of a sudden, he changed his mind and got run down by one of them tanks. He didn't even get out of Aldershot. That was a shock.'

'What?' Charlie froze.

Edna looked up and smiled quite brightly. 'Bernard, dear. It's Bernard, I mean.'

'Hang on, Mum, what are you saying?' Charlie gripped the back of a chair.

'It was instant. That's one relief anyhow.'

'Mum! This is my brother you're talking about!'

'That's right, Charlie, and you weren't here, were you?' Arnold answered Charlie's shout with a bark of his own. There was a silence as Charlie looked from his father back to his mother. 'What happened?'

'I'll just make the tea, Charlie. She's a beautiful girl, your new wife. I hope she don't have to cry.' Edna picked up the kettle with a dishcloth and poured the boiling water into the pot. Violet wanted to get up and hold her.

'Please.' Charlie looked back to his father. 'Tell me. Is Bernard . . . ?' He couldn't finish.

'We had to carry it ourself, son, because we didn't know where you were.' Arnold nodded towards Edna. 'Your mum, you can see for yourself.'

'Wait a minute, Dad! Tell me, will you? A tank? A bloody tank? He was run over by a bloody tank?' Charlie looked from one to the other.

Arnold nodded. 'Aldershot, Charlie. They was training.'

Charlie slowly sat down on the chair he had been holding and Violet reached out and touched his arm. Edna began to put out cups and saucers on the table by him. She seemed completely unaware of his state of shock. She looked at Violet. 'You could have the attic, dear, if you wanted it.' She smiled. 'It's where Bernard lived. Very nice curtains. Don't cry up there, will you? It's a relief.' She went back to the cupboard over the sink to fetch the milk and sugar as Violet tried to work out what she meant by, it's a relief. Was it a relief to cry or not to cry?

Arnold spoke as if Edna wasn't in the room. 'She hasn't cried. Not

205

once. I did though.' He turned away with tears in his eyes. Violet noticed he was tensing his body and could see that he must have suffered very badly.

'Dad?' Charlie's voice was cracking.

'We carry it, son. We bloody carry these things, don't we?'

'Jesus Christ.' Charlie looked down at the lino trying to take it all in. Violet desperately wanted him to go and hug his father, but he didn't. The two men stood separate and lonely in their grief as Edna poured the tea and Violet looked round at her new family.

'These you judge?' asked Mihr.

'They bring their own suffering,' said Sorush. 'Who caused their war? And who caused the violence and anguish that results from it?' She turned. 'Kasbeel!'

It was about ten years later. Young Arnie was nine years old, and if anything his big nose and ears seemed even more protuberant on his young and unformed face. He sat at one of the café tables playing with the cap of an HP Sauce bottle. A coloured comic lay on the table in front of him as he stared out of the window, daydreaming. He turned a page of the comic, then suddenly got up and went out through the passage at the back.

He passed Edna, who was behind the counter, slowly picking up cake crumbs one at a time and placing them carefully in a saucer. Edna lived in a dreamworld too, although doubtless it wasn't full of the vibrant heroes of young Arnie's imagination. Hers was dull and faded like a blanket and she kept it wrapped around the precious wound of her grief for her dead son. For this suffering to cease would be to admit that Bernard was gone, so instead she wrapped the injury like a hot coal and surrounded the scream with an absolute attention to a million irrelevant and suffocating details that repressed all thought. One crumb at a time was more than enough for Edna.

Violet came in from the scullery and watched her. She sighed. Over the years she'd come to love her mother-in-law, but her continuing decline was becoming too depressing to bear. She moved from the door and picked up a cloth. 'I'll do that, love.' Violet's voice had changed. She'd picked up some of the roughness of Charlie and the tonal edge of the neighbourhood. Not that she would ever have admitted it. In her mind she fought an eternal battle against vulgarity and slovenliness. Some of the women around here would as soon drop an aitch as their knickers and there was still enough of Lucretia in Violet to want to pull them up for both. She began to wipe the counter, but Edna didn't move and said, 'I like to help, Vi. Charlie says, help you.'

'Well can you go and wipe a table then, dear?'

'No, I'll do the counter. You do the tables.' Edna stood solidly in the middle of the counter and picked up another crumb.

Violet held the cloth and watched her repeat the action. For a second she wanted to shove Edna hard out of the way and send her flying back against the shelves at the side of the counter, but knew that it was her own anger she wanted to dismiss, not the old woman. She breathed in deeply, then threw the cloth down in exasperation and went through the passage to the back of the house.

Young Arnie was spreading jam on a piece of bread, having his tea with his father and grandfather at the table in the centre of the scullery. She stood in the doorway and looked at the three generations of Lacks and wondered, not for the first time, what she was doing there. She moved towards the table. 'Charlie, talk to your mum, would you?'

The old man, Arnold, looked up. He'd grown sour with age and although he appreciated the efforts of Violet in the café and the ever more dubious business skills of his son with his generous wad of readies, he still felt narked most of the time. It was probably akin to Charlie's reaction to Lucretia. Violet somehow made him feel small. There was something about her that implied he didn't know his own world and she knew something better. And here she was having a go at his wife again. His tone was sharp. 'Why?'

Violet's eyes flashed for a second and she replied in kind. 'She's in my way.'

'How can she be in your way in her own bloody house?'

'I can't do my work!' Violet was getting angry now, and then she spied her son licking jam off the blade of his knife. 'Arnie! How many times have I told you! Learn some manners please, and don't do that!'

It was exactly that kind of remark that got to the old man. Her and her manners; what was wrong with eating off your knife? He was about to make a sarky comment when Charlie looked up and said, 'We're having our tea, Vi.'

Violet tried to be more reasonable. 'She's under my feet. Can you . . . ?'

Arnold cut her off. 'Sort her out, Charlie. I'm having my tea.'

Charlie usually took a half-amused back seat at these subterranean war games between his father and wife, but this time the old man looked as if he might go too far, so he decided to mollify. He smiled at Violet. 'Put up with it, sweetheart.'

'Charlie . . .' Violet started then stopped. Edna had just walked in behind them. She smiled sweetly.

'There's a lady for you, Vi. She's got a hat on.'

Even though she hadn't seen her for ten years, somehow Violet knew who it was even before she'd walked into the café. Lucretia was standing by the counter, dressed in a tweed suit and narrow-brimmed green trilby with a small brown feather in the hatband. It wasn't for Lucretia to admit the torture of years of filial absence. She sounded almost bored as she spoke in the near-deserted room. 'Hello, Violet. We were on our way to Hastings.' She nodded towards her rotund companion, also smartly fitted out in suit and hat. 'This is Albert. A friend.' Albert creaked a smile.

'Mum?' Violet felt a surge of love and self-pity wash over her. She held out her arms and went quickly round the counter towards her mother, but Lucretia had already retreated to a table and Albert followed quickly, coming between her and her daughter, so Violet was forced to stop, unembraced. She stood over them, uncertain and a bit shaky, as they took seats by the window.

Lucretia gave her a small smile, as if to say, 'No hugs today, dear,' and put her handbag on the table. 'Just a quick tea and perhaps a custard tart.' She looked around the room without bothering to hide her distaste. There was a group of West Indians on the other side of the room, soberly dressed and on their best behaviour. One of them gave Lucretia a huge bright smile. She turned away and immediately wished she hadn't. She was facing Charlie.

'Well, bugger me. Lucretia.' He stood in the passage from the scullery with his hands in his pockets, jacket undone and collarless. His appearance increased Violet's apprehension, although she instinctively straightened her back. She had her pride and Charlie was her husband after all, and her mother hadn't even managed a peck on the cheek. Charlie walked towards Lucretia. His head was up.

Lucretia clasped her hands tightly behind her handbag. 'Mr Lack. We're on our way . . .'

'To Hastings. And this is Albert.' Charlie looked down at him, the mockery in his voice unmistakable. 'A friend.'

Lucretia caught the aspersion as Albert reddened. She glanced over at the immigrants. 'I'm not sure that hygiene and coloureds go together, Mr Lack.'

For a second Charlie felt the pointed stick of guilt. Not for his remark about Albert, that was just playful, but because the immediacy, tone and edge of Lucretia's response had revealed her anger, and he knew instantly that his strategy over the years had caused her more suffering than he'd imagined. Nevertheless, the bitch was insulting his living and his custom. 'I don't care if you don't think fish and chips go together, Lucretia.' His eyes were hard as he said it and Violet saw the first flash of the battle that she knew was probably inevitable.

'Charlie?' It was a plea, and perhaps he would have heeded it if his father and mother hadn't come in behind him.

'Who's that?' Arnold was as pugnacious as ever in the face of the uncertain.

'It's Vi's mum, Dad.' Charlie couldn't backtrack in front of his father, despite the look in Vi's eyes. If anyone knew how he felt, it was his old man. 'She's bestowed us a visit after ten years.'

'What's that on her head?' Arnold picked up his son's tone and smirked.

Lucretia's neck arched. She'd known this wasn't going to be easy, that the fool of a husband would try to be clever, but she hadn't been prepared for his father's outright rudeness. 'I beg your pardon?'

Violet stepped in quickly. 'This is Charlie's father, Arnold.' Then she smiled back towards the counter where Edna was hovering and simpering. 'And this is his mother, Edna. This is my mother, Lucre . . .'

'Mrs Green.' Lucretia wasn't prepared to be on first-name terms with these people.

'Pleased to meet you, I'm sure.' Edna half bowed.

Violet could see that his mother's ingratiation wasn't going to help Charlie's mood. She said quickly, 'I'll make some tea. And Edna, would you mind getting two custard tarts?'

'Yes, Vi, two custard tarts.' Edna went slowly around the counter as Violet caught her mother's triumphant eye. Every prejudice in the book was in that look. So this is where she'd got herself, was it? Living with the ill-mannered and the simple, not to mention the coloureds? Violet followed Edna to the counter to make the tea as young Arnie squeezed past his grandfather.

'Come here, Arnie.' Charlie put his arm round his son's shoulders. 'This is your grandson you've never met, Lucretia. Say hello to Grannie, Arnie.' The boy was aware of the tension and moved slightly behind his father, who immediately made it worse. 'Incidentally, Lucretia, why did you never answer my wife's letters?'

Violet was filling the kettle. She turned quickly to her son. 'Say hello, Arnie.'

'Hello.'

'Hello, Arnold.'

Lucretia insisted on the propriety of his full name, confusing the old man. 'What?'

'Don't worry about it, Dad.' Charlie stepped back as Edna shakily took two plates with two tarts on them to the table.

'Here's the custards. Thank you.'

'And thank you, Mrs Lack.' Lucretia openly patronized the old woman.

'Yes, thank you,' Albert echoed.

'Thank you,' Edna repeated, as if the first time hadn't been un-necessary enough. She might have gone on saying it all day. It was too much for Charlie. 'Dad, why don't you take Mum into the back.'

'What for?' Arnold began to bristle.

'Dad.' Charlie gave his father a sharp look.

'Edna, come here. We're not wanted.'

'What did you say, dear?'

'Come here. Out.' Arnold angrily took his wife's arm and led her away. She gave Lucretia a small wave of her gnarled hand as she went.

'Goodbye, dear.' And then she disappeared down the passage with a last, 'Thank you.'

There was an uneasy silence as Violet put out cups and saucers onto a tray on the counter. All she wanted was for things to be normal. 'How's May?'

Lucretia was beginning to feel better. Perhaps the stop-by hadn't been such a bad idea after all. With parents like that the idiot husband would never be able to feign superiority again, would he? She adopted her highest tone. 'May's doing very, very well, Violet. She's become the manageress of a tobacconist just off the Tottenham Court Road.'

The comparison and implied slur to Violet were too much for

Charlie. 'And Vi works in an unhygienic caff in Streatham, you mean?'

'If that's what you call it, Mr Lack.'

'There's nothing wrong with it, Mum.' Violet picked up the tea tray. She wanted to get cups, saucers and her own presence between the two combatants. But she never made it. The West Indians laughed loudly before she got there and Lucretia looked over at them.

'It's not an establishment I'd be proud of Violet.'

'Why don't you piss off?' Charlie said it quietly before Violet had turned the corner of the counter.

'Charlie!' She stopped dead, the tray still in her hand.

Lucretia smiled. The idiot had shown his true self in all his discourtesy and utter lowness. 'One very good reason for not corresponding, Mr Lack, is your implacable and quite unreasonable hatred of myself and my family.'

Charlie leaned in, his neck muscles were bulging. 'Don't mess about with me, Lucretia. I can see you.' He leered at Albert. 'And your friend.'

'You cannot see me, Mr Lack! No-one such as you can see me!' She pressed her palms onto the table top and stood. 'We won't stay for tea, Violet.'

'Mum, no . . .'

Lucretia snapped open the clasp of her bag, fumbled furiously within it and held out a gloved hand to Arnie. 'Here's five shillings, Arnold.'

'We don't need your money!' But Charlie was too late, Arnie had taken the two half-crowns in amazed delight and jammed them quickly into his trouser pocket. He grinned. 'Thanks, um . . . ?'

'Mum, please sit down,' Violet pleaded.

But it was too late, Lucretia had already walked to the door. She opened it and turned. 'I won't see you again, Violet, not until you have removed this obscenity from your life.' She walked out, leaving Albert, who, mustering as much dignity as he could, picked up his hat and gloves. 'Good afternoon, all.' He attempted a haughty smile and followed Lucretia, closing the door carefully behind him.

Violet took a few paces towards the centre of the room, still holding the tea tray. 'Mum?'

'Talk to me about mothers.' Charlie leaned back on the counter and sneered.

'Shut your filthy, bloody, fucking mouth!' Violet turned back to him

211

and threw the tea tray violently down onto the floor. Then she walked out quickly before she burst into tears. A teacup rolled around on the floor as Charlie looked up at the faces of the embarrassed West Indians.

Violet didn't see him for the rest of the evening. In her fury she'd walked through the scullery and out into the alley behind the terrace. Her first instinct had been to go round the house to the front to see if her mother's car was still there. She caught sight of a black sedan turning the corner on the next street, but didn't know if it was Lucretia's or not. She stood and watched it go, then started walking as the row between her mother and her husband went round in her mind.

She walked fast as her feelings flared, but then began to slow as the overcast sky and dull uniformity of the poverty surrounding her gradually muffled her indignation. There was no way to understand anything in this place, no room for thought here, no way to describe herself to herself. The filthy brick, the dirty clouds, the grey faces, deadened everything. All the pavements were the same, the streets were the same and Violet's life was the same. She'd had months and weeks of it, days and days of the grind of the cloth and feasts of fry, pub nights of Charlie with his deals and brutal love, drunk Christmases and drunker new years, the occasional visits of Harriet from uptown, the tinkers and traders charming her and driving her mad, a childbirth and the growth of her darling Arnie, the ever-present sniping of his grandfather, all the lewdness and decay of the south in all these houses, these streets, these hours, these minutes and these years.

It had been an entire decade of Lucretialess life. Charlie had succeeded. He'd stained her past with insult and made her reject it. It hadn't been too difficult. Violet had never liked her mother much and her attitudes less. But she knew now that he'd turned her from a past she didn't want, to a present she didn't like, and ahead of her was a future she couldn't envisage. In breaking her from her home, Charlie had left her rootless with no real sense of herself, and even after ten years she still felt as if her path was a dream and that she really, properly, belonged somewhere else, to some third place. Often she wondered if this place really existed, and if it did, what was it like? Perhaps it would disappoint her or like the green field it would always remain somewhere out of reach. Charlie had talked of getting out and perhaps soon they would. The café was doing well and Charlie's plans were getting bigger, and maybe the move would be to somewhere she could name as her own. Where was it? What was it?

She walked on through the streets and houses of sameness. The scene in the café came back to her. If her mother wasn't capable of something as simple as a hug, then her mother wasn't a mother. How can you connect with something that shows no desire to understand you? How can you know what any of it means? She had a sudden thought: I am Lucretia. The idea had crossed her mind before and she let it pass. It was too slippery and dangerous to countenance and she imagined Arnie instead. She ought to go back soon and put him to bed. Arnie was Arnie, he was the only, and he was central to her. If anything could provide root and sustenance it was him. That certainty brought her to a junction and she turned left, knowing she was heading back towards the café.

This made her think of Charlie again. He would always fight with Lucretia and that was that. These were class wars and neither had the strength to move up or out of them. She shuddered as she realized she was beginning to think of her husband as she thought of her mother. She turned into the alley at the back of the house. She ignored Arnold in the scullery and went up the stairs to find her son.

He'd already tucked himself into his bed and was rubbing his two half-crowns together in his palm. Violet was slightly irritated at his juvenile glee and avarice, but smiled as she sat on his bed. 'You're a good boy, Arnie.'

'She gave me five bob.'

'She's not all bad, you know.'

'Dad thinks she is.'

'Well perhaps he's right.' She sat back on the bed and said suddenly, 'I think I might be worse.'

'Mum? What you talking about?'

'Nothing.' The thought had come from nowhere and she was as shocked by it as Arnie. It was some kind of guilt, she supposed. If she couldn't accept the life she'd chosen, the life bestowed, then she must be . . .

'You're not bad, Mum.'

'I might be.'

'No!'

She leaned forward and kissed him. 'I love you, son of mine.' She

213

took the coins out of his hand and put them on the chest by the side of his bed. 'You can spend it tomorrow. Good night.' She turned off the light and went out.

The landing was quiet. She guessed Charlie was in the pub and couldn't face the rest of the evening with Arnold, so she took the narrow stairs up to the attic and the tiny bedroom she had shared with Charlie for ten years. She thought she'd have an early night and think about things. As she flicked the light switch in the room she was suddenly jerked backwards and slammed against the wardrobe. Charlie's face was inches away from her own and she could smell the booze on his breath. 'Don't you bloody ever talk to me like that in front of people!'

'Get off, Charlie, you're drunk!'

He held her tighter. 'I'll drown in it before you ever do that again!'

'You're hurting me! Get off!' She managed to break free and moved towards the bed. He turned as if to go after her. 'Don't touch me! Don't you dare touch me again.' All the fury of the afternoon was filling her up again. 'You insulted me and you insulted my mother.'

'You hate the fucking bitch!'

'That's my business! You keep your foul mouth out of it! You don't own me!'

'You what?' He moved towards her again. His face was black.

'I said, you don't own me!' And she understood in that one broken second that her torment of the afternoon was caused by her resentment at being some kind of pawn in the awful game of possession played by her mother and her husband. She knew then that she belonged to neither of them and would never find herself until she was free of both.

'Course I bloody own you! You're my wife!'

'Oh sod off, Charlie.' The words were hardly out of her mouth before the flat hardness of his palm was across it. The slap was loud and painful and she fell back across the bed.

'I'll teach you who owns what.' He stood above her and started to undo his belt.

'No, Charlie!'

'It's all you ever wanted from me. So, have it.' He unbuttoned his fly and began to push his trousers down. 'It's all you've ever wanted. You're a bunny rabbit, Violet, and you'll fuck all the way to heaven. Like your mother.' He pulled his underpants down.

214

'No!' She wanted to look up into his face, but couldn't help staring at his thighs. His cock was hard. 'Please, Charlie.'

He pushed his legs between hers and pulled up her skirt. 'You want it. You want it all the time.' He was pulling her knickers down and she knew she was lifting her body to help him. 'Every night, every morning. In, out of bed.' He threw her knickers to the side and began to lie on top of her. 'Don't you?'

'No!' But she didn't mean it. Even as her arms were pushing him away, her hands were grabbing at his jacket, pulling him down.

'Don't you?' His thighs were pushing at hers and she could feel herself opening and becoming wet.

'Yes.' She moved to adjust herself and help him penetrate.

'You want it now, don't you?'

'Yes!'

'So have it.' He pushed the tip of his cock into her and she groaned, trying to spread her crotch to ease the pain.

'Yes!'

'It's all yours.' And he was in her. She could feel him fill her up, thick and wide, pushing the sides of her cunt apart. She slid her hands down and grabbed at his buttocks, gripping hard and pulling him into her, squeezing and kneading his thrust further and further up into her body. Charlie, Charlie, the word ran round and round her mind. Now she knew why she was with him. It was this and nothing else and she couldn't do without it.

'No, Charlie. No . . .' She pulled down the neckline of her blouse and scooped her breast from her brassiere in her hand. She held it onto his mouth as he began to fuck her. 'No, Charlie, no . . .'

In the bedroom below Arnie looked up. He could hear the sound of his parents' bed as its legs scraped the floor above him. He heard the sound of his father's grunts and his mother's cries as the pounding increased.

'No, Charlie . . .'

Charlie fucked into her as she held her legs wide and open above him. 'And as for that bitch, you hate her, admit it, you hate the bitch!'

'Don't ever leave me, Charlie! Don't ever leave me . . . !'

'You hate her!'

'Yes!'

*   *   *

Arnie pulled the blankets over his head as he heard their headboard rattle against the wall above and his mother cry out as if she was in terrible pain.

Violet felt the waves of orgasm spill over her as Charlie came. She felt each thrust and each ejaculation burst inside her, driving all thought from her mind, leaving only her hands pulling at his arse, trying to heave every last ounce of him into her wide and heaving cunt. Her thighs heaved up to suck him in as his spasms increased. She felt as if her body was electricity, groin engroined, tight-locked, shaken in rock-hard unmovable muscle, as their energy pulsed between them, creating itself over and over, its growing, groaning sum far more than their two separate parts. They lay bonded, a still, single mass of the two of them, until the spasms died and she gasped as her body eased and the energy began to flow away, leaving her weak and lost, her being just the softness of her white skin around the pulsating heat of her thighs. Her hands fell to the side as he shuddered and then she put them back around him as he seemed to shiver. 'Oh, Charlie.'

He lifted himself onto his elbows and looked down into her face. His anger was gone and he leaned down and kissed her. 'Hello, my darling Vi.'

'We're animals. That's what you've taught me.'

He laughed and, raising himself, eased his cock out of her as she sighed. Then he lay gently by her side. 'What else is there? It's the truth. All we've got to look up to is the stars in the sky.'

'I want another baby.'

'I think you might have got one.'

'So do I.' She turned and licked the side of his face. 'It's the stars in the sky.'

'If it's a boy we'll call him Ronnie.'

'I want a girl!'

'No, it'll be a boy.' He turned and smiled at her. 'That was a nice fuck, Violet. Perhaps your mum should come more often.'

'Can we do it again, please? And can we take our clothes off this time?' Her hand was already reaching down to his thigh. He was still hard and she wanted it in her mouth.

*   *   *

'See his violence, Mihr.'

'And his love.'

'His love is for himself.' Sorush rose, she was growing and filling the street with her anger and darkness. 'And that destroys everything, including himself.'

'How can he know that?'

'He is not asked to know, he is asked to try.' Sorush was by now level with the rooftops. 'To try and recognize his God within himself. He sees only stars in the sky.'

'His belief is in his fate,' said Mihr.

'His fate is not his concern.' Kasbeel's voice cut through the enveloping night of the Dark Angel. 'His only concern is his duty to his God, his God-created self and mankind.'

'And all we ask is,' Sorush was now sixty or seventy feet high and level with Mihr, 'did he make the best of himself? Did he do any good?' Her darkness was by now reflecting the White Angel's light and she seemed like a vast and spreading black diamond shining over the street. 'Kasbeel.'

The Ancient Angel, still on the rooftop, tiny and almost invisible in the shadow of Sorush, opened the book and began the incantation again.

It was over a year later. Charlie had been right, the second child born to Violet was a boy, and as he'd said, they'd called him Ronald. Violet held the six-month old-boy by the door of Edna and Arnold's bedroom. Charlie's mother was dying. She lay still and pale on the bed as the local doctor, a good old boy in his seventies called Porteous, sadly packed his instruments back into his black bag. He looked up at old Arnold, who was standing lost and forlorn on the other side of the bed. 'I'm sorry.'

Arnold clasped and unclasped his hands. He had no idea what to do or say. 'I . . .'

'Do we need a priest, Doctor?' Violet asked.

Porteous had barely nodded before Arnold croaked, 'Where's Charlie?' It was a strange sound halfway between a shout and tears. 'Where the bloody hell's Charlie? He ain't going to leave us to do it ourselves again, is he?'

'I'll find him, Grandad.' Violet felt enormous pity for him.

'And where's Harriet?'

'I'll find Charlie.'

'Don't go, Vi. Don't you go an' all.' Arnold was getting gruffer as he fought back his panic and tears.

'I'll send Arnie.'

'Just don't you go. I can't do it all on my own again.' Violet could see how much the death of his son all those years ago had affected the old man and how the pain he carried had made him what he was.

Porteous moved to the door. 'I'll wait downstairs.' He gently touched Violet's arm as he passed and whispered, 'Give him the baby.'

Edna was literally deathly still and her breath was no more than an unheard whisper. She had become so translucently beautiful in her repose that Violet felt an ache of regret that she hadn't had the wisdom to have seen it before. She wanted to hold and hug the dying woman before it was too late. Arnold began to cry.

'I can't stand this, Vi.'

'Here. Sit down. You hold Ronnie.' Arnold did as he was told and sat on the chair by the bed. 'And I'll find Arnie.'

'Vi?'

'I'll send him for Charlie. I won't be a minute.' She touched the old man's arm and went out leaving him with the child and his dying wife. Ronnie began to cry.

Charlie was having it off with a woman behind a lorry in the pub car park when Arnie found him. It was the worst possible of all accidents. When he'd gone out it had seemed as though Edna was recovering; in his heart of hearts he knew she wasn't, but in truth was less able than his father to face the fact of her death. He'd got drunk, not knowing how to feel or react. Since the birth of his second son his wife had withdrawn from him. He'd met, by chance, a woman he'd known from years before and she'd been sympathetic. It was the first time he'd felt the need to unload his own feelings and he did so; the woman had a big heart or was a bitch, either way she wanted sex with him and led him on. He got drunker and decided he was going home. She followed him out of the pub. They had sex behind a lorry. That day a part of the car park fence had fallen down and Arnie took the unexpected opportunity for a short cut. Charlie had just reached orgasm when his son found him. Such are days of death.

'Dad.'

'Bloody get out of here!' Charlie still had his cock in the woman as he shouted it.

'Dad!' Arnie didn't go and Charlie knew why. It was his mother, he was sure of it. There was no other reason why the boy would just stand there. He shoved the woman into the darkness behind the lorry and awkwardly zipped his fly.

'You tell your mum and I'll kill you.'

'Dad, I think you'd better come home.'

Charlie ran from the car park with Arnie. For years afterwards he tormented himself with the thought that his mother had died at the precise moment that he'd ejaculated into the woman in the shadows.

It wasn't true, Edna had passed away the second after Violet had left the room to find Arnie. Arnold, trying to stop the baby on his lap screaming, hadn't noticed and it wasn't until Violet came back that they realized she was dead. Porteous had returned and closed her eyes with the palm of his hand. Then he went quietly back downstairs to write the death certificate and leave them to their grief.

Violet took Ronnie from Arnold and the baby immediately slept. The old man sat on the chair with his hands clasped in front of him, staring through his tears at Edna's masklike profile. He said, 'She was mad, wasn't she?'

'No, dear.'

'Yes she was. Truth is, I've been waiting years and years for her to go.' He looked up at Violet. 'That's the truth. You see, I thought when she was gone, I'd have another life.' He was beginning to sob. 'Now she's gone, I don't want another life.' He couldn't talk any more, his grief was bubbling and belching out of him in ugly, rasping squeaks and shudders.

'Here, here. Take Ronnie again . . .'

'No . . .'

'Take him.' Violet knelt by his side and put the baby in his arms. 'He's your grandson. He's Edna's too.'

Arnold took Ronnie and let his tears drip down onto the baby's face. 'Your gran loved you, you know, little boy. She loved you and I loved her.' His tears were choking his voice. He could hardly speak. 'She was my relief and . . . she was my bane. That's the truth.' He looked up at

Vi for a second, then back down to the child. 'She was my broken heart, son. She was this café, you know. She started it all.' He broke down again.

'Dad.' Violet touched his shoulder. It was the first time she'd ever called him that.

'She was my dead boy, Vi. I got over it, but she carried it for both of us. That's what made her mad, see? Now I've got to do it and I'm not strong enough.' His mouth opened. For a moment Violet thought he was going to howl.

'Yes you are,' she said.

'Dad?' It was Charlie. He was by the door.

'She's dead, son.' Arnold didn't look up.

Charlie came in with Arnie behind him. He stood at the foot of the bed with his hands hanging down by his side, then he clasped them together in front of him. 'I'm sorry. I'm so bloody sorry. I'm sorry, Dad.' He looked up at his wife with tears in his eyes. 'It's those bloody stars, Violet, those bloody stars.'

Although Arnie never told her, Violet could guess something of what had happened. She could see it in her husband's face, and she knew even then, ten years before she ran away, that it was the beginning of the end.

The Dark Angel was gone. Mihr was surprised that Sorush hadn't gloated and poured scorn on Charlie. Perhaps she thought that her case was won and the father was destined for the chasm. Either that or this investigation was merely the means by which to pursue Mihr and uncover her real mission, in which case there was hardly any need for debate.

┌─────┐
│ 18 │
└─────┘

Mirabelle looked round the huge factory and sighed. She was a dot of a waitress perched high and alone in a vast, dirty and hostile world that seemed to have no edge or centre. In the life of Charlie and Violet she could see the lies forming at the root of the family and she knew that they would fester and grow until they were revealed by understanding and extracted by acceptance. She felt depressed. If there was such a thing as angel school, then written bold above the door would be, 'Lies Destroy The World, Starting With The Liar.' But these were liars that she had come to love and she didn't want them destroyed. And anyway she knew they didn't know they were lying; they were surviving, justifying themselves, being what they were and using what they'd been given as best they could.

If it wasn't for the pulse of Mihr beating within, Mirabelle would have felt very inadequate. She'd known when she'd received her instruction to leave the Bridge that her mission was of some ultimate importance. She felt sure it would somehow be to change all this, to be part, in some way, of yet another wave of light coming to clean and brighten; but now, as she sat high in the factory, she shivered in her isolation. Perhaps the journey she was on with the brothers would itself give her the strength she needed to complete and understand her mission. She sat quietly and listened to the factory. A sound began to fill the walls of her mind. Bernie was dreaming.

The sound grew louder. It was the sound of horses' hooves and she could see he was dreaming of the end of the street where the café had been. Becoming slowly visible through the dark were the two black knights from his picture book. Their visors were down and their massive shoulders hunched as they spurred their ebony chargers. They lowered their lances as they gathered speed and began to gallop towards the factory. Their pennants were rags, ripping and tearing against the air, and the jet plumes on the dull metal of their helmets flattened against the wind as their huge black cloaks flew up behind them. Their chain mail beneath was jagged and it tore, razor-sharp, into the flanks of the horses as they charged, spraying black sweat against the windows of the houses either side. These were giants of threat and peril, dwarfing the street and filling Bernie's head with the horror of cracking, splitting thunder, as their lances came at his eyes with unnatural and terrifying speed . . .

Mirabelle heard his cries and scrabbled to her feet to run to him and then stopped dead. Below her on the deserted, dreamless street was the squat shape of a black Mercedes van coming slowly towards her. She stood rooted to the spot as the Mercedes pulled to a halt in the shadows of the houses fifty yards from the factory. The hairs on the back of her neck stood on end. Every instinct warned her of hazard. She'd never seen the van before, but its shape, its silence, its standing there, heralded only terrible danger. She knew this was them, the black knights made flesh, and some subterranean perception in Bernie had known of their coming. He was protecting them all, and his dream had issued the warning. She turned fast and ran back along the catwalk.

She clattered down the steps towards the offices. She needed the brothers. Ronnie was already coming out of the office doorway with Mathilda behind him, as she reached the bottom of the stairs. Bernie was still crying out. 'Meebelle, Meebelle!'

'Mirabelle, can you get in here? He's going crazy!' Ronnie looked as if he was coming to the end of his tether.

'Tilda, hold him, tell him it was just a dream . . .' shouted Mirabelle.

'A what?'

'A dream! I'll come in a minute. Ronnie, get Arnie!'

'What for?'

But Mirabelle was already running back up the steps to the catwalk and Mathilda, sensing her agitation, immediately ran back into the office to Bernie, leaving Ronnie alone on the workshop floor. He did as he was told and headed quickly towards the loading bay and the Snipe.

By the time Mirabelle got back to the window she was more circumspect. She hid in the shadows to one side and looked down. The van was still there and as far as she knew its occupants were still hidden inside. She waited, nothing moved. Arnie came up behind her with Ron. 'What's going on? What's . . . ?'

'Ssshh.' Mirabelle pointed down to the van. 'There.'

'It's a van, so what?'

As if to answer Arnie's question the driver's door slowly opened, followed immediately by the passenger door on the other side. First one, then a second pair of identical shiny black shoes descended to the ground, then black-suited legs, followed by lean muscular bodies, and finally the jet-black hair and impassive faces of Chan and Gerard McCarthy.

'Jesus fucking Christ.' Arnie went pale. 'That's the McCarthys.' The twins stood either side of the van and silently stared up at the factory.

'You don't believe all that, do you, Arn?' asked Ronnie.

'Course I bloody do!' Arnie stared down. 'What are they doing here? It must be Riss.'

'What are you talking about?'

'Them, Ron, them. He's got them to come after us. It must have been them who killed May.'

'I don't believe this.' Ronnie turned away. He'd vaguely heard the rumours of some apparently legendary Chinese killers. 'It's all bloody crap, Arnie!'

'Look what's in front of your eyes, Ron!'

'You ever seen them before, Arn?'

'I don't have to, do I? Look!'

Ronnie started to feel nervous. 'Well, I knew it couldn't have been the Riss mob.'

'It was them, wan' it?' Arnie couldn't take his eyes off the twins. They were still by the van looking up at the factory. 'They must have thought May was Mum.'

'So what are they doing here then?'

'They want us to lead them to her, don't they?'

'Arnie!' It was Lucy yelling up from the workshop floor below.

'Shut up!' Arnie turned fast and leaned over the iron railing and whispered fiercely, 'Keep your mouth shut, Lucy!'

'What's going on?'

'Get back in the office and keep everyone quiet. We'll be down in a minute.'

'Arnie?'

'Do it now, Lucy!'

She walked away, her high heels making an unnecessary racket on the concrete floor. Arnie turned back towards the twins through the window. 'How'd they know we were here?'

'Riss?' Ronnie suggested, but he couldn't understand it either.

'How'd he know?'

Ronnie suddenly thought. 'That priest! That evil bastard Horn!'

'How could he get to the McCarthys, Ron?'

Ronnie shrugged and gave up; the existence of the fantasy twins was bad enough, the reason for their appearance would have to remain a mystery.

'Look.' Mirabelle pointed down. One of the McCarthys was moving slowly towards the factory gates.

'He'll see the Snipe.' Ronnie looked up at Arnie.

'Get everyone into the back and keep them quiet. I'll see what's going on.' Arnie moved away quickly along the catwalk and came down the stairs. As he quietly passed the giant machinery on the workshop floor he realized they'd already made more than enough noise to alert the twins, and his heart was thumping as he slipped into the shadows of the loading bay. The rain had ceased and there was no sound except for an uneven drip of water onto the roof of the Snipe. Arnie moved forward into the darkness as quietly as he could and then stopped, frozen by the thought that maybe the twins had already found some way in, and at any moment he could suddenly come face to face with oriental death and mayhem. He had visions of swords, meat axes, deep cuts and blood and wanted to turn back and run to the offices for the comfort of the others, but managed to force himself to take another step into the blackness. He was so close to the wall and its shadow that he couldn't see anything in front of him. He kept his hand outstretched and felt his way along. For a moment he went through a patch of light and he could see the huge gates quite clearly. They were twinless and he went forwards with more confidence, again using the wall to his right as a guide. Then suddenly he stopped dead.

A foot and a half in front of him was the face of Chan. For a second Arnie was completely disorientated. He didn't know why his exploring hand hadn't touched the man's face. He stood, literally petrified, as he watched Chan's eyes flick across him. Nothing in Arnie moved, no heartbeat, breath or thought. His gut was knotted up as far as his throat and his head was just a ton of dead-weight terror pushing down. He was paralysis in thrall to gravity, and as silent as the grave opening up beneath his rooted feet. Chan's eyes flicked the other way. The gap between eyeball-left and eyeball-right could have been a lifetime and four sermons as far as Arnie was concerned. It was then he realized that no silver blade had materialized, his gut was unslit, no blood oozed and his face was still whole. His brain moved again and he worked it out. He'd come through the darkness to the gates themselves and the Chinese was standing on the other side looking through a four-inch gap in the wood. And more to the hysterical, life-saving point, he hadn't seen him. Arnie could have called the priest and shouted for joy, done a little dance and wiggled his fingers in front of his nose. Instead he began to half-inch backwards and then he stopped again. Chan's face was getting smaller; he was moving away. Arnie shifted forwards once more and watched through the hole in the gate as the twin walked slowly back to the Mercedes. He opened the passenger door as his brother opened the driver's. They both climbed in and slammed the two doors in perfect unison. Arnie couldn't see them through the windscreen. There was nothing except the parked van, silently facing him across the street from the factory. He assumed they had seen the Snipe and would sit there waiting until the brothers made a move. He turned and ran quickly back across the workshop floor.

19

Two-Pin hadn't heeded any calls for silence. She stood under the flaking plaster in a corner of the office, defending herself and her brother against Mathilda's charge of betrayal. 'Uncle Horn don't know no Mr Riss! And he don't know no Chinese boy neither! He's a holy man!'

'He ain't no holy man!' Mathilda shouted back.

'He speak the truth, and these boys know so!' She glared at Ronnie and Bernie. 'And so do she!' She pointed her finger at Lucy, who began to redden, and then she pointed it back at Mathilda. 'And so do you!'

'No I don't, Two-pin!'

'Don't you Two-pin me, girl! You telling me the Lord in all his wisdom comin' through the vessel o' Horn is a betrayer?'

'Someone told those twins, Auntie.' Mathilda's attack was losing ground in the fierce face of Two-pin's righteousness.

'Lord moves in mysterious ways.' Two-pin was rolling her eyes in holy ecstasy when Arnie came in. As he stood in the doorway he realized he'd pissed himself in fear and had to quickly readjust the bottom of his suit jacket to cover the wet patch. He moved sideways.

'They're out there, waiting.'

'Waiting for what?' Bernie was still upset over his dream. 'What are them geezers doing?'

Mirabelle took his hand. 'It's all right, we'll think of something.'

'So they going to be there all night?'

'The McCarthys'll wait for ever, Ron.'

'Arnie?' Lucy had noticed his damp trousers and touched his arm in sympathy, which embarrassed him. 'Get off, Lucy!'

Arnie's anger set off Bernie's panic again. 'This is blessed madness this is!'

Two-pin set her gaze firmly on the anguished giant. 'As my brother says, you is the lamb and the Lord will provide!'

'What's that meant to mean for fuck's sake?' said Arnie.

Two-pin gave him her haughtiest stare. 'Even if you is a sinner, I get you in here, so I get you out.' She was a diminutive ball of rags, colours and feathers, who had her own faith and knew her destiny. 'Why don't you just follow me?' She turned and walked out of the room.

'Arnie?' Lucy wanted to know what to do, but was equally enquiring about his state of mind.

'How should I know?' He followed Two-pin, as did the rest of them.

As soon as they entered the loading bay Two-pin went directly to the gates and looked through the rotten planking. The Mercedes was still there across the street, facing them. She turned back and whispered, 'So get in your car and leave it to Two-pin.' They watched in amazement as she walked to a corner of the bay and tore a ragged tarpaulin from an ancient petrol-driven, dirty yellow, fork-lift truck. 'This old monster personally kept in tip-top repair by my cousin Romeo for the lifting out of machinery parts no longer required by the owner.' She climbed up into the driver's seat and gave them a wide grin, her teeth gleaming in the moonlight. 'So why don't you get in that car and leave the rest to the servant of the Lord.'

'Auntie?' Mathilda suddenly felt protective of the old girl.

'You don' come from no family of traitors!' Two-pin turned the ignition and the truck fired into life with a roar. 'Get in that car, and you open them gates, Tilda!'

'We can't use the Snipe, Arn, every copper in . . .' Ronnie was seeing too many angles as usual.

'What else we going to do?' Arnie started to open the doors of the car.

'Arnie, this is blessed crazy!' Bernie shouted.

'Get in, Bernie.' Arnie was beginning to see what Two-pin was up to. 'And you, Mirabelle, Lucy. Get in as well, Tilda, I'll do the gates. Ronnie, start her up.' He left the car and ran towards the huge gates, then turned to instruct Ronnie, who was still standing by the car. 'Two-pin goes out first, we follow, all right?'

'She's going straight for the McCarthys in that?' Ronnie looked at the fork-lift.

'Get in, Ron!' Arnie seemed to be taking some kind of command again and Ronnie got in and started the Snipe. Arnie lifted the iron bar across the gates and was just about to pull them open when all Two-pin's plans went awry. Maybe faith in the Lord would have been sufficient for someone who knew how to drive a fork-lift, but for Two-pin, who didn't have the first clue, it clearly wasn't enough. She had a vague notion of the first principles of steering and had seen her cousin start it and then somehow he'd just driven off and the damned thing had just gone where he wanted it to, but as for these pedals for your feet and this stick in the middle getting in the way of your legs, how was she to know? She jiggled a pedal here and a lever there and the forks rose but the truck froze. She jiggled again and suddenly she wasn't where she'd been when she started jiggling. The truck was flying across the loading-bay floor, heading straight for Arnie. He dived out of the way as a couple of tons of yellow metal with two enormous prongs sticking out of the front collided with the sodden, rotten wood of the gates. It was no contest, and the fork-lift went straight through them as if the factory had been guarded all these years by mere splinters and air. Flying matchwood and the great bulk of the truck's back end disappearing through a cloud of blue belching exhaust smoke was the last the brothers saw of Two-pin.

Ronnie had jammed the Snipe into first, and Lucy held the passenger door open to pick up the dazed Arnie as the car careered towards the escape hatch in the shattered gates. Ronnie spun the wheel as Lucy managed to slam the door on Arnie. The Snipe skidded across the street outside with the boot in dire danger of disconnecting from the bonnet as it swayed from side to side. After a great screaming sliding curve, beginning inside the loading bay and ending 100 yards down the road, the bucking Snipe calmed herself and Ronnie got her into second gear, then third, and then down again as he took the corner at the end of the street in another great screeching swerve that sent the old girl rocking on her springs once more.

'Fucking hell, Ron!'

'I'm doing my bloody best, Arn!'

The car shot up a following straight at fifty and Ronnie finally got her into top and under some semblance of control. 'I think we lost them, Arn.'

Arnie looked back over Mirabelle's head through the rear window. There was no-one there. 'Yeah, we have.' Ronnie gunned the car and they disappeared towards the dark haze of smog that lay over the river.

20

A little later two pairs of black shiny shoes slowly picked their way across the rubble of the smashed gates and moved carefully across the greasy floor of the loading bay. They didn't slow or hesitate as they crossed the workshop floor and they passed the heavy machinery with confidence and certainty.

Two-pin was sitting on the ragged bed in her cubicle, nursing her wounds and singing a hymn of gratitude. Her voice echoed round the vast cavern of the factory as the two approached the old office and went through the door. The shoes stopped for a second outside Two-pin's cubicle. They seemed to be listening as her voice soared praising the Lord. Then, as one, both pairs of feet ran at the door. Two-pin stopped dead in the middle of her chorus as the door crashed down flat in front of her and she scrabbled back to the wall behind her as the two pairs of shoes stepped delicately over the flattened wood.

'What do you want with me?' She was very frightened.

Fairfax flashed his badge. 'We are police officers. We have a warrant to search these premises. We have reason to believe . . .'

Two-pin breathed a sigh of relief. The police was no threat. She cut off the sergeant in mid-official flow. 'Ain't never a reason to believe, Officer. You got to have faith.'

'Madam, there is a seriously vandalized factory gate and a fork-lift truck appears to be embedded in the wall opposite.'

'You see a black van?' Two-pin asked as she began to get up. It wasn't easy, she'd been been pretty banged about in the crash.

'You seen the Lack Brothers, madam?' Fairfax had dealt with women like this before.

'Or their mother?' Hooper added hopefully.

21

It was three thirty and they were speeding alongside the empty river road. Mathilda was looking through the back window. 'It's all right, Ron. We definitely lost them.'

'I'm pleased to hear it.' Ronnie put his foot down. 'Now all we got to do is keep out the clutches of the law, ain't we?' They were approaching a brilliantly lit suspension bridge crossing the river to their right. 'What do you want to do, Arn?'

'Take the bridge.'

Ronnie swung the wheel. The bridge was illuminated by thousands of plain white bulbs and stood, deserted and eerie, against the dark black of the sky.

'Where we going then, Arn?' Bernie, crushed between Mirabelle and Mathilda in the back, was cheering up.

Arnie watched as the lights flashed by. 'We done it, mate. We've gone west.'

Ronnie remembered what Harriet had said on the phone and felt fearful. It looked like they were going in the right direction.

'It's a quest, bruvs.' Bernie grinned and looked down at the picture of Galahad in his Arfer, which was open on his knee. Then, as if he knew exactly what he would see, he turned and looked through the back window. And sure enough, there was the white knight, dazzling in his silver armour, visor down and lance lowered, thundering through the brilliance of the light as he spurred his charger across the bridge behind them. Bernie grinned and whispered, 'Galahad! Come on you Lilywhites!'

PART FOUR

WEST

1

Hooper couldn't sleep. He'd decided not to go back to his flat. He'd known that if he had, he'd have spent the night staring through his window engaging in fantasies of Violet. This other world of daydream was consistently at the back of his mind, kept at bay, but not obliterated by the events of the day. If this had been the usual pursuit of the villain, he'd have been able to separate his professional life from his interior, and the day would have been uniform in both senses of the word. There'd have been procedure to keep him warm and coffee to keep him awake, and after such just endeavour he'd have returned home to his window to seek his reward: the sunny vision of a life with a wife he'd never had.

But now he was actually seeking Violet, how could he keep these worlds of fantasy and reality separate? The more determined he was to plant his feet fully into the filth of this inquiry, the more this other innocent reverie would intrude. It was as if he saw all these events through a Violet haze which fizzed constantly on the edge of his eye. The two worlds were beginning to merge and he'd started to panic. He'd once heard a forensic psychiatrist talk of the encapsulated psychosis of a serial rapist, who in his day-to-day life hid his madness as much from himself as from the world. It was only when the madness leaked out from behind the walls of his mind and seeped into the ordinary actions of his life, dislocating and corrupting them, that he began to realize he was insane. A serial rapist? He was a superintendent in the Met for God's sake!

One thing he knew for sure, this confusion couldn't continue. Fairfax

233

was already giving him strange, and worse, sympathetic looks. This was why he'd booked himself into a small hotel in the centre of the city, a good ten miles away from the back window of his dreams. He had to clear Violet from his thoughts. He'd sat up in his single bed, screwed his eyes tight and held his hands over his ears in an attempt to block out anything that was not relevant to his police work. He tried to think of it as not being a pursuit of Violet but an investigation into the murder of May Green. He clasped his hands tight and tried to review the day.

He must find the brothers because they would lead him to . . . It was no good, everything was going to lead him to . . . He clasped his hands tighter and moved on. The key was the twins. Or was it? Were they real or were they rumour? 'There's no smoke without fire, Superintendent,' he told himself. His policeman's mind began at last to click and turn. He would collect all gossip, check all tales, no matter how apocryphal, and do his best to separate fact from legend. There could be no more daydreams of any kind. He was adamant and would screw himself to the sticking place. But almost as soon as he'd legislated for this, he began to wonder if a man could exist without dreams? His mouth hung open for a second considering it, then he banned questions like that too. All fancy and reverie was prohibited and so were any thoughts, musings or philosophies concerning them.

He tried to concentrate again on the distressing reality and Scotch Jock came immediately to mind. He didn't know much about the movement of the mobs in this part of the city, but his boss, Luis Riss, needed to be checked and interviewed. He'd leave that to Fairfax. He was tempted to get up and go to the next room where he could hear the sergeant snoring and tell him to get on with it right away, but then he thought he'd look stupid issuing that kind of instruction at three in the morning and decided to wait for breakfast. However, it had helped him feel a little better. At least he was beginning to think clearly. And this man, Tom Cherry. What was he in all this? He was a successful manufacturer of women's clothing who worked with Violet's sister, and almost on the very day of the killing he had disappeared. This was something else that needed looking into much more carefully. He cursed himself for his lack of concentration throughout the day and resolved to do better tomorrow. He sat up straighter in his bed. This was more like it.

He moved on to consider his and Freddie's interview with Two-pin in the factory. There was nothing much there, apart from a ranting and almost unintelligible sermon on the sin at the heart of every man and especially the Lack Brothers. Although something she'd said about them being on their own path to damnation had struck him. Why were they any more damned than anyone else? Were they any more damned than him for instance? They were all pursuing the same thing, weren't they? And what was that? He knew what it was and could have screamed. It was no good. All paths led to Violet. There was no getting away from it.

'All right, Superintendent, there's no getting away from it, that's quite right, so face it.' The sudden sound of his own voice shocked him and he jerked up on the bed and found himself staring at his own image in the wardrobe mirror. He couldn't help thinking that he looked old and his eyes were red. 'You, Hooper, are a bloody idiot and you've wasted your life.' He'd almost shouted it out and the statement stunned him. Where had it come from? The words were hard, they echoed and hung like solid lumps in the cold air of the room. Was this the horrible, undecorated truth? Was this something that was actually correct, like a report or evidence was correct? He stared. It was, wasn't it? He was an idiot and he'd wasted his life.

He paused, time passed, nothing happened; then he felt himself slump back against the pillows, but couldn't take his eyes off the life-wasting idiot in the mirror. He'd seen himself and was devastated. He saw the bones of his face and the stoop of his shoulders. He saw he was thin and grey. He saw he was just a shell, a pathetic repository for meaningless and vacuous dreams. How the real Violet would have laughed at him if she'd known. He spoke aloud again. 'You foolish stupid bastard, Hooper. All this time she's lived her own life and never given you a thought.' He stared into his own eyes and saw such pain that he began to feel frightened. He'd been right, a man without dreams is no man at all, just flowing blood and declining cells, indicating life but containing nothing. And there he was, an empty husk staring at his own eye sockets in the wardrobe mirror of a dingy room in a cheap hotel. That was it, he'd finally faced the facts as any good copper should. This, here, was Hooper, an empty shell of an idiot who'd wasted his life.

He might have stayed that way for ever, but was saved by a bang on the wall. It was Fairfax who'd turned quickly in his sleep and accidentally thumped the thin plasterboard between them with his hand. Hooper looked up and away from himself. Then, to his surprise, he laughed. His sergeant had unconsciously knocked some sense into him. In the raging fire, the rising phoenix wasn't so much hope as the simple recognition that if you could still see the ashes then you hadn't been burned to a cinder. His sergeant's knock had told him that there was another human being dreaming in the room next door. Hear it, Hooper? There's someone else out there. He's breathing, farting and banging the wall. It was like coming back from the dead. Life was real; you could touch it and you could hear it. Hooper looked around his own room and began to see everything again. The wall was real, so was the wardrobe, the bedside table, the sheets and so was Sergeant Fairfax. And in sight and hearing of them so, therefore, was he. He was Superintendent James Hooper, a man who had suffered. That's it. It was the truth. What else was there to say? He'd sought clarity and found it in the detritus of himself. This day had been a kind of fire; he'd burned and now he was beginning to brush the ashes away. There could be no further fantasies of Violet. He was a policeman. He would do his job. And what was his job? To find the real Violet before she was attacked and quite possibly murdered like her sister had been. And he'd start where he'd started that morning, with her mother, and then with the man her sister had worked for. He'd go back to the tower and pay Mr Cherry a visit. He lay back and smoked his eleventh cigarette since midnight. The idiot would find the woman because that was his job, even though, admit it, James, he loved her and, admit it, James, she didn't love him. But in the real world you never knew for sure. Hope hangs eternal and in the real world you could dream properly. He'd made a little discovery. Dreams can replace life or they can make it happen; it's up to you. He stubbed the cigarette out, turned over and went to sleep.

$$2$$

Bernie looked out through the back windows of the Snipe as dark houses and streets flashed by. There were a few all-night stores open and people around. It was better than the south, that's for sure. 'This the west then, Arnie?'

Arnie was deep in thought. 'That's right, Bern.'

'Oh. Where we going then?'

'See a friend of mine.'

Lucy, jammed in beside Arnie in the front of the car, suddenly caught on. 'We're not going to Henry, Arnie? Not bloody Henry the Hippy?'

Arnie seemed to wake up. 'No, you're not.'

'What?'

'You and Tilda are getting out.'

'I am not, Arnie!'

'You are. Ronnie, stop at the next phone box will yer, I've got to make a call.'

'Ronnie?' Mathilda leaned forward from the back.

Ronnie wasn't sure of Arnie's reason for ditching the girls, but he agreed anyway. 'Arnie's right, Tilda, this ain't no place for you.'

'There's a phone box, Ron!' Bernie was trying to be helpful but Lucy wasn't appreciative. She screwed herself round to face Arnie. 'I am not bloody going anywhere, Arnie!'

'Lucy, we got to sort this out ourselves.'

'So, what you want to go and see Henry for?'

'You never met him, Lucy.'

'But you told me what he is, Arnie.'

'Leave it out, will you?'

'So why you going to see him?'

'Because we can't drive around in the Snipe all bloody night! We're bloody lucky to have got this far!' Ronnie pulled up by the phone box. 'And you're leaving, Luce. Sorry, mate, but that's how it is.' He put his arm behind her and opened the car door. She almost fell out.

'Arnie!' She managed to stand herself upright on the pavement.

Arnie got out after her. 'Thanks for all your help, Luce. I mean that.'

'I'm not bloody well going home!' She followed Arnie towards the phone box. 'I'm staying with you.'

'Get yourself a taxi, all right?' He went into the box and closed the door.

Lucy pulled it open. 'And you promised me you'd never go anywhere near Henry and all that!'

'I will go, Lucy, where I intend to go.' He pulled the door closed and then opened it again. 'You got any change?'

'What?'

'For the phone, Lucy.'

'Why can't I come?'

'Because we have to do this on our own.'

'Do what?'

'I don't know, for fuck's sake! Leave me to it, will yer?' He closed the phone box door and opened it again. 'Got a coin?'

'You're a big bastard!' Lucy hurled a fifty-pence piece at him, which narrowly missed his left eye and ricocheted around the inside of the box.

'Thank you.' Arnie closed the door and finally began to dial as Lucy paced angrily outside.

Mathilda's response wasn't so voluble. She stared at the back of Ronnie's head as he sat in the driving seat. Mirabelle held Bernie's hand in case the tension got to him. After a minute of silence, Mathilda said, 'Ronnie?'

'It's not safe, sorry. You got to go.'

'Is that all you got to say to me?'

He turned in his seat. 'Sorry, Tilda.'

'I said, is that all you got to say to me?'

It was. Ronnie turned back and stared out of the windscreen until Arnie came back. He didn't even comment as Arnie opened the back door for Mathilda and said, 'That's it, Tilda. Thanks for everything.'

'Ronnie?' Mathilda leaned forward and tried one last time, but he didn't reply and she got out of the car in tears.

'You as well, Mirabelle.' Arnie leaned further into the car.

'No.' It wasn't an argument, it was a plain statement of fact, and Arnie knew he was beaten even before Bernie started, 'Meebelle ain't going nowhere! She bloody ain't! She bloody ain't! She bloody . . .'

'Well shut your bloody trap then!' Arnie slammed the back door and got into the front.

'You're unforgivable, Arnie!' Lucy shouted through the window. 'You're just like your old man. You're completely unforgivable!'

'You're probably right, Lucy. Sorry.' He wound the window up as Ronnie put the Snipe in gear and let out the clutch. Ronnie couldn't look at Mathilda. 'I feel bad,' he said as they began to move forward.

'I don't feel anything,' Arnie lied.

'I feel hungry.' Bernie thought he should feel something too, and as that was what he always felt, he thought he might as well mention it. Then he looked down at his Arfer, as the Snipe pulled away fast and left the girls standing in the road.

Mathilda stared at it as it disappeared. She'd have forgiven Ronnie anything except walking out on her and she couldn't believe that's what he'd just done.

'All gone.' Lucy watched the Snipe disappear. She sounded more philosophical than she felt. She looked up the road for a taxi. There was nothing. 'Come on, sweetheart, there's more to life than a Lack.' They began to walk. Lucy stomped ahead, propelled by her anger, and Mathilda trailed behind, weighed down by her grief. 'Forget him, Tilda.' Lucy tossed it back over her shoulder.

'I can't, not just like that, Lucy.'

'Forget all of them. We're on our own, girl, always have been, always will be. Taxi!' She threw her arm up, but the taxi didn't stop and the driver showed no discernible sign of having noticed them. 'See what I mean,' said Lucy. She walked on. 'I'll tell you something. My mistake has been to believe in romance. You may not believe it, Tilda, but it's true. I always thought that if I gave everything, girl, including the blood out of my heart, then one day someone, preferably a man I fancied, would take out a tissue and mop it up. Well you know what they mop up with tissues, don't you? And it ain't my bloody tears!' She could feel the anger rising and it was pushing those very tears up out ahead of it. She couldn't help it, she was very unhappy. 'Let's face it, I'm an old whore and that's all there is to it.'

Mathilda stopped crying because Lucy had started. She thought it was at times like this that you have to be brave for your friends. 'You're not a whore, Lucy.'

'Yes I am. I'm a drunk and tired old whore. That's why the taxis won't stop; they think we're pissed and we're prostitutes. And they're right.' She began to walk faster, not wanting Mathilda to see her wet face. 'I'll tell you, I have this place between my legs, and they come along and they spit in it and then they fuck off. And I hate them!' She was almost running in her rage and Mathilda was having trouble

239

keeping up. 'Well it's all going to change. I may be a whore, but from now on I'm going to be a very cold and hard bitch as well. And so are you.'

'I'm not a whore, Lucy!' Mathilda didn't like where this conversation was going. She had her own grief and as far as she could tell it wasn't the same as Lucy's.

'Yes you are! We all are, because that's how they treat us!'

'It's because of how we behave!'

'No it's not, Tilda! I wouldn't have thrown a dead dog out of my car and left him on the street!'

'But I love him, Lucy, I still love him. I love him through thick and thin!' Mathilda's heels were making it difficult for her to keep up.

Lucy suddenly stopped. She wasn't having that. If she was going to hate the male in general, then so was the rest of womankind, and that included Mathilda whether she liked it or not. She stared at her friend in the gloom of the street, her face full of tears and rage. 'You love him? Are you out of your mind? You said he's gone gay!'

'No, I said that he didn't know!'

'You said that's what you thought, Tilda!'

'No! I said I didn't know if . . .'

'He's hurt you, Mathilda. Why don't you admit it?'

'I don't think he's gay anyway.'

'Yes you do. And you're a fool, girl!' Lucy walked away.

'I love him!' Mathilda ran after her.

'No you don't! You're just in love with the idea of him!'

'No, I'm not!'

'Well he doesn't love you, does he, or he wouldn't dump you in the street, would he? Taxi!' She shouted it again, but the taxi passed without slowing down. 'And fuck you too!' She folded her arms over her skimpy blouse and walked furiously along the street. 'We're on our own, Tilda!'

'I love him!' Mathilda lagged behind. 'And he loves me!' She looked up the road. It seemed a very long way to somewhere and Lucy had put all sorts of doubts into her mind. And so had Ronnie.

3

Bernie couldn't believe his eyes. It wasn't just a doughnut, or a plate of doughnuts, or even a tray of doughnuts, it was a whole wooden box of them, and there were other crates as well, and there was this geezer Henry, who had long blond hair and was a big mate of Arnie's and was a baker. He was hugging Arnie with his arms round him by the big table with flour on it, and there was a big oven with flames up the back and another baker was sliding big trays of bread dough in it. 'For crying out loud, I ain't never seen so many doughnuts.'

'Go on, mate, have as many as you want.' Henry grinned. The tall, thin proprietor of the bakery was delighted to see his oldest friend. He'd known Arnie for years, and with his flowing locks and ravaged face, it wasn't hard to see what Arnie had meant when he'd told Lucy he was an old hippy. He looked like some zonked-out rock star and it wasn't difficult to guess that drugs, hard, heavy and multifarious, were never too far from his vein or lip. He had a rasping, deep, city accent and laughed a lot with huge off-white teeth. Henry could love you like a brother, but you never knew quite where you were with him. Nor did he. There were bottomless chasms of paranoia and rolling foothills of affection and sometimes extraordinary peaks of generosity, but he never quite knew in which landscape he walked. There was a time he'd scared himself almost literally to death by becoming accidentally involved in one of the biggest cocaine scams in the history of customs and excise, but somehow – he was going too fast at the time to ever discern the real story – he'd evaded arrest and kept the profits. Hence one bakery for Henry, which, as he liked to say, was his hearth and his dough and he'd kept it through thick slice and thin, because without bread, man, we're lost, know what I mean? Then he'd laugh like he did now. His pleasure at seeing Arnie was tempered by amazement. He hugged his old friend again. 'Shit, I knew it, man. I knew you'd come. We're like one, man. How'd you know?'

'Know what, Henry?' Arnie didn't understand what he was talking about.

'Even like with what you're going through. I read about you in the paper, you know?' He looked round with sympathy at the brothers and Mirabelle. 'And you still come. That's fucking amazing, man.'

'What are you talking about, Henry?'

'Hey?' Now it was Henry's turn to not get it.

'Listen, Henry, is there anywhere we can stash the Snipe?'

The baker stared at Arnie for a second, realizing that Arnie hadn't come for the reason he thought he had. He suddenly said, 'You don't know, do you?'

'Know what?'

'Shit, man.' Henry didn't reply. He was going to have to tell Arnie himself.

But Arnie couldn't wait. 'Henry, we got to get that motor off the road.'

'Yeah.' Henry seemed pleased to change the subject. 'Jackie,' he called over to his fat and beaming assistant. 'Show them the yard.'

'Thanks, Henry.' Arnie touched him on the shoulder.

'Yeah, fanks Henry,' Bernie grinned with his mouth full of doughnut.

Henry looked at Arnie. 'If you don't know, man, it's crazy you came.'

'We needed help, man,' said Arnie, beginning to revert to their old lingo.

'Well you came to the right place,' Henry grinned.

Ronnie went out to the Snipe with Jackie. It was about four in the morning and the night rain over the city had stopped. It looked civilized here, more like home. There was a department store over the road, a boutique and there was even a bloke in evening dress staggering away from him on the opposite pavement. He was drunk admittedly, but at least his mouth wasn't full of damnation and he looked as though he'd had a meal in the last fortnight. He got into the car, started the engine and waited for the baker to slide open the gate to the yard. For some reason the smell of the Snipe's leather seats made him think of Mathilda. He even looked over his shoulder to the back seat where she'd been sitting. He knew he'd been cruel and unkind and he couldn't stand feeling like that about himself. He was wishing she was still there as he drove the car through the tiny gap and didn't look back as the gate closed behind him.

Henry took Arnie, Bernie and Mirabelle up the stairs to his small flat above the bakery. His little living room with its tiny kitchen off it

242

looked as if it hadn't been touched since the Sixties. It was neat and tidy with a low table in the centre surrounded by huge faded cushions. There were tapestries on the wall and a giant poster of Lou Reed. Candles, sprays of incense and an old hookah stood next to the sound system, and as if to underline the impression that they were entering some kind of psychedelic museum, Henry stabbed a finger at the cassette deck as soon as he came in. Arnie heard the Stones' 'Paint it Black' and felt as if he'd entered a time warp, or more to the point, come through that old green door into his own past. He slumped down onto the cushions. 'Fucking hell, Henry, who said things change?'

Henry grinned in nervous pleasure. Whatever Arnie knew, or whatever he'd come for, it was good to see his old friend back again. He turned to Bernie. 'Want a kip? Through here, mate.' And he led the big little brother and Mirabelle through a door on the far side of the room.

Bernie followed him into the bedroom and for the second time in about half an hour couldn't believe his eyes. First a million doughnuts and now this. The room was almost entirely filled by a vast four-poster bed, its sides draped in velvet. Its pillows were a hundred colours and the sheets were red and blue, with a big eiderdown on the top which was all patterned. He looked at it in amazement. 'It's King Arfer's bed, Meebelle.'

'And you can sleep in it, mate.' Henry patted him on the back. 'I work all night making the bread, see?'

'And the doughnuts.'

'See you in the morning, brother.'

Henry went out as Bernie threw his Arfer onto the bed. 'I'm blinking knackered, Meebelle.'

She smiled and moved round to the other side of the bed and looked out of the window. Opposite was a row of shops and behind them she could see the flash of car headlights moving along what must have been a major road beyond. Bernie was sitting on the bed and grumbling in his tiredness as he took his shoes and socks off. He lay back on the bed, still in the white shirt that Two-pin had given him. 'Night, Meebelle.'

'Good night, Bernie.' She moved round and pulled the eiderdown over him. His eyes were closed and he was almost immediately dead asleep, as he would have said, and wasn't dreaming. She felt a relief at that and stood at the foot of the four-poster, watching him as he slept surrounded by Henry's exotic drapes and luxuriant bedding. He was breathing evenly and his skin seemed translucent, hardly able to contain the beauty of the child within the man. She vowed nothing, but nothing, in this universe or beyond, would be allowed to touch him. She looked up at the window. Sorush had come.

4

Her legion crowded the roofs opposite and rose like a wall up to the sky. It darkened the starlight and cut out both sight and sound of the traffic on the far road. Sorush herself sat opposite on the burnished and weathered copper roof of a department store. Kasbeel sat by her feet in the face of the huge store clock.

Mihr filled the street with her opposing light in a dazzling display of power and pride. The fierce brightness of her beauty forced Sorush to shield her eyes and the angels above to turn away, flickering and fluttering their giant wings to hide themselves from the light.

'I know your beauty, Mihr,' said Sorush.

Mihr calmed and the light level fell.

The old angel began the incantation and Mihr saw that they were back in the Soho of the 1960s.

Arnie was eighteen and Ronnie, nine. They were standing under the newly framed pictures of filmstars in the basement club bar. The place was packed and Charlie was standing on a chair near the stairs up to the restaurant, addressing the crowd. He had a bottle of champagne in one hand and a huge cigar in the other. It was obviously the grand opening of the club. He grinned round at the upturned and laughing faces below him. They included a slimmer Geoffrey and a less bitter Martin. O'Dare, at twenty years younger, looked exactly the same. Violet was near the bar looking nervous. Harriet, standing close, beamed with pride as Charlie spoke. 'Ladies and gentlemen, welcome! My friends, you've been eating my food upstairs for eight years, and you looked so bad I thought I'd better give you a drink!' He beamed at the crowd. 'This is my house and therefore it's your house, and today it's on the house! Welcome to Charlie Lack's basement boozer!'

This was the moment Charlie had been waiting for all his life. He'd look back when things got worse and realize that standing on that chair on that day was the highest he'd ever got. He had his own business upstairs to gather the cash and the bar below to dispense it. As far as he was concerned it was perfect economics, you took with one hand and gave back with the other. In the months to follow Harriet would sometimes wonder if there wasn't a pipeline from the till in the restaurant down to Charlie's pocket below, but at the moment she was as delighted as he was. He had so many friends and such was his credit that, if things got bad, he could borrow as much as he needed. And anyway what were all those years of slog in the south for if he wasn't allowed to enjoy himself a bit now he was uptown.

The truth was that he'd never slogged much in either place, rather he'd charmed, dealt and connived. The old wine warehouse they'd converted into the restaurant had been paid for by the sale of his parents' café. Old Arnold had only survived Edna by a few months, and Harriet being an absentee daughter, Charlie had inherited most of the estate. A few years before their deaths Charlie had given a hand up to Sayeed Sayeed, at the time a newly arrived immigrant, and as in the world according to Charlie, what you give you more often than not get back, Sayeed and his sons had prospered and the old man had become a kind of father figure to Charlie. When Arnold and Edna died, Sayeed had lent Charlie the extra money he'd needed to top up his endowment and pay for the renovations to the restaurant. And now the restaurant had finally paid for the club.

The old Indian, dressed in his usual mustard yellow, stood in the crowd below Charlie as he finished his speech, and although it wasn't likely that he would become a regular boozer, he applauded warmly as Charlie stepped down from the chair and yelled at his eldest son, 'Arnie, get behind the bloody bar!'

Arnie was stoned. He'd been heavily into dope for at least two years, and although it was still only early afternoon, he'd already put together a little five-paper number of enormous proportions. The world, and especially his old man, was looking crazy to Arnie. Alternating between the giggles and paranoia he headed shakily to the bar, *en route* to becoming, for the moment, the slowest and most concentrated drink dispenser Soho had ever seen.

Charlie, despite his display of confidence and *bonhomie*, was nervous. He turned to Violet and whispered with an anger that few of his clientele had ever seen, 'Bloody boy! Look at him. I need help, Vi!' He watched as Arnie filled a beer glass, half inch by half inch, his paranoid imagination had proceeded to froth and overspill before his hand had even touched the pump. He was being very, very careful and had no intention of spilling one drop. 'Christ Almighty, Arnie, will you get a move on!' Charlie turned back to Vi. 'This'll only work, Vi, if I get the help I require.'

Young Ronnie had crept up and put his arm round his mother's waist, trying to get her arm round him. Charlie let him have it too. 'What are you doing down here? I told you to stay upstairs!'

'Dad!'

'Get out of here!'

Violet took her husband's arm. 'It'll work, Charlie, because I love you.' She tried to peck him on the cheek but he moved away.

'You've changed your tune, haven't you? For years all I've had is, let's get out of here!'

'Not now, Charlie . . .'

He turned away from her and Violet hardly felt there was any point in talking to him any more. Ronnie was clinging on to her and making her feel even more irritated. She angrily pushed the boy away and was moving on when she noticed Charlie wink at a blonde woman, who was standing by the door to the basement steps. Violet had seen her in the club before and knew she was an out-of-work actress called Mavis, who'd been coming on to Charlie for weeks. She was grinning at him and he started to push through the crowd towards her as Violet came back and grabbed his arm. 'I'm sorry. I was nervous, Charlie, that's all.'

He turned back and put his face close to hers. 'You were nervous? What do you think I've been feeling? Bloody hell, Violet, have you got any idea of the size of the investment I'm making here?'

'I'm sorry . . .'

'I needed support!'

'Charlie . . .'

'You didn't believe in me, Vi.' He stared at her for a second to make sure she understood what he was saying. There was a rage and disappointment in his eyes and she looked away. Maybe he was right, maybe she didn't believe in him. She watched as he took a bottle of champagne from the bar and moved through the crowd, filling glasses and heading for Mavis.

'Mum?' Ronnie was still holding on to her waist and looking up at her. His voice was so plaintive that she stroked his hair with the palm of her hand, as she saw her husband putting his arm round the actress on the other side of the room. Violet smiled down at her son. 'It's all right, dear.'

'Ever hear of Pierre Cardin?' She turned quickly and saw Tom Cherry standing in the crowd behind her. He was a laughing, charming, middle-aged man, with a moustache and thinning hair. He looked rich and splendid in a made-to-measure three-piece with a carnation in his buttonhole.

'Tom! Oh, you came! Tom!' She threw her arms round his neck and pulled him towards her. 'Oh, Tom.' She kissed him. 'I thought you were in Paris!'

He put his arms around her waist and smiled. 'I've done it, Vi.'

'Mum? Hello, Tom!' Little Ronnie looked up through the heaving stomachs around him. Someone had spilled beer on him and his shoulder was wet.

Tom put his hand on the boy's neck. 'Hello, Ronnie.' He was rewarded with a huge smile. 'How are you?'

'Tell me, Tom!' Violet interrupted. 'Tell me what happened!'

'They want me to sell for them, Vi.'

'In your shop?'

'Anywhere I can. I'll be running backwards and forwards to Paris from now on.'

'Oh, Tom, I'm so pleased!' And she was. She laughed and held the sides of her face in sheer delight.

'I'm going to need some help.' Tom was having to shout above the noise of the crowd. Arnie had decided to just hand the bottles out over the bar and they were being emptied by Charlie's mates as quickly as possible before they ran out.

'What do you mean?' Violet looked up at Tom.

'I'd like you to manage my shop, Vi.' He stroked Ronnie's neck again. 'You'd like that, wouldn't you, Ron?'

'Yes!'

Violet was stunned. If standing on the chair and announcing the

247

opening of his new club was the zenith of Charlie's hopes and dreams, then what Tom Cherry was offering Violet was what she imagined to be hers.

'Champagne!' Arnie slammed two bottles down onto the bar counter. He'd noticed his father slide his hand briefly over the blonde's arse and a shot of rage had forced a reaction before his drugged brain could interfere. 'Old bastard said it was on the house!' He stared at his father.

Violet had turned quickly from Arnie to Charlie and, although he'd moved his hand, the guilt was still on his face. She smiled at Tom. 'Let's go up to the restaurant.'

As they moved towards the stairs she could hear Charlie retrieving the awkward moment with a laugh. 'Course it's on me. Drink it! That's what it's there for!'

Later that night Charlie did what Mavis was there for. The bottles were empty, the place was a wreck and he fucked her on the floor amidst the debris in the club at one in the morning. Violet heard him do it. She sat upstairs in her dressing gown at one of the tables in the darkened restaurant and listened as the actress panted and groaned in the club below. She felt no desire to go down and interfere. She didn't want to shout or scream or cause a scene. She sat still and watched the shadows on the wall made by the lamp at the end of the alley.

She'd gone up to the flat earlier and put Ronnie to bed, then she had undressed and got into bed herself. She'd wanted to be on her own to think about the offer Tom had made. She'd been thrilled, not so much because of the challenge of running her own shop, or because it would get her out of Charlie's cheap restaurant and club, or even because it would remove her physically from him for most of the day, but because she sensed it was something to do with the mythical third place she'd always dreamed of. From home with Lucretia to home with Charlie, she'd always known there was somewhere else she would go.

A dress shop was something she would never have imagined, but the more she thought about it, the more she realized it was obvious. Occasionally in the past she'd helped Tom out, or sat with him in the back room of the shop. She'd loved the materials, the cut and design of the fabrics, she knew what looked good and what didn't, and knew the women who came into the shop liked and trusted her. As she lay in bed, she began to understand that her third place was perhaps not

248

another home, it involved no dreams of domesticity, it wasn't a place at all in that sense; it was something within her. It was a feeling, or an idea; it was a life she needed to live. She'd heard someone say, once, that in order to go a thousand miles you have to take the first step, and all her instincts told her that the shop would be just that, a first foot out of the door.

She'd been so excited she couldn't sleep, and although she knew Charlie would react angrily to the idea, she'd come down to find him, and even if he was drunk and wouldn't talk about it, at least she would have mentioned it. As she'd come into the restaurant, she'd seen that Harriet had locked up and everyone had gone. She'd no idea how much time had passed and realized that she must have been lying in bed dreaming for hours.

It was then that she'd heard Charlie downstairs with Mavis. She'd stood very still for a moment. She'd thought she was going to explode with rage but she hadn't. She'd remained at the top of the stairs down to the club for a long time, listening as Mavis giggled at her husband's inane whispers. She'd been able to hear the sound of clothes coming off, zips being unfastened, shoes being thrown down and Charlie laughing while he poured himself a last drink.

She'd turned and sat at one of the tables in the dark in the corner of the restaurant as they'd begun to have sex. She'd listened and was surprised to realize that all she felt was relief. Something was telling her that this was an answer to a prayer. She hardly heard as her husband came to orgasm. She thought maybe that, as this was a sound she was so familiar with, perhaps it had just passed her by unheard, like the other noises from the streets outside. Then she heard a bang and had to think for a moment to work out what it was. Charlie had closed the basement door to the club. He must have let Mavis out. She heard the actress's footsteps on the iron stairs outside and then she heard Charlie as he came up the inside stairs from the club. She watched as he came into the restaurant, staggered slightly and went straight towards the stairs up to the flat. He passed within five feet of her and didn't notice her in the gloom. She listened as his footsteps crossed the overflow room above her and then disappeared as he went on up. It was only then that the pain hit her. It came quickly through the quiet of the night, causing her to bend forward on the chair and clasp her arms around her stomach. She sobbed; waves of silent, wet convulsions racked her as if she was vomiting. She cried like this for an hour, until the front of her dressing gown was sodden and her heart was empty; empty of Charlie and of herself.

'I heard you with her.' Violet stood in the middle of the club room. It was mid-morning and Charlie had already been up for four hours cleaning the place out after the party. He was vacuuming the floor as she came in. He'd only had a few hours' sleep and his energy never ceased to amaze her.

He didn't turn off the Hoover. 'Heard me with who?'

'The actress, Charlie. I sat upstairs while you did it with her.'

'Don't be bloody stupid.'

'I just wanted you to know. I heard everything.' She walked towards the stairs as he switched off the machine.

'Vi?'

She stopped and turned back. 'You're a fucking bastard.' He stood in the centre of the room holding the handle of the vacuum cleaner as the sunlight dappled in through the basement windows. He could see she was white with rage. There was nothing he could say. 'You're just a ghost to me, Charlie.' She went up the stairs, leaving him there.

He looked down at the cleaner and began to feel sorry for himself. She'd never understood him. Never really seen him. She was like her mother and ultimately only contemptuous of him. He'd built all this; why couldn't she see what it had cost him? He'd come from nowhere hadn't he? No-one had ever given him a chance. He'd had to make everything from nothing with his bare hands and his brain. He began to feel angry. Why didn't she see what he was? Why didn't she believe in him? Then he began to feel his cock go hard under his trousers. He was thinking of Mavis and wanted to fuck her again. He flicked the switch of the vacuum and began to hoover. Violet would get over it. Fuck her, she'd have to. She would remain his, in his clutch and his palm. She had no alternative and nor did he. He hoovered up the butts and the ash. He knew he loved her, but he also knew he would throw her away. He was beginning to grieve a loss he knew he would somehow cause. He was already doing it. He hardened and tightened; these things were in the stars and beyond his control.

*   *   *

A few days later Violet was in the back room of the dress shop with Tom. She could see Ronnie through the door. He was sitting by the window in the shop itself, watching the street go by.

'My offer's still open, Vi.'

'Not yet, Tom.'

'You will someday.'

'Will I?' She turned to him.

'Oh yes.' He covered her hand with his. She'd never quite understood Tom. He seemed to love her, but she knew the attraction wasn't sexual. She pulled her hand away and slid Ronnie's drawing book towards them across the table. It was full of childish drawings of his pretty ladies.

'You should ask Ronnie; he's got all the talent.'

'And what about you?'

'I'm married, Tom.'

He seemed angry. 'And he messes about with actresses, doesn't he? Why don't you leave him?'

'I can't.' She looked away. 'I will. I suppose I will. I don't know how it will happen, but I suppose I will.'

'When, Vi?' He took her hand again. He was an attractive man, just the kind she'd always wanted: cultured, gentle, capable, without being threatened by the world. Tom was success.

'I don't know.' She looked down at her hand in his. 'Charlie thinks it's all in the stars. Perhaps he's right.' She looked up, her face suddenly full of anger. 'When I go, he'll know it.'

Tom was shocked. He'd never seen this in her. 'Vi?'

'He says, I don't believe in him. Well he's right. I hate him. He knows what's coming to him. He'll make it happen too. I'll make sure he does.' She'd spoken very quickly, spitting the words out.

Ronnie walked in from the shop. 'Mum?'

Violet got up. 'Stay here with Tom for a while, will you?' She turned and smiled at Tom. 'Look after him for a bit, will you? I'd like some time to think.'

'Of course.'

'Mum?'

'Do your drawings, Ronnie.' She walked out as Ronnie sat at the table by Tom.

'Can I use your pen, Uncle Tom?'

Tom put the rapidograph onto the table in front of him. 'Don't tell your dad you come here with your mum, will you?'

'Why not?' Ronnie had his head low over the page and was drawing carefully.

'I think it would upset him. I don't think he likes drawing.' Tom put his hand on the boy's neck and began to stroke up and down. 'He doesn't like to think of your mum doing other things. You understand that, don't you?' Ronnie nodded. 'You can keep the pen if you like.'

'Oh thanks, Tom!' Ronnie bent even lower, concentrating on the drawing as Tom's hand moved lower onto his shoulders and under the collar of his shirt.

Violet hadn't done much when she'd left Tom. She'd merely walked the streets of Soho, pretending to do some shopping. Something was building up in her and she knew that all she could do was wait. Later that evening she was making the boys' tea in the tiny kitchen of the flat. Arnie was in the living room, stoned as usual, lying with his feet up on the sofa, watching *Popeye* on the TV.

Ronnie, paler than usual, was hanging around the kitchen, getting under Violet's feet. He stood by the door holding the rapidograph that Tom had given him.

'Ronnie, you're getting in my way!' He seemed withdrawn and didn't move. Violet squeezed past him. 'Ronnie, will you get out of here!' She went to push him out of the door.

'I want to stay here with you, Mum.'

'Where did you get that pen?'

'Tom gave it to me.'

'Why would he do that?'

'I don't know, Mum.'

'Did you steal it?'

'No!'

She snatched it out of his hand. 'This is going straight back!'

Ronnie burst into tears. 'Mum!'

'Get out of here, Ronnie!' She shouted through the door to the living room, 'Arnie!' He didn't respond. 'Arnie, are you deaf? Can't you help me!' She was close to tears herself.

Arnie half lifted himself on the sofa. 'What?'

'For Christ's sake!' She pushed Ronnie out of the kitchen and slammed the door so hard that the glasses on the nearby shelves rattled. 'Charlie, I'm going to kill you!'

'You investigate the mother also, Sorush?'

'We look at the effect of the father. Remember what you've seen. His wife and his eldest son left him. The boy didn't return for ten years and the wife, never.'

'Why do you pursue this family?'

'Because you guard one of them. If you have come, there must be a powerful reason, Mihr. It will be profound and exist only in the deepest point of the past.'

'You mean where the hurt begins?'

'Or where the crime is greatest. Kasbeel! The mother.'

It was the morning after Violet had left Soho for the last time and they were back in the east. She was dressed in the same coat and carrying the same small case that she'd carried when she'd walked out on the new-born Bernie and finally deserted Charlie. She was walking along the side of Kitchener Square. It had dilapidated over the years, several of the houses were abandoned and empty and most were in a state of disrepair. One of the worst was her mother's. She came to the front of it, looked up and seemed to be making up her mind. Then she walked up the steps and lifted the still-polished brass knocker. She heard a door open and then slam inside the house and footsteps in the hall coming towards her. Lucretia opened the door. They hadn't seen each other since Lucretia's unfortunate visit to Arnold and Edna's café in Streatham. That was over ten years ago and Violet was surprised to see how her mother had aged. Her hair was now grey and she walked with a slight stoop. Her eyes were dull as she looked up and Violet immediately felt a pang of remorse at how much she must have hurt her, but was so full of her own anguish that she almost immediately dismissed it. Her voice was hard. 'Hello, Mum.'

'Violet?'

There was a silence, then Violet said, 'I'll only come in on one condition. That you'll swear you'll never tell Charlie I've been here and you'll never ever tell him where I am.'

For a moment Lucretia felt like crying. She held up her arms and Violet leaned forward into her embrace. Even after all that time there was no kiss, just cheek to cheek, and as Violet felt the old woman's thin back and bones in her arms she knew she wouldn't stay long. May appeared behind her mother in the hallway. 'Vi?'

'Hello, May.'

Her sister saw the look of triumph on her mother's face. 'What have you done, Vi?'

'I've left.'

'Charlie?' May looked down at the small case. 'For good?'

'Yes.'

May was stunned. She'd occasionally seen her sister over the years, but had never been close enough to her to know of her frustrations and the problems with Charlie. 'What about your boys?'

'I don't want to see them again.'

'Vi!'

Lucretia spoke for the first time. 'They should never have been born.' Her tone was as crusty and mean as the remark, and for a second Violet felt like slapping her face.

'There's another one now.'

'Another one?' May held her hands to her face.

'I didn't tell you. He was born a week ago. He's called Bernie.' As Violet said it, she marvelled at her own coolness and restraint. 'Can I come in, or am I going to stand on the doorstep all day?'

'Come in, Violet.' Lucretia stood to one side. 'I knew you'd be back.'

Violet went in and her mother closed the door after her.

Charlie was devastated. It was as if a cable had snapped inside him and the power still running through the split wires, fused and sparked, sending directionless shocks of pain throughout his body. He'd cried for the first time in thirty years. The tears, long repressed, had spurted from his eyes and he'd howled in a high-pitched whine like an abandoned puppy. Now a day and a half after she'd gone he was quieter, and sat by the table in the living room, looking down through the window at the alley below. Sayeed Sayeed had come and was sitting opposite him with his hands clasped. He was as sad as he'd ever been. Sometimes the torment of a loved one is harder to bear than your own. He'd held Charlie as he'd cried and would stay for as long as was needed. He said, 'She'll come back.'

'She won't, Sayeed. I know she won't and maybe I don't want her to either.'

'Charlie?'

'Harriet's coming over. She'll look after the baby.'

'Will you go and look for Violet?'

'No.' Charlie seemed to harden. 'What's right is to keep the business going. Perhaps I'll be able to do what I want with it now.' He watched a couple of women walk through the alley below him. 'This is my vineyard isn't it? So I picked a few grapes every now and again. So what?' He banged his hand on the table and looked as if he was going to cry again. 'You remember that night I came down to you? I said there would be blood. I was right, Sayeed. I smacked her. I gave it to my own fucking wife, mate. I'm a bad man, let's face it, Sayeed. I'm a very bad man.'

'What happened that night?'

'I don't know, Sayeed.'

'Why did she go, Charlie?'

'I said, I don't know!'

'Do you think it is something to do with Tom Cherry?'

'I did once, but I don't now.' Charlie shrugged. 'I don't know.' His voice cracked again as he raised his hands and looked up. 'The Moon and Mars and Charlie Lack. It's beyond me, mate.' He put the heel of his palms into his eyes trying to force the tears back. 'She did it, didn't she? I knew she would. She took a carving knife to my bloody heart.' He looked away as Sayeed reached out a hand.

'Dad?' Ronnie had come in through the door.

'Come here, mate.' Charlie put out his arms and hugged the boy close to him.

'Where's Arnie, Dad?'

'I don't know. Gone missing as usual when he's needed.' He suddenly looked up, his voice was cracking. 'What's happening, Sayeed?'

Violet didn't stay long with her mother. This was certainly no third place and she wasn't even sure if her mother wanted her in the house. It seemed to be enough for Lucretia that she had washed her hands of Charlie. He'd telephoned of course and Lucretia had extracted the greatest of pleasure from screwing the lie into him. 'No, I haven't seen her and don't want to.' Violet had watched her as she stood erect in the hall holding the receiver, or deceiver as Violet had thought. The stoop in her mother had gone and she looked twenty years younger. Revenge was sweet. 'I'd appreciate it, Mr Lack, if you don't call this number again.'

Violet imagined Charlie at the other end. It amazed her to think that she'd hardly thought about him until this moment and even now she felt cold. She'd not really considered Ronnie either, and as for the baby . . . she shuddered and put him from her mind. She'd been horrified when she'd discovered she was pregnant and had only stayed those last months in order to drop him in Charlie's lap. If she'd gone before she'd literally have had to carry the child with her, would have given birth to him on her own, would have borne responsibility for him and retained an inevitable link with Charlie. And a link with Arnie too, with the hated baby and Ronnie pining and isolated in the middle. It was all too big and too horrible to be contemplated. All she knew was that where she'd come from was intolerable and the very thought of returning was loathsome. She'd committed her own crime and this was her own personal burden. She accepted that she had to carry it, but that didn't mean she could bear to think about it, and she was far, far too weak at the moment to even try. She walked quickly from the hall as Lucretia turned from the phone.

She hoped that her mother wouldn't follow her into the kitchen and was relieved when she heard the front-door knocker. It would be Albert. He'd remained Lucretia's companion over the years and came round every afternoon for conversation and a glass of sherry, which lately had become several glasses and even, one day, a whole bottle. May had said that in all the years he'd been coming round, he'd never been known to refuse any offer: biscuits, tea, cakes, lunches and count-less dinners had all disappeared into Albert's little round mouth. He'd even found an old suit that had once belonged to their dead father and he had worn it beneath a hat belonging to the same that he'd found the previous month in what was left of the garden shed. May was sure he was after their mother's house, and then she'd laughed and said, 'He'd better be quick and get it before it falls down.' It was true too. Violet had been appalled at the state of the place. A doodlebug had exploded in the road behind the back garden in the last days of the war. It had destroyed two houses there and badly shaken the foundations of Lucretia's. She'd been told by a surveyor that it was irreparable and had seemed to almost welcome the decline. She watched the bricks fall and the fissures widen as if the whole deteriorating edifice mirrored the state of her own malicious interior. After a few days back, Violet couldn't wait to leave again.

She heard the front door open and May's footsteps in the hall. If one good thing had come out of these terrible events it was that she had found her sister again. May had been sympathetic, and in her own way understood that Violet was in a state of shock. May hardly dared question her. Her sister's abandonment of her family and her walk into this unknown future required a courage, a desperation, or at the very least, a burst of energy that May could barely imagine. She'd led a dim manless life, dominated by her once overbearing, but now uncaring, mother. She saw everything as magazine pictures or as a series of images from the TV serials she was addicted to. They were real life as far as she was concerned, so Violet's act of leaving was seen in the same terms, as either an extraordinary romance or a fool's tragedy. One night she'd sat and listened as Violet slowly began to talk. Sometimes it was almost incoherent; others, cold, dispassionate and strangely detached. When she began to speak of Charlie, May could see the hatred, but was given no detail. Violet clammed up if asked. It was as if her rancour was abstracted, and although directed at her husband, lived only within herself. Charlie as a man, as another human being, as a real thing in her life had ceased to exist. And so it seemed had her sons. Violet's rage was all her own and as yet could hardly surface. She said nothing of the events of the last year and the baby was a subject not to be mentioned. At the end of the evening Violet had looked up to the ceiling with tears in her eyes and said, 'I have to leave here.'

May came into the kitchen. 'Hello, Vi.' She'd been at work and was shop-manageress smart. 'Had a nice day?'

'I called Tom Cherry.'

'What did he say?'

'He's going to help me, May.'

'Oh Vi!' May put her arms round her sister. 'What's he going to do?'

'He's bought a boutique. He wants me to manage it for him.' She was flat, as if the offer hardly interested her.

'Oh Vi!' May excitedly hugged her even harder, but Violet looked dull and grey. If she couldn't stand on her past, how could she see the future?

'Where did she go?' asked Sorush.
Kasbeel returned to the incantation.

It was two years later and Violet was working for Tom. She was standing by her sister at the back of his boutique in Kensington and was watching as a small group of well-dressed men and women drank wine and celebrated. Violet had changed. She'd lost weight, her hair was now her natural brown and was, as May put it, up-to-the-minute styled. She poured champagne into a glass held by a large Jewish woman draped in a pale grey fur coat, and then moved on through the gathering. There was a new air of confidence and refinement about her, although behind the charm there was also a sense of sadness that seemed to permeate her every smile. If anything this distant, vulnerable shadow added to her appeal. It made customers trust her and the buyers and designers she dealt with want to put their arms round her and help her out. Not that she'd needed it. She'd walked into the trade as if she'd been born to it. She wasn't even nervous. From the very beginning she'd made decisions on the basis of some extraordinary and unconsidered instinct. What she'd bought, she'd sold. She'd known what the women wanted and she'd known how to treat them. She seemed to say that no matter how you feel about yourself, you can be beautiful. In a particular kind of flattery there is truth and not surprisingly the customers loved her for it. Violet had become a success. She'd found her third place. She looked round at the decorations she'd put up on the door and ceiling of Les Quatre Saisons. They'd been the most expensive she could buy and that in itself made her happy. She knew you had to spend to make and who would argue? This was the second boutique she'd opened for Tom and he certainly wouldn't have. He put his arms round her. 'I knew you were a natural!'

'It was your idea to come here.'

'Two outlets in as many years, Vi. I couldn't have done that without you.' He raised his glass. '*Salute!*'

'Thank you, Tom.' She touched her glass with his as the Jewish woman began to look through the racks.

'Mrs Klein! My dear Mrs Klein.' Tom went quickly over to assist her as May came up behind Violet.

'He's so proud of you. And so am I!'

'Here.' Violet poured champagne into her sister's glass.

'Vi.' May looked sheepish. 'Tom has asked if I'd like to work in the office.'

Violet was delighted. 'May!'

'I can type, I know I can do it, Vi.' She stopped, needing her sister's approval.

'Well, why don't you?'

'I'm not treading on any toes, am I?'

'What do you mean?'

'I mean, um . . . You and Tom.' May looked over to where Tom was laughing with Mrs Klein. To her mind he looked very debonair.

'Tom isn't that kind of man, May.'

May looked at her sister and then back at Tom. 'You mean, he's . . .' She was beginning to catch on. 'I thought he was married.'

'He was divorced six years ago.'

'Oh Vi.' May was only now beginning to see this other world she was in. 'You mean he's queer?' She whispered it. Violet shrugged as May looked over at Tom yet again. 'Oh God, Vi.'

'Does that mean you don't want to work with him?'

'No! I mean . . .' May didn't know what she'd meant. She'd left Kitchener Square to live with Vi nearly six months ago and had found her sister's new ways glamorous and exciting, but there was so much to learn. Life with Lucretia hadn't been the best preparation for swinging London. 'I mean . . .'

Tom was coming back towards them with another bottle of champagne. He grinned as he started to open it. 'Has May told you, Vi? What do you think?'

Violet put her arm round her sister. 'I think it's wonderful!'

'And so do I!' May held her glass out for more champagne as Tom popped the cork and Violet laughed, looking radiant and happy.

Sorush remained still and silent on the burnished dome of the department store, as Mihr turned away and the angels waited.

5

Having implicitly consented to a widening of the investigation, Mirabelle knew that as the relentless saw of the Dark Angel's perception cut its circle through the past, down and round to the beating heart, it would almost certainly lead to Bernie. She felt that this was as inevitable as was the final battle that would come between her and Sorush. But she was now realizing that in order to fight this she needed to know more of Bernie, and therefore of his mother.

She looked away from the window. She could see the power of the seeds that Violet had sowed in her sons and could sense many matters unresolved. Bernie didn't remember her at all and instead had created a fantasy of a gentle and perfumed maiden, like something out of his Arfer; a Guinevere with flowing, golden locks, who would sing him to sleep and stroke his hair when he cried.

But for Ronnie she was a distant, constantly dismissed ache. Mirabelle had the feeling that of the three, he was probably the most like Violet, and although he wouldn't have admitted it, he was the one who missed her the most. She wondered if a similar pulse or talent didn't beat in both mother and son. His ache, perhaps, was the absence of her encouragement and guidance.

And then Arnie? Why had he disappeared at the same time as his mother? He was the loudest, the most commanding and sometimes the most gregarious of the three brothers, and at the same time, thought Mirabelle, he was also the most unhappy. Violet was a closed book as far as he was concerned. If he ever mentioned her, it was aggressively, and then he would shut up. She was like a wound in him that wouldn't heal. Why?

She turned and looked through the half-open bedroom door to Henry's living room beyond. She could see Arnie's legs as he lay back on the cushions talking to Henry. Ronnie had just come in from stashing the Snipe.

Ronnie sat on the cushions near Arnie as Henry opened a small wooden cabinet, half hidden by about 500 neatly stacked vinyl albums on the other side of the room. He turned and smiled at Arnie. 'Same cabinet, same drawer, Arn. Same stash. You're right, man, nothing changes.'

Arnie grinned. No-one knew Henry like he did. Henry looked round. 'See, Ron, me an' your brother crashed together for years. I don't remember any of it, tell you the truth.' He laughed and tapped the cabinet. 'Want some black?' He took out an inch cube of hashish wrapped in cellophane. 'Yeah?' He offered it to Ron.

'No thanks, mate.' Ronnie looked away.

'Bernie's asleep, isn't he?' Arnie looked at Ron and then round at the doorway into the bedroom.

'No thanks anyway,' said Ronnie.

'Look at this, man.' Henry had poked through his drug drawer and was holding up a small tin. 'Does your acid mature with age?' He opened the tin and held it out for Arnie to see the small blue tabs inside. 'California Sunshine. It's the original.' He carefully placed the small tin on the table in front of Arnie. The tone of his voice became serious. 'These were Stella's, Arn. Her last bequest.' He kneeled on the floor on the other side of the table, picked up cigarette papers and began to roll a joint with the Paki black. It was time to tell Arnie what he didn't know.

Arnie had pretty well got it already. 'What do you mean, her last bequest? What are you talking about, Henry?'

Henry tried a smile, but it cracked and froze on his lips. He said, 'She's dead, man,' and then looked away and began to break up a Silk Cut and sprinkle the tobacco onto the papers.

Arnie tensed. 'Stella?' There was a quiet in the room.

'She went under a train, Arn. Piccadilly Circus. About two weeks ago. That's why I thought you'd come back, see? I thought you'd come back 'cos you'd heard about it, man. It was in the *Standard*. Just a couple of lines, not much.' He stopped and looked up at Arnie, his face full of doubt and pain. 'Acid flashback, man, on Red Leb. Straight under, no fucking about. Instant death.'

'How do you know?'

'What?' Henry was getting upset. 'They told me, man. I was at the fucking funeral.'

'I mean how do you know it was a flashback?' Arnie felt like he'd just walked into a wall and was numb with shock.

Henry looked at him squarely. 'I lived with her for seven years, Arn. I knew what was going on in here.' He touched the side of his head. 'It was a flashback. She took the jump, you know?'

There was a silence. 'Oh.' Arnie couldn't speak. Stella had been his girl for such a long time.

'She came back, see, a couple of years after you'd gone back home.' Henry looked guilty. 'You didn't show up, Arn. You didn't get in touch. You didn't seem interested, man.' He stopped, uncertain. 'I didn't think you'd mind.' He lit the joint with the flame of his Zippo and inhaled. 'I mean you didn't even bother to call me, did you?' He looked hurt.

'Stella's dead.' Arnie stated it and looked up at Henry as if it was a question.

'Yeah.' Henry took an acid tab out of the tin and put it on the table in front of Arnie. 'That's for you. The last will and testament of the Acid Queen.' He took a toke on the joint and handed it to Arnie. Then he got up and put the little tin of acid in his pocket. 'Got to go and make bread, you know? Sorry about everything.' He wanted to hug Arnie, but he went out. After a second Arnie slowly leaned forward and picked up the little tab of acid.

'Don't take that stuff, Arn.'

'Why not, Ron?' Arnie placed a tab on his tongue. 'It's from Stella.' He swallowed and lay back into the cushions. 'Starship Stella.'

Mirabelle turned back to the window. Now she also wanted to know.

$$6$$

Mihr looked up at Sorush. 'And the eldest? Where did he go?'
The Ancient Angel began the incantation.

Arnie was in his twenties. It was a few years after he'd left the restaurant. His shoulder-length hair was the same as it had been, but it was dirtier and his beard had grown longer. He was very drugged and swayed uncertainly as he tried to walk along the corridor of the damp and filthy high-rise. Every now and again he fell against a graffiti-covered wall and then pushed himself back upright as he slowly made his way towards the red light and pounding sounds coming from an open doorway at the end of the corridor.

'This is a long trip, Henry!' He laughed at the tilting walls and ceiling, announcing himself to no-one in particular, including Henry who wasn't there. Then he fell through the doorway into the light and the blast and Henry came through the doped-out throng. He was in his twenties, like Arnie, but more beautiful. The hair, the flares, the velvet, even the lapels suited him. It was an age and fashion he never grew out of.

'Too late, man.' Henry giggled through a head full of chemicals.

'Too late for what?' Arnie leaned back against the wall by the open doorway and could feel himself sliding slowly down towards the booze-washed lino.

'Too late to get wrecked, man.'

'You can't be too late to get wrecked, Henry.' Arnie continued the slide.

'You can, man.'

Arnie had reached the floor and began to speak perfect sense. 'See, man, getting wrecked isn't like getting a train you know? I mean there's no timetable for wrecking the train, man. You can do it any time.' He began to giggle with Henry, who'd joined him on the lino.

'I see what you mean, Arn. But it's too late for you.'

'Yeah?' Arnie considered it. 'Why?'

'We done all the acid.'

It seemed perfectly reasonable to Arnie. 'Oh right.' But that old brain-train wouldn't stop working. 'Er, Henry, I just thought of something.'

'What's that?'

'It's not too late for me to get wrecked, man.'

'It is, man.' Henry had his theory and was sticking to it.

'It's not.' Arnie watched his finger as he wagged it.

'Why not?'

'Because I'm wrecked already.' He looked at Henry and they both collapsed against each other in hysteria. 'We're so fucking wrecked!' Arnie shouted it out and then stopped in a weird and immediate moment of paranoia. The most beautiful girl he had ever seen in his life was standing over him and looking directly down. Her shoes were stacked five inches high, her dress was deep orange velvet, stretched over curved thighs that were on a level with his eyes, her neck and shoulders were covered in beads that twinkled, her eyes were round and blue, her lips were red and wet, and there was a pink flower in her thick red hair. Arnie couldn't move.

'You know who this is?' Henry had caught the moment.

'Stella.' She announced herself in a husky northern voice and crouched in front of Arnie.

'This is the Acid Queen,' said Henry.

Arnie couldn't speak. Stella placed a hand on either side of his face and pulled him towards her. Then she kissed him and then she kissed him again, running her tongue round inside his lips and then pushing it into his mouth. After the wrap-around of the century, which seemed to Arnie to have lasted about as long, she pulled away and looked at him with her huge stoned eyes. 'Hello.'

Arnie couldn't remember speaking again until the next morning. Stella had pulled him from the floor and then held his hand as she'd led him out. He found out later that she had a flat in the same shit-block, but he didn't recall the journey, just her swaying backside and serious eyes in front of him. A door had opened and closed and he remembered the smell of incense, the sound of 'Honky Tonk Woman' and her patchouli. She gave him a tab of her own acid, which he remembered was pale blue, then she gently pushed him onto the bed against big cushions and slid out of her dress and underwear, but kept her beads on. His clothes were coming off. He couldn't take his eyes off her. They fell naked onto the bed and rolled over and over each other, their lips and hands were everywhere, and it took hours; the acid turned her into an Indian queen, she was alive with power, she tingled with colour; lights flashed behind his eyes, his erection came and went and came again; she was wet in his mouth and he was huge in hers; her skin was fluorescent, his was pink and then red, then white; she was curving, swaying flesh, he was softer than he'd ever been; then he was thick inside her and didn't come; she moved like a silver eel, she gasped and he groaned; his head was between her thighs, he could smell her; she was sweet and perfumed and left her saliva on his stomach so it gleamed in the moonlight; he wanted to eat her because she was marshmallow and slipped his tongue between the curve of her buttocks; he took her breasts in his hand and squeezed and squashed and smothered, then filled his mouth as her nipples hardened and softened; and then they rolled over and over again as his hardness went and then she licked the limpness back into the shape she desired; and finally he penetrated her body of mountain fullness and everything and began to rock back and forth on top of her, faster and faster as she clutched at him, pulling his thighs into her, bucking beneath him as he felt his come begin its journey from the pit of his gut into his balls, that he thought were going to explode, and his cock got harder and bigger than he believed possible, and stiffer and thicker, and strained to break into her totally as he gripped her shoulders, pulling on them to bring her onto him and split her apart if he could, as she heaved up until she was a foot off the bed, opening herself, her legs a yard apart, her toes pushing down on the covers and him fucking back at her, trying to pierce her soul-breaking loveliness with his dick and then force all of him into her cave of a cunt, because his gut throbbed like he'd never known, and she shouted from the back of her throat, and he gasped and then cried as everything went and he came like that old wrecked train, blowing burning-bright scalding spasms of sperm, scream, spunk and the extreme cream of unrestrained and nuclear force into the great cavern opened before him, sending the torrent in tidal waves up through her intestines and belly to drown her inside heart in white, as her body turned pink neon beneath him and the wires fused and he saw only the pale-blue light of her eyes, sparking and scary, as her thick hair grew and caught fire, taking him by the shoulders and wrapping them and his quivering arse in a scarlet, smoking haze, and holding him there as he shook and shuddered and blew a load he never imagined he carried and which left him as completely and utterly empty as a sea that had drained; and slowly, over the hours, he subsided back into her and down onto the bed again, until the shivering stopped and he felt her hands fall slowly from his back, and his cock, little, limp and wet, fell out from the ledge and he felt cold. That's all he remembered. Until he opened his eyes the next morning.

She was standing by a hotplate on the other side of the room, making tea. She was still naked and her skin was very white in the midday light. Arnie squinted and watched as she bent to throw away a tea bag. Her arse was full and glorious, her waist was small, there were a few moles on her back, which was covered by her thick curly hair, and he could see the edge of her breasts under her arms as she straightened. She turned and looked at him.

'Hello, Arnie.' He didn't hear anything for a second because the full-frontal sight of her tits and thighs just about blocked out the rest of the world. 'I said, hello.' Her voice was heavy but soft.

'Hello.'

'You were nice last night.'

'Come back to bed.' He couldn't take his eyes off her and was hard again already.

She put the teapot down. 'All right.' And she got back under the covers and took his balls and cock into her hand.

'Where are you from?'

'Manchester.'

Then they fucked again. It was slower than the night, nothing oral, just a straight and delightful cruise back into the woman he had fallen totally in love with. He felt himself being enveloped by her. Her arms were strong, her heart beat with a deep thud, her mouth was big, her eyes bigger and her hair bigger than that. He knew she was much stronger than him and when they had finished he had to turn away so she wouldn't see him cry. She stroked his back as he said her name: 'Stella.'

'It means star,' she said. He turned over towards her. She was lying on her side, facing him, with her elbow on the pillow, propping her head on her hand. He put his face into her breasts and his arm round her waist, pulling himself into her, feeling the warmth of her body all the way down his own. 'You can move in if you want,' she whispered.

He moved his head back. 'I thought you were Henry's.'

'Well, what are you doing here then?'

'Uh? I don't know.'

'I don't belong to anybody.' She stroked his hair. 'But I like you, Arnie.' She said it like 'Arneh' in her thick accent and he smiled.

'Arneh,' he mimicked her.

She rolled out of the bed. 'You'll learn not to take the piss out of me.' She stood in front of him, pulling on a deep-green satin dressing gown and wrapping up her body out of sight.

'Don't do that.' He wanted to see her some more.

'Want some tea?' She smiled.

'Yeah. Stella. Thanks.' He was very happy and watched as she turned and went back to the hotplate. He liked the way she did things. Everything about her was certain. This girl knew where the mugs went on a tray. He lay in her bed and smelled her sweat and sweet scent

266

on the sheets, as the chemical sludge began to drain from his brain. 'I like you, Stell.'

She turned holding the milk. 'Have you got a job?'

'Ah? No.'

'Do you want one?'

'Ah? No.'

'You can work for me if you like?'

'Ah? OK.'

She brought the tray over and put it down on a chest by the bed. 'Milk and sugar?'

'Both.' He watched as she poured the tea.

'You can deal for me.'

'Deal what?'

'Where've you been, Arnie?'

'Ah?' The question seemed to upset him and he didn't reply for a moment. 'I don't know.'

She sat on the bed and held out his tea. 'Sit up.' He did and took the mug. 'I bring them home and you buy them from me at a cut rate, then you take them out and sell them for what you can get.' She sipped her tea. 'All right?'

'Acid?'

'Speed, some hash sometimes. Whatever you want really.'

'Where do you get it?'

'That's my business. We all have to have our little secrets, don't we?' She smiled. 'What's yours, Arnie?'

'Ah?' He turned away and looked out of the window. Outside was dull and grey, just shitty, rainy tops of houses. 'Don't ask.'

'I think you've got a very big one, Arnie.' She giggled and he turned back to her with a grin. 'Secret, I mean.' She kissed his shoulder. 'I'll find out, won't I? When you move into Starship Stella.'

Arnie looked worried. 'Will you?'

'Of course I will. You move in with someone you find out everything, don't you? All the little weaknesses. That's what secrets are, aren't they? That's why we hide them. Because they're weaknesses.' She looked at him. 'I doubt if you'll be able to hide anything from me.'

'Won't I?'

'No. Aren't you a lucky man?'

He looked down at his tea. For a second he wanted to get out of the bed and run, then he looked back up at her. Her eyes were quizzical and blue. He didn't know whether she loved him. 'And I live here?'

'If you behave.' She smiled. 'And if you fuck me like you did last night.'

Which is what he did for days and years, or was it months and hours? Arnie, man, didn't know if up was down, or what a clock did, or which one was sideways. He fucked Stell though, and every now and again said, 'Right on,' and took one fucking big heap of dope and acid and . . . ? And sold so much that he was the biggest dealer on the block, which would have made him happy if he could have remembered. Sometimes he screwed his eyes up tight and stood in front of Stella's mirror and wondered who he was. It was not a question that made much sense. A lot of the time he had bread and then didn't again, and she bought him shoes and maybe a spangled shirt, or like this jacket in chinoise, or some pink thing that was far out or outasight. He was in a place where he'd marooned himself because he was so desperate and unhappy if he ever stopped to think about it, which he couldn't afford to do. Acid took him to the edge and he peered over into the molten orange and red of his own insanity, daring himself to take the jump and fly down and never come back – and he knew he wouldn't if ever he leaped, which was why he didn't, because something, some centre of Arnie wanted to stay onside here and now and know it.

For a long time Stella pursued him, trying to get inside, crack the nut and eat the kernel. But his fruit was his own and had gone rotten, and he wouldn't let anyone near it in case, without it, the shell shattered and he'd retch at the stench and sickness he knew was inside. Anyway, Stella was too powerful and her questions too blunt. He needed her warmth, not her control, and she was too tight and too driven to see it. She made him hide even more. He was static, unmoving, staring at the ceiling for hours on the cushions, while inside he ran and ran until his head went completely. And it was dope for breakfast, dinner and tea, with acid down the pub, in the squat, on the street, in his brain, arms, legs and feet. Arnie wasn't cracking up, he was cracked up already and was in free-fall down the deepest chasms of his psyche; voice croaked, thoughts awry, head skimmed, blown by the sweet breath of little blue pills, sometimes into purple hurricanes, other times on the perfumed breezes of grass and apple trees. Stella was his parachute, even though he knew she would detach some time and take her silk elsewhere. Without her he was a split-vein, bloody suicide in the bath, and maybe he kind of looked forward to it.

He went crazy one day when he saw Stella fucking someone else. He destroyed her flat and threatened to kill himself. Even the Acid Queen was scared and began to understand and so reject the responsibility she'd taken on. All this was leading somewhere and Arnie knew it could only be down. This was just a rehearsal. It all crashed on a dope deal.

Arnie sat in the passenger seat of an old Ford Anglia. His head lolled back and his mouth was open as he looked out at the dark night and the rain splashing hard onto the windscreen. Stella jumped into the driving seat. She was drenched, her red hair plastered around her face, and she was furious. 'They've gone, Arnie.'

'Who's gone?' He didn't so much see her by him as feel her energy, and he began to put up the walls, fearing the worst.

'Arnie!' Stella wasn't fucking about. 'I want my money!'

He giggled. 'He said it was outasight.'

'Fucking stop that, Arnie.'

'He did. It's true. I gave him the stuff and I said, "Where's the bread?" And he said, "It was outasight."' He giggled again. 'It's true, Stell.'

She drew back her hand and hit him hard across his face with the flat of her palm. It made his nose bleed. 'Arnie!'

'Look what you done,' he said as he looked at the blood on his hand.

'I gave you a hundred tabs and I want fifty pounds!'

He whispered, 'Don't hurt me, Stell.'

'Money!'

He looked up at her, the snot from his nose beginning to mix with the blood on his hand. He was getting pathetic and knew it. 'I haven't been straight for so long, Stella.'

'You don't have any chances left, Arnie.'

'Please, Stell.'

'Get out.'

'Stell.'

'Get out.' She meant it and sat, perfectly still, both hands on the steering wheel, looking at him. There wasn't much he could do. He became aware of his left hand rising and then coming slowly down on the door handle. These were like the last moments, or at least coming close, and should be concentrated on properly. The door opened and he felt the rain on his knee. He took a quick look at her, then turned his head away so he could see the water skimming the gutter below him. He waited a second, then put his left foot into the gutter and half rolled out of the car. He didn't have time to slam the door; she'd leaned across and closed it herself, then keyed the ignition and pulled away, leaving him there, getting pissed on and wondering what had happened.

He walked for a while, feeling the water seep down inside his collar, probably giving him pneumonia. Cars flashed past sending up sprays of couldn't give a fuck, so why should he? He felt in his pocket, he still had most of the tabs. He'd lied to Stella as usual. Even as he was pleading for her not to throw him out, he knew he could make it better by giving her at least some of what she wanted, but he couldn't do it, lying had become his real habit. Anyway these tabs were his lifeline. Not her. He wouldn't be Stelled-up any more. Good night Stell. Then he had a notion. He'd sell the stuff and give her the money. Simple. And he'd save a few for himself. Simpler. Except there was a problem. Not much of what he'd been doing in the place back there with the banjy man had anything to do with the tabs, had it? This was all another lie, a lie beneath the lie. How many lies were there in this house of lies? He tried to count them, starting with the roof and going down through the floors until he reached the basement. For a moment he stood there, seeing little lies crawl around on a shitty concrete floor. Then he started to giggle in the drizzle. This is fucking all right! He had what he needed in his pocket. Yeah! He felt like a man who truly didn't know where he was going, which was OK by him in that kind of yeah-man, know-what-I-mean, kind of way. His way. Henry's way. This way. He walked down the road as he popped a pill and estimated he had about twenty minutes before he'd be in some other time zone.

Which was where the band played. He arrived at the cash hole and fumbled around for something to give the girl. Then he found a fiver in his pocket, which helped him remember that he'd made some money from the deal with the man, and that was another lie he'd told Stella, but the notes were in his hand and he could see them and that made him feel better. Or did it? It was so fucking confusing. What was Stella talking about? Tabs? He didn't get it. That wasn't what it was about. He hadn't gone to Mr Banjy for anything about acid. It was another thing. This other thing was another lie which wouldn't quite surface. The girl was trying to give him some change. Inside the band was crashing about and there was a weird smell of wet and incense as beardy freaks paraded past him in damp Afghans. He leaned against a cream wall like he was the dealer he imagined himself to be and kind of knew he was. Some acid-head had recognized the fantasy and was trying to do a deal as Henry came up and said, 'I'm so paranoid, man.'

The acid-head who wanted to do the deal had taken his tab but wouldn't go away. 'You owe me five bob,' he said.

'You want change?' Arnie looked at him.

'I'm so fucking paranoid,' said Henry and he really was.

'Er, yeah man. Five bob,' the acid-head said.

'You want a receipt, man, or what?' asked Arnie, being cool.

'That rain is real, you know? I was so paranoid,' said Henry.

'Give me five bob.' The acid-head was getting heavy in a kind of minor way.

'I thought like a hundred little guys were tapping me on the head, you know. Pitter-patter, pitter-patter . . .'

'. . . pitter-patter,' said the acid-head.

'What?'

'I knew what you were going to say next, man,' said the acid-head.

'Were you in the rain, man?' Henry thought he'd found someone who understood.

'See you, man.' It was all getting too heavy for the head, who took off, forgetting his five bob.

Henry turned to Arnie. 'I came in here and it stopped, you know?'

'What did?'

'The pitter-patter.'

'I owe him five bob,' said Arnie.

'Who? I'm so paranoid. I need some acid.' Henry looked at Arnie. 'You got any, man?'

'You got to pay me for it.'

'Why?'

'It's Stella, man. You know, I got to try and get some bread for her. It's her acid, right?'

'Give me one for free,' said Henry.

'All right.' Arnie gave Henry a tab. There was one wire in his mind that sparked, all property is theft, and one that went nowhere and another that ran directly into Stella's head. They were beginning to fuse.

'Why don't you have one?'

'Yeah. Why not?' Arnie put a tab on his tongue and the fusion was complete. Property, nowhere and Stella. He felt happy about it.

Henry stared at him for a while. 'You know that's my third tab today, including yesterday, and one of them's so speedy, you know? Why are you standing here?'

'I'm selling acid.'

'Are you? What's going on?'

'I don't know.'

'That's what I thought. See you, man.' Henry disappeared into the hall and stood in front of the band until they stopped playing an hour later. Arnie stayed at the back. He'd cleared himself a yard or two and began to freak because the band was getting to him, driving him crazy. He began to come apart as he danced, mania on skids. Faster and faster, he reeled and split as his insanity became physical and his body spreadeagled. His brain finally exploded a foot off the ground as he was trying to leap up into a heaven of blue sky, clean air and fluffy blanket love. He came down with his knees by his chin and crashed hard onto the ridge of floorboard reality as the lead guitar climaxed a riff. An hour or two later Henry dumped him in front of Stella.

She sat cross-legged on the floor, leaning against the wall in their flat, surrounded by candles and incense. Something weird came out of the stereo as she smoked a Rothmans and stared at the heap of Arnie in front of her after Henry had staggered away. Arnie's eyes blinked and he saw his crimson Stella/Shiva with bangled arms and legs of desire, he saw his empress of hell and destiny, his henna'd goddess in all the illuminated glory of the starship, his one and only Acid Queen. And she was full of wrath. He pressed his face into the floor, scared shitless.

'I know your secret,' she whispered.

'What's that?' His hand began to crawl across the rug towards her.

'You've been dealing heroin, Arnie.'

'Sorry.'

'You've had your chance.'

'Sorry.'

272

'You can have the flat. Stella's gone.' She stubbed her cigarette on the back of his hand and got up. 'Bye, Arnie.'

He hadn't noticed the boxes and cases already packed by the door and didn't look up. He lay with the pain of the burn on his hand as she went. He was trying to concentrate on the weave of the rug. This was a real last moment and every detail was important.

Henry found him there the next day. The place was empty except for the table, a couple of chairs and the mattress on the floor reeking of patchouli, Stella's reminder of what he'd lost.

'Stella's split, man,' said Henry.

The saw of the past cut deeper and deeper. Mihr was surprised at what came next. It was the fates, as she knew the father would have said. How else could it be that after all those years the eldest would meet both his estranged parents, and on the same day?

Arnie'd become a fully-fledged, needle-scarred and decorated junkie. He'd evened it up and got it normalized, so it was a way of life, just like any other. He made his needs by dealing mostly, some minor thieving and a bit off the state. He and Henry lived together in Stell's old flat. Sometimes he felt better. The heroin was like marshmallow. You put your head in it and couldn't see, or even better, couldn't feel. It even stopped the flashbacks from the acid. He got it routined. Hash for breakfast, first smack around midday, second vein evening, and usually that was about it, except for tea and cornflakes every now and then, with a continuous supply of reefer, which usually just came his way because of the company he kept. Henry was the man, a good man, Henry was his brother, because he didn't want to think any more about that other brother and that baby and all that over there in some distant universe. It was better to just deal the horse and let the years slide by.

Seven years after Arnie had left the restaurant, Charlie found him. He parked the Snipe, got out and stood at the base of the block in the west, looking up at the grey concrete and peeled green paint on the frames and balconies. He wasn't sure why he was there and hesitated. Did he need this? He was a survivor and he knew that sometimes you had to be ruthless, so why didn't he just let Arnie go? He was bound to bring

273

trouble. And he'd had enough of that since Vi had gone. There was Bernie for a start. She hadn't only left him holding the baby, but one that wouldn't crawl until he was two, or talk until he was five. They'd said it must be brain damage, but no-one knew for sure. Fucking doctors; if they couldn't work it out, who could? But Charlie had survived; he was the captain of the ship and with Harriet and Sophie and a succession of girls he'd brought the boy along and accepted him and then accepted him some more, until he'd become what he was, a normal boy whose brain didn't grow but whose body did. Even at seven he was a giant. And everybody loved Bernie, all the custom, the piss artists in the club, the reps, the merchants; for them the kid was a mascot, a good-luck charm, always had been and always would be. He'd helped Charlie, too, that was for sure. When Ronnie had withdrawn, not knowing how to deal with things, Bernie had grinned or farted or just been around like a ray of sunshine. He'd warmed up the cold of Violet's absence. Charlie hadn't searched much for her, he'd let her go. He knew that to look for her was to imagine, and to imagine was to tap the core of his rage and allow the burn to seep like acid into his stomach and throat, making him feel sick. So he turned away. Everything was anguish anyway, so what do you do but get on with it? It was simple enough, life was to be lived and lived well. If he ceased to believe that he would cease to be what he was. Charlie Lack didn't whine, he didn't moan and he wasn't short of friends or courage. Whatever else, he would survive.

So he looked up at the blocks and asked himself again why he was here. It was by chance that he'd heard where his son was. A whisky salesman had seen him first on the street and reported it back. Knowing the rough location, Charlie had put a word or two into the ears of some coppers he knew. Apparently Arnie wasn't hard to find; the local police knew him well. A few weeks later, after a few late-night drinks for the uniforms, he'd been given the address in the high-rise. It had taken him a month to decide to come, and now he'd arrived, he was suffering a bad attack of the nerves. He started towards the entrance of the block, still not clearly understanding what he was doing or why. But a son was a son and the eldest more so, so he kept going, and then had to climb the stairs because the lift wasn't working.

He hit Arnie at a bad time, in both the general and the particular. In general because his deal structure was breaking up. His first connection had got busted, the area supplier had done a runner and Arnie was back on the street like every other smackhead looking for a fix. In particular this time was bad because, having finally scored, he'd just wrapped the ligature, pumped the vein and the needle had broken, so he'd had to jack with the broken end, which was bloody and messy. He'd taken the hit, but had the idea that he'd lost most of it and so felt edgy that he wouldn't get the release and the fade. He lay back on the mattress and closed his eyes, hoping for impact, but feeling bad. When he opened his eyes his father was standing over him.

'Hello, son.' It was difficult for Charlie to speak, he was so shocked. Henry hadn't so much let him in as opened the door and then staggered back out of sight. The place looked like a doss-house and couldn't have been cleaned for months. As for Arnie, well that was the worst. There was no hiding what was going on. The syringe had fallen by the bed, there was silver paper, a spoon, matches, a bottle of water and an empty paper wrap. Charlie was a boozer but he'd been to the pictures. His son was a junkie. The boy looked about twenty years older; his clothes were filthy and his beard and hair were knotted and bedraggled. Charlie looked down and waited. Arnie stared back with blank eyes and didn't reply.

'Arnie?' Charlie tried again, then turned and saw Henry had come in behind. 'How long's he been like this?'

'Ah? Dunno man. Long time. Who are you?'

'I'm his father.'

'Oh right.' Henry couldn't think of anything else to say.

Charlie crouched by the bed and touched Arnie's arm. 'Arnie? Can you hear me? It's me. Dad.'

'Go away.' Arnie's voice was dead and Charlie wasn't sure he'd been recognized.

'Do you know who I am?' Charlie asked. Arnie didn't reply, just looked. 'I should have come before, I know that. I'm very sorry.' Even as he said it, Charlie was beginning to understand why he was there. The love for his wife and son that he'd decided to crush all those years ago hadn't gone away, it had lain locked in some deep place and was now hammering like his heart on the door, desperate to be out, breathing and living. 'I was angry, son. I'm sorry. You know Mum went, don't you?' Arnie hadn't known. He stared at his father, nothing much was sinking in. Charlie went on, 'You haven't seen her, have you

275

son?' It was all coming out, his denial was creaking and cracking. 'We're still a family, mate.' He touched his son again, but this time it was as if his fingers were electricity and Arnie recoiled in shock.

'Get out!'

'Arnie?'

'Get out! Get the fuck out! I don't know who you are!' Arnie scrabbled back on the mattress. 'Henry, what the fuck d'you let him in for?'

Charlie stood, not knowing what to do. 'Arnie, hang on a minute ...'

'I know who you are, you're my fucking old man. Why'd you think I left? 'Cos I didn't want to fucking see you again, that's why! So fuck off! Get out!' Charlie didn't move. If he'd have spoken he'd have cried. Arnie shouted again, 'Get out!'

Charlie turned back to Henry, who looked away and said, 'You heard what he said, man.'

Charlie didn't know what to do. He said again, 'Arnie, it's me.' Arnie just stared. 'Talk to me, son.' There was nothing but hostility coming from Arnie. After a moment Charlie lowered his face, turned and walked past Henry, who said, 'See you, man.'

After Charlie had gone, there was a silence. Arnie looked down at the stained sheets, the mattress and his works littering the floor in front of him. The front door had slammed before he said, 'Dad?' Charlie was at the end of the corridor and beginning to descend the stairs before he began to scrabble off the bed. 'Henry?'

'Yeah?'

'Help me . . .' He fell as he stepped off the mattress and Henry watched as he unsteadily stood again. 'Help me.' Henry couldn't cope and sat down on a crate as Arnie staggered across the floor to the door of the flat. He tried to pull it open, but lost his grip and fell backwards. He got up again and this time managed to pull the door towards him and then tumble through it. He half fell into the corridor and hit the wall on the other side. He pushed himself upright and turned. The corridor was empty. He looked towards the window at the far end. By the time he'd got there Charlie had come out of the entrance below and was walking towards the Snipe. Arnie looked down through the glass. 'Dad!' He hammered on the window. 'Dad! Dad!' He couldn't believe it, Charlie was getting into the Snipe. 'Dad!' He started to thump at the glass with the side of his fists, then his elbows. 'Dad! Dad!' Charlie was reversing the car. 'Dad!' Arnie punched at the window, desperate for a hole in it to let his words through. 'Dad! I'm sorry, Dad!' He stood back and started to kick, then punch again at the glass. 'Dad! I'm sorry.' The window finally smashed and he lunged towards it as the glass fell and Charlie, too far below, pulled away in the Snipe. 'Dad! Dad!' Arnie flailed at the window as if the remaining glass was preventing his plea getting out. Blood began to run down his arms and wrists. 'Dad!' He yelled it as far as he could across the air, but the Snipe was moving away. Arnie smashed and punched some more, the skin on his arms was being torn to ribbons by the glass. 'Dad! Wait!' The shout echoed round the blocks, but the car turned a corner and disappeared from his view. 'I'm sorry!' Arnie fell back against the wall and slid down as Henry came out of the flat doorway.

'Fucking hell, Arnie.'

'That was my dad.' Arnie covered his head with his arms and his blood ran over his face and down his neck. The heroin had finally hit and the next thing he remembered was waking up in casualty.

Violet knew nothing of this. She'd worked in the boutique all day and hadn't noticed as Charlie had passed within yards of her, on the way to the high-rise in the Snipe. He'd come back the same way. He was feeling very, very bad, and the vision of his damaged son burned so deep in his mind that to defend himself was the only option. Sorry Arnie. The door on you must be shut, locked, bolted, bricked up and let the weeds grow over it. He was actually in a deep state of shock, but by the time he parked the Snipe in the backstreet garage, he'd encapsulated the burn, breathed in and forced a lightness into his step. 'He wasn't there,' he lied to Harriet as he walked into the restaurant.

A few hours later Violet locked up the shop. As she'd got older, she'd grown into herself. Tom had been right. He'd seen the jewel inside her and mere recognition had been enough to make it gleam. She'd opened three shops for him over the years; she'd had the nose and bought and sold successfully, but the rag trade was for merchants (like Charlie) and she wanted something else. She was beginning to design the clothes herself, and although it was still early days, her style was beginning to evolve. She wore her own clothes. They were simple and elegant, with a spice of danger. She was her own best mannequin, her accessories tasteful, and the style unobtrusive but undeniably

European sexy. It hadn't taken long for the custom to notice. 'Where did you get that? Can I . . . ?' Orders were taken and Vi had begun.

She put on her coat, stood by the table in the basement storeroom and looked down on her latest series of sketches. Samples of material, weave and print were stapled onto the heavy paper. She was proud of them, but they frightened her too. This path was high and clear, but her very shine of success seemed to cast deep shadows of terrible loneliness. She was scared that to achieve anything else might make her feel worse. She tucked them under her arm and went quickly up the stairs, through the shop and out into the bleak and crowded street.

It was beginning to rain and she shielded her sketchbook under her coat as she walked. For some reason she began to think about Arnie. At odd times, when she least expected it, unsought images of her past would come to the surface of her mind, triggered by some sight, or scene, or smell. Sometimes she'd allow them to dwell and could smile or shed a tear, unless they were of Bernie. These were refused admission and her mind's eye would refocus fast with a blink and a shudder. This time it was Arnie. As usual with her eldest, the memory was accompanied by a sharp shaft of guilt and desperate remorse. She walked on quickly along the crowded pavement trying to shake him from her mind. Someone nudged her and she nearly dropped the pad. The sketches were loose in the covers and she had to stand still for a moment to repack them inside. As she was about to move on, she stopped.

She was by an intersection and five yards ahead of her, waiting to cross the street, was the son she'd just been thinking about. He stood sideways on to her and she was shocked, as Charlie had been, by his unkempt and filthy state. His hair and beard were wet from the rain, his jacket collar was torn and the arm she could see was bandaged. She stood, unable to move as the crowd moved quickly past on either side of her. She didn't know what to do and there was nothing in her experience to help her. How many mothers had done what she had done? Finally she turned and walked a yard away from him, then stopped again and looked back. This time he was looking at her. Now it was his turn for confusion. He turned away to cross the street, but the traffic wouldn't allow it. She began to walk towards him, at first tentatively and then more quickly. By the time she had got to him, her momentum was almost enough for her to hold out her arms and hug him to her. But not quite. The shame in her refused the contact. She stood facing him and then touched his arm with her free hand. 'Arnie.' He didn't reply and she looked down, noticing that both his arms were bandaged. 'What have you done?'

This was all too much for Arnie. It was the second time that day he'd been confronted by sudden and unexpected horror. He felt as if he was in some kind of screwed-up, primal nightmare. He'd been in the hospital for five hours and all he wanted was his next fix. He stared at her as if she'd come from some other planet.

His silence drove her on. 'Would you like a coffee? Or a drink?' She tried a smile but the normality of it cracked in the face of such extreme circumstance. 'I think there's a pub down there.' She pointed but he still didn't answer. They stood on the corner, jostled by wet commuters and angry skirmishing traffic. She tried again. 'Arnie?'

As with Charlie, his first reaction was to shout, run and get this obscene flashback out of his sight, but his state had changed and now his drug count was shakily low. This time he was more vulnerable. He said, 'You don't want to see me, do you?' He was right, he could see it in her eyes. 'You wish this had never happened.'

'It's a shock, Arnie.'

There was another silence between them in the clamour as pedestrians pushed past trying to cross the street. Arnie suddenly spoke. It wasn't anything he meant to say. 'We had a family once.'

'Don't, Arnie.' She looked away.

'I had a mum and a dad, and I had brothers.'

'Please.' She suddenly realized the meaning of what he'd said and looked up at him. 'Don't you see them then?'

'Course I don't.'

'Not at all?'

'No.' His tone was bleak and final and what he said hit her very hard.

'Go and see them, Arnie. Please go and see them for . . .'

He interrupted her. 'Why should I do anything for you?'

'For yourself.'

'Why should I do anything for me?' He asked her directly, as if his value was hardly worth her considering.

She didn't know what to say. 'I . . .'

'You can go now.' Again it was flat. She could have understood anger, but this bleakness was defeating her.

She tried to reach him again. 'Do you want a coffee?'

'No.'

She felt like she was in some kind of carbon monoxide hell. They were bumping into her, horns were blasting, a news-vendor was screaming. 'I can't talk to you here, Arnie!'

'So go.'

Tears came to her eyes. 'It was my fault, Arnie! Go home. Please go home. It was me!' Someone hit her full in the back and she dropped her sketchbook into the road. The drawings scattered under the wet tyres of the passing cars. 'Oh no!' She ran a few yards along the street and managed to rescue a sketch from the gutter as a bus ran over the bulk of the pad, breaking its spine and squashing it into the road and rain. She came back towards Arnie holding the one sketch she'd retrieved.

'Mum?' Arnie hadn't moved, but the word, unheard for so long, had such a resonance that she stopped and looked up at him, clutching the rain-soaked drawing to her wet coat. 'Have you got any money, Mum?'

'Money?'

Arnie had remembered he needed his fix. 'You got a hundred quid?' He was trying his luck, but so what? Who was she anyway, some mother he'd forgot? First things first. 'Or two hundred?'

She was so shocked and desperate to please that she immediately opened her bag. She gave him all the bank notes she had.

'Thanks, Mum. See you.' He walked off into the traffic. She stood on the corner and watched him go as the sketch slid out of her hands into the gutter. She looked down and watched as splashes of rain made the ink run.

Sorush smiled but said nothing. Her wings unfurled and were black against the crimsons and brilliant orange of the dawn sky behind. Kasbeel and the thousand or so of the legion that were visible to Mihr were silent too. Their sharply defined statuesque iron shapes were silhouetted against the brilliant rising sun and spread across the city like a dotted blanket of static menace cutting out all other sound. They surrounded the blazing pinpoint of eternal light that was Mihr. All was still. And then they were gone, leaving the bright rays of the sunrise and the sound of distant traffic.

7

Mirabelle was as sad as Arnie and as lonely as she had sensed Violet had been. It was as if some deep-rooted memory in herself had been ripped open and had left her unbalanced, incomplete and needing love as much as they had done. She was surprised to feel sorry Sorush had gone. She was beginning to feel the ancient need of Mihr for the Dark Angel; not for its own sake, but to cloak and assuage the fear that ran through her. For a second she found herself yearning for those golden times of security and certainty on the Bridge, when she and Sorush had complemented each other so well. There, they were the queens of heaven, and the earth and all its planets were for ever in their thrall. Here, with this family, nothing was sure and there was only the vaguest notion of success or failure. Their lives were the sum total of their action and no more. Could they climb to the sun and leave the material universe behind? This was the question asked, and on the answer given, judgement was made. She'd wanted for a moment to return to the warm interlock with Sorush, but she knew that these she'd come to, these the imperfect, these that exasperated her, these that could be foul and criminal; she knew that these were the source of her being. Their hope was her hope and their desperation, their desire and their failure was what love was. To stand above and judge was to be apart and was to see love, to know it, but not to feel it. Much as Mirabelle wanted to return to the security of her opposite, she knew that her growth and her mission were dependent on her being separate from Sorush. She breathed in and then denied herself the desire that had suddenly overwhelmed her.

She turned and looked at Bernie asleep on Henry's bed. He was snoring gently and his Arfer had become enfolded in the sheets. In some way he had come out of this darkness of the family, and as she watched him she began to think about what Sorush had meant by the deepest point of the past. This point, if it was anything, was the beginning, the moment of cause, and being so, it would touch the profound and therefore release the new. Perhaps it was a moment that was beyond angels.

She leaned forward and touched Bernie's hair, then she turned and looked through the open door into Henry's sitting room. Ronnie was curled like a baby, asleep on Henry's cushions. Arnie lay close to him. He was stretched out and staring at the rising light through the window. Stella's acid was still gliding through his mind.

Ronnie stirred and then opened his eyes. For a second he didn't know where he was and Mirabelle could see the pain cross his face as he recognized the room and the predicament they were in. He sat up and rubbed his face with his palms. 'Arnie? What we gonna do?'

'Dunno.'

'I've been thinking,' he said. 'I think we've definitely got to find her, Arn.'

Arnie stared at the window and said, 'It's all out of control, mate.'

'Arn?'

'Like the old man used to say, it's chaos in the heavens today.' Arnie still hadn't turned from the window. He was watching the sunrise. The reds were turning pink and the oranges, yellow, like those molten chasms of insanity he remembered from years ago. He still had the crazy desire to take the jump and never return, but the colours were bleaching as day rose and he was coming slowly down from the heights of the trip. Thank you, Stella. She was still the star.

Ronnie leaned forward. He needed to talk, even if he wasn't going to get much sense out of Arnie. 'I've been dreaming, Arn. I don't know...' He stopped. It was all sounding pretty stupid already. 'I got to find her. See, I...' He hardly knew what he was talking about. 'It's nothing to do with the restaurant or the flat, I got to talk to her that's all.' He stopped again. 'And I got to get Bernie out of this.'

'Tom Cherry,' said Arnie. Maybe it was the colour in the sky, or perhaps the drug was finally giving Arnie focus.

'What about him?'

'We'll get to her through him.'

'I don't want to go anywhere near Tom Cherry!'

'All right, don't.' Arnie went back to the sky.

'There's things you don't know.'

'There's things you don't know either.' Arnie turned directly to his brother for the first time. 'There was another night once when there was chaos in the heavens and I done a terrible thing.' He turned away again. 'It's an unspeakable thing, mate, and it was a horrible, bloody mess. It's all going to come out. We're going to find her and it's all going to come out.'

'What will, Arn?'

'What I done.' He closed his eyes; the acid was taking a final spin and he didn't need the light from outside any more.

Ronnie pushed himself up from the cushions. 'Arnie?' There was no reply. 'Are you listening? Listen to me, mate, I can't sit here. I got to go out.'

'Take care of yourself, bruv,' Arnie whispered.

Ronnie looked down on him for a second. He had no idea what to do. He looked at the door and then back at his brother. He needed someone to help him. He put his hands deep in his pockets, sunk his chin into his neck and stood for quite a while. Still not knowing what he was doing, he walked to the door and went quietly out.

Bernie woke up immediately. He raised his head from the pillows and looked through into the living room. From his angle, he could just see Arnie's feet and no-one else. 'What's up?'

Mirabelle was still sitting by the window. 'Nothing.'

'Yes, there is. I heard the blinking door. Who done a runner?'

'It's Ronnie.'

'Ronnie? Where's he gone?'

'He's gone for a walk, that's all.'

Bernie sat up. 'The bruvs have got to stick togever.'

'He'll be back soon.'

'How d'you know?'

'I know.'

'He better be.' He raised his voice. 'Arnie!'

'I think he's asleep.'

'That's all right then.' He lay back on the pillows. 'Read us a story, Meebelle.'

'You should go back to sleep.'

'I will in a minute. Read us a story first.'

She picked up the Arfer. 'Which one?'

'Lancelot.'

'You know them all off by heart anyway.'

'Yeah, but now I'm putting in other bits as well.'

She turned the pages. 'Sir Lancelot was alone . . .'

'Poor old geezer.'

'He rode through the gloomy forest thinking of the gorgeous delights of Camelot that he'd left behind . . .'

'All that meat and mead and all that.'

'Ahead of him was a castle belonging to an old and friendly knight . . .'

'Who had a saucer.'

'A sorceress. Go to sleep.'

'What was he doing with a saucer?'

'I don't know! I haven't read it yet!'

'Yes you have, thousands of times. Keep reading.'

'The old knight entertained him royally with all manner of delicacies, but Lancelot's heart was heavy. The old knight said to him, Go to the chapel to relieve the burden on your soul . . .'

'But beware the saucer . . .' Bernie's eyes were beginning to droop.

'So he went to the tiny chapel in the courtyard of the castle and knelt on the stone floor to pray. After a while he fell into a reverie . . .'

'What's that?'

'You know what it is. Don't pretend to be stupid with me, Bernie Lack.' Bernie wasn't paying much attention, so she read on, 'First a beautiful maiden came to him in his dream and he was bewitched. Then he saw a white dove rise from behind the altar, and as it flew up, two wondrous and glistening angels descended. Between them they held a gleaming cup that shone like the rays of the sun. Suddenly the cup burst into flames and hovered above the altar, for it was the Holy Grail. The angels looked to Lancelot to rise and take it into his hands, but he lay weak and sick on the stone floor. Slowly the fire ascended and was gone. It was the closest that Lancelot ever came to the Lord.'

Bernie was snoring again and Mirabelle gently closed the book. She could see Arnie lying quietly in the living room. These lives seemed so wide and so deep. They carried such a weight, not only from their own pasts but from the past of all of them. She looked down at the Arfer and then at the sleeping Bernie. What was he trying to tell her?

8

Ronnie walked through the early morning streets. He knew what he had to do, or at least what one of them had to do, but why did it have to be him? Tom Cherry. He didn't want to call Tom Cherry, did he? He couldn't get the bloke off his mind and it pissed him off. It was bleeding well over twenty years ago. Tom Cherry, Tom Cherry; the name seemed to echo in his footsteps as he walked. That's why he wanted to talk to Mum, wasn't it? He had a little bone to pick there. She was the one who left him up the back of the dress shop with the dirty bastard. Why didn't she work it out? The bloody geezer's hands all over him, up his trouser legs. He was only ten, what was he supposed to do about it? His mum didn't help because she was always asking him to go back! 'What's wrong with Tom?' and all that. How was he supposed to tell her? And why didn't she see what was going on?

And how was he supposed to tell Mathilda when she kept on about things like that? Half the time he couldn't even tell it to himself and there was still a whole bit of it he was blanking. Up his trouser legs, down the back of his shirt, opening his fly, the bastard. He blanked it again and walked. He wanted a word with his mum, that was for sure. He wanted something explained. Not Cherry. Cherry had his own problems. But her, she had to explain herself to him. Explain what? He didn't know what. She'd have to work that out. That was her job. She was his mum, wasn't she?

He stopped. Over the road, by a gents' convenience, was a phone box. He glanced at his watch. It was only six, too early to call yet anyway. He walked on. Maybe he'd come back this way. And he had to keep an eye out for the bleeding law, didn't he? But he wasn't too worried about that. Sooner or later they'd find her and the coppers would have to wait. And they would wait, not because they wanted to, or because the brothers wanted them to, but because they were usually too stupid to do anything else. And it was too early to call the bastard yet, so he wouldn't. He'd walk.

9

Harriet was coming painfully down the stairs from the flat in her dressing gown and nose splint. She'd heard the far-off tinkle of the piano five minutes ago and jerked up in her bed, suffering a searing spasm of nasal distress in the process. She'd glanced at the clock, seen it was six thirty and got up and out of the bed. Passing through the flat living room she'd noticed that Sophie was gone, and for a second entertained the cruel but quickly discarded thought that her greatest friend was a co-conspirator. No, it could never be.

She arrived downstairs in the restaurant to find Sophie cleaning the tables, with a look on her face as angry as her own. She'd heard the piano, too, come down and didn't know what to do about it, so she had picked up a cloth until Harriet joined her, as she was sure she would. They listened. The piano was louder now and there was the sound of a tuneless Italian voice rising in a cracked heartfelt crescendo. They both looked towards the stairs leading down to the club room. Harriet's gasp of rage nearly dislodged her splint. 'They've been down there all night!'

'Careful, dear,' said Sophie.

'Careful, my rump!' Harriet, ignoring agony, strode to the stairs.

Below in the club room, Porchese was posing as a tenor with one hand outstretched and the other clutching a half-pint jug of crème de menthe. He was repeating the climax of 'Ave Maria' as Martin began to hammer out his own half-remembered chapel version of 'Land of our Fathers' on the old upright near the basement steps. O'Dare was swaying in the centre of the room. He'd got tired of going to the bar every time he wanted a drink and on the last trip had decided to pull the upturned bottle of Scotch from its clips on the shelf and bring it back with him. Now he was holding it above his head and pushing the optic down onto his teeth every time he needed a squirt of the liquor. Geoffrey stood close by with tears in his eyes. He was a sentimental drunk. Was this humanity in all its courageous failure and tarnished beauty? Yes it was, and the fat, black-leathered old drunk couldn't help but cry at the poignancy of the moment. He was even considering a poem on the sheer loveliness of doom when Harriet came in from the stairs.

'Out!' No-one noticed, except Geoffrey, who wanted to hug her. He was opening his arms and moving towards her, as she shouted it again. 'Out! Out! I said out!' Her splint wobbled but she didn't care.

Martin's raised hand stayed that way, mid-chord; Porchese choked on a high Ave and O'Dare did the same on the optic.

'Do you know what time it is?' asked Harriet. No-one seemed to. 'Why are you still here?' No-one knew. 'Haven't I enough on my plate with three nephews on a murder charge?' Harriet glared and heads dropped. 'Haven't I had my nose bashed?' She looked round as the weight of Sophie appeared behind her at the bottom of the steps. 'And hasn't my good friend had her head caved in?'

'Sorry, Auntie.' Martin was genuinely contrite.

'And now what?' Harriet hadn't even started. 'Fat fools, Welsh drunks and unfrocked priests who should know better spend the entire dark swallowing my dear dead brother's last alcohol and testament when his very offspring are running from threat and evading arrest!' Martin was about to fall off his chair and grabbed for the keyboard to balance himself. The resulting chord was not to Harriet's ear. 'I find myself let down!' She stared at Porchese, whose legs were slowly bending under the strain of remaining upright. 'And how dare you corrupt my chef?'

'Ave, ave, ave Maria . . .' Porchese did his best, but was still sinking.

'Pack it in, Porkie! Kitchen please. First breakfasts in half an hour.' Harriet pointed an imperious finger, but she may as well have tried to reverse gravity. Porchese hit the floor and fell back against the piano, producing another chord, this time so deep and resonant that Geoffrey wondered if the sheer loveliness of doom wasn't already upon them.

'You see, Auntie,' Martin was swaying on the piano stool, doing his best to remain vertical, 'we stayed to guard you.'

'Guard me!' Harriet exploded.

O'Dare, having only just reluctantly pulled the optic like a baby's dummy from his spittle-spattered gob, spread his arms wide and overdid it as usual. 'Auntie, dear old Auntie Harriet. Listen. What eejit would inveigle your skirts again with such battalions of fine, fine men at your . . .'

'Shut up!' It was too much. Thoughtlessness, carelessness and drunkenness may well have been the ways of the world, but impu-dence, not to mention utter sodding impertinence, was a pain worse than her nose and not to be tolerated. 'You are banned!'

If there'd been silence before, now it was deader than the graveyard on a black Monday in January. 'Banned, Auntie?' Martin repeated it in a whisper.

'You are nothing if not banned!' Harriet knew she had them. This was their refuge, this was their heart and this was their home. And Harriet knew it. She'd never felt such power. 'You are banned!' Her splint shook. 'All of you! I shall see you east, west, north or south, but I shall not see you in this club again! Show them the door, Sophie.'

'No, no and never no!' Geoffrey was a bulk that refused to be moved. 'I will not be treated as a slattern in my own place of ah . . .' He was about to say worship, but then remembered where he was. 'My club!'

'Whose club?' Harriet asked with her eyebrows arched.

'My club, madam.' He put such a heavy emphasis on the first word that his jowls shuddered. 'Invited as a member by a very special man!' He held his head as high as he could without falling over backwards. 'A man who understood when no other would.' His voice boomed in shaking reverence. 'Your brother, Charlie Lack! A man who opened his arms to us!'

'His wallet, Geoffrey.'

'No, Harriet, his heart!' The sentiment so moved him that he shifted from lofty bombast to nauseating humility faster than any actor should ever contemplate. 'I admit I am a debtor. I admit I am a profligate and something of a tart. I admit . . .' He was descending to the tacky recesses of whining self-pity. '. . . I am what no-one else wanted.' He shook his head in simple wonder at his own searing, poetic honesty, and having created art, raised his tumbler of neat gin. 'But your brother wanted, Harriet. He did. He wanted! He wanted me! And I drink to him in this, his house and therefore my house!'

'Then consider yourself evicted.'

'You are breaking faith, Harriet!'

'And hope too and I'll certainly shatter charity! Now will you leave?' Harriet folded her arms.

Geoffrey was incensed. He turned in a small circle and his flabby white hands flapped at his sides. No words came, so he decided to stomp to the door. He went in the wrong direction, veered, then staggered, then righted himself, then staggered again and finally turned in fury, spraying the room with tears, whine and blubber. 'It's broken! All broken! You have betrayed us, Harriet Lack!' He raised himself to his full height. 'I shall never return! I shall die in a pauper's grave before I return!' He turned again, found himself facing the wall, and stepped neatly sideways to the door. He pulled it open and immediately felt faint from the inblast of cold air. He shook his head; this last, last exit was not to be spoiled by a swoon. 'I shall go north!' He pointed west, swayed backwards and fell forwards. As he crawled up the steps, he shouted, 'I shall never spit in here again.'

Martin had finally achieved the vertical. He leaned on the keyboard and Harriet stoically turned away from the sound of the third unwanted chord in as many minutes. Then he took a few unsteady steps towards the door and did his best to make a small bow. 'Auntie, I'm contrite. Pissed, you're right, but true, Auntie, always true.' He looked up then down again as he realized that he had vomited down the front of his suit. He wiped off the stench with the inside of his sleeve and turned to the door. 'Good night.'

'Good morning.' Harriet was relentless.

O'Dare plucked the optic from the Scotch and placed it carefully on the bar, then he put the bottle in his pocket as if he owned it. He gazed at the cold world through the open doorway for a second and, without a word, went out.

They were gone and it was very quiet. Harriet sat slowly on Martin's chair by the piano. She glanced at Sophie and knew she'd made a mistake. To ban them from the club was a cruelty too far and she knew she wouldn't be able to live with it. The club was what they were; it was how they defined themselves. Charlie had always understood that these men, despite their vainglory, were little more than pathetic, old and lonely drunks, and without the sodden walls of the club to soak up their failure and self-loathing, they would be bereft of all they had, which wasn't much – just each other. 'Oh dear, Sophie, what did I do?'

'I don't know, Harriet. It's a world turned upside down, if you ask me.' Automatically Sophie began to clear the glasses from the top of the piano and take them to the bar. 'Good's gone bad and the past is catching up.'

'Whatever shall we do?'

Porchese looked up out of his stupor and began to sing 'Ave Maria' again. This time he wasn't out of tune and Harriet didn't try to stop him.

10

O'Dare walked to the end of the alley and disappeared from view, probably following the invisible tracks of a hundred all-night boozers to the one bar in town that, known only to them, was always open at seven in the morning. Geoffrey and Martin wandered the early morning streets, the former intent only on packing his case into his sidecar and roaring his bike home to Mother in Hampstead. Martin dreamed of the mist in the valleys of home. They passed the front of Emil's slots arcade and neither of them noticed that the door was open, which was unusual at that time of the morning. If they had gone in and walked past the slots they'd have found another two suffering the raging ripples of Charlie's death pond.

Lucy and Mathilda sat over a one-bar electric fire in the tiny back office. After seven taxis had given them the cold and shiny boot, they'd given up and walked on their stilettos. They were so footsore and depressed by the time they'd returned to familiar streets that they'd counted themselves lucky to bump into Scotch Jock on the corner. He'd had his best night for months. The little bint with the mauve shoes and leather miniskirt who worked the back alley by the underground car park had been so pissed she'd given it to him for free and he'd spent the night in her kip. She'd kicked him out early in case her pimp paid an unexpected, and let's face it unknown, early morning visit. Jock, ignoring the look of disgust on her face when she woke up, had taken her at her word, hitched up his pale-blue jeans and departed down the alley with a swagger. Now who could say he was too ugly to get a fuck every now and then? He turned the corner and came face to face with two who said it all the time. He stood on the street with a big self-satisfied grin. He was a ready-made, jubilant, balls-on-empty, tartan, one-man welcoming committee. He greeted Lucy and Mathilda like old friends. 'Why don't you come into the slots and warm yourselves up, girls?' He rubbed his crotch. 'And let me tell you about my night.'

And so he did. Lucy and Mathilda were too tired and preoccupied to show their contempt. They sat in front of the electric fire rubbing their feet and dreaming their separate dreams. Jock mistook their silence for admiration and, with the true magnanimity of the conquering hero, made them tea. Then he sat on the broken swivel chair with his legs wide apart hoping for covert glances at his rampant groin and sweet sighs of desire. He even imagined for a moment that he could take the pair of them right there on the office floor in a magnificent three-up orgy of the slots; such are the wild fantasies of a satisfied prick. 'And so, girls, how was your night?' He emphasized the penultimate word in a grand beam of self-love.

'Fuck off, Jock, we're knackered.' Lucy leaned back on the ancient vinyl sofa.

'Excuse me, Lucy, you are in my home . . .'

'Fuck off.'

Jock thought about it. They were obviously intimidated by him. He would try charm and understanding. 'So the Lack Brothers pissed you off, did they?'

'Jock, for the last time, will you fuck off?'

The orgy obviously wasn't on for the moment so Jock closed his legs and caught his balls on a broken spring sticking up from the seat of the chair. 'Ah! Fuck!' He stood and rubbed his bollocks as Lucy laughed. 'Fuck you, you flabby whore!' He walked around in the cramped space with his legs bent, pulling the crotch of his trousers down to let the pronged testicle swing in the fetid air inside his pants. 'You're a bitch, Lucy, and as for the Lacks, there's no mercy. When those twins strike . . .'

'We lost them.'

'You what?'

'We lost them.'

'You lost the twins? Wait a minute, are you saying the brothers lost the twins?' Jock had forgotten his bollockular distress. This was big news and could even get him a stroke and a pat from Raphaella. He checked his facts like any good slots manager would. 'The brothers lost the twins?'

'That's not all they lost.' The more Lucy thought about how Arnie had treated her, the angrier she became.

'The time has come!' Jock grabbed at the phone. 'I'll piss on Arnie Lack!'

'I already have and look where it got me.' Lucy folded her arms in disgust.

'Shut up, you flabby whore . . . Boss!' Jock stood rapidly to attention with the phone to his ear while Emil woke up. 'Tell your sister the twins are off the map!' Then Jock recited Lucy's words to the son of Riss.

'Lucy?' Mathilda touched her friend's arm. 'I don't want it any more.'

Lucy turned to see that Mathilda was crying again. 'Tilda?'

'What's love meant to mean anyway?'

'Hate!' Jock slammed the phone down. 'We're going to find these Lacks ourselves. You know?' He grinned. 'I can feel a black mist descending.'

$\boxed{11}$

Arnie had been down to the bakery and found Henry with fat Jackie his assistant and another baker, a tall thin man with a droopy moustache called Alex. They were standing over a huge blue-iced cake in the shape of an acid tab. Across the top was written in white, 'The Acid Queen. With Love.'

Henry had pointed at the cake and smiled sadly at Arnie as he came in. 'California Sunshine. I thought she'd like it.'

'I took her tab. It doesn't change, does it?' said Arnie.

'I put the rest of them into the cake,' Henry said proudly.

They both looked down on it for a while. Jackie and Alex moved away as a mark of respect. After a while Arnie said, 'Is Stella dead, Henry?'

'Yes, mate.'

Arnie came back up to the living room and lay back down on the cushions trying to remember the night. He'd taken acid, Ronnie had gone out and now he'd seen Henry's cake for Stella the Acid Queen. Stella was dead. It still wasn't going in. He decided it must be because the drug was still moving, so he lay back to enjoy the last of the trip. He was still very speedy and everything seemed vibrant. Stella kept coming back. He thought of the sex he'd had with her and began to feel randy. Then for some reason it all got philosophical and he started thinking about death. This was what had happened before in those glory days of California Sunshine. He'd think about sex, then go to the edge of the chasm, have a look at the molten insanity down there, decide not to take the jump and sit on the edge thinking about death. His death. He wanted to die. He'd wanted to die for years, he knew that. He lived with it. Everything he did was about dying in some way. Even smoking fucking cigarettes was about fucking dying, wasn't it? Fucking Stell, fucking Lucy, fucking everybody else was about dying too, wasn't it? There were those who said that fucking was about love and creating life, but maybe he was turned the wrong way round and couldn't see it. He began to think about being gentle and kissing and the weight of Lucy's breast and the softness of her lip, and he wished that she was there with him so he could love her, but he knew if he started all that he'd get unhappy. A picture of Stella's corpse under a train came to him and he finally realized she was dead and started crying. He turned into the cushions and had the weird feeling that Mirabelle was watching him through the door of the bedroom. Slowly he calmed and began to think of his mother and all that. No wonder he was a fucking suicide. Then he could feel Mirabelle watching him again and began to feel sleepy. His last thoughts were that he loved Mirabelle, not for any of that old hokey-cokey, but just that he loved her and wanted her around. He felt a bit like crying again but didn't. He fell asleep.

Mirabelle had been watching and she'd calmed him. She feared for Arnie and waited to see his dream, but it was nothing but falling. He fell and fell down a deep shaft and then it went blank into something that he couldn't give shape to. Mirabelle felt his terror and prayed for him. Her white hand passed through his sleep and stroked his heart, neutralizing the acid static and taking the throb and pain away for a while. What did Arnie hide? she wondered. She waited. There was nothing but silence. Then Bernie began to stir in his Camelot bed. Soon it would be breakfast and every fry under the sun.

12

Ronnie picked up the phone and dialled. He'd taken a circular three-hour route since he'd last seen the phone box by the gents. The walk had taken him down by the river. He'd stood on the bank and looked out in the direction of the estuary and the sea. For a bit he felt it might be a good idea to be on a boat bobbing about out there, but then he decided it wouldn't be any good because even sailors have to come home some time. The river was the furthest from the bakery he'd got and he kind of knew it was where he had to turn round, not only with his feet, but with his brain. All the journey so far had been about hating Tom Cherry and not calling him. Most of the journey back was about what he would say when he picked up the phone. He'd just ask if they could see their mum, that was all. What was the point of getting involved again with Cherry? He was a swine, wasn't he? He was a child abuser. And what was he going to do about that? Take him to court twenty years later? He suddenly had the thought that Cherry might be as scared of him as he was of Cherry. He could threaten him with arrest if he needed to, couldn't he? But even as he thought it, he knew he'd never do it. Cherry scared him too much. It was like this bloke had got hold of him when he was too young and stopped his muscles growing or something, and so now, like he'd said to Mathilda, he was scared of everything that moved. And that was something else. Mathilda. He felt really bad about her, too, because he knew she loved him. Maybe it was because Cherry had taken his muscles away that he couldn't love her back? He decided he didn't know what he was going on about. He'd got to the phone box and stood outside it for a moment, expecting to have second thoughts, but he didn't, so he went in and picked up the phone.

13

Hooper had overslept by twenty minutes. By the time he'd shaved, failed in a bowel movement, dressed and arrived in the shabby three-table dining room of the hotel, Fairfax had finished his slimmer's breakfast and read the *Daily Express* twice. He was even contemplating turning the pages of the *Sun*, because his ambition was to be an inspector, but he'd only got as far as the front-page headline when Hooper walked in. 'Sir?' He stood up.

'No breakfast for me, Sergeant. Pay the landlord and we'll get on with it.'

'You want me to pay, sir?'

Hooper gave him a sideways look. Fairfax took the point and went out. Hooper stood in the middle of the empty room with his head down and hands behind his back. Time to reassess. Point one, he was Superintendent Hooper. That was as far as he needed to go. The name told him who he was and the rank why. It was enough. He'd decided to be as easy on himself as possible. Anyway, he knew what he had to do. First stop, Lucretia Green.

It proved to be a waste of time. On the journey there Fairfax had predicted as much. Having heard his superintendent's description of the old girl after the attack, he'd said that he wouldn't be surprised if her mind turned out to be so addled with hatred that her sight was affected. Hooper was impressed by the thought. He'd been through roughly the same thing in the hotel room the night before. His mind had been so besotted by fantasy that his view had been corrupted, not to say blocked entirely. As they walked the hospital corridors he couldn't help wondering, as the unhappy generally do, if his condition of entirely subjective perception wasn't, in fact, universal. These doctors rushing about with their stethoscopes for example. Wouldn't their medical diagnosis be affected by their state of mind in much the same way as his dream state of Violet affected his? And if everything was indeed always entirely personal, how could we ever be certain of assessing anything correctly? All conclusions, he concluded, could never be much more than a temporary expression of the being of the concluder. Hmm? He walked on, his mind whirring. He'd almost decided that the only way to survive in an insane world was to go mad, but changed his mind immediately the moment he saw Lucretia, who had quite clearly got there before him.

The assault had driven her well beyond the brink. Her existence had been to erect, day by day, brick by brick, a vast wall of prejudice and spite around her, to keep the nasty and vile outside at bay. Little by little these defences had become everything she was, so when they had been attacked by the twins she had been smashed completely, and what sat in the white hospital bed staring at Hooper was no more than shattered flying hatred and broken bits of bile. They seemed to be skimming the air around him as he looked down on her sagged white skin, draped like stained muslin over her skull. The venom, spat out like poison darts, seemed mainly to do with Charlie, the worm who'd entered the apple of good; but surprisingly May was attacked just as viciously. Hooper wondered if she knew her daughter was dead. In fact Fairfax tried as delicately as he could to mention it, but it wasn't clear if Lucretia heard. She spoke only of deserters and betrayers, then looked up with some degree of rationality and suddenly said, 'The worst wounds are the first wounds, Constable!' Her eyes glared to such an extent that Hooper was worried for a second that they might fall out. Fairfax dutifully noted down most of what she said, but later, when they tried to decipher it, they recoiled as if they had tasted acrid fumes from some deep neanderthal pit neither of them wanted to believe existed. They left her there, nodding her stream of invective at the bed-sheets.

At least Hooper had realized he wasn't insane. In fact he would have felt quite wholesome as they drove towards the tower and Tom Cherry if he hadn't almost at once had more news of his dream state, as he was now beginning to call her. On their way out of the ward, Fairfax had telephoned Cherry's office and had been told by a secretary that apparently Cherry had been in Rome with Violet for the past two days (Hooper's heart pounded as his sergeant related this), and apparently, on a whim, they'd decided to attend a fashion fair in Milan on their way back. As it was a holiday, Cherry hadn't informed anyone of this and the secretary had only heard about it by chance from an Italian business contact who'd called up on other matters. She'd also discovered, by way of a routine fax from the company's travel agents, that Cherry was on an early flight back from Milan that morning. Only one ticket had been booked. 'What, no Violet?' asked Hooper. Fairfax shrugged. The secretary he'd spoken to had sounded as exasperated as they were. She had said, however, that it was his habit to always call in at the office as soon as he returned, so she was expecting him at any time. And as far as she knew, he wouldn't be aware of anything that had happened to May Green. Fairfax had asked her to tell Cherry to wait for them at the tower, and having escaped the acrid fumes of Lucretia, they immediately ran into much the same thing on the South Circular. They were stuck in a traffic jam for ninety minutes.

14

'Where's Ron, then?' Bernie was sitting at the table in the tiny kitchen and as usual wanted to know the whereabouts of everybody. He could see Arnie's feet as he slept in the living room, so that left Ron, didn't it?

'I don't know. He hasn't come back.' Mirabelle cracked the fourth egg into the pan.

Bernie saw Arnie's feet move through the doorway. 'I won't wake him up, 'cos he's been burning the candle at both ends again and he's total conked out.'

'Leave him for a bit.' Mirabelle began to slice the tomatoes.

'He's a mad prat you know.' Bernie folded his arms on the table, looking serious. 'He drinks too much. And he takes drugs.'

Mirabelle turned. 'How do you know?'

'I've seen him, ain't I? And he told me. He paid sixty quid for coke once and I said, sixty quid for coke? You must be a mad prat. You can get it down Mister Supersave for fifty pence and anyhow the fridge is full of it. So he winked and said, "Shut up, Bernie, you don't know what you're talking about." But I did. I thought his coke was probably drugs, and then I thought, What a mad prat you are, Arnie.' He looked disgruntled. 'And he is. That's what he is sometimes. I know he's my big bruv and I love him, but I think he's a bloody mad prat!' He hit the table with his hand.

'Did you get out of the wrong side of bed this morning?'

'No. I'm just very worried, that's all.'

'Why?'

'I had this weird dream and it was all wrong. It was about Arnie and he was Sir Lancelot and that ain't bloody right, is it? He's Sir Bors! I am Sir Galahad, Ronnie is Sir Perceval and Arnie is Sir Bors! Not Lancelot! It's all wrong. And if you can't get things right in your dreams, what's the world coming to, Meebelle?' He looked up. 'And another thing. I'm very worried about these coppers and getting banged up in one of their slammers. I think all of this is getting too much for me, as a matter of fact. I've only got a low mental age, you know?'

'No you haven't!'

'Yes I have! Auntie Harriet told me, and Dad, and Arnie. So don't argue because I should know. It's my mental age, isn't it?' He held his hands palm up like an advocate.

Mirabelle turned from the frying pan and smiled. 'I just meant that you could be surprised. You might know more than you think.'

'How'd you know?'

'Well you knew your dream was wrong, didn't you?'

'Oh.' He considered the matter. 'You might be right, you know? I think something's going on to tell you the truth, Meebelle. I'll tell you that for nothing. I think I'm getting cleverer for a start.'

She smiled and put the plateful in front of him. 'Here's your breakfast.'

Bernie was horrified. 'Where's the bacon? And the sausages? And the black pudding?'

'I think Henry's a vegetarian.'

'Oh no, a bloody veggie! That's all I need. A bloody veggie! That has totally ruined my day that has . . . Arnie?'

His big brother was in the doorway, looking bleary, but still feeling speedy. He was coming down from the drug, but the colours of the kitchen were edgy. Mirabelle could see he still felt strange; his eyes were glaring more than usual and he took a long time to look at things. 'Do you want some tea?'

'No thanks, Mirabelle. I'll have a glass of water.' She went to the tap. 'I dreamed about you.'

'Was it nice?'

'Yeah.' She put the water in front of him. 'Thanks.'

The door opened and Ronnie walked in with Henry, who immediately noticed the water. 'Still suffering, Arn?'

'Suffering's the word, Henry.'

'Where you been, Ron?' Bernie wanted to know.

Ronnie sat down at the table. He was still feeling shaky. The phone call had upset him in a way that he didn't understand. 'I called Tom Cherry at his office.' He looked at Arnie. 'You hear me, Arn?'

'Yeah. What he say?'

'He said we can see Mum.'

'Yeah?' Bernie froze, his fork an inch from his mouth.

'When?' asked Arnie. The news had jolted him back into a reality he would have preferred to have avoided.

'There's some do. She's gonna be there tonight.' He looked at Henry. 'It's a place called the Crystal Rooms. He said he'd leave tickets for us on the door.'

'Fuck.' It was all Arnie could think to say.

'What do you mean, fuck?' Ronnie was getting testy.

'Well it means she ain't dead anyhow, dunnit?' said Arnie looking away. He'd never seriously imagined Violet was, but he felt a relief all the same. Then on top of that came a quick hate. 'I mean she might have . . .' he stopped. He was going to say 'been in touch', but he knew she could never have been and he wouldn't have wanted her to anyway. 'Anyhow,' he finished lamely.

Ronnie was getting angrier. He turned away from Arnie. 'What's the Crystal Rooms, Henry?'

'It's an exhibition place, mate. Full of lardies. They have shows there, you know? Rock 'n' roll, fashion shows, dinner and dance, stuff like that.' He shrugged, aware of the tension between the brothers and wanting to keep well out of it.

'Fashion shows? It's the rag trade in' it?' Arnie looked at Ron.

'What's the rag trade?'

'It's clothes, Bernie.' Arnie turned back to Ron. 'That's it, isn't it? Cherry's game.'

'I don't know.' Ronnie didn't want to talk about it.

'What's the matter with you?'

'I don't want to see Cherry, I told you that. And I didn't want to call him either; I told you that an' all. But you was too full of drugs, Arn, to take any notice!' Bernie looked up at Mirabelle. He'd been right about the coke then. Ronnie went on, taking it all out on Arnie. 'Why don't you wrap up your brain in a carpet, or an eiderdown, or clouds or something! It won't go away, Arnie, will it?'

There was a pause. Arnie didn't know what to say, probably because Ronnie was right. Bernie wasn't helping. He said, 'I had to come to terms with your drugs problem an' all, Arnie.'

'Shut the fuck up, Bernie!' Arnie blew it.

It was a mistake. Bernie had been on edge all morning and wasn't in the mood to be shouted at. He banged his hand on the table and stood up. His head wasn't far away from the ceiling. 'I had enough of this! I had enough!'

'Bernie . . .' Mirabelle tried to calm him.

'No! I had enough! I don't want to be here! I don't even get sausage for brekkers! I had enough of all this sleeping in funny beds and factories and all that. And I had enough of all this waiting around!' He looked down at Ronnie. 'And wass all that taking hours and hours to make a phone call? All you got to do is pick up the handle and put the cash in! That's it, in' it? I was worried about you!'

'Bern . . .' Ronnie put up his hand.

'Shut up! Who's Bob?' Bernie shouted it; he wasn't trying to be funny.

'Bob the birdbrain.' Arnie was exasperated. 'Be quiet.'

'I ain't gonna be quiet! I had enough. I wanna go home!'

'You have to try to be strong, Bernie,' said Mirabelle.

'I am bloody strong. I'm stronger than anyone I know! I'm just getting bloody nervous!'

'Eat your breakfast.'

'I don't want to eat my bloody breakfast! It's all bloody veggie! I want to go home!' He shoved the chair back out of his way and walked out into the living room, and then on into the bedroom. Ronnie looked at the uneaten eggs and tomatoes. 'That's a bad sign.'

There was a silence, then Arnie asked, 'What time do we have to be there?'

'He said, half-past eight, tonight.'

'The Crystal Rooms?'

'Thass right, Arn.' Ronnie was tight and clamped. Arnie was only just beginning to realize how upset his brother was. 'There's still the law, Arn. We can go in and tell them what happened.'

'No.' Arnie didn't want to go through all that again. 'We discussed it. No law. What else did Cherry say?'

'Nothing. He was polite and really helpful, wasn't he? He said, "Of course I'll give you a hand, Ronnie." Bastard.'

Arnie still didn't get it, but decided it wasn't the right time to push. At least the emotional rush of knowing they would see their mother had cleared his mind of the drug. Perhaps he was getting ready to finally face things, or perhaps it was because he knew he had to be strong because he could see Ronnie wasn't; either way he leaned forward and apologized. 'Sorry, mate, I know I let you down. I won't get like that again.'

Ronnie nodded, grateful for the support. 'You don't want to go either, do you?'

'No, mate. Nor does Bob. But we're going anyway, aren't we? All of us.'

'And what about these twins you was talking about?'

Arnie looked up at Henry. 'You see a couple of Chinese anywhere?' Henry shrugged and Arnie turned back to Ron. 'We must have lost them or they'd have been in here, wouldn't they? Or maybe I made a mistake. Anyhow, we'll keep an eye out.' He looked up at Henry. 'Do us a favour, Henry, will you? Send someone to get some sausages for Bernie? Won't be long, mate, then we'll be out of here.'

'You're welcome, Arn.' Henry went out with his cup of tea, leaving them to wait until the evening and to think about what might happen.

$$15$$

By the time Hooper and Fairfax had arrived at the tower, Cherry had gone. As his secretary had predicted he'd come straight from the airport to the office. He'd been told about May and had been utterly distraught. He'd made a few calls, taken one, and then left the building without saying where he was going.

As Hooper heard this, he looked down at the dried blood on the office carpet and cursed himself for not coming here before seeing Lucretia. He was so intent on lacerating himself yet again for irregular and illogical operational procedure that when Cherry's secretary came in and mouthed 'telephone', he didn't notice until Fairfax had already gone out. He looked at the blood splattered on the wall and wondered what to do next.

Fairfax didn't supply the exact answer to that but came in with news that was about to give his superintendent another dream state battering. The call had been from their own operations room in the east. Apparently Cherry had called the station from his office here before he left. He'd said that he'd been telephoned by Ronnie Lack and had told him that he could see his mother that evening at eight thirty at the Crystal Rooms in Chelsea.

Hooper went white. See Violet? Tonight? Already? This was all too quick. He had to sit down and grip his knees hard to avoid flinging himself back to a new fifth house and what colour to paint the study. Violet in the absolute flesh? He'd need at least six months to prepare himself for that. As it was, it seemed he had until eight thirty that evening and he didn't want it any earlier either. Fairfax smiled and said, with what he considered to be a fair degree of intuition, 'Cherry didn't mention where she was now.'

'And what about him? Where do we find Mr Cherry?'

'Didn't tell the station that either, sir. Although the secretary thought that the first thing on his mind would be to contact er . . . the deceased's sister and tell her about the deceased's er . . . decease, sir.'

'Tell Violet about May?'

That was it. 'Yes, sir.'

'Did this secretary say she had a home number for him?'

'She's tried it, sir. No reply.'

Hooper gripped his knees tighter. So this was it. He would see her tonight at the Crystal Rooms.

'So we'll have the brothers, sir.' Fairfax was thinking along another track.

'I beg your pardon?'

'They'll be at the Crystal Rooms too, sir.'

'Yes and . . .' Hooper stopped. He'd suddenly been struck cold and certain by a nightmare premonition. He didn't know where it came from, or why, but it suddenly flicked on in his mind like – there was no other way of describing it – a Chinese lantern. He looked up at Fairfax. 'Don't worry about the brothers, Sergeant.'

'Sir?' Fairfax gave him a sympathetic look, and for the second time that day Hooper felt the sea of madness lapping at his mind, and it terrified him. 'I want to go to Soho, Freddie. See if we can head them off.'

'The twins, sir?' Fairfax caught up.

'Yes.' Hooper looked down at the blood on the carpet. He'd suddenly realized what he was up against.

'We don't even know if they exist, sir.' Fairfax was ever the pragmatist.

Hooper laughed. It rang hollow from his dry mouth in his pale face. 'Don't be stupid, Sergeant.'

16

Raphaella glared at Emil across the table. She'd just got out of bed and heard about Jock's phone call from the peep. Emil was grinning. She'd decided to leave it all to the twins, and now they were off the case and there was nothing better than seeing your know-all sister with her pants in a pincer. Raphaella looked across the room. Luis was leaning forward on the sofa engrossed in the TV. He gave her a surreptitious glance and then turned away. She didn't know what to do. Her mind was stuck, the needle quivered and the dials registered zero.

'So what's the scam, mob girl?' Emil leered.

'Shuddup!'

'I only asked . . .'

'Shuddup!'

'I mean you want a restaurant or you don't want a restaurant? Ain't no twins gonna get it for you. What you gonna do?' Emil raised his shoulders and hands like a man who knew.

'Shuddup!' Raphaella knew that if she had to repeat the holy word three times, then her power was decreasing. This was her first real test and it was crisis already. There was only one thing for it. A make-up job. She turned and walked out of the room.

She sat opposite her wall-size mirror in her bedroom surrounded by her eighty-three pink teddy bears. They each had their own age, name, personality and make-up chart, but this was no time to be consulting soft toys. This was serious. This was cosmetics. She opened the drawers of her dressing table and lifted the lid of her make-up trunk. This was her larder of loveliness, personally hoarded by the beauty and paid for by Papa. She could be the most desirable object ever known to man as long as she didn't go out of the front door and meet any of them. And Raphaella had struck the hardest and most pouting of bargains for over ten years. Now she had everything. There was no powder, paint or palette, stick, brush, cleanser or base, colour, gel, tint, hint or rouge, that had ever been manufactured by male for female that was excluded from her collection. If there was ever a museum of twentieth-century vanity, this would be the most prized exhibit and crowds of thousands would queue, crane and be dazzled by the array.

She clipped her hair back, then rubbed her fingers together over the trunk, warming them like a surgeon before she began the operation. This was transformation; the ugly duckling who didn't know the answer to Emil's question was going to become the swan who did. As she began to cleanse, she estimated. Two hours on the face and half an hour to go through her wardrobe. A further hour to change her mind and then she'd be ready to do whatever was necessary. There was nothing on this earth that would stop her claiming her natural widow's rights. The Empress of Rouge and Powder would have her restaurant.

17

Mathilda sat on the desk at the peep. She hadn't known where else to go. Anywhere was going to be as bad. You couldn't leave your thoughts behind, could you? So she sat with them as the desultory early afternoon trade passed through, dropping their quids into her palm and heading for the Kleenex and Lucy inside. Normally she smiled at the punters because they were sad and she quite liked them really; today she was sour and there were no laughs in the air. It was all over with Ron and she knew it. Or did she? She was as confused and as depressed as she'd ever been, but now there was a new and strange feeling growing inside her. It was like anger, but she'd been angry before and this was harder and it was saying, 'I won't be contained.' This was a kind of desperation and it was demanding she did something about it before she went mad. And the more it rocked her the more still and silent she sat.

She hardly noticed as Raphaella swept past with Jock and Razor. They were probably going through into the back room to do whatever they did in the back room, and it was none of her business and she didn't care anyway. There was this other thing on her mind. She sat explosively sad and quiet by the till with her brown eyes cast down as they passed her.

Lucy was swinging her tits in the barrel. Her anger was passing as she danced. The events of the night were getting submerged into a thousand and one tales of a thousand and one other nights of scrambled lust and disappointment. It was always the same and always would be. Arnie was what they all were. They all came to her because of what she was and that's how she'd always be. And anyway she enjoyed it, making the tassels twirl, sticking her arse out and helping some poor John come into his fist.

'So where they go, huh?'

Lucy hardly heard it at first, but Raphaella's voice on the top note could have given a pneumatic drill a run for its money. Lucy stopped and looked round. It wasn't hard to find the slit of Miss Riss. There was a flash in her eye that beamed across the barrel like tracer. Lucy instinctively covered her nakedness with her hands. 'How should I know?'

'You tell us what we want to know, you bitch, or I'll cut your tassels off!' Jock's voice echoed from beyond the barrel. He was beginning to sound psycho, but Lucy wasn't impressed.

'Which is about as close as you'll ever get, Jock.'

The low door at the back of the barrel burst open as the music went dead and Raphaella ducked through into the circular space. She stood in her furs, staring at Lucy with a contemptuous look in her heavily painted eyes. Razor Jam came in and stood behind her as Lucy heard Jock grabbing her one punter and throwing him out.

Raphaella opened the front of her fur and placed her hand on her hip, revealing a pastel-pink designer silk suit. Lucy stared back and, aware of her defensive posture, defiantly dropped her arms from her breasts and revealed them as weaponry. She put her hands on her hips too and thrust her G-string forward as Raphaella slowly circled the barrel, looking her up and down. Scotch Jock came in and stood by Razor at the entrance, grinning like the obsequious thick prat he was. Having taken the full circumference of Lucy from buttock to nipple and back again, Raphaella deigned to speak. 'Maybe you want to be big shot in Raphaella world, huh?' She stood in front of Lucy. 'Assist Miss

Riss? Hmm?' She smoothed her skirt with a heavily ringed and sparkling hand. 'You like designer dress, like me?'

'Not a lot.' Lucy was beginning to wish she had a skirt to smooth.

Raphaella began to circle again. 'You want silk pantihose? I get it for you. You want tip-top lifestyle? You want night on the town with blue-chip businessman? You want great sex?'

'Are you kidding?' Lucy couldn't help but laugh.

Raphaella's tone didn't change. 'So what you want?'

Lucy looked up at the silent speakers hanging down into the barrel. 'What about a tune so I can get on with my job?'

Raphaella had once again come titside and she hissed into Lucy's face, 'So where is he? This dumb Lack who kick you off the street?'

'Arnie?' Lucy eyed her with a superior smile. 'Wouldn't you like to know?'

Raphaella cursed herself. She'd implied she was interested mainly in the eldest brother and let the dog out of the kennel, so to speak. 'Arnie!' She squeaked with derision. 'Arnie Lack? I don't want to know about no Arnie Lack! I pick better men out of my nose! I hate Arnie!' She stared eye to eye at Lucy, daring contradiction.

'He wasn't too keen on you as a matter of fact.'

'What? He want to screw me so much out by the garbage can he almost bust his trouser!'

'Not what he told me, Raphaella. As a matter of fact, he said you were too fat for him.'

'What you say? Are you kidding?' Raphaella was trying desperately to laugh it away. 'You telling me he want a wrinkled slut like you?'

Lucy smirked. 'He also said he didn't want to screw a cosmetic job who used every dick in town for lipstick.'

That was it. Raphaella exploded with a scream. 'Wha'!' She raised her talons. 'I scratch your . . .'

'Shuddup!' It was that magic Riss word again and this time it had reverted to its ancient master. Luis came quickly through the low door and stood in the crowded barrel with Emil smirking behind him.

Raphaella stood with her false nails raised, ready to strike. She couldn't believe her eyes. 'Papa?' She turned. 'You go home and watch TV.'

Luis, impeccable in his best suit with his cashmere coat draped over his shoulders, took a menacing pace towards his daughter. 'Sure I watch TV, Raphaella. I ain't done nothing but watch TV.' He spoke directly into Raphaella's face and there was a craziness in his eye that scared her. 'And you know what I see?' He looked round; there was a kind of white round the edge of his pupils that pinned everyone back to the sides of the barrel. 'I see a papa with a little girl in a little house on a prairie. And Papa says, do this little girl, do that little girl, and the little girl says, yes my papa, and no my papa, and looks at her papa with respect!' He'd suddenly barked and Raphaella flinched. 'Sure I watch TV and I learn about life. Real life!' He looked scornfully round the barrel. This was a man who'd seen the light in blue neon and who was going to argue? 'One thing I don't see on TV, Raphaella, is little boss girl who don't have no clue in her head!' He thrust his own at his daughter. She flattened against the wood behind.

'Sorry, Papa.'

'The day of the daughter is over! I watched and I waited, you get me? I wait for you to fuck everything up!' He grinned like a mad maestro whose crazy scheme had succeeded beyond his wildest dreams. Then he turned and barked, 'Jock! Razor!' He pointed at Lucy. 'Take this tart and cut it up in slices!'

The mood had changed instantly. Lucy could see this was no cat fight any more. Luis had gone over the edge; this was the time of the tough guy for real and bones could be broken. She backed away from them, but there was nowhere for her to go. The psychopath and the Sikh grabbed her arms hard and slammed her back against the side of the barrel.

'Give it to her, Papa! Compound interest, right?' Emil shouted.

'Get these animals off me!' Lucy shouted. She was getting very scared and pulled hard away from them, but she was held by the Jock and Razor she dreaded. They weren't playing about any more, and Jock suddenly turned and smashed his fist into Lucy's naked stomach. She gasped in pain, doubled and began to retch.

Luis ambled forward and stood over her. 'So. OK, slut. These twins is off the case, so now you look at me. Where is these Lacks?'

'I don't know.'

Razor grabbed her hair and jerked her head up so she was looking directly at the diamanté tiepin of the little Maltese Caesar. He said, 'I don't fuck about. I ask you one more time. Where is these Lacks?'

'They gone west.' The voice had come from behind them and Lucy

307

looked over Luis's shoulder and saw Mathilda standing by the door to
the barrel.

'Tilda?'

'They gone to Henry the Hippy. He's a baker.'

'No!' Lucy yelled.

Jock pulled her face towards his. 'Shut your fucking mouth!'

'Oh, what you done, girl?' Lucy was falling down in pain.

'Ronnie don't love me any more!' Mathilda burst into tears. 'He broke
my heart!'

18

It took Lucy half an hour to recover from the punch. She lay on the
floor of the barrel. All the lights were out and she'd heard them
lock the doors when they left. She didn't know whether that was
because they wanted to imprison her or just because they'd forgotten
she was there. She forced herself into a sitting position and wrapped
her arms round her stomach. All her thoughts were now with Arnie.
She began to realize that over the years his family had become hers
and she didn't want them to be hurt. She knew she had to get out
somehow and do something.

She began to heave herself up onto the wall and stood in the dark
trying to breathe properly. She was worried about Mathilda too. As
soon as she'd blurted out the whereabouts of the brothers, she'd fled.
Razor had run out after her, but had come back without her as Luis
and the others had left. So where had she gone and what state was she
in? Lucy felt her way round the barrel to the low door. The first thing
she had to do was find some clothes. This nudity was getting her down
and for the first time in her life she began to wonder if she wasn't going
to give it all up. The thought quite surprised her as she reached into
the cupboard they called a dressing room and felt for her coat. As soon
as she had it on she felt better. She made her way to the toilets at the
back. Someone must have left a window open. She didn't fancy the idea
much with the way her stomach ached, but she'd do it for Arnie. She'd
even give up the barrel for Arnie. She'd come to a conclusion in the

dark. She wasn't going to wait any more for him to become what she wanted. She was going to take him as he was and whatever he said she was going to change him. The certainty made her feel happier as she felt her way along the wall. She pushed open the door ahead of her. The ladies' toilet was light. The grey day filtered through a high open window. She raised a shapely leg, put her stiletto onto the toilet seat and began the climb.

19

Hooper and Fairfax had been in Soho for four hours and drawn a blank. Fairfax had warned that there'd be no-one at the Peking Palace who would admit to speaking English, but the superintendent insisted they went anyway. Fairfax was becoming even more concerned that his superintendent's train had left the rails somewhere on the journey up from the tower, but had decided to keep his mouth shut. It had occurred to him that his function in this investigation was not only to catch killers but also to keep his superior sane. This wasn't something to worry him; he was big-hearted enough to relish the responsibility and, truth to tell, was quite fascinated by this degree of lovesickness. He'd never seen such a bad case before. This brought out his protective side, and far from damning Hooper for his weakness, he decided he admired him even more because of it. To be such a warrior of the heart was something way beyond the imagination of a mere sergeant, whose only love had been a Norton.

Unfortunately, once inside the Chinese restaurant it proved to be him who'd been correct. Not only did no member of the staff admit to the mother tongue, there wasn't one who attempted speech in any language. With his new-found sympathy for his boss, Fairfax was all for calling in immigration and getting the lot of them transported, but Hooper put a stop to it with a gentle wave of his hand. This is humanity, he seemed to be saying. My own crushed state leads me to empathize with even these, the most obstructive of souls. Fairfax did wonder for a moment how this concept of compassion would help them apprehend two of the most ruthless killers they'd ever heard of, but he let it pass and they went back to the Soho station.

There was nothing more on Violet, but the forensic reports on her sister's death had come in. The scientists weren't optimistic of any worthwhile result because too many people had trod the room since the attack. Constable Plod again they assumed with superior and witty forensic irony. In conclusion, they reported, it was their view that the victim had had her throat cut by more than one assailant. Thanks very much, thought Fairfax.

They'd decided to pay a call on the family Riss, but no-one was at home and all their Soho businesses were strangely, temporarily closed. In fact they'd banged on the front door of the peep show as Lucy was falling out of the window of the ladies' toilet at the back. Not knowing what else to do they were reduced to wandering through Chinatown hoping for an idea. *En route* they passed the alley and the Lacks' restaurant. Hooper felt the pull of Violet, but resisted another call on Harriet. Fairfax led him away to a tea bar, where he sat and chain-smoked with his heart thumping as he waited for the evening and the appointment with the love of his life at the Crystal Rooms.

20

Lucy missed Hooper and Fairfax by about thirty seconds. They were walking away from the Lacks' restaurant and were probably in sight as she crossed Dean Street and passed by the lamp-post at the end of the alley. She was limping and didn't know what hurt most, her stomach still suffering from Jock's blow, or the gash on her leg she'd received when she fell out of the toilet window. The beating in the barrel had badly frightened her and she was terrified of being seen by any of the mob, so she slipped as furtively as she could on her heels along the alley. Things were getting straight, sharp and true. Sides were having to be taken, and she knew which one she was on. She opened the door of the restaurant.

Fortunately, apart from Sid the Slurp with his daily, three-hour cup of tea up the back, there was only Sophie in evidence. She was wiping a table as Lucy came in and immediately put her back against the plasterwork between the door and window. 'Is there anyone behind me?'

'How can there be, dear, you're standing against the wall.'

'In the alley, Sophie! Look! Please! Can you see Jock? Or Emil? They beat me up, Sophie!' For the first time Lucy felt close to tears. 'Look!' She opened her coat. Sid at the back nearly drowned in his tea as he caught sight of the tassels and G-string, but Sophie was quicker and saw at once the huge black bruise spread across Lucy's stomach.

'What happened to you?' Sophie's eyes bulged.

'Where's Auntie Harriet?' Lucy needed to get to a quicker intelligence.

'She's gone to bed, dear, with nerves and depression.'

'Oh no!' Lucy was getting desperate. 'Where's Geoffrey?'

'Oh, Lucy, we had such an up and down. They've gone north!'

'North!' That was it. Lucy leaned back against the wall in despair. Who was going to help her now?

God struck in the unlikely, booze-ballooned shape of O'Dare. The door burst open and he crashed in straight onto his knees. Anyone else might have thought that he'd decided on a quick prayer for the establishment, but Sophie could see that he'd continued drinking since the morning and the only thing he had to offer up was vomit. 'I thought you was going north!' She put her hands on her hips and glowered.

O'Dare managed to regain his feet and stood at the fullness of his entire five foot three. He swayed dangerously. 'I shall go when I am ready.' He was attempting dignification, and Lucy could have laughed if it wasn't for the severity of the circumstance. O'Dare pomped on, 'And tell me now, who wouldn't take his departure without a decent farewell at the Empress of China.'

'The Empress?' Lucy asked. It wasn't over yet!

'And what's the matter with that?' O'Dare's eyes bulged in hostility.

'Is Geoffrey there? And Martin?' Lucy closed her coat.

'Where else would they be, you stupid slag?'

'Tell Harriet, Sophie!' Lucy ran out of the restaurant, knocking O'Dare back against the till. As she ran down the alley she realized she could, of course, have found Henry's number in the book and picked up the blower, but this was personal. She wanted to be there to see Arnie give Jock what he deserved.

'What's the matter with the eejit?' O'Dare could feel himself falling

311

again. 'Where's me grub, Sophie? Where's me tot? I'm not going north, am I?' He suddenly looked very old and vulnerable. 'I can't be heading to cold places at my time of life.' Then he immediately collapsed onto Sophie's just-washed floor.

'Oh Lord help us.' Sophie looked down on O'Dare. The Lord ignored her. There was only Sid the Slurp and he'd seen it all before.

21

An hour later and the Riss Daimler was heading west. Emil had done what Lucy hadn't and looked up Henry under the bakery section of the Yellow Pages. They had the address, but this didn't prevent Jock, who was driving, from getting lost. 'Which way's west, boss?'

Luis, in the passenger seat beside him, decided it was expedient to explode. 'This is a navigator? Why am I surrounded by people with heads in their own arseholes?' He pointed an angry finger straight ahead through the windscreen. 'That way!' He leaned back into the soft seat, shot his cuffs and admired his pearl links. This was more like it. Just like the old days.

Raphaella, tucked in the back between her brother and Razor, listened to this crap with contempt. She'd been impressed by her father's rise from her fall, but was by no means defeated by it. She had the feeling it was nothing more than a temporary sense of grandeur ballooning from his crack-up. She could see that his various insanities were piling up and she was pretty sure that given time the whole lunatic edifice would pile too high and then implode, leaving a collapsed paternal mess in an expensive suit. In the meantime, she'd do what was necessary: she'd shift from battery to flattery and back, she'd play the old boy on the end of the line like he was a trout with a tiepin, and in the end she'd get her heart's desire, which was a restaurant with candles on the tables and good-looking boys in tight pants as waiters. So how did she start this angling? She became a ten-year-old again. 'Oh Papa! I'm so hot for a big daddy who ride like a stud in a saloon and gets his little baby daughter pretty presents like a restaurant!'

Luis beamed. 'We got the Lack place. I know we got it! I can feel it!'

'Me too, Papa!' Emil didn't want to be left out and he knew Raphaella was up to something again.

'Shuddup! I feel it better! No-one feels it like me!' His father rubbed his hands in warm wet joy. 'Luis is back! Riss has risen!' He laughed. 'No more hole in the corner, no more head in the balls. I want blood! I want the blood of a Lack!' He looked up to the soft vanilla roof of the Daimler and said a word to his dead wife. Ecstatic or depressed, it was something he often did when he felt manic. She was the only one who had ever understood. 'Oh Josephina, see me now.'

'But remember, Papa, I won't never give up.' Raphaella's tone was smoother and more dangerous.

Luis turned in his seat, his beam beginning to crack. 'What?'

'That restaurant is mine!' Raphaella snapped, pulling hard on the line. Luis blinked and for some reason his mouth hurt. There was a momentary silence as the Daimler continued west. The rift in the Riss was as riven as ever.

22

However, the split in the club room had been papered over. By the time Lucy had dragged Geoffrey and Martin out of the Empress of China, Sophie had pulled Harriet from her bed. The parties met in the restaurant and stood over O'Dare, asleep in his bacon and egg at the front table. Harriet began to apologize. She was tight-lipped to start with and grew frostier as she realized that neither Martin nor Geoffrey had any idea of what she was talking about.

They'd drunk through the hangover from the morning, then got drunk again, suffered a second hangover in the afternoon and decided there was nothing for it but to drink through that too, and having done so, surprised themselves by realizing that they'd come up sober. This was a Soho phenomenon known as falling out of the bottle. Charlie had once postulated that the riotous behaviour of drunkenness was caused by clean blood fighting the alcohol, but once the booze had scored a resounding and overwhelming victory, the blood gave up and there was no more fighting and hence no more drunkenness. It was as good a theory as any, but the concluding sobriety had so astonished some inveterate boozers that they'd immediately taken the pledge. After all, what was the point of spending all that time and money to end up where you started? Geoffrey and Martin, of course, were far too experienced to have any sympathy with views of that kind. As far as they were concerned, being sober was the perfect state because it meant that you were about to start drinking.

They'd arrived at precisely this point of re-embarkation, when Lucy had burst in on them in the Empress. She had other plans for their new-found temperate state. How about driving their motorbike and sidecar west to warn the brothers of the impending descent of Riss? To give them their due they responded immediately and enthusiastically. This sudden loyalty to the Lacks might have been seen as due to their forgiving nature, but the truth was that as they'd spent the last eight hours in and out of said bottle, ricocheting dizzily from drunk to hung-over and back again, the morning's débâcle with Harriet was merely a blurred dot on some past and hazy horizon, and as far as they were concerned relations with the family Lack were as they'd always been.

They hurried to the restaurant with Lucy to pick up their crash helmets and had found the brothers' aunt standing over the sleeping O'Dare. Their veins conveyed only alcohol, they were perfectly normal and seemingly suffering complete amnesia about the events in the club room earlier in the day. Harriet couldn't believe it.

'You mean you banned us, Auntie?' asked Martin. 'What for?'

'What do you mean, what for?' Harriet's lips tightened.

'Auntie! We haven't got time!' Lucy turned to Martin. 'Hurry!'

Martin ran down to the club room for the helmets as Harriet oscillated between fury and gratitude. 'As you are doing what you are doing for my nephews I'll put it behind me, Geoffrey.' He looked blank. 'You are unbanned.'

Geoffrey considered that this must be roughly the equivalent of falling through the bottle, inasmuch as you'd returned home without remembering the excursion. 'Thank you, Auntie.' Martin came back and gave him his crash helmet. He put it on and for a brief moment thought he'd gone blind. Then he took it off and put it on the right way round. 'Good night.'

'We'll call you.' Lucy pushed them towards the door. She was no idiot and could see that this seeming sobriety was just a state of mind. They were as plastered as brewery walls and she was already dreading the ride west.

Harriet watched them as they passed the window. 'I am amazed, Sophie. Is there nothing that can put a dent in these?'

$$23$$

Bernie had lain on Henry's four-poster all day. He'd even turned down the sausages Mirabelle had fried for him, which had worried her at the time, but now as she sat at the end of the bed she began to realize that something very powerful was happening to him as he lay there, half sleeping, half daydreaming, tossing and turning on Henry's multi-coloured sheets. It was as if he was expanding inside himself. Thoughts, dreams and words were coming to him that he didn't understand and they were pushing out, filling spaces in him that he didn't know he had. She watched as his brow furrowed and black confusions crossed his face. His body was reflecting his inner turmoil, and although she knew she was imagining it, he seemed to be getting bigger. It suddenly came to her that he was growing, not physically, but up. The man with the eight-year-old brain was putting on months by the hour.

For Bernie on the bed it was bloody terrible. He didn't seem to understand nothing any more. He didn't want the bangers or even the cornflakes, and he always liked cornflakes. Why didn't he like cornflakes no more? And why didn't he even feel hungry for any grub at all? What was happening? It was like his head was on blessed fire! It all started with thinking about Sir Lancelot lying on the floor of the chapel being sick and feeling ill. What was he so ill about anyway? He was like Arnie with those bloody drugs but he was pretty sure that Sir Lancelot didn't buy coke for sixty quid a can. Bloody mad, that's what that was. But perhaps Sir Lancelot was bloody mad too. It all gave him the bloody creeps to tell you the truth. And all this Mum business. She kept appearing in his brain like she was Guinevere or something, and then his dad came up like he was King Arfer with a sword in his hand,

bright and gleaming, and then Arnie, who he knew was definitely Sir
Bors, kept roaming all over the place and going sick and ill like
Lancelot! All his old pictures were getting torn up and he was forget-
ting all the words he used to use. And in the middle of it all, coming
back all the time, was this cup and this dove. What was that for? It was
the Holy Grail. Well what was the Holy Grail when it was at home?
Well, like, it was peace and comfort and things like that. Well where
did that thought come from? He didn't have thoughts like that, did he?
He had thoughts about Spurs and breakfast and that's bloody all mate.
There was something bugging him all right and it was getting bigger.
And Mirabelle was sitting on the end of the bed watching him.
Mirabelle? What was that? He didn't say Mirabelle, he said *Meebelle*.
What's happening? His words were doing a runner, that's what, and
how can you talk or think proper without words? And what was he
doing over here in Kensington or somewhere anyway? He was from
Soho for blessed, blinking sake. He'd been east and he'd been south and
now west? What was this, a round-the-world trip like you got on *The
Generation Game* or something? Was Bruce Forsyth going to show up
in a minute with the Holy Grail in his pocket? What's it all coming to?
And one day he was going to pick up a sword like Excalibur. What?
Where'd that come from? One day he was going to pick up a sword like
Excalibur. There it was again. This is bloody madness, mate. Blessed,
blinking crackers this is. And one day he was going to pick up a sword
... It just kept on coming and coming. And his dad was dead. So what?
It was going round and round. Where'd his dad go then after he was
dead? Mirabelle said he'd prob'ly go to heaven. Mirabelle? Meebelle,
Meebelle, *Meebelle*. He turned over again and tried to practise saying
his old words, but nothing was working. They just kept turning up
again like new words. *Bernard*. What? Bernard. That was another one.
He wasn't Bernard, he was Bernie. And suddenly he was standing in
some road somewhere and he could see these black knights again. Who
were these geezers anyway? And why was their visors always down?
These were bloody devils these were and he didn't bloody like it. And
they was charging about all over his brain and he wanted to think
about Galahad but he couldn't. And he was going to pick up a sword.
Shut up about that blessed sword! He didn't want to know about no
sword. He wasn't a sword fighter, was he? He supported Spurs.
Tottenham Hotspur. What? It wasn't no Tottenham Hotspur. It was

Spurs. It was *Spurs*, *Bernie* and *Meebelle* . . . Spurs, Bernie, Meebelle and the *Holy Grail*. What? Shut up about the bloody Holy Grail! And he was going to hold a sword . . . Shut up about that too! He sat up in the bed. 'Mirabelle.'

She smiled. 'We'll have to go soon.'

'Sooner the bloody better we get out of this place, Mira . . . Meebelle. I'm forgetting everything I know lying here and I don't bloody like it. Do you think I'm a conquering hero?' What? Why'd he ask her that? It was something else that was just popping out from nowhere.

Her grin broadened. 'Of course I do.'

'Well bugger me, it's news to me.'

'Do you want to comb your hair before we go?'

'Suppose so. You got to look spruce, ain't you? It's not every day you meet a mum you never met.' He got off the bed and stood up.

'You look like a conquering hero.'

'I don't care what I look like. It's not eating those bangers that's bothering me.' He lumbered out of the bedroom with his head aching with all that thinking, and went through to the bathroom wondering if Henry had any hair gel.

Mirabelle looked down through the window. The early evening rush was coming to an end but there were still plenty of people on the streets. She was relieved to see that the rooftops were empty. She didn't want to see Sorush again now, she had too many thoughts of her own. She'd caught glimpses of Bernie's daymares and a terrible pattern was beginning to take shape in her mind. Arthur, Lancelot, Guinevere and the black knights. These were the clues as to what Bernie was, what he was becoming and what she was here to protect. Was this leading to the profoundest point of the past? Perhaps it was and perhaps that was what the Dark Angel was here to destroy. How much did Sorush know? Did she have her own secret? And was the investigation into Charlie really just a sham? Mirabelle prayed for guidance as she meditated on the frailty of the streets below. She noticed that it was beginning to get foggy.

Ronnie had spent the day in a trance. His conscious mind seemed to have packed up in the face of the unintelligible, or at least the inadmissible. His mother, Cherry and all that had become as grey and impenetrable as the mist descending outside. What was it all about?

He didn't know and didn't have the energy to try and find out. He'd spent most of the time lying on Henry's cushions not listening to the music Arnie played on the old stereo. Stones, Moody Blues, Floyd, it was all part of some past that Ronnie was feeling increasingly disconnected from. In the end he'd had a bath and washed himself more thoroughly than he'd ever done in his life, first with a sponge, then a flannel and finally scrubbed with a loofah. He wanted to be cleaner than he'd ever been. He borrowed shampoo, then a razor, then a toothbrush, then a dressing gown. He ironed his shirt, then sponged and pressed his suit. Ronnie had always been neat, now he was going to be precisely neat as neat can be. He didn't know why, it just seemed to him to be the right thing to do. He even ironed his shoelaces.

Arnie hadn't really come down off the acid until midday and had spent most of the afternoon asleep or listening to Henry's sounds. There were hardly any dreams and, like Ronnie, very few thoughts. He looked a mess and felt a mess. While Ronnie cleansed, Arnie dirtied. He knew he was doing it too. He heard his brother in the bathroom and felt like getting some kitchen garbage out of Henry's bin and smearing it on his neck. He smoked a lot of cigarettes and deep inside felt the old dope tiger stir. He wanted to take more acid, but didn't because of Bernie and what he'd said in the kitchen that morning. Arnie had been shamed and didn't like it. Now he was empty. There was just the smoke he inhaled swirling round the big striped tiger in a hollow tube of dread. Finally he got up. It was time to get on with it. He needed to ask Henry one more favour. The Snipe had served its purpose and they needed another vehicle. He went down to the bakery.

Henry had been a good bloke and had slept down there in the office during the day. Now he, fat Jackie and thin Alex were running up again for the night shift. He took Arnie out into the yard and showed him their second van. It was an old, high-framed, clapped-out Commer with 'Henry's Bakery' painted in chipped yellow letters on the sides and back.

'She still runs, man. Can you have her back by tomorrow?'

'Sure, Henry, thanks mate.'

'When all this is over, come back, Arn. We got a lot to talk about, you know?'

'I will, Henry.' They embraced for a moment and patted each other's backs in an awkward show of deep affection. Then they went back into the bakery as Ronnie came down from the flat above with Bernie and Mirabelle.

Arnie moaned, 'You seen the fog? We don't hurry up, we won't bloody get there and we'll bloody miss her.'

'Sorry, Arn.' Bernie assumed it was his fault.

'Yeah, well get in the van, Bern, will you? It's out in the yard,' said Arnie and he started to walk back towards the door as Henry held up the blue-iced acid cake he'd made in memory of Stella.

'Take some cake with you, boys?'

'Oh yeah.' Something about the hair gel had given Bernie his appetite back and he reached for the cake.

'No.' Arnie turned from the door and snapped, 'Don't you touch that bloody cake.'

'Sorry, Arn.' Bernie withdrew his hand.

'Why don't we go then?' Ronnie had moved uneasily after Arnie.

'Yeah. Thanks, Henry.' Arnie touched his friend's shoulder and they went.

'Look after them, won't you?' Henry winked at Mirabelle as she followed, then wondered why he'd said it to her.

24

The van had been gone for three minutes when the Riss Daimler pulled up outside the bakery. Luis looked up at the old wooden sign above the doors and grinned. 'My time has come.' The family and their minders descended from the car and walked five abreast towards the unsuspecting Henry. If nothing else Luis and his boys knew how to cross a road mob-handed. They held their heads high, splayed their feet and their long coats flapped. Luis pulled the brim of his trilby down. This time his daughter was going to see such a man, such a father, such a fearsome and downright hood it would be enough to keep her an infant for ever. He pushed open the doors and walked in. Jock and Razor followed, one at each of his shoulders. Emil was, as usual, seeking glory behind, and Raphaella tried to look coy and mollish at the rear.

The bakers had lit the huge oven and were preparing their first tray of dough. Henry turned as they came in. 'Hello, man.'

Luis walked directly to him, stopped inches away and looked up from beneath his brim. 'Who you think I am?'

Alex and Jackie, sensing threat, hovered behind Henry as he foolishly tried to brazen it out. 'A geezer who needs a loaf?'

'Wha'!' Luis exploded. This was not his anticipated welcome. 'Razor!'

The blade flashed and before Alex knew what was happening blood ran down the left hand side of his face. Luis gave Henry a tense grin. 'Don't have cheek, Mr Baker.'

Emil got the joke and laughed uproariously. 'Hey Papa!'

Luis, pleased with himself, decided to extend the gag. 'Too much mouth! Jock!' Jock smashed his dustered fist into Jackie's mouth and the fat baker fell back against a wall cupping his hand to catch the blood and splintered teeth. Luis sneered at Henry. 'Don't no-one ever talk to me like that!' He turned to his minders. 'Get rid of them.' Jock looked baffled for a second. Did his boss mean homicide? Luis, on top form and ahead of the game, pointed to the cold-room door. 'In there! They can cool off!'

Emil hooted again and spread his feet, shooting his shoulders back like the bad boy he knew himself to be, as Jock and Razor pulled the bakers towards the huge fridge. 'Cool off! Hey Papa! Cool off!' He turned and grinned at Raphaella, who stood and watched, learning all the time.

'So.' Luis prodded Henry in the chest. 'Where's the Lack Brothers?'

Henry was very shocked. This kind of violence was something he'd spent his life avoiding. He tried to look surprised. 'The Lack Brothers?'

'The Brothers Lack!' Luis shouted and prodded him again.

'I don't know who they are, man.' Henry was thinking as quickly as he could. He'd taken a step back from Luis and his poking finger, and as he put his hand down onto the table to steady himself, he touched Stella's acid cake. 'Hey, you want some cake? This is the best we make!'

'I don't want no cake! Why should I want . . . ?' Luis stopped. He'd found himself staring directly into the huge gaping mouth of the long low oven. Flames were burning bright along the sides and back, and the space in the middle was just about man-size. He had a flash of

320

inspiration he was going to regret for the rest of his life. 'Hey! Hey!' He laughed; this would show Raphaella once and for all. 'You bake the cake and I bake the baker! Geddit?' Luis winked at his daughter, then turned delightedly to Jock. 'Put him in the oven!'

Emil started to get worried. 'Hey, Papa?'

But Jock had no such qualms. Thumping Lucy in the barrel had got him started up, then smashing his fist into Jackie's face had released all the necessary chemicals for full, unsummoned, uncontained psychorama. He tingled with the energy of destruction, a man made only for menace and mayhem, cruelty knotted in Scotch muscle and head-banging bone. This was what he waited for every day of his life. 'Yes, boss.' He grabbed Henry's right arm and leg.

Razor on the other side was blank. Nothing moved beneath the turban except the true teaching and instruction of Mr Riss. He took hold of Henry from the left.

Henry yelled as he was lifted bodily into the air, 'No!' But once off the ground, he had no purchase and there was little he could do but try to grab the sides of the oven as he was pushed through the door. He yelled, 'No, wait, I'll tell you. The brothers . . .' Jock slammed the door with a burst of power he hadn't felt in years and turned and grinned at Luis. Razor stepped back quietly to one side. They couldn't hear Henry any more.

There was silence. Luis stepped back with a slanted smirk, uncertain of what he'd done. Emil was more sure. 'Hey, Papa, he was going to tell you where they were.'

'Shuddup!' Luis looked at Raphaella and said, 'So, what do you think, huh?' He was preening as deadly Papa and he wanted her to beg him to let the baker out of the oven.

'Papa, he's going to burn up to fucking death!' Emil was getting very worried.

'Shuddup!' Luis couldn't break now. He stared at Raphaella and she wasn't going to either. She said, 'Hey you know, Papa, I think we give this baker his last wish, you know?'

Luis looked at her suspiciously. 'Like what?' He wanted to let Henry out of the oven, but couldn't find out how to do it. He stared at Raphaella and she stared back, not letting him off the hook.

She shrugged. 'Eat his cake,' she said sweetly. 'It's what he asked us to do.'

'Uh?' Luis was out-bluffed and he knew it. What could he do? He laughed like a hyena and said, 'Why not! Good idea! He want us to eat cake, so we eat cake!' He looked down on Henry's iced testament to Stella and read, 'The Acid Queen. With Love. Acid? What's this? Indigestion?' He tried a laugh, but the baker burning in the oven behind was getting to him. 'What's this? Some long-haired fandango!'

'Papa, for Christ's sake!' Emil was hearing in his mind, '. . . charge you Emil Riss with murder.' He was seeing a little cream-painted cell; he was beginning to cry. He yelled out, 'Papa!'

In the oven Henry's overalls caught fire and they heard him scream through the heavy iron door.

'Papa!' Emil shouted again.

Luis turned and didn't know what to do, then he suddenly plunged both hands into the cake. 'Eat! Eat!' He looked at Raphaella. So this was what she wanted; she could have it. 'Eat! Eat! Faster!' He walked round quickly like a demented dwarf, stuffing handfuls of cake into their holes and forcing it further in with his fingers. 'Eat! Eat!' He was laughing manically. 'Then we can get him out! Right, Raphaella?' She smiled sweetly and took a handful of cake herself as her father jammed more of it into Emil's mouth. 'Eat! Eat, Razor, eat! It's good cake!' He jammed a huge mouthful of it into his own gob and stared round with crazy eyes as they all chewed. 'Yum yum!'

'Papa, get him out,' Emil spluttered, spraying crumbs.

'OK. Jock, we eat the cake for Raphaella, now we can put out the baker!' Luis tried another laugh and then stared at his daughter as Jock opened the oven door and a huge cloud of black smoke billowed into the room. He and Razor took a foot each and jerked Henry out of the oven and onto the floor. He was black from top to toe. His hair was gone; his skull bubbled in huge blisters; his skin was purple black and flaking; his hands were charred and his once white overalls were little more than cinders. He lay very still as the mob stared down at him through the smoke. Luis crouched and put his ear close to the scorched, lipless mouth. 'So, where are they?'

'Crystal Rooms.'

They were Henry's last words. Not that Luis seemed to care. He stood up, and with his mouth still full of cake, he grinned at Raphaella. 'Crystal Rooms. So now we got the Lack Brothers for pudding, huh?' He buttoned his coat with shaking fingers and led the mob out of the bakery, leaving Henry where he lay. Jackie and Alex were still incarcerated in the cold room. Luis's last sane and reasonable act was to turn out the lights and lock the door behind them. Henry's revenge, not to say Stella's, was the acid. The cake was drenched in it. The mob sat in the Daimler as it began to work. It took Jock three hours to remember to start the car and even then it was only in extreme circumstance.

25

The fog was thick, Geoffrey was lost and Lucy, behind on the pillion, still wearing only her thin coat over virtually nothing, was freezing. Geoffrey brought the bike to a halt at traffic lights on the cold West Road. He turned back to Lucy. 'I've no idea, really no idea.'

'Shut up, you fat queen, and keep going,' Martin shouted up from the sidecar.

'Go where, Martin?'

'Look!' Lucy couldn't believe her eyes. Crossing the junction ahead of them was a van with 'Henry's Bakery' written on the side. 'That's it! Follow that! We'll ask them! Go on, Geoffrey!'

'I can't go now! The lights are against me!'

'Never ask the silly bitch to do anything!' Martin looked up scornfully.

As Martin and Geoffrey bickered on red, Arnie, unaware that he'd just passed his half-naked girlfriend on the back of a motorbike, turned in the driver's seat of the van. Next to him was Ron, and in the back, Bernie and Mirabelle, sitting on a couple of upturned baker's trays and hanging on to the empty wooden racks.

'All right, Bern?' Arnie shouted over the loud throb of the engine.

'Yes thanks, bruv.' Bernie's voice wasn't clear and Arnie turned back again. 'What's that you're eating?'

'A doughnut. I found it in the back. I din't eat them sausages today, Arn!'

'You didn't eat none of that cake?'

'No!'

'You sure?'

'Yeah, Arn, it's just a doughnut. I'm starving hungry!'

'That's all right then.' Arnie was quiet for a second, then he yelled over his shoulder, 'Listen, mate. You're going to meet your mum and probably a whole lot of other flash Harrys, so no farting and Who's Bob? You understand?'

'Yes, Arn.' Warnings always made Bernie nervous.

'We'll see her', Arnie went on, 'and Ronnie will sort out all this restaurant roundabout. All right?'

'Why me?' Ronnie turned in his seat.

'You wanted to talk to her, Ron. You said so.'

'Don't you want to?'

'I just want it all straightened out, mate.' Arnie avoided his question.

'And I don't want to see no coppers!' Bernie pulled himself up the racks, having a sudden panic attack.

'You won't. You leave it to me.' Arnie gave him a thumbs-up sign in the mirror and Bernie sat back down on the wooden tray with his legs spread on the metal floor. They drove on in silence, each wrapped up in their own thoughts. The fog was beginning to lift and Mirabelle looked out of the back window. She saw, a long way back on a curve, a motorbike and sidecar, but didn't give it a thought.

<hr>

26

The Crystal Rooms were beginning to fill. It had once been a grand hotel, but now its public rooms were used for prestigious public functions, and their most famous and impressive features, the giant crystal chandeliers, hung above, blazing with sparkling light and giving the place its name. London's finest and most glamorous were assembling in evening gowns and dinner jackets below. The occasion tonight was to publicize the city's new look. The top half-dozen of the capital's up-and-coming young fashion designers had been invited to show. One of these was apparently a protégé of Violet's, and that was why she was here.

Hooper stood behind the balustrade at the head of the stairs leading up from the grand reception. He was at about the same level as one of the glittering chandeliers and he couldn't help getting depressed as he watched the dazzling crowd below moving under its brilliant light. What was a grubby copper like him doing in a place like this? This is where Violet was. This is where she'd arrived for real. It wasn't, let's face it, where he came from, or exactly where he would end up, was it? His life was peeling paint, chipped furniture, Metropolitan police wanted posters and, if he was lucky, a gold watch and a booze-up after forty years' service.

He squinted into the dazzle of the chandeliers, getting more nervous by the second. Violet was, he'd been told, at this very moment in the backstage area of the main exhibition hall, helping her young designer to prepare the girls. Not being able to face her himself, Hooper had sent Fairfax to check and ask a few questions; primarily, would she talk to the superintendent later? Hooper needed this time to stabilize himself. He'd made sure that Fairfax had mentioned his name. Perhaps she'd remembered him? Perhaps she'd been waiting for him all these years? He could hope, couldn't he? It wasn't against the law, was it? And as one who should know, he allowed himself to forget himself for a minute. False dawns could be eternal on Hooper's horizon.

He glanced at Tom Cherry standing on the landing next to him. He hadn't liked him on sight. He was a small man; what was left of his hair was cropped and grey and he was dressed in an elegant blue suit. He spoke with a confident ease. Suave was the old-fashioned word for it. Slick was a more modern one. Is this what Violet had come to? And what was his relationship with her anyway? Hooper was fairly convinced that Cherry was homosexual, which was a relief, and his heart had lifted momentarily when he'd discovered from him that Violet had never remarried, but then it had sunk again as he gazed at the glitterati below. Apparently she'd been very successful in this world of fashion that Hooper knew nothing of. As far as he was concerned, clothes were something you took off the peg in Marks and Spencer and then hung up in your wardrobe. Shirts were white, suits were grey and ties were a problem. He may well have been a respected policeman, but in the world of haute couture he was hardly a speck beneath a lacquered nail. He sighed. Perhaps the truth was that he and Violet were never meant to be. The Crystal Rooms were her, and it just wasn't him, was it?

He looked down at the reception, aware of Cherry's aftershave, as he waited for Fairfax to return. Cherry had told him that Violet was in a state of shock over her sister, but had insisted on coming anyway. 'She's a very strong woman,' he'd said, looking Hooper in the eye. The superintendent immediately took this as implying that he, Hooper, not only wasn't strong, but was also playing in the wrong league, so why didn't he take himself back to his grubby police station and pound his grubby beat and issue parking tickets. Hooper was about to reply to this series of imagined slights when he saw Fairfax coming up the stairs towards him.

If Violet was in a state of shock, then so was Fairfax. He'd just come from a room full of the most beautiful women he'd ever seen, and most of them had been in a state of undress! Fairfax hadn't so much gone red as become red itself. You could have lit your fire with him, or used him as a beacon in a North Sea gale. He'd stood a yard from a woman that the *News of the World*, only last Sunday, had described as 'the most lovely girl in the world'. She'd looked at him and she'd scowled! His knees had pretty well gone entirely and he'd hardly been able to speak to Violet. The only way he'd managed to survive at all was by forcing himself to imagine the cylinder head and brake linings of his Norton parked up in his garden at home, in the forlorn hope that a passion contained would obliterate the one flaring in front of him before he self-combusted.

'Did you see her?' asked Hooper.

'Yes, sir.' Fairfax did his best to relate his conversation with Violet as faithfully as he could, although his heart, mind and loins were still elsewhere.

Hooper whispered, 'Are you sure she didn't say anything?'

'How do you mean, sir?'

'That may have indicated she remembered me?'

'She didn't, sir.'

'Are you absolutely certain?'

'Yes, sir. Sorry.'

Hooper tried to conceal his disappointment and looked down at the packed entrance hall beneath them. 'Are we ready?'

'Yes, sir. But we don't have too many of them,' said Fairfax. The local nick had pleaded manpower shortage to disguise their disinterest and lent them six detectives and three uniformed constables for ninety minutes. He'd kept the constables in a back room as reserve and had positioned three of the plain clothes in the exhibition hall itself, close to the doors to the reception area, and told them to keep an eye open for anyone oriental, as well as three men who could be brothers coming in with a girl. The coppers had raised an eyebrow and given him the patronizing smirk of the west to the east, but had done what he'd said. Another three plain clothes were below them by the reception entrance doors with the same instructions. They stuck out as Woolworth's against Armani, but there were too many eyes ogling prestige, flashbulbs popping and necks craning for celebrity, for a few hole-in-the-sock coppers to be noticed.

'No sign of the Lacks yet, sir?' asked Fairfax.

'No.' Hooper pointed down to a doorman in a pink braided uniform. 'They'll have to collect their invitations from him. Make sure you let them get in. I don't want a chase on the street.'

'Yes, sir. We'll keep between them and the main doors.' Fairfax was planning to arrest the brothers at the large, double-doored entrance to the main exhibition hall and auditorium. With three coppers coming from the reception behind them, three in the hall ahead of them, and himself and Hooper in attendance, it should be enough.

Cherry walked over to them. He spoke with a debonair ease. 'I hope you're going to arrest them before we start.'

'They're not here yet, sir.' Fairfax immediately picked up his superintendent's dislike of the man.

'I'd prefer there to be no disturbance once the show has started.' Cherry showed his teeth in what Hooper immediately took to be a patronizing smile.

It occurred to Hooper that Cherry hadn't told Violet. 'Does she know?'

'Know what, Superintendent?' asked Cherry.

'That she might see her boys for the first time in years, Mr Cherry?' Hooper was beginning to snap and he warned himself to be careful.

The question caught Cherry off guard. 'No, I thought it best not to tell her.'

Hooper turned to Fairfax. 'Sergeant, did you?'

'Uh? No, sir.' Fairfax had thought she already knew, and what with the half-naked 'most lovely girl in the world' scowling at him, hadn't thought to check.

'Can I ask why you didn't tell her?' Hooper asked Cherry.

'She's been through a great deal, uh, Superintendent.' Cherry was being more respectful now, Fairfax noted. 'And I was hoping you'd at least save her from having to deal with sons she hasn't seen for twenty years on top of everything else. I'm sure she'll see them in her own time.' He glanced quickly at his watch. 'If you don't mind, I'll leave you to it and make my way inside.' He began to leave and then stopped. 'I would appreciate it . . . I ah . . . have helped you, Superintendent. There are many important people here. Please be as discreet as you can.'

'Yes, sir.' Hooper did his best to be polite, then stood back as Cherry perfumed past him and descended the stairs below. Hooper waited until he'd gone, then turned to Fairfax and said, 'Are you sure she didn't recognize my name?'

'Sorry, sir.'

Hooper was going to have to wait. But what was a few minutes compared to all those years?

Arnie parked the baker's van in a street adjacent to the Crystal Rooms. Ronnie opened the back doors and Bernie and Mirabelle got down. From where they were they could see the brightly lit entrance, the red carpet, the press photographers and the crowd. Ronnie immediately began to worry. 'Bloody Ada, we're not dressed for it, Arn.'

Arnie was revved. This was it, he'd decided it on the drive. He looked down at his own mess of a suit and started to walk. 'Bugger the flutes and strides, Ron. We're not stopping now.' The others followed him. 'We're getting it straightened out for good and all.'

'All right, Arn.' Ronnie came up to his shoulder.

'And me.' Bernie came up on the other side and the three brothers crossed the road, with Mirabelle behind. As they disappeared into the crowd, a black Mercedes van cruised slowly past.

PART FIVE

NORTH

1

Fairfax was the first to see the brothers as they came in. He was still standing on the balustrade with Hooper, looking down at the packed reception. He pointed to the crush at the doors. 'There, sir. Three men. And there's the girl.' They watched as the brothers spoke to a doorman, who pointed them over to his senior in the pink braided uniform. 'There you are, sir. They're going to pick up the tickets.'

Hooper looked down. This was his first glimpse of Violet's sons. He turned to Fairfax. 'All right, Sergeant.'

Fairfax spoke into his small handset. 'Can you see them?'

He was answered by the bored, disinterested voice of one of the detectives in the reception area. 'Where?'

'By the bloke in pink,' answered Fairfax.

'What, the orientals?'

'No! The brothers!' Fairfax raised his eyebrows at Hooper. This is what came of using unknown officers from foreign parts. His thoughts were interrupted as the handset stuttered into life again, distorted by unbelievable static.

'Wha ... they ... in ... here ... alread ... ?' Fairfax managed to work out that it was one of the officers from inside the exhibition hall, wanting to know if the brothers had passed into the auditorium already. Before Fairfax had time to answer, there was another voice: 'You want us yet, Sarge?' It was one of the reserve force of three constables speaking from the back room behind the hall.

'No,' Fairfax replied sharply. He was trying to connect up with the detectives in the reception area, but instead heard, 'at . . . you . . .

mean . . . to . . . here . . . ?' It was the auditorium again. If the men were useless, their equipment was worse. He turned to Hooper. 'I'm going to have to go down and sort it out myself, sir.' He sounded apologetic.

'Get a move on, Sergeant.' Hooper watched him go, then looked back towards the brothers. They were moving away from the doorman. What seemed to be the eldest, Arnold, had the tickets in his hand.

'Over here.' Mirabelle pulled Bernie into a corner of the reception area, out of the crush.

'For crying out loud, it's all blessed, blinking snobs and snotties,' he said, looking around with his eyes wide.

Arnie joined them with Ronnie behind. 'And none of them's better than you. You remember that, Bern.'

'Yes, Arn.'

'I'm bloody stone-cold scared shitless.' Ronnie was pale.

'I could do with a drink myself.' Arnie wasn't too happy either.

'I could do with another doughnut,' said Bernie.

'How are we gonna find her in here anyhow?' Ronnie looked round. If anything the crowd was increasing.

'Through there. Look.' Mirabelle pointed to the high arch of the double-doored entrance to the exhibition area. 'She'll probably be in there.' But before any of them could make a move, they were suddenly crushed by the crowd as it seemed to turn and swell back towards the front door. There were shouts, flashbulbs started popping again at an alarming rate and necks were craning at even more extraordinary angles. The star, whoever he or she was, had arrived. Not that the brothers or Mirabelle could do much about it. The irresistible movement towards the door had been met head on by the unstoppable force of the star's party coming in the other way, and the brothers, with countless others, were being squeezed out at the sides. Fortunately they were being pushed in the direction of the exhibition hall and towards Fairfax, who was himself trapped in the crowd three yards away from them.

He watched over bobbing heads and shoulders as they swept past him. He cursed. He hadn't managed to make contact with either of his men in the foyer and looked round desperately, trying to locate them. He managed to get his handset to his mouth as yet another evening suit barged past, banging the radio hard into his lip and making it bleed. He restrained himself from making a fast and angry arrest for assault – it could have been the mayor of somewhere for all he knew – and spoke quickly into the handset, wiping the blood away with the back of his hand. 'They're moving into the exhibition hall. Don't do anything! Repeat, nothing! We'll get them after the show!'

It took him five minutes to make his instructions clear. By that time the brothers were standing at one end of the exhibition hall. From where they stood they could see the scaffolded back of one of the seating blocks of the horseshoe-shaped amphitheatre that had been erected for the show at the other end of the huge space. The half of the hall in which they stood had been turned into a large bar area, covered in white-topped tables, and was already full of elegantly dressed guests waiting to go into the auditorium for the show.

Mirabelle took a pace to one side and could see round the side of the seating block that ran across the hall. Beyond it was a long, shiny, red catwalk running between two other seating blocks and coming to an end in a T shape in front of the third block they were standing behind. At the far end of the catwalk was an entrance draped in dark crimson velvet, overlaid in places by a taut pink gauze. This, she guessed, was where the models would enter from. Either side of this shrouded entrance were two massive stacks of speakers. They'd also been wrapped, shrouded and incorporated into the design. She suddenly realized that she was looking into a giant mouth, and the catwalk, where the girls would walk, was the long wet tongue. The speakers were already emitting a deep bass thump, and she saw that audience members were beginning to give their tickets to ushers standing at the two open corners of the seating blocks and were taking their places. She turned back to Bernie, who was looming above her, looking around their end of the hall. Guests were standing around the tables that were dotted about the polished wooden floor, drinking champagne. At the far end was a long bar with yet another crowd of socialites congregated around it.

Bernie wasn't impressed. 'Stone me, more of them! Does this nightmare never end!' Mirabelle smiled. Bernie's capacity for confusing what he imagined to be maturity with the overdramatic always made her laugh.

Arnie eyed the bar. 'Where's Ron?'

'He went round for a shufti, Arn.'

'Look, I'm going to have a quick one. Here's your tickets. I'll see you inside.'

'OK, Arn. I give it to the geezer over there with the jacket on.' Bernie nodded wisely at one of the ushers.

Arnie winked at Mirabelle. 'That's right, mate. I won't be long.' He started to move away, then came back. 'Listen, Bern. I wanted to say this before. I'm sorry about the drugs last night, all right? You just got me at a bad time. Henry and all that.' He paused. 'Sorry, mate.'

'Don't worry about it, bruv. We all got to live and learn.'

'Yeah. And don't you ever do it or I'll bloody kill you. Got it?'

'I ain't going to do no drugs, Arn!'

'Good, 'cos Mirabelle'll kill you an' all.' Arnie smiled. 'Who's Bob?'

'Bob the Slob. And no farting!'

'That's it, Bern. I'll see you in a minute.' He winked and went through the crowd over to the bar.

'He's a bloody good bruv, Mirabelle. He looks after me, don' he?' Bernie grinned. 'Even if he is a prat sometimes!' He was pleased with himself for a second, then Ronnie came back, looking worried, and so Bernie looked worried too.

'Where's Arn?' Ronnie looked around.

'What's wrong?' Mirabelle could see his concern.

'I just seen Cherry. An' there's a couple of coppers . . .' It was the wrong thing to say. Bernie immediately started to panic.

'Coppers!'

'I don't know, Bern, maybe they wasn't . . .'

'I ain't going down no cop shop, Ron!'

'No-one's saying that!'

'You're not going anywhere.' Mirabelle took his hand again.

'I mean they was probably dressmakers.' Ronnie tried to limit the damage. 'I mean, look around you. You don't need no law here, do you? You find the law down the sewerage with the rest of the scum.'

'What, like us, you mean?' Bernie was still unsure.

'Well, something like that, Bernie, yeah.' Ronnie turned away. It was bad enough seeing Cherry. And he was pretty sure there were coppers about. The point was, had they seen the brothers? He looked up at Bernie towering above them like a lighthouse and couldn't see how they'd miss him. 'Where the bloody hell is Arnie?'

'Why don't we go in? He'll join us in there.' Mirabelle was getting nervous too. The crowd by the tables in their half of the hall was thinning and she could see that Ronnie was beginning to feel vulnerable.

'Yeah, let's go.' Ronnie walked ahead of them towards the seating blocks.

'Well strike a light,' said Bernie, following, 'we've had bakers, snobs and snotties, and now dressmakers and the boys in blue! What's coming next, for crying out loud?'

Two pairs of feet in black shiny shoes came quietly and quickly up the red iron fire escape at the back of the building. Chan McCarthy carefully inserted a crowbar into the join between the double emergency doors and jerked hard. The doors splintered open and he threw the iron bar over the side of the fire escape. The twins were in the building before it hit the ground.

Arnie wouldn't have heard the clang of the bar on the concrete even if he had been listening. He certainly wouldn't have heard the footsteps of the McCarthys as they came silently through the building behind him. He hadn't even noticed as the bass thump in the giant speakers began to quicken and deepen, and hadn't looked up as the chandeliers above him slowly dimmed. He was leaning on the bar with his big nose in his third large Scotch, feeling sorry for himself because he was more nervous than he'd ever been and didn't know how to deal with it. Why didn't someone give him a hand once in a while? The only one who could was probably somewhere in here and called Violet. And she was about the last person in the whole entire universe he wanted to see. He realized his hand was shaking as he held his glass up for the barman.

'You all right, sir?' asked the barman.

'Don't ask me, mate.' Arnie put a note on the counter. 'Keep the change.' It was a ridiculous tip and he wondered what he was up to.

The barman didn't seem to mind. 'I'll make it a double double, shall I?'

'Yeah, do that, will yer.' He got the drink and drank again, trying to shake the anger and sense of failure out of his system. He told himself that where there was tragedy, there was always light, and there was probably always a laugh too. It was the old man's philosophy. Well a lot of bad had been said about the old man, most of it true, but there was his other side as well, wasn't there? He helped people out, didn't he? And only Arnie really knew that, because the same thing was deep within him too. He took another drink. He was timing it. A double double meant three good gulps, and he'd had two. He'd wait a second for the last, then go in and see what he'd see. He suddenly thought of Lucy and wished she was with him. Why didn't he just let her love him? He didn't know. He took the last gulp and turned towards the seating blocks.

Fairfax watched Arnie as he walked quickly across the polished floor, threading his way through the empty tables in the low light. He'd been discussing the situation with Hooper. It was awkward to say the least. The operation was badly undermanned, not to say badly under-planned. They were also surrounded by about 500 scented socialites and if they weren't careful any precipitous action could become an haute couture incident. There were certainly enough press boys and photographers around; there were even two TV crews. There seemed to be only one option: to wait until the end and tail the brothers back to the foyer, hopefully to arrest them as they left the building. In the meantime Fairfax could get on the blower to the local nick and beg for more support. He was about to take off for the exit and a payphone when he spotted Arnie. He was fifty feet away and alone, heading across the empty floor towards the amphitheatre.

'Sir?' Fairfax turned to Hooper. This seemed to be a chance that was too good to be true. 'Sir?'

But Hooper wasn't paying any attention. He was staring through a gap in the scaffolding and there, across the catwalk at the front of the farther seating block, she was, the Violet of his life. She was being helped to her seat at the last minute by Tom Cherry. Hooper's knees quivered, his heart pounded and his skin instantly prickled with sweat. He didn't know what to think; he didn't know how to think. His brain was shaking. He heard a voice: 'Sir?' He ignored the voice. What sound can pierce a thirty-year reverie? Fantasy houses, fantasy cars and fantasy children were beginning to revolve in his mind, getting faster and faster as the stuff of his rapture began to centrifugally disintegrate in a hail of holiday homes, hairdryers, hubcaps, hula hoops and income-tax forms for newly-weds. He heard the voice again. It was saying, 'Sir, there's one of them, sir.' He ignored it. Violet, the very Violet, was there, real and in front of him. As the detritus of his dreams crashed, bounced and fragmented as if in slow motion all around him, he realized with a soaring spirit that he'd been right! She was what he'd always wanted! He felt a tug at his sleeve and pulled his arm away. He was in terminal delight and about to faint. 'Sir!' The voice was getting louder. 'Sir!' It was shouting. He became aware of the mouth and chewy-mint breath of his sergeant. It was Fairfax; he knew it was Fairfax and he was screaming in his ear, but Violet was there! He sucked her up into the vacuum of his empty heart, as Fairfax pulled at his arm. Finally he turned through a haze of perfumed reverie to see his sergeant's anguished face. He took a second to focus and then said, 'Yes, Freddie?'

Fairfax looked across the polished floor. It was empty. 'It doesn't matter, Superintendent.'

2

It was too late for Arnie to get to his seat, so he stood at the corner of two seating blocks with the ushers as the sounds from the speakers reached a violent, pulsating climax and the first girls came up onto the catwalk from the great red mouth at the far end. They were greeted by a wall of dazzling light from the spots above and camera flashes below. There was a barrage of sound from the speakers behind them and rapturous applause from the audience in front as they strode towards Arnie through the sparkle and strobe, heads high, hips bouncing, mouths in great rictuses of gleaming white. They reached the T of the catwalk and turned, preening, posing and pouting as the creations on their backs flowed and swirled.

Arnie looked up through the dazzle of the light, the spin of gleaming shoes and the shining, twirling limbs. He could see his mother sitting by Cherry at the front of the seating block, diagonally across the catwalk from him. She was silent amidst the glamour and applause around her. Occasionally she smiled and sometimes there was a look of pride in her eye, but the overwhelming sense was one of vulnerability and sadness. Arnie could see that she'd seen Ronnie and then was looking at Bernie. They were seated directly across the catwalk from her, several rows up into the block. Ronnie was just staring back at her and Arnie could see that his mother didn't know where to look. She glanced at Cherry and then back up to the girls.

More of them came prancing down the catwalk as the music shifted and pounded on. The clothes were becoming more bizarre; feather and skin, suits in brocade; the girls had long thighs and small bobbing tits, they were trailing silk, swirling satin and revolving velvet, they had love-me eyes, suck-me lips and soft, swinging, sweeping hair. Arnie could have been in paradise. He could have taken 10 per cent of any one of these sweet and vacant shells and dined on it for ever, but then he remembered Lucy and smiled. All that shit was over and fuck these in front of him for the titsy-bitsy, squealing, cuntsy little coquettes that they were.

He glanced away from the girls down the side of the catwalk. He was wondering whether he'd have a quick Scotch or three, then a brief word with Mum, leave Ronnie to sort it out, and maybe even have a word with a solicitor and get this Bernie business done, when he saw a gleam which didn't seem to fit. He saw another brief sparkle and couldn't work out what that was either. He strained to see through the lilt and stride of the girls on the catwalk above him. What he was seeing weren't spotlights and they weren't camera flashes. He suddenly went cold as he realized that he was looking at a pair of knives.

They were ten yards away in the shadow of the speakers by the great mouth of the catwalk. He began to make out two shapes, identical in black, each slowly raising an arm. A tilt of a follow-spot splashed light into the dark corner and caught, for a fraction of a second, two oriental faces and then two white hands, each holding the shining blade of a throwing knife. Arnie was rooted to the spot. The hands were rising. Another flick of light and he could see the twins were looking directly at his mother. She was their target and they were slowly coiling, waiting for a gap between the girls that would give them a clear sight of her. Arnie turned in cold panic, not knowing what to do. He started to yell, 'Mum!' but the pulse in the speakers and the noise of the crowd was too strong for him to be heard. Violet was looking down, then up again at Ronnie through the models parading between them.

Arnie began to run towards the catwalk. An usher grabbed his arm, but he shook it off and leaped up onto the platform as a girl screamed. He fell and then scrabbled to gain his feet and barged into another girl, who overbalanced on heels too high. She crashed to the ground. Arnie kept going. 'Mum! Look out!'

Violet looked up to see her crazy son flailing through the girls towards her. Two more skidded and fell directly onto the catwalk above as Tom Cherry stood and leaned across her to offer protection from this unknown lunatic. The crowd were on their feet, most of the girls on their backs, and in this screaming, squealing mayhem the twins unleashed their knives. Arnie dived in desperation as the blades flew. He came plunging down the other side of the catwalk to land on his mother and half turn to protect her at the same time as Cherry desperately tried to push him away. At precisely the same instant, Chan's dagger hit Arnie in the centre of his chest and Gerard's pierced Tom Cherry's throat.

A roar of sheer panic swept the seats. Girls on the catwalk scrabbled on their knees in their suddenly ridiculous costumes. One shrieked and thrashed as red blood spurted onto her legs from the split jugular in Cherry's throat.

Bernie rose as a giant fifteen feet across the catwalk and roared, 'Arnie!' He began to clamber down the seats like some unchained colossus, increasing the terror and chaos in the screeching audience below him. He roared again, 'Arnie! Bruv!' and crashed down towards the girls screaming and squirming on the wet crimson catwalk.

Arnie was losing consciousness and falling back into Violet's lap, soaking her dress with his blood. 'Mum?' She looked away, reaching for Tom Cherry. She was shouting and trying to staunch the red flood from his neck with her hand. 'Tom! Oh no, Tom!'

Bernie came careering down, his huge feet and hands driving through the terrified frailty of the dinner jackets below. Mirabelle followed as best she could. Ronnie couldn't move. He stayed in his seat with his head in his hands. He didn't see as Arnie fell choking across his mother's legs while she tried desperately to wrap her scarf round Tom Cherry's neck.

Hooper and Fairfax were recklessly trying to battle their way through the audience stampeding away from the mayhem. A dozen half-crazed photographers pushed the other way trying to get at the scene of the crime and the story.

Fairfax yelled, 'Police! Police! Let us through!' It was no good, there was nowhere for the audience to go except towards them and nowhere for the photographers except past them. Soon the superintendent and his sergeant were engulfed by a mass of flashbulbs and perfumed panic. Hooper began to fall and slide down the side of one of the seating blocks and Fairfax reached for his hand. 'Sir! Hold on, sir!'

'Violet! See to Violet!' Hooper yelled, and then was separated from Fairfax by another surge in the crowd and he disappeared into a jumble of overturned seats at the side of the block. Fairfax tried to reach down towards him, but was thrust forwards by three photographers, themselves caught and helpless in the maelstrom of flying elbows and yelping, frightened mouths.

But nothing could stop Bernie. He had single-mindedly forced himself onto the catwalk through a crush of squealing starched shirts, and now was stepping across the bruised and blood-spattered limbs of the swooning mannequins who were spread over the catwalk like broken dolls. Mirabelle had slipped down the seating block in his wake, nimbly passed him on the catwalk and managed to jump down from the platform ahead of him. She was the first to reach Arnie. She leaned down over him.

'Get them out, Mirabelle,' Arnie gasped. Mirabelle could see he was beginning to spit blood.

Bernie leaped down from the catwalk with a crash. He crouched beside them. 'Bruv! What's up, bruv?'

'Nothing, mate. It's all right.' Arnie could hardly breathe. He half turned to Violet, who was holding Cherry tight in her arms and sobbing. Then he looked up again to Bernie and saw Ronnie who was standing above them on the catwalk. Arnie tried to talk. 'Get out . . .'

Ronnie gazed down at his mother and his brother. He didn't seem to be able to do anything.

'Police! Police! Out of my way!' Fairfax was still yards from them, but had been joined by two of the reserve uniformed constables and was beginning to have some success in fighting his way through. From where he stood Ronnie could see them quite clearly. They had moved up to the top of the seating blocks and would soon begin to descend towards them. He shouted, 'It's the coppers, Arn!'

'Get him out of here! Get Bernie out of here!' Arnie gasped.

'Coppers!' Bernie panicked. 'Coppers! I ain't going down no nick!' Before anyone could stop him he had reached down and shoved his huge hands under Arnie. 'Come on, bruv. We ain't staying in this place!'

'No, Bernie!' Mirabelle tried to stop him but it was too late.

Bernie had stood and was holding Arnie in his arms. 'We're getting out, Mirabelle. We're getting out! I'm in charge now!' He began to run along the side of the catwalk towards the speakers, carrying the six-foot Arnie as if he were a baby. Mirabelle sprinted after him as Ronnie stood still, staring down at Violet holding Tom Cherry. She looked back up at him, wet-faced, her voice full of anguish.

'What are you doing to me?'

'It wasn't us!' Ronnie shouted. 'What the fuck are you doing holding him?' It was a scream that he'd suppressed for twenty years. He moved to the side, then back along the catwalk, and not knowing what else to do, he turned and ran out after his brothers.

Bernie hit the steps leading down from the catwalk at a run, went straight up onto the platform and was immediately swallowed by the velvet lips of the gaping mouth above. He had only one thing on his mind: he wasn't going down no cop shop and that was that. He burst into the changing room behind the auditorium like a tank through a wall. The girls, their designers, their dressers, their stylists and their assistants were still bent, bowed and quivering from the twins' initial attack. One had sprained an ankle, some had grazed their shins and the rest were in a state of shrieking hysteria, when Bernie, six foot five, weighing fifteen stones and carrying a half-murdered man with a knife in his chest, charged like a bull gone berserk into their pretty pink sanctum. He had demolished three racks of hanging designer glory, wiped out two tables of sequins and pins, stamped flat an antique hatbox and bellowed, 'I ain't going down no cop shop!' twice, within seconds of his arrival. As he charged through them, several of the girls left the ground in sheer panic. Furs literally flew, gloves came off of their own accord, necklaces snapped, knickers dropped and urine ran down waxed calves. Mirabelle, with the speed of light – some later said she actually disappeared – ran round the lunging giant and got to the emergency doors at the back of the room ahead of him. She had hardly snapped the bar before he was through them, with Arnie's head and feet lolling over his elbows as he lumbered forward. Mirabelle followed fast with Ronnie coming up quickly behind her, leaving two girls clinging to a wall, a stylist who couldn't speak for three weeks and a manicurist gone half mad. Bernie had come and gone. And so had his brothers.

3

Bernie had reached the parked Baker's van before Fairfax managed to get to Violet through the hysterical crowd. She was still holding Cherry, but even to Fairfax's untrained eye, he was clearly close to death. One of the constables crouched down by him, hoping to staunch the blood, but he was too late. Cherry died with a horrible gargle in his throat and a terrified, bug-eyed, pleading look at Violet. It was the second death Fairfax had seen. The first time was a road accident and he hadn't been too sure that life had left the body. This time there was no doubt.

Violet was still on the floor, her legs under Cherry's body. She leaned back against an overturned chair and closed her eyes. Suddenly everything seemed quiet. The majority of the audience were standing pale, shocked and very still in the larger half of the exhibition hall near the bar. No more screams or cries, no movement, just the temporary silence of life passing. It had been a little over two minutes since the twins had struck.

Fairfax leaned forward, and with the help of the constable, gently lifted Cherry so that Violet could move her legs. She did, but didn't try to get up. She sat on the floor with her hands in front of her, leaning back on a chair. Fairfax could hear a low murmuring beginning from the other side of the seating block. He knew from experience that it would soon increase to tears, cries and a secondary wave of panic. Before long there'd be recriminations and anger, a few would start to try to get drinks from the bar, and then, even worse, some of them would want to leave. They were witnesses! Fairfax, training intact and procedure instilled, got up quickly. He nodded to the constable to take care of Violet and moved away, talking quickly into his handset. The first thing was more assistance, second, not to let anyone go without leaving a name and a contact number. He was instructing two plain clothes and a second uniform, who were by now, and at last, paying proper attention, when he saw Hooper. He was standing amidst the debris of the seating, looking dazed and holding his head.

'Sir?'

'I'm all right, Freddie. A mild concussion. Nothing else.' Hooper looked round to where Violet was sitting. 'Is she all right?'

'He's dead, sir,' said Fairfax. Hooper didn't seem to be listening and began to lurch towards Violet. Fairfax reached out and took his arm. 'I think you'd better sit down, sir.'

'Yes. I think I had.' Hooper sat heavily on a still upright chair about two yards along from where Violet was sitting. He had been badly winded and was breathing heavily. He put his elbows on his knees and leaned forward looking at her. Slowly she turned towards him. Her dress was covered in the blood of Cherry and that of her son. Her face was white and tear-stained. Hooper fell forward onto his knees from the chair, and with Fairfax's help half crawled the few feet towards her. He held out his hand and she took it. He looked into her eyes, hardly knowing what he was doing. 'Violet, I'm so, so sorry.'

Her face creased and she began to cry. He didn't move towards her. He held her hand while she sobbed. Fairfax moved quietly away and left them to it.

4

Even Bernie's huge frame had grown tired holding Arnie. As they'd rounded the van, the first thing they'd seen was a huge bright light bearing down on them. Bernie immediately feared the worst and yelled, 'Coppers!' Still holding his brother, he'd started to run, breathless as he was. 'Buzz off, coppers!'

But then Mirabelle had heard a voice she recognized. 'Bernie! Bernie! We've been looking everywhere for you!' It was Lucy and the light they'd seen was Geoffrey's motorbike headlight.

Bernie turned and held out Arnie for Lucy to see. 'It's bad, Luce, we got to get him to hospital, quick!'

Arnie still had the knife in his chest and Lucy had screamed, but

Mirabelle had run quickly to the van and opened the doors. 'Hurry, get him in.' Then she'd turned to Ronnie, who was standing in a daze by the side of the road. 'Ronnie, are you going to drive?' He didn't answer. 'Ronnie?' He hung his head. 'Where are the keys?' Mirabelle held out her hand.

'Arnie's got them.' Ronnie turned away.

Mirabelle followed Bernie and Lucy as they took Arnie into the back of the van and felt through his pockets for the keys. She shouted through the back doors as Geoffrey came up with Martin. 'Geoffrey, lead us. We need a hospital!'

'What happened?' Geoffrey was pale. He was imagining this must have something to do with the Riss family.

'I'll tell you later. Please, hurry!' Mirabelle had found the keys and jumped down from the back of the van. She closed the doors as Geoffrey ran back towards his bike with Martin.

Inside, Lucy was bent low over Arnie. She assumed it must have been Jock or Razor who had done this. 'Arnie! Oh my God, Arnie. I'll get them bastards!'

'The knife.' Arnie clutched at her sleeve.

Being carried by Bernie had dislodged the blade from his chest and Lucy hardly had to touch it before it fell onto the floor of the van. He didn't seem to be bleeding too badly. 'Just hang on, Arnie!' Lucy held him to her as Mirabelle got into the front and started the engine. Ronnie got in the other side and sat staring out of the front window in a state of shock.

'Git going, Mirabelle, git going!' Bernie shouted to her from the back. Perhaps it was his faith that showed her what to do. She'd hardly driven before, except for a couple of jokey hours with Charlie in the Snipe nearly a year ago in a backstreet on a Sunday morning. She remembered vaguely about the clutch and gears and put both hands on the stick and shoved. Then she released the clutch too fast and the van shot forward with a jerk and stalled. She restarted it and again it jerked forward. Fortunately there was nothing parked in front of her and she managed to steer the Commer out into the road.

Geoffrey was already ahead of her and haltingly she followed, pulling at the gear lever again. More by luck than judgement she managed to get the van into second. She looked at Ronnie by her side for help, but he was sitting silently, staring at his hands in his lap.

She pushed down on the accelerator and prayed as they turned the corner onto the main road. They passed the Crystal Rooms, where police cars and ambulances were already screeching to tyre-burning halts with their sirens wailing. A crowd was beginning to form as Geoffrey's motorbike and Henry's baker's van shot by, heading north.

After a few minutes of gear crunching and one accidental brake instead of a declutch, Mirabelle got the van into third and left it there. She could see Martin's face and the black bulk of Geoffrey's back in the beam of her headlights and turned quickly to look into the back of the van. There was no sound. Lucy was still holding Arnie and Bernie was sitting on the floor, holding the wooden racks either side and staring down at his brother. Mirabelle wasn't sure, but she thought she could see Bernie's lips move. Perhaps he was praying. She concentrated on the road and Geoffrey ahead.

The traffic was getting lighter as it began to rain. They drove in silence. Even if anyone had anything to say, they wouldn't have dared. It was as if Arnie's life was in a balance and anything, even a hushed word, could have tipped it. Ahead Geoffrey and then Martin signalled left. Mirabelle saw briefly, in the headlights of the bike, a sign reading hospital. She jerkily slowed the van and made the turn. They were in what seemed to be a huge park. Perhaps the hospital was sited in the middle of it . . .

'Stop! Stop!' It was Lucy. She'd suddenly looked up from Arnie. 'Stop!'

'Stop, Mirabelle!' It was Bernie joining in.

Mirabelle could hear Arnie coughing and pushed the brakes as gently as she could. The van came to a halt under a tree and she turned in her seat. Arnie was forcing himself up. In the half-light she could see a black stain on his chin. He was coughing blood. She vaguely heard the roar of Geoffrey's returning motorbike as Lucy wailed, 'I don't know what to do! I don't know what to do!'

Mirabelle pulled up the handbrake with both hands and got out of the van. She ran round to the back as Geoffrey and Martin got off the bike and came towards her. By the time she had opened the back doors Arnie had stopped coughing and had lain back onto the floor of the van. Mirabelle could only see his feet. She stepped up into the back and looked down. Arnie's chin and throat were covered in blood. He was looking up at Lucy. He said, 'Hello, mate.'

'I love you, Arnie.' Lucy was crying and her tears were falling onto Arnie's face.

He raised his hand to Bernie. 'Bern.' Arnie was smiling. Bernie leaned in close. Arnie laid his hand on his collar and pulled him closer. 'Come here, come . . .' He began to whisper and it was difficult to hear what he was saying. Bernie put his ear close to his brother's mouth as he spoke. Then Bernie pulled away and he stared down for a second, as if he was stunned by what he'd just heard. Arnie smiled; his teeth were red from the blood. He said, 'I'm proud of you, mate.'

'I'm proud of you, Arn,' said Bernie.

'God . . .' Arnie didn't finish. His head fell back. There was a dry rattle in the back of his throat.

'Arnie!' Lucy clutched at him. Her cry rang in the air as his body went limp. Arnie was dead.

No-one spoke for a long time. Lucy remained hunched over the body, as Mirabelle stepped down from the back of the van and stood in the rain, head bowed with Geoffrey and Martin. She felt the wind and water on her face and began to cry. She looked into the back of the van. Bernie hadn't moved. He was looking down on the death of his brother. His huge hands gripped the racks on either side and his head hung low between. His left leg was crooked over the body like a shield. His back was an arc of sorrow, his every breath a sigh. Mirabelle could hardly bear it, she felt as if her heart was going to burst. If she'd ever been unsure as to why she'd left the Bridge, she was certain now. She would never make judgement again.

Lucy raised her head and looked out of the back of the van to Geoffrey standing in the rain. 'Can we do something please?' She stopped, catching a sob. 'I don't want to sit with him in a baker's van all night. Please.' She looked down as she began to cry. 'Geoffrey, take us away.'

Geoffrey looked over her head to Ronnie, who'd turned in the front seat and was looking down on Arnie. 'Ronnie?' Ronnie looked up at Geoffrey for a moment. There was nothing he could say. He turned away again and stared ahead through the windscreen at the rain spattering the glass.

Geoffrey wanted to help, but didn't know how. 'Well . . . ? I . . . ?' He glanced at Martin. 'Martin? Ah . . . ? First we must telephone Auntie and . . . tell her. And we must make arrangements.' He stopped and looked at Martin again. 'Martin?'

Martin took over. His harsh, high-pitched Welsh voice cut through the uncertainty. 'All right. First, we must get out of this awful place.' He looked around the dark park. None of them knew if they were still being followed by whoever had done this to Arnie. Both Geoffrey and Martin were very frightened.

Lucy was relieved that someone was saying something practical. She said, 'Yes, Martin?'

'So . . .' Martin wasn't sure where they were to go. He looked nervously back down the road again. He did his best to think quickly. 'So. I know a place. Follow me and Geoffrey. Mirabelle, you drive. And . . .' He stopped again.

'Where are we going, dear?' Geoffrey was at a terrible loss.

'You leave it to me,' said Martin. 'We need time at the moment, don't we? Yes. Time to think. Get off the road anyway. Leave it to me.'

'Thank you, Martin.' Lucy had confirmed his leadership and no-one was going to argue with her at the moment. Mirabelle least of all. She knew it didn't matter where they went. She looked up at the bleak and windy sky. Somewhere in the heavens she was sure there was a fire that had been started years before. Now it was beginning to flame and flare and it would follow them like a blazing star until it had burned itself out and its cause was seen. And Sorush would come soon. There were two deaths in the family now and the Dark Angel would investigate them both. She looked at Bernie, who still hadn't moved. He seemed to her to be like a great power about to break from the earth. She gently closed the back doors and went to the front of the van as Martin climbed into the sidecar.

'Where are we going?' asked Geoffrey.

'We'll think of somewhere,' said Martin.

Geoffrey started the bike, revved and pulled in front of the van. Martin turned in the sidecar to check that Mirabelle was following them.

5

Hooper was hoping, but after Violet had held his hand and begun to cry, she'd said nothing more. They'd led her away from Cherry's body and taken her to an office at the back of the building. Hooper had stayed with her for ten minutes, but she was silent and sat staring vacantly out of the window. A medic had come in, given her a cursory examination and mouthed the word 'Shock'. Hooper had tried to take her hand again, but it was lifeless and so he had let it go. Then he had whispered, 'Do you remember me?' She hadn't answered. He waited for a moment, looking at her sad unseeing eyes. He knew that he had to get her out of there; he wanted her somewhere safe and warm. He wondered where it would be best to take her. As if in answer to his unspoken thought she suddenly said, 'I want to go home.'

'Don't worry, Violet, I'll look after you now.' If Hooper had meant nothing else in his life, he meant that. She didn't move and showed no signs of having heard him. He knew he had to act and for the first time in days he was clear as to what he was going to do. He got up quickly, went out of the office and detailed a WPC to sit with her. He ordered two uniformed constables to guard the door under the absolute instructions to allow no-one, but no-one, into the room. Then he went to find Fairfax.

If there had been any benefit from the killing it was that it had been public. Within minutes of his call for assistance, Fairfax had been swamped by it. The local force had sent everything they had. Even the Soho nick had come on the line offering help. It was known as front-page policing. This was a celebrity event and there wasn't a superintendent in the capital who didn't want his face on the late-night bulletins. They also wanted to please Hooper and deflect any possibility of reports of their previous lack of interest. Fairfax was so inundated by uniforms, plain clothes, scientists and the upper ranks being helpful, not to say servile, that he found himself with little to do.

The first witness reports hadn't been useful. No-one had seen the attackers. In fact, most observers seemed to think that it was the wild and unshaven man who'd been seen drinking heavily at the bar a few minutes earlier who had suddenly thrown himself at Violet, stabbed Cherry and then for some reason plunged a dagger into his own chest.

Then an equally crazy giant had carried him off. Most of this Fairfax discounted. He had seen Arnold charge across the catwalk with his own eyes and was sure he held no dagger. And anyway, he'd observed the handle of the blade in Cherry's throat; it was short and flat. Fairfax knew a throwing knife when he saw one. This was an attack from an external source and Arnold had been doing his best to protect his mother. Fairfax was prepared to bet next month's overtime on it. So who'd done it?

'The McCarthy Twins.' Hooper had come up behind him in the auditorium. Ever since he'd sat staring at May's dried blood on her office carpet in the tower he'd known that they were up against something outside the usual realms of the Met. His head began to spin because he had a fair idea of what that something was. He also knew full well why no ordinary, sane or reputable citizen had ever reported the twins. It was because no ordinary, sane or reputable citizen could ever entertain their existence. And why was that? Because the twins came from beyond us, that was why; and more than that, Hooper had begun to realize, in his own weird way, that they also lived within us all. They were the seeds of our own destruction made manifest, weren't they? The twins were not only death, they were inevitable death. And Violet was their target. He shuddered. What could he do about inevitable death? He knew the answer, but it terrified him. The inevitable was rational. In order to defeat it, he would have to be otherwise. And he knew how to do that. He would have to occupy the fifth house and the rose garden after all, wouldn't he? Because in the rose garden nothing was inevitable unless he willed it.

'No-one saw anything, sir,' Fairfax said.

'They're not likely to have done, Sergeant.' Hooper's eyes were wide.

'Sir?' This was news to Fairfax. Invisible killers?

'The twins are not seen, Freddie.' Hooper looked at his sergeant with a meaningful eye. Like a man on the edge of a deep and uncharted sea he had at last begun to understand. You can't fantasize for thirty years without some kind of shift in perception, and he'd made it. In a sudden false burst of elation he grinned. This was the case that he'd been made for. He was entering the realms of the angels.

'It could have been Riss, sir,' said Fairfax, trying to ground his superior.

'Two knives, Sergeant, two assailants, two twins.'

'The Scotsman and the Sikh, sir?' In fact, Fairfax was coming round to Hooper's point of view, but where did you even begin to find a pair of twins whose very visibility seemed to be in doubt?

Hooper surprised Fairfax. 'You're right.'

It caught the sergeant out. Put absolutely on the spot, he knew in his heart of hearts that an idiot like Scotch Jock was more likely to throw up than throw a knife. He was sure Hooper thought that too, so what was he getting at? 'You've changed your mind then, sir?'

'No, Sergeant.' Hooper put his hands in his coat pocket and thought about it. 'You see, Sergeant, the McCarthy Twins are at a distance from us inasmuch as they exist in a world we can't conceive.'

'You mean like on another planet, sir?' Fairfax was trying to be helpful but knew he was sounding facetious.

It didn't appear to worry Hooper. 'Could be.'

Fairfax asked very seriously, 'Are you serious, sir?' All around them was the heavy, painstaking plod of police work. SOCOs were screening off the catwalk, police photographers were shooting roll after roll of film, and the scientists were already laying out their gear. How could he be standing in the middle of this, talking with his superintendent about the possibility of murderers from Pluto?

Hooper went on, 'You see, Sergeant, I am beginning to understand that there is an area of conduct, not to say being, that is very far removed from us.' He looked up at his sergeant. 'Let's assume it for a moment anyway. Let's assume that it is so far away from us that we cannot see or even begin to understand it.' He stopped. Fairfax waited with bated breath. 'If it is the fact of the matter that we cannot come close to understanding it because it is removed from our plane of consciousness, then what do we do?'

'Ah?' Fairfax hadn't got a clue.

'It's obvious, Sergeant.' Hooper looked up at the work going on around them. 'We do what we can and we proceed towards the unknown by first examining the known.' He sighed as he realized Fairfax wasn't following him. 'You see there is a link between us and what we don't know, isn't there?'

'Is there?'

'Yes, Sergeant. The unknown has in fact trodden on known turf, it has come into our realm: in the restaurant, the attacks on the aunt and grandmother, the murder of May. These are all tangible, are they not?

These are all points of contact between us and the unknown. These are where we begin to see the unseen. Could be their mistake.' He paused, thinking about it.

'Sir?' Fairfax definitely wasn't getting this.

'Ordinary police work, Sergeant.' Hooper looked at Fairfax. 'The Riss family, Freddie. They are our first step. They are the link between us and the McCarthy Twins. Find them.'

'Yes, sir.' Fairfax cheered up. This was something he could appreciate.

'I also want you to provide an escort for Miss Green to her apartment, and then maximum, and I mean maximum, protection.'

'Will we be able to protect her from the unseen, sir?' Fairfax asked logically.

The question perturbed Hooper. 'Good point, Freddie, good point.' He inhabited the rose garden, considered for a moment and immediately had the answer. 'Yes. Yes we will.' He looked directly at Fairfax. 'Because, you see, where the unseen becomes seen is where it takes action in the world that we know. And that's where we will be waiting for them: at Violet's apartment.' He smiled. He was beginning to get the hang of this.

'We have a car waiting, sir,' said Fairfax, who wasn't.

'Good. And the brothers. My instinct is that they are an innocent party, but they may well be able to help. I want them too. The eldest was wounded. Hospitals, doctors, Freddie.'

'Yes, sir.' At last his guvnor was back on track.

'You have the full force of the Met at your disposal, Sergeant.'

'Yes, sir!'

'I'll take her to the car myself.' Hooper walked away towards the rear of the auditorium. As he held open the door of the office for Violet, she seemed to smile. Did she know that in his mind he was holding open the door of the restaurant and leading her to a pre-booked table to celebrate their wedding anniversary? Perhaps she did. With everything else that was going on in him, Hooper considered that thought transference, fantasy connection and a mutual swim in the deep waters of the unconscious were all little more than everyday events. The unknown, let's face it, was normal.

Violet was shrouded in several blankets. She was escorted to the waiting car by a woman police sergeant and two plain-clothes officers, besides Hooper. Waiting for her in the car were two other officers. In the car behind there were a further four, and in front were two motor-cycle outriders. Fairfax had done his job well. Violet gave his superintendent barely a glance as the convoy pulled away from the Crystal Rooms. As he observed the protection he could provide Hooper felt proud. He had no doubt that the interior bubble of joy he'd known all these years was going to expand and swamp this ugly world of screaming crowds and ambulance sirens with the smiling faces of their children and Christmas-tree lights. He was so happy and so convinced that the unreal and the unknown were one and the same thing, and that his acceptance of the first would reveal the second, that he failed to notice the black Mercedes van that pulled out of a side street and silently followed the squad car carrying Violet as it went away up the Great North Road. Maybe Hooper was right and it was invisible, not to say inevitable.

$\boxed{6}$

If Hooper was slowly losing his mind as he put his toe into the great and dark sea of the inexplicable, then Mirabelle was hardening hers as she swam into the depths. She knew she had no alternative. This was all going to get worse before it got better. She had no doubt that the Mihr within would remain absolute in her faith and would show her how to adapt to meet whatever Sorush would throw at them. Even so, she was unprepared for what happened next.

She had been driving the Commer for twenty minutes and was beginning to feel at least a confidence in that. No-one in the van had spoken. Lucy was still hunched over Arnie's body and Ronnie sat silent by her side. Ahead in her headlights was the motorcycle and sidecar. She could see Geoffrey's staunch, black-leathered back and Martin's pale worried face as he constantly turned to ensure that she followed. There was silence apart from the muted rasp of the ancient engine. Then suddenly the sound disappeared and she could see nothing at all out of the windscreen except plain grave black. The dark seemed to penetrate the van and it was even becoming difficult to see Ronnie, head bowed and listless by her side. Instinctively she braked, but couldn't tell if the van was slowing or not. She began to panic, pushing her foot down against the pedal, then putting both hands onto the handbrake and trying to pull it up. It wouldn't move. The van, as far as she knew, was out of control and plunging through the darkness.

Suddenly the windscreen was crowded with the faces of angels. Their heads had shrunk and their pale ceramic faces were no more than two or three inches from brow to chin. There were over a hundred of them, moving ceaselessly across the screen. Their wings pressed against the glass like a horde of horrible giant insects.

Their tiny grey faces completely shut out the road ahead and then, as quickly as they had come, they disappeared, to be replaced immediately by the grossly distorted face of Sorush. Her huge eyes filled the windscreen and there were thousands of cracks in her manufactured skin. She spoke in triumph. 'The eldest is dead. I shall have him.'

The light of Mihr filled the interior of the van. 'You shall not,' she shouted and the Dark Angel was gone as quickly as she had come.

Mirabelle grabbed at the steering wheel again. She was shaking, but at least she could see through the windscreen again. They were on a fast dual carriageway and she had no idea how they'd arrived there, or how she'd managed to get through the last few seconds without crashing the van. Ahead there was Geoffrey and the motorbike. He was slowing and Martin was manically waving his arm and indicating left. Mirabelle realized that her foot was still on the brake pedal and the van was coming to a halt. She turned the wheel and brought it to a dead stop in what seemed like a deserted car park. She fell back into her seat and wanted to cry as Ronnie looked up and said in a dull voice, 'What's going on now then?'

Mirabelle didn't answer. She watched as Martin got out of the sidecar and walked over to what seemed to be an abandoned pub. The windows were boarded over and covered in torn curling posters and graffiti. The place seemed to be derelict. Martin hammered on the huge wooden door and after a few seconds it was opened by a small man with grey cropped hair, a moustache and an earring. Mirabelle smiled to herself. She might have known that Martin would have brought them to his own. He spoke to the man for a few seconds and came over to the van. 'We can stay for a couple of hours. At least it's off the road, isn't it?' He looked up at her from the gloom of the car park and added, as if he'd heard her thoughts, 'They're Buddhists.'

Geoffrey had gone round to the back and opened the rear doors of the van. Bernie and Lucy were perfectly still. Arnie lay where he'd died, stretched almost the full length of the van. Geoffrey said, 'Perhaps it would be better if we left him?'

'No. He comes with me, Geoffrey.' Lucy looked up. 'I'm not leaving him.'

'It's all right.' Martin had appeared by Geoffrey's side. 'We can take him in, and . . .' He looked uncertainly at Lucy. 'Make arrangements. They have a phone.'

'I'll take him, Luce.' Bernie heaved himself up and got out of the back. He pulled his brother's body gently towards him as Lucy held his head off the metal floor, then he heaved him up and took him towards the door of the old pub.

The interior was in the process of being ripped out. The old saloon and public bars had been knocked into one and the tables and chairs cleared. The resulting space was dark, uneven and lit by temporary working lights on long cables. There was the smell of incense burning. Several shaven-headed men stood around in the uncertain light holding hammers and saws as Bernie brought the body in. Two of the men immediately cleared a large old pub table and pulled it to the centre of the room. Bernie carefully laid Arnie down. Not a word was spoken as the short man who'd opened the door produced an old white sheet and laid it carefully over him. Then everyone stood silently around the corpse, not knowing what to do next.

'I . . .' Martin had turned to the short man.

He felt the need to explain, but the man held up his hand and whispered, 'Never mind. I'm sorry we're in such a mess.'

'Thank you.' Martin smiled at him, then turned to the others and said quietly, 'They're turning it into a temple, you see.'

'It's like a chapel.' Bernie's deep voice resounded around the big, quiet, half-renovated room. Up above it was all getting painted white, behind there was a huge statue of a big fat geezer with a big bald head, who sat with his legs crossed, and he had robes on, and in front of that there was some heavy bits of concrete brick. Maybe there was gonna be an altar. Maybe it was one like out of the Arfer. It seemed to give him an idea. 'Excuse me.' He lumbered slowly over to Arnie and stood at the head of the body with his hands clasped in front of him. Everybody watched him and waited quietly as he looked down. They felt the instinct to clasp their hands, too, as Bernie began to speak very slowly. 'This is Lancelot who lay sick with illness and grief on the cold stone floor. He was the bravest knight of them all. He had the biggest shield and the sharpest sword and everyone agreed he was the best of the lot. He also suffered the most pain in his heart because of Guinevere. God bless you, Lancelot. All you have to do is look up. I promise you, you will never die.' Bernie bowed his head. 'I will pray for you.'

There was a silence as those who wanted to pray prayed and those who didn't stood still as a mark of respect. After a while, and one by one, they spread to sit on the old chairs and benches scattered around the room. The short man asked each of them gently if they'd like tea. No-one did. Lucy laid her head on Martin's shoulder and Ronnie sat quietly in a corner. Mirabelle could see that the shock had incapacitated them all. She motioned to Geoffrey and slipped out of the room. She whispered to him for several minutes in the dark of the hallway and then made her way further down to where she'd seen a payphone as they'd come in. It was going to be the most difficult call she'd ever made. She'd thought of asking Martin to do it, but decided it would be better if she made the decisions herself from now on. Geoffrey had reluctantly agreed to take her, Bernie and Ronnie to his mother's house in the north for the rest of the night. Harriet would have to come and take Arnie home. She picked up the phone.

7

After she'd replaced the receiver, Harriet sat with Sophie in the cold of the darkened restaurant for a long time. Both of them were in their nightdresses and gowns. Sophie was slumped, Harriet sat straighter. They held hands and didn't speak. Perhaps they would have stayed that way for the rest of the night if it wasn't for O'Dare. Ever since he'd passed out earlier in the evening he'd lain asleep on

355

Charlie's chequered restaurant linoleum. He'd been wakened by Mirabelle's phone call and had tried to go back to sleep, only to be jolted back into consciousness by Harriet's howl of grief and the scrape and clatter of a chair as she'd fallen back into it. He'd listened to the rest of the phone conversation, the tears of the two women, and then witnessed the silence. Now he thought it was about time something was done.

'Now girls, it's time for faith!' Harriet and Sophie both half screamed as the shadowy figure rose from the dark in the corner of the room.

Harriet sank back into her chair as she realized who it was. 'Not now, if you please.'

O'Dare came over and sat quietly by them. After a second he said, 'Don't you have to collect the body?' Harriet looked round at him. His tone was very gentle. 'I heard the call, Auntie. What do you have to do with Porkie?'

'I . . . ?' Harriet tried to recollect what Mirabelle had told her.

'Try and think now, Auntie, because I'm going to come with you to help.' This was a version of O'Dare that no-one had seen before and such was Harriet's dull shock that she didn't think to question it.

'We have to pick up the Snipe from Henry who is a baker. And we have to go . . .' She picked up the piece of paper by the till. Apparently she'd written down both addresses.

O'Dare took them from her and held them up to the light. 'Well, Henry's in the west and this other one's north. In your state you don't want to be travelling to all points of the compass.'

'No.' Harriet turned to him, grateful for his assistance. 'What shall we do?'

'So. If you'll agree to this, we'll get two taxis.' And O'Dare, new man of action, outlined his plan. Extraordinary to say, but beneath the reservoir of booze that made the man, there lay a heart of cunning and gold that perhaps made something else altogether. Maybe it's how he'd survived so long. They did exactly as he said. Harriet and O'Dare would go straight to Arnie in the first taxi. Sophie would go west with Porchese in the second and pick up the Snipe. Then they'd meet at the old pub and all come back with Arnie in the car and call the undertaker.

Porchese was dragged from his heavy crème de menthe dreams on the bench at the back of the club room, Harriet and Sophie had dressed, O'Dare had called the cabs, and within fifteen minutes they were in them and heading in different directions from the end of Dean Street. Harriet and O'Dare didn't think about it, but as they went down Great Windmill Street, they passed directly beneath the window of Mathilda's room.

8

Having betrayed the boys in the barrel of the peep, Mathilda had run onto the streets and kept going. She'd walked for hours along the embankment, fuelled by her rage at Ronnie and his betrayal of her love. But as the day came to a close she'd slowed and slowed, her shoulders slumped and her feet began to drag as her real feeling surfaced. It was the dull and heavy pain of shame; shame for her betrayal of the brothers. There was no power in shame to get you walking, there was no energy to burn, it just smouldered and threatened to choke. She'd hardly been able to move and stood staring at the river for a long time. And then the idea came; it was so brilliant and simple she couldn't believe it.

She'd moved away quickly and walked into the first chemist she'd come to. As she'd bought the first pack of paracetamol, she'd noticed how cunning she was being. Just the one box. She hadn't wanted to give anyone the impression that it was for anything other than a headache. In the second chemist she'd bought another pack, and then in another street, a third, and so on. She'd also decided to add brandy to the list, but that was easier because you didn't have to lie about booze, everybody assumed that it was natural to buy enough to kill yourself. Her spirits had begun to lift as she'd done her round of suicide shopping. She could have carried on all evening and begun another round of the chemists, but the brandy had cost more than she'd expected and she had run out of money, so she'd decided to leave it at that and go home.

She didn't know that two days before the twins had been in and wrecked the place. She stood on the door that had been ripped from its hinges and flattened to the ground. She looked around at the emptied drawers, the tipped-out cupboards and her clothes scattered across the floor. In ordinary circumstances she would have cried. Not now. In her present state of mind all this seemed perfectly natural. She didn't even stop to think about who had done it. She put her plastic bag of drugs and booze on the bed and calmly picked up the door and leaned it back into place. Then she began to clear up. She'd decided she didn't want to leave a mess.

When she'd finished she sat on the bed and looked round. It was fine. Apart from the door and some bits of glass on the carpet, you'd hardly know that anyone had smashed her place up at all. She turned on the TV. It still worked! She watched a late-night news programme as she emptied the five canisters of paracetamol she'd bought into a plastic bowl, which she placed carefully on the bedside table. Then she took an old and dusty silk flower that her mother had once given her for her hair and pushed the stem down into the pills so the flower stood perfectly beautiful, sticking up out of them. She placed the two bottles of brandy behind the bowl of drugs and draped a necklace and a purple cotton scarf around them. Then she got up, found a mug that hadn't been broken and opened one of the bottles. She poured herself a good three inches, put the bottle back under the necklace and plumped up the pillows on the bed. She was very happy. On the TV there was an item about unemployment. She scoffed and wondered why everyone didn't just get themselves a job, it was easy. She scooped up a small handful of pills from the bowl and took a sip of brandy. This was going to be the best night of her life.

9

'Hahaha!' Emil had started to laugh. He didn't know why; he just felt like it. They'd been sitting in the Daimler outside the bakery for over four hours. Stella's acid was the best, and more to the point, immediate.

When they'd come out of the bakery, Jock had opened the unlocked door of the car, got in, taken the keys from his pocket and held them by the ignition. Then he'd stopped and looked down at them. Two

358

hours later he'd still been looking at them. He liked the way they glinted in the light. He'd licked his lips and tasted something sweet. As he'd brushed his mouth blue cake crumbs had fallen into his lap and he stared at those for another half an hour. Some of them had gathered together in a crease in his trousers. They were like tiny blue people in a black valley. How come he'd never noticed things like this before? He looked up. The night outside was orange. He looked to his left and noticed that Luis was staring at it too. What a night this was.

For Luis the night was more red. He was staring at a kind of perspex, static hell. For a while it seemed like one of those Day-Glo pictures of an inferno he'd seen in a shop that sold posters to teenagers, but occasionally it seemed to move, and every now and again black shadows wandered through it. When they came closer he realized that they were human beings with bright pink faces and they looked at him in a peculiar, not to say hostile, way. He had considered this for a while and then these thoughts disappeared as he was taken by the way the red-feathered parrots were materializing from the streetlight up ahead. They kept coming and coming, and if he really concentrated he could make them fly towards him and keep them in view until they disappeared over the roof of the car. They were magnificent. 'It's better than the peep,' he'd heard himself say at one point, but the sound seemed disjointed and no-one had answered, so he'd let the words fall with a soft thud onto the dashboard and then slide down to his feet. He'd felt them on his ankles for a little while, but then forgot all about them and went back to watching the parrots.

Razor had stared down at the road by the side of the car. After a while he'd lifted his head and realized that it continued ahead of them. The thought came to him that it would probably connect with another road and then another one. He'd had the sudden insight that all roads led everywhere, and it pleased him as much as if he'd found his uncle's gold that he was sure was buried somewhere under the little house in Balsall Heath. He kept following the roads in his head and at each junction he had a little thought about his life. His mum and dad, his brothers, his cousins were all very clear and had big noses and beards and liked the same things as he did. He began to imagine murdering them. One at each junction on this extraordinary map of roads that had seemed to have taken over his brain. He'd go all the way from this bit of road here to the street where his cousin lived in Selly Oak. He'd murder him too. It was amazing, all you had to do was follow the map, like a trail of blood, and it was just murder all the way.

Emil had stared at his watch for four hours. So far, he had tried to count under his breath about fifty times exactly one minute in seconds. When he'd finally done it he'd felt overjoyed and started to do mental arithmetic with the figures on the face. Ten times five, forty-five times twenty-five, and fifty times five past. Each calculation had taken him into abstract realms of pure number that seemed to come alive in his brain. He decided to try to count his brain cells and for half an hour thought he knew how to do it, but then he forgot all about it. He'd looked at his precious watch again and tried to understand what time would be like without numbers. He'd realized that we wouldn't know it existed. Then in an extraordinary leap he decided that without time we wouldn't know we existed either! Because thoughts and ideas came one after the other like time, didn't they? And he knew all this because of his Riss watch! He was beginning to giggle at his own delicious brilliance. It didn't seem to surprise him. It was like he was a natural. This was it. He was a counter and his life was just a lot of numbers, like the slots, which he'd known all along! Now he knew how to count his life! He knew what it counted for too! You could definitely count on Emil because he was a right guy! Someone who counted for something! He was starting to laugh out loud.

Raphaella had her head back on the seat and had been staring up at the stitching in the upholstery of the inside roof of the car. She liked stitching and cotton and she didn't know why she'd never realized it before. It held things together. She followed the seams as they ran the length and breadth of the roof, and sometimes she leaned forward or arched up to study them more closely. She looked carefully at the little holes made by the upholsterer's needle and wanted to dive in and go on the journey with the thread. She'd be able to travel the whole car, wriggling in and out of all the holes and holding the thread between her legs like a rope. At one point she'd begun to scratch hard at her inner thighs to simulate the feeling. As the peak of the acid had passed, she'd begun to realize that she wanted to be fucked more than she'd ever wanted to be fucked before. She'd slipped her hand up her dress and silently begun to masturbate, but didn't get anywhere because her fanny didn't feel like it was hers. She'd tried kissing her fingers, but they didn't seem to belong to her either. She'd realized that she was in bits, a sum of all her separate parts that just floated around what she was thinking about, and that it was only when she had the correct thoughts that she'd be able to connect herself up again. She was in true dispersal and was beginning to feel panicked when Emil laughed.

It was fortunate he had. Because in the front seat Luis's static red hell had started to come alive and was about to move in on him and burn him up. Emil's laugh jerked him away from the creeping, molten world outside and he suddenly looked around. 'Where am I? What is this? What are we doing?' He stared round the dashboard and then an extraordinary thought came to him: Why is this car?

Jock woke from his crummy reverie and turned as if in slow motion. 'Boss?'

'Why is this car?' Luis said, his eyes bulging.

'This car is why, boss.'

Luis seemed to find this hysterically funny. 'This car is why!'

Jock hadn't finished. 'This car is a Daimler.'

Luis stopped laughing. 'A Daimler?' This was something altogether more serious. He turned in the seat and addressed the back row. 'You know I got this Daimler off a tiny black spider widow woman called Anita Wolfenburg!' This was funny again and they all laughed, especially Emil who became hysterical. There was something about his son's gaping, slobbering, laughing mouth that terrified Luis and suddenly he went pale. 'Her husband wasn't even cremated and I took his Daimler!'

'Cremated!' Emil yelped with laughter again.

'Aaaghh!' Luis suddenly screamed. 'May I never be forgiven!'

Razor leaned forward with a brilliant smile. 'Don't worry, Mr Riss, all things come to pass.'

'That's what worries him!' Emil's sides were splitting.

Razor looked at Emil and said, 'I am blank.'

'What?' asked Emil. Paranoia hit him like a punch. Razor was terrifying. Emil's mouth sagged. 'Wha'?'

Razor turned away, his mind travelling roads again. Raphaella had looked out of the window and seen some lights above the bakery; they reminded her of something. She suddenly remembered the baker's last words: 'Crystal Rooms'. She spoke them aloud. Then she said, 'I want Arnie. I want nookie.'

'What! What she say?' Luis suddenly jerked up. 'I am on the edge, you hear me? I am on the fucking edge! Look at me! Aaagghh!' He had looked down over the front seat to the floor below and began to scream. 'I'm so high! I'm on the cliff and I see seagulls below me and I see the sea! The sea is burning. The sea is red! Why is the sea red?' He looked around, his jaw was still working and some terrible words were trying to force themselves through his gullet. Finally, as if he was being sick, they came up in hot gobbets: 'The sea is red because we burned the baker.'

'Burned the baker!' Emil was off again, laughing fit to bust. But then he stopped as he saw his father's terrified eyes.

'You see,' said Luis slowly, 'we get fried in the oven for bakers and widows.' He looked round slowly. 'You get me?' He turned fast and looked at the orange and red hell out of the front window. The number of Day-Glo parrots had increased and they were flying straight towards him. 'They're coming to get us!' He scrabbled back against the seat, then leaned over into the back again and grabbed his son's knees. 'This is serious. Listen to me. I tell you something.' There was a hush in the car. 'We put them on to us. We hired our own hell. We hired the twins! They're coming to get us!' He began to whine. 'You see any Chinese in the bakehouse?'

Jock shifted sideways. 'I see McCarthy on every plane of existence, boss. In the street, in my dreams, in the mirror.' His voice became hushed. 'I see them twins everywhere.'

This was the most important and profound conversation Luis had ever had. 'In the oven? You see them in the oven?'

Jock turned to Luis, full face. 'Twins in the flames, boss.'

There was quiet as they all digested this extraordinary statement. Jock had become, for this one second of his miserable life, a great leader of men. Up until then they'd thought he was a psychopathic, drunken arsehole, but now they could see he was a prophet.

Luis's mouth sagged, then he stuttered, 'The twins in the oven, don't you get it?' No-one did. 'This is life and death! I am guilty!' Luis roared with tears in his eyes. Then his voice dropped to biblical profundity as he stared at Emil, who had begun to giggle again.

'Can't a papa get to feel his own poor self, ungrateful son?'

Before Emil could think of an answer, Jock said, 'Excuse me, boss …'

Luis took no notice of his soothsayer. He turned, like Moses, to Raphaella. 'A man has a kid and you know what?' His voice quavered. 'It's suicide.'

'Boss!' Jock's eyes were fixed and staring madly out front through the windscreen. He suddenly shielded his face with his hands. 'It's all over!'

Luis turned and saw two huge and dazzling lights coming at them fast. He couldn't believe it! 'Aaaaggh! It's them!'

Raphaella screamed too as the lights grew bigger. They began to fill the windscreen and flood the car. Emil thought it was all his fault and scrabbled up the seat towards the back window. 'I'm sorry, Papa! I'm sorry!'

Outside the lights came to a stop. They'd never seen anything so dazzling. They sat frozen in panic as two silhouettes appeared either side of the brightness. Jock curled back in his seat. 'It's them! The twins from hell!'

'Go,' Luis whimpered, then suddenly yelled as he'd never yelled before in his life. 'Go! Go! Go!'

Jock jerked upright, turned the key in the ignition, slammed the Daimler into reverse, and jammed his foot down. The car shot backwards, burning rubber.

'Keep going, keep going! Don't look, don't look!' Luis turned in terror away from the lights out front and stared manically through the back window. The others all did the same thing, hoping that what they couldn't see wouldn't come after them, as the car lurched backwards away from the bakery and down the street.

The two figures watched as the Daimler disappeared. Two hundred yards from where they stood it did a crazy three-point turn, hitting a hairdresser's signboard and a rubbish bin, then it careened away, rolling madly from side to side, until it was out of sight.

'They think rubber's cheap?' Sophie gave Porchese one of her big looks.

'It was them Riss people,' he said, sounding scared, as he stepped to one side and their taxi pulled away.

'What? Ain't it enough we got dead bodies every way we turn, we got to have Riss too?' Sophie looked up at the bakery. 'What next?'

$$\boxed{10}$$

Mirabelle looked over at Arnie's white-shrouded corpse. It was now surrounded by candles. Everybody was quiet as they waited for Harriet. Bernie prowled alone in the dark near the back of the room. Mirabelle had never seen him so agitated or so isolated. She remembered what he'd said when he'd stood over Arnie earlier: 'God bless you, Lancelot. All you have to do is look up. I promise you, you will never die.' What did that mean? And then, 'Lancelot suffered the most pain in his heart because of Guinevere.' If Arnie was Lancelot, who was Guinevere? And who was Bernie? That much was obvious. She knew he was Galahad.

She looked around. Ronnie sat close to the wall with his head on Geoffrey's shoulder. Lucy was on a wooden chair with her head in her hands close to Arnie's body. Martin and several of the men sat silent in the darkness at the edge of the room. Nothing moved. It was as if they were all held fast in the aspic of time. Was this some ancient story being acted out yet again? Perhaps this was Camelot too, and the past was always, the present was the same and the future held no change. The clock would run through and beyond these immobile figures; their bodies would fail, but their spirit was eternal and immutable. She looked again at Bernie, still prowling in the shadows, deep in thought. It was as if he swam in some psychic torrent that ran with and through the deepest legends of himself and these others. Was this why she had come? To further this truth of Camelot? To protect Galahad? Or was it to be protected by him? She knew she must discover more of the history of this family; of Arnie, his father and Violet, and the extraordinary break-up that had happened around the time of the birth of Bernie. She suddenly turned and went out.

As she came into the car park the moon had partially appeared from behind dark, blustery clouds and was giving the wetness a yellow sheen. She immediately saw what she'd expected.

Sorush was leaning on the wall by the entrance. She was as human as Mihr had seen her, and at her most beautiful. The cold breeze gently whispered through her black hair and blew softly at the thin material of her coat, which hung open, revealing what could have been jet-streaked silk beneath. Her lips were red and her eyes shaded. She stood in a coquettish way with her hands in her pockets and her shoulder against the brick. She could have been a whore.

Her legions were on the dual carriageway. There were thousands of them, hanging suspended and semi-transparent as the traffic hissed through them on the wet tarmac. The light of the moon made their wings appear to be in shades of brown. They could have been a vast cloud of bees or moths. Kasbeel sat beyond them on the roof of one of the great houses opposite. His book was open on his knee.

'The eldest son,' said Sorush.

It was what Mihr had come for. There was no argument as the angels stared at each other across the car park, and Kasbeel began the incantation, 'O Lord Jesus Christ . . .'

Arnie was thirty. His hair was long and matted and his beard filthy. He had a twist of charge in his pocket as he stood at the end of the alley, looking down towards the restaurant. It had been ten years since he'd left; a decade of drugs, booze and abuse, extraordinary times with Henry and all the pain of Stella. He'd decided to come home. He didn't know why. It wasn't as if the previous weeks or months had been particularly bad. There'd been no horrendous trips, no unusual violence, no insanity at all that he could think of. In fact it had been quite peaceful. He'd re-established his regular score and he'd even held down a job as a decorator to pay for most of it. And then he'd walked out. Perhaps it was because he'd stabilized the habit and achieved enough solid heroin equanimity to see the horizon, perhaps some beat of family within him had never really died, or perhaps there were no more veins to pierce. As he walked he knew he was heading back to Soho, but hadn't admitted it to himself. After a few hours the sun had begun to come up ahead of him. He registered the light, its pinks and its reds, but not the significance. This was no new dawn for Arnie, it was just a walk he needed to take because he'd decided he didn't want to kill himself any more. He'd arrived in the alley at around ten in the morning.

Charlie was in the club room, clearing up from the night before. He'd achieved an equanimity too. He ran the place, borrowed too much, spent too much, drank too much and didn't have quite enough sex, but that wasn't bothering him a lot these days. He was living how he wanted and if it had to be without Violet, then so be it. He'd thought about her every now and then and had the odd twinge or occasional dull pain on grey days, but as with indigestion when you watched what you ate, so he kept an eye on what he allowed himself to think and avoided heartburn in both cases. He'd never been able to see Violet clearly in the present and so wasn't able to imagine any future for her. Consequently she'd begun to fade in his memory. But Arnie was another matter. He could still imagine Arnie. After all the boy was half of him, wasn't he? Perhaps he'd given up the drugs now. Perhaps he had a job, perhaps he was in another country, perhaps . . . ? But, truth to tell, even these thoughts were going the way of all things, down the old porcelain tube. It was time to leave it all alone and let it heal.

He was whistling as he wiped the bar. He threw the cloth into the sink and reached up behind him for a full bottle of Scotch off the top shelf. He had unscrewed the top and was pushing an optic into the neck when he heard a sound behind him and turned. His son stood at the bottom of the basement steps. The winter sun filtering through the window flicked round the edges of his silhouette making him look better than he did.

'Hello, Dad.'

'Arnie?' Charlie was still holding the optic half in and half out of the bottle.

'I thought I'd see if it all still was.' Arnie tried a grin and shuffled uneasily. 'Still fiddling the optics then?'

'No, mate, straight forward now.' Charlie put down the bottle. 'Same old place though.' He couldn't move from behind the bar and stood there, just staring at the prodigal.

'Same old world, hey?' Arnie didn't know what to do either. They stood and faced each other across ten feet of worn club-room carpet. The silence was broken by the sound of heavy feet on the stairs down from the restaurant. Arnie looked up.

'Dad!' Bernie jumped down the last three steps and stopped. He was ten years old and already huge for his age. His arms hung loosely by his side as he gawped at the two men, aware of the tension.

Charlie smiled at him. 'This is your big brother.'

Bernie turned with his mouth open. There was spittle on his lip. 'What, Arnie?'

'This is Bernie, Arnie,' said Charlie.

The big boy took a pace towards his elder brother. His voice was already deep and sonorous. 'Hello, Arnie.' He looked up with steady eyes.

Arnie looked down at his feet and then away. The black and white filmstars were still there on the wall. Nothing had changed, except this boy standing in front of him. He was beginning to wish he hadn't come. 'Hello, mate.' He didn't look at Bernie as he said it.

Bernie came another pace closer. 'Will you read my book to me? It's King Arfer.' He stared with big eyes. 'Mum gave it to me when she went away.'

Arnie was thinking that there was something about him. He was standing odd, his arms were awkward, his voice didn't seem to fit his body. Charlie put him straight. 'He's a fit and healthy boy, Arnie. But he never got over her going.' He coughed. 'That's what I think anyway.'

'What are you saying?' Arnie was beginning to sweat. Charlie wasn't sure how to answer.

'I'm retarded.' Bernie said it very simply. 'That's what they say down the school.'

'He's learning to read though, aren't you, Bern?' Charlie was feeling defensive. He wanted Arnie to like his young brother because he wanted Arnie to stay.

'I read a little bit, but mostly I do it by heart.'

'Harriet's been good to him.' Charlie was smiling, but Arnie could sense his desperation. He could also sense his shame, which was worse. He was beginning to wish he'd fixed before he'd come down, but he

367

knew if he had done he'd never have made it. It was as much as he could do to stop his voice shaking. 'I don't know how long I can stay, Dad.'

This made Charlie move. 'Have a drink anyhow. What do you want?'

'I don't think I can stay, Dad.' It was getting more definite. He had to go.

'Come on, son.' Charlie was pleading and grinning at the same time. 'We haven't seen you for ten years.'

'And I don't remember you at all.' Bernie said it very seriously, like it was a true and ancient fact that needed to be considered.

The last person Arnie wanted to see was his younger brother. Why hadn't he thought about that? 'I've got to go.'

'You want to get a haircut, mate.' It was Bernie again, and he was still just as serious. Arnie could see already that his brother had no defences. He would say what he had to say and never understand the consequences.

'You're here now,' Charlie intervened quickly. He didn't want Arnie to think that he had any problems with hair, beards, or what he looked like. 'Have a drink with us.'

'No, I've got to go, Dad.' Arnie took a step back towards the base-ment steps. He had to get out of there. Bernie was looking at him with a sincerity and a need he couldn't bear.

Charlie wasn't having it. 'No.' He finally moved out from behind the bar. All those years of repressing it, stuffing it down, waiting for it to go away; well it was still bloody there and he knew it. He suddenly shouted, 'You're not going again! No-one's bloody leaving me again!' He stopped with one hand on the bar. The words had come out in a rush. He'd told the truth and wasn't sure if he could handle it. His head dropped a little. 'You don't know what I've been through, Arnie.'

There was a pause, then Arnie made up his mind. 'I'm going.' He turned and headed for the basement door.

'Don't go, bruv,' Bernie said very quietly and simply. Arnie had to stop and look back. 'It's good here. And we got Ron. We'd all be together.' There was no emotional content, no blackmail, no personal need in his voice. It was just kindness and it was horribly flat and real.

Arnie tried to explain: 'I've got to go, Bern.' He shot a glance at Charlie. 'You don't understand.'

'Yes I do.' Charlie moved towards him from the bar. He was remem-

368

bering the time he'd found Arnie in the high-rise and seen the needles by his bed. He thought it likely his son was still a junkie. 'I understand more than you think.' He stopped a pace from Arnie. 'Come back, please. You don't have to live here, although you'd be welcome if you want to. All things are past and forgotten. All right?' He put his hand out. Arnie didn't move. 'If I've insulted you, or offended you, and I know I've done more than that, then I'm sorry.' He put his hand out again. There were tears in his eyes. 'Please accept my apology, Arnie, as Bernie's my witness.'

Arnie looked down at the proffered hand. 'It's not that, Dad.'

'If it's not me, well what is it?' Charlie raised both his hands, palms up, in a kind of plea.

'It's not you.' Arnie looked away from his father.

'Well come here then.' Charlie moved forward quickly and took his son in his arms.

Arnie had a drink with his old man. At first it was a small Scotch, but then Charlie pressed another larger one on him. Arnie had to smile to himself and admit that the old boy had always been easy on the despatch of alcohol. As far as he was concerned the sun existed permanently over the yard arm and never rose on a boozeless hour. Drink was life, life was drink, don't fall over if you can help it. Charlie grinned and poured another. By the time Arnie had tipped back three doubles he was feeling better. The twist of junk was still insistent in his jacket pocket, but the alcohol in his brain ensured that he was strong enough to keep it there for the moment. He carried on drinking.

Around midday some of the old regulars turned up. Without exception none of them made any comment on his appearance and all gave him an unquestioning welcome. These were drinkers who understood because they came and went themselves; disappearances were never noted or remarked upon. Anyway he was Charlie's son. If you couldn't say hello to the offspring of the benefactor of booze who could you greet? Arnie liked this impersonal bonhomie. They recited the latest chapter of their daily round with a confidence that assumed that somehow he must have heard about the last ten volumes that he'd missed. Charlie had given him a clean slate on the bar, he could drink as much as he liked, and there was something about the smell of the old place that made him feel warm. He looked around. His old man's clientele were as no-hope as anyone he had met in the west and merely filled their particular vacancies in heart and brain with their own particular poison, which was booze – but no smack. Sitting on the pan and pumping a vein would be anathema to them. So what was the difference between glass and needle? There wasn't any, he concluded. They were just various routes to hell (or from it), so he may as well pour his old man's largesse down his throat until he fell over. Then he'd sleep somewhere up in the flat for a few hours and that would be most of the day gone. After that he would see what he would see.

Around four in the afternoon he crashed on the battered sofa in the living room of the flat. Charlie had been delighted and had half carried him past a pained but equally pleased Harriet, seated at the restaurant till up the stairs from the club. On the way Arnie had blurred impressions of what had once been his life. Nothing seemed strange, all was normal and how it had always been, except for the massive moon face of Bernie sitting up in the overflow room staring at a picture book. He'd looked up as Arnie had passed him on Charlie's shoulder. 'Hello, bruv!' He was as happy as everyone else, and given his overemotional state, Arnie might have cried as Charlie left him stretched out on the worn cushions. He might also have looked round the room and been deluged in a flood of brutal memory. He might have experienced again his despairing anger of a decade ago; he might have remembered his mother's tears and her blood on his cheek. But none of this came back to him. He was too dizzy. His drunken brain spun in circles for a while and then he slept.

It was nearly nine o'clock when Bernie woke him up. 'Dad says do you want to eat somefing? Ronnie ain't here yet, but prob'ly won't never come back till midnight 'cos thass what he's always up to, so d'you want to have a bite now with me and Dad and Auntie?'

Arnie blinked. The place was dark and he could hardly see Bernie, but the voice was close and warm. He immediately felt panic and decided to get out of there fast.

'You got to eat some time, mate. I eat tons of it. Bangers mostly.' Bernie stood there like a giant wall between Arnie and where he wanted to be.

'All right, Bern, I'll come down.'

'In the restaurant.'

'Yeah.'

'Shall I wait for yer?'

'No. Go down.'

'I'll wait, case you get lost.'

'It's all right, I'll . . .'

'I'll wait, Arn.' Bernie went to the door. 'Case you get lost.' He stood there.

Arnie rolled upright on the sofa. He felt terrible. It wasn't just the hangover and it wasn't because he wanted to untwist the grief in the packet in his pocket and inject it into his arm, right now; it was because he already knew that Bernie had begun to bind him. And every second he stayed would be another loop, and soon he'd be trussed and trapped and then what? Held up to ridicule for the failure he was? Scorned by Bernie? He turned on the sofa and saw him waiting by the door. No, that wasn't it. He'd be loved by Bernie and that was the tie he dreaded. He heaved himself up. He knew he couldn't leave yet. He'd eat with them anyway.

They were down at a table in the empty restaurant. Harriet plonked a huge plate of fry in front of him. 'Porkie says good night.'

Arnie looked at the food and knew he couldn't eat it. 'Thanks, Auntie.'

She folded her arms and stood above him, looking down with a piss-take in her eye. 'I can't say I haven't seen you looking better, Arnie. You're thin as a blade, dear. Where've you been?'

'Ah, over in the west, Auntie.' The smell of the food was making Arnie feel sick. Bernie was grinning at him. He felt really bad. He wanted to get out of there and jack up.

'Did you ever see your mother?' Harriet still stood above him. What was this, an interrogation?

'No, I . . .' Arnie didn't want to talk about his one time with Violet in the rain.

Charlie helped him out anyway. 'I don't want to hear about Violet, Harriet.'

She persisted as she was wont. 'I thought you might have seen her, Arnie.'

Arnie was beginning to sweat and shake. 'I didn't see her.'

'Do you know why she went in such a hurry and without a word?' This had been worrying Harriet for years.

'Harriet.' Charlie looked up again. He was starting to get pissed off. 'I want to know, Charlie!'

'That's enough, Harriet. I went looking for her, didn't I?'

'Hardly at all.'

Charlie tried to be reasonable. 'She's gone, isn't she? Arnie's back and welcome. If she walked back through that door now, she'd be welcome too. But she hasn't done, has she? And I don't think she will, so that's an end to it.'

'Hope springs eternal, dear.'

Charlie slammed his hand onto the table. What she was saying was a denial of his ten-year pretence and he couldn't allow it. 'I don't hope and don't say I do hope, Harriet! I am here, Arnie's here, we're all here, and that's all there is to it!' He looked up bitterly at his sister.

The anger in the room triggered resolve in Arnie. He could use it as a barrier against Bernie's affection. 'I don't think I can stay much longer, Dad.'

Charlie pitched a forkful into his mouth. What could he say? He certainly couldn't plead after what he'd just said to Harriet. He kept his mouth open and chewed.

He hadn't bargained for Harriet's certainty. She raised an old-fashioned eyebrow at Arnie. 'Oh you'll stay, dear. Men may roam, but men come home.' She sighed. 'Women of course are another matter.' She sat heavily at the table, resident in her own house of truth, then picked up her knife and fork and began to eat.

After a while Bernie said, 'You read me my book later, bruv? Ron ain't here see, an' Auntie's too busy 'cos Porkie's gone home.'

'Bern, I . . . ?'

'Go on. Just a bit of it.'

Harriet watched Arnie. She didn't say anything because she knew that if she did, he might say no.

'Just a bit then, Bern.' Arnie pushed his plate away from him. If he was going to read books he didn't have to eat.

It was gone eleven by the time Bernie was ready for bed. He was in the bathroom for three-quarters of an hour, while Arnie was in the living room going insane. The shaking had turned to shivering and his sweat was running cold. Three times he took out the twist and laid it on the table next to a syringe. Three times he returned the works back to his pocket, promising himself the fix as soon as Bernie was asleep. The old man had said to join him in the club; maybe he'd do that later when he was charged. Finally Bernie appeared in his pyjamas, holding his Arfer.

'Read my book, Arn?'

'Yeah, get into bed.' Arnie was getting desperate. This was going to have to be quick.

Bernie must have sensed his brother's panic. 'Won't take long, 'cos I'm really tired. I can't keep my bloody eyes open.' He disappeared into his bedroom and Arnie followed. 'Won't be a minute, Arn.' Bernie switched on the bedside light, carefully folded the bedcovers back, got into the bed and then neatly tucked himself in. Arnie could feel the sweat in his eyes. Every movement Bernie made seemed to be taking an eternity. Bernie lay back on the pillow and opened the Arfer. 'It's the one where Lancelot is ill in church because of all his crimes. Here y'are.'

Arnie took the book with unsteady hands and began to read, 'So he went to the tiny chapel in the courtyard of the castle . . .'

Bernie took over: '. . . and knelt on the stone floor to pray. After a while he fell into a reverie.' Bernie lay back with his eyes closed and recited as Arnie watched. 'First a beautiful maiden came to him in his dream and he was bewitched. Then he saw a white dove rise from behind the altar, and as it flew up, two wondrous and glistening angels descended. Between them they held a gleaming cup that shone like the rays of the sun. What's next?'

'Ah . . . ?' Arnie looked down at the book. 'Suddenly the cup burst into fire . . .'

'. . . and hovered above the altar, for it was the Holy Grail.' Bernie was off again. Listening to him made Arnie feel calm. There was something about his voice that soothed at the same time as bringing tears to his eyes. Bernie went on, 'The angels looked to Lancelot to rise and take it into his hands, but he lay weak and sick on the stone floor.' Bernie's voice was getting slower. 'Slowly the fire ascended and was gone. It was the closest that Lancelot ever came to the Lord.' He stopped, his breathing was even. 'Night, Arn. I'm glad you came back.' He lay still with his eyes closed.

Arnie didn't move. He knew he was going to get up, go into the living room and stick a needle in his arm, but he didn't move. After a while he leaned forward and switched off the bedside light, then he sat and watched as Bernie dropped off to sleep. If anything was going to help him it was this retard. He felt tears mix with the sweat on his cheek and he wiped them away with the back of his hand. If anything was going to fuck him up more it was this retard.

He got up and went out into the living room. He didn't turn on the light, he didn't have time. He ripped his jacket off and pushed his shirtsleeve up. He was moving very quickly. He undid the twist and realized he didn't have a spoon. He went fast into the kitchen and scrabbled among the crockery on the draining board looking for one. He pushed the plates and cups out of the way. They landed in the sink with a crash. 'Shit. Fuck.' He turned and realized he couldn't remember where they kept the cutlery. He opened a drawer and started hunting through plugs and wire. Then he realized he was being a stupid cunt because they wouldn't keep spoons with the electrics would they? He opened another drawer and found what he was looking for. He was almost running as he arrived back in the living room with the spoon. He shook some of the stuff onto it and heated the spoon with his lighter. He was scared his hand was shaking so much that he'd drop the fucking lot. He dipped the needle and filled the syringe. Then he grabbed a tea towel that was lying over the back of a chair, pushed his sleeve back up again and twisted the towel around the top of his arm as a tourniquet. He held the end in his teeth to keep it tight, then began to flick at his inner arm, trying to get a vein. He was glad he'd been doing the stuff in his leg lately to give his arms a break. He struck lucky and found a juicy one quickly. He picked up the syringe to inject.

'You doing heroin then?' Ronnie stood by the door.

Arnie didn't move. He was going to shoot up in front of his brother, he knew he was. He didn't have any alternative.

'Dad said you were back. Hello.'

'Hello, Ron.'

'You look the same.'

'You look bigger, Ronnie.' Arnie still hadn't moved.

'Can I have some of that, Arn?'

'No. Fuck off will you, mate?'

'I've done it before, but I haven't jacked it up though.' He was standing talking calmly as if he couldn't see Arnie's panic.

Arnie moved the needle fractionally away from his arm and straightened. 'I packed it in, mate,' he lied.

'Why you doing it then?'

'I had to have some to come here.'

'Give some to me then.' Ronnie moved closer to him.

'No.'

'Why not?'

'It's not for you, Ronnie.' He took the needle back to his arm, but now he couldn't see the vein. 'Fuck.' He put the syringe back on the table and began to flick at his arm again.

'You read to Bernie, did you?' Ronnie was matter-of-fact. He stood and observed Arnie as if he were some poor alien.

'Yeah, I read it to him.' The vein wouldn't reappear.

'We all have to share it out.'

'I told you, I read to him!' This was getting fucking worse, he pumped his arm again trying to get the vein to bulge. Then looked up, beginning to feel a prat. 'Go to bed, will you, Ron?'

'Dad said you were in my room.'

'I'll sleep in here.' He nodded towards the sofa.

'No, it's all right, Arn, you can have my room. You can have it permanently if you want. You can even do that in there if you like.'

Arnie dropped his arm. This was no good. He had to get rid of Ron. 'Give me a break, bruv, will you?'

'All right, mate, I'll go and leave you to it.'

'Thanks Ron.'

'Night then, Arn.' Ronnie stood for a second then went.

Arnie pumped again and the vein reappeared. He shot up. The rush was immediate and heaven. He staggered back towards the sofa and sat heavily with his head on the backrest. His eyes flicked up and his mouth fell open as the joy spread. His hand fell onto his knee, still holding the syringe.

About half an hour later, Ronnie came back in. The room was still dark, but he could see that Arnie was still on the sofa, but now he was in Charlie's arms. Their father looked up and smiled. He held up the syringe. 'We're going to have to help him, aren't we, son?'

'What I see is kindness, and kindness is eternal,' said Mihr.

Sorush moved away from the car park wall. Up close her skin was cracked and her eyes glazed, but from this distance, as her body flowed within her silk and she preened and posed with one hand on her hip, she exuded earthly sexuality. Her dead eyes flashed. There was a silence in the air like danger. Mihr had seen Sorush like this before when she sensed the kill.

'Kasbeel.'

The incantation continued. Now they were to see the mother.

It had been four years since Violet had seen Arnie with his arms bandaged in the street. The wind, the wet, his haggard face and filthy hair, the unpitying street corner, his bleak and bitter voice drowned by the uncaring traffic, and most of all, his cruel indifference to himself, had all merged into such a picture of misery and self-loathing that she couldn't get him out of her mind again. It was as if they were both being told there was no escape. Her shadow was Arnie and his was hers. From the time of that accidental sight of him, her son's desolation had become an echo of her own.

When her sketchbook had been crushed under the grinding tyres of the bus, she hadn't cared. She'd got the message. Don't try again, Vi, your day is done and there's no way out. Such was her guilt that any achievement felt like a repudiation of real justice. The small chain of shops she'd built up for Tom was now reduced to one, and it was enough for her. But despite herself, she sometimes found a pen in her hand, and worse, discovered she was doodling. Bits of card, brown paper, old envelopes and wrappers found themselves screwed in the bin with her black marks creased, scrunched and abandoned. Until one day her shop girl, Rachel, carelessly left in the basement room a company sketch pad she'd been given by a lecherous rep, who'd seen it as a first marker in his lonely expedition to reach the summit of her long, lithe and lovely legs. Violet had seen the pad and thrown it onto a shelf. One night three weeks later, when Rachel had gone, she'd taken it down and started sketching again. She'd filled eight pages when May found it on one of her infrequent late afternoon visits.

Her sister's renaissance was complete. She was Tom's personal assistant now, and as his empire had grown, so had her confidence. She dressed city-smart and expensive, her hair was coiffed, as was her view of herself. She had done well in the business, had the occasional man friend, and most of the time was too pleased with herself to be anything more than an irritation. She stood by the table in the basement. She'd immediately seen Violet's sketchbook and opened it. She was very impressed. Organizing an office was one thing, but this was art. 'You should show these to Tom.'

'No.'

'Why not?'

'I . . .' Vi couldn't answer her. It was the same old feelings of guilt. She didn't deserve herself or what she could do. She closed the book and put it back on the shelf. 'Do you want some tea?' She went to the kettle in the corner, wishing May would go away. Like most converts her sister never got things quite right. 'Why have you come anyway?'

May took the pad back off the shelf. 'Show them to him.'

'He's not interested in any of that now.' Violet ran the tap.

'He still reads the journals.'

'Aren't you supposed to be at work?' asked Violet. There was a coyness about May that she knew was a cover for something.

'Can't I visit my sister?'

'What do you want, May?' Violet folded her arms and faced her.

'Would you like to eat somewhere later?'

'Not tonight.'

'Come out with me. I want to take you out.'

'No thanks.'

'What are you going to do? Stay in and watch the telly?'

'I might.'

'You can't stay in every night, Vi. Before you know it you'll be an . . .'

'Old maid?' Violet stared at her sister with clear blue eyes. There was something about her that sometimes frightened May. 'Good. Then it'll all be over, won't it?'

'Vi!' May was shocked. 'What's happened to you?'

'It took you long enough to ask!' Violet couldn't help the anger, although she knew it wasn't fair.

May looked away. She was aware of how much she owed her sister.

Violet said, 'I'm sorry. Nothing has happened. I want to spend the evening at home, that's all.'

'Home?' Sometimes May could give what she got.

Violet's eyes flashed. 'Are you going to tell me why you came?'

May looked up at her. 'All right.' She fingered the sketchbook. 'Tom's moving the investment company back east.'

'May?' Violet waited. There was more to come and she knew it.

'He's thinking of selling the boutique.'

Violet was stunned. 'What?'

'It's the last one, Vi. I don't think he's interested any more.'

'Why didn't he tell me himself?' Violet's anger was as much to do with a resentment at May being so clearly in Tom's confidence as it was with losing her livelihood.

'He wanted to.' May, having been in her sister's shadow for years, was aware of the jealousy and couldn't help being quite pleased by it. 'He hasn't made up his mind.'

'Where does that leave me?' Violet moved towards her.

'He'll look after you.'

The collusion this implied between May and Tom made Violet even more angry. 'I don't want looking after!'

'We all want looking after.'

'I don't!'

'When did you last have a man, Vi?' May picked up the sketchbook and folded her arms over it.

'When did you?' Violet didn't feel like one of these conversations now.

'I'm happy. You're not.'

'What difference does a bloody man make?'

May shrugged. 'Quite a lot, I'd say.'

'I don't want to talk about it.' Violet faced away from May, watching the kettle boil.

'Don't bother about the tea, I just wanted to tell you.' May moved towards the door. 'That's all. Don't worry.'

'Bye, May.' Violet was relieved she'd gone and didn't look round as she went. It wasn't until Rachel had left and she'd closed the shop that she realized her sister had taken her sketchbook. In one way it was a relief. The book was a kind of hope, a symbol of the third place that she'd once imagined. And she was too tired for all that now.

She didn't see or hear from Tom for five weeks. She didn't know what this meant. Had he decided to sell the boutique or not? Occasionally the question surfaced in her mind, swam briefly, then sunk unanswered. What would be, would be. She wasn't unaware of the fact that this was essentially little different from Charlie's philosophy of the fates, but she had to admit that, whereas his view was optimistic, hers was more or less joyless. The longer she waited, the less she expected, and by the time Tom turned up unexpectedly at her weekly visit to one of her wholesalers, she'd concluded that dullness was best, and if things could continue roughly as they were, she'd be as happy as she would ever be.

She was sifting through a rack of blouses when he suddenly appeared in front of her, holding up a blue cotton striped top. 'This one?'

It was so awful she couldn't help but smile. 'No thank you. Put it back.' She watched as he did and started to feel nervous. Was he going to tell her now? 'What are you doing here anyway?'

'I called Rachel. She said you were coming here today.' He looked around the racks. 'You're not thinking of putting any of this in the shop, are you?'

'Occasionally they have something I can use.'

'You haven't lost your touch, have you, Vi?' He moved to the other side of the rack and she couldn't make out his mood. He turned and looked at her over a row of coats. 'I know May's told you.'

'You're selling up?'

'Yes.' He nodded and moved away. 'Yes, I am.'

'Couldn't you have told me yourself?'

'I've been busy.' That was all he said, which she didn't think was particularly graceful considering that she'd worked for him for more than ten years. 'Do you want a coffee?' he asked.

'What?' She was inclined to say no.

'A coffee. Come on.' And with that he left the wholesaler's. She was getting angry as she fetched her coat, but thought she may as well go with him. There wasn't much point in buying anything if she now officially no longer had a shop to sell it in. She caught him up on the edge of the pavement. As they crossed the road, he said inconsequentially, 'The retail end's over, Vi. You were always much better at it than me anyway.'

'What are you going to do then?' She didn't know why she should be so concerned, but nevertheless she crossed the road with him.

'Manufacture. Some wholesale.' He nodded back to the place they'd just left. 'I don't think I could do much worse than that, do you?' He began to walk along the pavement. He seemed preoccupied and didn't speak for a while. They passed a coffee shop.

'Here's a place,' she said.

He stopped. 'Would you mind? Ah. I'm sorry, Vi, I've just remembered something . . .'

'Do you want me to wait?' She indicated the coffee shop.

'No, come with me.'

'Where?'

'I'd like to know what you think.' He turned and walked on.

'Think about what?'

'I'll show you.'

She pursed her lips and followed. It wasn't far. He stopped at a small door between two shops and pushed an unmarked bell. Although there was an entryphone system, no-one asked who they were. Violet heard the latch click and Tom pushed open the door. They went into a narrow hallway and Tom began to climb the steep stairs ahead of them, looking up at the peeling wallpaper either side. 'It's not pretty is it? What would you do with it?'

'I don't know, Tom.'

'I do, you'd have it painted white.' They continued to climb. 'There's no room for a lift unfortunately.'

Violet assumed he was talking about his new offices. 'I thought May said you were moving east.'

'Oh we are. I'd say it was a bit grander than this.'

Tom came to the head of the stairs and pushed open a door. They went into a large open space. Bright sunlight streamed in from three huge skylights. Tom put his briefcase down on the large table that ran the length of the room. 'What do you think?'

Violet was impressed. There was a simple beauty about the place and she liked the light. 'It depends what you're going to use it for.' She walked down the other side of the table. 'It's a perfect studio.'

'Good.' He was beginning to smile.

She turned. 'Good? Is that what you are going to use it . . .' Before she had finished a door had opened directly opposite her and May appeared carrying a birthday cake with lit candles. 'Happy birthday, Vi!'

'May!' Violet put her hands to her face. Rachel and Susan, who was another occasional assistant in the boutique, came through the door behind her sister.

'Don't you even know the date?' May laughed and began to sing, 'Happy birthday to you!' The others joined in as May shouted, 'Trust you not to remember!'

'Happy birthday, dear Violet.' Tom raised his hands and indicated the studio. 'Happy birthday to you!'

Violet couldn't believe what he meant. 'Tom?'

'It's yours.' He opened his briefcase and took out the sketchbook May had taken. 'And so is this.' He put it on the table. Vi looked round the room. She didn't know what to say.

'That will be the office.' May pointed back to the small room she and the girls had just come out of.

'A five-year lease. Thank you for all you've done, Vi.' Tom was coming round the table towards her.

'Quick!' May pushed the cake towards her. 'The candles! Blow them out.'

'No, I . . .' Violet stepped back from the cake.

'Yes, Vi. It's the least I can do.' Tom picked up the sketchbook and moved it closer to her. 'I want you to give it a try.'

'The candles, Vi. We didn't put all of them on!' said May.

Violet had no alternative. After a second she leaned forward and blew them all out as they sang 'Happy Birthday' again. Then Tom explained. If he was to start manufacturing, he would need one or two of his own designers. Why didn't she at least advise him? He smiled. She could do some of her own commissions at the same time. Perhaps he could even help her market some of them if she wanted him to.

'Why are you doing this, Tom?'

'I told you. It's a thank you for all you've done.'

And that's all he would say. Violet squinted at him through the sunlight across the bright reflecting surfaces of the studio. May and the girls were laughing as they opened a bottle of champagne. After a while Tom turned to her and said, 'I have to run. We'll wind down the shop over the next three months. The studio is yours from now.' He smiled. 'Thanks, Vi. Do accept it, please. It makes me feel better, that's all.'

'Thank you, Tom. Thank you so much.' She kissed him, and after more kisses and thank yous he went. She sipped her drink and listened as May and the girls ran round the studio making plans for her. Not long after they left too, and she sat on the table with the last of the champagne and tried to take it all in.

Why had he done this? The question wouldn't leave her alone. Tom had frequently been generous, but never foolishly so. He was a businessman, and although she knew that she'd been useful to him, he would consider that he'd repaid her by giving her the opportunities he had. It was as if there was something between her and Tom that she didn't fully understand. She had the strangest feeling that she had just entered into a pact with the devil. Or maybe it was a pact between two devils? She knew what she had done, but what about him? She'd always known that connections between people were never quite as they seemed. Opposite poles never truly attracted and trouble was drawn to itself. Maybe that's why she'd married Charlie? She smiled to herself. She didn't want to think about that now, or come to that, ever again. She emptied her glass and looked up at the windows. The sun was still shining and she began to allow herself to feel excited for the first time in years. Her own little studio! She was going to have to start to make plans of her own. Was this it, after all this time? Was this the third place?

'A pact?' asked Sorush. 'Devils?' There was triumph in her voice and the question of Violet flashed between the two angels like gleams of light.

There was a silence, then Sorush said, 'I have been too proud, Mihr. My own vanity has prevented me seeing your cause. I thought you left the Bridge because of me, but now I see it isn't so. There is a power in this that is beyond you. No angel as glorious as Mihr would ever have been asked to leave the Bridge to guard a single soul, whoever it was. This is another thing.'

'I am engaged in the business of God.' It was a standard reply.

'So be it, Mihr.' There was a sound like rushing wind as the angels behind Sorush seemed to increase in volume; their wings beat and fluttered and then they were gone.

Mirabelle turned from the car park and walked back into the boarded-up building. She still needed to know more. This had begun and she was sure it would somehow end with Violet. Why had she left Bernie? And why had Arnie left at the same time? These questions filled her mind as she passed down the gloom of the passageway and went into the candlelit bar.

Bernie was still sitting in the darkness behind Arnie's shrouded corpse. His huge shoulders were hunched and his head hung low. He was going mad. There were too many thoughts rushing through his brain like an express diesel with its hooter blowing. And that was just his head, what about the rest of him? He felt like the muscles in his arms were getting bigger and his backbone was getting stronger, and his legs felt like thunder thighs, and he had too much bloody energy and power, which was rippling all over the place like some whirlwind gone mad making his whole body bubble up and down. What the blessed, blinking, stone the crows was going on? He was like full of strength he didn't particularly want. His arms were beginning to ache because they were so big and his head felt like it was going to go bang . . .

And here comes Auntie Harriet, and oh no, she's got that bloody O'Dare with her. And now Auntie's crying and that made him feel sad and want to cry himself, but he didn't because there was no tears and then there was this funny smile which came onto his face. He didn't know where it came from, but Auntie reached up and kissed him and he put his big arms round her and he could feel her crying again on his shoulders, and he thought that was a bit weird, because usually it was the other way round and it was him having a bawl into somebody else's neck. And then Mirabelle's having a bloody go too. She's smiling at him like he's footballer of the year or something. What the bleeding, blinking hell is going on? And that O'Dare is wandering around trying to be a priest again and saying we've all got to kneel down and say a prayer, which is really easy. He found himself saying his own, which was, 'Oh Holy Father, bless us all. With your help and guidance we will be what you wish us.' He kept saying it over and over again, then it changed a bit. He was saying instead, 'Oh Holy Father, bless me and help me. I am your shepherd.' Which was all blinking mad, because he wasn't no shepherd. That was what God was, and he was a sheep like everyone else, wasn't he? But he kept repeating this one over and over again and he didn't get it at all.

And then O'Dare's standing up and he's gone out of the place, just leaving Arnie there on the table. And now he's come back with Martin and one of the gay or Buddhist or whatever it was monks and, yes, he bloody thought so, the bloody O'Dare had found a bloody bottle from somewhere and him and Martin and Geoffrey are having a swig out of it. But then the thoughts started to change again and he found himself laughing a bit at O'Dare and thinking what a sad old man he was. Even Lucy and Harriet didn't seem to mind. They was getting bloody hysterical or something. They was all at it now, having a swig. Bloody Martin even passed the bottle to him, so he had to have one too. It was red wine, which he drank for the first time, except for when his dad had given him a Scotch three years ago and he'd hated it, but the red wine was all right and it made him feel better. It made him feel like he was full of the Lord, which was really weird, and he started praying again. 'Bless me Father and give me a hand.'

And now bloody Porkie's turned up an' all with Sophie. What is this, Waterloo Station? They're all running around and they're crying and hugging each other and he's got to hug Sophie an' all. And now Porkie's getting out of order and he's telling them about some geezer who got burned to death. He's saying it's a baker! It was time he stood up and asked a few questions.

'What's all this? You saying Henry's burned to death or what?' Everyone stopped and looked at him.

'A baker in a white coat and burned to buggery!' yelped Porchese. It was the catering gear that had got to him. 'Two men in the fridge, bloody blood running on their face and no teeth!' He was looking at Bernie in the same way as he might have once looked at Arnie, or even at Charlie before that.

'And Riss.' Sophie stared with huge round eyes. 'We saw them in their car. And the frozen boy was saying there was five of them and one was a woman!'

'Iss Raphaella!' Porchese was very frightened.

'What did you do?' Lucy asked.

'We call an ambulance, got in the Snipe and come here!' Porchese was going out of control.

'All right, Porkie.' Harriet tried to calm him down.

'One baker burned and two frozen!' Porchese's teeth chattered as he said it.

'An example of death that is hard to beat.' O'Dare took a last swig and drained the bottle.

'It's evil! And Evil don' do no-one no good!'

'You may thrill with the grill but leave the theology to your betters. That's enough thank you, Porchese.' Harriet was priming herself up. Grief would have to wait, someone was going to have to sort this out. 'We gain a foothold while we can. Did you say you'd repossessed the Snipe?'

'*Si.*'

'Good. We'll take Arnie to his own home and enlist an undertaker.' She dabbed at her eyes. 'And as you've offered, Geoffrey, I'd much appreciate it if your mother would shelter the remaining brothers until this storm is over, or at least until Mr Riss and family are behind bars.'

'Of course, Auntie.'

'And . . . And I'm sorry I banned you,' she added.

'Oh Auntie . . .' Geoffrey held his arms out and Harriet's brief control collapsed. She wept on his shoulder, which triggered Sophie, who began to wail, and then Lucy, who sobbed on Arnie's cold shoulder. Porchese knelt in some kind of Italian prayer and Ronnie sat silent in the corner. He'd hardly moved for the two hours they'd been there. Bernie went over and touched his shoulder. 'It's all right, bruv. We'll just stick together.' Ronnie looked up with blank eyes. Bernie may have had five thousand thoughts an hour, but Ronnie had none.

'I think we'd better get him out before he starts to stink,' O'Dare, ex-expert in ceremonies of death, stated. The wine had given him a new lease of life and he wanted to get back to Soho quick before it expired. 'Bernard there, take up your brother and put him in the car.'

'We must be brave, dear.' Harriet nodded her assent, although her opinion of O'Dare was beginning to revert back to what it had always been.

'I know that, Auntie.' Bernie moved towards the table and gently lifted Arnie. Martin held the door as he slowly carried him out with Lucy behind, followed by Harriet and then the others in a slow procession towards the Snipe that Porchese had parked by the baker's van.

┌─────┐
│ 13 │
└─────┘

Fairfax had already issued details of the brothers' car and the Riss Daimler to all stations and mobile patrols. He had all the assistance he required and was beginning to enjoy himself. Officers from other sectors were asking him what they should do and he could see there was a glint of jealousy in their eyes. This, he had already realized, was his star turn, and if he could bring it off he'd hear the applause of instant promotion. He turned to the remaining witnesses with renewed zest.

After he'd seen Violet into the car, Hooper had found an empty room at the back of the auditorium, sat for an hour and smoked eleven cigarettes, trying to calm himself down. The fact and fantasy of Violet was confusing him again. As he'd sat staring at the back of the door, the Violet that he had witnessed covered in blood here in the Crystal Rooms had stridden, pale, vulnerable and unasked straight into the kitchen of the fifth house and asked him to look after the children for half an hour while she pulled herself together. Before he knew where he was, Tom Cherry had vanished from events altogether, and he, the dashing superintendent, had single-handedly driven to the Peking Palace and arrested the McCarthy Twins after a heroic gun battle. In the fraction of a second that it took to create this new scenario, his wife, who in his previous fantasy had never worked before, had gained an eleven-year career in haute couture and he had dressed better all his life.

This was not on, was it? He shook his head and gazed down at his shabby suit. 'Stop it, Hooper! Stop it, you prick!' He'd almost spoken it aloud and was pleased he hadn't, as when he looked up, he noticed that an attractive young WPC was standing by the door.

She said, 'Excuse me, sir, we have rather a considerable amount, or number, of press and reporters, including photographers and the BBC, who have requested a briefing on events and procedures and, if you wouldn't mind sir, follow-up inquiries, and what would you like us to do with them?'

Her attractiveness went down the pan with her use of the language. Hooper stood and found himself wondering why police officers and those who spoke to them couldn't speak simple English. He had arrested a Jamaican once who'd stated, 'I arose from my sleeping place at eight thirty hours man and proceeded to the bathroom, wherein I witnessed the distinct aroma of an illegal substance in the possession of another person of whom I am innocent of being.'

Hooper turned to the WPC and said, 'Press? Where?'

He walked down the corridor seeing only Violet, and soon found out. There were about thirty of them in the reception area. They were all shouting at the same time, waving cameras at him and shoving microphones under his nose.

Three uniforms pushed them back and Hooper cleared his throat and did what he considered to be necessary. 'We are engaged upon an inquiry in which two persons have been unfortunately attacked in a manner deemed to be illegal, of which one of them has been removed by a suspect whom we would like to interview as soon as possible, who is known as Mr Bernard Lack, his brother Ronald, and a Scottish serving girl, name at present unknown, er, no, called we believe, Mirabelle, at this time thought to be proceeding to destinations also unknown in a black Humber Snipe, of which the registration number will be announced shortly by a further colleague or officer.' He took a breath. 'In addition and most likely we are seeking and have sought, in order to apprehend, two twins, that is one pair, in other words two men, identified as McCarthy, who are of Eastern origin and, we believe, can help us with our inquiries, which are proceeding as of at the present time, and as such, therefore, we are appealing to the general public not to approach these men in any particular circumstances whatsoever, whom we believe to be dangerous. Exceedingly.' He stopped and then added, 'Over six feet tall.'

He looked up at the idiots writing it all down, then turned quickly and walked away towards the exhibition hall as the pack howled out further questions behind him. He felt utterly disgusted with himself and couldn't face turning back; he'd said 'proceeding' twice! He was worse than the Jamaican!

Once inside the area of the wrecked seating blocks, he did his best to thrust all further thoughts of his inadequacy from his head. The last witnesses had gone and he gazed dismally down at the dried blood on the floor by the catwalk being meticulously scraped and sampled by a couple of scientists. He looked around at the overturned chairs and began to feel disorientated again. Fairfax suddenly arrived, panting, overexcited and out of breath. 'Sir! They've attacked a baker!'

'A baker?' Hooper looked at him with glazed eyes.

'I've had a call, sir. It looks like another killing. Four men and a woman, answering to the description of Riss.' Fairfax waited for it to sink in. 'Shall we go, sir?' There was no movement from Hooper. 'Sir?'

Hooper raised his head, stared ahead for a second and then said, 'Of course.' He walked quickly towards the doors, not entirely certain of where he was going. Fortunately Fairfax overtook him and led the way. He was shouting over his shoulder about two men in a fridge. A fridge? Violet? A bloody throat? Twins of death? Grandmothers and bleach? Bakers? Hooper began to feel as if he was looped into some surrealist film. His mind began to overheat. He decided to close it down as he got into the back of the car. He stared blankly at Fairfax and the driver in front of him. It wasn't until they'd driven a mile further west at high speed that he thought it was safe to start thinking again. 'Riss? Did you say Riss?'

'Yes, sir.' Fairfax turned excitedly in his seat. He was about to expand when the radio burst into life. The Snipe had been sighted in the north. It was travelling south back towards Soho and was being tailed at this very moment by an unmarked police car. 'We've got the Lacks, sir!'

$$14$$

Porchese wasn't too sure of the way, but didn't feel like mentioning it. Harriet sat pale and pursed beside him on the passenger seat. There had been a terrible performance outside the pub, in which O'Dare, Sophie and Lucy had all insisted on accompanying the body. It had ended up with Arnie being laid across all of them in the back of the car with his head in Lucy's lap and his feet out of the side window.

Harriet knew it was a disgrace and a macabre one at that, but what could she do? She'd decided that they'd go straight to an undertaker she knew and knock him up. She had no doubt there would be questions and the police would poke their noses in again, but she couldn't face laying Arnie out in the restaurant, and at least the other brothers would be out of the way until this whole horrible state of affairs was over. Geoffrey had promised her that they would be in touch first thing in the morning. Bernie had cried as they left and Ronnie had said nothing.

They drove in silence until O'Dare, with the gay boys' wine igniting the vast dormant pool of alcohol already stored, started to hum a little tune. First Sophie, then Lucy couldn't believe their ears. The sound spread to Harriet in the front and she slowly turned as O'Dare finally burst into song: 'Love and marriage, love and marriage, go together like a corpse and carriage. You can't have one without the . . .'

Lucy screamed, 'God will get you, you bastard!' As soon as she said it, they were suddenly all violently jerked forward. Arnie's body was thrown up and hit the back of Harriet's neck. For a second O'Dare thought that God had heeded Lucy's words and his well-deserved end had come. He was already beginning a complicated Jesuitical defence of booze and whoring, when he realized that their motion had been caused by Porchese's foot slamming down hard on the brake, and coming at them fast through the rocking, swaying front window of the car was a police roadblock.

If the officers manning the block had known that at the wheel of the Snipe was a half-drunk Italian chef from Leytonstone, whose experience of driving for the past twenty years was primarily confined to sitting on the top deck of a red bus, they would perhaps have stood a bit further back. As the Snipe came at them, it executed what one of them later described as the longest and most acrobatic handbrake turn without the handbrake ever witnessed by the Met. First it broadsided left, then skidded right, then did a complete circle, then straightened going forward, then broadsided again, and was on its second full circle when it crashed, rear first, into the side of a panda car. No-one was hurt. Porchese's skid pan technique, known from then on as the Roman Rhapsody, had started so far back down the road that the brave officers of the law had had enough time to scatter. They were a minimum of twenty yards away when the Snipe impacted. It sat quiet and smoking, facing back the way it had come.

Porchese was actually still at the wheel, although you could have fooled him. All he saw was a whirring, spinning world that stank of burning rubber, and he wondered for a second if he wasn't back home on a dance floor in Perugia. O'Dare had shot forward over the front seat and had come to rest sitting astride Harriet and facing backwards. Sophie had traversed the length of the car and ended up with her head down on the clutch, her feet up by the back window and her backside flat against the roof. The only person who could be said to be reasonably happy was Lucy, who lay along the back seat with Arnie's corpse on top of her, reminiscent of some old and more pleasurable times.

As the one person looking forwards through the rear window was O'Dare, he was the first to see Fairfax coming towards them with two uniformed constables. At first he was relieved. At least it wasn't God. Then a more secular reality took hold. 'Ah, Jesus, who needs the law at a time like this,' he groaned.

Fairfax, who was expecting to find three brothers and a girl, rapped on Harriet's window with his knuckles. 'Excuse me.' He said it as if he was making a mild inquiry of a courting couple behind steamed-up windows in a lay-by, then he looked into the back seat, saw Arnie between Lucy's legs and silently congratulated himself on being exactly right as usual. O'Dare, still astride Harriet, looked ahead and behind the car at the crunched panda and wound the window down. 'Now would you care to tell me, officer, what kind of eejit parks a police car like that?'

'Would you mind getting out, sir?' Fairfax opened the door and O'Dare toppled into his arms, revealing Harriet as Hooper came up from the direction of the roadblock.

'Miss Lack?' Hooper was, as ever, solicitous of Harriet. By far and away the worst aspect of the crash for her had been to find herself beneath O'Dare. Now that he was gone and pretending to be mortally wounded on the tarmac, her old self immediately revived. 'Can you not leave us to grieve in peace, Superintendent?'

Hooper wasn't sure what she meant until other officers had opened the remaining car doors. One of them patted Arnie on the back. 'Excuse me, sir. I think it's time to stop that now.'

'He's dead!' wailed Lucy. The officer looked down on her upside-down, tearful face, half hidden by Arnie's unmoving shoulder and

Sophie's swaying thighs, and immediately realized his mistake. 'Sorry, madam.'

Hooper helped Harriet out of the front, while other officers untangled Sophie and Lucy. Porchese had gone stiff with shock and had to be lifted from the car. They sat him upright on the road. As he was still facing away from the roadblock, he remained unaware of what had happened until he was being breathalysed twenty minutes later. Arnie was left lying on the back seat.

Harriet refused Hooper's assistance although she needed it. She was shaken but unstirred by his predicament. 'You cannot arrest the dead, Superintendent!'

'This is a murder investigation, Miss Lack.'

'Whose murder? My nephew?' She glared. 'Can we not even bury him?'

'I'm afraid we'll require the body for forensic examination.'

'Torture him, cut him up, even when he's gone! You are animals, Superintendent. Animals in blue!' Hooper looked away. How could things be going so wrong?

'Where are you going to take him anyway?' asked Harriet.

Hooper didn't know. 'Ah?'

A local officer came to his assistance and whispered in his ear, 'The Sarras Hospital, sir. It's the nearest morgue.'

'Thank you, Constable.' Hooper looked back to Harriet. 'I'd appreciate it if you'd tell me where you came by er . . . him, Miss Lack.'

'Tell the bastards nothing!' O'Dare rose from the dead at Harriet's feet. He began to brush himself off as he looked round the officers. 'And couldn't anyone have the Christian generosity to give a road victim a drink?'

He was led away, complaining, to an ambulance as Lucy stooped awkwardly into the back seat and kissed Arnie's forehead. 'Goodbye, my darling.' Her frailty and courage in the face of this barbarism was too much for Harriet and she began to cry. Hooper instinctively touched her arm in pity. She shook it off with a woeful glance at Arnie.

'We will never be able to love him again, Superintendent. That's what breaks our hearts, don't you understand?'

'I am very, very sorry.' And Hooper genuinely was.

'It's not your fault, is it?' Harriet stoically dabbed her eyes with a handkerchief she'd found in her pocket.

'It's Mathilda! It's that bloody Mathilda! Riss would never have known where they were if wasn't for her!' Lucy suddenly blurted out on her way to the ambulance. 'I hate her!' She was led away in rage and tears.

Hooper turned back to Harriet. 'We need to protect the others.' He was being as gentle as he could. 'There's something out there, you see?' A siren suddenly stopped, emphasizing the silence of the dark road and underlining the significance of what he'd said. For a moment everybody stood still. Two constables looked round as if frightened that the shadows cast by the high quiet moon held some threat they couldn't imagine. Fairfax looked at his superintendent with renewed respect. Once again the thought crossed his mind that the clear lunacy of his superior was perhaps all they had going for them as they waited for the invisible McCarthy Twins to strike again.

'Perhaps we could speak later?' Hooper said to Harriet. He indicated that she should get into the second ambulance.

'Perhaps. And perhaps not.' Harriet walked slowly across the road, leaning on the green of a medic.

That left Porchese, who failed the breath test. Arnie was taken to the morgue at the Sarras Hospital for an autopsy as soon as it could be arranged.

$$\boxed{15}$$

Geoffrey's mother's house was on a wide, tree-lined suburban avenue in the north of the city. It was big, semi-detached and dowdy. The front was hidden by huge trees. Mirabelle brought the van to a stop behind the motorbike and sidecar on a driveway of unraked and rutted pebbles covered in dead leaves. Geoffrey went quickly to the front door. He let himself in and turned a dim light on. He motioned for them to follow him and they soon found themselves in a large hallway that obviously hadn't been decorated for years. The walls were covered with military paintings and prints in heavy brown frames. Mirabelle glanced up at an antique grandfather clock looming above them to their left. It was half-past four. Geoffrey opened a door to his right and they went into the living room.

The walls were papered in faded cream and brown, and hung with more military prints and sepia-tinted photographs. Mirabelle looked closer and realized that many of them were of the same man dressed in an army officer's uniform. Was this Geoffrey's father? He seemed embarrassed as he switched on the heavy mahogany lamp stand and then two other sidelights. Their shades were all made of a yellowing parchment, cracked and stained with age.

'So this is where you disappear to, is it?' Martin asked sweetly as he looked around at the heavy brown furniture.

'Shut up, Martin, Mother's asleep.' Geoffrey seemed nervous as he showed them to a cavernous and antiquated chesterfield opposite a monstrous, dark-wood mantelpiece. The room was cheerless but clean. It was as if over the years some hand had rubbed, polished and swept the life out of it, leaving a brittle, dust-free shabbiness that could crumble as they stood. 'Sit down, please.' Geoffrey turned as if to go and then stopped.

An old woman stood in the doorway behind them. She was dressed in an ancient flock nightgown. Her short grey hair stuck out at the back and her face was lined and yellow. She smiled gracefully. 'Good evening. How nice of you to come. Geoffrey has told me so much about you.'

'Mother!' Geoffrey was mortified. Martin was already smirking.

'Introduce me, Geoffrey.' The old woman came further into the room, not seeming to notice that her nightdress was open at the front revealing thin, spindly, naked legs and bare feet. She went straight to Bernie and held out her hand. 'I am Mrs Vera Arkwright. How do you do?'

'Very good, thank you, Mrs.' Bernie took her tiny frail hand in his giant paw.

'And what's your name?'

'Bernard.'

'Good evening, Bernard. How nice to meet you.'

'And you, Mrs.' Bernie seemed quite taken by the old girl and watched with a stupid grin on his face as she introduced herself to everyone else.

Mirabelle felt for a second that she should curtsy, but gave the old lady a brilliant smile instead. She was rewarded with, 'What a charming girl.'

Martin wanted to guffaw. If he'd ever had one over on Geoffrey, he had it now. He kept a straight face and said, with not a trace of irony, 'I'm very, very pleased to meet you, Mrs Arkwright.'

'And you, my dear.' Vera nodded gracefully and continued to Ronnie, who merely nodded and looked down at the threadbare carpet.

Vera stepped back and addressed them all. 'I'm so thrilled you've been able to visit me at last. Geoffrey's told me all about your secret world of Soho.' She stood in the centre of the room, seemingly completely unaware of her undress. 'Now, we should have refreshment, shouldn't we, Geoffrey? Gin and tonic? I have a very fine Madeira. Would you like peanuts in a dish?'

'Mother, may I have a word?' Geoffrey's face was very red.

'Sherry before dinner?' Vera looked round with a broad smile.

'Mother, it's four in the morning. Please.' Geoffrey put his hand on her shoulder and turned her as if she were a leaf.

'Geoffrey?' Vera was still smiling. 'What shall we have to eat, darling?'

'This way.' He led her from the room.

'Shall we start with oxtail?' Geoffrey ushered her through the door and they could hear her continue with the menu as they mounted the stairs. She was wondering if they shouldn't have something steamed for dessert when a door closed above them and her light tremulous voice was cut off. Martin fell back into the chesterfield, laughing and banging his knee with delight. 'I knew it! I knew it!'

'I didn't!' Ronnie suddenly shouted. His eyes blazed with anger out of his white and drawn face. 'I didn't bloody know it, Martin! I thought Geoffrey was supposed to be brassic lint! Look at this bloody place! Every day of my bloody life, I've had, "On the tab, Ron, give us a tenner, Ron!" It's been a tenner a day for bloody Geoffrey or nothing! And now look at this bloody place! He's soakin' in it, in' he?' He glared at Martin, all his feelings of the night tumbling out. 'And you're the bloody same! Hanging on to us, hanging on to every bloody penny we got! I've bloody had enough of it, mate!' He looked away. There was a silence.

Martin stopped laughing and stood shamefaced as Ronnie sat down on a huge wing-backed leather armchair by the fireplace and stared at the floor.

'You all right, bruv?' asked Bernie.

'No.'

Ronnie didn't speak again. Bernie sat down on the armchair opposite him and they waited through the long silence until they heard Geoffrey's feet on the stairs again. He came back into the living room.

'Martin, could I have a word, dear?'

'Oh, he wants a word now.' Martin got up and went towards Geoffrey at the door.

'Please don't be cruel,' Geoffrey pleaded as Martin passed him, and they went out into the hall and then into some other room on the ground floor. Ronnie, Bernie and Mirabelle sat and listened as their voices rose. Geoffrey defending and Martin being a bitch. Mirabelle closed the door. She'd hardly got back as far as the sofa when it opened again and Geoffrey came in looking very flustered. He closed the door behind him and leaned against it.

'I'm so sorry.' He came further into the room, his jowls shaking with embarrassment. 'I have been remiss. I wanted to explain to Martin, I ...' Whatever it was he wanted to explain to his friend, he couldn't tell them. He suddenly changed course. 'Beds! I must show you ... Bernie?'

'Thanks, Geoffrey, I'm really tired.' And as if to prove his point, Bernie stood up and yawned. 'It's all been really bad and I want to ...' he stopped, looking confused.

'What, Bernie?' asked Mirabelle.

'I dunno. I got to think about things.'

'Sleep.' Mirabelle stood up ready to go with him.

'It's all right Mirabelle, I'll go to bed on my own these days.' He turned to the door. 'Fanks, Geoffrey.'

'Of course, I'll show you,' said Geoffrey and they went out. It seemed right to Mirabelle that Geoffrey had automatically assumed that Bernie should be taken to his bed first. It was as if they were admitting to themselves that his strength was something they were going to need. The thought made her nervous and she sat on the chesterfield and looked over at Ronnie. Since his outburst at Martin he had remained silent, staring down at the carpet with his head in his hands.

'What do you want to do, Ronnie?'

'I don't know.'

He didn't move for a moment and she said, 'I'll do whatever you want.'

'Yeah. Thanks, Mirabelle.' Ronnie turned away angrily. There was something going on in him that seemed about to come out. Mirabelle waited. He suddenly shouted, 'That bloody Cherry lying there, gushing blood!' He stood up suddenly and started to walk quickly round the room. 'I bloody wish I'd killed him myself!'

Mirabelle turned to look at him. 'Why?'

Ronnie stood by a window and looked out into the dark night. He spoke more quietly. 'You know what got me? He was so bloody small! That's what got me! He put his arms round me when I was a kid and I thought he was a bloody giant. I couldn't move, you know? And I haven't been able to move all my life because of him.' His head dropped. 'And he turns out to be a puny little bastard.'

'Tell me,' Mirabelle said gently.

He turned to her, his eyes full of tears. 'You don't need three guesses, do you? He did it every Friday afternoon when she left me with him. Then *she's* there, isn't she? Hanging on to him! Bloody Arnie's dying and she's hanging on to bloody Tom Cherry!' He brushed the tears away with the back of his sleeve. 'Sorry.' He looked back out of the dark window again. 'I mean, what's she playing at, Mirabelle?'

'Perhaps she doesn't know.'

'Doesn't know!' He turned in fury. 'Why doesn't she fucking know?' Mirabelle looked away. 'I'm sorry. It ain't your fault.' He moved away from the window and sat back down on the leather chair. 'I can't even think about Arnie.' He stopped for a second, holding back a wave of self-pity and confusion. 'I think I'm going to have to get out of all this, Mirabelle. Sorry.'

'Don't be sorry. It's not your fault.' She leaned back on the chester-field and looked out of the window. There was a faint pale glow behind the darkness. It would be daylight soon.

16

Half an hour later and for Luis the day had begun. He was still sitting in the front seat of the Daimler. He knew that because he could see the walnut and smell the leather. As for the rest it was, well . . . it was white. He turned in his seat. Everything outside the windows had disappeared. There was nothing except white. White? He tried to screw his mind against the last swirling flares of the acid and looked to his right. The driver's seat was empty. He turned. Razor was behind him on the back seat. He had his mouth open and was snoring. Raphaella and Emil were asleep next to him. Then Raphaella ground her teeth as she turned her head, and Emil, leaning on the door, began to snore too. What was this, a bunch of pigs? He shouted, 'Wake up! What's going on?'

Razor reacted first. With the speed of light, his second-best knife appeared in his hand at exactly the same moment as Emil jerked forward, opened his eyes and saw the glittering blade three inches in front of his nose. 'Aaaaghhhh . . .' Emil's yell slowly subsided as he felt something damp on the seat between him and Raphaella. He looked down.

'I think you pissed yourself, Mr Riss,' said Razor.

'What!' Raphaella woke immediately. She felt the wet on her dress, yelped, and pushed herself as far away from her brother as she could get, which was virtually onto Razor's lap. 'Get away from me before you do the works, you aimless prick!'

Emil tried to lever himself up and away from the spreading puddle. 'My suit, my suit!'

'Shuddup! Shut that razor, Razor! Shuddup!' There was something about Luis's tone that was more than usually insane. They quietened and stared at him as he slowly pointed around all the car windows. 'Look!' Luis motioned out of the car. 'It's all white.' He turned back with his eyes wide. 'There ain't nothing except white.' They all followed his finger. He was right. 'Where are we? Heaven?'

'Us? You kidding?' Raphaella was trying to be flip, but the sight of the white disconcerted her too. 'This ain't heaven, Papa, this is hell.'

Luis was in no mood to be surrealistic. 'Hell? What are you talking about? Hell is fire and red!'

'We don't know for sure, Mr Riss,' said Razor.

Emil looked round. 'He's right, Pa. This could be hell. Just another version, we din't never hear about.'

'You think so?' Luis craned round. 'And you can't hear nothing either!' He listened to the quiet for a moment. Maybe it was hell. So what did that mean? He was stuck in hell with . . . ? He stared at the three of them in the back. Raphaella was motionless up on Razor's knee and Emil was pushed up against the door, still half levered six inches up above his piss puddle. Luis said slowly, 'You know, I heard it in a business meeting. Hell is other people.' Then he said, even slower, 'Especially the kids.'

No-one could think of anything to say to that. They didn't move. Their eyes flicked round. There was no break in the white, and no sound.

Luis suddenly became aware of something else. He turned like a cunning barrister. 'If this is hell, why don't we got Jock in it?'

Emil tried to be more reasonable than he felt. 'This ain't no hell, crazy guy?'

'We burned the baker!' Luis shot back.

'Heaven, hell, who cares?' Raphaella was suddenly bored by the theology.

'So where's Jock?' Luis wanted to know.

'So why don't you look?' Raphaella proposed the obvious.

'Because I'm in crisis!' Luis shouted.

'Emil, big brother, piss pants, do Daddy a big favour and open the door.' She leaned across him to do it herself and Emil was so squeezed against it to preserve his suit that he immediately fell clean out of the car.

'Where'd he go?' Luis blinked, it was as if his son had disappeared into thin air. Suddenly another shock. The front door opened and Emil leaned in, covered in mud and dripping water onto the driver's seat. 'Why can't you get a driver who can ride the street? Huh? He already ducked my Corvette! Now it's the fucking Daimler! What is he? A sailor?' To Luis it was an apparition. His son, previously pale, had gone brown. 'We're in another river, Papa! This ain't white!' He gestured around him. 'This is mist, you fuckhead!'

'Mist?'

Emil flapped his drenched trousers. 'And look at my suit!'

Raphaella laughed. 'At least it don't look like you pissed yourself no more!'

'Shuddup!' Luis was in a fury. 'This is my Daimler! In a river! Are you kidding?' He leaned forward over the driver's seat and looked at the water lapping gently at Emil's shoes. Then he shouted, 'Where's Jock? I'll kill him!'

As if on cue they immediately heard the whining tones of the missing Scot. 'Here, boss!' He seemed to be somewhere behind them.

Emil turned and peered through the mist. Slowly he made out the bulging form of Jock on the river bank ten yards away. Emil was about to tell him what he thought when he noticed two other figures with weirdly pointed heads looming towards him out of the fog. He realized what was happening too late to do anything about it. He shouted into the car, 'Papa! It's the cops!'

The effect on Luis was electric. He scrabbled for the door handle and leaped out of the car. Razor, as always perfectly in tune with his boss, followed out of the back. They immediately realized their mistake. Both had landed up to their ankles in thick mud. It was like those Mafia concrete boots Luis had read about. He was shackled by his own feet.

The two uniformed constables were quite clearly in view now and as Luis peered through the mist he saw that there were more on the bank behind. Two were holding Jock. Another figure stepped forward and shouted, 'I am Detective Sergeant Fairfax. I am arresting you on suspicion of the murders of Thomas Cherry and Arnold Lack . . .'

'Arnie!' Raphaella screamed and jumped across the back seat. She leaped through the already open back door and into the same wet footcuffs that held her father. 'Arnie? What do you mean, murder of Arnie?' she yelled. She managed a few paces through the mud towards the bank. 'What are you talking about?'

Hooper stepped from behind Fairfax. 'Perhaps you should tell us, miss?'

Raphaella lunged forward towards him and fell onto her knees into the mud, then flailed and splashed as she tried to get up. 'Look at my dress! You know how much this cost me?' Then she fell again, this time onto her face. She surfaced with her mouth full of brown water and pushed herself up, spitting and clawing at the sludge in her mouth. 'Get this off me!' she yelled, then half turned, slipped and ended up sitting on her backside, engulfed and held fast by a grateful river bed. Then she started to scream.

Luis put his hands over his ears. 'I knew it, widows and bakers.'

Emil yelled at Jock, 'What you done to us, crazy guy?'

Jock was upset. 'Sorry, boss, I went for help.'

'What you do? Call a policeman?'

Jock hung his head. He couldn't deny it. At the time it was more because he thought his brain was being eaten by a swarm of antlike blue cake crumbs, than for any concern about Luis and his car. He'd had the strangest notions all night.

The mob were sucked out of the mud and deposited, wet, cold and argumentative, into the back of a police van. The Daimler wasn't so lucky. The tide had come in and gone out again before it was rescued. Luis's pride and joy, like Emil's Corvette before it, had joined the navy. Stella had had her revenge.

Not that Hooper cared about any of it. He'd been at the hospital, unsuccessfully trying to elicit the whereabouts of the other Lacks from Harriet, when they'd heard that a mad Scotsman had phoned the emergency services. He and Fairfax had been on the scene within twenty minutes. He got into the back of his car behind a triumphant Fairfax and they began the drive to the station to begin the interrogation of the family Riss. They'd hardly gone 150 yards when the call came through.

$$17$$

Violet lay on her bed in a silk robe. Since having been driven back from the Crystal Rooms, she'd been in shock. A young WPC had asked her for her clothes for forensic examination. She'd undressed and given them to her. The WPC had told her kindly that she was under full police protection. There would be an officer outside her door night and day and a further two downstairs in the foyer of her apartment block. If she felt in any way frightened, panicked or merely in need of a cup of tea and a biscuit, all she had to do was ask. The superintendent would be round to speak to her first thing in the morning. Violet had nodded, although she hadn't heard a word of it. She'd locked the door behind the WPC and turned and looked at the quiet, simple beauty of her living room.

From the drapes, to the furniture, to the prints on the walls, Violet's taste was expensive and exquisite. This was her third place, all she'd ever dreamed of. It was silent, it was simple and it was lovely. And from now on it would for ever echo with the sounds of the screams in the Crystal Rooms. She could hear them already. Had they always been

400

there, silent in the walls, waiting to emerge one day like horrible whispered cries of reminder? She let her robe fall to the ground and stood naked. She'd achieved her dream and realized it only existed to taunt her with its emptiness. Her sister was dead and now her son was dead too. And so was Tom Cherry. She was empty, like the room. She had everything she desired and stood in the middle of it all with nothing at all. She bent, picked up her robe and went into the bathroom.

She lay in the bath for hours and soaked away all thought until she was just dull pain. She'd come to where she deserved, naked in water; her crime, as yet unseen, but revenged nevertheless. She gazed at the tiles and wished she were as white. She watched the soap slide from her skin and knew she had to accept defeat. Arnie was dead. That was all that really mattered and it didn't matter at all. It was like wet heat evaporating, soon to be gone and cold. She felt the beginnings of a tear as she regretted that she'd held the wrong man as he'd died. But it wasn't important. Accept defeat, there's nothing more to be done.

Below her in the foyer of the apartment block were two policemen, Sergeant Carr and Constable Jarvis. They'd been there most of the night. They'd admired the sumptuousness of the place and wished they lived there, then they'd mocked it and were glad they didn't. They'd laughed a bit about Constable Cockrell sitting upstairs on the fourth floor outside Violet's door. They'd placed bets twice on whether or not he was having a kip. Jarvis had even gone up in the lift once to catch him at it. Unfortunately Cockrell had been awake and Jarvis had lost a quid.

Carr had been dying for a piss for hours, but there was no gents' toilet in the foyer and he didn't feel like he should knock on someone's door at this hour. It was nearly half-past five and getting light, and they were off at six. He'd wait. They'd taken another couple of bets. One on whether a Ford would pass them on the road outside before a Vauxhall did, and the other on the gender of the next person to enter the foyer. Jarvis had lost again on the Ford, and this time he thought it would be safe enough to bet that the next person through the doors would be a man. Unfortunately he would turn out to be right.

Carr had decided he couldn't hold it in any more. He decided to go round the back and have a piss in the garden. Jarvis sat down to wait for him. Carr hadn't been gone for more than thirty seconds when

Jarvis felt his eyelids droop. It had been a long night. He was thinking he'd close his eyes for just a minute. He was doing so when the male he'd bet on coming through the door first did exactly that, and slammed him on the side of the head with a hammer. He fell forward onto the floor and a thin trickle of his blood ran between the cracks in the polished parquet. Constable Jarvis never opened his eyes again.

Chan McCarthy, who'd hit him, ran quickly towards the elevator at the back of the foyer. Gerard followed him, but didn't wait as Chan pushed the button for the lift. Both twins carried a long blue bag. Gerard went quickly past the lift and out to the back of the building. Sergeant Carr, intent on emptying his bladder, didn't turn or notice him as he went quietly up the iron fire escape behind him. By the time his brother had stopped the lift on the fourth floor, Gerard had reached Violet's kitchen window overlooking the fire escape. He unzipped a compartment on the side of his bag and took out a flat blade which he inserted into the window frame.

The lift doors opened on the corridor outside Violet's apartment and Chan looked out briefly to see Constable Cockrell sitting with his legs crossed on his chair. He was singing softly to himself. It was his favourite tune, 'All Things Bright and Beautiful'. Chan quickly slipped to his left, along the corridor and away from Constable Cockrell. He hid around a corner waiting for his brother.

Violet hadn't got into her bed; she'd lain on top of it in her robe. Occasionally she'd dozed, but hadn't slept. She raised her head as she heard a sound from the kitchen. It was Gerard slipping the catch on the window. She heard nothing more and laid her head back on the pillow. Gerard silently climbed onto the sink beneath the window and then dropped quietly to the floor. He passed quickly from the kitchen into the loveliness and empty quiet of her living room. His shiny shoes softly crossed the deep pile of her carpet as he went and stood behind the front door. He waited a second and could just hear Constable Cockrell's hymn from the other side. Suddenly he raised his fist and knocked hard on the inside of the door. He did it loud enough for Chan, who was still waiting at the other end of the corridor outside, to hear him.

Constable Cockrell immediately looked up and, assuming the knock was Violet, stood and opened the door. He hadn't got over the shock of seeing Gerard, when Chan's hammer came down on the side of his head and crushed his skull from behind. He fell sideways, knocking his chair over. He'd hardly hit the ground before Gerard had grabbed his feet and pulled him inside the apartment. Chan followed them in, closed the door and carefully locked it from the inside.

Violet, of course, had heard the bang on the door and sat up quickly on her bed. The sound had come from the front of the apartment. She wanted to shout out but couldn't. She knew somehow that this was what she had been waiting for. She stared at the bedroom door.

Sergeant Carr came back from the garden, zipping his fly and whistling. He saw the blood on the parquet before he saw the body of Jarvis. He stood for a second, stunned, with his hand still on his zipper, then his jaw dropped and he felt his shoulders sag before he heard himself release a long low groan. He knew Jarvis was dead without touching him. His fingers were shaking, but he managed to get his radio from his belt at the same time as turning fast to protect his back from the empty foyer behind. He shouted into the radio.

His call was relayed to Hooper and Fairfax as they were still in sight of the misty river. There was already an all-car alert to Violet's apartment. Fairfax turned from the front and looked square into his superior's eyes and knew he'd been dead wrong to ever doubt him. He said, 'Sir?'

Hooper's face was contorted. He screamed the scream of thirty years' pain, 'Drive, you cunt! Fucking drive!'

The driver said later that he'd been so shocked by the madness in the superintendent that he'd shifted that Rover like he had a rocket up his arse. He said he'd clipped two bollards and a milk float, he'd hit ninety on the wrong side of the carriageway on the Great North Road, he'd cut a minimum of fifteen reds, and on the third left at the M1 roundabout he burned three tyres down to the rims. It still wasn't enough for Hooper. 'Drive, you cunt! If she dies . . . !' The driver had said he was more terrified of Hooper than of having a crash.

Fairfax was terrified too. 'We need a SWAT squad, sir . . .'

'Fucking get them!' Hooper sprayed them with the froth on his lip when he was thrown halfway up the side of the car as the Rover spun yet another corner on two wheels. 'If she fucking dies . . . !'

Violet stared at the bedroom door. Keep still. They will come. Accept defeat. Even as she was saying this to herself she was getting off the bed and instinctively moving quietly. She moved quickly across the white rug at the end of the bed. Accept defeat. She got to the door and looked down at the lock. Keep still. Let them in. They're what you've been waiting for. Her hand came down fast and locked the door. She backed away, staring up and being aware of the white satin paint-work. Keep still. Let them come. She moved fast away from the door. Accept defeat. She was gone.

In the living room, the twins turned as they heard the click of the lock. Chan dropped his blue bag softly onto the carpet, unzipped it and took out a sledgehammer. He took three steps down the passage towards the bedroom door as Gerard unzipped his own bag and took out two four-foot bamboo swordsticks, then followed his brother. Chan swung the heavy head of the hammer and hit the door six inches above the lock. The wood dented but didn't give. Gerard stepped back to give his brother room. Chan swung the sledgehammer again. This time he hit the brass knob of the door and smashed it flat. The door still didn't open.

It was pretty well the end for Fairfax and Hooper. As the driver said later, 'It was this fucking truck. One of those big ones, eighty fucking tons going to Amsterdam or somewhere, coming straight at us. I kid you not, my fucking pals, I had six feet to get through and half of that was fucking pavement, and I was doing eighty. Don't ask me. It makes me fucking cry to think about it.' The Rover shot the kerb, went through a litter bin, smacked the back of the truck with the rear wing, spun left, skidded right and came back to earth on the onside front as the back end crunched down throwing them all up onto the roof. 'It could have fucking gone anyfuckingwhere!'

'Drive, you cunt!' screamed Hooper.

The third time Chan hit the door with the sledgehammer it burst open and violently swung back. The twin looked from the broken door into the bedroom. It was empty. Gerard passed his brother a swordstick and they unsheathed them in exact and perfect unison. They entered the room silently together. Their three-and-a-half-foot-long, three-quarter-inch-wide, tapering silver blades shone in the pink light of the dawn that was filtering through the closed pale-blue blinds. They stood on the white rug at the end of the bed and looked round.

Violet was in the closet. She could see through the slats as the twins went slowly into the bathroom opposite her. She could see the light glinting on their swords, like sparks against the white of the tiles. She could see as they turned and walked back out of the bathroom. She could see as Gerard looked towards the window and checked behind the blinds. Then she could see as they looked straight towards the closet where she was hiding. And she saw the blank look in their eyes as they came towards her with their swords held up at shoulder height. She pushed herself back into the rack of her clothes and pulled them round her. They felt as light and flimsy as the world she'd spent her life creating. The breath caught in her throat as she saw an eye peering in through the slats. Then she heard the rattle as a hand tried to pull the closet door open. She'd locked it from the inside. The eye was flitting back and forth across the darkness that hid her. She knew those eyes could see in the dark. She had no protection. She saw the tip of a blade coming slowly through the slats. There was no urgency in it as it slowly prodded the gowns hanging in front of her stomach. She shifted slightly to her left and felt the blade graze the right side of her robe. Then she saw another blade coming through another slat a few inches lower down. This too was slow. Please go away. I do not accept defeat. I am Violet. Whatever I have done, I am me. I'm sorry. The second blade brushed past also on her right side. The first blade withdrew and then reappeared in a higher slat. This time it was coming towards her chest. She couldn't go any further right because the other blade was still there like a rod across the closet. She went left and watched as this new blade passed to her right. It stayed where it was, as the further blade withdrew. Then that was coming in again, this time closer to her. Again she couldn't go right, and realized with an utter terrified certainty that they knew she was there and were gradually, intentionally driving her across into the corner of the closet. Slowly the blades kept coming and slowly she retreated, all the time going to her left towards the corner. She wanted to pray. She realized she was crying. She couldn't make a sound. The blades kept coming, one remaining static preventing her going right, as the second drove her further left. They were coming so slowly, as if they were feeling for her. She did pray. Please God. I'm worthless. Help me. The blades came closer. The wet on her cheek was silent. She was in the corner of the closet. There was nowhere else to go. The furthest blade was withdrawn. The nearest pinned her into the corner. She knew that when the next blade came through it would find her. She waited, one hand over her mouth, the other held fractionally in front of her in a hopeless attempt to stop the steel as it came through the slats. She was expecting it to come slowly like the others. It didn't. It came through with the speed of light and pierced the left hand side of her abdomen. She'd never felt such pain. She began to scream.

Sergeant Carr knew that once he'd seen Jarvis dead on the foyer floor and once he'd called up reinforcements, he'd have to go up and check Cockrell in the corridor. He took the lift with his knees shaking. He wasn't a brave man, but this was a colleague up here. He gripped hard on his truncheon. The lift door opened on the fourth-floor corridor. He came out of the lift at a hundred miles an hour and crashed against the wall on the other side of the passage. He turned and immediately saw Cockrell's upturned chair. He ran towards the apartment and tried the door. It was locked. He began to hammer on it with his fists.

The twins heard him but took no notice. They were engaged in killing. Their previous stealth was only to corner their prey. They knew that their blades would easily pierce the closet doors. They stood shoulder to shoulder moving the hilts of the swords from thigh to head height as they plunged the blades at lightning speed through the thin wood. Violet hardly saw them coming. There was just a crack of wood, a flash of light on steel, and then the excruciating pain as she was speared. She screamed and rocked backwards and forwards across the closet, turning first one way and then another as the wood in front of her smashed and splintered. She'd been stabbed twice in the stomach, once in the shoulder, three times in the leg and now the blades were coming at her higher. One grazed her cheek as she flew across the back of the closet, another pinned her shoulder again. She screamed louder, becoming hysterical. The silk of her robe was wet with her blood, and still the blades came. The twins whirred the steel like the wind. They were unstoppable. They were cutting the wood and then Violet to ribbons. Blood splashed back at them through the jagged holes appearing in the closet doors. Violet was close to the end. She turned away from them screaming as blades pierced her back and buttocks. She was being hacked like a piece of meat. She turned again and another caught her in the stomach and penetrated to her spine. She began slowly to slide down the wall at the back of the closet as Chan finally leaned forward and ripped the remains of the doors away with his hand.

He looked down as Violet, little more than pulp, fell forward at his feet. Gerard touched his shoulder. They could hear the sound of police sirens and Sergeant Carr's hammering on the door was getting louder; it sounded as if he was trying to break it down. Gerard turned and wiped his sword on the bedcovers. Chan looked down at Violet and slowly pushed his sword deep into her side. He pulled it out, and following his brother, flattened the blade on the silk sheets of his victim's bed, smearing them with her blood. Then they walked back towards the living room to pick up their sledgehammer and blue bags.

Hooper's car had been overtaken by two police outriders as they neared the apartment block. His manic drive was soon to be legendary, but already his insane calls over the radio had inspired or terrified the rest of his descending force.

One of the outriders, desperate to be first on the scene, having thrown his bike round the last corner at an impossible fifty, had slewed, then toppled and slid the last thirty yards with sparks flying to the sound of screaming metal. His bike had come to rest on its side exactly outside the foyer entrance. He'd made it there first, but would spend the next three weeks in hospital, having left half his right leg spread along the skid mark on the tarmac behind him.

Hooper's driver threw out all his anchors and brought his battered Rover screeching to a halt inches from the fallen outrider's head. There were already countless sirens coming from all directions as Hooper and Fairfax leaped from the car and ran pell-mell into the foyer. Hooper hardly noticed the hapless Jarvis, dead in a pool of his own blood on the parquet. He ran straight for the lift and hit the button. 'Where? Where?' he shouted.

'Fourth, sir.' Fairfax arrived breathless behind him.

The lift opened and Hooper ran in with his driver and another sergeant who'd also just arrived. He punched four and yelled at

Fairfax, who was still outside the lift, 'Back! Back, Sergeant!'

The lift doors had closed on Hooper before Fairfax understood what he meant. He yelled to three uniforms and a plain clothes as they ran into the foyer behind him. 'Back of the building! Rest of you, up!' He pointed to the interior stairs and then turned from the lifts, trying to work out how to get behind the apartment. As the plain clothes ran up the interior stairs, a uniformed constable found the door to the back and they ran through into a large tree-lined garden. Fairfax saw a figure on the far wall and stopped dead. A uniform, not expecting it, ran into his right shoulder from behind and knocked him sideways onto his left knee. Fairfax turned quickly and shouted up, 'I saw one of them! Black suit. He looked at me! I've seen a bloody McCarthy!'

On the fourth-floor corridor, Hooper joined Carr at Violet's apartment door. He didn't need to tell his driver, who immediately began to kick at the heavy wood with Carr.

'Heard screams, sir,' Carr panted between kicks.

'Together! Do it together!' Hooper shouted.

The two men stepped back and then lunged forward in unison, smashing at the door with their feet. It splintered around the lock, and as the two men backed off to try again, Hooper hit it with his shoulder. The door immediately gave way and he almost fell into Violet's apartment.

The sight of the living room and its quiet, undisturbed tranquillity in the streaming dawn light stopped him for a second. He looked around as Carr, the driver and other officers crowded into the broken doorway behind him. They saw Cockrell on the floor at their feet and two of them went to him. Hooper heard a low moan, hardly more than a sigh, and turned towards the short passage to the bedroom. He was shaking as he walked down it, terrified of what he would find. The bedroom door hung on its hinges and he touched it with his fingers as he walked slowly through into the room.

Violet lay on the floor in front of the disintegrated closet doors. At first she was hardly recognizable, a bundle of pale mauve silk, soaked in crimson. He knelt by her on one knee, bent his head to her blood-splattered face and whispered, 'Violet?' She didn't move. 'Please don't die.' He took her hand in his. This was what he'd wanted to do all his life. He'd never let go now. He waited, crouched over her. There was no point in shouting or issuing instructions. The medics would come and they would save her. He was sure of that because there could be no world without her. The strength running from his fingers to hers would keep her alive. He knew it.

Fairfax had come to the back garden wall too fast. He'd assumed that speed would get him over the eight-foot obstacle, but all it had done was give him a painful bang on the elbow and grazed his knee as he slithered back down. He stepped away from it. 'Give me a hand!'

Another officer made a back for him and he clambered up onto the man's shoulders, then to the top of the wall. Behind it was a leafy alleyway. Fairfax rolled over the summit and jumped down, jarring his ankles. A plain clothes had found an easier way over via a tree and landed close to him. They quickly looked up and down the alley. There was no sign of the twins. 'Split!' Fairfax shouted, and he ran off to the right in a direction that he hoped would bring him to another alley at the side of the block. He knew the McCarthys could only be seconds in front of him, but within yards he came to a dead stop.

In front of him was another wall. He was in an alley cul-de-sac. He looked round and was about to turn and run the other way when he heard the sound of footsteps moving away from him. Two uniforms had run up behind him and he put a finger to his lips and pointed in the direction of the sound. The three of them looked at the wall. Without a word the two constables made a bridge of their arms. Fairfax stepped up as they heaved and he had to clutch at the top of the wall to save himself being thrown completely over it. He landed on his knees on the other side in a patch of four-foot stinging nettles. He stood, rubbing his smarting hands and face, and realized he was in another garden. Ahead of him was a trampled path through the under-growth. He ran towards it as one of the constables landed behind him. The garden obviously hadn't been tended for years. Fairfax found himself ducking beneath heavy gnarled boughs and avoiding brambles not too successfully. He felt his suit trousers rip and tear, but kept going. Soon he came to the side of an old house and looked up and then behind him. It was the building next to the apartment block. The constable caught up and pointed to a narrow passage at the side of the house that clearly led back to the road. Fairfax charged down it with the constable breathless behind.

They came to a sudden halt on the road, thirty yards along from the entrance to Violet's block. All they could see was police. Three squad cars had arrived and an ambulance was coming wailing to a stop as Fairfax looked desperately up and down the road. There was nothing except blue uniforms and the howl of sirens as more patrol cars and pandas converged on the apartment. 'Shit!' Fairfax looked back down the passage behind him. Maybe he hadn't heard footsteps? Maybe he hadn't even seen the twins? Doubts were crossing his mind faster than the instructions he began to issue to the arriving officers.

He was about to run towards the cars when a plain clothes tapped him on the shoulder and pointed. 'There!' Fairfax looked and saw a black Mercedes van pull out of a side street 200 yards down the road from him. He could just see two men in the front. As the van turned right and away from them, the passenger slowly wound the side window up. It was enough for Fairfax. He'd just caught his second glimpse of a McCarthy. All doubts gone, he screamed, 'It's them!' Then he looked madly around for a means of pursuit.

Most of the squad cars were obstructed by the ambulances that had arrived. Their cabs stood empty as the medics had already gone into the building. The one car that could still get out was facing the wrong way. Fairfax ran one way, then the other, not knowing whether to get the squad car to reverse or order a medic out of the building to shift an ambulance. Then he saw the crashed outrider's bike still lying on its side in front of the building and visions of his Norton flared in his mind. It was as if it was meant to be.

He ran quickly to the fallen bike and wrenched it up, praying it would still go. He jumped astride it and jammed his foot down on the kick-start. The engine was dead. He leaped off, flicked it into gear and frantically began to push it down the road. He pounded his feet into the tarmac, gaining as much speed as he could, then he let out the clutch. The machine roared into life and shot away beneath him. He managed to hang on to the handlebars as the momentum lifted his feet from the ground. More by luck than judgement he landed in the saddle, and his sudden weight on the back lifted the front wheels. The bike wheelied almost vertical for forty yards as Fairfax battled to control it. He was heading straight for an oncoming squad car as he managed to get both wheels on the ground and change up to second. He accelerated and the sudden shift forward almost threw him off the back, but he hung on and hunched down in pursuit of the van as other cars began to rev and reverse behind him.

The road ahead was very straight and wide. As yet there was very little traffic and Fairfax could see the black Mercedes about a quarter of a mile ahead. He changed up again to third and felt a thrill at the power of the bike as he sped after it.

The twins must have seen him in the rear-view mirror. The driver had shifted back down to third and the van burst forward with squealing, spinning wheels. Behind them Fairfax accelerated. He knew they didn't have a chance. The bike was faster and there was nowhere they could go that he couldn't follow. The wind rushed past him. He was exhilarated. The twins were his. Suddenly, 200 yards ahead, he saw the brake lights of the Mercedes. It was slowing and he began to brake. He shifted the bike to one side and could just make out two squad cars abreast of each other much further down the road coming directly towards the Mercedes. They must have heard a radio alert from someone at the apartment and decided on their own action.

The brake lights of the Mercedes flared again and Fairfax realized that it was going into a violent handbrake turn. He saw he was gaining on them too quickly. He desperately began to pull the bike up, and then began to feel it slide beneath him as he sped towards the van, now broadside to him on the road ahead. He put his foot down on the rushing tarmac in a desperate attempt to keep from losing it and going over. He was within five yards of the side of the van when it shot away across the road and accelerated past him going the other way. Now he could see the two squad cars ahead of him were only 100 yards away and bearing down on him fast. He was aware of their sirens and flashing lights, as he managed to lock his wheels and complete his own spin. He pulled back hard on the throttle and the bike spat out a cloud of blue exhaust fumes. His wheels spun in a cloud of black smoke as he gunned the bike after the twins in the opposite direction.

He was sure they'd had it now. They were headed back in the direction of the apartment and he could see a solid phalanx of squad cars coming straight at them. He began to slow and looked behind him. The two squad cars were there. The twins were trapped. He had them at last, coppers fore and aft. He pulled back on the throttle, wanting to be the first at the van. But no sooner had he accelerated than he was having to brake hard again and this time he knew he wasn't going to

411

be able to stop. The twins ahead had suddenly broadsided again, the van rocking and almost flipping over as it came to a dead stop across the road. Fairfax was flying at it. The bike was going down under him and there was nothing he could do. He was half a second away from impact when the van disappeared. The bike became a sliding, riderless quarter ton of smoking, screaming metal as it skidded on its side, carving deep ruts in the road. Fairfax followed, slithering across the surface where the van had been. His skin was being ripped apart by the tarmac and he could see that he was heading straight for the centre car of the three coming down the road towards him from the apartment block. He was helpless as the middle car braked and slewed to its right, trying to avoid him, and crashed into the wing of the car on its offside. The third car mounted the opposite pavement, missing Fairfax by inches as he continued sliding helter-skelter down the crown of the road. As he slowed he was aware of the sound of the squealing tyres of the squad cars who'd just missed him and those who had been following him. As he came to a stop he looked up to his right. There was a high arch between two buildings. Above it was a sign reading 'Builder's Supplies'. The twins must have taken the only way out and accelerated into the yard beyond. They must be in there now. He slowly pushed himself up from the road surface and began to hobble towards the entrance to the yard.

'No, Sergeant, stay where you are!' It was a plain clothes yelling at him from a doorway. He was holding a revolver. Fairfax assumed that one of the cars must have been carrying a SWAT team. He kept walking.

'Sergeant! Get out of here!' It was another armed officer. 'Leave it to us!'

Fairfax kept walking. If anyone was going to take those bastards it was him. He walked between the police cars as armed officers shouted for him to get back. He took no notice and limped painfully through the arch.

The yard was small and dark. Building materials were leaned against the walls. He saw the van immediately. It had crashed into a low wooden structure at the far end of the yard. Fairfax could see windows and what remained of a door. It must have been used as an office. They'd probably stored scaffolding poles on the roof because hundreds of them had rolled onto the top of the van and had now formed an extraordinary steel web around it. The back end was still smoking as Fairfax approached it.

'Wait, Sarge, wait!' It was one of the SWAT team. They came up behind and to either side of him, taking cover where they could find it. They held their pistols with both hands, training them on the back of the van. Fairfax saw that they were all pale and frightened.

He stood, tattered and bloody, with his hands hanging by his sides, facing the back of the van. Then he shouted, 'We are armed police! Do you hear me? We are armed police!' There was no response. 'I want you to lay down any weapons you may have and make yourselves known to us.' The yard remained silent. A scaffolding pole rolled and then clanged to a stop as if to emphasize it. He shouted again, 'I am coming to the doors of the van. We are armed police. Lay down your weapons. We will open fire.' There was still no response and he began to go towards the van. The SWAT team inched forward around him. He could feel their tension as he slowly moved closer to the doors. He stopped a foot away. The back windows were blacked out. He looked at the team around him and leaned forward to the door handle. He shouted, 'I am going to open the back door.'

'Wait a minute, Sarge!' One of the SWAT team came right up to his shoulder and aimed his revolver over it. Fairfax slowly gripped the door handles, waited a second, then yanked open the doors. All four members of the SWAT team hit the ground as the doors swung back. Fairfax stood where he was. The van was empty. He didn't move as two of the team leaped past him and up into it. He could see that the front of the vehicle was relatively undamaged. They'd crashed through the flimsy wooden walls and arrived unannounced in the office as the first call of the day. Then they'd opened the driver's door of the van and got out. Fairfax was prepared to bet that the SWAT team would find there was a back way out of the offices too. He stood and waited until they came back. Yes, there was a corridor that led to a passage, that led to the road on the other side of the block. He could hear squad cars on the road behind him pulling away to try to cut them off, but Fairfax knew they'd lost them. He turned and slumped down on the back of the van. 'Bollocks.'

The medics had a drip into Violet as they brought her, as fast as they could, out of the front of the apartment block on a stretcher. It was a miracle she was alive. Hooper came quickly behind. He looked up at the grey sky that had overtaken the dawn. The clouds were swirling above him as he whispered, 'Please God, keep her alive.' Then he got into the back of the ambulance and sat over her as the doors closed on him and the sirens began to wail again.

Fairfax watched as the ambulance pulled away. He felt bad. It wasn't just the absence of skin on his leg. He'd heard what had happened in the apartment block. Now Constable Jarvis had to be added to the list, not to mention Constable Cockrell, who had a cracked skull. A medic asked him to lie down in the back of the last remaining ambulance. He refused. He wanted a painkiller, a perfunctory bandage, another suit, a cup of tea and that was that. He had too many things to do to mess about. He looked up at the sky as Hooper had. He had a feeling it was going to be a very strange day and he didn't want to miss it.

PART SIX

UNDERGROUND

Ronnie hadn't slept. He'd sat in the wing-backed chair in Vera's living room all night trying to work things out. He thought it was a weird thing when you didn't know who your mum was. Not only had she been dumping him around on child abusers, whether she meant to or not, and not only had she not bothered to concentrate when he was telling her in one way or another what was going on – and he was only bloody ten – she'd also bloody left him and pissed off before he'd worked out who she was and therefore who he was. And it was no good Mirabelle going on about trying to love them through it because they'd had problems just as big as his. How can you love someone who'd done what she'd done?

And Arnie was dead. He didn't even try to work that out. Sometimes Arnie was a pain in the arse, but at least he got involved in things. But him, Ronnie, well, he was the geezer who stood up the back and waited to be told what to do and then moaned about it. What were you supposed to do anyway, keep your mouth shut and look after yourself, or mind other people's business and half the time piss them off? He didn't know. But he did know that Arnie was a presence, like a shadow in his life which wasn't around any more, and it really hurt him and made him feel at a full fucking loss.

He guessed that this was what grieving was. He remembered he'd felt the same when his mum took off. So he'd probably do the same thing again, which was keep his mouth shut tight and mind his own business. But he didn't want to this time. He wanted to stand up and bloody scream and shout, but he didn't know what to say and he thought anyway he'd probably make a fool of himself if he did. So he'd have to deal with it on his own again, wouldn't he? He'd have to live without Arnie and that was that.

Same as he'd have to live without Cherry, which was a thought that came suddenly and shocked him, because if you'd asked him who was the one person in the world who he'd want to live without, it would have been Cherry. He couldn't believe he was going to grieve over that bastard too! Arnie was one grief, but Cherry? He thought about this for a while and began to understand that he was feeling bad about Arnie because he couldn't love him any more. So did that mean he was feeling bad about Cherry because he couldn't hate him any more? He wondered if you could seriously hate a dead man? But the only thing he could come up with was that he hated Cherry because he had gone and therefore he couldn't hate him any more. Did that mean he needed to have something to hate? He didn't think so. He'd hated Cherry for what he'd done, and quite right too. So did that mean that he was now hate free? That thought quite pleased him until he thought that if that was true then it was also true that he was love free because Arnie had gone too. But then he thought that wasn't right, was it? Because there were plenty of people around he loved: Bernie, for a start, and Auntie and Mirabelle and . . . it was a long list. So then he realized that although there could be an absence of hate, there could never quite be an absence of love . . .

Which brought him with a crash to Mathilda. Why hadn't he considered her? She was the best of the lot. It was weird. He sometimes thought that the more she loved him, the less he could manage the same thing with her. Why? He didn't know, but he suddenly found himself standing up and staring at the phone, which sat on its own round table by the window with the directories stacked neatly on a shelf underneath. He realized with a shock that he was going to call her and tell her he loved her. Then he thought again. Was he really going to do it? What would she have to say about that? As per bloody usual he didn't know what to do. He was staring at the phone with his legs shaking when Geoffrey walked in.

He was dressed in a bathrobe and had a brave but broken face. He closed the door behind him and stood with his back to it, sighing. It was an extravagant pose, slightly ruined by the protuberance of his

418

large hairy belly through the front of the robe. Ronnie could tell an announcement was coming.

Geoffrey finally spoke. 'I think I should tell you that Martin has gone. It is now . . .' He raised his wrist to look at his watch and realized he wasn't wearing it. 'What time is it?'

Ronnie told him it was half-past eight.

'Then I should tell you that in an hour and a half Martin will be on a train to Swansea.' Geoffrey's voice was self-pitying and larded with manufactured courage. He wanted Ronnie to know that he was absolutely ruined, struck down, disintegrated emotionally, but also that he, the bravest man on earth, could, amazing as it may seem, cope with it. 'We have decided to separate.' He sucked in on his cheeks as he prepared to tell the witheringly simple truth. 'It's not surprising really, as we've hated each other for years.' Only a real actor and poet could speak honestly thus. He blinked back tears as he awaited Ronnie's reaction.

'Sorry, mate.'

It wasn't quite the response Geoffrey had anticipated but it was all he had, so he worked with it as well as he could. 'So am I.' As Ronnie didn't seem inclined to say anything more, he turned to the door, adding stoically, 'It's a ramshackle life. I shall make myself a pot of tea and take a bath.'

'Geoffrey.'

He turned back. 'Yes, Ronnie?'

'As long as Martin stays alive you'll love him or hate him. It's only when he's dead that you'll know which one it is. It's the one you keep, you see?'

Geoffrey didn't know what to say. He puffed for a second, trying to think of a deep, dramatic and philosophical, not to say poetic, response that made sense, and then looked up and saw Ronnie's face. It was full of pain and confusion and Geoffrey felt ashamed of himself. He said, 'I'm sorry to have burdened you . . .'

Ronnie didn't seem to be listening. 'Mind if I ask you a question, Geoffrey?'

'Not at all, my dear.'

'When we were in the south we met this preacher called Horn who kept telling us to spill the beans. What's that mean? What beans are

419

you supposed to spill? And what do you do when you've spilled them?'

'I don't know.' Although Geoffrey had no clear idea of the circumstance or even existence of this Horn, there was something about Ronnie's demeanour that immediately made sense. The question could just as easily have applied to him. He said sadly, 'Spill them all. What else is there?' Then he bravely opened the door and went out to run his lonely bath. After a second Ronnie walked over to the phone, picked up the receiver and dialled.

$$2$$

The ring was muffled. Having cleaned up after the twins' search, in preparation for her suicide, Mathilda must have messed up her room again. All her cupboards and drawers had been emptied on the floor and a pile of clothes were heaped over the phone. It had been a long night. At first she'd felt warm and happy. This was going to be just OK. She'd watched the TV and sipped brandy from the mug. She'd wanted to make the event last and so had taken the paracetamol in twos. She'd estimated she had about 500 of them and patted the top of the bowl in an affectionate way and adjusted the silk flower she'd stuck in the top. She'd thought it looked really pretty. Then she'd started to take the paracetamol in threes. And she'd poured more brandy, then watched more TV, taken more pills and drunk still more brandy. At some point the flat had been wrecked again. Perhaps she'd been bored by the TV. Maybe she'd decided this was no longer a happy time, and if she'd had a knife maybe she'd have done the same to her face as she'd done to her room. She'd have sliced her cheeks, made the blood run, then split her mouth and cut her heart out. These were the dark hours, when she went a long distance inside herself and lost who she was. She didn't see the dawn; she was unconscious. She lay on her back on the bed, her right arm was crooked and her hand was near her face. The other hand lay limp across her bedside table near the overturned bowl of pills. Many of them were scattered across her body. One bottle of brandy was empty, the other had fallen over and disgorged its contents onto the floor, soaking the silk flower her mother had given her. She didn't hear the muffled ring of the phone.

┌─────┐
│ 3 │
└─────┘

They'd taken Violet to the Sarras Hospital. When Fairfax heard this, he'd hoped they didn't tell her that her son was lying in the morgue in the hospital basement, not that she'd have paid much attention if they had. There'd been no-one who'd seen her after the twins' attack who'd have given any odds at all on her ever hearing anything again. She was just something off a butcher's hook, mate, someone had said. The way things were, it looked as if the only way she was going to find out about Arnie was by joining him on the slab.

Having left the hospital, Fairfax was being driven to the station in Hammersmith where the Riss family were being held. He knew that Hooper would be even now pacing the corridor outside the operating theatre. He was aware that Violet's death would probably destroy his superintendent and said a prayer for the first time in twenty years. He also had to admit that he felt partly at fault. Her protection in her apartment had ultimately been his responsibility, and he felt he had let down a man who he'd always respected, and who, deep in his own unreason, knew more about this case than anyone else. Fairfax was beginning to feel inadequate. Who were these twins anyway? And how could you apply procedure to shadow? He shook his head and tried to clear his mind, then turned back to the road. One thing was for sure. No-one was going to come anywhere near Violet again. Half the coppers in London were packed into the Sarras Hospital. He hoped that someone there would have the wit to organize them. He had a feeling that Hooper wouldn't and was desperate to get back himself. But he'd decided that he was going to have one last go at getting to the twins before they tried again, and if anyone knew where they were it had to be one or all of the Riss family. He moved uncomfortably in the front seat of the car. The medics had dressed his wounds as best they could and given him an injection to kill the pain in his legs, but they couldn't do much for his state of mind. As they pulled into Hammersmith police station car park he was in no mood to be pleasant.

For reasons unknown, the alcohol consumption in the west of the city during the previous night had broken all records. All along the Fulham Road and King's Road to Kensington, even as far as Harlesden and Kilburn further north, there was hardly a public house that hadn't had to call in the meat wagons at least twice to control the resulting mayhem. No-one could remember anything like it since the last World Cup. Must be something to do with the stars in the sky, thought one old sergeant as he made his seventh arrest.

At Hammersmith the cells were full to overflowing and by the time the Riss mob had been brought in there were none left available to take them. They'd been slammed up in a temporary holding area just off the charge room. The bars that contained them were wall-width and floor to ceiling. Consequently they had a good view of Sergeant Hilary Braine the custody officer and weren't slow to let her know how they felt about being locked up. Raphaella especially. 'Whassa matter with you? You think I killed my own lover boy! You crazy? Look at my shoes! Hey and look at yours! How you gonna go around in great cluds like that? You a girlie or what?'

Braine sat at her desk trying to ignore them and deal with the night's overload. She'd been irritated with them since they'd been booked in. They sat in a row along the bench behind bars and hadn't stopped shouting since the key had been turned. Raphaella had wanted the bathroom twice and then she needed her lipstick, then her mascara, then the bathroom again. Jock had demanded a solicitor, Emil wanted a dry-cleaner and the Sikh had asked for breakfast. At least he'd been polite. Now they were all pleading their individual innocence.

Emil stood and pushed both his hands through the bars and clasped them together. 'We didn't do nothing! I'm being straight with you! It was Papa!'

'Wha'?' Luis looked up out of the furnace of his mind. 'Wha' you say, Emil?'

'It was my father! He done it!' Emil yelled.

Luis couldn't believe it. 'I conceive my own torturer! Ahh . . .!' He sat on the bench with his head in his hands.

'So you should've kept your fly zipped. Who knows what comes out?' Raphaella stood up next to her brother and looked back down on her father with contempt.

Luis leaped up and put his own hands through the bars. 'It was them! My son did it. And my daughter! They did it!'

Raphaella turned on him. 'It was you! You killed my little baby, Arnie!'

'Witch-bitch!' Luis leaped at her across Emil, who was standing between them. Raphaella screamed and returned the attack, lunging with her nails. The space was small and Emil couldn't get out of the way. He struggled backwards as his sister scratched his face and his father inadvertently punched him in the stomach.

'Get off! Get off me!' He managed to push them apart. 'Who did it anyway?' He turned to Luis. 'What I tell you, piss-brain? Huh? Who called up the twins?'

'That's what I'd like to know.' They all turned. Fairfax was standing in front of the bars with his driver and another constable behind him. 'I want you all to sit down, please.'

'Hey, Inspector, listen to me . . .' Emil thrust his hands through the bars again.

'No don't listen to him.' Luis clutched at the air in front of Fairfax.

'Sit down!' the sergeant shouted and they could see from his face that he meant it. They all sat back down on the bench, except Raphaella who flashed her teeth, thrust her breasts and tried to smooth her mud-caked skirt over her thighs. 'Can we talk somewhere private, Superintendent?'

'Sergeant. I am *Sergeant* Fairfax. Now sit down.'

Raphaella tossed her hair, brazen and wounded, then squeezed onto the bench between Emil and Scotch Jock. 'Yes, Sergeant.'

Fairfax glared at them through the bars. He knew that this was irregular and he should be taking them one at a time into an interview room with a solicitor present, but as far as he knew there were no rooms available and he didn't have time to wait. 'You are being held on suspicion of murder.'

'Ah . . .' Luis's head disappeared between his hands again.

'Hey, Sarge . . .' Emil raised his hands.

'I got nothing to say without legal representation.' Jock folded his arms and tried to move away from Raphaella, squashing Razor against the wall at the end.

'Please, why don' we talk, Sergeant?' Raphaella flashed her eyes again.

Fairfax ignored her. 'The McCarthy Twins. Who hired them?'

'He did!' Raphaella pointed at Luis.

'And who went back to insult them?' Emil stared at her.

'No, Emil. Not me. I never seen no McCarthy Twins,' said Raphaella.

'Wha'? What you talking about, crazy woman?' Emil gasped.

'You tell me, big brother. Maybe it was you done the whole thing.' Raphaella had decided if she was going to blame a father, then she may as well include a brother. Two made a bigger target. 'Whoever it was, it wasn't me, Sergeant.'

Fairfax was already beginning to think it was hopeless. He wanted to return to the hospital. These would have to wait. He decided on one last try and moved along the bars until he was standing opposite Razor at the far end of the bench. 'Who hired the twins?' Fairfax asked abruptly.

Razor couldn't tell a lie. 'Mr Riss.'

'Shuddup! Shuddup!' Luis stood, but the magic words had lost their power.

Emil pulled him back down onto the bench and said, 'Thass right. Thass what my papa did.'

'Emil, shuddup . . .' Luis struggled.

'Why did he hire them?' Fairfax asked Razor.

'To kill the restaurant woman.' Razor spoke in his own tongue.

'Speak English.'

Razor obeyed. 'To kill the restaurant woman.' Fairfax cursed himself for not demanding the obvious when he'd arrested the Sikh the previous day. He quickly moved away from the bars and whispered to Sergeant Braine.

'He don' know! He don' know nothing!' Luis was in despair. He stood up and put his hands through the bars again. 'He don' know . . .' But it was too late. The custody officer and the constable were moving towards them. They unlocked the door and Razor stepped from behind the bars.

'Listen to me! Listen . . .!' Luis wailed as Razor was led away.

Braine put Fairfax and the Sikh into a superintendent's office and asked them if they wanted tea. The Sikh nodded and sat relaxed and blank across the desk from Fairfax. The injection was wearing off and his legs were beginning to feel sore, but there was something oddly soothing about the Sikh. He didn't seem to have anything to hide. If Fairfax had asked him, he'd have been quite precise about himself: he was a killer, at the moment in repose, who would sooner or later end up incarcerated as his father had been before him. He was a man made for the bin, and as long as his tea had three sugars in it, he was quite content.

Fairfax leaned forward on the desk and came to the point: 'Keep speaking English.' Razor nodded and Fairfax went on. 'Where are the twins?'

'Killing the restaurant woman.'

'Where?'

'Where she is.'

'Where's that?'

'I don't know.'

'Where were you last night?'

Razor furrowed his brow. 'I don't remember.'

'Were you at the bakery?'

Razor thought about it. 'Yes.'

'Did you kill that man at the bakery?'

'Yes.' Razor's eyes were dead.

'Did you go to the Crystal Rooms?'

'No.'

Fairfax believed him. Having admitted to one killing what was the point of denying another? He stared at the Sikh. It was clear Riss had started the whole thing but hadn't finished it. Hooper had been right – as usual – it was just the twins. 'I want to ask you again, Mr Singh. Do you have any idea where the McCarthys might be?'

'Yes.'

'Where?'

'Wherever the restaurant woman is.'

'Supposing she's dead?'

'You won't see them again.'

'And if she's not?'

'That's where they'll be.'

'Why are you so sure?'

'Because they'll kill her. That's what they're paid for. And that's what they'll do. What else is there?'

425

Razor's flat Birmingham accent, his glazed eyes and immobile face, were beginning to scare Fairfax. He realized that the Sikh had something of the same quality that he had sensed in his two brief glimpses of the twins. It was an utter acceptance of who they were and what they did. He wondered if the twins would admit to murder as easily as Razor and suspected that they would. There were no secrets in this world of killing. What they did was inevitable. What was the point of trying to disguise it? But if they were the same as Razor, why weren't the twins as easy to catch? There must be some difference between them. He could see that the cause of the evil in Razor was a weird insanity, stemming from some personality defect. It was also the reason for the ease of his capture. Personality connects; it's the form of the relationships between us, it always leaves traces and so can be seen, or at least sensed. And there was the difference. The twins had no personality, they left no trace and that meant no connection could ever be made with them. They existed somehow outside of us. And, he realized with a shudder, they were locked on to Violet, and if the Sikh was right, would pursue her for ever.

He stood quickly. He needed to get back to the hospital. He arranged for Razor to be given his tea in a cell that had become vacant and told him that he would be charged with murder. The Sikh didn't react and Fairfax limped away along the corridor looking for his driver. As he passed through the charge room, he heard Luis yell from the holding area, 'It was my daughter!'

Then it was Raphaella, 'It was my brother!'

And finally Emil, 'It was my sister!'

Fairfax was too depressed to comment. As he got into his car, where his driver was waiting for him, he remembered one of the officers at the Soho station saying of the twins, 'You can't stop the wind.' Well that was probably true, but he'd do his best. It was his duty. They drove north.

4

Bernie wasn't hungry. He turned down his breakfast, even if it was midday. Mirabelle, standing at Vera's sink in her large, tile-floored kitchen, wanted to know why.

'I'm going on a fast.'

'What for?'

'I don't know.' He was looking worried.

'Bernie?'

'It's like Sir Galahad did. Before he saw the Holy Grail.'

Mirabelle sat opposite him at the table. 'Do you think you're going to see the Holy Grail?'

'I might.' He set his jaw. 'I don't know, do I? I might know more than you think. I might know more than I think. That's what worries me.'

He turned away as Geoffrey's mother walked in. She'd taken two hours to prepare herself for her first house guests in ten years. She wore a prim navy-blue dress with white epaulettes and too much lipstick and her hair was severely parted at one side and had been flattened by water. It seemed as if she'd forgotten the introductions the night before, or at least wanted to make a fresh start. 'Good morning, I'm Geoffrey's mother, Mrs Vera Arkwright. Geoffrey's asked to be excused as he's taking the air in the garden.' She beamed and held out her hand to Bernie. 'You must be Mr Lack the Younger.'

'That's right. Good morning, Mrs.' He stood and shook her hand.

'And you are Mirabelle. Such a pretty name. My husband was a brigadier.' The statement came out of the blue, but was evidently of the highest importance to Vera because, having made it, she stepped back, put her heels together, clasped her hands in front of her and dropped her shoulders in a little sigh.

'Your son's a monk,' said Bernie.

'I beg your pardon?'

'Bernie?' Mirabelle cocked her head to one side.

'I worked it out you see.' He looked up at Vera. 'We was in this old battered pub and there were these other geezers who were monks, and then I realized that so were Geoffrey and Martin, because they're full of prayers and shelter. They're not brothers in arms like me and Arnie and Ron.'

Vera didn't seem at all confused by this. 'You mean you're fighting men?'

'Well, Mrs, being as you asked, I wouldn't be surprised. My big brother was the bravest of them all, as a matter of fact.'

Vera sat opposite him at the table and leaned towards him. 'I know all about fighting men, Mr Lack.'

'I thought you did,' said Bernie, clasping his hands in front of him. He stared straight at the old woman as if he had known her for years. Mirabelle looked on. There was something about the pair of them together that made the sum of their deficient parts seem much greater than the whole. Bernie said, 'You see, Mrs, my brother whispered something to me before he died.'

'Did he, Mr Lack?'

'What was it, Bernie?' Mirabelle came closer to the table, remembering Arnie's last seconds in the back of the baker's van.

'Well.' Bernie paused, pondering. 'What he said was . . .' He looked up, paused again, then said, 'He said, Bernie; that's me, Mrs. He said, Bernie, your dad wasn't your dad.'

'Oh I say!' Vera sat back with her hand covering her mouth.

'Did he say that, Bernie?' Mirabelle leaned in towards him. This was extraordinary. All she knew of Charlie, Violet and the history of the family flashed through her mind. 'He said that Charlie wasn't . . .'

'That's what he said.' Bernie was very serious.

'Did he say who your real father was?' asked Mirabelle.

'No. He died before he could mention it.' Bernie looked round at them both and then said, 'Which means I might probably be a basket.'

'A basket, Mr Lack?'

'That's a bastard, Mrs.'

'Oh I see.' Vera sat back and deliberated, as if she were going over the ramifications of this new information in her own peculiar way. 'I see,' she said again. It was as if she somehow understood the real nature of what Bernie had said. Mirabelle certainly hadn't. She watched fascinated as Bernie waited for the old woman to speak again. She spoke slowly. 'Do you know, Mr Lack, there are many bastards who have become kings.'

'Are there?'

'Oh yes.'

'Well that's exactly what I mean then. See, that's why I'm having a fast and turning down my breakfast.'

'I don't understand, Bernie.' Mirabelle could see that the questions she'd been grappling with were in realms of lore and custom that she'd no knowledge of.

'It's because things are happening, Mirabelle,' said Bernie. 'See, one of us is gone and that leaves two. And one of us is the basket, which is very dangerous.'

'Why?'

'Because it means I might be up for the Grail.'

'Why, Bernie?'

'Because it does, Mirabelle. You don't understand.'

'I do, Mr Lack.' Vera raised her head. She seemed to glow with pride.

'I know you do, Mrs. I knew it the first time I met you. You're like the wise old crone, you are.'

Vera didn't seem at all put out by the description. 'Oh I'm so pleased!' She clapped her hands in delight as Mirabelle looked on bewildered.

'Bernie.' Ronnie came into the kitchen. He stood nervously in the corner by the door. He'd tried Mathilda again, but there was still no answer, so he'd finally called the restaurant and Lucy had answered. She'd told him she'd found Mathilda in her room. Ronnie was pale. He looked over at Bernie from the doorway. 'Can we have a chat, mate?'

'Am I in the way?' Vera got up and stepped back from the table.

'It's all right. You can stay if you want.' Ronnie was past caring. He told them what he knew, which was the shorthand version of events as related to him by Lucy. Mathilda had taken some pills, but was still conscious when Lucy found her. It seemed that the brandy had saved her life. Lucy reckoned that she'd passed out before she'd been able to take enough pills to kill herself. The news had badly shaken him. 'I got to get back there. Geoffrey's going to take me on the bike.' He was worried about how Bernie would react. 'I'm sorry, Bern.'

Bernie looked up. 'Don't worry about nothing, Ron. I'll take care of everything here.'

'Perhaps it's time to call the coppers, mate?' Ronnie asked.

'No.' Bernie banged his hand on the table and stood up. 'I don't want no coppers. This ain't their business.'

'The police know it wasn't you now,' said Ronnie.

'That ain't the point, Ron. I ain't scared of no slammer no more, as a matter of fact. I jus' got other things to do, and I got to do them here.' He looked over at Vera. 'If you don't mind, Mrs.'

'Of course not, Mr Lack.'

Mirabelle was in a dilemma. She knew that once Ronnie had gone her whole position would become clear and Sorush would know who she was protecting. How could she not? Bernie would be the only one left. She looked at him. 'You could go with Ronnie.'

'If you want, Bern,' said Ron, 'you could get in the sidecar.'

'No thanks, Ron. See, sometimes you fight with other knights beside you and sometimes you're on your tod. Depends on the adventure.'

'Bernie?' But Mirabelle knew it was hopeless. Bernie's face was harder and more certain than she'd ever seen it before.

'I'm staying here, Mirabelle. And don't get no coppers, Ron. Not yet.'

'I'll sort it out for you, Bern.' Under normal circumstances Ronnie would have demanded that Bernie come with him there and then, but those days seemed a very long time ago.

Geoffrey followed behind him to the kitchen door; he was holding two crash helmets. Ronnie promised to phone as soon as he could and then turned into the hall following Geoffrey to the front door.

Vera, Mirabelle and Bernie went after them and watched as they got onto the motorbike. Geoffrey started it with a roar and they pulled out through the trees to the gates and then away down the road.

Vera stood on the drive as they left. 'How is it that my son didn't say goodbye to me?'

'He's prob'ly got other things on his mind, Mrs,' said Bernie.

'That's right, Mr Lack. How wise you are.' Vera put on her bravest face and turned to him. 'Would you care to stay for dinner?'

'Thanks very much, but I'm fasting.'

'Oh, but after the fast comes the feast!'

Bernie thought about it. 'I think you're dead right, Mrs. I'll have a turkey on a spit, if you don't mind.'

'Turkey?'

'If they're small, you better make it two, Mrs.'

'Then I'll have to telephone my butcher.'

'Do you have any mead, as a matter of fact?'

'I have Madeira, Mr Lack. Or perhaps you would prefer a chilled Châteauneuf-du-Pape?'

'I'll have both, thank you. I have to prepare myself, you see?'

'I do, Mr Lack, I do.'

'What for?' Mirabelle didn't.

'My adventure, Mirabelle.' He nodded, then Mirabelle realized with a shock that he hadn't nodded at all. He'd bowed. 'Excuse me please, Mrs. I've got to go and think about it. May I use your garden?'

'Of course you may, Mr Lack.'

'You're very kind.' Bernie bowed again and went into the house.

'What a remarkable young man.' Vera followed Bernie inside. She was as elated as she'd been for years. Geoffrey was forgotten. She was going to give a dinner party! Mirabelle watched her go to telephone her butcher and then turned and looked up at the sky. Still nothing. She was sure it wouldn't stay that way for long.

5

Hooper stared at the doors leading to the hospital operating theatre. He hadn't moved for three hours and had even let an unknown inspector telephone Harriet to give her the news of the attack. He stood a yard from the doors with his hands in his coat pockets, his shoulders hunched and his eyes fixed. Other officers had moved carefully around him. They were somehow aware that they needed to protect him as much as Violet. Maybe it was because his life was now nothing other than projected love, and even the toughest, most streetwise, seen-it-all copper couldn't but respect that. A nursing sister had tried to coax him to a chair. He'd refused. He'd decided that he was Violet's link to life. While he stood there, she would not die, and therefore there was nothing that could move him. Nursing sisters, inspectors, even chief constables could come and go, but Hooper would remain as the heart-beat of his love.

The surgeons in the theatre did their best to save her in their own rather more practical way. They didn't hold out much hope. The twins' swords had pierced her more than seventy times in every part of her body. Such stabs, slashes and gashes were nothing to Hooper. He barely heard the reports on her declining condition. It was his faith against her mortality and he had no doubts as to which would be victorious. You can't murder a dream.

Fairfax had returned from Hammersmith an hour before, and rather than disturb his superintendent, had concentrated on a complete overhaul of the defences in the hospital. Now, as he limped down the hushed corridor to report his efforts, he sensed at once that there seemed to be some kind of aura around his superior. It was as if Hooper was engaged in a battle that he, a simple earthbound sergeant, could never imagine. He approached with care and the greatest respect. He whispered gently, 'How is she, sir?' Hooper didn't reply. 'Sir?'

'They shall not come, Sergeant.'

'I beg your pardon, sir?'

'I'll gouge out their eyes.' Hooper spoke very quietly. 'I'll carve them up. I'll split these twins in two.'

'We need to find them first, sir.'

'They'll come.' Hooper said it with such utter conviction that Fairfax knew his call on the Riss family had been a waste of time. He looked up at Hooper's lined and pale face and felt an immense surge of affection for him. He did nothing but stand there, but it was enough. The twins would come if Violet didn't die, and as Hooper was going to ensure she didn't, they'd better expect a visit. Hooper said, 'I am on guard, Sergeant.'

'I'd say she was better protected than the monarch, sir.' Fairfax said it not only to reassure Hooper, but also because he knew it to be true. There were over thirty men guarding all approaches to the theatre.

It didn't seem to impress Hooper. 'If I am here, Sergeant, then not even a shadow will pass through these doors.'

Fairfax pressed ahead anyway. 'If I may show you, sir. These are the defences I've organized.' He flipped open his notebook. He'd sketched a rough plan of the hospital floor that contained the operating theatre. All entrances and stairways leading to it were marked in different-coloured inks. 'You see, sir. We're on the first floor, here.' He pointed it out to Hooper, who wasn't paying any attention. 'The three stairwells leading to this point are marked in different colours: red, blue and orange. Each staircase . . .'

Hooper turned to him. 'I am the defence, Sergeant. Don't you see?'

'Yes sir, I'm sorry, but . . .'

'Now go away.'

'Sir, if I may say . . .'

'You're a good boy.' Hooper turned back to the operating-theatre doors. 'I am here. Wild horses are nothing to me.' He sighed. 'I doubt if anyone will ever understand.'

'I do, sir.'

'Thank you, Freddie.'

Fairfax waited a second, but Hooper didn't say anything else, so he went back down the corridor to refine his defences. He remembered the Soho sergeant again, 'You can't stop the wind.' Well if his superintendent thought you could, then so did he.

6

Geoffrey parked his motorbike behind the restaurant. He dismounted and followed Ronnie round to the alley. What was he supposed to do now? Go back home? What to? A mad mother, Madeira and peanuts in a dish? He sniffed the monoxide of Soho and heard a girl call. This was his home. How could he leave? But this was now his Martinless home. How could he stay? He felt his fat sweat under his creaking leathers and traipsed miserably after the silent Ronnie, who somehow, in spite of it all, was still dapper and neat in his dark suit.

All Ronnie wanted to do was see Mathilda. He increased his pace. They came to the restaurant door, walked in, and they had hardly arrived when Sophie told them about the latest assault on Violet at her apartment.

'Oh bloody hell.' Ronnie sat on a chair and stared at Sid the Slurp up the back with his daily cuppa. He had no idea what to say. When Harriet came down the stairs with the additional news that the police were sure that his mother's attackers had been the twins and nothing to do with Riss, all he could do was repeat, 'Oh bloody hell.'

'We ought to go to the hospital and see her, dear.' Harriet stood above him.

'That would mean the police.'

'I'd say we were well past all that.'

Ronnie said nothing, but at the back of his mind the idea was forming to telephone Mirabelle at Vera's and get her to take Bernie up to the hospital. They could see their mum and sort it out once and for all with the coppers. But as usual with Ronnie, practical matters came second. That's why he was a failure, he guessed. He stood up. 'I got to go out.'

'Where are you going, dear?'

'I want to see Mathilda.' Ronnie looked at the ground as he said it because he knew his voice was giving away his feelings.

'She's here, Ronnie.'

He looked up. 'What?'

'Lucy brought her from casualty in a taxi. She said her flat had all been smashed up to smithereens.' Harriet smiled making her nose hurt. 'She's asleep in Arnie's bed.'

Ronnie didn't wait for any more. He walked straight to the stairs and quickly went up them. Harriet turned to Geoffrey who was still standing by the door. He seemed lost. She said, 'Would you like a cup of tea, dear?'

'No thank you, Auntie. I need a drink.' He didn't really feel like a drink without Martin, but what else was there to do?

'You sure, dear?'

'I am, thank you.' He turned from the door. 'If you really want to know, Auntie, it was good to go home, but . . .' He knew he wasn't making much sense, but continued anyway. 'I adore my dear mother. However, I really don't see how I could possibly live with her. And anyway . . .' he tried to sound nonchalant about the *non sequitur*, 'Martin and I have parted. I . . . uh? It seems to be the case that two bitches can't mate.'

'He's in the Empress of China, dear,' said Harriet.

'Martin!' Geoffrey withered and his cheeks shook in delight. Then he calmly sat down. 'In that case, Auntie, I'd love a cup of your best char. Take your time.'

The first person Ronnie saw when he came into the living room was Sayeed Sayeed. He was in his customary mustard dhoti and touched Ronnie on the arm as he came in. 'I am so sorry.'

'Thanks, Sayeed.' Ronnie was pleased the old man was there. For as long as he could remember the Indian had always shown up when they

434

were in crisis. Sayeed half bowed and Ronnie went through to Arnie's bedroom.

Mathilda was asleep. He'd never seen a black woman look pale before. He felt like she was faint or grey or like a ghost. She looked so beautiful he wanted to cry. He stood by the door for a minute, then closed it behind him. The little cluttered room was very quiet and stunk of bedclothes. After a bit he sat carefully on the edge of the bed and listened to her breathe. He couldn't take his eyes off her. Her lips were black and her eye sockets kind of shaded and translucent. Her hand was outside the covers and he touched it with his finger, then held it.

He started to talk in a croaky whisper. 'I . . . I'm sorry . . . I just want to say I'm sorry for everything.' He stopped and looked at her. He could hear some talking coming through from the living room. 'I'm sorry for everything I said and everything else.' She stirred. 'Can you hear me?' She moved her head to one side. He didn't know if she was saying yes in her own sleepy way or not. He decided she was and went on. 'See, I had some bad times . . . Everybody does. I bet you did.'

He stopped for a second and looked at her sadly. 'I couldn't do anything about you. I'm sorry. It was like I was trapped in something. See, because I was trapped I couldn't do anything about anything as a matter of fact. Trouble is, you see, Tilda, as a matter of fact, there don't seem to be any facts. And that's what gets me. See, I mean, no facts to help you out. I mean, what are you supposed to do then?' He stared at her for a while, hoping she might give him a clue, and suddenly she turned her face towards him. If she opened her eyes she'd be looking directly into his own. It was as if she was waiting for him.

And then it came to him that there was a fact in his life, and he'd been such an idiot never to have seen it before. Maybe he hadn't because he'd been trapped, but he wasn't sure about that, and anyway he didn't care, because as he stared at her face he could feel the doors of his trap beginning to open. It was only a tiny crack, but it was enough to let in little pinpricks of light which scattered all over this raw and junior fact he'd just discovered. The light got brighter as the trapdoors opened a bit more and he could feel his fact begin to grow. He began to feel happy, which was strange because if you'd asked him five minutes ago, he'd have said that he'd never felt more depressed in his life. But not any more. He leaned down and kissed her on the forehead. Then he revealed his fat, pink, juicy, new-born fact. 'I love you, Tilda.' She opened her eyes.

7

Bernie had gone through the house into Vera's walled garden and sat on an old rockery near her overgrown pond. He had squatted there for hours. He had a look round at the high grey stone walls that surrounded him and the bleak sky above, then he closed his eyes. And he immediately started to see things which were like visions out of the Arfer.

The first thing was a ship parked up on a river with purple and blue mountains behind growing up to the sky. It was like a dream, but also stranger than a dream. He felt like he was walking towards this ship. He got up to it and it was old-fashioned and made of wood with big white sails, like a pirate ship, except it wasn't pirates, he sort of knew that from somewhere and he also had the feeling that the ship was a great beauty and somehow reminded him of a church, although it definitely wasn't a church; it was a ship with a high mast.

There was a notice on the side of the ship which said, 'I was built by Solomon.' He thought it might mean something like Solomon & Son boat builders. Then he looked underneath the sign and saw a big note. It said, 'I am Faith. Don't get on board unless you're entirely spotless and good, or it will be the worse for you.' He thought about this for a minute and had a little joke to himself about spotless meaning having no spots, but knew that it really meant being pure and all that, which he reckoned he was, so he walked up the gangplank and went on board.

It was even more beautiful inside. The wood was shiny and carved and there was a door which was open. So he went through it and down some steps and came into a giant cabin, which was even more lovely than everywhere else. He didn't know why it was beautiful but just knew it was. And there was this maiden standing there, and she said, 'Hello.'

And he said, 'Hello Maiden.'

And she said, 'Welcome.'

And he said, 'And you an' all.' And then he looked round and said, 'What's that?'

And she said, 'It's a bed.'

And he said, 'Why's it got three wooden posts, one white, one green and one red, holding up the curtains?'

And she said, 'They come from the tree which Adam and Eve slept underneath. It was white when they were pure and it was green when they had a baby, and then it was red when Cain killed Abel.'

'Oh,' he said. 'You mean it went red like because of the blood?'

And she said, 'That's right.'

'Oh,' he said and had another look round. To tell the truth the maiden was beginning to remind him a bit of Mirabelle, but he didn't mention it. Then he saw, lying at the bottom of the bed, a huge sword half in and half out of a sheath. The handle of the sword was made of jewels and sparkled. He looked closer and saw that there was a label on the sword which said, 'I am a marvel, because no-one can ever have a hand big enough to hold me.'

'I can,' he said, and he picked it up.

'Be careful,' said the maiden.

'What for?' he said.

'Look at the sheath,' she said.

And he did and there was some more writing, which he read out loud. 'Don't draw this sword out of the sheath unless you are stronger than everyone else.'

He had a think and then said, 'Well I think I am stronger than everyone else, prob'ly.' He was going to pull the sword out of the sheath and the maiden again said, 'Be careful.' So he read some more.

This time it was on the handle of the sword. It said, 'Don't ever change the belt of this sword unless a maiden gives you a new one made out of something that is precious to her and then ties it round your waist.'

'Oh.' He looked up at the maiden who smiled a tinkly little smile. Then he looked at the belt of the sword and saw that it was all frayed and tatty, so he said, 'Excuse me, Maiden, have you got another belt made out of something precious to you?'

And she said, 'I have made it already.' And she gave him a belt made out of her own shiny and glorious hair and then tied the sword round him, and he felt great, like he was really well sworded up.

'Thanks, Maiden,' he said.

'Don't worry about it,' she said. 'The sword is called Blood Mover.'

'What?' he said.

And she said, 'Blood Mover. And so off you go on your adventures, and don't worry about me because I shall be dead.'

'Oh no,' he said.

'Don't worry about it,' she said again, 'for it is God's will.' And then she disappeared. And so did he.

The next thing was he was in a much smaller boat and, surprise surprise, there was Arnie up the other end and he was looking pleased to see him. So they hugged each other and had a good laugh about all the old days. Then they rowed over the water for at least six or seven weeks.

Then one day they came up on a beach and there was this geezer standing there with a white horse. And this geezer said, 'Your time is up. You've got the sword and here's your charger, so go and have some more adventures.'

So he said, 'All right then.' And he got on the horse.

'Bye, mate,' said Arnie. 'I think you might see God.'

'What, you mean the Holy Grail, Arn?'

'Something like that,' said Arnie who was looking very unhappy. 'I wish I was you, mate.'

'Don't never wish you was anyone else, Arn. For you are what you are and that's that. And that's what God gave you.' Even as he said it, he was surprised at these odd words which were coming tumbling out of his mouth. But he decided to just forget it and he got up on the horse and rode away to see other places. And as he rode away he seemed to get bigger and bigger, and ended up so huge that he was looking down on this city like it was just a little Airfix model below the hooves of his horse. So he got off his horse and knelt down and had a closer look. He could see thousands of little people running around on the streets and somehow he knew the place was called Logris. He'd never heard of Logris but guessed it was perhaps London, but he wasn't sure. Then he saw that everybody was unhappy because the river that ran through the middle of the city was very swelled up and choppy. As a matter of fact it looked like it might burst its banks any moment. So naturally he just put his finger in the water and immediately it calmed down and flowed nice and quiet and all the people were overjoyed.

Then he saw a fire, which was burning very bright, and he looked closer and saw that it was a flaming gravestone and that there was all smoke coming out of the earth. And he thought, Hello, what's all this then? And so he pushed his fingers into the earth and the fire went out. And he prodded around a bit and he saw an old man at the bottom of the grave, who said, 'Thanks, my son, because I've been in hell down here and you've made me feel better now. I can be dead happy after what you've done. See what I mean?' The old man's voice reminded him a bit of his dad, but he didn't really look much like him because he was much older. And then he said, 'I am your ancestor.'

Blimey O'Reilly! he thought, and he pulled his hand out. And that was about the end of his adventures for now.

Mirabelle leaned forward on Vera's old-fashioned stone sink watching Bernie through the kitchen window as he stretched and yawned. She had seen his visions too and tried to work out what they meant.

The last was the easiest to decipher. The burning grave was clearly Charlie waiting in torment as his fate on the Bridge was decided by herself and Sorush. Bernie's cool hand of forgiveness descending into the underground fire had eased him in the same way as it had calmed the tumultuous waters running through the city of Logris. She guessed that this signified his power to bring tranquillity and peace to those around him.

The beautiful ship he had entered was clearly a sign of a journey. It was obviously the ship of faith, which was why only the pure in heart could enter and why there was no doubt that Bernie was acceptable. The coloured posts of the bed were the green, white and red symbols of the earliest garden and indicated Bernie's profound connection to the very beginnings of life. The beautiful, bejewelled sword with the hempen girdle she knew about. It was the legendary weapon made by Solomon and his wife as a sign of, and defence for, the last of his lineage. It meant that Bernie was being armed for battle, and Mirabelle shuddered at the thought.

It was clear that the maiden on the ship was herself. She touched her hair as she realized that she in turn would need to create a girdle or equivalent for Bernie's sword, whatever that may be, when the time came.

It was only the boat journey with Arnie that she didn't understand.

Where had Arnie come from and why was he so disturbed? Bernie had calmed his brother and brought him peace. What did this signify? She sensed that the man on the beach had been a servant of God and had given Galahad his charger for the next part of his journey. But what was that? Where was he to go next? Arnie had said Bernie would see God. From the Arfer she knew that Galahad had paid witness to the Grail. Would Bernie? Through the window she saw him slump back down again. He was deep in thought once more. And then Mirabelle saw red. Literally.

The walled garden was suddenly filled with billions of minuscule red dots. Sorush had returned. This time her legions were crimson and tiny. Each angel was barely more than a centimetre of detailed, intricate perfection. They were a massive, billowing cloud, filling the walls and surrounding Bernie with the smarting hum of beating wings as they swirled and slowly began to form themselves into a shape that Mihr couldn't fail to recognize.

It was the twenty-foot-high, arrogant and angry face of Sorush, made up of an infinite number of ceaselessly shifting, tiny, buzzing angels' bodies. Her image was red in every hue. It was brilliant and terrifying. Mihr panicked for an instant as Bernie was obscured, and she retaliated by shining her own genius into the dark red. But even her brilliance left him only as a rocklike shadow within the moving storm, making it seem as if he now existed physically inside the mind of her enemy.

'You have brought a false saviour,' said Sorush.

'He is not false.' Mihr fought back. She spun and reflected blinding white. Sorush burned and hurt, held fast and spat crimson in waves. The light between the two, the battleground of all time, held precarious balance, particle rearing to particle, and infinite power to its own opposite.

'Dark shall subsume light. I shall destroy you, Mihr.'

'Light will always be.'

'I shall have him.'

'You shall not.'

A million angels flew and made Sorush's lip curl. She flicked her hair and another billion cherubim rose then fell. Infinitely more condensed and expanded in eternal reformation as Sorush summoned her power and spoke again. 'This is now inquisition, Mihr.' It was a final state-

440

ment. The cloud of red seethed. They had been commanded. This was full battle alert.

Mihr said, 'Let it be what it will.'

'Inquisition.' The sound of Sorush was made up of the harshness of wings beating and echoing for all time, as if in some great shadowy black hole. And as suddenly as they had come, Sorush and her deadly, microscopic horde were gone.

Mirabelle leaned against the kitchen counter. Inquisition. Such a step, once taken, was absolute. There could be no doubt or debate. Inquisition presumed an assault on creed, a threat to the ultimate order of the faith, an ideological attack on the rock. In such rare and dangerous circumstances, the inquisition would have no parameters or mercy. Nothing, or no-one, could be allowed to escape its inexorable scrutiny, and destruction, whatever the extremity or consequence, was an accepted means of search and condemnation. Mirabelle knew that the legions she could see were insignificant compared to those that would come. Inquisition. Although she'd expected it sooner or later, the word sent a shudder through her. Inquisition was a prelude to war.

In front of her, on the rock in the garden, the great bulk of Bernie sat silently. He was unconscious of what had passed and she was thankful for that. She wondered how much he would ever know. Perhaps he was destined to be for ever a conduit: a huge and hulking half boy, half man, who would remain for ever unaware of his own power. Mirabelle realized it was probably so. Nevertheless she knew Sorush was wrong when she had spoken of a false saviour. He was far from that. He was as real as the rock he sat on. He was as real as faith. He was a re-injection of belief, and as such would have the power to split the traditions and revolutionize the creed that Sorush depended on for her existence. And Sorush knew it too. It was Bernie or her. Mirabelle's mission was now crystal clear. She was to protect this saviour until the time of battle. In the heavens it would be fought between her and the legions of Sorush, and on the ancient field it would be between Galahad and the black knights from the Arfer. And here and now? Bernie had seen Solomon's sword. Who was he to fight?

The garden was very quiet. A blackbird flew from the tree above Bernie. Behind, Mirabelle could hear Vera coming down the stairs. The phone rang. Vera called out and Mirabelle went into the hall. Vera handed her the receiver and she heard Ronnie's voice. He told her of the assault on Violet. Mirabelle put down the phone and sat quietly on the wooden chair by the umbrella stand. She had the answer to her question.

$\boxed{8}$

Two pairs of feet in shiny black shoes came ordinarily, normally, up the concrete steps to the front doors of the hospital. Above the shoes were identical black trousers and above those the green hems of surgical gowns. Once inside the glass doors the feet stopped and each pair turned to face the other. Then one pair stepped to the left and took two paces forward as the second pair turned full circle. The constable that passed them only saw their green-gowned backs and barely glanced at their jet-black hair beneath their surgical caps and masks as they stared at the noticeboard. Once the constable had gone by with his handset crackling and his mind on other matters, the two turned and moved into the main body of the hospital.

Three surgeons had operated on Violet for seven hours. They leaned back exhausted as she was wheeled from the theatre. Despite their diligence their hopes were low; although they didn't communicate this to Hooper, who knew for a fact that she would survive.

He followed the stretcher, as it was pushed into an intensive care ward, with his hands clasped in front of him like an old and wise seer. He watched as his love was connected to the various drips and monitors. He could have cried out that all this technology was worth no more than the momentary blips on the screens. What was invention, science, even genius, compared to the great blast of life that he felt waiting in his heart? But he kept his mouth shut, because in the soft steps, gentle hands and quiet concentration of the nurses he saw a dedication and belief that was similar to his own. There was nothing they wouldn't do to preserve this precious breath that blew on a path from nothing to dust. A tear came to his eye for a second as he thought that it was as much their faith in this growth and blossom within themselves as it was their machines that would save Violet. And the fact that they didn't even know her seemed to Hooper to add an almost unbearable poignancy. He brushed his eye with his sleeve and stood back. Violet's face was pale and bruised. Her eyes were closed. He waited, unmoving, then muttered to himself, 'I am here, Violet. They shall not pass.'

Fairfax looked into the ward through the glass portholes in the door. He could see Hooper's hunched back as he stood close by Violet's bed and said his second prayer of the day. Since Violet's move to the ward his security system had required readjustment. The staircase that he had previously marked as orange had now become redundant to his defence and he had moved several of his uniformed forces to another set of stairs. Blue was the same, but he had reorganized red to cover another corridor as well as their original, and then, to his horror, he had discovered that the position of the intensive care ward had now laid them open to a fourth line of attack from the rear of the hospital. He'd reshuffled his men yet again and now had a fourth bulwark against the twins which he'd called green. His notebook was now a mess of coloured lines and he'd run out of different-coloured pens.

Now that he'd rearranged everything he realized that he could re-rationalize it all geographically. East, west, north and south would be simpler and evidently easier to locate than the colour codes, as every staircase had the compass direction written clearly on them. However, knowing the minds of the men in the Met and their antipathy to change, Fairfax was fully aware that present complexity was always preferable to future ease, so he left it as it was. Even so he'd sent the sergeant, who was a thin man called Laurel and nicknamed Stan, to check that every constable knew the precise location of his own self and his colour. As Stan returned, Fairfax asked, 'All set and understood?'

'They're from the Met, Freddie, not the Royal College of Art.'

'Give me a break, will you Stan?'

'I did my best.' Stan sounded doubtful.

'Do me a favour. Check them all again, will you?'

'Come on, Freddie. They'll think I'm an arsehole. They're aware of the potential upshot, they've got their tea and cheese rolls; leave them to it.'

Fairfax sighed and looked at the ceiling. In the end, no matter the genius of man, it all came down to where the simplest boots trod. His handset burst into life.

'Suspects. Two orientals, ground floor.'

Fairfax fumbled for the radio. 'What? Stay calm. Which wing?'

The handset crackled. 'They're heading for the east staircase.'

'You mean heading blue?' Surely the system hadn't broken down already?

'What?' asked the handset.

'Blue? Is this blue I am talking to?' Fairfax wanted to know.

'Yes, Sarge,' said the handset.

'Blue!' Fairfax looked at Stan in a kind of terrible triumph. 'They're here. East staircase.' He punched the buttons on the handset again and shouted into it, 'All units. Blue! Blue staircase! Blue wing!'

A hundred and fifty yards away from Fairfax and down one floor a bearded constable, sitting comfortably under a sign that read 'East Staircase', nearly dropped his polystyrene beaker of tea as his handset burst into life. 'Blue! Blue! Blue!' He turned to his companion, a tall thin man with a beaky nose, and said, 'Where's blue?'

'Dunno, mate.'

'Blue? That's got to be west, hasn't it?' They both looked up at the sign reading East above them. 'I mean east is always red, isn't it?'

'Is it?'

'Course it is! Come on!'

They both leaped up and charged towards the west wing.

Fifteen seconds after they'd gone, two pairs of identical shiny black shoes came round the corner from the foyer and quietly went up the empty staircase. The clothes and faces of the two men were hidden by their green gowns, surgical masks and cotton theatre caps.

As they disappeared at the top of the stairs, the constable who'd first spotted them in the foyer and had radioed to Fairfax came to a breathless halt. He'd glimpsed them again as they turned at the top of the east staircase. He didn't get it. Why wasn't anyone there? He pulled out his handset. 'Suspects on east staircase, Sarge. Where is everyone?'

By this time the bearded constable and his beaky-nosed companion had reached the two constables guarding the west staircase. They were just coming sliding to a halt when they heard Fairfax screaming through their handset. 'Blue? Are you on blue?'

The bearded constable looked at the constables he had just joined and then up at the sign, which read, 'West Staircase'. He shouted back into his handset, 'Yes, Sarge, on blue. We're on blue.'

'Any sign?' Fairfax wanted to know.

The bearded constable looked up again. 'Yes, Sarge. It says West.'

'I mean any sign of the twins . . .' They heard Fairfax choke through the earpiece of the handset. 'Did you say west!'

The bearded constable, beginning to feel his east/west colour theory unravel, tried to brazen it out. 'You said blue, Sarge.'

Fairfax's voice came screaming out of the handset. 'Blue is east! West is red!'

'Thought it might be the other way round . . .'

'Get on with it!'

'We're on our way, Sarge!' The, by now, four constables sped off down the corridor in the direction of the east staircase. They'd gone fifty yards when Fairfax had a change of plan. The bearded constable's handset burst into life again. 'It's too late! Get up on to the first floor!'

All four constables heard it immediately and the posse came to a sliding halt; four pairs of boots leaving long black skid marks on the grey polished lino.

The bearded constable yelled back into the handset, 'First floor, Sarge, we're on our way!' He clicked off the handset and looked at his companions. 'Which way up's quickest? East staircase or west?'

One of the officers who'd been guarding the west staircase panted, 'Red!'

'Right! Red!' the bearded constable shouted as the group split and ran off in different directions.

By this time the two pairs of shiny shoes and dark oriental eyes were already on the first floor. They padded soundlessly towards the intensive care ward. The corridor was silent. A nurse passed by without giving them a glance. They came to a door marked 'Surgical Stores' and stopped. One of them tried the handle. The door was unlocked. They went in quietly and closed it behind them.

Ten seconds later, the constable who'd first spotted them in the foyer and had followed them up the east staircase came to the corner of the corridor twenty yards back from the surgical stores. He flattened himself against the wall, to the amusement of a passing porter, and peered fearfully round the corner. The corridor ahead of him was empty. He reached for his handset and whispered into it, 'Lost them, Sarge. They've disappeared.'

Fairfax could have kicked Stan Laurel in frustration. The tension was getting to him and he shouted into his radio. 'All units. Regroup. Secondary position. First floor. Corridor outside intensive care. I will repeat that. First floor! Where I am!' He switched off the handset and turned to look through the glass portholes of the door into intensive care.

He could still see Violet, quiet and still in her bed. Hooper remained standing over her with his shoulders hunched like an ancient eagle. Fairfax turned back to Stan. 'This is for the superintendent, Sergeant.'

'Don't worry about it, Freddie. No-one's coming in here.'

'We'll wait.' Fairfax glared both ways down the corridor. He could see various constables taking up secondary positions. There didn't seem to be any way that the twins could get through. But then he thought back to the Crystal Rooms and then to Violet's apartment. There hadn't seemed to be any way through there either. Like the wind, like the wind. He shuddered.

His handset crackled again. 'Sarge!' It was the constable who'd first seen them in the foyer. 'Got them again. They've come out of a door ahead of me on the east wing and are heading towards you.'

'Right.' Fairfax whispered hoarsely into his handset, 'All units proceed towards the intensive care ward. Cover all corridor intersections.' This was it. He could feel it. He was beginning to sweat. He turned to Stan beside him and they began to walk slowly away from the double doors and down the corridor.

The bearded constable, anxious to make up for his earlier mistake, was being extra vigilant. He was stationed with two others in a trolley bay on a corridor running at right angles to the one leading to the intensive care ward and Fairfax. He peered forwards and was about to move towards the intersection when he stopped and pulled back quickly. He'd seen the two figures in green. They'd crossed the intersection ahead and were, nonchalantly it seemed, heading for Violet. The bearded constable whispered into his handset. 'Got them, Sarge. They're coming towards you.'

Fairfax quickly moved towards the side of the corridor, pulling Stan and another constable with him. Two other officers slipped into an office doorway on the other side. Fairfax whispered across to them, 'They're on their way. Towards us,' then he carefully looked down the corridor. It was very long and, apart from the movement of various hospital personnel, he could see nothing. He realized he was beginning to shake. He glanced briefly at Stan by his side. He'd only known him for three hours but it seemed like a lifetime.

Stan's face was pale too. Suddenly he said, 'There they are.'

Fairfax looked down the corridor and could see two men in surgical green coming towards them. They were half hidden by a porter pushing a patient on a wheeled stretcher. Then the porter wheeled the stretcher into a side ward and Fairfax could see them clearly for the first time. They weren't as big as he'd imagined, but every bit as oriental as he'd been led to believe. They were coming straight towards him. There were no intersections between them and him and behind he could see other uniformed police on the corridor advancing and beginning to bear down on the two of them. They were barely twenty yards away. Fairfax couldn't believe their nerve. They didn't seem to care. They weren't speaking, just walking quietly towards him. He had them trapped and even now he couldn't believe it.

He glanced at the officers around him. The two were now ten yards away. Were they armed? Fairfax, after much anxious consideration, had decided not to bring in a SWAT team. Firearms were too dangerous in a hospital. They were five yards away. He was beginning to seriously regret his decision. They were three yards away. This was it. He leaped forward, holding his warrant card high. His tension erupted in a scream. 'Stop! Police! We are police!'

The two masked men stopped and looked down at Fairfax in front of them. He was almost on bended knee in anticipation of the weapons he'd become certain they would draw. The masked men looked behind them and saw six constables in various positions of anxiety and aggression waiting to pounce. In front was Fairfax and four other officers. They turned and looked at each other. They didn't move.

Fairfax screamed again, 'Police!'

The man on the left pulled his green mask from his face and said quietly, 'Gynaecologists.'

Fairfax couldn't believe it. They were oriental. There were two of them. They looked like twins. What was going on? It was too late.

The constables behind and in front, perhaps confused, but strangely comforted by the word gynaecologists, had gone in hard. The two doctors, who were later revealed to be Filipino surgeons, were given a brief battering before Fairfax could do anything about it. To his credit, he instantly put a stop to the rough-house and pulled the surgeons out. They were soft, they were human, and he immediately knew they weren't who he was looking for. He left them to Stan and stood back, leaning on the corridor wall to regain his composure and work out his defence for any complaints the surgeons might make against him. As he considered this, a thought came slowly creeping into the back of his mind, within milliseconds it was gaining speed across the middle of his brain, and before he knew what was going on, it had exploded with a bang in his frontal lobes. Intensive care! Unguarded! Christ Almighty! He leaped away from the wall and yelled at Stan, 'Come with me!'

Within an instant the Filipinos were abandoned and Fairfax was leading a flying wedge of uniforms at frightening speed along the highly polished floor of the corridor towards Violet's ward. Nurses, Zimmer frames, bottles and patients were scattered, smashed, or flattened against the walls as the phalanx of thundering black boots hammered back towards intensive care. They came to a scattered and tumultuous halt at the doors. One constable hit the wall to the side, breaking his nose, and another thumped Fairfax squarely in the middle of the back, forcing his face painfully hard against the glass of the porthole. He looked through.

It was very quiet, Violet was still, the monitors shed lazy green light and Hooper, as ever, stood hunched and on guard.

Fairfax pushed himself away from the doors. 'All right, Stan. Primary positions. This time it's east, west, north and south. Forget the colour coding, all right?'

Bernie felt one foot taller. In fact he'd gained exactly one inch. His experience in the garden had filled him out and straightened his spine. He now stood at six feet five inches and was having to bend as he hacked at the spuds on Vera's kitchen counter. It was getting dark outside and they were preparing for the dinner or, as he called it, the feast.

At just over five feet, Vera was considerably lower than the young man she now thought of as her hero. She looked up adoringly. 'I say, that's a huge lot of potatoes, Mr Lack.'

He looked down and eyed her seriously. 'I'm from the trade, Mrs, so I know what I'm doing.' He poked the potatoes with his knife. 'We got to cut them up into chips next.'

'I have more if you'd like them.' Vera began to move towards her vegetable rack.

'The more the merrier.' Bernie nodded his assent as she picked up three more huge King Edwards. 'Is the turkeys cooking?'

'They are,' said Mirabelle as she came in behind them with a packet of stuffing she'd found in Vera's larder.

'Why ain't they on the spit, then?'

'Because we have a modern oven, Bernie.'

'Oh. That's all right then.' He nodded his assent and turned back to Vera. 'Do you by chance have any beans, Mrs? I was always told by my brother, Arnie, that grub wasn't grub without beans.'

Vera looked up at him imploringly. 'Runner or broad, Mr Lack?'

'What? Oh, I should say baked. Arnie always had baked beans, Mrs.'

'He sounds a wonderful brother.'

'He was.' Bernie began to chip the potatoes. 'He was brave, you see, Mrs.' He looked at the knife in his hand for a minute. 'That's what bothers me. I'm not very brave, you see?' He looked at Vera and thought about it. 'Or at least I wasn't. I don't want to be scared of no coppers no more, Mrs.'

'Oh I'm sure you won't be, Mr Lack.'

'You think so?'

'I can see that you are without doubt the most courageous man I have ever met, Mr Lack.'

'Well thank you very much, Mrs.' Bernie nodded and Mirabelle could see that Vera's belief was having a huge effect on him.

Vera went on. 'And I should know all about it. Did I tell you my husband was also much decorated, Mr Lack?' Bernie was about to mention something about wallpaper, but she continued, 'He was a very big man, too, and I had a great lot of medals to polish, I can tell you that.'

'Did you?' Bernie was very interested in this medal aspect.

'I did.' She stood small and proud in the middle of her huge and rather bare kitchen. 'But let me also tell you, Mr Lack, that there's as much courage to be found amongst the lonely and the deserted as there is to be found amongst the militia.'

Bernie thought about it. 'You know, Mrs, I quite agree with you. There's lots of people deserves medals, ain't there? I mean, Arnie for a start. Then there's Ron.' He hacked at another potato. 'And my Dad deserves a medal as well for giving everybody food, and so does Sophie and Porkie for cooking it. And my mum; she probably deserves a medal for lying there in hospital and having an operation. And Auntie for keeping them monks in order. And the monks an' all!' He prodded the air with his knife. 'And you too, Mrs. You deserve a medal for being lonely and deserted!' Mirabelle winced, but he was too innocent to be offensive.

'Oh I say, Mr Lack!' Vera could have wept.

'And Lucy! And Tilda! And Mirabelle for looking after me! Bloody hell, Mrs! To tell you the truth, everybody in the whole bloody world deserves a medal!'

'And what about you?' Mirabelle asked.

'Oh no, I'm too thick.' Bernie bowed his head over his growing pile of chips, then he winked at Vera and whispered, 'I'm not really, Mrs. I only tell people that so I don't have to do the cooking.'

'But you are doing the cooking, Mr Lack.'

'I know. Exactly! I can do it really.' Bernie chuckled as the phone in the hall rang. Mirabelle turned to go out of the kitchen and answer it. 'It's all right, Mirabelle, it's about time it was me who done the phone calls.' He put down his knife. 'There y'are, Mrs, you can get on with the chips.' He went out.

'Oh what a wonderful, wonderful young man.' Vera picked up the knife. 'Do you know he makes me feel as I used to feel.'

Mirabelle smiled as she watched the happy old girl trim down Bernie's massive hunks of potato. She could hear his deep voice rumbling in the echoing hall as he spoke on the phone. She could tell he was being very serious and capable. After a few seconds he ambled back in and said, 'Ronnie says we should go up to the hospital tonight, and he'll talk to the coppers before we go so it all be OK.' He stood in the doorway.

'Is that what *you* want to do, Bernie?'

'It's what *we* are doing, Mirabelle, because I told Ron.' He winked at Vera. 'How you doing with the cooking, Mrs? Don't cut them chips up too small. You want to get a good mouthful, don't you? I'll show you how to cook them later, like we do in the restaurant. You got an industrial fryer?' He ambled back to the counter as Vera apologized for not having one. 'Don't worry about it, Mrs. We'll work it out. That's what Arnie used to say.'

And that's what Bernie did. He did all the cooking the Lack Brothers way because it was by far and away the best in town. Vera disappeared to lay the table in the dining room with her best silver, which had been going yellow in its canteen for several years, and she put two huge ancient candlesticks in the middle, next to the cruet her mother had given her. This was the feast of feasts, mainly because Bernie was in charge. Vera disappeared again and Bernie helped Mirabelle get the turkeys out of the oven, then he put them on two huge plates and carried them into the dining room.

By the time Mirabelle had come in with the chips, beans and bread, Bernie was standing at one end of the candlelit table laughing as Vera tried to force her dead husband's brigadier's uniform jacket over his huge shoulders. 'I found it for you, Mr Lack. The coat's in the hall.'

'I seen that. I already tried it on. It's good.'

'It's huge, Mr Lack.'

Bernie pulled at the jacket. 'But this is too small, Mrs.'

'No.' She pushed upwards at the collar. 'I do believe, Mr Lack, that it will go.'

'No, Mrs. It's just going to fall apart.'

'One last try, Mr Lack.'

'You asked for it then.' Bernie grasped the lapels and tried to heave the jacket up to his neck. It immediately split along both side seams. Vera stood back with her hands to her face and began to laugh. She seemed to find the sight of the wrecked jacket too funny for words.

'Don't worry, I've still got the hat.' Bernie reached down to the chair and picked up the brigadier's peaked cap. He put it on. 'That fits anyhow.' It was a bit small, but he could just about keep it on his head. 'And I got the coat outside. And look at this, Mirabelle.' He reached down again and came up with a ceremonial sword in a tasselled scabbard. 'See this. This is a blessed real sword for crying out loud.' He held it out to her.

'And I want you to have it, Mr Lack,' said Vera.

'No!' Mirabelle was instantly horrified. She put the tray onto the table. 'You're not having a sword, Bernie!'

'Why not? I can wear it with the big coat and the hat.'

'No!'

'Oh yes, Mirabelle. Them days are well past when you could tell me what to do.' He stuck his hands in his pockets and Mirabelle could see that there wasn't much point in arguing with him.

Vera smiled and said, 'Sit down please, Mr Lack. At the head of the table. It's my husband's chair.'

He sat down in the heavy, wooden, high-armed chair and surveyed the grub before him. 'Right, are you ready?' He picked up his knife and fork, then waited until Mirabelle and Vera had sat either side of him. 'Are you steady? Go!' He lunged towards the food, and then just as quickly, pulled back. 'No, wait. We should have grace. Because you see, Mirabelle,' he turned towards her seriously, 'that's what Galahad does.' He looked at Vera. 'That's true, Mrs, except he had monks doing it for him, but our monks have gone home. So why don't you do it, Mirabelle?' The request took her by surprise. It was the first time in her three years with the brothers that anyone had ever even mentioned prayer. Bernie warned, 'Not long prayers though.'

Mirabelle put her hands together. 'Close your eyes.' Bernie pretended to, but was still squinting at the food in front of him. 'Please God, bless us and our food, especially on this very important—'

'And sacred,' Bernie added.

'And sacred?' Mirabelle asked.

'That's right, and sacred. Get on with it.'

'And sacred night.' She opened her eyes and unclasped her hands. Never had a prayer been more heartfelt.

Bernie looked up. 'All over?'

452

'Yes.'

'Right! Go for it!' He reached forward with his plate as Vera began to carve huge hunks of turkey for him. 'And when we done this, we go down the hospital like Ronnie said.'

'You don't think it might be better to wait until morning?'

'Mirabelle, what's the matter with you? First you don't like the hat, then you don't like the sword, and now you don't like going down the hospital. That's the whole point! That's my adventure!'

'What do you mean?' Mirabelle looked up. There was something about going to the hospital that was unnerving her.

'Well I worked it out,' Bernie explained, at the same time as stuffing his mouth full of bread. 'Arnie told me my dad wasn't my dad. Then Arnie died. Then I had a fast. Then I did some thinking. Then I'm going to have a feast. It's all like Galahad before he went on an adventure.'

'What is your adventure, Mr Lack?' Vera handed him a plateful of turkey.

'I got to ask my mum, who was my dad. See, that's it. That's the quest. That's why I got the sword, Mirabelle.' He waited a second, as if thinking about what he'd just said, and then began to pile more chips onto his plate. On the other side of the table Vera pecked at the meat like a tiny bird. There was a silence as they ate. Between them was a candlestick and Mirabelle watched as the flame began to flicker. She knew it was the breath of Sorush. The Dark Angel had come.

Mirabelle quietly stood and went into the kitchen. The room was dark and she could smell the stench of judgement. She glanced behind her and could see Bernie hunched over his food in the candlelight in the dining room. She moved to the window and looked out into the moonlight.

$$10$$

Kasbeel sat quietly on the rock. He had his book open on his knee. He raised his head slowly and his chin dropped, revealing the black interior of his mouth. He was staring at Mihr, although it was difficult to discern his eyes. He spoke as if from the inner cave. 'I call upon the

Council of the Inquisition to witness this you call pure. Azza, Araqeel!'

As soon as he had said this two angels that Mihr immediately recognized appeared below him, half in and half out of the Earth. The first was Azza, who in ancient times had been dismissed from heaven for his knowledge of the carnal. Next to him in the ground was Araqeel. This was an angel who had once taught the signs of the Earth to the righteous, but he was now nothing more than a fallen judge. He held his hands as if in eternal plea.

Then the old angel looked up as a fire suddenly burst into the night above his head. He half growled, half sighed, 'Moloc.'

Mihr looked into the flame and saw the flickering shape of the fiery angel. She knew him to be one of the fiercest spirits, who had once glowed such bright gold that Solomon had built a temple in his honour. But his pride had tarnished his brilliance and now he burned, unhappy and angry.

'The great dukes, Uval and Askorath.' The Legendary Procurer and the Leader of the Infernal, the first in deep red, and the second in black with a viper in his right hand, appeared immediately behind Kasbeel and back towards the dark walls of the garden. They glowered as they stared in past Mihr towards Bernie in the dining room.

'The Great Pontiff, Balberith, and Raum.' These rose from behind. Balberith held a dark quill in his hand and was Kasbeel's master in the depths. Raum was in black oily feathers. She had been known to manifest herself as a crow and destroy great cities with the sweep of her tarred wing. Mihr detested her.

'King Pursan and Mammon.' These appeared even higher. Mammon the Prince of Tempters sneered. He was the demon of avarice and feared by all but the perfect. Pursan had once been one of the virtuous, whom ancient man had prayed to as a prophet of the future. Now he was King of the Backlands and existed in the swamps of shame.

'Caim.' This was an angel as a bird. Smaller than the rest, she flew above in front of the dull moon, her brown wings a blur of speed as she darted amongst her fellow fallen.

'Ezekiel.' The great augur who had failed to foretell his own future was transparent and even higher. 'And Meresin.' He came highest of all as chief of the aerial powers and Lord of Thunder.

Kasbeel recited, 'Azza, Araqeel, Moloc, Uval, Askorath, Balberith,

*Raum, Pursan, Mammon, Caim, Ezekiel and Meresin. These are the
Council of the Inquisition, Mihr.'*

*After he had spoken, and before Mihr had been able to assess
the disparate powers in front of her, they were combined in the terrible
being of the thirteenth angel, the untitled ruler of this abominable
council. Sorush, queen of nothing and everything, encompassed them
all. Her beauty was her terror, its each part the full horror of one of the
twelve within. Her eyes sparked malevolence, her lips were full red
malice, her breasts flowed rancour and her demeanour was hatred. She
said, 'I shall show you pure, Mihr. I shall show you from whence pure
came.'*

*This was the beginning of the end. Mihr knew that Sorush would
now show her the beginnings of Bernie. She was going to see the night
of the stars in the sky, as Charlie had said. The night he'd gone to
Sayeed Sayeed. The night when Violet's face was bloody.*

Arnie was nineteen. It was nearly a year before he and Violet would
leave the restaurant within days of each other. He nodded to Harriet
behind the till in the restaurant and went through towards the back
and the stairs up to the flat. His hair was long and his beard was
starting. He went up giggling to himself. He was stoned as usual and
had come back to the flat to pick up his stash. He had a good night
ahead and wanted to be out of his brains. As he came into the living
room he heard the raised voices of his parents in their bedroom. He
stood still for a bit and listened. Charlie was shouting, 'And this! And
this!'

Arnie went along with the beat of it and muttered to himself, 'And
that. And that.' He didn't care what was going on, but took a step or
two into the hall. The door to their bedroom was ajar and he could see
Charlie taking Violet's clothes out of the wardrobe and throwing them
onto the bed, one by one. 'And this! And this? Where do they come
from, Vi?'

Violet backed away from him. He'd been down in the club all
morning and she could see he was drunk. 'Tom gives them to me at a
cheap rate.'

Charlie threw more clothes onto the bed. 'Silk! And silk! What's this
one?'

'It's taffeta. What difference does it make?'

'And this?' He held up a dress. 'More bloody silk . . .'

'Satin . . .'

Charlie threw down the dress. 'What do you think I am? A fucking muggins?' He stared at her, waiting for a reply.

'No you're not a muggins, Charlie, you're a drunk.'

'I'm not asking you about that, Vi.' He waved his arm as though brushing her words to one side.

'And you spend night after night at the Leeds Hotel.'

'So fucking what?' He staggered a little, coming slightly closer to her.

'So what do you do there, Charlie?'

'Where do you spend your days, Violet?'

'At least I'm not a whoremaster!'

'A what?' He laughed out loud at her stupid term for it. 'A what?'

She retreated a bit. She knew she'd got it wrong. 'You know what I mean.'

He leaned towards her over the bed. 'At least I'm not the dress-maker's whore.'

Arnie moved away from the door as he heard his mother say, 'That's not true, Charlie.' He'd been hearing this for months and was getting bored by it. Ever since his mother had started working in Cherry's dress shop, the old man had been getting more and more jealous. Charlie was always a drinker, but now it was getting out of order. And there was something else, too, like there was like a chasm between them that had always been there. Arnie couldn't work it out and right now couldn't be bothered. He just wanted to get stoned.

And he was going to be out of here soon anyway. His mate Max had got his eye on a little place in Great Windmill Street over a strip joint. They'd move in there and push some dope and smoke a lid a week. Lovely. And then there was the acid. These were the days of the first trips; the first is scary, second is better, then you get onto plateau sublime for years, right?

He took the lump of hashish out of his drawer and dropped two acid tabs into an old envelope. He put the envelope in his pocket, went out and passed his parents' bedroom again.

Violet was saying, 'Why go to the Leeds Hotel? I'd be cheaper, wouldn't I?' For a second Arnie couldn't work out who was more

456

jealous, his mother or his father. 'How much do you pay them, anyway?'

Charlie raised his hands. 'What's here for me?'

'Why don't you look?' She said it in a way that meant he could look as much as he liked, but he wouldn't find anything.

Charlie attacked again. He picked up a dress from the bed. 'Silk?'

Violet smirked. 'Don't they wear silk at the hotel? Not even as underwear?'

'I bloody warn you!' Charlie was going red.

'Not even the stockings?'

'Are you listening?' Charlie was going to explode. 'I warn you!' He pointed his finger. 'On my heart and on my life, I am warning you! Your time is up. I'm going to get you!' He stared at her, his eyes full of rage. 'I mean that, Violet.'

Arnie, outside the door, wasn't giggling any more. He wanted to walk in there and smash the old bastard in the face, but he knew he didn't have the nerve. He could hear the bullying, harping tone in the old man's voice. Charlie was scared of his wife and that was the truth. And Violet was scared of him back, and that was the truth also. And so was Arnie, scared of it all. He moved quickly back into the living room and down the stairs to the restaurant.

He saw Ronnie, who was three days after his tenth birthday, sitting at a table, drawing on a big pad. Sayeed Sayeed was sitting next to him drinking a cup of tea. Then he heard a sound on the stairs coming down from the flat. It was the old man's tread and he moved quickly to the door. He said to Harriet by the till, 'I'm leaving, Auntie. Upstairs is not turned on, you see?'

He hadn't gone quickly enough. Charlie came into the back of the restaurant before he could open the door. The old man's face was full of fury as he came towards him. 'I'd like to see more of your face in this place. It doesn't run itself.'

'Hello, Dad.' Arnie was quite brazen but nervous too. He knew the old man was unpredictable in these moods.

Charlie didn't seem interested. He looked over to Sayeed. 'I'll buy you an orange juice, Sayeed. I've got to get out of here. I'm full, too bloody full of it. I'll see you there if you want.' Then he walked past Arnie and out of the door.

Arnie watched as Charlie went down the alley. 'It's yet another one of those days, Auntie,' he said to Harriet, and tried a grin, but it failed. He wanted to wait a moment until his father had disappeared. He turned to Sayeed. 'I thought Indians didn't drink.'

'I don't.' Sayeed smiled.

'Well what you following him about for then?'

Arnie turned to the door to go as Ronnie shouted out, 'Arnie?'

'Not now, little bruv, I got to see a man about a drug.'

'Arnie!' Harriet was outraged, but Arnie was gone. The door banged after him as Sayeed Sayeed came towards her to pay for his tea.

'Talk to Charlie, will you, Sayeed?' said Harriet as she took his money. 'He's my own brother, but if I was Violet I'd leave him like a dog out of a trap. Drink, women . . .' She became aware that Ronnie was listening and her voice dropped to a whisper. 'I can't see how he wants Vi to stay.'

Sayeed shrugged. 'Perhaps he doesn't.'

'What? Lose a wife and then what's he got?' Harriet looked up at the old Indian. 'Crisis? What sort of man wants that?'

'A lonely man?'

Harriet didn't understand what he was talking about. She rang up the cash on the till. 'Don't be silly, dear. He's not lonely. If you ask me, he's getting like one of those mob boys. I've never in my life known anyone surrounded by so many crooks and jibber-jabber.' She leaned forward towards Sayeed. 'I'll tell you something though, he's got life in him. I've never known anyone so full of it. You know what I always thought? I always thought he was a fighting man, Sayeed, without a war. And he'll come to a sticky end.' She gave him his change and pushed the till drawer shut.

'If you say so,' said Sayeed.

Harriet shrugged as if it were all obvious. 'He longs for it, doesn't he?'

'A sticky end?' Sayeed was faintly taking the piss.

'A crisis, Sayeed. So then he's got something to fight about, hasn't he?' She spoke the truth and Sayeed nodded. She smiled. 'I'm pleased we agree at last.'

Sayeed didn't smile back. He shook his head as if he was thinking about something. 'Good morning, Harriet.'

He went out as Ronnie shouted, 'Sayeed!'

'He's gone, dear,' said Harriet, 'so he can keep an eye on your dad.'

'I'm fed up.'

'You've got your chocolate and pens.'

'I want another brother.'

'Not much chance of that.' Harriet sighed and opened the till drawer to look at the money. She counted the notes and then counted them again. She looked around the restaurant. It was mid-afternoon and very quiet. The air seemed thick and heavy, like it was pressing down on free spirit.

After fifteen minutes Violet came in. She'd changed and coated her lips with thick, dark-red lipstick. She moved through the silence towards Harriet.

Ronnie looked up from his pad. 'Where you going, Mum?'

'To see Tom. Want to come?'

Ronnie picked up his pen. 'No thanks.'

'I won't be long.' She went towards the door.

'You look nice, dear,' Harriet smiled.

'Thanks. Bye, Ronnie.' She went out into the alley as Ronnie pushed the tip of his pen hard into the paper. He said, 'I hate Tom Cherry.'

'You're not the only one, dear.' Harriet opened the drawer and counted the money for the third time that morning.

She'd hardly finished before Charlie had seen Violet again. He was standing in the front room of the Leeds Hotel. The place was empty but for him, Sayeed Sayeed and a snoozing barman in a white shirt and waistcoat. Charlie was tipping back a pint of bitter when he saw his wife pass on the other side of the street. He held the glass away from his mouth and didn't bother to wipe the froth from his lips as he watched her. 'What I tell you?'

Sayeed turned on the old leather of the bench seat and looked through the window. 'Perhaps it's nothing.' They watched as Violet went into Cherry's dress shop. Charlie drank again, emptying the glass, which he put onto the bar for a refill.

'I tell you what, Sayeed, this is a very sorry day.'

Violet sat in the back room on the other side of the old wooden table from Tom. He was writing in a ledger and didn't look up. She sat in silence for a couple of minutes, then she said, 'Have you ever felt as though you were watching yourself?'

He didn't look up. 'Only when I've smoked marijuana.'

'I'm serious, Tom.' She looked away, thinking of the problems she had with Arnie, but after a second they seemed far away too. 'I feel as if I am tiny and small and my eyes are big.' Tom looked up from the ledger. She didn't often talk like this, but he was fascinated when she did. This was an unknown, childlike Violet who spoke from another place. She said, 'I feel scared. And I feel ashamed. And I feel excited.' Then she looked directly at Tom. There was something about her that frightened him. 'And nothing's happened, Tom.'

'What do you think is going to happen?'

She shrugged and pulled the corners of her mouth down like a little girl. 'I don't know. I thought I knew Charlie, but I don't think I do any more. I think he's going to go for me.'

'Why don't you leave him?'

'No.' She seemed to be thinking about it. 'That's not how to do it, is it?'

'So what is, Vi?'

'I don't know.' She leaned back in her chair. There were tears in her eyes. 'Are you my friend, Tom?'

'Of course. Do you want some tea?'

Charlie saw her again when she came out. He said, 'She knows you know.' It was a joke or a catchphrase from somewhere, but Sayeed Sayeed didn't get it. He turned to the window. Outside the afternoon was getting hotter and people were moving around as if in slow motion. There were smudges of filth in the air. Charlie raised his glass. 'Here's to the stars, my old teetotal Bombay buddy. It's all in them, which is something I know you understand.' He drank again, finishing his third pint since they'd come in. 'And so does she. That's why I love her.' He put the empty glass down on the bar.

'Charlie, come back with me. Come and eat with the family.'

'No, you go, mate. This is my place.' He put both his hands on the brass runner of the bar.

'Charlie . . .'

'No, mate. I want to drink. You have to, don't you? So you don't notice it's falling apart.' He turned with a smirk. 'Or maybe you do it to make sure it does.'

Sayeed's skin was grey with the worry. There was all sorts of dust flying in the sunbeams coming through the window. He knew there was nothing he could do. He stood up and gave Charlie a quick bow. 'Come and see me when you want to. Please, Charlie.' Then he went out into the shimmer of the yellow jelly air. He passed men in white shirtsleeves and women in heavy dark jackets on the way to the underground station. Sometimes it was very hard to be Sayeed Sayeed. He knew that up to now Charlie had sunk five whiskies in the club and was on to his fourth pint in the pub, and it was still the afternoon.

Arnie was probably in a worse state. He'd done a chillum or two with Max, and by the time he'd got back to the flat at nine that evening, he was into the first hour of an acid trip. When he sat on the sofa, he couldn't remember why he'd come back. There must have been something to it, or something he had to do. He tried to think about it, then forgot what he was thinking about. Violet stood over him, watching his head loll. 'How dare you come in here like that?'

'I wanted to see you?' Was that it? Is that why he was here? 'I feel a bit shaky, Mum.'

'What have you been doing?'

Arnie wasn't sure. 'I keep seeing blood or something.'

'What do you mean?' She still stood over him.

'Ah? Not enough drugs basically.' He knew he was talking rubbish, but couldn't think of anything else to say. 'I don't really think we're running fast enough, Mum.'

'What do you mean, blood?' Violet was getting worried.

'What? I don't know. Don't get angry, Mum.'

'I am, Arnie!'

He looked up at her, suddenly very vulnerable. 'It's horrible, isn't it?'

Violet folded her arms. 'I wanted you to help me.'

Arnie leaned back, exhausted. 'Forces beyond my control. It's all too much.'

'Go to sleep.'

He was mumbling. 'Sleep's out of the question. It's not even the beginning of the question.' He started to force himself up. 'I've got to go.'

'Arnie?' said Violet, then she heard a noise behind her and turned. Ronnie was standing in the hallway to the bedrooms in his pyjamas. 'Go to bed, Ronnie.' She turned back to Arnie. 'Don't go.'

'Too late, Mummy.' He said it as if he was three years old.

'What?'

'Mummy?' Now Ronnie was saying it as well.

Violet shouted at him, 'Go to bed!' Arnie was opening the door on his way out. 'Arnie?' she said again, but he'd gone. She breathed in as he closed the door gently behind him. Ronnie was looking up at her. 'Go to bed, sweetheart. Your daddy will be home soon.'

'Shall I go to bed now then?'

'Yes, you'd better.' Ronnie went and Violet sat down on the sofa. She looked round the room. She didn't trust the walls any more. Then she heard Charlie's voice from down below.

'Arnie!' It was dark. Charlie was leaning on the alley wall opposite and down from the restaurant. He was up to eight pints and ten whiskies. 'Where are you going, son? Why don't you come out with me?'

'I can't, Dad.' All this was just a blur to Arnie.

'Don't say that!' Charlie's voice was self-pitying. 'It's just the one night. Come out with your old man.'

'I have to be somewhere else, you know?'

Charlie shifted off the wall and went towards him. 'What's better than me? I've got plenty of cash.' He pulled his roll from his pocket and held it out to prove it. 'We'll make a night of it.'

'No, Dad.' Arnie stepped back. 'I don't want to.'

'You see, son.' Charlie staggered a bit. 'I don't want to go indoors. Don't let me down.'

'I've got to go, Dad.' Arnie started to move away.

'You're letting me down!'

'Sorry, Dad. Bye.' Arnie had reached the lamp-post at the end of the alley and for a moment seemed brilliantly lit, then he was gone.

'You useless bastard!' Charlie shouted after him and then looked around. The alley was empty. He waited for a second, staring at the restaurant door, and then walked towards it. He didn't seem quite so drunk.

Violet was still sitting on the sofa. She heard her husband's foot on the stair and got up quickly to close the door to the bedrooms and Ronnie. Charlie saw her there when he came in and thought she was going out. 'Don't go, Violet.'

She turned. 'I wasn't. I was closing the door.'

He leaned back against the wall, slightly breathless from the stairs. He was going to make his statement. He dropped his head and raised his eyes. 'I saw you come out of the dressmakers . . .'

'Where were you? The Leeds?'

'It doesn't matter where I was. I saw you come out of Cherry's. You don't need to deny it . . .'

'I'm not.'

'That's after I warned you, Vi.'

'Oh please, Charlie . . .' She was contemptuous.

He paid no attention. 'I'm going to get you now, Vi.' She stood there, wondering what he was going to say next. 'I'm going to get you. Not now,' he raised his hand in a placatory way, 'later. I'm going out again now to have a nice drink. And then I'm going back to the Leeds and I'm going to see a nice girl, which I haven't done before. Do you hear me, Violet? I haven't done it before, but I'm going to tonight. And then I'm coming back to get you.' He stopped. 'You know I'm telling you the truth, don't you?'

'Yes, Charlie.' She looked back into his eyes. This was a kind of ultimatum she supposed. She could wait and take whatever he had to give her, or she could be gone. She heard Cherry's voice in her mind: 'Why don't you leave?' She knew she wouldn't.

Charlie pushed himself away from the wall and fumbled with the door. 'See you, Violet. To get you. Later. Back about twelve, dear.' He went out and she sat down slowly on the sofa as his footsteps receded down the stairs. She reached over to the sideboard drawer and pulled it open. She fished around in the junk and pulled out a pair of dressmaker's scissors. She pushed the drawer closed, put the scissors on the arm of the sofa, sat back and waited for midnight.

11

The shapes of the Inquisition were translucent in the moonlight. Sorush was silent. The flow of images had stopped for the moment. Mihr sensed a similarity in this night now in the garden, to the one she was seeing from twenty years ago. Everything was still and stopped in order for the power to be released; then as now.

Mirabelle turned back to the candlelit dining room. Bernie's plate was clean and his chair empty. Then she saw the hall door open and he came in carrying the brigadier's huge greatcoat. He put it over the back of his chair and leaned down to pick up the sword and scabbard. Vera stood to help him buckle the belt.

Mirabelle remembered the unnamed maiden in the ship of faith who had made the girdle for Solomon's sword from her hair. She went quickly into the dining room. 'I'll do that.' She went behind Bernie, plucked a hair from her head and wrapped it into the leather as she pulled the belt around his waist.

He said nothing. Then he picked the coat off the chair and put it on. It was some kind of huge cape from the First World War. It completely covered the sword and made him look vast. Mirabelle realized with a shock that he seemed armoured. Vera offered him the peaked hat.

'No thanks, Mrs. Mirabelle says no hat,' said Bernie and he moved towards the door. Mirabelle was beginning to feel as if events were moving out of her control. She hurried after Bernie as he went out. He stopped and took Vera's hand, then he leaned down and kissed it. 'Thank you and God bless you, Vera.'

The old lady didn't reply as he walked away into the moonlight and then into the dark shadow cast by the fir trees at the side of the drive. Vera smiled directly into Mirabelle's eyes. 'He came for me. I always knew he would.'

Bernie stopped and turned back on the gravel. 'Got to go, Mirabelle.' Then he was walking away again and Mirabelle went quickly after him. 'Hurry,' he said. 'We got to see Mum in the hospital before it's too late.'

'What do you mean, Bernie?'

'Nothing.'

They walked on.

Mihr had already caught sight of the aristocracy of angels amidst the trees and abruptly Moloc burst into flame above, sending a dull red light down through the spiked branches of the fir. Higher still she could see Caim, Ezekiel and then Meresin. Their shapes came and went against

*the circle of the moon. Behind them, stretching up into the night sky,
were the rest of the Inquisition and their hordes, like thousands of black
glistening stars. Mihr realized that the air was literally full of angels and
the foul beat of their wings. Sorush appeared, walking parallel to them
on the road. She smiled but her eyes were dead. The night disappeared.*

Violet sat on the sofa in the living room. She reached up and touched
the blades of the scissors on the arm of the sofa. She glanced at the
clock. It was nearly ten o'clock. He'd said he would be back at twelve.
What was she to do for two hours? She leaned back into the cushions
and decided she'd do nothing. Whatever he did when he returned, he
would do. How could she stop him? She touched the scissors again, but
doubted if they'd be of much use. You had to have heart to stab, in the
same way that you had to have hope to leave. All she could do was
wait.

Arnie was about half a mile away from her and increasing the distance
as he walked. He was beginning to hallucinate. The night was still and
orange. Everyone was stuck in jelly. Their faces were slow and their
hands were pink. He didn't know where he was going, but he knew
perfectly well. The pavement was shining and the black cars ran in
their trough by the side sending up little sprays of silver water. Some
shops were open and bright, but no-one inside them moved because
they were trapped in the light. He began to see blood again, but didn't
know what it meant. It was like a mist that kept coming down and then
clearing up, then it was drops sliding down glass, then it was smeared
and messy on a wall. He kept going through the blood because he didn't
think that it was going to stop him doing anything. If anything it was
going to make him go faster. For a second he felt euphoric, then the
blank came down again and he felt heavy, surrounded by solid air and
things that were static. Buildings were high. He came to a side street
and turned down it as if he knew exactly what he was doing. He looked
up at the sign over a doorway. It read, 'Here Comes The Sun.' He
pushed open the door and walked along a narrow hallway that was lit
by a red bulb. The blood came back into his eyes, but was immediately
cleared away by the punch of some really heavy sounds. He went down
some stairs and nearly fell, but he hung on to the walls and a poster
ripped under his fingers. There was a pink face who grinned at him

over a table and a box of cash. He knew what that was and pulled a ten-shilling note out of his trouser pocket. It was red. The pink face shoved some coins into his pocket for him and said something like, 'Yeah.' Then he went down some more stairs and came into a room that was every colour and not too much red. He slumped down on some cushions and stared up at the oil slides flickering over the ceiling. The sounds started to explode in his brain in little puffs of pale blue and then long strands of silver. There was a purple thump to go with the bass and he began to feel the pulse. It was his own and it wasn't. His body was just sound. There was no flesh and there was no blood, just breaking, thumping, thrashing, crashing noise. He felt very, very happy.

Charlie sat hunched on the end of a bed in the top room at the Leeds. He was up to fifteen pints and eighteen whiskies, not that he was counting. He had his head in his hands as he looked down at the pair of red stilettos under his nose. They belonged to a prostitute called Sylvie. Above the shoes were a pair of legs encased in black stockings and then nothing else. She was skinny, but sexy, and her tits were good. She was smoking a cigarette. She blew out the smoke in a bored way. 'You've paid me.' Charlie couldn't open his mouth. It was like he was taken over by the booze or some other thing. He was only allowed to say certain words. She tried again. 'Don't you want what you've paid for?'

'Be quiet.' That was something he could say.

She decided to be formal. 'I have other custom waiting, you know?'

'Shut up! I'm trying to pray!' That came out and surprised him, because as far as he knew he wasn't. Then he looked up and saw a chest of drawers with a blue plastic beaker on top. He didn't know where he was, so he got up and went to the door. He seemed to be walking quite firm and steady.

He went out as she said, 'Well fuck you too.'

He didn't remember the next bit and only regained full sight and hearing in the back of the cab. He looked up at the glass ahead of him and wondered who the driver was. He could smell the leather. He said, 'What's the time?'

The bloke at the wheel turned and warned, 'Don't puke in my cab, mate.'

Charlie felt for the wedge in his pocket. 'I got the cash, brother.'

Next he was in the Bengali Star and he looked back out through the door he'd just come in through. The cab was still there, its black paint was shining in the moonlight and he could hear its engine ticking over. He turned back into the restaurant and straight into the face of the most beautiful girl he had ever seen. She was Indian. Her hair was black, she had dark-red lipstick, big silver earrings and kohl round her eyes. She was smiling. He rocked a bit and said, 'Where's Sayeed?'

And there was the man himself. 'Here, Charlie. Will you eat with us?'

He stood where he was. 'The meter's running, mate.'

Sayeed Sayeed took his arm. 'Send the taxi away.'

'I can't.' He couldn't move in any direction. 'I had to see you, Sayeed.'

Sayeed took his hand in both of his. 'Tell me, Charlie.'

He felt like crying. 'You found that place for me in Soho, Sayeed.' He could smell incense and there was Indian music. 'You found the restaurant and the club and the flat.' He didn't know what he was going to say next and then he did. 'You said it was my fate. Tell me, Sayeed.'

'Tell you what?'

'Tell me what you meant by it.'

Sayeed gripped his hand. 'Charlie, you are my friend.'

'What's going to happen?'

'I don't know.' Sayeed seemed very sad all of a sudden.

'What do I do, mate?' If ever Charlie had wanted to know anything, he wanted to know the answer to that. Sayeed didn't say anything so he asked again, 'What do I do?'

'Accept it.'

'What?'

'You heard me, Charlie.' Sayeed Sayeed was looking at him in that way he sometimes did.

'I can't accept it.'

Sayeed shrugged. 'It will happen anyway.'

'What will?' Charlie had suddenly shouted. 'There's going to be blood on my hands!'

'Charlie, please.' Sayeed looked round at the restaurant. There weren't many customers, but they were starting to look over at them.

'Fucking hell, Sayeed, I don't know what's happening.' He was starting to whine and knew it was because he was somehow coming off the path. If he stayed on it, he wouldn't whine and he'd be strong. He stepped back away from Sayeed and said, 'Accept it? No. Not yet.' Then he backed to the door. 'The meter's running.'

He managed to get back into the cab and close the door. 'Know a place called Kitchener Square?' There were some thoughts as they travelled, but they were confused. He remembered loving Violet and taking a swig out of the quarter bottle of White Horse he had in his pocket. Then the taxi was slowing down. The driver turned. 'What number, mate?' He looked out of the window. 'That one.' The taxi stopped and he got out. The house was falling down. Old bitch. Couldn't she afford paint? He fell up the steps and grazed his knee. The light came on as he took another plug out of the bottle. Albert was at the door. He must have said something about Lucretia, or Mrs Green, or the mother-in-law, or the old bag, because Albert, who was in a dressing gown, said, 'She's asleep.' His lips were pursed with distaste.

'Tell her I want to talk with her, please.' He tried not to be drunk.

'You're drunk.'

'I want to talk to her.' He imagined he was falling back down the steps, but he wasn't, it just felt as if he was.

'Good night and go to hell.' Albert slammed the door in his face.

He couldn't believe it. He'd come all this way just to put a stop to things. All this fucking way. Couldn't they help him? He just wanted to get off the path he was on. He tried to keep calm. 'Open the door, please. Please open the door.' He started to shout. 'Open the door! Lucretia, open this fucking door!' He pointed his finger at the peeling paint. 'Open up, or you will fucking regret it!' He fell back down the steps. He shouted, 'Lucretia, I know you can hear me!' He saw the light in the hall go out. 'Lucretia, listen to me! You're the fucking heart of it, you bitch!' He heaved himself up. He could hear the taxi driver telling him to cut it out, but he knew the bloke wouldn't drive off because he hadn't paid him. He staggered backwards through the gate, still shouting up, 'Lucretia, you're a thieving, lying bitch! From you to her, it's all the same! I came to you for help! You've stolen it from me!' He felt his gut begin to go and he realized he was bending forward crying it at the pavement. 'You've stolen it from me.'

'Come on, mate.' The driver was pulling him backwards and the pavement went up and then down again and it became the floor of the cab as he jolted backwards and it pulled away. Things were passing. It was all over. He'd tried to stop it; he'd asked them to stop it for him, but it was unstoppable. He knew where the taxi was going. It was taking him back now. He must have told the driver. He was going back to Violet.

12

Ezekiel streaked the sky ahead. Above him was Meresin. There was already the first sound of thunder, but it was low and far away. Mihr sensed the evil of Uval and Raum above her. The angels were a continuous presence of heavy air and the fire of Moloc seemed to be leading the way, although Mihr knew he was following them. Sorush remained parallel to them on the road.

Bernie strode along in the greatcoat. Mirabelle could see the tip of the sword as it poked out of the bottom of it. The avenues full of trees were slowly giving way to narrower streets. The smell of leaves was fading as the buildings closed in.

'Mrs said down here to the underground.' Bernie's voice was getting harsher. There was something about it that Mirabelle didn't like, but she knew she had no alternative now. She would protect him as best she could, but had the feeling that her work was done. She ran to keep up with Bernie's enormous strides.

Ahead was the red and blue circle and stripe of the underground. Everything was moving very fast. Bernie turned in at the brightly lit entrance. The place was deserted. There were no clerks in the ticket offices, no guards, no travellers. The floor was dirty, an old newspaper blew up from the escalators and the neon burned down. Bernie didn't stop. 'Mrs said north, one stop.' He went straight for the escalator and plunged down, hardly breaking his step. Mirabelle followed as quickly as she could. She was sure that the stairs were moving quicker than usual.

Mihr felt the cold behind her and knew the angels were following down. The black hair of Sorush appeared at the top of the escalator, followed by her shoulders, then the sway of her whore's hips and legs as she stepped down. Behind came a crowd of the old. Mihr turned away. She didn't need to see the forms taken by the council. They would be decrepit, arcane and rotten.

Mirabelle rushed after Bernie. He had turned onto the platform and was moving quickly to the far end. She shouted breathlessly after him. 'Bernie, where are you going?'

'Get on the front.' As he reached the barrier by the tunnel he turned. There was the roar of a train coming from behind them. Mirabelle ran towards him along the empty platform. The neon on the platform seemed to dim. The train's lights were brilliant and for a moment it was as if a golden ball was hurtling towards them out of the black mouth of the tunnel.

'It's the ship, see.' Bernie seemed to understand. 'I got the sword first off Mrs, that's the only difference.' He was having to shout as the front carriage rattled to a halt and the doors slipped open. The entire train, of course, was empty. Bernie adjusted his scabbard and sat down, legs wide apart. Mirabelle sat close. For the first time she felt as though she needed to be protected by him, rather than the other way round. His vision in the garden ran quickly through her mind. The golden ship of faith, the bed of Solomon, the beautiful maiden, the sword, the death of the maiden and the final journey of Galahad. In these, her last moments, Mirabelle wondered if she would have the courage to complete her mission. Or was it over already? The doors closed and the train began to move.

Mihr looked back. She could see Sorush slowly coming through the train towards them. Behind her was the pack of the ancient. Even at this distance Mihr was aware of their dry croaks and papery white hands. She could see the black eyes of Sorush burning through the glass of the connecting doors as she came ever closer. Then they entered the tunnel and the lights went out. There was just a rush of sound and blackness, apart from the twin pinpricks of crimson as Sorush's eyes turned red and the images started again.

Violet had remained on the sofa. She touched the scissors, then she glanced at the clock. It was a quarter to twelve. She clasped her hands in front of her and did her best to calm herself. She suddenly stood and then didn't know what to do or where to go. The thought flashed through her mind that she'd still have just enough time to throw a few clothes into a bag and get out. But she couldn't do that. She went into the hall leading to the bedrooms. She opened the door to Ronnie's room. He was asleep with his arms above his head. His mouth was slightly open and she could hear that he was catching his breath. She realized she was beginning to shake with fear. Her knees were actually beginning to quiver, which shocked her. She whispered, 'Ronnie, wake up. Ronnie, please wake up.' She knew she didn't want him to. This was the night of the stars in the sky and it was nothing to do with him. She backed away, closed the door gently behind her and went back through the hall into the living room. She sat on the sofa again and looked at the clock. It was nearly ten to twelve.

Arnie had begun to come off the acid. The cushions beneath him were damp and beginning to itch. The sounds were too loud and his limbs were aching. He held on to a wall and pushed himself up into a whirl of coloured light. He knew he had to get out of there. He staggered up the narrow stairs and into the hallway of red light. The air outside hit him like a wall of ice and he fell back against the brick behind him. He coughed and walked back along the side street. As he came to the junction he began to walk faster. Things were no longer orange. Cars were moving. He loped faster through the flashing light and was beginning to become aware of sounds defining themselves. Shouts, pinball thumps and rings, a rock 'n' roll band somewhere, then a milk bottle smashed. But as fast as these sounds came they faded again. The colours, too, started to disappear. He couldn't see red, there was just a rising tide of black. Little blips of light and pings of noise in a monochrome, silent place. He plunged through it, knowing he was going home. He stopped dead and stared at his reflection in a shop window. It was clear who he was. This was Arnie.

Charlie got the taxi to drop him off a few hundred yards away from the restaurant. It was his last chance to get off the path. Maybe someone he knew would grab his arm and haul him off it. He felt in his pocket for the bottle of White Horse and couldn't find it. He must have left it in the cab. It didn't matter. He was beyond the anaesthetic. He watched his feet as they propelled him forwards. All he had to look forward to was battle and he felt the first spring of joy. This was him in pure delight in pure destruction. This was him in pure and nature. Codes forgotten, barriers down. Just him, these feet, this pavement. Just movement, just breaking through into pristine, inviolable, all-powerful self. Into pure. Speak, hear, see no evil, be just taut and sacred on the sharp edge of terror as the shoes work the stone, as your life lights up for what it is, which is the unspeakable. And so the moment approaches. He stopped dead and stared down at his feet. Last chance, Charlie. He had no idea who he was. He was empty of all of that.

13

Sorush was coming through the train. In the reflected light of her red eyes Mihr saw the skin of the ancient grotesques begin to crack and peel as the darkness came through them and they began to reform into the true shapes of their abomination, all the time coming closer.

The train was still dark. Bernie didn't seem to mind. Suddenly it stopped in mid-tunnel. Everything was quiet. Emergency lights flickered on. To their right was the door to the driver's cab. Bernie stared at his reflection in the window opposite. He was thinking it was about time things got started. Mirabelle wanted to tell him. She spoke. 'You are pure.'

Bernie took hold of the hilt of his sword, which was sticking out from beneath the greatcoat, and stood up.

Mirabelle said, 'Remember that, Bernie.' These were almost her last words.

Bernie wasn't listening. He got up and moved along to the driver's cab and jerked open the door. There was no-one in the cab. He looked at the empty driver's seat and said, 'I thought as much.' He shuffled sideways across the cab towards the side door. The space was much too small and cramped for him. He ducked his head and squeezed past the dead man's handle. The weight of his coat pushed it down for a second and the train juddered forward another yard, then stopped again. Bernie didn't notice. He jumped down onto the track and reached up for Mirabelle, who had followed him through the cab. He plucked her from the train like a flower from an overgrown wall. She weighed nothing. He carried her for perhaps ten yards before putting her down, and they started moving quickly along the dark track, leaving the train behind.

Mihr knew that Sorush would be following. She kept her eyes ahead and her mind intent. There was hardly any time left.

Violet twisted fast on the sofa. She could hear footsteps on the stairs below. She looked at the clock. It was a minute to twelve. She breathed in and reached for the scissors and stood as the footsteps came closer. She tried to work out the weight of the tread. Was it Charlie or Arnie? Any other day, any other time, she'd have known immediately, but now all such senses had deserted her. These were just sounds, the weight of a man pressing down. They were halfway up the stairs. She backed away from the sofa and faced the door. Her hand was sweating as she gripped the scissors. She heard the scrape of the footsteps as they came to a halt outside the door. She watched the handle turn. She decided not to scream.

Mihr could feel the breath of Sorush. It was perfumed like the days on the Bridge of Sighs.

Mirabelle heard it first. Bernie was too intent on marching fast between the rails, and perhaps the crunch of his boots on the black stones drowned the sound out. She turned and shouted, 'The train!'

He stopped and looked round with big eyes over his shoulder. The underground train was coming towards them. All the lights were on. They blazed, illuminating the sides of the tunnel as the train picked up speed. Bernie started to run. This wasn't a joust he'd anticipated, otherwise he'd have turned with the sword. He picked up his knees and his feet smashed down on the sleepers between the track.

Mirabelle ran at his heels. She was soft and heavy, her angel's powers were gone. She was tripping, falling. He turned and pulled at her white hand flying through the dark, yanking her upright again. The train thundered behind. There was no way out. The tunnel was too narrow. The ball of light and iron behind was bearing down. The rails beneath them vibrated, juddered and screeched. The sound was immense and filled the tunnel.

The front of the train loomed high above them. Mirabelle sensed rather than saw the front wheels. They were three yards behind them. She screamed. A black alcove appeared in the spat-up spray of gravel and shale. As her last act, Mirabelle lunged and pushed at the back and bulk of Bernie. His left foot hit a rail and he fell as the train smashed into Mirabelle and threw her up into the air. As she came down, the wheels on the right-hand side carved their own track across her upper legs and thighs. She half rolled, but was caught unconscious and tangled beneath the wheels that followed, crushing and splitting her into barely recognizable pieces.

As Mirabelle died, Bernie had fallen back against the back wall of the alcove. His head had hit a rock and he momentarily lost consciousness.

As Mihr was released, she saw the beginning, as did Sorush and the Inquisition; but, unexpected by them, so did he.

As Bernie blinked back into sight, the train flashed past above him. He could see that all the lights were on and really bright, but instead of people being in the windows there were pictures, and they were going on and off like they were flashing, and they were weird. In the first window he could see his dad coming fast through a door and he was hitting this woman, and her lip split open with blood as he hit her again. Then he was hitting her with both his fists and holding her on the ground while he did it. And in another window, he could see Arnie coming in the same door. And then it was another window in the train and his dad was turning round and he had his fist up and there was blood on it. Arnie was shouting out, but the noise of the train was drowning out his words. He saw more windows and his dad was getting up and punching Arnie in the stomach. And it was the flat! It was their own bloody flat they was in! But why did Arnie have all this long hair? Then he saw this woman crawling away with blood all over her face. And his dad was shouting, and he couldn't hear him either because the train was still too loud. Then the woman turned round and she was saying something, but this bloody train was crashing about up there and he couldn't hear a blessed thing, he could just see it through the windows. And this woman was starting to try and get up. She had some scissors in her hand; and it was his mum. He knew it was her because he remembered the picture that Harriet had showed him when they was going up east to find the old grannie. And then he saw his dad pushing Arnie back towards the door and shouting and screaming at him. Then his dad turned and started to shout at his mum, and he held up his fists with blood all over them and started to laugh. Arnie was crying though and the woman wasn't saying nothing. Then his dad was looking like he wanted to cry, too, and he was looking really scared. And all these pictures were coming really fast, like one for each window of the train. And then his dad was gone and Arnie was staggering out of the living room into Dad's bedroom, and he was falling on the bed. And there was still more pictures up there in the train. And then there's this woman, who must have been his mum, and she's leaning on the wall in Dad's bedroom and there's blood all over her face, and she's looking down on Arnie and she's sort of smiling and crying all at the same time. And this bloody train is making more noise than before and throwing up sparks as well. And then there's his mum and she's lying down on the bed with Arnie. She's kissing him and the blood from all over her face is going onto him. And there's still more windows for crying out loud. And there's his brother with his face in this woman's titties and he's pulling her clothes off. And there's more windows and the noise is too bloody much. And now Arnie is on top of his mum. And this bloody train. This bloody train. And this woman is crying out and Arnie is shouting something because they're doing it. He knew what they were doing, too, because he'd seen it in the pictures. And his mum puts her hands up in the air and then down on Arnie's back and is pulling hard at him. She's scratching his back with her fingernails, and they're going mad. And his mother is shouting out in a big long scream, and that's the last window, except one, which is Arnie just standing there looking down on him like Lancelot.

And the angels had seen.

And that's the last of the train because all the noise is gone. And the rails are still ringing, but that's going too. And now it's just quiet. Just some dust still flying through the air in the tunnel. And there's

Mirabelle who's dead. She got hit by the train and her body's all mangled up.

He got up and wanted to say goodbye to her, or thank you. But he couldn't think of any of the words, so he just stood there looking down at her, which was all blood and mess. His fingers kept crushing up into his hands all by themselves, and he wanted to cry, but didn't bother because there were some other feelings that he didn't know about, which were that everything was very difficult but was going to be all right. And anyway Mirabelle wasn't dead; it was just part of the adventure. So that was that then. And what was Arnie doing with his mum up there in the pictures on the train? They was making love, wasn't they? So what was that then?

He saw that his Arfer had fallen out of his coat and was lying across the rail. One half of it was flattened and the other half was the picture of the two black knights. He looked down on the book for a moment, but then thought he didn't really want it any more, so he left it there. He was going to run, but he decided not to and walked away down the tunnel, knowing that wherever he was going to end up, it was going to be all sorted out anyway. It was weird, but he knew it for certain.

14

There was a clap of thunder (this was as the underground train left the empty station). Fairfax hardly heard it. By this time he had so perfected his defences that the officers were getting bored. How much hospital tea can you drink? On the other hand the nurses were providing a distraction. At least two dates had been arranged and a third was being negotiated. Why is uniform always attracted to uniform? He realized that he wasn't immune to it either. There was a particular sister in intensive care dressed in a blue that appealed to him, and although he could have done with a little loving attention, he'd made do with a few more painkillers for his leg and drilled his men yet one more time.

They were beginning to moan, having been at the hospital for over nine hours. Fairfax wouldn't have any of it and took the most recalcitrant constables one by one to witness his superintendent's ever-present vigil by Violet's bed. Hooper had remained hovering over her, muttering occasionally to himself. He wouldn't even take a cup of refreshment in case it caused a lapse in his concentration. He continued to pour the urgency of his life and love into his unconscious sweetheart as she lay quiet and scarcely breathing beneath the soft green of the monitors. The constables peered at him through the portholes in the door. There was something about his stoop and silence that moved them, and they went back to their defensive positions on the stairs with a renewed commitment, although Fairfax was beginning to wonder himself if the twins would attack again. He was kidding himself; he knew they would. Violet was their target and she would remain their target until she was gone. Their logic was absolute, that's what was so terrifying.

He was considering this when the hospital lights suddenly dipped. (This was the death of Mirabelle.) Fairfax thought nothing of it and decided to check his men again, and was walking away from intensive care when Stan came running up to him. 'It's the brother, Freddie. He's arrived with a party. They announced themselves in the foyer.' Fairfax had no idea which brother it was. One of them had called earlier and had spoken to the ward sister, but he'd only said he was the son of Violet Green. Fairfax vaguely heard another clap of thunder above him as he hurried to the stairwell (this was Mihr ascending from the body of Mirabelle). Whichever brother it was, it was about time he met one of these Lacks.

Ronnie had heard the thunder too. He'd borrowed a car and the first rumble had been when he'd pulled in to the hospital car park. Harriet was with him in the front seat. Sayeed Sayeed and Lucy were in the back. Ronnie hadn't really wanted to bring the latter, but she had wanted a last look at Arnie before they cut him up for the autopsy, and there was no way of arguing with the dull pain in her face. She looked up at the first spots of rain splattering the windshield as Ronnie parked the car. 'It's going to be one of those electric storms.'

'Oh yes, that's what it will be.' Sayeed Sayeed said it as though he knew what was coming.

'I think it's in memory of Arnie.' Lucy was beginning to cry again and Ronnie didn't think he could bear it. He turned away and opened the door. 'Let's go anyway.' He got out of the Snipe.

As they walked towards the main entrance Sayeed said he would wait for them outside, as this was a strictly family affair.

'You are family, Sayeed.' Harriet turned from the glass door.

'I will wait.' Sayeed stood his ground and looked up at another clap of thunder. It still seemed distant. 'It will not be for half an hour yet,' he said vaguely to himself. He remained looking at the sky. Harriet followed Ronnie and Lucy to the reception, leaving the old Indian to unfurl the collapsible umbrella he'd thoughtfully brought with him.

Hardly had Ronnie spoken the name of his mother to the receptionist than they were surrounded by policemen and asked heavily and threateningly to wait. They stood surrounded by a circle of six uniforms until Fairfax came down. As soon as he saw Ronnie's pale face and fragile bearing, Fairfax knew that he was innocent of any crime. He shook his hand with sympathy, and with hardly any enquiry led them up the stairs to intensive care. As they walked along the corridor on the first floor he asked if the third brother was coming. Ronnie nodded and said Bernie would be. He hardly looked at Hooper as Fairfax introduced them and the superintendent said nothing either.

Ronnie sat on a chair by his mother's bedside and tried to take it all in. Apart from the fateful few seconds in the Crystal Rooms it had been almost twenty years since he'd seen her, and now here she was with tubes sticking out of her and machines counting her heartbeats. She was hardly breathing and he wondered if she was dreaming; and if she was, what was she dreaming about? He thought that if she recovered she could come back to the restaurant and it would be her instead of his dad, but somehow he couldn't imagine it.

Harriet didn't stay for too long. The combined sadness of Hooper and Ronnie was too much for her. She stood at the end of the bed for a few minutes and looked down, feeling all the frustration of the living when confronted by the dying. Her head, heart and hands, all so full of the desire for aid and miracle, were useless. She nodded her respects and touched Lucy's elbow. They went outside, and as they drank the inevitable tea, Lucy told Fairfax everything she knew. For the sergeant it was the completion of many parts of the jigsaw he'd puzzled over in the past few days, but even as he felt matters were concluding he sensed that it was only a prelude to something else, and that could only mean one thing. There was another clap of thunder and the lights dimmed again. The twins were going to come. Hooper had always known they would, and now so did Fairfax. There was more thunder. The storm was almost overhead. Then there was the first flash of lightning.

15

Mihr, released from earthly form, exploded upwards in a ball of light, free, as the right-hand angel, to assemble her legions and join battle with Sorush. The Inquisition was done, the identity of the father known and the circumstance of the birth clear. Only the final question remained. Who, then, was Bernie? Galahad, the saviour pure, born as a pearl from pain? Or an evil source, the only and inevitable product of incest? If he was a saviour, he ran counter to perceived nature. How could good come from such bad? To accept such a doctrine implied absolute forgiveness and meant that the heart of faith was always, had always been, and would never be less than supreme absolution.

Where did that leave original sin, the Apocalypse, or the Last Judgement? Where then were the priests, their books, their churches, their creed and their structures of a thousand years? Their existence had always been founded in the imitation of a judgemental God that they had created in their own image; but such a purpose could only be irrelevant in this new theology. Forgiveness was all and judgement could only be man-made. It meant the horizon was pure. There were no chains, fire, hell, or any other invented condemnation. And there was no Bridge of Sighs.

Finally, then, Mihr had understood and could see full well the cause of the utter violence of the opposition of Sorush. This was a final tearing apart of the two-headed being of light and dark that had believed it could live in balance between opposites. Now Mihr could see that there was no equilibrium to be found between good and bad; there was only good. If the end of judgement was the termination of priestly power, then it was also the elimination of Sorush. And that, finally, was the purpose of Mihr.

*   *   *

How conscious Bernie was of such things is uncertain. However there was a power of sight that was growing in him by the minute. There were things he had never known that were appearing clearly and unquestioned in his mind. He stood motionless, spine stretched, neck arched and head back against the moon, as he stared up at the electric blue light and swirling clouds of the night sky.

He had walked through the tunnel in his armoured cape with his scabbard slipped and trailing on the iron of the rails. He had heard many strange sounds as he had come: the hard clash of iron on iron, like a hammer on an anvil; he'd heard the hiss of water vaporizing over fire; he'd heard shouts and curses, and sometimes, what seemed to him to be the heavy crack of a whip. Every now and again the metal of the track had begun to sing, but no other trains came. Sometimes as he walked it was so hot he'd had to put up his hands to shield his face. Then the temperature would drop, he would feel ice on his fingers and his feet would go numb with the cold. Then suddenly a wind would come, blowing up the dust and shale, but hardly had he had time to shelter than it was gone. He didn't know how long he walked, there didn't seem to be any sense of time in the tunnel. His big feet strode across the sleepers, his shoulders hunched and down, his eyes peering ahead, until finally he saw light. He trudged on until the tunnel was gone and he was standing on the track down between two huge banks of concrete with neon signs much higher up on the silver sides of the high-rise blocks that towered above. He clambered onto the bank on one side and pulled himself up on top of a culvert full of filthy brown water, then up higher by sticking his toes and heels in cracks in the concrete, until he'd come to a mesh fence, which he'd pulled away with one hand. He felt quite high up, although he was only on ground level. Then he stretched against the moon and looked up. That's when he first saw the angels in the sky beginning to array themselves for battle. Somehow he knew that this should be so.

He looked down again and saw ahead, on his own level, what seemed to be a vast canyon, except he knew it was only a very long deserted road between high and dark buildings. At the far end of the road, about a mile away, he could see the bright lights of a place he knew to be Sarras. He hitched his belt tighter, straightened the scabbard and began to walk between the buildings. His boots rang out on the road, the sound echoing around the unseeing windows on either side. There was no break in them, no side streets or alleys, just an unbroken stone and sometimes marble façade. The doorways were high and forbidding. The doors they protected were shut tight against him. He walked slowly towards the distant Sarras, his hand on the hilt of his sword. He could hear nothing but the sound of his own footsteps as he looked up again at the thin strip of sky between the tops of the buildings, where the angels were gathering for combat above him.

Sorush, in full battle order with wings a mile wide, was summoning her hordes across the darkness of the sky. Her angels were assembling round the blazing night fire of Moloc, standing motionless against the stars. Near him was Azazel, the standard bearer, with his seven heads and his pennant of rags. He flew over the Council of the Inquisition, who ranged around Sorush with their countless legions spinning high and wide against the dark caverns and peaks of the silver moonlit clouds.

Surrounding her closer were the angels fallen from the great celestial orders. On her left flank were the craven witches, Amy and Carreau, who were led by the malevolent Duke Procell with his forty-eight legions of dark and grotesque magic. To her right was Beelzebub, who was once closest to Christ, and the mighty one-eyed Prince Gaap, who had at least sixty armies in his own horrific image. And to the rear was Satan with his twelve dripping wings and his awful bride, Lillith, each commanding their own countless legions from the abyss.

Then, beneath the wings of Sorush and descending vertically a hundred miles to the Earth, were thousands more in full battle array, including: the prophetic Asmoday with three heads; the lawyer, Daniel; Gadreel, who had tempted Eve from the Garden; Kazdeya, Princess of Abortion, and Kawkebel with his two million foul just like him. These armies were so black, so vast and so loathsome that they sucked the light from the stars and the breath from the air.

And above all these flew Meresin on dark-grey wings. He pealed thunder as these appalling powers of destruction gathered across the heavens blocking the light from one half of the sky.

In front of Bernie the light was different and the gleam reflected golden in his face as he walked through the shadows of the chasm below.

Mihr was high above the cloud. She organized her forces by lightning bolt and moon. There were great and brilliant armies sweeping up as wide and golden winds from beyond the horizon. In contrast to the chaotic forces of darkness, these were ordered and led by the seven ruling princes of the great celestial orders.

On the right hand of Mihr was Archangel Michael, the saffron-haired Prince of Light. To her left was Archangel Gabriel, the spirit of truth and justice and Angel of the Annunciation. Deployed between them were the shining legions of Raphael, the healer; Uriel the messenger with his flaming sword that could strike thunder; Metraton, once King of the angels and Prince of the Divine Face. Then came Zadkiel, one of the nine rulers of the heavens; and finally, Camael, ruler of Mars and formed in the shape of a leopard. These legions rose as a whirlwind of bright fire.

Bernie was 100 yards from the gates of the Sarras when he saw a small figure in mustard yellow waiting for him. He began to walk faster as the familiar face of Sayeed Sayeed became recognizable through the darkness. When he was twenty yards away from the old man, and before he could speak, he heard the thunder of horses' hooves behind him. He knew that these would be the two black knights. He turned and looked back down the canyon. A quarter of a mile away he could see a squat Mercedes van coming slowly towards him. He turned back towards Sayeed, who smiled and half bowed. He knew the old man would say nothing. Then he turned back again towards the chasm. The Mercedes had stopped 200 yards away and the McCarthy Twins stepped down from it. They stood for a moment, perfectly still, and stared at him. The road was deserted. Only he and Sayeed stood between them and the gates of the Sarras. Slowly they began to walk towards him in their thin black coats. They stopped 100 yards away, and in perfect unison unzipped their long blue bags. Each took out his four-foot swordstick and unsheathed it. Bernie saw the flash of steel as they held the blades horizontal to the ground at shoulder level and began to advance on him. His mouth fell open as he quickly looked back at Sayeed, who smiled again and seemed to be telling him that all was as it should be. The twins were coming closer. For a moment he felt a great wave of doubt and fear and thought his legs would collapse under him, but then he heard the thunder of hooves again. He knew what he would see before it appeared in his mind. He didn't have to turn; he knew it was Galahad pounding towards him from the hospital. He knew that the white knight would pass through the gates behind him as if they weren't there. He knew that as Galahad came upon him they would unsheathe their blades and become one. And as Galahad attacked the black knights, so he would assault the twins. The thunder of the hooves grew loud in his head, his sword was out of his scabbard and came into his hand. Galahad passed through him and at that moment they were joined.

On the exact instant of this conjunction Mihr attacked along her right flank. Her princes, Metraton and Zakriel, released their legions into the left of Sorush, pushing back the carnal angels of Duke Procell. Kazdeya, the Princess of Abortion, who had commanded seventeen legions, was the first dark angel to fall as . . .

. . . Galahad rode full tilt at the black knights and there was an ear-splitting crash as his lance splintered the shield of the first and pierced his throat, sending a cascade of red blood sliding off white armour . . . and Bernie's blade whizzed the air, cut through Chan's collarbone and carved it blue like a chicken leg, and blood spurted again in another fountain, which left a great puddle on the tarmac which splashed and sprayed up . . . as Bernie and Galahad wound round their enemies, swinging their metal and fighting with their breath panting and . . .

. . . *Mihr's Metraton engaged the left of Sorush, and Michael and Gabriel attacked through the centre. The loathsome Pontiff Balberith fell in an implosion of 10,000-year decay, and seven of his legions plummeted through the skies releasing a million black dots, like splats of soot, to fall slowly to the earth. But Sorush was by no means defeated, and . . .*

. . . Gerard came back fast, thrusting his sword into Bernie's shoulder. He felt a sharp and burning pain and heard his own cry and was shocked. The air became crimson and filled up with bits of bone and drips of flesh mixed with soot falling from above . . . as Galahad clashed shields with the second knight and both of them fell from their mounts, and the pennant of rags came fluttering down in slow motion and bumped on the ground like it was . . .

. . . the ensign of Azazel, who was the flag bearer of Sorush, which began to slide down from the sky and slowly break up into strange pottery angel material and then into dust as it got closer to the ground and it began to rain black water which . . .

. . . made everything wetter than it had been, and Bernie counter-attacked and Gerard fell back. Bernie reached out and tried to grab his arm, but he also had his sword up in his other hand to keep Chan back, because he was getting up again with blood pouring from his neck. Gerard, pulling away from Bernie's hand, tripped and splashed down into the red water beneath them, and Bernie went after him on the deck in a steam of sweat which made it difficult to breathe, whilst above him . . .

. . . Mihr advanced from the left and sent the blazing legions of Raphael and Camael, with their spears tipped with light, into the fray. Archangel Michael, with Gabriel behind, drove forward into the centre and met Astorath, Earl of Mayhem, hand to hand.

This was a royal battle of electricity and jagged yellow, and Bernie thought he heard a trumpet, or maybe it was a car horn, but soon he was twisting violently away as Chan's sword scythed through the air causing a slipstream to bubble in the falling debris. And the rain of other things from up there was getting harder, which made the ground slippery. Bernie saw that the pain in his shoulder was a huge gash, but didn't have time to think about it because Gerard was getting up off the ground and coming at him with his silvery blade, so Bernie had to shift his sword away from Chan to hold it up and parry. He watched as the two blades clashed, sending up bright sparks and frizzled fire. Then he pushed forward again . . . as Galahad rose up and hewed with his Sword of Solomon into the black knights, and . . .

. . . Gabriel's armies lit a path for a thousand miles as they began a thrust deep into the witches, Amy and Carreau. Sorush spread her wings and rose fast, like a great ruffled bird whose nest has been attacked. For a second the whole sky was filled with the beating of her

feathers as she tried to hide from the dazzle of Gabriel's assault. But unbeknownst to him, there was coming from the dark below a whirlwind of Harbonnah, Daniel and the demon Arioc, with a mighty force that would shred Gabriel's sun with blades of dark.

Bernie had his right hand full keeping Chan off, and he could see that Gerard was also preparing to attack again. His heel began to slip in the wet stuff and he began to fall back as ... the second black knight ripped Galahad's visor open, which made the beautiful youth turn away to protect his eyes and gave the knights the momentary advantage they were looking for ... and even though Chan was badly wounded in the throat, he still had the strength to swing at Bernie, and if that wasn't bad enough, there was Gerard coming at him with a steel swing-blade haymaker from his left. For the moment things were looking bad indeed. Bernie was running out of strength in his shaky legs and the look on Gerard's face was scaring him because it showed no feeling or any true violence which could be understood. So he began to splash back through the pool, trying to get away from these crazy twins and their bloodlust, which was just blessed terrifying, and worse was to come as up above ...

... Gabriel fell and Michael's legions were destroyed by Agares and Paimon, who led her black battalions astride a camel made of falling rock. Then the hideous Prince Gaap launched an assault all down Mihr's right, sending Metraton with his divine and pretty face flying with his golden wings broken and his legions scattered, leaving their bolts of lightning aimlessly streaking across the sky, finding no target but empty black space.

This was like a bad, bad dream as Bernie's head began to explode and all the parts of his brain that had been opening up like the exotic flowers in his brother's drug-crazed brain were beginning to get crushed up together. And his huge body was cracking and falling as the twins drove down on him with their thin blades zipping the air and slashing through the armour of his coat like it was some old army material, which it was. He was beginning to bleed like his mother had done, as it seemed like a thousand razors a second were whirring and slicing through his flesh. He saw the black suits of the twins as he fell.

They were crowding in on him, making it dark like a nightmare . . . and Galahad was falling too as the knights stood above him in the pouring rain, which was turning all the blood into water and angel dust and soot and stardust, and . . .

. . . a bright angel fell, and then one ten times brighter, then another a hundred times brighter than that, then another a hundred thousand times brighter than all those preceding, all falling, falling, breaking glory, falling like broken light away from the cackle of Sorush, who began to spread her wings in hideous delight . . .

. . . and Galahad in the red pool was now weighed down by his armour and could hardly move as the great black swords of the knights hacked at his body, beginning to carve at the life he loved and had lived so pure. There was just the swish of blades as his white armour began to bleed red, and the sound of laughter rattling from inside the knights as they knew they could cut up his good and devour it later, and . . .

. . . Mihr saw that her shattered power was being drawn into the darkness of Sorush. She began to accept this as right and as it should be, but in that instant she determined that, if she was to be defeated, then her destruction would be bright and soaring and she would be light until extinction. So in supreme and burning power she turned and rallied with first Zadkiel behind her, then Camael in the shape of a leopard . . .

. . . and Galahad's arm came up out of the dead, and he saw through a gap in the black knight's visor the dark glint of eyes that wanted to cut him into pieces . . . and Bernie thought, Go for the eyes, go for the eyes, and his great legs began to draw under him and his great fist wrapped hard round the hilt of his brigadier's sword. As he rose, the flat blade of Gerard's steel swung and glanced off the top of his skull. Still he hauled himself upward from the red pool, through the rain and the sweat, now so hot it blistered his skin. Go for the eyes! There's a hole for the thrust! He pulled his sword back . . .

. . . and Mihr curled, coiled and shot across the sky like atomic white, igniting and flaming the air as she gained velocity. Behind her came the

486

*remnants of the legions of Gabriel and Raphael, set to fill the black hole
at the heart of Sorush with such a blaze that it could only expand until
it burst, shattering the spirit of the dark into infinite dust that would
fly and fall where it would. The Dark Angel, seeing the three-headed
bolt of power and surge coming at her, called unto herself the foul that
stenched the sky. They compressed, cracking, heavy and dense, to repel
Mihr's spinning sheet of blinding fury, speeding in extreme violation of
the laws of light, burning faster and faster towards the darkness as its
ultimate and best contradiction. They entered the black hole as . . .*

. . . Galahad hewed upwards with his blade . . . and Bernie's sword sped
forward and penetrated the skin of Gerard's eyeball, then further
through the grey of his brain until it felt the bone of the skull that held
it. Then he withdrew and plunged again, lower, into the softness of his
stomach, until he felt the blade cut, then snap clean, the spine behind . . .

*. . . and the legions of Mihr opened like dazzling blooms of heat, then
expanded as an infant fireball, pushing out at the heaving stomach of
this unconscious mother density, Sorush, who fought to contain the
light within her horrible, black-packed, infinity-deep wall of darkness,
as . . .*

. . . Bernie's hand shook as he held the hilt and withdrew the blade from
Gerard. Entrails dripped and writhed alive in the pool as the twin
splashed down onto the tarmacadam road, and Chan, immediately
halved because he was bereft of his brother, staggered to his left with
his throat bleeding, and . . . Galahad rose as the first black knight fell
back dead, and trumpets brayed elsewhere on a piece of old England
where maidens howled their praise of the mighty white knight and . . .

*. . . Sorush screamed across the arc of time at the exquisite agony of
this growth of light inside her, as it heaved and burned, mushrooming
out in bulbous riot and pushing the darkness back until it met itself in
its own disgust and bleeding rupture, for . . .*

. . . now was the moment of execution. Chan just dropped his blade and
stood there with his head bowed like he was expecting it . . . as did the
remaining black knight who knelt on the ancient grass. And the two

bloody swords of Bernie and Galahad were pulled back at shoulder height. There was a moment of nothing and then there was the final thunder from the fireball above as the swords, one of now and another of then, swung in brilliant, silver, celestial arcs, and two heads, one of now and another of then, severed from their necks, flew up in the air and became like everything else that had crashed and fallen to the ground. They thudded into the pools of water, blood, soot and stardust and splashed droplets of crimson moonlight which splattered Bernie's face as Chan fell headless, and . . .

. . . for an instant night was day as the walls of darkness disintegrated and Mihr and the princes of heaven erupted high on the edge of the fireball that was all that was left of Sorush.

Bernie's sword slipped from his hand and clattered onto the road. Sayeed Sayeed didn't move. The twins lay at the big boy's feet. His huge coat had been cut away or fallen off him during the fight and the white shirt that Two-pin had given him was torn and stained with blood. He stood still over their twisted bodies. It was very quiet. And Violet died. In their death the twins had taken her with them.

And for this moment there was a silence in the sky.

So that was that, except for one thing and he knew what it was.

$$\boxed{16}$$

Hooper didn't move as the nurse covered Violet's face with the sheet. He'd sat down on a hospital chair on the other side of the bed from Ronnie. They both stared at the corpse with its face shrouded by white cotton. The outline of her nose and lips was quite clear. She looked like any other human being with a sheet over her face, except that she didn't breathe and somehow the air seemed cold. The nurse had asked Harriet and Lucy to come in. They stood at the end of the bed with their hands clasped in front of them as a mark of respect.

Harriet cried because of the old times she could remember and also because of Charlie. Lucy cried because of Arnie. Ronnie was wondering what might have been if his mother had lived. Maybe he could finally have had that conversation with her, but it was too late now. And because he hadn't had it, he wasn't too clear who she was; just someone who was dead and bandaged up and who he hadn't seen for twenty years. He could feel the churning in him begin to subside. It was getting to be all over.

The real grief should have belonged to Hooper. But grief for what? For this real woman who lay dead only inches from his hand? Or for the end of the vision he'd had for all those years? But how can a dream die? He could already feel himself slipping back to the fifth house. He could already hear the shouts of the children in the garden and the clink of the lemonade on the tray as Violet came smiling through the French windows. Violet would live in him as she'd always done. She would be happy and bright. She would laugh and they would plan sixth and even seventh houses. He knew a man who could advise them on a very reliable pension scheme. What about a little surprise holiday in Malta? He'd heard Valletta was very pleasant at this time of year. He` sighed and looked up at Ronnie, then round at Harriet. He stood and nodded to them in a professional way. 'I'm sorry.' He'd said it before like that to the relatives of other victims. Ronnie didn't react, Harriet returned a small smile and Hooper walked out of the room, leaving them to grieve over this unknown woman.

Fairfax was standing outside and saw his superior coming towards him through the glass of the door. The moment he glimpsed Hooper's face he knew that his mind had gone. It struck Fairfax as all being too tragic for words. He opened the door for Hooper and was about to attempt a sentence or two of condolence when his handset crackled into life. 'Two men, Sergeant! Foyer!' Fairfax couldn't believe it. He couldn't be that wrong already. He yelled back into the mouthpiece.

'What do they look like?'

'Big one covered in blood and a Paki in yellow. They're in the service lift.' Fairfax looked round at Hooper, who was by this time standing next to him with a strange smile on his face.

'Sound like the youngest brother to you, sir?' asked Fairfax.

'I don't think it's quite over yet,' said Hooper.

'Sir?'

'Life goes on, Freddie. It always does, you know.'

Fairfax was flummoxed. Hooper had raised his head, and although his chin was shaking, the strange smile didn't leave his face. All around them constables were running towards the huge industrial-sized lift at the far end of the long corridor and taking up defensive positions. Harriet came out of intensive care with Ronnie behind her. 'Did you say the youngest?'

'I don't know, madam.' Fairfax left her and ran towards the lift doors. As soon as he got there he knew they'd cocked it up again. He yelled, 'Why didn't you tell me the lift was going down?' He ran towards the stairs with half a dozen constables behind him as the hospital lights dimmed again and came back on at half power. Everything was dull yellow and seemed quieter than it had been. Harriet wondered for a second if it was Violet's soul leaving her body, but kept it to herself. Ronnie looked round as Lucy ran up to join them by the lift doors. 'What's happening?

Ronnie didn't know, but something told him that whatever it was he should be there. He ran quickly after Fairfax down the stairs.

Lucy looked at Harriet. 'Oh Christ, Auntie, what now?'

Bernie had known where to go. If he hadn't Sayeed would have told him. They came out of the lift doors in the basement and walked straight ahead down a very long and dimly lit corridor. His hands were by his side and still sticky with blood. His shoulder hurt but he hardly noticed the pain. Out there in the battle zone everything had melded and you couldn't tell what was what, except there was some explosion in the sky which had put power into his arms. But even as he was wielding the sword and taking away the McCarthy Twins he'd known that there was one other thing he had to do, and it was about Lancelot lying there cold and sick on the cold stone floor. That's what he was doing now, so he kept walking.

Fairfax hurtled down the stairs with the constables behind him. They arrived breathless in front of the open lift doors. The basement corridor stretched ahead of them. There was only one way to go and they began to run again as Ronnie arrived at the bottom of the stairs behind them. As they came to the end of the corridor, it turned sharply left and they found themselves facing the heavy steel door of the mortuary. Fairfax pushed at the door and slowly it swung open. He walked in with the constables and Ronnie, who had caught them up.

Bernie stood with his hands bloody and limp by his side, looking up and out of the narrow grill that ran along the top of the blue-lit room. His head was arched back, his mouth open and he seemed to be looking up at the moon. The old man in a yellow dhoti stood to one side with his hands clasped in front of him and his head bowed. By him a mortuary drawer had been pulled open. Arnie lay on it. He was naked and his body was a grey white. The wounds on his chest were small and deep dark red, surrounded by yellow. His eyes were open and he was smiling. As he began to sit up, Fairfax fainted. Slowly Ronnie shakily and tearfully approached his living, breathing elder brother. But Bernie took no notice; he was staring up into the dark sky seeing something else altogether.

$\boxed{17}$

Mihr was cold. She pulled her thin white coat tighter around her shoulders and looked down from the steeple of the old brown church at St Aldgates to the cemetery below.

The brothers were carrying their mother's coffin up to the grave next to Charlie's at the top of the hill. Father Cassidy was in front, behind came Harriet, Lucy, Mathilda and others from the family, club room and restaurant. The gathering was much smaller and more restrained than the riot of Charlie's funeral a week ago. Not so many had known Violet, although there were a few additional faces from Kensington and her life that the brothers had never seen.

Fairfax stood at the back of the congregation. His thoughts were with Hooper. That morning he'd tried to gently explain to him that Violet had died and as far as he knew the twins had never come to the hospital; they seemed to have disappeared off the face of the earth, but the retired superintendent had just smiled. He appeared contented enough looking out of his window, but it made Fairfax feel sad. He'd spent the rest of the day on the paperwork involved in charging Luis Riss and his minders with the murder of the baker. Emil had been done as an accessory, but it looked like Raphaella was going to get off. Well you couldn't win them all. Or could you? He looked over at Arnie and wondered. Apparently in the confusion of that strange night no-one had ever made out a proper death certificate and so he should never have been in the morgue in the first place. That was what the hospital manager had said anyway. Fairfax didn't believe a word of it. He watched as Bernie helped his brothers lower the coffin into the grave. It was said that his wounds had been caused in some incident on the underground when the girl had fallen under a train, but he'd leave others to deal with that. Bernie seemed to be well enough now.

Sayeed Sayeed glanced up at the angel on the steeple. He was an angel, too, descended years before as guardian to Charlie, and now he would remain to keep a watchful eye over the youngest son. He looked up at the steeple again. Mihr had come for the last time and now she was smiling.

The big boy stood at the end of the grave and slyly grinned when Arnie winked at him. Ron was over there, too, in his smart new suit, next to Tilda. These were the bruvs, together again. Bernie wanted to be with them and he didn't want to talk to no coppers no more 'cos he didn't have anything to say 'cos he couldn't remember nothing. He looked round and about at all the people with a daft look on his face. He hoped they'd hurry up 'cos he was starvin' hungry.

Around the streets, they were already starting to talk about him. The boy who was a retard up at the café. There was something about him, wasn't there? Everyone said it. There's something about that geezer. He's barmy and he don't talk much, but there's something about him, don't you think? Know him, do you?